DOG AND DRAGON

DAVE FREER

Dog & Dragon

This is a work of fiction. All the characters and events portrayed in this book are fictional, and any resemblance to real people or incidents is purely coincidental.

A Baen Books Original

Baen Publishing Enterprises
P.O. Box 1403
Riverdale, NY 10471
www.baen.com

ISBN: 978-1-4516-3885-1

Cover art by Bob Eggleton

First Baen paperback printing, April 2013

Library of Congress Control Number: 2011053038

Distributed by Simon & Schuster
1230 Avenue of the Americas
New York, NY 10020

Pages by Joy Freeman (www.pagesbyjoy.com)
Printed in the United States of America

This one is for my Old English Sheepdog, Roland, loyal companion, faithful friend.

═══ Acknowledgments ═══

My thanks go to the many readers who asked for this, and to my editor, Toni Weisskopf, for listening. To my agent, Mike Kabongo, for getting me to write a high fantasy in the first place. As this is my first entirely Australian-written novel: To the Australian immigration authorities for letting us come here to our own enchanted island, Flinders, and to all those who saw our animals (Roly, Puggles, Wednesday, and Duchess, Robin and Batman) safe through quarantine and here with us. To the friends who helped us settle in so that I could write, and the ones (that's you, Jamie) who came up with good ways to kill monsters.

And, as always, most thanks to Barbara, for editing, supporting and driving through Melbourne traffic.

Characters

Queen Gwenhwyfach	Last queen of Lyonesse.
Lady Cardun	Chatelaine of Dun Tagoll.
Neve	Tirewoman to Meb.
Lady Vivien	Widow of Cormac, the late captain of the Royal Guard.
Lady Branwen	Wife of Earl Alois, not of the House of Lyon.
Owain	Alois and Branwen's son.
Gwalach	Second-in-command of the Army of the South.
Mortha	Wudewasa wisewoman.

— OTHER —

Sir Bertran	A knight of Brocéliande.
Avram, Dravko, Mirko	Travelers who trade between various planes.
Mitzi	Avram's dog, and Díleas's light o' love.

Chapter 1

Back to the sunset bound of Lyonesse—
A land of old upheaven from the abyss
By fire, to sink into the abyss again;
Where fragments of forgotten peoples dwelt,
And the long mountains ended in a coast
Of ever-shifting sand, and far away
The phantom circle of a moaning sea.

—Idylls of the King, Tennyson

"WHO ARE YOU?" HISSED THE LITHE, DARK-EYED man with the drawn sword.

Meb blinked at him. Her transition from the green forests of Arcady to this dark, stone-flagged hall had been instantaneous. The stone walls were hung with displays of arms and the horns of stags. Otherwise there was not much to separate it from a cave or prison, with not so much as an arrow slit—let alone a window—to be seen in the stone walls.

In Tasmarin from whence she had come, she had known just who she was: Scrap, apprentice to the black dragon that destroyed the worlds. You could call her anything else, but that was who she had been. Now...

1

"Cat got your tongue, wench?" he said quietly. "Well, no matter, I'll have to kill you anyway."

He swung the sword at her in a vicious arc.

Moments ago, before she'd made the choice that swept her magically from Tasmarin, from the green forest of Arcady, she'd thought she might be better off dead rather than leaving them behind. Leaving *him* behind.

Now she discovered that her body didn't want to die just yet. She threw herself backwards, not caring where she landed, as long as it was out of reach of the sword.

She screamed. And then swore as the blade shaved along her arm to thud into the kist she had fallen over. She kicked out, hard, catching her attacker in the midriff, knocking the breath out of him in an explosive gasp. Trying to find breath, he still pulled weakly at the sword now a good two-finger-widths deep into the polished timber of the kist. Meb wasn't going to wait.

But it looked as if she wasn't going to run very far either. Her scream, and possibly the swearing, had called others, and the great iron-studded doors were flung open as men-at-arms with bright swords and scale armor rushed in.

As she turned to run the other way, her passage was blocked by a sleepy-looking man—also with a sword, emerging from the only other doorway.

There wasn't a window to be seen.

She wanted one, badly.

And then she saw one, in the recessed wall to her left. She just plainly hadn't spotted it before.

She ran to it, and realized it wasn't going to help

much. In the moonlight she could see that it opened onto a hundred feet of jagged cliff, to an angry sea, frothing around sharp rock teeth far below.

Some of the soldiers surrounded the man she'd kicked. They'd blocked her escape too, but you couldn't really call it surrounding her. Not unless that included "getting as far from her as possible, while not leaving the other prisoner, or the room."

The man who had looked so sleepy moments before didn't anymore. His sword was up, ready, his eyes wide as they darted from the window to her, seemingly unsure which was more shocking.

"Who are you?" he asked.

There was something weaselly about him that made her very wary about answering, in case her words were twisted against her.

And why did they all want to know something she wasn't too sure of herself?

There was a narrow bridge across the void. Along it walked a black-and-white sheepdog, followed by a black dragon. The dog never looked back at the dragon, just forward, his questing written into every line of his body, from the mobile, pointed ears to the feathered tail.

The bridge itself was narrow—made of vast, interlocking blocks of adamantine—or at least that is the way it looked. Reality might be somewhat different, at least to the eyes of a planomancer. Such eyes would see deeper than the ordinary spectra of light, and could see patterns of energy. Fionn, the black dragon, saw it all as the weave of magics that made the bridge between the planes of existence. He knew the bridge was fragile and fraught with danger. That did not stop him walking along it, any more than it stopped Díleas the sheepdog.

The bridge was barely two cubits wide and had no rail. Far, far below seethed the tumult of primal chaos. The only way the dog could go was straight ahead. He kept looking left though.

That was where he wanted to go. Sometimes he would raise his nose and sniff.

Fionn knew there was nothing to smell out here. The air that surrounded the bridge was drawn and melded by the magics of it, from the raw chaos. It was new air, and Fionn knew that it did not exist a few paces behind them, or a few paces ahead.

He was still sure Díleas was following the faint trail of something. A something which even a very clever dog could best understand as scent...even if there was nothing to smell.

At least he hoped that was the case.

Hoped with ever fiber of his very ancient being.

Fionn had long since given up on caring too much. He was not immortal, as far as he knew. He could certainly be killed. But compared to others, even of his own kind, the black dragon was long-lived. Time passed, and so did friends. His work was never done, fixing the balance, keeping the planes stable. He moved on.

He'd been hated. He'd been worshiped, though it irritated him. He'd been laughed at and reviled. He'd been feared.

He'd even been loved.

He had never loved before, though.

The black-and-white sheepdog was more experienced at love than the dragon, and he was a young dog still, maybe eight months old. Barely more than a pup. But Díleas—whose name was "faithful" in an old tongue, long forgotten by most men—would go to the ends of the world for her, and beyond, as they were now. His mistress was his all and he would search for her until he died, or he found her.

Fionn knew that he'd do the same. His Scrap, his inept apprentice, had been plucked from them by magic. Her own magic and her own choice, made freely for them, and for Tasmarin, the place of dragons. Fionn knew, however, that it had cost her dearly. For him, left here without her, it was a worthless sacrifice.

So now, somewhere, back in some place that she'd been torn from as a babe, they had to find her again.

Fionn had no idea where that might be. A place of magics, where human magery ran strong in the blood, that much he could be sure of. But there were many such places in the interlinking chain of worlds, and they themselves were large and complex places.

It was a good thing that Díleas seemed to have some idea where to go, because Fionn didn't know where to even start, except by trying everywhere. He would do that, if need be. He had time. He would never give up.

The only problem was that she was human and very mortal. And, if he had to be truthful with himself, she was able to attract disaster toward herself, just by being there.

Fionn had never known love. He'd never really known worry either. Pain, and the avoidance of it, yes, fear, yes, but now he was afraid for her. Worried.

The end of the bridge was now visible, if wreathed in smoke or mist.

Fionn wondered if it would be guarded, or if the bridge was too new. The transit points often had their watchers, or barriers.

As the other side of the void came closer, Fionn realized this place would not need such things.

Most travelers would turn around and go back just as quickly as they could.

Gylve was a place of fire and black glass.

Fionn had been there before, and wouldn't have minded if he'd never had to go there again. A planomancer needed to visit such places and straighten things out. Last time, it had glowed in the dark, and he'd had to do some serious adjustment. He was pleased to see that the radiation levels at least had dropped. Still, you could see fire dancing across the sky as the methane jets caught.

On the silver collar on Díleas's neck hung a bauble. A little part of the primal fire, enclosed in what merely appeared to be crystal. It should keep the dog safe from demons and from actually freezing. It wouldn't keep his feet safe on the broken volcanic glass in the place they were coming to; only dragon hide would do for that.

Fortunately, he had some with him, available without the discomfort of slicing it off himself. He could have done that. Dragons were tough . . . even if they really didn't like making holes in themselves any more than the next creature. But every now and again a dragon died or was killed. If a dragon was sharp about it, they could get a piece of hide before the humans did. Honestly, thought Fionn, for a species that was afraid of dragons, humans had a habit of sticking their necks out.

It was one of the things that he liked about them.

The bridge was beginning to widen ... to open onto the jet-black clinkers of one of the fire-worlds. Fionn stopped.

Díleas didn't.

"Díleas, come here!"

The dog did turn and look at him, with a "what do you think you're wasting time at?" look. And then began to pace forward.

"This muck will cut your feet to ribbons. And then you won't be able to walk to her." Fionn had to smile wryly at himself. Talking to the dog. Just like his Scrap of humanity had.

The dog turned around and came back to him. Lifted a foot.

Fionn's eye's widened. He'd have to do some serious reevaluation. And yes, now he could see that the dog was substantially magically ... enhanced. Curse the dvergar and their tricksy magics. He was supposed to be the practical joker, not them. His Scrap had *wanted* Díleas to understand her. And she wore a very powerful piece of enchanted jewelry, which bound the magics of earth, stone, wood, fire and worked metals to her will.

Not surprising really that her power worked on sheepdogs. They were clever and loyal anyway, or so he'd been told.

"It won't be elegant," he said, "but then there won't be other dogs out here to see you. He took the section of dragon leather from his pouch and rent it into four pieces, and then made a neat row of talon punctures around the edge, before transforming his own shape. Human form was one of those he knew best, and it allowed him to wield a needle well. It was of course partly a matter of appearances, and a useful disguise. He was far too heavy and too strong for a human—but hands were easier to sew with than clawed talons. A piece of thong threaded through the holes and Díleas had four baggy boots.

Díleas looked critically at the things on his feet. Sniffed them.

"Dragon hide," said Fionn. "I wouldn't show them to any dragons you happen to meet, but otherwise they'll do. And really, scarlet boots match the bauble on your collar."

Díleas cocked an ear at him. Fionn wasn't ready to bet the dog didn't grasp sarcasm, so he merely said, "Well, let's go. The only thing we're likely to meet are demondim, and they like red anyway."

They didn't like dragons, but were suitably afraid of them, so that was the form Fionn assumed, as the two of them walked into the badlands. It reeked of sulphur and burning, and Fionn knew the ground could collapse under their feet, dropping them down hundreds of cubits to white-hot ashpits. Vast coal measures had been pierced by ferocious vulcanism, and deep down, somewhere, it burned still. Fionn blinked his eyes to allow himself to see other spectra, patterns of energy, that might allow him to spot such instability before it killed Díleas. But the dog seemed aware and moved with a slow caution that he hadn't showed up on the bridge.

It was, as befitted a fire-creature world, hot and waterless. Fionn noticed that Díleas was panting. He'd have to learn to carry water for the dog, or to somehow carry the dog while he flew, because there were worse places than this, in the vast ring of planes that Fionn had once maintained the stability of. He was a planomancer, made by the First for this task, and there was plenty of work waiting for him.

Right now, it could wait. All he did was to make a few preliminary marks with his talon and tail.

And simply because he'd said to Díleas that they would see nothing here but demondim, right now he could hear noises that were very unlike those beloved of the creatures of fire. A jangle of bells, and, clearly, a bark. And human voices.

Díleas, panting, could hear them too. Dogs could hear more keenly than humans, but not dragons.

Fionn changed his form again, becoming human in appearance. A dragon would almost certainly be an unwelcome sight. He could, and possibly should, leave the demons to their nasty games. But he had some sympathy for humans these days. She'd taught him that. He would help, simply for her sake. They moved towards the voices and sounds.

The caravan of carts was moving, slowly, along a causeway of blue-black hexagonal blocks. Probably the safest place around here, reflected Fionn, although you had to consider just what had flattened the top of the columnar dolerite dyke into a narrow straight road across the ash fields and lava lands. Bells tinkled from every horse's harness strap. Whoever they were, they were not ignorant of demondim and their dislikes, or quite the helpless lost travelers Fionn had expected. The fire creatures liked to mislead and torment those. But whoever had made those bells knew a thing or two about the demondim. They'd been made either to very precise mathematical formulae, or been shaved very carefully into making an octave.

"Go on, Díleas. We might as well see just who they are and what they're up to and cadge you a drink, panting dog," said Fionn, prodding him with a toe.

Díleas dropped his head and looked warily . . . not at the advancing carts but at the trail in front of them. He gave a soft growl. So Fionn looked closer. It was a well concealed little trap, the clinker plates hiding the thing's lair. The Silago wasn't a particularly intelligent predator, but it didn't need to be. All it did was to make a bit of a trail and lie in wait. Eventually something—if there was anything—would choose the easiest trail and walk into its maw, just as he nearly had. Half-rock, half-animal, it didn't need to eat more than once every few years anyway. Fionn found a piece of glassy rock and tossed it at the clinker plates. They collapsed inwards and a segmented creature with long snapping jaws reared out, lashing about, looking for prey.

Fionn stepped back, Díleas had already neatly moved up against his side. And then the tossing Silago head sprouted an arrow shaft. And a second. Fionn paused, wondering if he should take refuge behind a rock spike. Any bow that could push an arrow hard enough to penetrate a Silago might even get an arrow into him.

The dark-skinned, white-haired man on the lead cart—with his recurved composite bow in hand, arrow on the string, and perky-eared dog growling from the seat beside him—was smiling, though. A suspicious smile, but better than fear or anger, while he held that bow. And there were plainly others, because of that second arrow. "You ain't one of the Beng," he said, "because they don't like dogs and they don't walk on the ground. And they don't like our bells or garlic. The question is who or what are you, stranger?"

Finn touched his hat. "Finn. I'm a gleeman. A traveling singer and jester. I juggle a bit too."

The man didn't put the bow down. "Not many inns or villages around here. Where are you from, gleeman? Abalach? Annvn? Carmarthen? Vanaheim? The Blessed Isles or . . . Lyonesse?"

Fionn was an expert on tone. Lyonesse was probably not a good place to be from. He'd been there. He'd been everywhere, once upon a time.

In front of him the Silago still thrashed about. "None of those, recently," he said cheerfully. "A place called Tasmarin. Back there."

"Didn't know there were any Ways over there," said the traveler.

"It's rather new, and I don't think it's going to see much traffic, judging by this charming countryside," said Fionn, waving at the ash lands. "And anyway, Tasmarin is quite full of dragons. They're not overly friendly." The Silago was threshing rather more weakly now. Fionn could simply have jumped over it, but not if he wished them to believe he was human. He slowly, calmly, reached into his pouch, took out three balls and began to juggle one-handed. He'd found it very good for distraction and misleading before. And those little balls were made of osmium, both a lot harder and heavier than observers might guess. Fionn could throw them fast enough to knock an armored knight out of the saddle. "To tell the truth I am a little lost. And my dog could use a drink."

The cartman smiled again. "I think we could probably sell you some water. And the road should see you to Annvn, if you stick to it. You'll have to wait until the Beng-child is dead, though. They usually put themselves in the middle of the only safe path. It's surprising you got this far." His tone said that alone was reason for not putting aside his bow, just yet.

Fionn shrugged, not stopping his juggling. It was good for hypnosis too. "The dog is good at finding safe ways."

"I like his footwear," said the cartman.

"Worn by all the best dogs in the capitals of many great lands. It also keeps his feet from being cut up. Purely as a secondary thing, you understand," said Fionn. He pointed to the Silago. "It's dying, whatever it is." There was no point in admitting to knowing too much.

"Give it a little more time, gleeman. Even half-dead, the Beng-child will have your arm off, and might scratch the dog's boots. When it's dead we'll have the jaws off it. They'll fetch a good price where we're headed."

Fionn nodded patiently, which was more than Díleas was showing signs of. "Where did you say you are bound for?"

"Annvn. Well, if it's there. You never know these days."

Fionn raised an eyebrow. "And where else might it be?" He was a planomancer. There was a logical consistency to where the various planes of existence interlocked. It was not variable. The multidimensionality and subplanes of it all meant it was more complex than a mere three-dimensional ring would be. It was possible that points of departure and arrival could be geographically close. But until Tasmarin had opened up a way to multiple planes, one link point did not lead you elsewhere. Had Tasmarin changed it all?

"Last time we took the giant's road we found ourselves in Lyonesse. If that happens we'll head back," he said, putting the bow aside, and getting down from the cart. He pulled a long metal stake and a hammer from the cart. Looked for a crack, found one and hammered it in. "How far to this Tasmarin place?" he said casually, in an I-am-not-fishing-for-information tone.

Fionn was amused, and used to human ways. "Not far. I could tell you in some detail . . . in exchange for a drink for my dog."

"Ah, you're a sharp one," said the cartman, grinning. "Worth a trading venture?"

"Probably," said Fionn. "What are you selling?"

"Things which are exotic in one place and cheap in another. Peacock feathers and pepper, bottles of mermaids' tears, amber, narwhal ivory, and carved walrus tusks this trip."

"I'd say pepper would sell." It was a game, and Fionn played it well.

"Ah. One of those places," said the traveler. "Magic, and the creatures of it are more common than pepper. Hey, Nikos, Dravko. The Beng-child is ready for you to butcher the jaws out of. You might as well come across, stranger."

Fionn could see things they could not. The Silago was not dead. He patted Díleas. "The dog thinks it is faking, mister. And he's a sharp dog." He caught all the juggling balls in one hand, and picked up another rock and flung it at the open jaws, which snapped closed viciously and sent splinters of rock flying.

The white-haired man looked very thoughtful indeed. "Sharp dog he is. And earned himself a drink, I'd say, gleeman. Maybe worth asking you about the way across to this place."

"I made marks." He had. With a talon. They were

not intended as trail markers but they could work as
that without undoing his purpose. Energies needed
to flow, and the travelers could be vehicles for that.
Travelers tended to be a cunning lot though. Over the
years he'd known and journeyed with a fair number
of these sort of folk, too many to believe them to be
easily fooled or used without them knowing.

"Ah. It's a sharp master too. A wonder you don't
cut yourself, gleeman. Nikos, come and give the Beng-
creature a good poke with that black iron spear of
yours."

Someone knew—or had known—a great deal about
demondim and the few creatures that survived just
what they had made of their worlds, thought Fionn,
looking at the spear in the next swarthy man's grasp.

It wasn't iron-edged and had a fair weight of magework about it. Antimony might·not be the ideal metal
for edging anything, but it was deadly toxic to the
silicate sulphur of the Silago.

Soon Fionn and Díleas were able to pass the two
traveler men cutting at the dead Silago. The dog on
the seat of the lead cart growled and bristled. "Hear
now, Mitzi. That's no way to greet a dog with smart
red boots," said the lead cartman. Díleas was studiously
ignoring her. The cart driver got down, and tapped
some water out of a small keg into a bowl. Held it
out to Fionn. "Here, gleeman. Best if your dog drinks
a little way from Mitzi. It's her bowl."

Fionn gave a little bow. "Thank you, goodman.
This place was hotter than we expected. Dustier too."

"Ah well, you've a fair distance to travel in it. Best
to be prepared. My name is Arvan, gleeman. I only
look like a good man."

"Call me Finn. Most do," said Fionn, taking the water and setting it on the ground. He noticed the watchfulness of the lead cart driver. The watchfulness of the dogs on the seats of the other eleven carts. The fact that they had at least two other men hidden in them, and they weren't watching him or Díleas. The water smelled all right, wasn't bespelled . . . Díleas sniffed it too, and then drank with a great deal of tongue splashing. He had needed that. Well, he was wearing a good thick coat of black-and-white fur.

"And now, Finn, if you'd tell me a bit about this Tasmarin place, I could offer you a mug of beer," said Arvan. Fionn knew the name was a small part of the traveler's true name, which suggested that the travelers knew of the importance of those too. Well, they did accumulate knowledge or fail to survive.

"It's an hour's walk from here. See the double smoking peak? Bear just left of that. You'll find this symbol scratched on the rock here and there." Fionn scratched it with his toe in the dust. "There is a narrow white bridge that you will have to cross. Not much room for a cart on it. And the dragons on the other side are fond of gold, so I'd take care to appear poor."

"Oh, we are," said Arvan, tapping Fionn a small flagon of beer. It was good beer.

"They can smell gold at twenty paces," said Fionn, who could smell theirs, above the beer. It was under the front end of the cart. Probably a hidden panel or something.

"Ah. There haven't been many around for a while. People wondered where they'd got to. Some of us wanted to know."

"There, that's where," said Fionn.

The jaw cutters had finished their work by now, and they carried them back to the causeway and roped them onto the back of the cart, still dripping black ichor. The little caravan set off again, Fionn and Díleas walking alongside the lead cart. It was, it appeared by Díleas's behavior, the direction they needed to go.

A mile or so later the causeway was interrupted by what might have been called a river, if rivers boiled, and did not run with anything anyone could have called water, although scalding water diluted it. It ran through a fresh fracture in the dolerite, and the steam reeked of brimstone and the almond smell of cyanides. Arvan scratched his head. "That's a new one."

Fionn tried to work out the least obtrusive way of changing the situation. Energy and fire magic abounded here. There was even an ancient water pattern. The place had been verdant once. A tweak here and there . . . But it would all take time, and by the way that fool-of-a-very-clever sheepdog was pacing back and forth and bunching his muscles, he would try jumping soon.

The beautiful crone-enchantress, the queen of Shadow Hall, stared vengefully at her seeing-basin. Dun Tagoll—dark stone towers silhouetted against the moonlit sea—seemed to stare back at her. He'd protected it as well as he was able, and she could see no further into the castle on the cliff top. She had stared at it, the same way, for over fifty years now. Eventually, she would win. A few hours earlier she'd felt a surge of magical energy, and wondered if he'd finally died. But no, the tower still resisted her vision—it would not if he was dead, she was sure.

So, the fight must continue. She was busy mustering her forces, yet again. She worked with her unwitting allies' fears, and she had the Cauldron of Gwalar. It brewed and bubbled now. Soon she would cast pieces of yet another dead hero in the seethe of it. They had to be boiled apart, or at least finely diced, before she could reassemble them and reanimate them. And then dispatch them . . . to whichever of the nineteen worlds Lyonesse would try to leech off this time.

She stared at the image in the seeing-basin. The tallest tower and its highest window. There was a light there. He would be working away, creating falsehoods and illusions. Working on his simulacra and devices. Bah. Machinery. She had been fascinated by it once, the cogs and springs and the mechanisms for harnessing the tides themselves. The smell of oil, and magic . . .

He was not a summonser, but one who worked inanimate things and the laws of contagion and sympathy. She used that, but drew on higher powers too. The powers of life . . . and death. She learned as much of his craft as she could, of course. In those days Dun Tagoll had been the place to learn and to practice magecraft. He'd stopped that. He didn't like competition.

To think she'd loved him once. Trusted him with their secret. Sworn eternal faith to each other and their secret. Dreamed that some day . . . She spat into seeing-basin, shattering the image.

Death would take him one day.

And it could not be a day too soon for her.

In the meanwhile she had to finish the warrior in her cauldron. And then get onto making more mury-ans. Shadow Hall would have to walk again, to follow

Lyonesse, to raise war and chaos and foes against it. She followed Lyonesse's progression across myriad leagues and subplanes in her palace of shadows.

Her hall moved. It did so on tiny ant feet. Many, many ant feet.

═ Chapter 2 ═

"MY NAME IS MEB," SHE SAID, CLINGING TO A PART of her youth.

"Mab?" It was said with a narrowing of the eyes. The sword came up a fraction and Meb wondered if the jump might be more pleasant. She had no idea if her untrained magical skill would work here.

It sounded as if "Mab" wasn't too popular. "No. Meb. E, not A. My real name is Anghared. But I like Meb more." Really, she preferred Scrap.

This had some rather unexpected effects. The oddest was from the man who had tried to kill her—who was now pinned down by three burly men-at-arms: he started to laugh. Several of the soldiers knelt. The sword tip threatening her dropped. "I suppose you can prove that?" said the once-sleep-addled man facing her.

"What proof does she need, Medraut? She is a summonser, able to work in cursed Dun Tagoll itself!" shouted the man on the floor.

If looks were poison, the prisoner would have been dead instantly. "Take him away," said the man called

Medraut. "I ask you again, stranger. Who are you, dressed like that, in my outer chamber? How did you get here?"

Meb shrugged. The bleakness of despair was settling over her again. She'd assumed the magic would send her back to the place where she'd been drawn to Tasmarin from. She'd assumed that it would be a place she somehow recognized as home. In truth she hadn't cared. She'd simply known it would mean banishment from all she knew and loved. However, innate caution instilled by dragonkind's hatred of human magic stopped her going too far with explaining. It might be different here. But it might not. "I don't know. I was in Arcady and then I was here. But I'll go away if you don't want me to be here. I think I just stopped you from being murdered in your sleep." She gestured toward the prisoner being dragged from the room.

"It is almost as if she was sent to save you, Prince Medraut," said one of the guards, wonderingly. "The door wardens are dead, the door unlocked... and had this stranger not given the alarm, Earl Alois would have killed you. Alois nearly killed her."

Prince Medraut blinked. "You... you are the Defender?" and part of the tone said: Why me? But there was hope there too.

Meb wasn't sure who "the Defender" was. But she was pretty sure that it wasn't her, anyway.

"I don't think so," she said, exhaustion, doubt and misery warring in her breast. "I am just someone who is hungry and tired, and going to jump out of this window, if you try anything with that sword."

The prince suddenly realized that he was holding

a naked sword...and that she was on a window sill.
He looked faintly embarrassed. "Your pardon, lady."

How did he know she was a woman? With a
cropped head, boy's clothes and tight breastband, she'd
passed for a boy for months and months. Well, said
her inner voice—the sensible pragmatic voice that
overrode village thought, and overrode daydreams too:
maybe the name Anghared is a clue. That and the
fact that, somehow, her hair seemed to have grown
to waist length in the transition here. The clothes
remained, of course.

The prince put the sword down, on the floor, as
that was the only surface available to him. "We will
have chambers and food prepared for you immediately.
We are deeply honored by your presence and pray we
have not caused you any offense."

She'd trusted him more when he'd been pointing
a sword at her. It must have showed in her face. But
the soldiers sheathed their swords, and they at least
appeared to believe him. "I swear by the House of
Lyon that we mean you no harm, lady."

Reluctantly Meb came down from the stone sill.
She hadn't liked falling last time, and it looked as
if the rocks would get her before a merrow could.
Besides, she might as well die well fed. What worse
could happen to her than certain death?

She knew some answers to that one, too. But she
allowed the guards to respectfully escort her away
to a small withdrawing room, where a generous fire
burned in the grate and the hangings were rich and
old. There was a riven-oak table that must have
weighed as much as ten stacks of stockfish, painstak-
ingly smoothed and polished. It was set with two

branches of good beeswax candles, with a chair that was more like a throne than the three-legged stool she'd have considered luxury a twelvemonth ago. The guards bowed. "The old queen would dine here, Lady Anghared. They will bring you food and wine, very soon," said a grizzled captain, very respectfully.

If there was one thing that was really intimidating, Meb thought, it was all this respect. But she was hungry, as well as miserable and a little confused. Just where exactly was she? Somewhere called Dun Tagoll? A castle hanging above the sea. The place where she had come from as a baby, presumably, before being magically snatched away to Tasmarin, to a world that had become her own, that she'd loved and had given all to Finn and Díleas. So this must be her world. But, if she'd ever thought about it, she'd expected to return to a fishing village.

She'd never thought of herself as a castle kind of person. That was the place of alvar, after all.

It would seem that was not true here. These castle people were all human. She closed her eyes, and sat back in the chair, remembering. Remembering walking behind Finn in his ridiculous "notice me" lilac and canary-yellow silks and satins, juggling tasseled balls in the palace of the alvar at Alba, with its high arched roof, alv-lights and the butterflylike flitting of the courtiers, as she pretended to be dumb and tossed the balls.

Something landed in her hand. Instinctively she caught it. And the second, third and fourth. The sight of the balls, summoned out of nowhere, was enough to prick her eyes with tears. Someone cleared their throat. There was an elderly man, in neat clothing, but plainly a servant by his mein, with a silver salver, a stemmed goblet, and a chased jug. He was staring, rather wide-eyed, at the juggling balls. At her. He suddenly realized she was looking at him. "Er. I have brought the wine, lady. May I pour for you?"

Meb set the balls down, carefully. They were as precious as . . . no, more precious than the rubies of the Prince of Alba. She'd helped Finn to salt the sea and the river with those. She smiled at the thought. The servitor thought she was smiling at him and smiled back tremulously. "We're so glad to see you, lady. People were praying for your coming."

It only got more complicated.

He poured wine, looked around quickly. "Don't trust him, m'lady. The old king hated Medraut even when he was a little boy. And I changed the wine Aberinn poured in the cellar," he said quietly.

Prince Medraut had dressed himself hastily, not waiting for his manservant to return from calling Cardun. There were few others he could trust in this place, but the chatelaine would lose her place and probably her life if he lost his position here.

The woman arrived, as he was attempting to dress his hair. "Pellas told me the story," she said, taking over. "I think it is a trick, Medraut." In public of course she gave him the honorifics he was due. In private . . . she was still his aunt. "One can't be sure, yet, of course. But this is similar to the way Aberinn got rid of Regent Degen. The false feint and the death thrust, if you like."

"It's hard to see just what sort of death thrust a young woman could manage, Aunt. And the sea-window is restored."

"There could be several ways a competent practitioner could arrange that," said Cardun, who was far better at the theory of magic, even if her practice was feeble, for one of the house of Lyon. "The stones have the memory. Aberinn could set it up very easily. So could several others, but with the spells set to suppress magework within the castle, Aberinn is your principal suspect. And you know as well as I do that it is really his voice that stands behind the silence of lords. He is the reason the nobles' houses do not call for you to become the king."

Medraut sighed. His aunt was driven by that ambition. It had its attractions, but being the regent was quite adequate in this dying, riven kingdom. He just wanted to stay that, because the alternative was to lose his head to a successor regent. "I was there. If it was trickery, Cardun, she must be the greatest actress in the world. She might be this Defender, and in some ways that might a relief. And now, I'd better go. Some fool will have called Aberinn, and I'd rather be there when they meet."

Few guards were courageous enough to go and disturb the mage in his tower, no matter what had happened. And thus the guard sought his peculiar out, telling her the story.

Vivien was just as afraid of Mage Aberinn. And she had even more reason to be afraid, for with Aberinn, that which she knew,was worse than the guards' imaginings. Part of her hoped, though, that what the man-at-arms said was true.

She went to the tower. Knocked on the heavy door. It opened by itself. He liked those sorts of small

displays of power. He was sitting at his workbench...
but he had been waiting, she was sure. "So Prince
Medraut is dead. And they sent you to tell me. There
are no secrets in Dun Tagoll," he said, smiling his
humorless smile.

"No. Prince Medraut is alive. The Defender has
come! The first part of the prophecy..."

"What?" He stood up, disturbing the model he had
been at work on. "The royal chamber..."

"The sea-window is back. And a young woman
calling herself Anghared has saved Prince Medraut."

"Anghared! Who would dare use a name like that?
Don't tell me—our all too clever manipulative regent.
The commons will assume that the royal names are
worn by the royal house," he walked to the door,
shooing her out in front of him, like a hen. "What
has happened to her?"

"They've taken her to the old queen's withdrawing
room. They fetch her food and drink. She said she
was hungry."

"I'd better see this convenient miracle," said the
mage. "A neat ploy by Medraut. I wonder if she has
any real skills? You are to watch and befriend her."

"But the queen's window..." protested Vivien.

"A trick that could easily enough be done...once.
She could even merely spring the spell, without any
skill herself."

There was a sound from the doorway and the
servitor straightened up, bowed, as Prince Medraut
entered with another man in once-white robes and a
beard that he should have washed after eating egg,
and of course the obligatory couple of guards. Meb

sipped the wine. If this was good wine...she'd had worse in her travels with Finn. But not much worse.

More servants came in, carrying platters. It did look something of a feast.

Medraut bowed his head politely. "Ah, Lady Anghared. May I introduce myself more formally. I am Prince Medraut ap Corrin, Earl of Telas, and Prince Regent of Greater Lyonesse. And this is our court magician, Aberinn. I trust you are enjoying your wine?"

Meb had always been a poor hand at lying. So she stuck to a nod and a smile.

"Allow me to cut you a piece of this bird," he said, slicing into what appeared to be a plump roasted pheasant and placing it on the trencher that another servant had set before her. Meb knew it was a high honor to be served with choice portions cut by the lord of the hall, with his own dagger. And besides she wasn't sure she still had one to eat with. Mostly a rough hand-carved wooden spoon would have done for the pottage of most inns and fingers and a knife for the meat they might have grilled on the way. Here...there were platters and silver salts.

They were watching her rather carefully. She picked up the slice of breast and ate...

It wasn't pheasant. It wasn't even bird. It was bread. And stale, at that. Fortunately, she eaten a fair amount of that in her time. The pickings as a glee-man's apprentice had often been slim, but they were still better than they'd been growing up in Cliff Cove. There was always enough fish, of course. But bread was quite a luxury at times, and a girl-child often got the stale crusts. She washed it down with some wine.

The magician and prince relaxed visibly.

"If we might ask, lady, where did you come from?" said the magician.

There seemed no harm in telling him. "A place called Tasmarin."

They looked blank at the name.

"Ah. A far-off realm, no doubt?" said the prince.

Meb was tired. The stale bread was better than nothing, as was the sour wine. But her stomach, and temper, were set up for more. "How would I know? I don't even really know where I am now."

"You are in the Kingdom of Lyonesse, in the great fortress of Dun Tagoll, the crowning-place of the Kings of the West," intoned the magician as if reciting a poem.

"Never heard of it, I am afraid," said Meb with a yawn.

"Er. Perhaps more wine. Some of these little cakes?" asked Prince Medraut, into the awkward silence.

She had no doubt, now, that those too would turn into stale bread. "No, thank you," she said curtly. "Why are you doing all this?"

The two looked at each other. "Because it was foretold that the return of the sea-window would come with the guardian against the sons of the Dragon," said Prince Medraut.

Meb decided not to tell them that Tasmarin was a place ruled by dragons, or just how she felt about a specific dragon. "What do you mean 'the return of the sea-window'?"

The magician shrugged. "There has not been a window in the antechamber since Queen Gwenhwyfach leapt from it with her baby son. She was the greatest of the summonsers, a powerful mage and much loved. The king was heartbroken, and had the window walled up. The masons closed it off, and then, when that was not enough for the king, they knocked out part of the wall, tore out the lintel and the sill, and built it again so there was no trace of the window."

"Oh." It seemed a very inadequate response. But Meb couldn't think of anything else to say, so she sipped her wine, and thought about it instead. She didn't want to tell them that their prophecy was wildly inaccurate and the window, she now realized, had been something she needed to escape through, and that the magic of the dvergar artifact on her neck obviously still amplified her own magical skills, even here, far from Tasmarin. She didn't want it! A hand went to her throat. And then Finn's words about the dragon necklace with its wood-opal eyes came back to her. It wouldn't stay lost, not even if she buried it or threw it into the sea. And would it be better used by the likes of either of these two men? She already trusted neither.

Someone knocked on the door. It was a warrior, in a dripping cloak. "Prince Medraut. The enemy have been sighted from Dun Argol. They look a great host, burning and plundering as they come."

The prince tugged his hair. Sighed. "M'lady. We will talk further, later. I must consult with my war leaders and wizards. The women will come to escort you to your chamber. You have not come at a time of peace, I am afraid."

It looked more like she'd come at a time of murder, war and conspiracy. She sipped the wine. Looked at the "feast" she had largely ignored. Out of the corner of her eye she realized the far items looked

like hunks of bread. So she turned her head. Yes...
on the periphery of vision it was all various shaped
lumps of coarse bread. She had to wonder why, and
about the wine.

Was this what they had? Was it just for her? She
hoped it was the latter, if they were facing war and
probably siege. So... this was where she'd come from
as a baby, was it?

It made Cliff Cove seem quite attractive.

A stiff-looking matron came in, her washed-out
blonde hair done up in tight coiled braids and disapproval written on every line of her plump face. She
had plenty to write the disapproval onto, but the
application of powder and paint plastered over some
of it. She looked Meb up and down as if examining
a side of stockfish from a not-very-reputable dealer.
"You are the Lady Anghared?" she said in a chilly
voice. "Lady" was definitely questionable. "I am the
Lady Cardun, the Chatelaine of Dun Tagoll. I was
told that you would require a bedchamber and water
and suitable attire."

Given the matron's attitude, it was clear she felt
Meb should be sleeping in the attic on a straw pallet
with three others and a lot more fleas, and given a
kitchen trull's castoffs. Meb had already begun to think
she might be better off leaving, even via the window
that had once been blocked off, no matter the sharp
rocks below. Maybe her face showed it, because one
of the two women in the chatelaine's wake, the one
with the spare, lined face smiled sympathetically at
her, and said in a quiet, much kinder voice. "Oh, Lady
Cardun, she looks about to fall over. And so young
too. Come, child. We'll see you safely bestowed."

Obediently Meb stood up. Tears pricked at her eyes. She hadn't had much female sympathy, or company, since the raiders had destroyed her home. And even there . . . she'd been an outsider. "Thank you," she said gruffly. "I am very tired. It's been a long and awful day."

"With Prince Medraut and Mage Aberinn at the end of it," said the sympathetic one.

= Chapter 3 =

A CHEMICAL BRINE STEAMED AND FROTHED AS IT gushed through the new tear in the black road that crossed the shattered ash lands. Something hissed up from a fissure, taking shape into one of the elemental creatures of the smokeless fire. Díleas backed away, barking. So did the travelers. "Back on the carts, men, it's one of the big Beng!"

Fionn had spotted what he had been hoping for, deep down. This dolerite dyke had blocked it, and now the creatures of smokeless flame had cracked that. The bells that were ringing from the carts helped to hide the sound he made, as he sat down next to Díleas and scraped rock-sign onto the stone.

The fire-demon was less easily fooled than the travelers. "What does one of your kind want here in our demesnes?"

"Yours? I thought you liked places of ash and smoke and flame," said Fionn mockingly, answering in the creature's own language. "Not such a place as this is about to become. I am one of the advance surveyors."

31

"Surveyors?" hissed the creature.

"Yes, that is what they call those who make accurate measurements and determine the boundaries. Those are busy changing," said Fionn, with exaggerated patience, as if explaining to a simpleton.

"We changed them, in order to stop this endless incursion into our lands!"

"You did, did you?" mocked Fionn. "I was of the impression you liked incursions. Devoured their essences or fed them to your pets."

"These have protections. We seldom get one. So we have broken their road."

"And that has broken your land. You should have guessed that when you got the brine-boil instead of the lava," said Fionn, with all the confidence in the world.

"We frequently have fumaroles," said the creature of smokeless flame.

"Do they usually get cooler?" asked Fionn, his voice even. He had redirected sufficient heat downward for that to start to happen. All that heat was cracking the dome far below now. When there had been tiny fissures . . . the water had boiled and picked up minerals on the way up. But, if those fissures grew, more water would flow from the strata below. Water that had been trapped down there for millennia, under increasing pressure. A lot of water. Fionn chuckled to himself. The fire creatures would hate it, but it might help their ashpit world regenerate. They were running out of coal measures, and once, after all, it must have been wet and warm here to grow the forests to make the coal. It would ease the balance of forces here. So good to achieve two things at once. And seeing the look of startlement on the creature of smokeless flame's features—you couldn't really say "face"—was a joy.

Ah, he'd forgotten the pleasure of being the trickster in the last little while. The wider worlds *needed* him. Aside from rebalance, there was the pure delight in overturning the expected and changing the order of things.

The creature of smokeless flame left hastily, with no further words, not even of farewell, or of threat. No doubt it had gone to consult with its superiors. They had a habit of doing that, whenever confronted with something different. They were so hierarchical they struggled with independent thought. It was their weakness. Which was just as well, really. They needed some weak points.

Fionn watched its departure with some satisfaction. And went on talking. He did the fire-creature's speech part too, while he backed up to the cart, and felt for the catch to their hideaway with his foot. The travelers would be hiding their heads from illusions, most likely. And anyone peering out could see his head and hands. He was just as dexterous with his feet as with his hands, and he'd a lot of experience with hide-aways. He deserved a fee for this, besides the sheer pleasure of doing it.

In a way, he thought, he had taught his Scrap of humanity, and she in turn had taught him. He told her that there were many ways of solving a problem. She'd showed him that his ideas were still quite constrained to maintaining the status quo. His purpose was retaining the balance, but it didn't have to be same balance—just so long as it was balanced.

A few moments later he was back at the edge of

the flowing, fuming stream through the blue-black stone of the causeway. It was running stronger and fuller now, and definitely not as hot. He put his hand on Díleas's head. "Wait. It will get cooler."

So what was it about him, and her, that would have unbalanced Tasmarin, that meant she had had to go back to where she came from?

It didn't make much sense to the planomancer.

There was a need for balance, but why the two of them? In terms of energy all things were different, but not that different that they could not be balanced out.

The traveler Arvan emerged from the cart. Fionn noticed he had his bow again, arrow on the string. "What were you talking to the Beng about, stranger?"

Fionn had spoken in the tongue of the creature of smokeless flame. There was no need of course. They were nearly as adept linguists as he was, but it unsettled them to have someone address them in their own tongue. He wondered how the Scrap was coping with a language that would be strange to her . . . only that dvergar device might just help. She'd learned to read fast enough with its help. He grinned at the traveler, cheered by that thought, and pleased with his bit of work here. Force-lines were realigning already. "I just ruined his day. What did you want me to say to him?"

"Nothing. They're tricky, those ones. You know his language, though." That was outright suspicion.

Fionn shrugged. "Rather a case of he knows mine. They have the gift of tongues, those ones. All the better to lie to you with. So I told him a truth, and made him very unhappy."

"And what was that? You have a spell against them?"

"I wish. But they have a dislike for water. The merrows could sell you a few charms, if you had goods they were interested in. I've a protection I bought from them for a song and some entertainment. The Beng tried me, and the merrow spell has brought a counter to the demon. I pointed out to the creature that water is wet. Wet, and cooling down, and spreading out. It didn't like that and has probably gone to consult with its master. We'd best be away before the master comes here too. They can put powerful compulsions on people, and the bigger they are, the stronger they are. We'll have to contrive a bridge of some kind, but we'll be able to cross it. The dog and I can swim it if need be. By now it'll be like a very hot bath."

Díleas growled and shook himself. Looked suspiciously at the water.

"He doesn't like baths," said Fionn, grinning.

The traveler burst out laughing. "Same as most dogs. Usually when the Beng find us here, they torment us. Send their creatures to attack us. We've got the bells and other protections on the carts, but the best we can do is to stay in them and keep moving until we get out of the local lordling's territory. Never seen anyone chase one off before."

"I wish I could chase them off. It was just the merrow spell doing it, and a lucky happenstance. But the chances are next time I won't be near a lot of hidden water, and the merrow spells need water. You don't happen to have a plank about those carts of yours? And maybe a rope? I could get you a start on a way across the water. It's cooling, but I wouldn't swim it for a while."

"Plank?" asked one of the other travelers, curiously.

"Yes," said Fionn, pointing. "There is a rock there, see. I could put the plank out to it, and then another— or maybe a long jump and I'll be over. I can take a rope over and tie it off for you. There is some rock on the other side you might make something of a bridge with. Or you could take a cart apart and make one. But you probably don't want to hang about here too long. The Beng will come back."

In a place where time ran slowly enough to at least sustain the illusion of immortality, where even free energy danced slow minuets, and the beings called the First dwelled, occupied by and large with passions of immortality, beyond most mortal ken. The First were not a matter for easy understanding. The dragon Fionn was one of the few beings that actually remembered them, which was . . . less than desirable. They had become distant and disconnected observers of their immeasurably vast creation.

It had taken a human glimpse within their roil of energy, interconnected as all energy was, to let them know that after millennia there might be a problem that they had not foreseen. That they had taken no steps to prevent. That a group mind made of the descendants of fractions of themselves could exist briefly. That something rather like their own power could be exerted by it—temporarily, it was true.

They didn't like that.

But there was a worse possibility. And they always looked at possible futures.

The situation could become permanent.

Food did not interbreed with its predator. They had designed it like that for that precise reason.

Paradoxically, the very powers they had built into Fionn made him quite immune to their manipulations, and near invisible to them as a result. The same could not be said of the dog.

But if they destroyed the dog, they would be blind to Fionn's doings and movement.

The dragon would not be easy to destroy, and the human had taken a part of them into herself. That made her difficult to deal with. The energy that flowed into her had been supposed to take control, not become a slave itself.

It would have to destroy all of them, by proxy.

Fortunately it had an almost infinite supply of proxies.

Unfortunately, the planomancer would be able to detect and counter their movements. They would need to be subtle.

"Right," said Fionn, looking at the rocking plank he'd set up. "Come, Díleas. I'll have to carry you."

"You're out of your mind, gleeman," said Arvan.

Privately, Fionn agreed with him. But he knew humans too well. When they stopped to think about it, they'd start getting even more suspicious about his dealings with the fire creature. And they had weapons that could hurt the dog. He could kill them if they tried, of course. Had he been any other dragon, he would have been free to devour them anyway. Had he been any other dragon he might have desired to do so. But he was Fionn: the last of those who were made first, to see intelligent life flourished. Best to get on the narrow board and away. The water running through the gap would not kill him. Not now.

The acids and toxins were already much diluted. But it might still be too hot for the dog. He'd have to throw Díleas if he fell. "Ach. I was something of an acrobat in a traveling show once." He looked at the plank. It was twelve cubits long and none too wide, or thick. It came from under the canvas of the cart, from the arch where it helped to spread the load. Now it stretched to a rock in the middle of the flow. "Let's put it on edge, and jam it. It'll be narrower, but stronger."

"You're definitely mad. Leave the dog here. He's a good, valuable dog," said Arvan.

Díleas growled at him, as if to prove he might be valuable, but he wasn't good, and danced onto his hind feet. Fionn reached down a hand and said "up," and Díleas jumped up, putting his front feet over one shoulder. He really still was a pup with more fur than body.

"It's like he understands every word you say!"

"You wouldn't say that if you knew how long it took me to teach him that trick," said Fionn, sticking out a hand for balance and stepping out onto the narrow plank. And falling off it. He was still above the rock so no harm was done.

"Give up, gleeman," said the caravan leader, shaking his head.

"I have hardly begun to try and you want me to give up!" said Fionn. "No. I can do it, I'll wager."

One of the younger travelers snorted. "How much?"

"Well," said Fionn. "I haven't got much." He stuck his free hand into his pouch, felt about, past the nine golden coins he'd removed from their hidden trove. They had plenty more. Never pluck a peacock bare naked, and he'd give you plenty of tail feathers over time, was Fionn's feeling. He fished out some coppers. Counted them with great show. "Nine. I'll give you nine coppers if I fall in. What do you dare wager? A silver for my copper?"

"Huh. Gold, I reckon," said the traveler. It was Dravko, one of the men who had been discussing what price he'd fetch as a slave in Annvn. "But what's the point? You fall in there and you're not coming back, you fool."

"I'll set the coins on the rock here," said Fionn, suiting the deed to the word. "Then you get them if I lose. Give me a coil of rope, and I'll tie it off and toss the two ends back, and you can tie them onto your cart. With one line for my hands and one for my feet I can walk across easily."

"And then we lose a coil of rope when you fall in," said Dravko scathingly, but looking at the coins.

Fionn shrugged. "No entertainment for nothing."

"A coil of rope is worth nine coppers," said Arvan. "Give him one, Nikos."

So Nikos did. It was a finely braided rope, and worth, Fionn reckoned, at least eight coppers.

Fionn took a few dozen steps back and measured it all carefully with his eye . . . and sprinted at the plank. It was only three long strides to the rock, with a bit of a wobble in the middle, and he was on the midstream rock. The tricky part had not been crossing, but stopping in time to avoid landing in the water beyond—or dropping the twisting dog, who squirmed loose and bounded around on the lump of rock. Fionn leaned out and levered up the plank—a feat of strength most humans could not have managed, and swung it over.

The other bank was not as far off—a mere nine cubits or so. Fionn laid the plank on the widest edge, with a good overlap.

As Fionn inspected it, Díleas ran over it, nearly but not quite falling in. He stood on the far side, and barked at Fionn. Fionn shrugged. Walked along it. It bent quite alarmingly, but did not break.

On the far side, Fionn, not quite off the plank, did an artistic stumble and jumped for the rock, kicking the plank off its rest and into the water, but gaining the far side, rolling. It was pure showmanship, but the fool dog was not proof against arrows. Someone could still decide they were demons. He stood up and dusted himself off. "Now I just need somewhere to tie the rope to, and I can come back and fetch my coins, and my winnings. Come, dog."

They walked off. They must have been a good seventy yards further along the causeway when one of the travelers said: "I don't think he is coming back." Fionn had keen enough ears, even at this range, to hear them, just as he'd heard the quiet talk on the price that he might fetch as a slave.

Fionn whistled cheerfully and lengthened his stride. "I'd run ahead, dog," he said quietly. "They might not have gone through with selling us, but soon someone is going to work out that I didn't leave nine copper coins for no reason. They didn't cheat me too badly for the price of a rope though. It might be useful. And you nearly fell in, you fool dog."

Díleas looked at the red, dragon-hide boots as if to say, "they have poor grip," and then bounded away along the hexagonal stones. Fionn walked still faster. He did hear distant yells, but there were no arrows.

And it was comforting to have a little gold about him again. It always made a dragon feel good, in a way that coppers did not.

The causeway was an interesting thing. He'd never run across it in his many earlier wanderings across the multidimensional ring before, and yet it apparently led to places he once used to visit, and visit quite often.

Had the structure changed? And what would reintegration of Tasmarin do to it all?

If Fionn had not had to walk the worlds looking for his Scrap of humanity, he'd have been dead keen to find out. He rather liked changes, after millennia of the same.

═ Chapter 4 ═

MEB AWOKE TO THE SOUND OF SOMEONE IN HER room. She had only vague, exhausted memories of how she got to this bed. Of the women, talking around her. But the sound of someone there, now, trying to keep quiet was enough to make her instinctively nervous. She opened her eyes just a crack. Unless she was due to be murdered with a ewer by a young, scared-looking female, she was in no danger. There were towels and a basin set on the tall kist already, and a wisp of steam suggested that the water was hot. It brought back to Meb that her last wash had been in a horse trough, and that had not had warm water in it.

Once, not so very long ago, washing herself all over had been something undertaken only when unavoidable. Usually in spring. Now she itched to do so. Well, maybe just itched. The bed linen was fine, but there was undoubtedly a flea in bed with her.

Her doing something about that itch nearly had the young girl pour the ewer down her own front. "I am sorry, your ladyship. I didn't mean to disturb! Only, Lady Cardun said..."

Meb blinked. Your ladyship? "I don't bite. I've got a dog who does, but he's not here." She swallowed. Díleas. How she missed his unswerving, unquestioning loyalty. But he couldn't be here. She'd told him to look after Fionn, when she'd hugged him farewell. It was almost as if he understood. Obviously, the distress must have showed in her face.

The serving wench forgot her own fear in seeing it. "Is . . . is something the matter, lady? Can I do anything?"

"Just missing my dog," said Meb, her voice cracking a little.

The serving wench nodded. "We always had a dog, too. And then, when I came to take service . . . he ate a blowfish and died. You'd think a dog living on the foreshore would know better. But he always was eating some rubbish."

Meb nodded. "There was always trouble with Wulfstan about dogs and the stockfish. I grew up in a fishing village."

The serving wench gaped. "You, my lady? But you've the power!"

"I'm not too sure what you're talking about," said Meb, although she did indeed have a very good idea. It struck her that it might be a reasonable idea to find out a little about this world she had exiled herself to. The misery of that exile struck her again. Best to distract herself. "Tell me about this place."

The servant wench looked puzzled. "What place, lady? Dun Tagoll?"

"That's this castle, right? I know that, but it means nothing to me. I've never heard of it."

"But . . . but it is the greatest castle in all Lyonesse!"

said the maid. "Everyone knows that. Even the forest people."

"I'd never even heard of Lyonesse until last night. And now I am here," explained Meb.

"So, where are you from, my lady?" asked the maid.

The "my lady" was beginning to irritate her. "I was from the island of Yenfar, the demesne of Lord Zuamar—but he's dead and no loss. Tasmarin was my world. And my name is Meb."

"Oh. They said you were the Lady Anghared. That's one of the royal names, lady. They don't use it anymore after Queen Gwenhwyfach died. Only the royal line were called that. It's usually used by . . . by the daughters of kings."

"Oh. Finn said that was my birth name. But no one ever called me that."

"Not even your mother, lady?" asked the maid.

"Hallgerd called me Meb," said Meb resolutely. "And she was the only mother I ever knew. The sea spat me out on the beach at her feet when I was a baby."

The girl wrinkled her forehead. "But your father Finn knew your name was Anghared?"

The very thought of Finn as a father made Meb laugh. Not that he hadn't helped her grow up a bit. "I think you should put the ewer down. What's your name? Are you needed elsewhere?"

The girl shook her head. "No, my lady. I'm to wait on you. I've never attended a lady before."

Someone didn't think much of the "Lady Anghared" then, thought Meb, sending her a tirewoman who was so new she still had fish scales on her hands. Well, the girl suited Meb better than someone she couldn't talk to. "So I am supposed to give you orders, am I?"

The girl nodded, looking worried.

"Well, my first order is to put the ewer down before you spill any more of it. And then to tell me your name."

The girl set the ewer down, carefully. Curtseyed. It was plainly not something she had done often. "Neve, m'lady."

Meb smiled. "Now come and sit down on the bed and answer my questions."

"Oh, I can't sit on the bed, m'lady!" said Neve, horrified.

"You can. I just told you to. And I also told you my name was Meb."

"But . . . but I'll get into terrible trouble from Lady Cardun."

Meb got up. The stone floor was strewn with rushes, but still cold on her feet. The door was heavy and had a bar. So she closed it, and put the bar down. And took her cold feet back into the bed. "Now she won't know," said Meb. "Sit." She'd hold off on the "m'lady" a little.

The girl giggled nervously and did, at the very foot of the bed. On the very edge. "I . . . I'm very new to this work, lady . . . um, Meb. I don't want to lose my place. Times are hard."

"I'll do my best not to lose it for you. I promise I won't tell anyone you sat on the bed while I asked you questions," said Meb, smiling at her. "I just . . . I'm just lost. I don't know anything at all about this place. I should be doing your job if anything. I'm not a lady. I can't dance, or play music, or do embroidery or even ride. I rode a donkey once. I fell off that. I should be a kitchen maid, if they didn't turn me out. I don't know why they're doing this to me. Who do they think I am? I . . . I don't want to be turned out either. There's an army out there." Armies had a certain reputation. Meb decided that if she couldn't have Finn . . . they wouldn't have her either.

The girl shrugged. "Ach, there is always some army. Every few months, it seems. They'll be gone in a week or two when the moon is full. Or we will. Then we try and get our lives back together. The nobles send messages and play at politics and we try to make a living again."

That seemed a rather fatalistic acceptance of war. "You're always at war? Who are you at war with?" No wonder they were enchanting stale bread. Growing crops and farming during a war were going to be difficult.

The girl, her round face serious, started counting on her fingers. "Albion, Brocéliande, Albar, Annvn, Vanaheim, the Blessed Isles. There are more . . . My gamma said in Queen Gwenhwyfach and King Geoph's time it wasn't so, but it has been almost ever since. And there was much magic then, and there was peace and plenty."

"Hmm," said Meb. "I bet she also said us young people don't know how lucky we are."

The girl giggled so much that it shook the bed. Nodded. "It was all rich and wonderful and we're soft and disrespectful, and don't know what hard work means. I love my gamma Elis, but if you believed her, there were spriggans in every pile of rock, piskies in every field and bog, muryans everywhere, knockers underground, and even dragons on the hilltops. Dragons, I ask you!"

Gradually Meb began to build a picture of the place she had ended up in. A craggy coastline to the west, with Dun Tagoll in its center, with a fertile plain bounded by mountains to east and north, and the shifting sand coast across the bleak moorlands, to more mountains in the south. Ruled by men—not the alvar, or the dragons. Under almost constant attack from the forces of darkness itself, cursed because the kingdom had to be ruled by a regent, and its magic needed a king. And the king needed its magic . . . not Prince Medraut.

"Him? No, m'lady. He's scarcely noble enough to raise a magefire on his blade. Without Aberinn the wizard, Dun Tagoll would have nothing magical. You'd barely think the prince was of the old blood, but he's good at turning troubles to his advantage, as they say."

"Why?" asked Meb. "I mean why would you say you'd barely think he was of the old blood?"

The girl looked puzzled. "Because he has the magic, m'lady. Only the House of Lyon has that. That is why they rule."

Men ruled. Meb shook her head. It was just so different from Tasmarin. And then the fact that magical ability marked the noble house. On Tasmarin the use of magic by a human would have gotten one killed. Here . . . It turned out that even the court magician was a royal by-blow. A very ancient and much feared by-blow.

"He's awful, m'lady. Been here through three regents. They say he keeps dead men's bones in that tower of his. It stinks enough, and no mortal ever gets in there to clean, unless it's the prince himself sweeping the floor. You be very careful of him, m'lady. You can't lie to him. He pounces on you the minute you offer him falsehood. He has the power. It's his great engines that keep Lyonesse free."

Meb avoided saying she didn't think much of the freedom. "Engines of war? Great catapults?"

"Oh no. Magical engines. They defend us from the magics and the enchantress of Shadow Hall and her dead creatures. And it's there the great engine of change is, m'lady. We hear it clanking, but it's few who have seen it."

That all left Meb none the wiser. Dead creatures and sorceresses were something they accepted as sort of normal here. So was magic by humans. Dragons were not. "So what's this bit about the sons of the dragon? This prophecy?"

The girl looked at her, openmouthed. And then recited:

> Till from the dark past, Defender comes,
>   and forests walk, the rocks talk,
>   till the mountain bows to the sea,
> Till the window returns to the sea-wall
>   of great Dun Tagoll,
>   beware, prince, beware, Mage Aberinn,
>   mage need.
> For only she can hold the sons of
>   Dragon,
> Or Lyonesse will be shredded and
>   broken and burned.
> Only she can banish the shades,
>   and find the bowl of kings.
> Mage need, mage need.

"Er. So who are the sons of the Dragon?" asked Meb. Neve shrugged. "It could be the Vanar—that's who I think it is—in their dragon ships, or the Saxons under the white dragon banner or there are princes of the middle kingdoms who call themselves the sons of the dragons, whose banner is a red wyrm. No one knows. Not even Aberinn. They say he fitted and foamed at the mouth when he spoke the words."

"I wish I could have seen that. I didn't like him much. He had egg in his beard."

Neve snickered. "My father says men with beards should only eat boiled eggs. Or have a wife to watch them."

Someone knocked on the door. A sort of perfunctory knock . . . and pushed it. And then knocked harder. "Lady Anghared. Lady Anghared, are you within?" By the look of terror on Neve's face it could only be the chatelaine. What was her name? Cardun. She was nearly enough to frighten Meb, and best on the far side of the door.

"Who is it?" said Meb, grabbing Neve's arm as the girl wanted to run to the door.

"It is I. Lady Cardun," said a chilly, haughty voice from outside.

"I am busy with my ablutions," said Meb, very proud of that word. She'd heard it on their journeying, and had to ask Finn what it meant. And then she realized . . . it wasn't the same word by shape or sound, coming out of her mouth. It was not the language she had spoken all her life. Neither was the rest of what she'd said. And in this language, Díleas actually meant "faithful." How . . . how had she learned another language? Learned it as if she had spoken it all her life.

There was a moment's silence from outside the door. "Do you need any assistance? A message has come that we are to take you to Mage Aberinn's tower."

Meb looked at the window. It was far too narrow. She touched her throat, and the hidden dragon that hung there, and courage came to her. "Thank you. But no. I have my tirewoman to attend to me. I shall be out when I am finished," she said, doing her best to sound like a spoiled alvar princess.

It must have worked. Cardun sounded slightly chastened. "The girl is new. Is she satisfactory? I could send some of my women..."

"She is exactly what I want, thank you. A perfect choice. I would like her to continue to attend to me," said Meb, trying not to laugh at Neve's expression. "And now, I will need to finish washing and robing, if you do not mind."

"Oh. Yes, my apologies," said Cardun from outside the door, sounding as if the words would choke her.

It was a good, thick door. Meb was at it, listening. No footsteps. Huh. She motioned Neve—who looked like she might just burst—to silence. She tiptoed back to the bed and poured water from the ewer into the basin. "Next time," she said loudly, with a wink to Neve, "see the water is hotter."

"Yes, m'lady," said Neve. "Do you want me to fetch more?"

"No. Just remember in future," said Meb, in what she hoped was a suitably long-suffering manner for a noblewoman, putting up with inferior service.

Meb washed, and went to see what clothes she had. And then she was truly glad of Neve, because she had absolutely no idea of how to put the garment on. The woolen cloth was fine-woven, and while, as far as she was concerned, gleeman colors were her colors, not this pale blue, and breeches were more practical than skirts, and anything was more practical than this dangly robe thing, it was still rather nice to have fine new cloth against her skin.

Neve brushed her hair. "How would you like it put up, m'lady?" she asked, nervously.

Meb had absolutely no idea. She had a feeling her fisherfolk plait and pin would not do. Anyway, she'd lost the wooden pin to the sea, before the merrow took her hair. And she was willing to bet Neve was not much of a hand at it either. She needed something like that combination of comb and hair clip the alvar women had used at the Alba soiree she and Finn had walked through disguised as elegant alvar butterflies. It was something that could look beautiful and keep the hair out of your eyes. She'd truly envied one. She recreated the filigree curlicues of it in her mind, thinking of the details.

It would appear she could summons small items to her; she marveled, looking at the intricate, ornate piece of silver in her hand. She hoped the alvar that had owned it would forgive her. She also hoped she wasn't unbalancing things too much, as Finn said her magic did. She'd never understood that aspect of the black dragon's work. She handed the pin-comb to the startled Neve. "It's worn at an angle." She shook her combed hair forward. "Slide it from the front, to pull the hair away from my face, and then slide the pin in, once the back corner is past my ear."

Neve did. "Oh, it's beautiful, m'lady," she said, holding a mirror so that Meb could see. "But . . . but it's not how it is done here."

Meb looked closely at the reflection. Of course she'd remembered it perfectly, capturing the details in her mind's eye. But she'd not really realized that it was filigree dragons—very Tasmarin alvar. The silver of them showed bright against her dark hair. Looking at Neve's tight braids, here at least she was no longer the wavy-haired brunette among the straight yellow thatch heads of the fisherfolk of Cliff Cove or Tarport. "I am not from here. I don't think I could pretend to be."

She stood up, and Neve held the mirror. She wasn't sure she recognized the stranger in it. "Well. That will just have to do. What do we have for footwear, because I don't think my water diviner's boots will do, will they? They're the best boots I've ever owned."

Neve looked at them, critically. "They're good boots. But, well, they look like, well... men's wear. Lady Vivien—she sent the clothes and the combs with me, sent some lachet boots for you. They're good boots."

Meb tried them. "They'll do. But they're too narrow. I have wide feet. Finn said it was from going barefoot. He had to get the cordwainer to change his lasts to make them for me."

Neve looked impressed. "Specially made just for you? This Finn, he was your father?"

"My master," said Meb quietly. "I love him very much. But..."

Neve nodded understandingly, although Meb was absolutely sure she did not even start to understand. But Meb wasn't going to try to explain. Instead she walked to the door. "Do you think I get to break my fast before going to see the mage? Or does he feed me on the bones of dead men?"

Neve shuddered. "I don't know, m'lady. No one goes to his tower. I told you. I don't know what is in there."

Meb took a deep breath. "Time to find out, I suppose. Can you show me where I have to go?"

"Well, there's an inner door, but it's locked. I'll have to take you into the courtyard."

Meb let Neve lead her down the flagged passages and up the stone stairwell, onto the battlements and up the stair to the door of the mage's tower. It faced the narrow causeway of land that linked the almost island of Dun Tagoll to the rest of the lands beyond. Meb looked out at those, across fields and forests toward the distant high fells tinged purple with blooming heather.

The door swung open abruptly, before she'd even gathered herself to knock. Neve squeaked and retreated behind Meb as Mage Aberinn loomed out at them. His beard, in daylight, was longer and less clean than she'd realized the night before. "I didn't know I had sent for two of you," he said curtly.

Meb knew she ought to be afraid, but instead, his manner just made her angry. "My mother told me not to go alone into strange towers with men I did not know," she said coolly. Actually, Hallgerd had not ever quite said that, but variants of the same usually involving bushes, huts or fishing boats. And she hadn't been too concerned about whether Meb knew the men or not. But it would do.

Aberinn raised his eyebrows. "Your mother. And who was your mother? Do you remember her?" he seemed to find that very important.

Meb remembered what Neve had said about not being able to lie to him. She thought . . . well, she should try it. "I ought to. I lived with her for seventeen years," she said.

It seemed to take the wind out the mage's sails a little. "Ah. Well, I suppose your reputation should be considered. Yes, bring her along."

Neve looked as if she might faint in pure terror. "Me? I was just showing m'lady the way," she squeaked.

"Just think what stories you'll have to tell the others," said Meb, smiling an unspoken "please" at her.

"Of course, she'll do as she's told," said the mage, an edge coming back to his voice.

The fisherman's daughter took a deep breath. "For you, m'lady."

The first interior room of the tower, reached after climbing a short stair was rather a disappointment after all that. It was a large and comfortable room, with a fireplace, and a number of tables, and book- and equipment-filled shelves lining the walls. It was, unlike the magician's beard, very tidy and ordered. No spider webs, no dust, no disorder. The tables were full of various items being worked on, but even the tools were set out in very precise neat rows, and components tended to be set out in what almost seemed geometric patterns. There were no dead men's bones. In fact, Meb couldn't even see a thing made of anything that was not metal, let alone human remains. The nearest to "human" anything was a model—a very precise and carefully made model—of part of the castle. It was opened so she could see into the rooms, with every item in them exact. It looked like a child's—a very rich child's—dream dollhouse.

That was not to say that the room looked like anything but a magician's workshop, because it didn't. The objects being worked on were strange. Some glowed with their own inner light. Odd clicking noises came from somewhere. And some things looked as if they might almost be alive. There was a bird in a gilded cage. A crow. Only it too was gilded, and appeared to be made entirely of metal.

Meb had seen dvergar artifice, and that was finer. But the magician was better than most humans at mechanical contrivance. She identified the source of least some of the clicking—a device with a series of globes suspended from thin brass rods. As it clicked, the globes moved. "What is it?"

"An orrery. It allows me to predict the positioning of certain celestial forces for my work," said Aberinn. "It is essential for the Changer. Unfortunately I have found certain inaccuracies in the movement. There may be factors outside of my knowledge operating on the spheres."

"How...how does it move?" Part of her was impelled by the peasant fisherman fear of the unknown, to not want to know, to fear the worst, to believe it demonic and evil. The other part of her mind was already imagining small imps on treadmills, or perhaps magical recitations of spells that would command it to move...

"Springs, counterweights, and various cogwheels. My magic is confined to working on things of a higher order," he said, as if reading her mind. "But I asked you to come here to establish some of your own history."

Which, thought Meb, I don't think is a good idea to tell you too much about. But she smiled. "I will be glad to answer the questions of the High Mage of Lyonesse." She wondered how much of alvar life in Tasmarin she could get him to swallow. Finn, gleemen and fishing villages seemed good subjects to avoid.

Oddly, she didn't need to. His questions seemed

designed to catch her out. To betray a knowledge of
Dun Tagoll or the people and politics of Lyonesse.
He asked about the view from home and the plants
there. Meb was happy to describe the cliffs of Cliff
Cove in loving detail. He asked about the rulers of
Tasmarin. Meb didn't think it necessary to point out
that the dead Lord Zuamar and Prince Gywndar were
a dragon and an alvar princeling. Or even that they
were both now dead. And then someone came knocking on the door. In obvious irritation Aberinn went to
open it. "What is it?" he asked the wide-eyed page.

"A message from Prince Medraut, high mage. The
prisoner . . . Earl Alois, has escaped. Magic, the prince
believes. And the woman has vanished from her chambers!"

Aberinn sighed. Shook his head. "The young lady—
and her maid—are right here. And it was obvious Alois
must have had some accomplices to get so close. This
is not magic. It is treachery." He sighed again. "Tell
the prince I am coming. Send messages to the other
Duns. He won't get far on foot."

═ Chapter 5 ═

FIONN AND DÍLEAS WALKED ON DOWN THE HEX-
agonally paved "causeway." Now out of sight of the
travelers, Fionn stuck to being a dragon. While it
was fun to tempt the creatures of smokeless flame
into folly, they tended to see too clearly to be easily
fooled. Besides, he had other things to do.

It was inevitably hot. Fionn began wondering if he
should have relieved the travelers of some water as
well as some of their gold. The smoky air was still and
thick, and Fionn traced more flows of energy rushing
through it. It felt like a thunderstorm—not just dry
lightning, but a real cloudburst of rain—was coming.
It even looked like it, with black thunderhead clouds
forming. The creatures of smokeless flame would not
like that! They'd be exerting all their power to stop it.
Things were definitely in a state of flux here, although
the causeway itself did not seem to be a problem. The
weather could always be a side effect of Tasmarin
rejoining the great planar ring of worlds. That would
have an effect on all the planes and all the sub-rings

that spun off those. Had others of his kind kept the energy of the planes balanced, while he was trapped in Tasmarin? Would Tasmarin itself remain truly stable without him? That could be awkward, as his hoard was hidden there. The few pieces of gold he had with him were a poor replacement for that.

Just when Fionn thought he'd have to carry the drooping dog, who was still determinedly pushing onwards, two things happened: firstly, it began to rain, in thick hot drops; and secondly, they came to a large stone trilith set over the causeway, which had narrowed down and become stones in the dust here. The trilith—made by hauling a huge megalith onto the top of two other upright megaliths—was big enough to have required several giants to move the vast, shaped stones. There was considerable magic about it, but yet it did not disrupt the flow of energy. Either the builders had consulted another planomancer or this was a relic of the First.

The dog wasn't waiting to examine it. He found the energy to scamper towards it.

And did not emerge onto the causeway beyond. Fionn could see that. It was singly devoid of dog.

So he lengthened his stride to walk though himself.

On the other side there was still a trilith. It was just much lower and entirely surrounded by forest. And darkness.

It was also cold, and wet. Fionn's dragonish eyes saw further into the various spectra, and also rather well in the dark. He could spot the white patches on Díleas. The dog was sitting there, looking back at the trilith. Waiting. Plainly not with much patience, by the way he stood up. There was obviously a time difference here. That happened in transitions between the planes. It was usually more gradual though.

"I am so sorry to keep you waiting," said Fionn. It occurred to him the dog probably did not understand irony, even if he understood entirely too much speech, by the way Díleas butted his hand with his nose, and started to walk down the rough track. The dog seemed to know where he was going, and there wasn't much to keep Fionn here, even if he might be tempted to have a closer look at that trilith. Human worlds had once abutted those of the demondim, so that was not that surprising, but to find a path he did not know...worried him.

Also, he was sure, just by the feel of the place, that this was not the cool damp of night in fair Annvn, but the cold terror damp of night in Brocéliande. Mind you, in the dark it was hard to tell. If they were attacked by monstrous beasts or wolves it would be the vast primal forest of Brocéliande. If it was mere bandits, it was probably Annvn. The beasts or bandits were more likely to attack a human, and Fionn had nothing against helping himself to their booty, so he altered his form accordingly. If it turned out to be Brocéliande, he'd probably regret that. It was, either way, one of the Celtic cycle. His Scrap's true name suggested she might have come from one of those.

They walked on, the wood even darker than the cloudy night sky, with trailing branches drooping over the track. A sliver of watery moonlight peeked out from the cloud as they came to a stream with a shallow ford. Díleas ran forward to drink as if there was no other water ever to be found.

Fionn was beginning to wonder whether he had

been wrong, and this was somewhere else entirely, or that times had changed for the bandits or wolves or monsters. He was also thinking about the trilith-gated road, and wondering about the mathematics of joining planes thus, and how it could be that the outcome was uncertain. He was so deep in thought he almost didn't see the afanc slithering closer to the dog. He barely had time to yell and leap as the crocodilian jaws clashed shut...

...On Fionn's cloak and the arm rolled in it, giving Díleas a chance to utter a startled yelp as he leapt back and pulled his head aside. Without Fionn's yell the monster would have had the dog, and even with it, the afanc would have had Díleas by his nose, except Fionn had stopped the jaw closing on the dog with his arm.

The downside of this was that the water monster had Fionn instead. And while dragon skin is tougher than human skin by several orders of magnitude, and the thick woolen cloak would have stopped a knife thrust, the afanc still had a truly viselike grip, and it was using all of the strength of its massive legs and beaverlike paddle tail to haul its prey back into deep dark water to drown him.

Dragons are not easy to drown, and the afanc would need more than just patience to manage that. But no one told Díleas that. The crazy dog latched itself onto the afanc's nose, burying his sharp teeth inside the sensitive nostril.

The afanc was now trying to get away, shake off the agony attached its nose, and deal with Fionn. And Fionn knew that he wouldn't drown, but there was no such guarantee for that obstinate dog.

So he stuck the fingers of his free hand into the afanc's eye, and at the same time hauled with all the strength of his legs.

And got wet. Fell over and got showered. The afanc did not like having its eye poked out. It loosed its grip briefly and, with a ripping of cloth, Fionn pulled the arm and cloak free, and dealt the afanc a wallop alongside the head that would make the monster regard anything bigger than a field mouse as hard chewing on that side for a month. As Fionn fell backwards he grabbed Díleas by the scruff of the neck and flung him back up the bank, before scrambling that way himself.

A minute later he was sitting high above the stream, wet and a little wary, with a sheepdog nearly on top of him, inspecting the damage to himself and the dog. Fionn could feel Díleas's heart pounding. Fionn realized that under all that fur, he was still not a very large dog. He was not too sure if the dog thought he was defending the dragon, or seeking a safe spot. "I think," said Fionn, "that we're in the forests of Brocéliande, dog. Which makes that thing one of the nicer creatures that inhabit these dark woods. I think my dragon form is probably wiser and safer. The blasted thing has half shredded my cloak and given me a rather sore forearm. But that could have been the end of you. And I do not want to have to explain that to your mistress. So, could you cope with riding over the water on my back? And I should probably take those boots of yours off. You've got them full of water."

Díleas held up a foot in the moonlight. The thongs were wet, easier to cut than untie, but the dragon-leather hide was still good.

Fionn became the black dragon, and was sure that

the eyes watching from the water, and quite possibly the woods, would sheer off. He wondered, as always, just what happened to his clothing and gear in such changes. For years he'd set them aside. He still was wary about a pack, but it appeared that somehow all his clothing and gear were with him, yet not with him. He could still feel the ghostly touch of them, as a dragon.

The logical answer now was to fly across the water, but he had no idea how the dog would deal with that. And it was unlikely the afanc would seek a second encounter just yet. "Up on my back," he said, wondering what would happen. The answer was readily supplied. Díleas jumped up. Stood between his wings. "If I have more trouble with the afanc, you're to jump off and make for the bank. I can deal with it, but not if I am trying to stop you getting drowned or bitten."

Díleas growled at him.

It was a good thing, reflected Fionn, that he'd taken the dragon-skin foot coverings off Díleas. The dog was getting far too big for his boots. Fionn walked slowly into the water of the ford, trying to keep his back even and steady.

He was prepared for Díleas to fall off, or even for the afanc to make another try. They really weren't very bright. What he wasn't expecting—and it nearly had him lose his footing on the slippery rocks—was for Díleas to bark at the water the whole way across. A sort of "come and get me if you dare" bark.

Fionn had to try and ignore it and concentrate on keeping his balance on the slimy, shifting, round rocks.

On the far side, having had enough of barking in his ear, Fionn said, "Off."

"Hrf?"

There was definitely a questioning note to that bark. Or was he beginning to imagine speech from the dog too? "Yes, off. You enjoyed that, didn't you? You were taunting him. Well, I suppose he did very nearly snap your nose off, and possibly would have eaten you. But—although this advice may seem odd coming from me—make sure the beast you taunt is not merely making you advertise yourself to the rest. Because unless I am very much mistaken, those are wolves howling a reply to you. You had better stay up there after all. But no barking in my ear unless you're warning me of something. My foreleg is somewhat tender from the last effort."

They walked on, and the only sound Díleas made was an occasional low growl. Looking behind himself briefly—one of the joys of dragon form was that he could, while humans could not without turning their entire bodies—Fionn saw that the dog was alert, questing, tasting the air with inquisitorial sniffs. The white fur made him quite visible, as did the glowing red bauble at his throat. There might be a need to do something to hide it.

The wolves, and anything else watching from dark woods—and there would have been things there, Fionn was certain—left the dragon alone. At length, after perhaps an hour's walk, dragon pace, they spotted a light. And smelled a more welcome scent than that of a manticore or wolf—woodsmoke.

"I think food and sleep, indoors, is called for. If you sleep outdoors in the forests of Brocéliande, something digestive, or even nastier, can happen you. The trick is going to be persuading anyone to let us in at this time of night. I think it is time for me to become a gleeman and you a gleeman's dog rather than a dragon rider. I don't think those are much more welcome than dragons. Of course in these parts you never know just who might own the farmhouse. They could be just as keen on eating us. And finding space can be an issue out here. Even the cows have to sleep indoors."

Díleas received this speech by lifting his leg on a roadside bush, from which something sneezed and retreated, making Fionn laugh and Díleas growl. "Even half the trees in Brocéliande have some sort of awareness. And many are not going to enjoy that kind of shower, dog." They walked on.

As it turned out it was not a farmhouse, but an inn at a crossroad, catering to travelers who didn't want to chance spending the night out in the forest. In these forests men traveled in groups and, as none had arrived at the inn, it had plenty of space. The crossbow-armed innkeeper wanted a vast sum to let them in, which as far as Fionn was concerned, was both iniquitous and, worse, up-front. "I should have slept under a bush," said Fionn, grumbling as he counted out silver. Copper would have been more appropriate and normal.

"You're welcome to, and the dog'll be extra," said mine host. "They make work."

Fionn sighed. "And not much chance of juggling for my supper, I suppose?"

"Supper will be another silver penny. You can juggle all you please, but half your takings will come to me. Anyway, there's no one here but a pack-peddler and a pot mender, both waiting for a group going West. The rest of their party was going to Carnac."

Mournfully Fionn fished out a coin from the corner of his pouch. Rubbed the edge of it, with a good imitation of regret. It was larger than the pennies, and gleamed. "I only have this. I'll go hungry before I give you all of it. Make change for me."

The innkeeper took it. Looked at the unfamiliar face stamped onto it—the silver pennies were so thin and worn, it was hard to tell what they were. "Where is this from?" he said suspiciously.

"How would I know? Some drunken merchant gave it to me in a tavern as payment for my juggling. The light was bad and he probably thought it was a copper. I did, then. I didn't go looking for him in the morning to ask. It's silver. Worth at least twenty pennies. Give it back if you don't want it."

The innkeeper slipped it into his pocket. "I'll give you ten for it."

"Eighteen I'll take. No less," said Fionn.

"What's money to a corpse? You're lucky to be alive out there, on your own in the dark. Wolves or monsters get most such fools."

"I didn't plan it," said Fionn. "The others ran the other way when we had our little run-in with the afanc at the ford. It ripped my cloak, curse it."

"You're lucky it was just your cloak."

"Ach, the dog gave me warning. I sleep sound enough knowing he's there," said Fionn. "Now either give my silver back or give me eighteen silver pennies for it."

For a moment it looked like the innkeeper was weighing up whether simple murder would not solve this dilemma. Then he sighed. "Seventeen. And that's merely because the dog looks hungry."

"I haven't let him eat a rascally innkeeper for weeks,"

said Fionn, sardonically. "Seventeen. Provided you feed him too." Twenty silver pennies was still far too little for the weight of the coin—had it been silver, or going to be staying in the innkeeper's pouch.

The beer was good, the squirrel stew adequate. Fionn found the quarters less so. The window was thoroughly barred with heavy iron bars and a fair amount of magework too. In fairness, Fionn had to admit it did seem directed less to keeping him in than to keeping the various forest denizens of Brocéliande out. Only he had thought a little fly-around would help to orientate himself, and quite possibly make the denizens of the forest a little more wary. With self-mocking virtue, Fionn laughed at himself. There was nothing quite as easy as performing a public service, while actually looking for the sort of magical chaos his Scrap of humanity would be generating, just by the way she was. So he sat down and took out a fragment of the coin he'd given the innkeeper, and called it back to itself to be whole again. He was rewarded a few moments later by the coin squeezing itself under the door, and rolling across to him. The dvergar coin would follow its heart piece for miles. Fionn had once thought he'd lost it, when it had been trapped in an iron strongbox. But sooner or later, someone had opened the box. Besides, it wasn't silver, but actually a great deal harder. Dvalinn said it would burrow its way out of anything in time.

Díleas growled at the coin, as Fionn put down a hand to allow it to roll up to his pouch. Fionn shook his head at the dog. "Tch. After it paid for your dinner, too."

The dog informed him—by jumping up onto the bed—just where he was planning to sleep. Fionn suggested he try curling up under his tail. Díleas thumped the bedclothes with said tail, and ignored him.

Later that night—by the feel of it, approaching dawn—Díleas woke him with a nose in his ear, and a low growl.

No human would have heard it . . . or smelled it. But someone was talking, and there was a faint smell of wolf. An odd smell of wolf. And it wasn't coming in through the window. Fionn got up. So did Díleas.

"I think you should wait. Those claws of yours make a noise on the wood," said Fionn quietly, and slipped out. He moved as quietly as only he could, through the dark building and down to the landing of the stair to the main room and kitchen. From here he could hear them, and smell them. Ah. Mine host was talking to something that smelled . . . both like a wolf and a man. That was worrying enough without the faint smell of decay too. Fionn had dealt with enough skin changers before to know how those smelled. They were dangerous, in that they had the strength and skills of their beast side and the cunning of men. It was fortunate that men were not always particularly cunning. He listened.

". . . too much money for what he pretends to be. He gave me a silver coin, from a realm I've never heard of, worth five times what I gave him for it. Also there were no other travelers on the Malpas road. Leroy would have let me know, and I would have let you know," said mine host, the innkeeper.

Fionn had to swallow his snigger at the mention of the coin, now safe back in Fionn's pouch, and go on listening. So the innkeeper—and his friend along the trail—kept the skin-changers informed of good targets. Such things were always useful to know, eventually.

The wolf-man's voice was gravelly and deep. "We saw no men on the road between here and Hunger ford. Just a mighty wyrm and a dog."

"This one had a dog. A sheepdog."

"A black-and-white dog. It rode on the wyrm. I think you have a magician here. Our mistress will reward you well for such a one, Gore. Let us see the coin he gave you."

Fionn did not wait. It was time to leave. He moved quietly upstairs, picked up Díleas and was back down the stairs while the innkeeper was still searching and swearing. Fionn took himself into hiding next to the fireplace breastwork. A few moments later, the innkeeper, candle in one hand and club in the other, exited from the kitchen with his companion—heading upstairs for the room Fionn had just vacated. If Fionn had waited, he'd have met them on the stair. As it was, he was able to duck into the kitchen, and close the door. Most conveniently, it had a bar, perhaps for when the food displeased the patrons. In the light of a bunch of rag wicks in an oil jar, Fionn scanned the shelf, and helped himself to a jar. The travelers must bring the spice here, as it would have been too precious and rare for anyone but royalty otherwise. He put Díleas down, tipped an oily crock of olives onto the floor, opened the outer door and left.

Of course at this stage, like most slick plans, it went awry. There was a pack of wolves waiting only a few yards outside the door on the roadway.

Fortunately, they were as surprised to see Fionn and Díleas as the dog and dragon were to see them. Fionn had a moment, as Díleas barked, to fling the fired-clay spice jar at the roadway just in front of them.

Fionn flung the jar with all his considerable strength, so it literally shattered into flying fragments, releasing a cloud of the precious pepper within.

He grabbed Díleas and ran the other way. The sheepdog was blinking and sneezing and trying to rub his eyes with a paw, so Fionn had a feeling that the wolves would not be doing too well in pursuit. Nonetheless, he preferred to deal with them in dragon form, so he underwent the short discomfort of changing his shape. It was not ever something particularly pleasant to do to one's body, especially in a hurry, but . . . needs must. Thus it was that the first angry, sneezing wolf got a bat from Fionn's tail that sent it thirty yards back down the road. The others retreated hastily and Fionn realized that Díleas had not waited on an invitation but had leapt up onto his back and was now barking defiance at the chastened pack.

"Enough, Díleas," said Fionn. "It's time to leave before this escalates into an angry innkeeper with crossbow bolts. We'd better go." He started down the trail. And Díleas leapt off, ran ahead and turned and barked at him.

"Not really playtime, boy," said Fionn, pushing on. Díleas growled at him and stood resolutely in his path. And then, when Fionn would have snagged him with a foreleg, he grabbed a talon with his mouth, but gently, holding, not biting, and pulled Fionn back the way they'd come. Whining anxiously between his teeth. Wagging his flaglike tail furiously.

"I don't think we should . . ."

Then it occurred to him that he'd already seen enough evidence of his Scrap's magical meddling in this very intelligent dog's nature. "You're trying to tell me something, aren't you? Do you know where your mistress is?"

Díleas tugged at his arm again. And then let go and sat down. There was little light—it was still grey predawn. But Fionn would swear the dog was nodding. Then he got up, danced a little circle and darted back down the road. And then ran back. And whined.

Fionn sighed. "Up on my back then. I can't chance flying with you. But my skin is more proof against arrows than yours. At close range, crossbow bolts could still be a problem."

Díleas leapt up, and they turned back toward the inn. The innkeeper, when they met him at the next bend, did have his crossbow, but Fionn had learned how to fling rocks with his tail, years ago. The result was very bad for the crossbow, and Fionn simply barreled past, down to the inn at the crossroads. And here Díleas leapt off his back—a flying leap that had him doing a somersault—before running a little way up the left-hand fork, and then coming back to make sure Fionn was following. So he did, into the dawn and off toward the distant sea at Carnac, because now that it was light, Fionn recognized this trail. He'd been down it before, many years back, before there had been an inn at that crossroad.

As it grew lighter Fionn could see more of the ancient forest surrounding him. The trees there must have been old when he'd last been free to walk this road. He looked for signs of imbalance, and also back for signs of pursuit. He could—and often did—change his appearance to avoid that sort of problem. The dog however, well, that might be a bit more tricky. Of course, this being one of the wildest and most dangerous of the Celt-evolved cycle of worlds, Fionn was also cautious about the road ahead. There would almost inevitably be wood dwellers who would try anything once, especially with a dog, although probably not on a dragon.

The road could provide problems of its own for walking dragons, though. The Brocéliande knights would probably not respond well to sharing the road with him. And they fought monsters of various sorts here.

Well. He'd deal with it. Right now the one problem he was most troubled by was breakfast, or rather, the lack of it.

So when he saw a knight in full armor, barring their way, he regretted the conditioning set on him by the First. His kind of dragon could not combine moving the obstacle with having breakfast. Knights apparently broiled well in armor. It kept the flavor in, or so he'd been told. Armor being what it was, and having epicurean tastes, Fionn suspected that knights were probably too gamey for his liking anyway.

The knight was no coward. Well, in a place like the forests of Brocéliande, cowardice might let a knight survive, but did poorly at making them acceptable to potential mates.

It was selective breeding that made the knight lower his lance and put his spurs to his horse.

It was the sight of a black-and-white sheepdog on the dragon's back that made him pull up the horse and stare.

"I am a knight under an enchantment," said Fionn loudly.

The knight almost fell off his horse. But he was a superb horseman, and recovered himself. "Which one of you spoke?" he asked.

"I did," said Fionn. "And I am afraid if you bar my path I must fight you, although I have no quarrel with you. I need to go to my lady's rescue. She was plucked from me by magic, the dark workings of the same enchanter that bound me to this form. I must free her, and then I can be free of this curse."

The knight stared. "Is having a sheepdog on your back part of the curse?" he asked, still not entirely putting up his lance.

"Considering the dog barks in my ear, you might think so," said Fionn. "But no. He was my lady's loyal companion, and he guides me in my search."

The knight shook his head. "I have seen various monsters and fearsome creatures. But never a dragon. There has not been one seen in all Brocéliande for many a year. I thought great honor had surely come to me this day. But I had not heard that the fell beasts could speak or, well, that they would put up with a dog. Methinks it is an illusion."

At which Díleas leapt down and trotted over to the knight. The horse paced warily, sniffing at it. "Your horse does not think it is an illusion. And to be honest with you, I could flambé you, right now, before that lance got near me, should I wish to. Actually, all the dog and I wish is to go on our quest, and to find some breakfast."

Díleas had by now walked around to the stirrup and stood up against it, reaching his nose up. The knight reached down and his chain-link-covered gauntlet got a lick.

"If he's an illusion, he's a remarkably friendly and touchable one," said the knight, somewhat more mildly. "What is your name, Sir Dragon? And where are you from and whence bound?"

Anything rather than another fight on an empty stomach, thought Fionn. And besides the wolves and monsters, Brocéliande was known for the ideals of chivalry. Fionn had found these often crumbled when closely examined, but there were exceptions. "Might I know yours, Sir Knight? I hail from a far land, and I am bound I know not whither, because I cannot speak the language of dogs. The dog knows, but I do not. I merely follow, but will follow until I find and rescue my lady. My name is Fionn of Tasmarin, and my style, Earl of Laufey." Which was true, in a manner of speaking. It was one of the advantages of having assumed many personas and having been a fraud for so many years. It was unlikely that the knight would know Laufey, which was in the Nordic cycles somewhere.

The knight raised his lance in salute. "Well met, Earl Fionn. I am Sir Bertran, son of Ywain, guardian of the fountain of Escalados. I had hoped this day to fight a great battle against some foul creature, to gain honor. But instead I have met something so passing strange that I can at least have a tale to tell my grandchildren one day. It would be ignoble for me to fight someone on such a great quest. Is there some way I can aid you?"

"Breakfast, and to allow us free passage, would be good." Fionn never forgot geography. Escalados fountain was a place he'd had occasion to visit. It was a pinch point for water and electromagnetic energies he'd had to adjust before. It was close enough to here.

Díleas barked in agreement, and danced on his hind legs. Fionn had realized that the dog was quite good at the manipulation of humans ... and dragons.

=== Chapter 6 ===

"I THINK, M'LADY," SAID NEVE FIRMLY, ONCE THEY were out of earshot of the tower, "that I am going to faint."

"Must be the lack of food," said Meb, grinning. "I'm hungry enough to fall over myself."

"Oh, I am sorry, m'lady. I'll run to the kitchens . . ."

"You'll do no such thing, Neve," said Meb, grabbing her. "Without you I'm lost. I'd probably end up down the well or wandering in on Aberinn and Medraut in counsel and get executed on the spot. Show me the way instead."

"But . . . but you shouldn't go there, m'lady. The nobility don't. Only Mage Aberinn goes down to the kitchens and cellars to magically replenish supplies."

"He does?"

"Yes," said Neve, cheerily. "Otherwise we'd be eating our shoes, m'lady. The wars have been that fierce. And the Vanar raiders have burned most of the fishing boats. That was why I came to the castle seeking a place. At least the food is wonderful. There are times that it looks better than it tastes, though."

Meb was willing to bet that those were the times that it really was old boiled shoe. "Well, if I can go into his tower, I can go into the kitchens. And if anyone asks I will say he told me to, and I'll bet not one of them will ever check."

Neve giggled, which, the sensible part of Meb knew, was just the sort of encouragement she did not need. Without Finn to keep her out of trouble . . . That nearly made her cry again, so she resolutely thought about other things until they came to the kitchen of Dun Tagoll—with spits and hobs and great cauldrons . . . and most of them idle. There was, however, new bread. That much her nose told her. There was also a sudden shocked silence at her presence there.

The cook, large ladle in hand, approached tentatively. "What can we do for you, Lady Anghared?" he asked.

So even here they knew who she was. "I have just been speaking with Mage Aberinn in his tower." Someone would have seen them going there, unless castles were vastly different from villages. By the gasps and nods she could tell that the two weren't that different. "I came to see the state of the provision of the castle. And also to get a heel of that new bread." Neve's struggle to keep a straight face definitely made her worse. "And a jug of small beer."

"The . . . mage put a stop to brewing. There is wine . . ."

Meb didn't need to be a mage with great powers to tell that that hadn't happened. "I won't mention it to him. Or to those in the hall," she said with her mouth as prim as possible.

She got the bread and small beer. And smiles as the two of them retreated to her chamber.

"I'm not eating or drinking this alone," said Meb.

"And small beer is the only kind of reward I can give you for coming into the lion's den with me. He didn't seem to know that I wasn't telling him the whole truth all the time, either."

Neve shook her head. "Eh, my lady, I had a friend back in our village like you. Always up to some mischief."

"Oh, dear. What happened to her?" asked Meb, already expecting a homily.

Neve shrugged. "She got into a fair amount of trouble, got a few beatings, but mostly got away with it, I suppose. And then she got pregnant."

"Ah." It had to end badly.

"Yes, she married the miller's boy. She was the strictest mother in the village," said Neve. "You wouldn't think she was the one who got up to mischief. Or led the rest of us to do such."

"I was a mouse back in my village most of the time. I was too different. Then the pirates burned our boats, and, well, I had to learn," she said quietly, trying not to think of who had taught her. Never do the expected . . .

"I just came here when that happened," said Neve, equally quietly, helping herself to some of the bread without thinking.

"Well, that's learning too. So you'll help me? Tell me, quietly, when I am doing something too crazy? I just don't know. I don't know where I should be, and what I should do."

Neve nodded. "When you've eaten, m'lady, I'll take the plate and jug to the kitchens. You should be in the bower. The ladies would be sewing and weaving there now. Maids too. I'm not very skilled."

"Oh good. That's two of us." Meb ate another piece of bread and tossed her tasseled juggling balls in the air, doing a simple one-hand routine, keeping all four balls in the air while Neve stared. "I think this is about all I'm really any good at. Will that do? Mama Hallgerd also showed me how to set stitches and weave flax, and tie netting knots."

"Don't show them the juggling! They'll think you're... I don't know, m'lady." They won't like it. I think it's wonderful. Like magic. Can you do other things?"

"A few," said Meb, taking a drink and wiping her lips with the back of her hand. Grinning she said: "I can belch pretty well, too," and she demonstrated, "but I don't think that'll impress Lady Cardun."

Neve looked as if she might giggle herself into apoplexy as she shook her head.

Aberinn attempted to look at Prince Medraut without his contempt showing. Medraut was a schemer and plotter. That was normal for the House of Lyon nobles. But it also normally went with courage and mage-power. Aberinn had kept vacant the throne of Lyonesse through two other regents, and seen that the old king never had any heirs to claim it. The mage had kept it for his own son or no one. And as the spell from the cord-blood showed, the child still lived. Aberinn had devoted an entire table to drawing-spells to call the boy back here to claim his own. And he'd seen to it that no one could be anointed as the new king ever since the old king had died. Only those of Aberinn's line could ever find the ancient font now, for all that it was in plain view.

All of the regents had planned to take power, of

course. But none had been as eel-like about it as Medraut. Aberinn was even more certain now that this woman had been Medraut's plant. The window was a simple trick and could easily have been hidden. And at a stroke, Medraut was free of Earl Alois—his worst enemy from the South—and the royal mage. Aberinn knew there were no other mage-workers of his ability in Lyonesse—but that was unlikely to worry someone as shortsighted and power hungry as Medraut.

"Do you think she's really the Defender?" Prince Medraut said, plainly attempting to cover his tracks.

Aberinn wondered just where the regent had found her. She did have some power, he suspected. There were Lyon-blood children conceived on the wrong side of the blankets all over the kingdom. His mother had been one, which had made Queen Gwenhwyfach his cousin. Well, if Medraut wanted to play this game, so could he. "It is possible. Magic will find a way. Of course, if she is, your regency is over, Medraut."

Medraut shot a quick glance at the royal mage. "That . . . would depend on the rest of the prophecy coming true. Or of her being the true Defender. The real Defender was supposed to come from the past, not this . . . Tasmarin place. Everyone knows that. And anyway, she did not come to be king." He laughed at his little joke. "She could hardly be that, eh?"

Aberinn decided it best to ignore that attempt at humor. "It is possible that she deceived us as to where she came from. Her accent speaks of the south."

"She hasn't got much of an accent," said Prince Medraut, confirming the mage's suspicions. "And anyway, I thought the wine was bespelled to make her speak the whole truth?"

"It is possible to magically proof someone against enchantment," Aberinn did not add "as you know, full well." After all, who would know better than Medraut about that? The man could lie like a flat fish.

"Yes, but why?" demanded Medraut, with a good show of puzzlement. "Alois would likely have killed me, without her."

"Really? You had no other safeguards?" asked the mage.

"Yes, but he had already got through the outer ones. If he had that much knowledge, and that much skill... and look how he escaped from the dungeon before the torturers could put him to the question. You said you had proofed that cell against enchantments and magics. You told me it would hold the sorceress of Shadow Hall itself. You told me I was safe!"

That was nearly a scream. Perhaps Medraut really was worried? If the girl were not Medraut's plant... maybe she was Alois's tool? But surely that was too extreme. She could, of course, be the tool of the enchantress in her Shadow Hall. The woman was mad. "No crowned head is ever safe, Medraut. No regent either. I'll watch her."

"I think we should kill her quietly," said Prince Medraut.

"It would have to be subtly done. The commons are already very full of the story. Your hold on Lyonesse is not a strong one, Prince," said Aberinn.

"Tell me something that I do not know," said the prince, sourly. "And now they expect me to lead the troops against this latest foe. Can we not change earlier?"

Aberinn shook his head and got up to leave, not

trusting himself to speak. Thinking about it with the benefit of hindsight, perhaps his freeing of Earl Alois had been a mistake. Or premature.

The ladies' bower was all Meb feared it would be. For a start, it was a-buzz above the clicks of weaving shuttles—like an angry beehive—with woman talk when she came around the corner, following Neve. She grabbed Neve's shoulder, and they stopped. And Meb proved that eavesdropping is a sure way to prove that you do in fact never hear anything good about yourself.

"... she has the magic, but she is not noble. Look at the way she was dressed."

"And she did not even put her hair up or cover it. Wanton, I tell you. She was in Aberinn's tower this morning."

"She does seem very young."

A gentle voice. The one who had been sympathetic the night before.

"Hmpf." That was Cardun. "I have never believed that prophecy of Aberinn's. He's never done the like before or since. It just came when Prince Medraut had the Royal Council and the earls ready to agree to the vote."

"Oh, no one could have faked that, Lady Cardun. Why, there was foam coming out of his mouth. It was terrible."

"It was as real as this 'Defender.' She's a common trollop who was wearing a man's breeches!"

Meb took a deep breath and walked on into the room. The comments about Aberinn's fit or the reality of the prophecy—or her—died. Vanished into silence and false smiles.

She gave them one which matched theirs very well, and did her best to look down her nose at them, which was difficult, because she was not very tall. "So this is what the ladies occupy themselves with in Dun Tagoll. How nice." She hoped that sounded condescending. She'd never really had a chance to do condescension before. There were tambour frames, a bigger loom than she'd ever seen, women sitting and stitching where the light was best. Meb loved fabrics and loved fine embroidery. They just weren't things that had come her way. She was saved from deep embarrassment, or finding some way to squirm out of this, by a call from outside. It was a panting page. "The prince's troop is about to ride out, ladies."

So they all went out to the collonaded cloister above the courtyard to see the brave colors hoisted above the cream of Lyonesse, before they rode out to do battle. The little woman who had been kind to Meb the night before looked as if the sight of it cut her to the quick. She did not go down and bestow favors on the men of the troop. Instead she looked as if she might start crying.

Meb had no one to cheer on either, so she just stayed looking out from between the pillars too. "What is wrong?" she asked, looking at the tight face.

The woman made an effort to smile. "Nothing, Lady Anghared. It just brings back old memories. Painful ones. Cormac, my husband, rode out like this, with my favor on his sleeve...oh, more than ten years ago."

"And he never came back," said Meb quietly.

"Yes. They say they saw him fall...but they also say he's been seen with the hosts of the Blessed Isles."

Meb did not know what to say.

"And with the armies of Ys. He was a very recognizable man. But he was as true as steel. He would never betray Lyonesse."

The "he would never betray me" was left unspoken. But she did not have to say it. "I have two young sons. They too will ride out one day," she said fatalistically. The "and maybe fight against their father" was also left unsaid.

Desperately looking for something to say, Meb came up with: "You chose my clothes, didn't you? I'm sorry... I don't think I know your name."

The woman nodded, looked her up and down. "You were so pale last night I thought the blue might suit you. I think yellows and greens would bring out your color better, dear. I do like the comb, even though I imagine Lady Cardun won't approve. I'm not surprised you don't remember much from last night. My name is Vivien. My husband was once captain of the Royal Troop."

"I think if I wound my hair up just like hers, she'd still say that it didn't suit me." said Meb, looking down at the chatelaine in the courtyard, a safe distance off.

Vivien shrugged. "She's worried about her place. She's the prince's aunt.

Meb wrinkled her forehead. "What does that have to do with me? I am sorry... I just don't know what is going on here, lady. I'm... I'm out of place. I was... living in another land. In what nearly was a war to end all of it... we... Finn and me, stopped that, and then suddenly I was here."

"It sounds a rather momentous history for someone who looks... How old are you, Lady Anghared?" It was asked kindly, with a gentle concern.

"Um. I think eighteen. It was rather hard to keep track this last while. Might be nineteen," said Meb, who was better at dealing with outright conflict than this. Was it a trap of some sort?

"They say you're too young to be the Defender. But at nineteen I had two children. They're saying a lot of...things about you, dear. Don't give them fuel."

It was actually meant kindly, Meb decided. And Vivien was plainly more careworn than actually old. "I don't know if I am this 'Defender.' I don't think so. I think I am just an unhappy person dropped here, far from everything and everyone I love. I don't want to be here. I don't want to be your Defender."

"You saved Prince Medraut from death, and you brought back the queen's window, a great magic, and Dun Tagoll is defended in every way against those. You frightened Prince Medraut into giving up his sword. You spoke of dealing with dragons...The men-at-arms...well, I heard about it from my boys. They are both squires. But the haerthmen and the men-at-arms are full of it. So are the servants. Also you've been into Aberinn's tower. Almost no one does that. Don't let...spitefulness hurt you."

Meb realized that Vivien, too, believed. Or wanted to. She feared for her sons. "I don't...Lady Vivien. I can't *be* a lady, let alone your Defender. I don't want to be."

"What do you want?" asked Vivien.

Meb sighed. "Something I can't have, either. Ever. I am not even sure I want to be alive, half the time."

"I think I understand," said Vivien, holding her. "I'm sorry."

"I've lost everything I ever had. Everything I ever

loved," said Meb quietly, tears starting to form and flow. Vivien said nothing. Just hugged her. There were others weeping and being comforted, so it was not that very obvious. Somehow Meb found herself being taken back to the bower and shown embroidery stitches. She was given an ivory frame, and she concentrated fiercely on it. Trying to lose herself in it. She did love the threads' silkiness and the bright colors of them.

A little later someone looked at what she was doing. "I thought...you said you had never done this before?"

Meb looked at the picture that had started to form out of the tiny stitches. There had been a carefully drawn pattern there, but after a while she had somehow lost the simple flower pattern, and gone on setting stitches according to a pattern in her head, not on the stretched fabric. The dragon was perfectly detailed on the white lawn, and his flame was orange and red and bright, almost seeming to burn out of the material.

The dragon was black, and its eyes were wicked with mischief.

Meb got up and left, her eyes blind with tears again. Neve and Vivien led her to her room.

"When I saw the stitchery...I thought you were making a fool of me, getting me to show you the basics. That you knew far more than I could ever learn. But that was magic, wasn't it?" said Vivien. "Magic here, in Dun Tagoll."

Meb nodded.

Vivien shook her head, eyes wide and worried. "I thought that maybe Cardun and the others were right. I thought maybe you were just here by accident. But Anghared...that is magic, and straight out of the prophecy. Now I think you are the Defender, whether you know it or not. I think you have come to save us, even though you didn't know it, and don't want to do it." The woman paced a little. "Anghared. I know... I can see you are heartsore. I remember my own heartbreak when they told me Cormac had joined the fallen. But, please...there are so many of us. Others who see their men ride off to a war we can't escape and can't win. Can you not...try to spare them the heartbreak too? We need you."

"She's right, m'lady," Neve said quietly. "The boy I was, um, sparking with. The Vanar killed him when they burned our ships. Lyonesse is..."

"Dying slowly from a thousand cuts," finished Vivien. "Every time there is a little break, people try and plant crops, messengers go to the outer marches. Life starts. And then the next invasion comes."

Meb sighed. "I don't even know where to start."

"By washing your face," said Lady Vivien, practically. I don't think you need to know. I think this is a sign. You will defend us against the black dragon."

Meb started to laugh, maybe a little hysterically, but laugh, all the same. Eventually she stopped. Smiled a little at Vivien's worried face. "Whatever I don't know, I know I won't be defending you against that dragon. And even if I wanted to, I couldn't." She got up from her bed. "Let me wash my face. And then let's see if we have dry bread and sour wine again."

"We eat well here, Anghared. Not quite siege rations yet."

Meb pulled a wry face. Well, maybe this was not the right time to tell them. They needed her, or something. And she needed something. Anything. This would do.

=== Chapter 7 ===

"I HAD NOT," SAID THE KNIGHT, SIR BERTRAN, "BEEN aware of the usefulness of dragon fire in kindling a fire in these wet woods." He was eyeing the dragon with a little more respect.

That was a good thing, probably, Fionn thought. He was a nice enough lad in a society where the nobility had to prove themselves with deeds of courage. Ignorance of dragons—and some might leave Tasmarin now—could be rapidly fatal. It was small repayment for the fact that Bertran was sharing a hind he'd shot earlier with them. Besides, the dog approved of him. Of course, Fionn admitted to himself, Díleas was a shameless beggar from anyone who had food, but he had gone trotting over to the knight before he'd known about the knight's nearby camp and the deer carcass strung in the tree next to it.

"I had hoped," said Sir Bertran, "that it might serve as bait and bring the fearsome beasts to me. They are more numerous in the woods than in my father's time, but still, they are wary of an armored knight. But if not bait, then food, if I can get a fire to kindle." Fionn had been happy to oblige. Díleas had been perfectly content to eat it raw, and had been provided with a few slices of meat to keep him going while it cooked. If Fionn understood soulful doggy looks, a little drool, and the occasional *hrrm* noises, it had been wholly insufficient, at least in Díleas's opinion, and "cooked" should be a relative term.

And then, of course, something scented the bait. The knight's horse gave first warning, before the distracted dog. But even without that whicker of fear, they would have known soon enough.

The giant broke trees and shook the earth with his tread. The forest life fled before him—birds, deer, a unicorn, foxes, a cockatrice, squirrels and an ogre.

The giant wasn't interested in them. It was hunting, in Fionn's opinion, a dog and a dragon.

In Sir Bertran's opinion, it was hunting him, and thus the company he was in.

There was nothing wrong with the young knight's courage, or the agility of his horse. He did manage to place his lance tip in the bellowing giant's eye, and the horse danced aside from the giant's club—a ripped-up tree—as the lance tip snapped. Unfortunately it had five other eyes—as it had three tusky heads.

Fionn had yelled at Díleas, "Run!" before taking to the wing himself. Dragon fire singed the giant—as he kicked over their fire and sent the partly cooked hind flying.

Dragon fire carbonized the club, but the giant itself merely bellowed in anger and lunged at him. It didn't burn. It was a siliceous giant... A rock giant, as opposed to the frost and fire ones Fionn knew for their bad temper. Normally the rock giants were slow to anger, and slow of reactions. This one was neither. In fact, thought Fionn, as his wings bit air and pushed him higher, this one was a rock giant in its resistance to dragon fire, but looked fire-giantish, with its three heads and brutish nature. And it smelled . . . odd. Like something had died and it had stood in it. That was always possible.

The fool dog, however, was not running. He was standing and barking. And the fool knight wasn't running either. He'd drawn his sword—which was not going to be a lot of use against the giant. Fionn swooped down and slapped the left outer head with his tail. It might be a rock creature, but a blow from a dragon tail was enough to make it stagger. And bellow again, and plunge towards him.

The dog and the knight, instead of running, followed.

So Fionn had to taunt the giant again, because it narrowly missed seizing the teasing dog. Spiraling up again, Fionn looked for answers. He could lead it off and lose it—if the knight and dog would back off. The dog might . . . possibly. The knight wasn't going to. Which meant that he had to deal somewhat more permanently with the giant. One could poison them— the silicate organic chemistry was quite susceptible to arsenates, and to some of the powerful acids. Heat would not work. One could bog them down, sink them in a lake, but they'd just keep walking, or toss them over a cliff. Or he could smash the giant apart with a hammer bigger and heavier than itself. Or bespell them. Looking at the energy flows, Fionn thought he saw another answer. This was Brocéliande, and this young knight was, after all, the son of the guardian of the fountain of Escalados. Escalados, the red fountain that drew the storms...and the stone giant dragged his feet as he blundered through the trees.

Fionn swooped down. "We must lead him to Escalados. To the fountain."

"I must defend that! And my mother, the Lady Laudine, is within the manor there. There are no tall walls..."

"He's a stone giant. It is the only way to kill him. He wants us, not the manor or anything else." The giant proved that by ignoring a small herd of deer that bolted from in front of it, and by plunging after the three of them.

The knight nodded. "It is the better part of half a league!"

Brocéliande's ancient, ferny, mossy forests, full of vast trees and twisted branches, were no place to play catch-as-catch-can with an angry, hunting giant. The giant was capable of going straight, rather than around. Still, the trees slowed him, as they might a man pushing through thick brush.

The giant had by now decided that the knight, sheepdog, and the dragon were all part of its target. And it had three tusky-mouthed heads to feed. It must want one each, Fionn decided. The knight was at most risk, as Fionn had the open sky and Díleas could dart through gaps that were too narrow for a horseman. Perhaps it was the color, but the giant was fixated on the dog...who in turn was determined to prove that he was as capable of herding giants as he should be of herding sheep, darting behind it—even between the tree-trunk legs, to snap at the giant's heels. Of course his teeth could not make any impression on the giant's flesh, but the giant itself seemed far more interested in trying to reach the dog. On several occasions when the knight was trapped, the dog drew off the giant before Fionn could flame its eyes or bat its heads.

Then they broke from the woods into what was obviously the home farm of the knight. They'd cleared a bit of land since Fionn was last here. You could see the thatch of the walled manor house, low down along the shallow swale that ran from the standing stone against the ridge. There was a good reason for the house being low down and far from the standing stone, Fionn knew.

The magic fountain was at the base of the standing stone, some half a mile across the fields. The knight's tenants were in the fields—or at least running from the fields. Someone had the ability and courage to flight an arrow so Fionn took to the ground, making it very obvious—with shouts and cooperation—that the dog and dragon were working with their overlord, dealing with—or at least taunting—the three-headed giant. It would seem to Fionn that the giant had no understanding of human speech, which was odd, as most other giants did. It was either that, or it was very stupid, because they kept it away from the mill and away from the barns and away from the cattle, leading it on—on towards the bleeding fountain. The bleeding fountain was once nothing more than iron in the rock the water oozed through—but superstition and magic often built on each other, and Fionn wouldn't be surprised if it really was some kind of blood now, with all the belief in it being that.

It was a numinous spot, with the squat misshapen

monolith and its altar stone above the old stone-carved basin into which the ruddy water seeped. It was surrounded by blackened and dead oaks. That, Fionn knew, had nothing to do with mysterious powers, but everything to do with the energies channeled here.

"It's your fountain, Sir Bertran," he yelled. "You'd better scatter the water."

The knight leapt from the saddle of his steaming, tired horse as Díleas and Fionn teased and taunted the giant. It was, Fionn knew, a dangerous game. They were still faster than the giant, but they were both tiring.

The siliceous creature was not. He would pursue them relentlessly. Fionn was willing to bet he now had the scent of their essences, and would follow, no matter how fast or far they fled. Eventually it would catch them.

This smelled, and not just faintly of dead things.

Sir Bertran scooped a handful of the red water and poured it out on the altar rock, respectfully. He ignored the giant as he did this.

And then he mounted again and charged back towards the fray.

Above, already, the thunderheads built, as with a magical speed the sky darkened. The air seemed to thicken.

"We need that idiot in the iron suit off the horse and further away from the giant," said Fionn, sotto voce, to Díleas. "Because any minute now..."

Then lightning, blue-white and so close there seemed no pause between it and the terrible rattling boom of thunder, carved a ragged, jagged line to the tallest point.

The giant.

Sheeting rain began to fall.

But that was of no concern to Fionn because he was under a shivering dog, and he had to pick up a knight who had fallen from his horse, as more lightning hissed down, hitting the giant again and again.

Nothing, not even siliceous proteins, could survive the lightning bolts. Dragons had found out the hard way that lightning could be survived in the air . . . but not when they landed.

Now Fionn just had to deal with minor problems— an unconscious knight and a dog that really, really didn't like thunderstorms. And he had torrential rain to cope with, of course.

That was still a better deal than the three-headed giant had gotten. Fionn was fairly sure it was now dead, the neural circuits fried. It was probably a large lump of glassy rock now, for people in later years to laugh at the superstitions of their ancestors.

The rain began to ease off, and Sir Bertran sat up. "What happened?" he asked muzzily.

"I think I'd tell your adherents that you struck it a thunderous blow. Some of the braver ones are approaching now, and I'd appreciate it if you told them that there is no need to pinprick this particular dragon with arrows and that the quivering sheepdog is no threat. It's all right, Díleas, the storm is over."

Sir Bertran stood up. "My mother," he said resignedly, looking at the palanquin approaching. "Sir Fionn, you and your dog strove bravely with me today. I give you thanks. I am in your debt, as I am aware the giant could have caught me on several occasions had the two of you not drawn him off." He patted

Díleas. "Seldom has the world seen a braver, cleverer dog, Sir Fionn."

"As long as there are no thunderstorms," said Fionn. "Anyway. One of your grazing paddocks now has a new rock formation, I think. Let's go and inspect it before they come and fuss about you. You took a quite a toss there. Got something of a shock, too, I shouldn't wonder." Fionn didn't point out that he thought the knight had got off quite lightly, all things considered.

They walked across to the late three-headed giant, now a vast tor of blackened glass, with the evil tusky faces distorted and twisted into something even uglier. The giant glass statue was somewhat the worse for having suffered multiple lightning strikes, but that didn't stop the peasants and men-at-arms approaching cheering their lord, or Díleas lifting his leg on its foot. He was still rather new to this lifting of a leg instead of squatting puppy- or girl-dog fashion, and nearly fell over in the process. That could have been awkward, as the foot was still cracking with internal heat.

Maybe the loyal retainers might have been approaching a little less fast than they might . . . if their lord was not being supported by a dragon. And even from here Fionn could hear the hero's mother. He was a brave lad, this Bertran. Best to leave him to be brave alone, decided Fionn, but it appeared he was not going to be that lucky.

= Chapter 8 =

ALOIS, THE EARL OF CARFON, HAD BEEN RIDING
south by night, hiding by day for more than a week
now. He was exhausted and hungry and he was in
a better state than his horse. He knew he should
be grateful for the horse. Grateful for the magical
intervention that had plucked him from the cell, while
waiting for the torture chamber, and dropped him next
to the horse in a half-ruined stable, a good fifteen
miles from Dun Tagoll, where months of planning
had all gone so wrong.

And he was glad. Glad that he would see his son
and wife again. Glad, in the last few miles, to see
signs that he was returning to farmed lands and not
anarchy and banditry. Only Dun Tagoll had wholly
abandoned any effort to farm the lands. Only they
could. All of the Duns tried to keep at least some
agriculture and livestock farming going. It was usually limited to fields just outside the walls. Too few
fields, feeding too many mouths. Only in the South
had they managed to keep a reasonable amount of

land under cultivation, and that by building a great many more forts and having as nearly as many men-at-arms as neyfs working the land. And as he'd said to Branwen when he'd rode out on this venture, the Gods above and below alone knew how much longer they could survive. That was why he'd taken up the offer from the plotters. They'd be dead for their pains, he had no doubt.

So close. So very close to seeing Medraut dead.

And then . . . He mulled it all in his mind, as he had a thousand times since.

He rode slowly along the lane. It was muddy, but at least not overgrown too. And bandits were rarer here.

"Halt. Who rides after the curfew bell?" demanded a voice.

"Earl Alois. And I am truly glad to see my own land and my own men!"

Six hours later, after a sequence of fresh horses, and with a troop around him, he rode into the gates of Dun Carfon—he'd never thought to see it again—and then into the arms of his wife, and to gaze on the sleeping form of his son. "We'll have to wake him," said Branwen. "I'm afraid . . . like most of us, he believed you were dead, Alois. It's . . . its been hard for him."

She was a jewel. A mere local chieftain's daughter, not even of the House of Lyon. He'd married her against the politics and calls for alliance. Married her just because he was a headstrong young lord and he'd looked at her and known what he wanted. In earlier years it would never have been permitted. But if one good thing had come out of this chaos of endless war, it was her. "Yes. Hopefully he'll see a better Lyonesse before he grows up."

She blinked, holding him, as if to reassure herself he was real. "I thought Medraut still sat on the throne?"

"He does. But the Defender Aberinn forecast in his prophecy has come. I was there. I saw it. She made the sea-window reappear."

"Really?"

Earl Alois sighed. "Yes. I saw her appear from nowhere, I saw the sea-window reappear. And I heard her name herself as Anghared. I believe it is her. That was magic of no low order. She has come to set things to rights. She even looks like the old queen in the tapestry hanging in the banquet hall. But the bad part, Branwen, is that she will want my head. And if that is what it takes to put Lyonesse back together again, I will go to the headsman."

"No!" she said, clinging to him. Clinging as to someone whom she'd loved, thought dead, and now had to face the fear and uncertainty again. Which was true, of course. "Why would she do that? It's Medraut who has brought Lyonesse to ruin. Not you, Alois!"

The boy woke up and stared at his parents, and rubbed his unbelieving eyes, as his father said: "Because I tried to kill her."

Meb wondered how long the state of tense waiting would continue in the halls of Dun Tagoll. Wars could go on for years. This one had, it appeared. But the answer this time was: not too long. The prince seemed to have developed a hit-and-run strategy, simply designed to hurt the foe, irritate them and make them plunge after the army, toward Dun Tagoll, rather than ravaging the countryside.

That might be good for the countryside, but right now

it meant that the attackers were setting up siege engines on the headland. "Last time they threw everything from dead horses to rocks at the castle," said Neve. "It looks like they're making bigger ones this time."

"And...will it break the walls?" asked Meb.

"No, m'lady. The walls are magical. Even if they break, they just pull together. But a dead horse...oh, the mess. And the rocks can kill people."

The causeway was too narrow and steep for a charge, but their foes had sent brave men across in the darkness, under their shields, carrying a brass-headed ram. So Meb woke to the pounding of the ram and a sudden, inhuman yowling and screaming. In the darkness of her room, it was terrifying. She'd never been in a castle under siege before. Had the attackers broken through? What should she do? Fight back, obviously. What was there in this room that she could fight back with? She needed a sword. Or better yet, an axe. You needed to have some skill with a sword, but an axe—one of those metallic-handled, narrow, wicked-bladed ones that the alvar gate guards used—surely didn't need much. She was afraid and imagining it in detail...and it was a great deal heavier in her hands than she'd thought. Summoning magic again...it seemed to work when she was absorbed enough and afraid enough...neither of which were easy to switch on at will, she thought as she wished for a light...and failed. She couldn't even find the pricket, let alone light it. So she went and opened her door by feel, alvar axe in hand. There was a tallow-dipped brand of rush on a metal wall sconce at the end of the hall. She walked down that way. To find a bored guard walking down the passage...

He was a lot less bored seeing a woman in her nightclothes with a silvery, two-handed spatha-axe in her hands. "M'lady," he took a grip on his own sword handle. "What's amiss?"

"The noise. That screaming. What happened?" she asked.

He looked a little startled. "Oh, just the Angevins getting a snout full of hot pitch, m'lady. Never man the ram. Aye, first at the loot, but also first at the hot pitch."

"Oh . . . I thought they'd got in," said Meb, feeling faintly foolish.

"No, m'Lady Anghared. We're safe enough within the walls of Dun Tagoll. Siege engines and rams won't do naught. Starvation neither. It'll take more magic than the Shadow Hall can throw against us."

Meb went back to her bed, leaving the axe next to it. It was a long while before sleep came again. What was this Shadow Hall? And why did the Kingdom of Lyonesse seem to have such an ample supply of enemies and, apparently, not one ally? Finn had said magic use inevitably made work for him, distorting energies. What was happening here? Were there other dragons, planomancers like Finn, moving in their shifted shapes, fixing things? Her dreams were troubled. Full of screaming and silver-handled axes with narrow, curved slicing blades.

She awoke to a troubled squeak. It was Neve, staring at the axe, looking as if she was about to drop the water she carried and run. Meb yawned. "Thank all the Gods you're all right, m'lady! What's that nasty thing doing in here?"

"I thought I might need it if you spilled all the

water on the floor...I'm only joking, for dragons' sakes. I thought we might have to defend ourselves. And I don't think I can use a sword. I've split wood with an axe, so I have an axe."

"Dun Tagoll is safe enough, Lady Anghared. It's those poor people outside who need defending. Where did you get it? I've never seen anything like it. It looks very sharp and dangerous."

Meb decided it was better not to answer that question, and began washing. She thought it looked just about sharp enough to slice stone, let alone armor. It wasn't a subject so easily avoided when Lady Vivien came in a little later.

"How did it get here?" she asked, warily, looking at the axe. "It has the look of a Finvarra spatha-axe... what are you doing with such a thing, Anghared? It's no weapon of the men of Lyonesse. Where did it come from?"

"Oh, um. The alvar guards use them back in my homeland. I was afraid in the night and wanted something to defend myself with."

"But you couldn't have had it with you. You...you had barely the clothes you were wearing, when you came here, Anghared," said Vivien, troubled. "I was there. I helped to put you to bed."

"Sometimes, when I'm really scared or just dreaming...imagining things deeply, they come to me. Fragments of things..."

"Fragments...aha! Summonsing magic. Here, in Dun Tagoll? You can't," said Vivien.

"I didn't mean to. I just heard the screaming. I was scared."

"No...I mean it is not possible. The Mage Aberinn,

by his craft, protects the castle. But while we're guarded, it affects us too. Only those of the greatest of power can manage the smallest working. That... that is a vast object for a summonser. It would take preparation and skill..."

"I don't know what I am doing or how I do it," said Meb, knowing this to be slightly less than the truth. The dragon-shaped dvergar device around her neck, the thing that carried some of the magic of all the species of Tasmarin, the device that would help her be what she wanted to be... tricky little dvergar! That would affect things. But... well, she summonsed far larger things, wanting to, needing or just... wishing to. A black dragon, once. And she'd needed him. She still did. She just hadn't known it, then. "I do summons big things sometimes. I summonsed a dragon once."

"Gods above and below. Well, I hope you don't do that again!"

"I can't," said Meb flatly. "Never ever again, although I want nothing more. It would kill him."

But that seemed to have washed right over Vivien. "You *are* the Defender, Anghared. Oh, thank all the Gods. I must tell..."

"No. Please, no," Meb grabbed the fluttering, excited hands. "Please. I want to help. But... well, Prince Medraut. Aberinn. Do you think they'd like it much?"

"The prince has honored you and respected you so far. And the mage called you to his tower. I should have known when we heard about the sea-window. I thought it must be stone memory. The embroidery... that was a small thing, and I was amazed. But, but summonsing magics. And so powerful. I'm Lyon, on my mother's side, and I can call things from across the room. Small things. A brooch like this one." She pointed to the thumbnail-sized one at her breast.

Meb sighed. "Vivien. I don't trust Prince Medraut, or the mage. I don't know how to make magic happen every time. And, and it goes wrong. My master said . . . he'd teach me. But now, I just feel it would be a very wrong thing to do. I am going to help. I promise. I swear. I swear by the black dragon."

"That . . . binds you?" asked Vivien.

"It binds me more than anything else ever could," said Meb. "And I think I'd better hide that axe before anyone else asks awkward questions."

"I could wrap it up in something and take it to the armory," said Neve, coloring slightly. "There's, there's a man-at-arms who might do me a favor. If I asked."

It made Meb smile a little, determined to find out just who this armsman was, and let him know that someone would make his life very unpleasant if he was anything less than good to little Neve. She could do that. Finn had taught her quite enough for that. "I think I want it a little closer. Lady Cardun might decide to do my hair. Stop laughing, both of you. It would make a wonderful mirror. We can slide it under the bed."

"They're very full of your embroidery in the bower, by the way. Even Lady Cardun was saying she didn't know how you worked so fast and set such precise and tiny stitches. Of course she said it showed a lack of discipline not to stick to the pattern, and you were a flighty, moody young girl; that the regent's guidance would be needed for many years, even if you were the Defender, which she didn't for a moment believe."

"I need to ask some questions about this regency,"

said Meb, who didn't see why it was up to her, but would not have left shifty Prince Medraut to look after a tub of jellied eels, let alone a kingdom. "Who is the prince the regent for?"

They both looked at her as if she'd suddenly started dribbling and gone simple on them. "The true king of Lyonesse, of course," said Vivien.

"Oh. And who is he?" asked Meb.

"He is the king anointed with holy water from the ancient font of kings. He alone can bind to the land and draw its strength to himself to destroy our enemies," explained Vivien.

"But who is he?" Meb pursued. "Does he have to be found or something?"

"No. It is the ancient font that must be found. It vanished just after Queen Gwenhwyfach and her babe plunged from the sea-window. It is believed that the enchantress of Shadow Hall summonsed it, somehow."

"So... do I get this right... the prince is not the regent for someone specific. It could be anyone that finds this font, and gets dunked in water from it?"

Vivien nodded. "Prince Medraut is regent for the Land, because the Land is the King and the King is the Land. Of course the king would have to be of the blood of the House of Lyon, because they have the magic. Normally the old king would take his son or chosen heir to the font and hand on the power. But the old king died before it was found. That is why the Shadow Hall has been able to raise everyone against us. That is why the Land will not destroy the invaders."

"So where do the women fit into all of this?" asked Meb.

The other two looked at her, faintly puzzled. "They say men make kings. Women make babies. We carry the bloodline. Some Lyon women are powerful magic workers too. Queen Gwenhwyfach was."

"They were wondering down in the kitchens if you were going to marry Prince Medraut," said Neve.

Meb snorted. "I'd rather marry a midden. I'm not..."

"But they were saying he was considering speaking for you. And he's a prince of the blood." By the tone, that was obviously all that was required. Well, it wasn't going to happen. She'd take the axe to him first. And the little logical part of her mind said, well, it happened to women here. And Fionn... she'd never see Fionn again. She should accept that and move on.

There was an enormous thud and the walls shook.

"What was that?" asked Meb, fearful.

"They've set up trebuchets and have started flinging rocks from the headland. Be easy, Dun Tagoll can withstand anything they can fling at it. And besides, Mage Aberinn has said he had something planned for them. Don't worry, Anghared. It wants but three days to the full moon."

And what did that have to do with it?

They seemed to assume she'd know. She hated showing her ignorance, but she needed to know. "So what happens at full moon?"

"The full tides power the Changer. Lyonesse moves."

"You mean...an earthquake?"

Vivien stared at her. "I forget, Lady Anghared, that you are not from here. You know that the land is linked to other places? Places which are not our world? We call them the Ways."

Meb knew that from Finn's talk of other planes. She supposed that was what was meant. "Yes."

"Well, back in the time of King Diarmid, the magic of Lyonesse grew much weaker. Magic flows in across the Ways. The king and his mages built a device, a magical device, that moves Lyonesse around the Ways. When we move, our magework is refreshed. It takes a great deal of power, and so the device was harnessed to the tide in caves beneath Dun Tagoll. It stores power from every tide, but it takes a full tide, usually the equinoctial tide, to do the change."

"These enemies outside . . . are they from these other places?" asked Meb, a light beginning to dawn.

"Of course," said Vivien. "Yes . . . I suppose you wouldn't know. They come storming in across the Ways to attack and ravage. It wasn't always like that, of course. When we had a king . . . and then it took a while for them to realize we were unprotected. The mage says the sorceress of Shadow Hall has turned them against us. But it could as easily have been the raiding."

Meb did not need that explained to her. And to be honest she could understand and sympathize with the army out there. Lyonesse had come and drained out their magical energy . . . and Lyonesse's raiders had gone out, and come running back to a land that the victims could not attack to punish. No wonder Lyonesse had no friends. She said as much.

Lady Vivien nodded. "King Geoph forbade the raids, but there were always some. But this land was also a refuge. Defeated tribes, persecuted people. They knew they could find shelter and safety here. The other lands hate us for that too. Then when the invasions began...well, Prince Medraut began counterraids. We needed the food. They burned the fields and ran off our kine and sheep."

And now they were left with a situation where everyone hated their guts, wanted to kill them, and they still could not farm, and had to eat ensorcelled scraps or rob their neighbors, thought Meb. *And I promised to help them. I thought taking on the dragon Zuamar was crazy. This is worse. And they don't even seem to see it will just gets worse, every time.*

There was another shudder, and a hollow boom, as a trebuchet-flung rock struck the castle...and a spectacular flash of violet light through the high window, and distant boom. It didn't rattle the walls but she felt that it should have. All the women took cover, diving down next to Meb's bed.

"What was that?" asked Vivien.

Meb managed not to say "how should I know?" but instead, "Maybe we need to find out?"

"Could we leave the axe?" asked Vivien, beginning to recover her calm. "I think we'd hear the call to arms if they'd breached the walls."

So the axe was placed under the bed again, and they went out. It seemed a fair number of others were doing the same thing. There were definitely no vast crowds of fighting men, or even the sounds of battle.

They went up a flight of stairs to be met by a bemused guard. "The stone," he said. "It flew back."

"What do you mean?" asked Vivien.

"They threw a stone at us with that big trebuchet of theirs. And it flew back from the castle with a big purple flash. Go and have a look."

Peering over the battlements, Meb could see the

enemy encampment on the headland short of the narrow causeway to the castle on its peninsula. The camp had probably been set up in good order. Right now it was in chaos, with that chaos centered around the huge, smashed wooden structure of the trebuchet and the plowed-up remains of tents beyond.

There were three other large trebuchets . . . but no one was near them. They were all—along with half the camp—plainly damaged by flying shards. The foe's engineers were busy seeing just how far from the camp they could get, and the soldiery looked to be, in part, joining them and, in part, under their knights' orders, trying to stop them.

Somewhere on the wall of Dun Tagoll, a cheer started.

Meb was walking back, deep in thought, when she came, abruptly, on Mage Aberinn. He stared narrow-eyed at her. "A word, young woman." He looked at the other two women. "Here in the courtyard. So you do not need a chaperone."

Meb didn't know how to avoid this so she walked a little way with the mage. "Did you interfere in some way with my working?" he asked abruptly.

"I wouldn't know how. I didn't even know you were doing anything. What am I supposed to have done?" asked Meb, alarmed by the ferocity of his tone.

He seemed mollified by hers. "I had built a device to mirror back the energy of their projectiles. To return them."

"But it worked, didn't it?" said Meb, puzzled.

"Yes, it worked. It worked far too well, with far more power than such a working could harness. Not since King Diarmid has such a thing been reported."

"Well, it had nothing to do with me! Ask the others. We hid behind the bed when it happened."

He sucked his teeth. "I do not like or trust this. Or you." And he turned on his heel and walked off without another word.

In the Shadow Hall, the queen stared at the viewing bowl. Where had Aberinn acquired such power? Lyonesse had been crumbling, slowly. Onslaught after onslaught it had lost more men, lost more ground. Once it had taken troops months to fight their way anywhere near Dun Tagoll. Now the borders were unguarded. West Lyonesse had become, effectively, a few fortresses along the seaboard, hated by its neighbors, with even the peasantry turning from their Lyon overlords.

Even if magically he had barely remained able to hold her out of the castle itself, it was failing.

Nothing was simple or quick. She'd learned that. And now to add to her irritation, the muryans had brought her hall too far while she had slept. So many years of working her magic on them, and they'd never been less than precise before, and right now she was not in the deep ravines of Ys, but somewhere near a noisome town in the lowlands.

She had her cauldron-men to send out. With the colors of Lyonesse flying at their head they'd go raiding and pillaging and burning for her. But was there any point in doing it here? The great Changer would not open these Ways this time. She knew its pattern. Aberinn had never guessed that.

Meb knew her curiosity about the Changer would have to wait. She'd done some subtle questioning and the answer to what it was and how it worked was simply that the women of Dun Tagoll did not know. Her attempts at being a good lady were being met with very mixed success, and she'd been getting the feeling that leaving the castle might still be the easiest way to help. Or at least, easier for her. They accepted that she could embroider. Her skills at the rest of the womanly arts, Meb knew that they considered as far below the salt.

Maybe this Changer would bring other changes? It was inside the mage's tower, she was told. It had always been, from long before Mage Aberinn. Yes, it was a device of some sort, which he worked with. And no, when they changed, nothing was really that different within Lyonesse . . . except that the attacking army could not return to its own country. Nor could they get supplies from their home. Their supply chain was cut, the country was picked bare, too bare to live off, and chances were good, any other invader would attack them too. And back in their own country, the people would know: attack Lyonesse and you are lost, forever.

Once that had been enough.

Now it wasn't.

When the change came it was silent and sudden.

Meb knew it had happened.

She could feel it. It was a little like some strange scents carried on the night air. Scents of faraway things, and of spices she knew the smell and taste of . . . but did not have a name for.

The association was not a pleasant one though; it somehow also smelled of cold, salt, decay, and other nasty things.

═ Chapter 9 ═

"YESTERDAY, ALL YOU WANTED WAS TO GO WEST,"
said Fionn as Díleas danced around him, barking.
Darting off southward, and then running back to see
if Fionn was following. Doing everything but to bite
the dragon's heels to get him to follow. "You'd have
been well served if I'd had have left you there for
the plump lady to pamper, forced to sit on a satin
cushion, and be fed sweetmeats for saving her precious
boy. It wasn't easy getting you out of there, but the
last thing we need is a young knight traveling with us
as well. He's probably trying to track us, and we're a
lot harder to follow moving down the roadway than
fighting our way through the forest."

Díleas was paying no attention to his eloquence,
so Fionn gave up and followed. He wasn't prepared
for the sheepdog to turn around and give him a lick
on the nose.

He also was not prepared for another trilith, some
three hundred yards into the forest. A low, squat one,
barely five cubits from the forest floor to the balancing

stone, and covered in enough moss and fern to blend into the woods.

"Now just how did you know that was there? And I'll warrant it leads to elsewhere," said Fionn.

It did. They came out in a long grassy dale, with the hills rising all around them. Fionn smelled the air. And then turned his back on the dog and went to have a long hard look at the trilith . . . which wasn't there. He walked back up the track past where they had stepped into this place. It did not take him back to the forests of Brocéliande.

"A one-way gate. And another I did not know existed. Either things have changed in the wider planes while I've been trapped, or I knew very much less than I thought I did." Fionn used his vision to peer into the currents of energy around the spot, ignoring the dog and his "come on" bark. There was very little sign of the vast flow of magic and other energies that such a displacement should cause. Someone or something very skilled had set up this gate.

Fionn preferred to be the one who knew more than others, to being the one who was still trying to understand. Why had the dog come this way? How did it know where the gate was?

And . . . did it really, somehow, as he hoped desperately, know where his Scrap of humanity was? He missed her fiercely.

Up the slope some white-grey shapes ran away. "Sheep. Yes, Díleas, I am coming. I don't entirely like it, but I am coming. And you should be a very happy sheepdog as there seem to be a lot of sheep, rather than wolves, afancs and giants . . . not to mention the mother of knights here. Lead on. Here I think the appearance of being human will lead to less problems."

It felt like Albar or Carmarthen. Which was illogical. Ys and Cantre'r Gwaelod abutted Brocéliande. But as the trilith-gated way had proved, there were places and things that he had known nothing of, linking places, obviously by some sort of different mechanism. Well, Groblek could be anywhere...

They walked on. Díleas seemed determined that only one direction would do, taking them cross-country and through a muddy stream, over several dry-stone walls and into some conflict with a shepherd and his dogs on the steep hill-path they were following. "What are you doing in this pasture?" yelled the shepherd standing astride the path next to some large boulders. "Here, Strop, Cam. See them off, boys."

Two black-and-white sheepdogs, remarkably like scruffier versions of Díleas, hurtled towards them, barking, dividing at the last minute, to flank them, and then suddenly getting the smell of dragon.

They weren't stupid dogs. They were a lot brighter than the shepherd, Fionn decided. Brighter than Díleas, who was regarding the two suddenly halted dogs with a display of fur, a curled lip exposing his teeth and a deep burring growl. "We're just passing through, fellow. Call off your dogs, and we'll be on our way."

"Not over my master's land you're not! Strop, Cam, gettim."

The dogs advanced. Not in a hurry.

"Díleas. Put your head between my legs," said Fionn quietly.

The sheepdog did, and Fionn whistled. He'd found

dogs—and animals who heard higher frequencies—did not like that whistle. People didn't even hear it.

The dogs did. So did the sheep on the hillside and quite a lot of mice and a fox. They all wanted to leave.

The shepherd did quite a lot of yelling and then some whistling. And a fair amount of swearing. "He lacks originality, Díleas," said Fionn, addressing himself to the sheepdog. "And you're a young dog. I don't think you should be listening like that," because Díleas plainly was listening, head cocked to one side, tongue a little out. Looking at his expression, Fionn was fairly sure Díleas was laughing in doggy fashion. "Now, shepherd, we're tracking someone we've lost. Will you get out of our way, or shall I repay the favor by letting Díleas bite you? Or I could toss you down this hill? I've no real desire to fight, but I'm in a hurry."

One of the sheepdogs had returned to behind its master, nearly crawling on its belly, tail between its legs. The other was staying a lot further off. "What have you done to my dogs?" said the shepherd, backing up himself. "I can't let you walk over here. My lord said I was to keep people off. They're stealing his game, he said."

"Don't be dafter than you have to be," said Fionn, his sympathy, as usual, with whoever was stealing the odd pheasant. "Firstly, you can see I'm not stalking or hunting anything, and secondly, I'm not going to tell him I met you if I happen to run across him. And who else will tell him? I'm just passing through."

"But...but there is nowt up there. Just devil's leap."

"Then maybe I'm the devil, going there."

The shepherd looked at him, wide-eyed, and then jumped down the rocks on the edge of the path and ran away as fast as his legs could carry him, followed by his dogs.

"Come on, Díleas. Barking at him is just rude," said Fionn. "I think we've started a new legend, which is enough chaos for one day. And it should make poaching up here a bit easier too. I do like doing public service, especially when it involves a mischief. And something tells me you're taking me to this 'devil's leap.'"

Indeed he was.

It was well-named, if you were human. A great plate of cap-rock had been eroded into a narrow tongue, while the softer underlying rock had been eaten away. It hung above the wrinkled valleys of the lowlands a thousand feet below.

To a dragon, of course, it looked like it could be prime real estate, especially if there was a cave somewhere close. The difference was that dragons had wings, and dogs and humans were a little short of those.

And that fool dog was simply walking towards the drop. It did seem to be giving him pause . . . well, he was slowing down. "Wait. Díleas, this is a better task for a dragon than a human. And better too for a dog to have a dragon for company. I really need to rig you some kind of harness. Aha! I have it. The coil of traveler rope. Let's tie it to you, because my talons might have a bad effect on a fast-falling dog."

So they stopped, high above the world, where along a distant roadway a cart toiled. Fionn could detect a minor perturbation in the energy flow here, but he would never have found it without getting so close. Whoever had built these Ways between worlds had been adept at hiding them from planomancers, also from others here, if reaching them involved walking over a cliff.

The dog got a long harness, which, Fionn could tell by his pawing at it and sniffing, was less popular than the red boots had been. "I haven't got you on a lead. You've got me on one," said Fionn taking the end in a dragon talon, and wrapping it around his leg. "So lead."

And Díleas did. One cautious foot at a time... stepping out into the air. And then, he leapt into space. Fionn followed. Either the dog knew more or could sense more than a planomancer, or it was just a really crazy dog.

They did fall.

But not far enough for Fionn to unfurl his great wings. Actually he had to do a frantic roll in the air so as not to land on the dog. And the turf they landed on was springy and covered in thick moss. There were trees—gnarled, huge, ancient trees—overhanging the dell. The air was sleepy, warm, and full of the gentle background sounds of bees.

Fionn was attuned to the use of energies and magics. He knew this for what it was. He turned to Díleas, who had flopped down, panting. "Come, dog. Don't even think of lying down. Think of rats, or rabbits, or better still, busy beavers. Or you'll end up like that." He pointed to a green-white curved dome, lying in the shade. It might have been a rock, except for the eye sockets. Díleas got up and walked with leaden feet, still with the rope leash on, too tired to even protest that indignity. There were other bones here in the forest. A rotten femur nearly tripped him. Fionn could feel the lethargy affecting him too. Dragons were not as much affected by the magic of other species, not even the magic of the tree-people. How many desperate humans had walked to the devil's leap to jump...and found themselves here? Spared to become plant food. They walked towards another long-dead human, with shreds of faded clothing and a rusted sword and hauberk. Fionn picked up the sword in his dragon talons. The dog was swaying on its feet. "That's enough," he said. "Stop this now or there will be trouble."

The dog sat down. Yawned. And Fionn threw the sword as if it were a knife, to peg in the nearest tree. The branches swung lower over them. "Dragon fire is next," said Fionn grimly, hauling Díleas to his feet by the leash. "Onwards."

The sleepiness lifted as they moved on. Fionn searched out the patterns of the working. It was a deep and old enchantment, that the trees had merely enhanced. But it had been intended as place of rest, not a final resting place. A place to comfort and allow the wounded in heart and spirit who fell into this place to recover.

Kindly meant. Not predatory.

The sprite-trees who had moved in had found it a good way of obtaining fresh nitrates. That irritated Fionn. Well, the tree-people irritated him quite easily. The First had created vegetative intelligence, but wood had shaped it. Fionn wondered if he should burn the place. But there was real beauty all around, so he settled for collecting together a small mound of skulls that could be seen from the entrance, and scratching a little symbol on each. The sleep spell did not work on insect life, but merely on vertebrates. And now it would still be a wonderful place to sleep...if not for the mosquitos that would infest it henceforth, and make it impossible. Fionn chuckled quietly to himself as they walked on. He saw Díleas stop and scratch furiously and attempt to bite at the base of his tail.

He looked anything but asleep. "Ah. Fleas too. They are an irritation, but at least you can get rid of them with a bath, Díleas. Those blackhearted old trees there wanted all of your blood, not just a few drops."

Díleas scratched and wrinkled his nose at Fionn. "You'll live through a bath. You would not live through that place. Let's move on."

A half a mile further and they merely had the fleas and not the tiredness. Fionn knew that that was a good bargain, even if the trees would not have thought so.

Díleas rolled and rubbed his back, and Fionn kept a lookout for fleabane plants. Dragon hide was hard for a flea to get through, but these ones were hungry and determined. It was a pity they didn't eat sprite. A little later Fionn and Díleas came on a stand of silver birch—with a sprite. There was something familiar about them. It was Lyr. All the tree-sprites on Tasmarin had been Lyr, part of the one tree that was Lyr.

The beautiful tree-woman bowed. "Fionn. We bear fruit."

"Ah. So he is still fertile, is he?" Plainly the sprites who had been trapped in Tasmarin were either leaving there or merely spreading back to other sprite places. His Scrap had given them back their male sapling, and brought the long-dead stick back to life. Male sprites had no intelligence, but plenty of sprite-pollen.

There was a joyousness in the "Yes."

"Good. He is growing well?" asked Fionn, out of

politeness. They made bad enemies, the sprites. The sisterhoods—and there were various forms, each associated with its own tree type, and some were more talkative and friendly than others, although all of them poorly understood animal life, and did not tolerate it very well. Lyr had been one of the worst... until his little Scrap had given them what they needed.

The sprite nodded her gracious head. They were beautiful. Humans, and alvar, found them almost irresistibly so. Dragons, and it appeared dogs, could take them or leave them. "The human chose well. The soil there is rich."

"I think she made it like that for him," said Fionn. "She had powers over earth, and she's, well, kind by nature. It's not something you sprites understand, but it is something humans possess from time to time."

"We had not understood humans. We need to cultivate more such. Where is she who gave us back our mate?"

"We're looking for her ourselves. She is no longer on Tasmarin."

"Lyr has not seen her. She has not been near living wood since the day the towers became bridges and some of us could return to sprite lands."

That was worrying. The sprites weren't everywhere of course. But they did have ties to forests, and all trees communicated. Mostly they did not say anything very interesting, except to other trees.

"Well. The dog is getting impatient, Lyr. It seems to know where it is going, and I am hoping it is to her. But if you find her... well, a bit of dragon gratitude would be good for the trees."

"If we find her, you will be told. We understand

your role too in saving our beloved. We have learned the value of that."

"The tree-women learn gratitude and wisdom," said Fionn. "Well, you'll have mine, if you help me find her and keep her safe."

"Word will go out."

Fionn and Díleas walked on. And on. As far as Fionn could establish, the dog walked as straight as it was possible to walk in the forest. That night they slept in a pile of dry leaves under the trees. It was warm enough for sheepdogs and dragons, anyway. Both of them would have preferred a comfortable bed, and a meal that consisted of something other than the remains of the food from Sir Bertran's feast. There was no other animal life, and Fionn had not seen any fruit. Like Díleas, he thought fruit was all very well for herbivores and omnivores. Not for dragons, unless it was a slice of melon wrapped in salty ham.

Drink was supplied by a stream. Díleas eyed it very suspiciously, and looked at Fionn a couple of times, before coming to drink thirstily. He was a very intelligent dog, to have learned the danger of afancs (and other water creatures he hadn't met) but he seemed to prefer walking in the stream and drinking downstream of himself. Perhaps he liked the flavor of the mud. Fionn wondered if they would be reduced to eating that before they got out of this Sylvan world.

The next day was more of the same. Fionn found flows of unbalanced energy to put right. There was a newness about them. He wondered if they'd come about as a result of Tasmarin rejoining the great ring. That had to have had an effect. Magic would grow a little stronger in places. Much had been tied up just in keeping Tasmarin isolated. That magic would flow now.

It should change a great many dynamics. It might well even change the way magical forces worked.

Most mages performed their arts by rote. They'd find this interesting, thought Fionn with a nasty laugh, imagining the consequences. Undoubtably, what he'd just done was going to make their lives difficult.

It was a full hungry day and a night later that they came to what Díleas had plainly been aiming for. As a way out of a Sylvan world, it was appropriate.

It was a row of trees...well, it had been a noble double column of lance-straight firs, standing in what could only be a planted line to the top of a round hillock. A mound, Fionn guessed. An ancient one, that trees had long since covered. Díleas walked up, until he got to the last pair of trees...which were different. They had been the same, but now they were just blackened stumps. That would put off the sprites, Fionn thought. They feared fire. Didn't even like its old sign. Just as the people of Brocéliande would superstitiously avoid triliths...

There was a pattern here.

Mysteries like this teased Fionn. He'd get to the bottom of it, just as he'd eventually work out how the dog knew where they were.

The other mystery was that, having got there, Díleas just sat down. He'd been eager to go through the gates to other places before. But now he was just sitting. Looking intently ahead. In a way that was worrying. The Sylvan worlds were slow-time worlds, not as much as the alvar ones, but still, a month might pass in human worlds while a day slipped by in the tranquil Sylvan forest.

Fionn tried walking past him. Díleas growled at him. A real growl. A "don't do that even if you are a dragon" growl. So Fionn sat down, and waited. He stared into the energy patterns around him. Most of the time he confined his vision to the ordinary spectra and a few others. Otherwise it simply became too much for his brain to process. Now he looked deep, trying to learn more. Trying to learn how to find these gates to other planes. They were magical workings, and yet . . . and yet showed little sign of their presence. The trees were centuries old at least. Had this been here when he'd soared over this forest looking for things to put right? The planes he patrolled were huge. He went to areas where the balance was disturbed. They often seemed to be the same places. That too was unsurprising.

Díleas suddenly got up, turned and barked at Fionn, and walked forward. The dog vanished from view as he stepped past a certain point. And there was quite a vortex of energy between the trees, right now. It hadn't been present, earlier.

Fionn followed . . .

. . . And was not surprised to find that they were elsewhere. And, pleasingly enough, in an elsewhere where he might find food for the two of them. That was undoubtably peat smoke on the air. Of course hearth fires had their own downsides, but it was better than hunting worms and bugs in Sylvan.

The problems the First had with the bauble of energy that hung from the dog's neck were twofold.

For a start, it gave a limited view of the world that the dog experienced. It was not impossible to track the dog and dragon by their energies, but it was harder. It had been many eons since the First had exerted themselves, and the time dilations and contractions were confusing and very rapid. Logically they lived where time passed slowly. Very, very slowly. Some of the movements of the tiny gobbets of energy seemed absolutely microscopic, to the First.

But this was better than the Sylvan worlds. Annvn was a slower world, and they could move plenty of pawns here. They were easier to move than trees.

=== Chapter 10 ===

"THE KITCHEN WORKERS HAVE IT THAT WE'RE GOING
to have a bit of a rest. Gather fresh food. Ys is slow to
arm and their Eorls are too busy fighting and robbing
each other to send much of an army," said Neve, "and
Queen Dahut does not care."

"And what of the army at our gate?"

Neve shrugged. "They go or are killed."

It was outside her knowledge, obviously. So Meb
asked Vivien. She had, with her contact with her sons,
and her dead husband's position, a far better grasp
of the military.

"Some of them fled after the rock thrower was
destroyed. But most of them are trapped here. Obviously their mages thought they had at least another
month before we could accumulate enough power to
change. It can take up to six months sometimes. I
know Prince Medraut was surprised. He expected it
to be another month or three. Anyway, the ones that
are left... the prince will offer them terms in a week
or two. These days they always refuse them. It's a

pity. The Angevins make good soldiers, my husband said. The army used to recruit most of its men like that. My Cormac's father was a gallóglaigh himself, trapped here with the armies of King Olain."

Meb shivered. Trapped, far from home, with no way out but to accept service in the army of your enemy. She felt a little bit like that herself. "It's cold this morning. Is it always this cold here?"

"No. In summer it is often too hot!" said Vivien with a smile. "It is only the start of spring. We still have bitter nights and occasional cold snaps if we have a cloud front come in from the ocean. You can usually see the warmer weather coming from the outer parapets, with the blue patches forming across the sea. Take your cloak and we will walk up there and have a look. You are looking a little confined."

"It'll be even colder up there," said Neve. "There is a fire in the bower."

Meb shuddered. "I'd rather freeze than face the bower right now," she said.

So they walked across the courtyard to the outer parapet on the western side. Here there was no cliff, but a steep green slope down to the foam-laced edge of the dark ocean. That was deep water. "You could get a line out to some big fish from there," said Meb expertly. She'd caught fish, along with all the Cliff Cove children at the foot of Cliff Cove's crags. She'd missed fish, she suddenly realized. She'd never thought she would.

Neve laughed. "They'd never lower themselves to fishing here."

Looking out to sea there was no sign of blue-sky patches in the slate grey. Instead there was a wall of cloud, right down to the water, stretching across the horizon. "That doesn't look good. If I saw that back home, in Tasmarin, I'd expect a sea mist for days. Cold and clammy and useless for fishing," said Meb. "The fishermen would stay home, drink too much and get morose."

Lady Vivien gave a little snort of laughter. "I thought you said you had no experience that would help you to live in a castle. It sounds like winter. We get freezing fogs in the winters. But I have never seen anything like that before."

It was apparent that not many of the castle people had, as others had come up to look at the cloud wall. Someone had even called the prince.

And the mage was called too.

His face became as bleak as a winter storm as he looked at it. He sent a soldier running along the battlement.

To fetch both her and Prince Medraut.

He turned to the women accompanying her. "You are not needed. Go." Before, Aberinn had made some pretense of abiding by the conventions. Now he plainly was simply too angry. "Prince. I do not know what meddling you are attempting, but you have led us to the very brink of disaster."

Medraut first looked guilty—which Meb had decided was his normal look—and then puzzled and worried. "What are you talking about, High Mage?"

Aberinn waved a hand at the western horizon. "That!" he snarled. "The Changer was set to take us to Ys. This is your doing somehow, Medraut. Ever since you brought this woman here, nothing has worked as it should."

"My doing? MY DOING?!" Prince Medraut snarled, roused to fury like a cornered rat. "I nearly got murdered in my bed, Aberinn. The assassin escapes, and we still do not know how he got in in the first place, although I've put the suspects to torture. You are supposed to guard me. To guard Lyonesse. Your precious prophecy says I need you. You brought this woman here, not me. Admit it. She could not lie to us without your magic supporting her."

"You fool!" shouted Aberinn right back, inches from his face. "There are records, ancient records of all the places the Ways link Lyonesse to, even the non-human places. This Tasmarin creation was a mistake. There is no such place. I do not know which of the Lyon have allied their magic to this prop of yours, but I will find out. I have means denied to you..."

Meb looked at the two madmen...and walked away.

"Where are you going?" demanded Aberinn.

Meb shrugged. "Away. Away from that," she pointed at the horizon, "and away from you two. Even that army out there has to make more sense than either of you."

"The gates are closed," said Medraut, tersely.

Meb shrugged again. "Then I'll go as far as I can. You're killing this place, both of you. And neither of you care, except about yourselves."

Aberinn snorted. "Well, you'll be glad to know that you have brought about its final destruction, you and this prince of plots. The Ways are not open to Ys. They are open to the Fomoire. And they come."

It looked like a wall of cloud to Meb, but it was enough to make Medraut's blood-suffused face go from red to white. "It cannot be. After the last time the Changer was set so that it could not link us to Fomoire lands."

"So see what your meddling has brought us to!" yelled Aberinn.

Meb did not stay to listen to them. She kept walking away.

Vivien and Neve hurried to her. "What is it? What do they say?"

"They say those are the Fomoire. They both accuse each other and somehow it is my fault too. I don't even know who the Fomoire are."

Vivien stopped dead. "In King Gradlon's time, when Lyonesse was near the peak of her strength, the Fomoire came. They nearly destroyed us."

"Who or what are they? It just looks like a cloud to me."

"The sea people. They come from under the sea and have much magic."

"Under the sea...the merrows?" Meb felt a shred of hope. She knew and got on with merrows. She knew she had to watch them, but she could trust them, deal with them. She'd liked them, for all their tricky ways.

"No...not water-creatures. They live in a land beneath the waves, and the waters are magically held at bay. They're human...well, giants, but deformed." Vivien shuddered. "And they are powerful and evil. They built great bridges of ice and came with their war chariots and mages. They don't have ships, so they must freeze the sea into a bridge to attack us."

"Um. What do they do when they get here?"

"It was said they brought disease and bitter cold, but I suppose that could just have been the ice. Their chieftain had the evil eye. He only had one eye, but if he looked at a man...he turned them to stone. Not that that is possible."

It was. Meb knew that. She'd done it once. But that had taken touch, on her part. The news was obviously spreading around the castle, by the frightened looks on many faces.

And a cold, stinking wind was blowing from their ice bridge. It reeked of staleness and of old smoke. Meb wondered for the first time if she could bring some kind of magical power to bear on these attackers. This was not her home and these were not her people. But they were so afraid.

The next weeks were fraught with fear, tension... and helplessness. They could see the ice bridges now, although the cold meeting the warmer water tended to swirl up a sea mist. The Fomoire mages were pushing them in three long tongues toward the shoreline. When the wind—bitter cold and dry—came blowing off the ice, the people of Dun Tagoll could hear the chanting and the drumming coming out of the sea mist. When the wind blew the other way they could see the black huddles of the mages walking circles on the ice tongues. And day after day it grew closer. And colder.

Aberinn had retreated to his tower, and although sounds of industry, hammering and metal shrieks came from inside, he did not.

The Angevins had broken camp and fled inland.

Meb wondered if they should not all just follow.

She did, finally, get out of Dun Tagoll herself. Hunting parties—those included the ladies, and the dogs and the hawks—sallied out on horseback to see what food they could gather in. She was invited to ride out with them.

Meb decided she liked the country a great deal more than the castle. And riding, which she'd been more than a little terrified of, she actually found she loved. She hadn't dared to tell anyone, except Neve, that she'd never even been on a horse before. A donkey wasn't quite the same, and she'd feared the derision that would bring. But like the language, riding came easily. So did being sore afterward, but the horse liked her as much as she'd liked it. She'd treated it rather like Díleas. She'd watched covertly as the other ladies had mounted, and realized she was being watched herself.

Either she was more athletic than most castle ladies, or she was mounted on a good mare, or her magic worked as well on horses as puppies, but those who expected her to fall off, or cling to the saddle, were disappointed. Meb spent a fair amount of time petting the dun, and talking to it. She had no idea if she was supposed to do that, but she wanted to, and did, leaning forward to whisper in the horse's ear, telling it quietly where she wanted to go. It seemed to work, which was just as well, because the reins were something she was less than sure about what one did with.

"You have a fine seat, Lady Anghared," commented one of the noblemen. "You need to watch that mare. She's nasty-minded."

Meb thought the seat could do with a bit more padding, if it was supposed to be so fine. And the mare seemed the sweetest-natured animal. But she knew very little about riding, so she settled for smiling.

The country near the castle showed signs of the devastation from the armies, but Meb could see it could be rich and fertile. There really wasn't much game left on it though, and of course the farmhouses had been burned and there had been no crops in the fields for years, by the look of them.

The day's hunting tally had been one feral pig, some songbirds and some rabbits. And, oddly enough to Meb, a glimpse of a nasty little grey-mottled alvlike face from among the rocks near a hilltop, grinning wickedly at her. No one else seemed to see it, but having seen one once, Meb saw several others. They vanished when they realized she was looking. Were they so normal here no one spoke about them? Or did no one else see them?

She wasn't ready to ask.

They dismounted in the blackened ruins of a village—something that tore at Meb, remembering Cliff Cove before the raiders. This was long gutted and burned though, and the wilderness was reclaiming it. There remained, however, a fountain that bubbled out of a central rock and down into a stone bowl set among the winter-dead ferns. It overflowed into a long horse trough. The hunters went to drink, as did their horses. And, leaning against the stone, being sniffed and nuzzled by the dun mare, Meb saw something walking across her hand. She'd stripped off her gloves to drink, and had not put them on again, as she was rubbing the mare's nose. It was quite a large ant. She nearly brushed it off but something made her pause at the last moment and peer closely at it.

It had an oddly human face, and it was staring at her as intensely as she was staring at it.

"Excuse me," she said to one of the nobles walking past. "What is this?"

"Your hand, Lady Anghared." He seemed to find that funny.

"I mean walking on it." Her tone told him she did not.

"It is an ant." He reached out to flick it off.

She pulled her hand away. "I mean it has a face. Look."

"It looks like an ant to me, lady. Mind you, the neyfs believe they're little people. They won't harm them. Call them muryans."

Meb put her hand against the rock and the ant walked off.

"Your steed has behaved?" asked the knight, seeing it reach out to nuzzle Meb.

"Oh, yes. She's lovely."

They rode back to the castle. That felt like oppression, even if it was not a devastated ruin. Up on the seaward walls there was a great deal of construction going on. By the robe, Aberinn had finally emerged from the seclusion of his tower. She would have gone for a closer look, but for the thought of meeting him up there.

"She's either ridden from an early age or we were misled about the horse," said Prince Medraut to his aunt. "Aberinn has it fixed in his head, or at least he claims to believe, that she is from the South, and it is somehow my doing to upset his prophecy. I think he is going mad."

"He's been mad for years," said Lady Cardun. "You need him, though, Medraut. There is no one else with his knowledge or skill in the working of magic. You know that as well as I do. As for that . . . woman, he plainly dredged her up as an excuse to seek changes. She's no lady. She has no knowledge of the feminine arts. She dresses her hair like a trollop and walks like a man. She cannot hold a conversation. The lower orders are fascinated with her, of course, just as Aberinn intended."

"I had heard she had some skill with a needle," said Prince Medraut, mildly.

"She couldn't even follow the cartoon, Medraut. Trust me, it was merely some magical trick of Aberinn's. Still, she is being watched all the time. She's no lady, whoever she is. I would guess at a Lyon by-blow, but maybe from one of the other worlds. The product of rape on a raid out on the Ways somewhere."

"I wish I could see just exactly how Aberinn plans to use her. Of course, the other possibility was that somehow she was a plant of Alois's faction. But I don't know how she dealt with that mare. That horse is supposed to be a killer. It even bit the groom bringing it to her."

The queen of Shadow Hall had stared into her seeing pond, still seething with rage. She had put in so much effort to get the Angevins into a treaty with Ys. Queen Dahut was an insatiable slut, and it had been almost impossible to get her to cooperate on anything that wasn't bedding her latest victim. Dahut killed them, which was something the queen of Shadow Hall could see the sense and value of. And then, just when Ys was seething with rage at Lyonesse, with the Eorls all demanding war, and not even fighting each other, which had taken her years of work and planning...Aberinn had somehow not opened the Ways to Ys.

But when she saw the cloud wall and the tongues of ice, she crowed and cackled and danced with glee.

What the mage had been setting up on the inner wall was a series of huge lenses. In the morning the men-at-arms were trying to aim the weak sunlight at the ice tongue, which was barely out of bowshot now. He was painting patterns around each of the devices, and in some way, they must be working because the chanting and drumming stopped, and what could only be swearing had started. Meb braced herself for the possibility of meeting Aberinn and went back to the wall.

The ice was dazzling with the brightness of the sunlight reflecting off it. It might just be spring here, but it was midsummer out there. The water around the floe was actually steaming, making the black-cloaked army on it look even more monstrous than nature had managed. Even from here she could see that they were somewhat bigger than most men. Not giants as Meb thought of giants, but eight or nine cubits tall, she would guess. And even from here she could see that they would not win any contests for handsomeness. Their shapes were just wrong. Arms too long, or they were too squat and broad in the torso.

The ice was black with them and their chariots. They were drawn up under various banners—here a severed head, there a blood-dripping axe, and in the center, a large eye.

The floe cracked. It sounded like a whip crack, but right in her ear.

The Fomoire broke ranks and retreated with as much speed as possible.

It still wasn't quick enough for some of them. The floe calved off the tongue and deposited half a dozen huge, black-cloaked warriors into the ocean with much bellowing and yelling.

And much cheering from the wall of Dun Tagoll.

That worked for the morning. But by the late afternoon, the chanting had returned, and the good work of the morning was being undone. Now the archers had begun firing at them. Only those capable of the longest of shots, true, but the Fomoire archers, bigger than the defenders of Dun Tagoll, had drawn mighty bows and were launching their heavy black-fletched arrows back at the defenders.

And the ice-making did not stop for darkness either. The chanting went on all night. By early morning, Meb could stand it no longer. She'd barely slept. She went out to see how close they were.

There were plenty of other women up already. In fact Meb wondered why she'd been left, until she was told that Neve was in the infirmary. "She'll have been overlooked by the eye, lady," said one of the other servants, fatefully. "By tonight we'll all be dead of it, I shouldn't wonder."

Meb made her way across to the infirmary. Already the women were carrying wooden buckets, and ewers, and bowls and anything else that would hold water from the central well to higher points. The buildings within the outer wall were almost all thatched, and plainly fire was a threat. So they labored up from the well with water. Meb wondered why they didn't take water from the worn rock-bowl next to the outer wall. That was still full and trickling its water into a clay pipe. But perhaps it was for some other purpose. It was a very scruffy spot in the otherwise tidy courtyard. There must be some reason it was ignored. The water was probably brackish or something. It would still put out fires, surely?

Neve was looking pale and wan, and had apparently been carried in from the battlements about midnight. "We're going to die, m'lady. I shouldn't have done it. But she told me I'd lose my p-place." Tears streamed down her little face and Meb could get precious little sense out of her, or little comfort to her. Somehow she must use her magical skill to get rid of these attackers. She knew she still had the power that she'd wielded on Tasmarin, only . . . only most of the time there it had gone wrong. She'd had Finn to fix it for her. She actually really had no idea what she could do, or what she should do. She knew she was a summonser. She could call things to her. What would turn the Fomoire back? A dragon? A troop of centaurs? It sounded like everyone had reason to hate Lyonesse. She wouldn't bet that that would not be true of anyone she summoned too.

So she went up to join the bucket teams. Like the men-at-arms, they were trying to stay out of direct sight of the Fomoire, but judging by the chanting, the ice bridge was not there yet. But the sky was slate-grey, and the sunlight through Aberinn's devices would not help today. Meb bit her lip. Well, there was no point in hiding the axe under the bed at this stage. And she could summons it . . . but best to save that. She went and fetched it instead. It remained the most deadly, sharp-looking thing she'd ever seen. She imagined she might cut a hair by dropping it on that blade.

No one questioned her taking it with her to where

a row of women huddled below the stone and mortar on the inner bailey with their buckets.

After a little while Meb's curiosity penetrated even her fear. The chanting seemed to have gotten far louder. She'd have to risk a peep soon. And then the idea stuck her: she had a perfect alvar-silver mirror in her hands. She held it up.

No wonder the chanting was louder. The Fomoire host was nearly at the least-steep edge of Dun Tagoll's peninsula. The monstrous, shaggy warriors had their big ovoid shields up to protect their chanting mages from the arrows being fired from behind the battlements without looking over—with their errant aim, quite a few were landing in the water. And lined up on the chariots just behind them and under the huge eye banner was a row of gigantic, misshapen men...all with only one eye...staring at the walls, from behind their shields. Meb changed the angle of the alv axe a little more to get a better view of them. Saw one stagger and fall sideways off his chariot.

And then someone knocked the axe down. "What are you doing, woman?" demanded the man-at-arms.

"Using my axe as a mirror."

"The evil eye will overlook you just as well in a mirror! Do you think it hasn't been tried?"

"It's as bad reflected as direct?" she asked.

"Yes, of course. Everyone knows that."

It was like a candle in a great darkness. A bright spark, in dry idea-tinder.

Meb picked up the axe. The blade was bigger than her face...she held it in front of her face, and stuck her head up above the parapet. She couldn't see anything. But she'd bet some Fomoire's baleful eye was hurting. And she was rewarded by a reverberating groan from outside the walls. She was aware that the women—a mixture from both the bower and the kitchen just here—were staring at her. "Every one of you! Quick. Go fetch a looking glass. Any looking glass. Anything that reflects. We'll give them their own back. Let them enjoy it."

Women looked, gawped, and then began scrambling away to run down the stairs.

Within fifty heartbeats, mirrors—everything from ladies' hand mirrors, with gold foil behind the glass, to polished pieces of copper sheet, to a shiny piece of plate—were being held up above the battlements. And even the chanting outside the walls had stopped.

Meb had to risk a peek. By the cheering from the walls of Dun Tagoll she wasn't the only one. The chariots which had held their one-eyed starers were being hastily driven back, pushing through the mobs. The eye banner had fallen. There was chaos in the Fomoire ranks, and quite a number of their men were down, and now archers on the walls of Dun Tagoll began aiming their shots at the rest.

Meb saw Aberinn come out on the lower battlements. She could recognize him by the robe, but his head was encased in a glassy, spiked helmet of some kind. He took in what was happening. Took in the mirrors. Spoke to some people.

Soon he was up on the inner battlement himself. "This was your idea?" he asked Meb, with no pretense of ceremony or politeness.

"Yes. Someone said the evil eye affected you even if reflected . . . so I thought we'd give them their own back. It seems to have worked."

"You are either cleverer, or more powerful, than I had realized." He turned on his heel. "Sergeant. Get me four men-at-arms and carry that lens down to the tower. We'll give them a mirror to avoid. I'll tin one of the lenses."

Even Meb's dealing with the baleful eye did not stop the Fomoire mages. They were back by late that night. And by morning the Fomoire warriors were assaulting the walls. But now it was just warriors against walls. And gigantic though the Fomoire were, they were as scared of hot pitch, and as easily killed by a dropped rock, as the Angevins had been.

What wasn't better was the sheer volume of warriors they had to fling at the task. Fomoire would climb dead Fomoire to get up those walls. If the sun shone in the mornings the mage's lenses poured heat at the ice bridge. The Fomoire mages tried to build the ice bridges, and when the sun did not shine from the east, turned the cold of chanting onto the castle itself.

It was bitter. So was the siege. The part that Meb really didn't understand was how it affected her. It seemed to have merely deepened the infighting among the women.

And Neve wasn't dying. She just wasn't getting much better either.

— Chapter 11 —

THE PEAT SMOKE FIONN HAD SMELLED CAME FROM a small village. It appeared that Fionn had reached the travelers' destination of Annvn.

The travelers might have wanted to go there for trade, but it was not one of Fionn's favorite places. Its hereditary rulers had always had something against dragons. That was not abnormal or unevadable. It just meant he'd have to stick to human or some other form. Fionn could, with sufficient study, do a passable imitation of most body forms that he could cram his mass into. Some, like human, he was so at ease with that it took little or no effort. Others were barely worth the effort it took. But for Annvn, human would be best, although an alvar would be respected.

On the other hand, it wasn't even the best of places for a human. Slavery was still widespread, and the law was petty and very carefully enforced. There were licenses required for almost everything—including being an entertainer.

In most planes silver was silver and copper copper, and the locals weren't too fussy about the coin's imprint.

Annvn really was picky. Fionn had none of the local currency and a very hungry dog and a fair degree of hunger himself. It was late afternoon, not the ideal time for him to be doing a gleeman routine for his supper, beside the fact that, no doubt, some officious little man would demand to see his license. Anyway, there seemed to be some sort of contest on. Annvn was sheep country, like quite a lot of the Celtic cycle. And right now, several of the locals were showing off their dogs' skill at herding sheep to the locals. By the looks of it there were some considerable sums being wagered. Fionn was a competent pickpocket. He just had a moral objection to it, and would in general only relieve thieves of their ill-gotten gains. He'd pushed the line of who were "thieves" to certain merchants, lordlings and tax collectors, too—and to the dvergar, simply because it was part of the game. You always paid them for what you stole or tricked them out of afterwards, or they'd get really nasty. But they liked the game. So did Fionn. "If you want to eat, you'll have to work," he said quietly to Díleas.

Several of those taking bets had the look of professional gamblers doing their best to look like passing farmers. Fionn relieved one of them of a silver penny. He'd give it back later, if the man proved honest. "I'd like," he said, assuming his best village idiot look, "to see how my dog would do."

He could feel the eyes of the "prosperous farmer" take stock of him. Apparently he looked enough of a rube. "Hey, Lembo. Stranger says he wants to try his dog at the sheep work."

"Aye," said what plainly was a shepherd. "He good with sheep, mister?"

"Well," said Fionn. "He's never worked with sheep before. He's young, see. But he's a really smart dog. He understands every word I say. I reckon he could be a champion."

"He looks like a sheepdog," said the shepherd.

"Well, his mother was. But his father was one of my lord's graze-hounds. He's but a pup. But you should see the size of his feet."

This provoked laughter. "And you reckon he can herd sheep? He'll be more inclined to eat them."

"Oh, not Díl!" said Fionn, patting Díleas' head. "He's a good dog. Sharp as a whip."

"It takes a lot of training."

"I'll bet my dog can do it," said Fionn. "Sharp as a whip, I tell you." He dug out the silver penny. "Here. Bet you my dog can get a sheep into that fold," he said, pointing at an enclosure made of hazel-withy hurdles.

"I'll take you on that," said the shepherd—who had not been Fionn's intended target.

Well, he could return it, once he'd worked over the money men fleecing the crowd. Fionn shrugged. "Which sheep, mister?"

The shepherd shrugged in turn. "Any one. But just one, mind."

So Fionn bent over Díleas and said quietly, "One sheep, in that pen. But don't make it too easy. We want to get the others to bet." He'd found Díleas could hear him perfectly at a pitch humans could not. He'd realized it could be useful some day.

Díleas trotted off as if he was the most obedient and smartest dog in the world. Started nosing one of the punters, pushing him out, with a wicked look in his eye at Fionn. Really. That dog. Showing off.

"Sheep, Díleas, sheep. Not a man," said Fionn. "One sheep. Up there. He hasn't had much to do with sheep before," he explained earnestly.

"Neither have you," said the shepherd with a laugh.

That was true enough. As a dragon, Fionn had regarded sheep as needing to be well seared to get the wool burned off, or it might stick between his teeth. When masquerading as a human he generally had it served to him roasted or stewed.

He rapidly began to appreciate that they really were best that way, and that he'd just lost the silver penny he'd wagered. The problem was twofold. Díleas was smart. Perfectly capable of understanding what was needed of him. The first problem was, of course, that sheep were stupid, and not capable of understanding his canine orders, and he'd never had any experience at herding them. The second problem was that sheep... didn't separate. They really, really did not like it. The minute Díleas managed to get one out of the bunch, the sheep would either desperately try and rejoin the others, or the others would try and join it.

Díleas was seriously unimpressed with the sheep and their lack of cooperation. He barked and told them about it, and they ran away. He had to run after them. The crowd, on the other hand, were delighted with the performance. Several of them were laughing so much they had to sit down.

Fionn sighed and relieved the pickpocket, who had thought to take advantage of the distraction, of a few coins, and gave the probing hand a squeeze that would put the thief off for a while.

"You'd best call him off," said the shepherd, wiping the tears off his cheeks. "He's chasing a month's grazing off the sheep. I'll not hold you to your bet. He's got potential, that dog of yours."

Fionn knew when to admit he was beaten or, at least, when Díleas was, and called the dog, who came back panting, looking hangdog. Ears down, and his self-esteem somewhat lowered. Well, it might be a stolen coin well spent, for that. "A bet is a bet," said Fionn, and handed the shepherd the silver penny. "I've learned something and so has Díleas. Worth the money."

The shepherd slapped his back. "Ah now. I'll buy you a mug of ale with it. Best laugh I've had for years. Here now. Watch and learn." He whistled up his dogs, and gave Fionn a lesson in how sheep should be handled. Fionn noticed Díleas studying the proceedings with intense care, head slightly to one side. "He's a bright one, that dog of yours," said the shepherd, noticing. "If you'd care to sell him, I'll buy him."

"Oh, I can't do that," said Fionn. "He's the lass's dog, really. And she'd eat me alive if I didn't come home with him."

"You watch some of those fellows then," said the shepherd, jerking a thumb at a pair of apparently well-to-do farmers. "If they think he's good, they'll try and steal him and sell him. Did it to one of my dogs a year or two ago. I got him back; he must have come halfway across the county to find me, and he was in a terrible way. But straight as an arrow he came to me. Don't know how he knew the way, but he did."

Fionn marked the two men down, and pondered what the shepherd had said. So dogs were known to have this ability, were they? She'd probably enhanced it without knowing.

They went across to the alehouse and the mug turned into two, and Fionn used some of the copper to buy a mess of pottage for both himself and Díleas. The shepherd's dogs were at least amiable—and also at his heel constantly. They, of course, were aware of the smell of dragon. But they were also fiercely loyal and very obedient. When told to shut up, they had. "You're a good man. Many's the fellow that might have sat quaffing and eating and left his dog hungry. Bella and Sly here, they eat in the morning. I'll not be running to a bowl of stew for them, Finn! I don't win silver every day."

"Well now," said Fionn thoughtfully, "it's possible that we could win some more of it. Those fellows who stole your dog are over there. Did you ever get your own back on them?"

The shepherd scowled. "They are talking to Barko. He's a gambler and a fixer. I have my ties to Old Persimmon. He's as straight as a corkscrew, but he's a fine man compared to Barko. They'll be drinking some fellows into the army tonight. You be careful with them, Finn. You can't touch them."

Finn smiled wickedly. "I thought they might like a little easy money. A bet with a drunk who is far too proud of his dog to have any common sense."

"Not your Díl and the sheep again!"

"Oh, he's not good with sheep. But I've taught him a trick or two with numbers. Enough to fool people he can count. Here, Díl. What's two and two? Tap your paw for the number of times." And speaking too high for the human to hear he said, "Tap each time I say 'now.'"

So Díleas tapped out four. The shepherd nearly fell

off his stool. "Now, that's clever. He really is sharp as a whip, Finn."

"Good," said Fionn. "Now all you have to do is tell me and the alehouse in general, loudly, what a fool I am. No dog can count."

"But he can," said the shepherd, puzzled.

"You know that. And I know that. But our friends over there don't. All they know is Díl and I made fools of ourselves earlier. If I'm willing to put my money down, they will be."

And indeed, they were. And oddly, simply because Díleas had made many people who were now in the alehouse laugh, some others were prepared to bet on him getting it right. "Any sum," said Fionn, slurring his words. "Shmartest dog inna world. Sharp, sharp as whatchamakillit. Whip. Whip. Bet you a piece of gold, he c'n add or shub...subtrac. As long answer's not over twenty-one. He only got his toes an' tail ter count on, see."

"It's a trick," said a skeptical individual.

"S'not. You make up the ques...questi'n. Smartes' dog inna world. Worth a fortune, see."

Fionn ignored the comments about how smart his dog had been at handling sheep.

Bets were taken. The alehouse silenced. "Make it up," said Fionn to the sceptic.

"Uh. Seven add three add four, minus nine, minus two."

"Ach. He can't count on his toes that fast. Write it down. Say it again slowly. An' then you count his barks."

"Seven...add three..."

There was a gasp. "He's looking at his toes."

Díleas was nothing if not a showoff. And it appeared

that he could count, at least well enough to fool a rural alehouse. When he barked three times, and then looked at Fionn expectantly, Fionn's "good boy" was lost in the roar. And quite a few people intervened to stop Barko and his friends hastily leaving before paying their bets. For the price of a few more bits of addition and subtraction from the smartest dog in the world, the shepherd's Bella and Sly got mutton bones, as did Díleas. And Fionn could have had enough beer to float in. Fortunately alcohol had almost no effect on dragons. He simply liked the taste and the company.

The shepherd, however, was a lot more worried than Fionn was. "They'll have marked you down, Finn. They'll not like you having taken money off of them. You'd best come with me. I'll see if I can sneak you and Díl out the back."

It was at times like this that Fionn knew why he preferred low human company to high dragon company. They'd bet on the underdog, and they'd help out a stranger. At least, some of them would. "I've decided I don't like them taking dogs off people either, my friend. Neither Díleas nor I are easy to catch. He's cleverer than most and I am nastier than most. Unless I am much mistaken they'll wait until Díl and I stagger out to sleep somewhere. And then I think they'll plan to relieve me of my winnings and of my dog."

"But there are two of them. Maybe Barko too," said the shepherd.

"Don't you worry," said Fionn. "I've got a little surprise for them."

"You're a thief-taker?"

His Scrap had once come to just that wrong conclusion. "By the First, no! But I have nothing against taking from thieves, and I have decided I really don't like people who steal dogs. Díleas doesn't either."

Díleas had started out very doubtful about the other two sheepdogs. But now that they had all finished the bones, and it appeared that the other dogs were now used to the dragon smell, and the treats that came with it, he was quite enjoying being one of the pack. They were all peacefully snoring together at the dragon and shepherd's feet. How to gain social acceptance with animals you were designed to eat: via the dog, thought Fionn, sardonically. He really would have to try it with horses, someday. It made traveling incognito very difficult in some areas. He prodded Díleas with a toe. "Come, boy. It's time to be bait."

"They'll likely use drugged food. There is a piece of meat from down the inside of a horse's hoof that dogs find irresistible. I've trained mine to only take food from my hand, now," said the shepherd, still looking worried. "They're bad men, Finn. Best to leave them alone. You've hurt them enough with the money."

"Oh, it's best, I'd agree. But we've come a long way today, and have a fair way to go tomorrow. And you might say I have a little training in fighting."

This plan was rather turned awry by a shout from the door of the alehouse. "Recruiters!"

There was a frantic press at the door, and they were a long way from it. Fionn's shepherd friend was very pale, and rapidly sobered by the situation. "Do you have a chit from your lord? Or are you a freeman?"

It was clear that the press at the door were only getting out one at a time. Fionn would bet the kitchen door was guarded too, but probably with a club rather than a demand for papers. By the way the shepherd said it, being a freeman was anything but free...or good. It appeared that Annvn hadn't gotten any more pleasant since Fionn was here last. Well, he worked on the energy flows of planes, not their social evolution. He'd seen plenty slip downhill. "No. And you?"

"Mine's out of date," said the shepherd, tersely. "And what'll happen to my dogs if I'm taken?"

"Well now," said Fionn. "The answer is you can't be. This is the work of our friends that we tricked out of robbing a drunk who was too proud of his dog. So now I'm going to work another trick or two. I will get us out of here. You call your dogs close, make for the hills, and I'll organize a distraction."

"What...?"

"Hush. Close your eyes. Cover your dogs' eyes with your hands. Díleas, eyes closed, boy."

Dragons were good with fire. The alehouse was fairly badly lit with tallow rush dips. The recruiters had lanterns—and they included the two who had been dealing with the gambling fixer. Fionn concentrated on the energy flow of tallow dips and especially those nice iron-bound lanterns. Iron oxidizes...usually as rust, but in the presence of sufficient oxygen, finely divided iron will burn. And when you can direct energy and focus heat, and speed chemical reactions...

The smokey tallow dips exploded into a bright flare, burning up instantly. So did the iron lanterns. Fionn could have made that reaction hot enough to consume the hand that held them too, but he cut it short, settling for sudden darkness and some burns. He could still see perfectly well, but he was the only one in—and probably outside—the building who could. A lot of people decided that this was the perfect time to panic and leave. Fionn held back his shepherd friend, who was all for joining them. "Wait."

When the bulk of the stampede had gone out the front door, they walked through to the kitchen. There was a burned-out lantern and an iron-bound club there, but no sign of any other watcher, so Fionn, the shepherd, and the three dogs slipped out. By the sounds of it there was an almighty fight going on in the village green. Fionn was quite tempted to go and join in, especially as it appeared that, having had the tables turned on them, a fair number of people were for tossing the recruiters into the river. Fionn and the shepherd instead skirted the backs of kitchen gardens, and cut onto the road just beyond the town.

"Finn, my dogs and me owe you," said the shepherd, looking back. "That'll teach me to come to town without a chit from my lord. But they were in town recruiting barely two weeks back. There was no reason to expect them here again, gods rot them. Ach, that was a neat trick with the light. Magic worker, are you?"

"Not really. I've picked up a few little spells." Fionn gathered by the tone that that, too, was something to be cautious about in Annvn these days.

"My grandmother had the sight. And she had nowt to do with Lyonesse, either," said the shepherd.

Lyonesse again. "Me neither. But people think that," said Fionn.

The shepherd shrugged. "If you're the demon himself, I'm grateful not to be a foot soldier and to leave my dogs to starve. I've no wish to be a soldier. And I'll say nowt if they come looking for you."

"Well, if they come looking, I'd stick to saying you fell in with me at the ale-house and claim I borrowed money from you, and left without paying it back, if anyone asks. Who are they fighting with that they need to use such harsh recruiting methods?"

The shepherd stopped and looked at him incredulously. "Where are you from, stranger?"

"Further than you can imagine, friend. And I have further to go. I'm just passing through. No real interest in your wars, I just need to know where to avoid going."

"We go to war with Lyonesse. They raid our lands, rape our women and steal our sheep. The mage has foretold the Ways will open soon, and we must be ready this time, to strike hard and fast before they do." It was plainly a recitation of a speech he'd heard, rather than a deep-held belief that could make a shepherd volunteer.

Given that the paths between planes that Fionn had once known were poor places to try and take armies through, Fionn had to wonder just how they did that. And just how this mage knew all this. But he was human. Probably therefore a charlatan. Fionn was one, himself. But he avoided starting wars.

That night they slept under a haystack. And the next morning they came to the coast, and the next of the spots that the dog seemed to know just where to find. This one involved swimming.

The dog could do that without any alteration or teaching, even if he still tried to bite the waves that splashed his face.

Fionn decided there were better forms for the ocean here. There were sharks big enough to try their luck with humans, and certainly dogs. And besides the water looked cold. Form gave some protection.

It took him a few moments to change into that of a large sea lion and plunge after the dog.

It was nearly a few moments too long. The dog wasn't paddling his way across the surface anymore. Heart full of terror, he plunged down, looking for Díleas, his eyes wide, staring, twisting over and over in the water to look all around him. Then he shot to the surface, propelling himself out of the water to look around.

There was no dog. No triangular fin cutting the water and no trace of blood either.

Forcing himself to calm down, to be systematic and sensible, Fionn began looking for telltale energy patterns, and, on the third pass, found them.

It took five more dives to find the exact point of transition, to somewhere beneath the waves.

In the strange dapple-shadowed world, Díleas greeted him with a bark and by shaking all over him.

"So kind of you to share," said Fionn, "but I was wet enough without your help." He wished that transformation did more than hide his clothes. They were wet. And it was cold here.

"This may be the way to your mistress," said Fionn, "but it's an awkward place to pass through," said Fionn, looking at the water-dappled "sky" above. "They don't have dogs like you, and it's not exactly a friendly place. I am hoping that we are just passing through, Díleas, because this would not be an easy place for her to survive. If anyone has harmed as much as a hair on her head, I am going to extract a vengeance that their great-great-great-grandchildren would remember. But I'd rather find her alive and well, and generating chaos."

"Hrf."

"So the issue is just how to travel where we need to go, without it turning into a running war. Fomoire lands are, shall we say, interesting: the effects of magical ideas meeting real physics. The locals aren't friendly either." He shrugged himself into a body form that would pass local muster. Díleas, who knew his smell, and was accepting of dragons, and of Fionn shifting to human form, still backed off and barked. Fionn was not that surprised. It was the extra head that did it, as well as the withered arm and the extra height and bulk.

"It's me, you fool dog," growled Fionn through his snaggled teeth. "Smell. I smell better than most Fomoire. The problem with most of their 'blessed plain' of the land beneath the waves is that it is abyssal plain. Cold and dark. And the magic needed to keep off the weight of the water produces some very strange side effects.

"You need lead underpants if you're going to live here rather than just pass through in a hurry. Besides that, they're inbred, which is why they look like this. I think you will have to be my fur. There are places where dogskin cloaks are very fashionable on people, not just on dogs, and this is one of them. I doubt if they'd realize, with you sitting on my shoulders, that you aren't a dead dog. They don't always bother to skin their cloaks here. They figure they can always eat the contents later. My glamour might affect you too. I look the part, thanks to learning a thing or two from the alvar about their magics."

Díleas stared at him. It was a disconcerting, intent stare. "And I know you were studying those other sheepdogs, but it's no use giving me the eye. I am a dragon, not a sheep, and I'll go with you without being herded. Up on my shoulders, and you can point me with your nose."

Fionn bent down, and the dog jumped up. It was rather odd to be that trusted. It was rather odd having his ear licked, too.

They began walking. Mag Mell, the blessed plain, or the joyous plain, or, as far as Fionn was concerned, the blasted plain, sloped steadily toward the dark depths. The sunlight that did penetrate down here made everything a twilight blue. The only fertile areas of the land beneath the waves were those parts which lay in the shallows, and the entire thing had a bad effect on marine life. It was a good example of how a need for security could blight a people, thought Fionn. Yes, the Tuatha Dé Danann could not reach them here... but that was all that was good about it.

It did not take Fionn long to realize that something was seriously amiss with the land beneath the waves. It was the first of the places he'd been recently where the energy flows were seriously adrift and in trouble.

The other thing, of course, was a lack of Fomoire. They farmed—as much as they could—the shallow lands, where the water-filtered sunlight still fell. Mostly they grew seaweeds, watered with salt water—the freshwater springs of this place were few and far between. Too precious for plants. And rain could not fall from their saltwater sky. They lived as much by hunting—harpooning fish and whales and other creatures in the sea above them, spearing them through the magic curtain that kept the sea off and dragging them through—as they did by cultivation. But the sea was wide, and seaweed could be nutritious, and fish were abundant, and one could feed a fair number off a whale, and most things washed into the sea. Some things were pretty dead and ripe by the time they got into the depths, but the Fomoire had long ago stopped being fussy.

Now they were not around. Not even their women, for which Fionn was extra grateful. They had ideas about the hospitality owed to visitors. Curiously, they hadn't been gone long. Fionn came upon a still-smouldering fire. Fires were precious down here, for all that they made the air hard to breathe.

He could simply fix a few things as they went. And it seemed like it was going to be a longish walk. It was cold here under the ocean, but not, Fionn realized, as cold as it should be. Nor was the air as foul as it usually was. It smelled of the upper world, and not just of salty damp.

That might be an improvement, but it meant something was not as it should be. And by the traces of the crude magic they were using it was easy to spot.

So he made a few changes.

Their mages were not going to enjoy that.

=== Chapter 12 ===

EARL ALOIS AND HIS MEN WATCHED FROM THE headland. Of course the water was warmer down here, and it must be taking the Fomoire ice tongue more time to reach here than it would in the colder waters near Dun Tagoll.

That was scant comfort. Well, the ice would spill Fomoire onto the land and those ill-formed giants would fight their way south—if there was anything to fight against—once they'd overwhelmed Dun Tagoll. If they did, which, considering history, seemed likely.

In the meanwhile they had to be stopped here. Straining his eyes, Earl Alois could only make out the outlines of their banners. His engineers were busy building siege engines, and he would add his art to their strength and accuracy shortly. But he wanted a better view. "I am going up there to have a look, Gwalach," he said to his second-in-command, pointing at the rock spike above the bay. There was nowhere up on it flat enough for the catapults, or they'd have been building them there.

"Supposed to be a spriggan up there, my liege."

A few months ago, Alois would have laughed. No one had seen a spriggan—outside their imaginations—for many a year.

The last while . . . it had been different.

"I've a mail shirt and a good steel sword, Gwalach."

He scrambled up the rocks and was staring at the ice on the sea, at the banners, when someone said, "One standard with the eye. I make it seventeen of the one-eyes under it."

"You've better eyes than I have," said the earl, still staring. "With any luck we'll land a rock on them."

"If the catapult doesn't break and drop it on you," said the the other observer with morbid satisfaction. "Mind you, I'd throw a sheep or two. Fomoire haven't seen fresh mutton or decent fleece for a long time. And they're loot-hungry. They'll fight each other for it."

Alois turned to look at just who was telling him how to wage war, and nearly fell off the rock he was sharing with a spriggan. Its skin was the same color as the etched limestone he stood on. He reached for his sword. And it stepped back into a crack and . . . vanished.

Alois stood staring at the rock for a long time. And then swore. Long and hard.

At himself.

Drawing his sword! That was nearly as stupid as trying to kill the Defender because she stood between him and Medraut.

Since she'd come, the land's fay had been waking. Scarcely a day passed without some neyf being piskie-led. Other creatures too had been reported—including the spriggans. He should have realized. Worked out the connection. The spriggan hadn't been there to kill him. It had been watching the Fomoire. Advising on what could be done.

Well, they'd have to drive some sheep up here. Slaughter a few ready for flinging. And drive the rest into the Fomoire horde, when they came ashore. Hopefully without their seventeen evil eyes.

Further north, the siege of Dun Tagoll dragged on. Meb was the only one unfortunate enough to be tasting and seeing just what the feasts consisted of. It was curious that no one starved on the food. It was real enough though, just not the rich fare it appeared to be. Meb decided that somehow Aberinn must multiply it from some little stock he kept somewhere, rather than making it out of nothing or summonsing it from elsewhere. That had puzzled her at first: if all the blood of the House of Lyon were skilled in magic, well, why then did they not use it? Finn had said it was a poor idea because it distorted the other energies, but firstly, she wasn't too sure what that meant, and secondly, she couldn't honestly see the castle people caring unless it hurt them. But it seemed that was Aberinn's price for the magic he guarded the castle with. Other magic was suppressed, only barely possible to the most powerful with great effort. And it seemed their magics were very different from hers, all tied up with long complex rituals and symbols and appeals to Gods. Well, at least they knew what they were doing.

She didn't. And she really didn't have anyone she dared ask about it.

Neve was still pale, weak, barely able to swallow gruel, and very inclined to weep whenever Meb was there. She didn't seem be able to speak anymore. That left Meb with Lady Vivien, as no one else in the bower was even speaking to her. It appeared there had been considerable trouble about precious mirrors being used without their owners' permission. Mirrors were valued and expensive items in this society.

On the other hand, she'd found that the kitchen servants, the stable hands, and the common men-at-arms all were, to varying degrees, her partisans. They would bow, and give her a smile and a greeting.

Meb also found she was desperate for space. Dreaming space, if nothing else. Space away from the cold fetid breath of the Fomoire host would have been good. Her room felt too...watched. Too small. She took to walking in among the buildings and along the inside of the outer wall. It was a much older wall than the main keep, built of precisely fitted dry stones that had later been plastered over with mortar. It had cracked in places, and, because it was sheltered from the wind and caught the morning sun, the inside of the west wall had some tiny plants growing in those cracks. Periodically they were scrubbed off, except down by the fountain and the rock-bowl. For some reason the neyfs left that area alone, and Meb liked to go and sit there, on the edge of the basin. No one had told her not to, and it seemed that when she was there, they ignored her, and left her in peace. It was the one place the reek of the Fomoire invaders didn't seem too noticeable. The water was sweet, and she'd taken to having a drink there and dribbling some off her fingertips onto the ferns. Even in the cold Fomoire winds, they'd put out some little curled green shoots. She had a drink and washed her face. It had been another restless night. She sat and thought about happier times. Before she'd known too much. When she'd had a dog and Finn to follow. And had slept rough and been nearly killed...and had been happy.

At last she decided there was no use moping, and she needed to go and do something. Anything.

She got up. Bent down, had a last drink, washed her face, and walked away, away from the little oasis next to the wall.

She was passing next to the washhouse when an uneven stone made her stumble and fall headlong into the muck. It saved her life. The arrow would have spitted her otherwise. She sat up and saw it quivering in the wooden washhouse wall. For a second she stayed still. And then she scrambled on hands and knees behind the nearest wall. And another arrow hit that.

Someone was trying to kill her. And it wasn't one of the crudely fletched big Fomoire arrows either. Those, she'd seen, had long multibarbed points. This was a normal arrow, with the single barb of the Lyonesse arrows.

Meb wondered just what she should do now... besides get out of there. "What's wrong, Lady Anghared?" Anxious voice, male...it was the elderly steward who had changed her wine from the one Aberinn had bespelled that first night. Was that why she saw and tasted what the food really was? She didn't care. He was help.

"Are you all right?" he asked, kneeling next to her.

"Someone shot at me. Someone tried to kill me."

"Are you hit?" he asked.

"No. I tripped over a stone. It saved me," she replied.

"The Fomoire have not managed to get many shots over the wall. Come, my lady. Let me help you..."

"It wasn't the Fomoire. It was someone in the castle. Look." Meb pointed at the arrow in the washhouse wall.

Only it wasn't there anymore. There was just a narrow hole where it had struck.

Having someone try to kill her was bad enough. That had her on her feet and sprinting for the shelter of the main keep, with the elderly steward running behind. She didn't stop until she had barred herself into her own room.

Panting, she sat on her bed. If magic was that difficult inside the castle—unless one was Aberinn—it could only be the castle mage who had had a hand in trying to kill her.

It took her quite some time to settle her nerves. She had to get out of here. She would have to wait until the siege was over, unless...well, she had no idea how to get herself magically anywhere else. And if mere wishing would do it, well she knew where she would have been now...except it would kill Fionn. And she'd rather die herself. She took a deep breath. Stood up. Well, she'd brave the bower. At least there, if anything happened, she had some kind of ally.

Walking down the passage towards it she met that smiling ally.

"Good news! I've just heard that the Mage Aberinn has nearly enough power for the Changer. We'll be able to escape the Fomoire, months before anyone could have expected it."

Several other women came down the passage. Now was no time to tell Vivien that she was going to flee this castle just as soon as the siege was lifted. Instead she made her best effort to smile and said, "I must talk to you later, but first I will go and see poor Neve."

She made her way down to the sickroom. The news had plainly got there too by the looks on the faces of the injured. She made her way to Neve's bedside. The poor girl looked, if anything, worse. Meb had heard that others—those who had not died—recovered. The only thing holding her here in this castle was this faithful girl.

Holding her hand, she said. "Neve. Someone tried to kill me. I..."

Neve squeezed her with a clawlike little hand. And then spoke in a little dried-up whisper. It was the first thing she'd said for two weeks. "I didn't want to do it, m'lady. They said I'd be turned out. Left to starve and be raped." She sobbed convulsively, wracking her little body. "So I told them. I... hate myself."

Meb looked at the weeping woman in puzzlement. "But you've been here in the infirmary for weeks."

"I...I told them about the donkey. That you couldn't ride. So they put you on the killer. I tried to run and warn you, but Methgin, he held me, put his hand across my mouth when I screamed."

Methgin was one of Prince Medraut's bodyguards. And some of the comments about the horse now made sense. "I didn't get killed. The horse liked me, and I liked it. So all their plans came to nothing. Stop worrying about it, and get better."

"I never told them about the magic. I told them things I thought would make you seem safe. They'd be scared by the magic, and want to kill you. But it didn't work. They told me I'd have to poison your wine. Prince Medraut sent the order... I couldn't.

So . . . so I went and looked at the evil eye. You must flee, m'lady. You must go."

Meb hugged her. "I am not leaving you here, you silly goose. You didn't have to do this to yourself."

"I'm dying, m'lady," said Neve. "You've got to go, as soon as you can. As soon as the Changer takes us from the Fomoire."

"Firstly, you're not dying. If you were going to die, you'd have been dead within hours. You've just been wishing yourself dead and starving yourself to death. That stops right now. I am going to need you to help me get out of this place," said Meb firmly. "I'll talk to Vivien . . ."

"She reports to the mage."

"What?"

"She's scared for her place and her children. Besides, her family are old queen's men. Aberinn is too," said Neve.

Meb swallowed. Friendship? All she'd had was spies. And Aberinn had to be behind the latest attempt, surely. And then she got a grip on herself. One of those spies had tried to kill herself, rather than go through with murdering her.

She hauled Neve upright, sitting her against the wall. "Let's get some food into you, dear. You'll need your strength, because we are going as far as possible from this nasty little nest of vipers."

"Me?" asked Neve, puzzled.

"Well, unless you'd rather stay here and starve yourself to death, while we could go and take a chance on just starving to death."

"You . . . forgive me?"

"There's nothing to forgive, and everything to be

grateful to you for," said Meb, kissing her. "And I probably would have done the same if it had been the other way around. Now, let's get you some food."

Neve ate, very little, but she ate. But one-handed, as the one skinny little claw hand held onto Meb. And Meb knew that the mending had started.

Now all she had to do was get the two of them out of here, which was going to be more complicated than just going missing during a hunting ride, which had been her half-formed plan up to now.

It did have one positive effect. Meb was so absorbed in thinking about it that she forgot to be afraid. She decided there was no point in trying to go through the motions with the bower—they knew who she was, and what she was, by now. Instead she went to the stables, something ladies did not do. The expression of the stable hands would have told her that, if she hadn't known already. "The horse I rode."

"Yes, Lady Anghared," said the chief groom, who had hastily swept up to see what she wanted. He had looked very wary before the mare was mentioned. "Leia. Um. a good bloodline."

"Can I see her?" asked Meb.

"Um. Yes . . . she's got an unchancy temper." The groom looked as if his own entrails might melt out of pure terror.

"She was lovely to ride," said Meb. "Who was kind enough to suggest her for me?"

"The . . . the p-p-prince's groom."

But you all knew, thought Meb. They'd arrived at the stall. And the mare rolled a liquid eye at her, and whickered softly and pushed her nose at Meb. Meb stroked it instinctively. "I wish I had an apple for you," she said, putting her cheek against the side of the nose, horsey whiskers tickling her neck.

And of course, she then had one. She just wished, earnestly, that she really understood this and could do it with intent—but that wish was not granted. And it was only right that she took a bite of the apple first. It was real food, not old castle food. The mare thought so too.

The chief groom shook his head in amazement. "They said you were a good rider, lady. Not that you were the Horse Goddess herself." Obviously she had stepped up several leagues in his esteem. "If you need anything of us, my lady, you just say."

There was a murmur of assent from around the stable. "Just look after her," said Meb. She couldn't ask them for what she'd need. Horses, and a way out of here. But . . . step by step. "You could show me how you put the tack on properly. I have never learned."

If she'd wanted to be shown how to fork dung they'd have shown her, even if she was supposed to be a lady. When she left the stable, she was floating on a sea of goodwill and feeling oddly happier than she'd felt since parting from Fionn and Díleas. Horses were not as clever as dogs, or certainly not as clever as Díleas—but they had some of the same kind of trust for humans.

Of course it was all too good to last. She had horse-hair on her dress, her hair less than well ordered, and she found Lady Vivien waiting for her, worry written all over her face. "Anghared. You look a fright. You mustn't go to the stables. You mustn't wander around without an escort. The women are in an uproar about it."

Meb wondered if now was the right time to challenge Vivien about being a spy for Aberinn. She decided she just couldn't face dealing with it right now. "What does it matter? They don't like me anyway. They won't like me, and won't accept me."

"They're saying you must be some kind of lowborn imposter."

"Well, I am, I think. I'm not what they thought I was, anyway. And the minute I can get out of here, I will leave. I know . . . I promised to help Lyonesse, but I can't do anything here. There must be somewhere else I could go."

Vivien shook her head. "Anghared!" she sighed. "Yes, there are some fortresses to the north, and down to the south where Earl Alois still has some following. But, well, they are leagues away. You can't just 'go.' Even the regent's messengers go with an armed escort of twenty men. There are the tail ends of armies out there. You can't feed yourself and there is nowhere safe or dry to sleep. And anyway, judging by the talk, they're more likely to throw you in a cell and question you than to let you go. You have to try to fit in, and you have to show them your power."

"That will probably make them want to kill me instead," said Meb crossly. As if they hadn't been trying to do that already. It was obviously no use asking Vivien for help in escaping. "I'll wash and change, and come and smile and try to be nice. And tell them I had left something in a saddlebag, and as I don't have a tirewoman to send, I went myself."

The queen of the Shadow Hall peered in puzzlement and anger at her glass. Not only had Dun Tagoll withstood the evil eye, but they were thinning the ice bridge. She'd worked hard, feeding pieces of the dead to her cauldron, mixing, blending and making her creatures. Filling their minds with her orders and sending them out. Spreading the fear of treachery across Lyonesse. She'd been able to preempt the false, treacherous Aberinn, because she'd known the patterns of the Changer. Known that the Ways between would open when next the mage used the ancient device in the tower. He did not understand it fully. His strength lay in protecting, cloaking and hiding. Who would have thought he could turn that against her skills? Of course he did have the legacy of the devices and the books in the tower.

She had the cauldron, her muryan slaves and the vision. He could stop her looking at Dun Tagoll, but that was the limit of his power. She sighed to herself. She'd fought this war for such a long time now, she would not let a little check stop her. There was work to do, the cauldron to be fed. The muryans brought a constant stream of material for it. She'd been getting behind, and some of it was quite ripe. Of course, when the muryans brought it in, some of it was overripe already.

= Chapter 13 =

IT WAS INEVITABLE, FIONN THOUGHT, THAT THEY didn't meet just one Fomoirian, but a good fifty of them, All waiting as they came out of the mouth of a defile, so there was no avoiding them. And they were in a filthy, fight-picking mood. In other words, their normal selves.

"What are you doing here?" their leader demanded. A number of them, Fionn noted, were walking wounded.

Fionn stared at him as if he was a large salad at a carnivore dinner. "It's more like what are you doing here? Here of all places."

"Why shouldn't we be? It's our hunting territory," said the burly, misshapen leader, scratching his vast paunch.

"Where have you been?"

"Killing Tuatha Dé children with the magic-stealers. But they've melted the south bridge, and the priests say they can't find the cold to send out."

"Ah. That explains it. Part of the sky is going to come down," said Fionn, pointing at the dark water

above their torch flares. He got suitable expressions of
terror from the Fomoire. It had happened, occasionally.
"They've drawn too much cold out. It got too warm
in here, and that's making the sky fall. I'm supposed
to be looking for fires. You better put those out."

"But . . . it'll be darker than the inside of a whale's
belly if we do."

"It'll be wetter than one if you don't," said Fionn.
"Keep one lit, and head out for somewhere higher."

"And you?" demanded one of the warriors. He was
quite well made for a Fomoirian. Could almost have
passed for a large, pallid man with very big ears and
horns.

"I can see in the dark. Been sent by my clan chief
to smell out fire. So that's what I'll do." And he walked
on past them, aware that his neck piece was twitching.
The dog was behaving as if it was going to sneeze.

"Who is your clan chief?" demanded one of Fomoire.

"Balor." There were always at least twenty Balors in
the evil-eye clans. And they had the most power and
the most respect as a result of the status of the evil eye.

"Huh. The Tuatha Dé children taught you lot a
lesson, didn't they?"

Fionn could only hope they had. The evil eye gave
him a headache, which of course was nothing to what
it did to creatures less robustly built than dragons.
The dog wouldn't survive it, even if it was about to
sneeze in his ear. "Yeah. But we'll make them pay,"
Fionn grunted and walked on. Fomoire were, because
of where they lived and because bathing was not a
cultural practice they'd ever been that keen on, always
a smelly bunch. But this lot had a real taint to them.
Dead meat. Rather like that giant.

"I don't think he is what he claims to be," said the fellow with the horns.

Most of them had been good little Fomoire and put out the torches. Fionn helped the surviving two to go out, and loped off.

They wouldn't manage to find him. But word would get around. That would cause panic. The Fomoire had retreated here to be safe from the cheerful genocide of their successor people. They had made repeated attempts to take their old lands back, in the earlier days anyway, secure in the knowledge that they had a place which was safe. Which could not be reached, let alone invaded, by others. It had meant that they didn't even have to try to get on with their neighbors. It also meant no one could get away, and they had to live with their own fire smoke and mistakes. The place didn't even have decent beer. Fionn hoped that the dog was leading them out of Mag Mell, and soon. They'd been walking in this direction for several hours now.

And then, abruptly, the dog sat up and barked in his ear. Fionn looked around. It was pitchy dark of course, but planomancer dragon eyes could still see a little. They were alone, in the darkness.

The dog nosed at his face.

"What do you want?"

Díleas jumped down and began walking...back. He turned around and gave his little "come along" bark.

Fionn wanted to sit down, put his head in his hands and use some very descriptive terms in several long-forgotten languages. "We just came from there," he said between gritted teeth. "Look. I followed you, principally because I didn't want you to get hurt. You're important to her, and one place is much the same as the next for starting a search. I'll spot her magic easily enough. When you started taking me through gateways between worlds that I didn't even know existed, instead of the usual transitions, *and* you brought me to the Celtic cycle...well, I assumed you had some way of knowing where she was, just as the shepherd's kidnapped dog found its way home. I'd heard of lost dogs tracking people who had moved before, but this is insanity. This is the second time you've just changed direction. Do you have any idea where you're going?"

"Hrf."

"Two barks for yes. One bark for no."

"Hrf. Hrf." A pause. "Hrf."

Fionn closed his eyes. "That's either 'yes and no' or 'maybe' or just me imagining things. Well, the only way I know out of here is a good two weeks' walk away...so is it back the way we came?"

"Hrf hrf."

So they began the long walk. That was one of the major drawbacks, as far as Fionn was concerned, of Mag Mell. The land beneath the waves had a magical "roof" a mere ten cubits up, which made dragon flight impossible there. It was shank's pony or nothing. Anyway, he had the dog to look after. He needed to see how he could fly with it.

Fionn was careful to avoid Fomoire. It was easier, because night had fallen above the water, and even in the shallows there was little ambient light. Smoke drifted up here and was trapped, polluting their best lands. One could, to some extent, understand why the Fomoirians were such a charming bunch, even if it was partly self-inflicted injury.

Fionn was glad the dog knew where to find the way out, because there were absolutely no marks on this side. Just gravel that had once been seabed and dead scallop shells in the water-filtered moonlight. Díleas jumped down and danced around him on his hind legs. So Fionn reached down and picked him up and held him above his head. Díleas jumped through the "roof" of dapples. Fionn, determined not to lose him again, used all his strength to jump up and follow. It was pretty much, Fionn decided, exactly where they'd entered Fomoire lands, only it was not dark out here, but late afternoon instead. Well, time ran at variable speeds in these planes. Fionn and Díleas swam back to the beach. The rocks provided some fresh oysters, and a driftwood fire dried them, and while Díleas did not deign to dine on raw oysters, he did eat them cooked; a small, slightly brackish trickle provided their drink. It wasn't ale and a good roast dinner, but Fionn was tired, and tomorrow would have to provide those.

They were woken in the morning by cockle pickers. Fionn had time, barely, thanks to Díleas's warning growl, to assume a human form. By the reaction of the cockle pickers he might have been wiser to let them confront a just-awakened dragon. It didn't help that one of the cockle pickers threatened to beat Fionn for poaching and trespassing, so Díleas bit him. Matters only went downhill from there, as there was a small army of cockle pickers arriving. And the terrain of low-sand hills and marrams did not lend itself to running away.

"Look, I'll go along with you to your lord. Just don't lay a hand on my dog." It was usually easier to talk his way out of situations than to fight or to run.

"He bit me," said the aggrieved cockle picker, carefully not coming close enough for Díleas to have a second try. "He'll have to be killed."

"No," said Fionn, patting Díleas, who was working on giving the cockle pickers the intimidating eye, as he had seen the other sheepdogs do to the sheep. It seemed to be working on cockle pickers too. "He should be fine," said Fionn. "I don't think he ate enough of you to poison him. Dogs have tough constitutions."

Fortunately—in a way—for both parties, an overseer came riding along to see why they weren't at work. He defused the riot by escorting Fionn and Díleas back to the lord's manor and promising his master's retribution.

Their overlord was faintly puzzled at the demands for summary justice. "How many bags of cockles did you catch the varlet with, Velas?"

"None, milord. He was trespassing in the bay, though," said the overseer.

The lordling turned to Fionn. "Well? Don't pretend you didn't know that it's my land and my rights. Where are you from?"

"Well, my ship was from Dun Arros, but it's sunk now. So I am from nowhere, I'd reckon," said Fionn slowly, as if this much speech was a chore.

"Your ship?" asked the local lord.

"Aye. She ran onto the sands last night. The dog mostly hauled me ashore, led me out. Was not my idea to trespass, milord. Just to stay afloat."

"You mean you were shipwrecked?" The local lord was sharp for an aristocrat, Fionn had to admit. Only had to be told twice, and not the usual three or four times.

"Aye, look at my clothes, all salt-stained," said Fionn, doing it for the third time anyway, just in case. "We ran

onto the sand and tore her keel off. Lost her masts . . .
She was heavy laden, poor old thing."

"Where?" demanded the local lord, a predatory
light in his porky eye.

"Out in the bay. I reckon that bunch of corpse
ravens are all over her by now. Fine woolens she was
carrying. That's why they wanted to be rid of you," he
said, jerking a thumb at the overseer, who had been
unwise enough to hurry Fionn along with his whip.

"Wreck rights are a lord's rights!" said the noble,
his jowls quivering at the indignity of it all.

"You had better go and claim them then," said
Fionn laconically, and sat down and put his head
between his knees.

"Velas! Get what men you can. Damn this levy for
the war. We need to get down there before they steal
me blind. What's wrong with this man?"

"I'd guess he's half-drowned, milord. I think he's
faint," said the overseer, shaking Fionn. Díleas snarled
at him.

"Well, leave him. Let's get down to the beach."

And in a flurry of shouting and yelling, they did.
Before the dust had settled, Fionn got up, walked to
the kitchen. "Your master said to feed the dog and
me," he cheerfully told the cook.

Well breakfasted, they were on their way a short
while later. Fionn wished the cockle pickers and their
masters the best of a miserable morning, and walked
really fast. It would take the local lordling a few hours
to establish he'd been gulled, but he was not going
to be very pleased when he failed to find the wreck,
or the sailor.

"The question is, Díleas, where we should go now?

And don't suggest 'back.' I think 'back' is going to be a bad idea for some years," said Fionn as they stopped to take a breather at the top of a hill a few miles from the bay. "You appear to have an instinctive idea, which I've been following. But I am reaching a few conclusions after a bit of thought about this. If she went back to where she once came from...well, that would fit with the Celtic cycle. Anghared was her name, and that could be from anywhere, with Annvn, Carmarthen, Abalach, and possibly Lyonesse being the more likely places. And she has the ability to stir things up around her, and to be in the very center of all sorts of trouble, and yet she's shifted from place to place. So right now my bet—if I was a gambler, which I am not, as I only bet on certainties, except where I am wrong about innate sheep-herding ability—is Lyonesse. On the other hand, your sense of direction indicates that either she is moving, or her world is, and as the latter is impossible, perhaps she is with an army that is moving? Or maybe some more of those travelers are with her."

He prodded Díleas with his toe. "Of course, I am open to your canine guidance."

The dog yawned, rolled onto his back, and exposed his belly.

"That's either a statement of trust or an invitation to scratch you. I think I should have investigated those travelers more closely. At least they would have been able to answer my questions," said Fionn, obliging Díleas with a scratch.

=== Chapter 14 ===

THE ONE POSITIVE THING WAS THAT NEVE, NOW that she'd started eating, recovered very rapidly indeed. It wasn't her body that had needed to heal. The other advantage was that Meb, having decided that she was going to leave Dun Tagoll, knew now that her purgatory was temporary. She smiled mechanically at the jibes and ignored them. She found there were several women in the bower who were mere general servants and she took one with her to visit Neve, or to take some air in the courtyard. They didn't like going with her, of course. But they didn't have to like it. Just be there. Ideally, Meb decided, between her and any cover an archer could shoot from. She did discover one odd thing. They all skirted the rock basin and its little weedy patch of wall. It was obviously a local shrine or something.

She had more important things to do than worry about that. She had to work out a way to escape from the castle for the two of them. And that was proving difficult, especially as she couldn't discuss it with anyone.

Vivien, in the meantime, kept pressing her to show the bower her magical power. Somehow Meb felt that would be a very poor idea. "It comes when I need it. Not when I want it," she explained. And that was partially true too.

Lady Cardun folded her hands in her lap and shook her head. "I don't know. She just does not say much, Medraut. And she's either a very good mimic or she was leading her maid on. She makes faux pas, she hobnobs with the servants, she wanders about without any chaperonage. Yet...she does some things in a manner well-bred. I'd suspect she was raised in a noble household. The daughter of a favored woman, maybe."

Medraut tugged his beard. "I think she may be cleverer than we suspected. Look, it turned out that she could ride. To ride that well...she must have had a great deal of practice. I know you said she was stiff and sore the next day, but that is still possible, if she had not ridden for some time. She claimed never to have ridden a horse. And she's been very close to Vivien. We know she reports to the mage." He sucked his teeth. "Having her fall from a horse or become sick and die would remove her from the situation. That was my thinking. Yet Aberinn appeared genuinely angry and distrustful of her. And she's immensely popular with the men-at-arms for some reason. To act openly to get rid of her would be foolish until I have more information, I think.

"There are those who believe she made the queen's window reappear. But the more I think of it, the more certain I become that the entire scene with Alois was contrived. It was Aberinn's doing. They may have fallen out since. I have spies in the south, still. We may hear something."

"Her maid is recovering. She has returned to work. She will tell us what we need to know," said Lady Cardun confidently.

"It would seem to me that she's guessed that the maid is a spy." The prince pursed his lips. "I may have to trump something up, to at least put her to the question."

"You cannot deceive me, Vivien."

The eyes bored into her. She wished the mage was wrong, just this once. "I've told you," she said, wringing her hands. "She did the embroidery as no mortal could. It's *sídhe* work. It's some kind of glamor. Some kind of deception, but I don't think she knows she's doing it. It's not like our magic at all."

Vivien hated this. Hated being in the tower. Hated being given orders. Hated reporting to the mage. Hated his touch. But she was trapped here. Trapped by chains of fear and her children. Trapped by the shreds of hope. Hope that had breathed in her when she'd seen that spatha-blade axe. She'd thought Aberinn would be pleased at the time. It would spell the end for Prince Medraut and his pretensions.

Aberinn rolled his eyes. "There is no secret magic. There is no unknown magic."

"I've tried to get her to use her magic again, so you could trace it. So you could see," said Vivien.

"She probably can't. There are ways around the protection on Dun Tagoll. But it is self-healing. Such tricks will work only once."

He toyed with the models on his workbench. The

interior of the royal chambers, perfect in every detail.
He was building a model bedchamber. The shape of
the chest showed that to be that poor child's room...
she looked away, at anything else. A miniature of
an Angevin crossbow, a tiny thread on the arrow, a
trebuchet...she had been taught some of the theory
behind symbolic magic and scalar spells. The magic
of Lyonesse had, especially among the males, always
been tied to mechanical symbols. But she had no idea
of how the compulsion on her worked or how to break
it. She stood, silently. Waiting for the orders. Finally,
she could endure no longer. "Maybe she is the one
you prophesied. Maybe she really is the Defender."

Aberinn snorted. "That she cannot possibly be. She
may even be less than human, as you suggest. But put
one idea from your mind. She is not this 'Defender.'"

"But how do you know?" asked Vivien.

He laughed. "She is the third fraud we've had. And
soon she too will be dead. Now go."

He walked away to the piece of bench with the
symbols and careful patterning as she turned away.
She knew, from her training as a child, what some of
those symbols were. She wished she dared stay and
make it permanent. But he would have his protections.
And she had her children, hostages to fate.

The mage had cheated death for so long by being
one with the dead for most of the day and night.
She'd recognized the symbols, even before she'd seen
him lying there, unbreathing.

Weeping to herself, she fled the tower.

From its cage the gilded crow watched her with
a jewel eye.

✧   ✧   ✧

Meb sat in her room as Neve brushed her long, wavy hair. Hair that at least was like the hair of the locals... she felt the dragon neckpiece of the dvergar gold, heavy, magical and yet invisible, its links cunning and perfect, full of what magic the dvergar had been able to bind into it, designed to enhance her own power, designed to draw on the magics of wood, fire, gold, earth... She must still have some of the courage of the centaurs' windsack about her... centaurs? Maybe that was why the horse had liked her? What was it that the dvergar had said about the piece of magical enhancement she wore about her neck? It would help her to be what she wished to be. Well, at one stage she'd wished to be dead, and it had nearly helped her there! Only she'd changed her mind. It had helped her, and Fionn, to travel unseen and unsuspected into Albar, she was sure.

So could it help her to get out of here? Just how would her master have done it? Besides outrageously? Well, maybe that would have to work.

"Is it a full moon tonight?" she asked.

"Yes, m'lady." Nothing Meb had done or said had ever been able to shake Neve from calling Meb that. Not even discussing gutting and gilling techniques.

"So tonight will be the night for the Changer?"

"Yes, m'lady. The Fomoire will have their ice melt under them," said Neve with grim satisfaction. "Except those ones already ravaging the country. They kill just because they can."

"I hope the next change is something better."

"Can't hardly be any worse, m'lady," said Neve.

Finn would have said that that was a sure guarantee that it would be.

He would also have walked into the stables and demanded that they saddle a horse for him and Neve. Meb didn't think she'd quite get away with that. But a little glamor... If the alvar could do it... "How do I look?" she asked, thinking of Hallgerd, dressed in her best go-to-market-in-Tarport clothes.

Neve dropped the brush. Backed away, fright on her face. "M'lady?" Her voice quivered tremulously.

"It's just me," said Meb, wondering if her appearance would stay like that. It didn't, it appeared. Neve hugged her. "Oh, m'lady. I'm sorry. I... I just got such a fright. There was this wicked old crone here. An old fishwife..."

"It was me. I just took on a seeming."

Neve shuddered.

"Tomorrow we will use it to leave," said Meb. "Or as soon as some ordinary women walk out of here. They must, sometimes."

"Once the troop rides out to clear out any last foes, m'lady. Could be a week or two. But the Fomoire will know something is wrong quick when their ice bridge goes. Then, usually after the men have gone, the kitchen women go out and collect rock samphire and birds' eggs on the cliffs with a couple of guardsmen."

"Excellent. Once we're among the cliffs and rocks we can slip away."

"Yes... but... those are the kitchen drabs," said Neve. "And you're..."

"A fishing village brat. Like you. How did you end up in the bower?"

Neve blushed. "My granny was a bower woman in the old king's court. Not to say anything, but my mother was born something like seven months after

the wedding, which happened soon enough after she
left service with a fine gift. She must have taken the
fancy of one of the lords here, because it was enough
to buy a house and boat and a cow, and to keep a bit
for spoiling us. The Lady Cardun, she remembered
my gamma. Took me for the bower. Didn't take her
long to find out that I didn't know much, though."

"Well, at least you know who your mother was.
Which is more than I do. Or my father," said Meb.
"Anyway. A seeming is easier with some props. Can
we get some baskets?"

"Easy," said Neve. "They're hung in the corner of
the kitchens. But, m'lady. I'm quite scared. And it
won't be safe for you out there..."

"I could probably look like a dragon, as easily as
a fishwife."

Neve squeaked at the thought.

It was hard to sleep that night, and then when she
did finally get to sleep, Meb woke abruptly again. It
was...different. The last time the air had held the
smell she'd come to realize was Fomoire. This...this
was a melange of new scents. Just hints of them, as if
carried by errant breezes from faraway places. Some
were of forest, mushroomy and moist, some of gorse
flowers, and some of Tarport on a hot day.

It wasn't all pleasant, but it was a lot sweeter than
the Ways to the Fomoire had smelled. She slept well
now, for the first time in weeks. She had such sweet
dreams too, dreams that involved her kissing Fionn
and didn't, in a rather confused fashion, entirely stop
there, so that being wakened was anything but welcome.
Neve was too full of the news to even wait until

Meb's eyes were properly open. "Oh, m'lady! The Changer. Something is wrong. It didn't work properly. The mage is up and in a rage. The prince is going to ride out with his troop soon to try and work out which of the Ways are open."

"And somehow it will all be my fault," said Meb. "We'd better go, and quickly."

She'd tried to think, last night, just how she could take the axe with them. Could she tell it to look like a stick? Could she rely on summonsing it again? She rather wanted it with her. She tried making it look like something else. An old stick.

It seemed to work, at least while she was holding it. Put it down, and it reverted to being an axe.

"M'lady! You can't take that!" said Neve, shocked, seeing her pick it up.

"But it's just the thing for cutting rock samphire," said Meb, swinging it about. "Anyway, it changes appearance with me. Look."

They made their way down through the passages of the castle. No one questioned the old woman, with her stick and one of the castle maids. Collecting two baskets from outside the back of the kitchen where Neve had stashed them, they walked down to the great gate, to sit and wait in the sun on a mounting block.

"The other women will be along presently. They were talking about it last night," said Neve.

"And best we got down here early. Mage Aberinn will be sending for me again," said Meb. "And somehow it's always someone else's fault. I'll be glad to be out of here."

"But . . . m'lady. Just where are we going to go? What are we going to do?" asked Neve.

And then Prince Medraut and his troop rode up, and saved Meb from answering something she had no idea of the answer to. Because things went badly awry, just about immediately. Medraut didn't recognize her. But he did recognize Neve. "You. Wench. Where's that mistress of yours?" he demanded, jigging his horse up closer, reaching down and raising her chin with his whip.

She dropped onto her knees. "P-please, your Highness Prince, I don't know. I just got told to go and collect samphire this morning."

"By whom? Your mistress?" demanded Medraut.

"N-no. Lady Cardun sent me to the kitchen. I'm not to work in the bower anymore."

The whip slashed at her unprotected face, and Neve screamed as it cut her cheek. "Don't lie to me. I spoke to Cardun not two minutes back. She said she had no idea where you were." He raised the whip again.

"Stop it," said Meb, standing in front of her. "Don't you dare hit her!"

The whip halted. Prince Medraut stared. "So that's where you've got to."

Meb realized she'd stopped concentrating on the glamor. She was no alvar, able to just to set a glamor in place and have it stay in place.

"Yes. I am leaving," said Meb.

"No one leaves Dun Tagoll without my permission," said Medraut. "Aberinn is blaming the latest disaster on you."

"Everything that goes wrong is my fault," said Meb. "What has he done this time? Just so I know what my fault is supposed to be, so I can be very sorry for it." She was seethingly angry now.

"We are not in the right place to intersect to the Ways," said Medraut, tersely. "Some form of sabotage is suspected. And you are the stranger in our midst, Anghared, as you call yourself."

Meb sighed artistically. "He got it wrong, and now it's my fault again. I think he is going senile. Or your machine is not right. It's the second time it has been wrong, and it has nothing whatever to do with me. Maybe he just needs a little more effort or more power. Magic is like that."

Medraut looked at her strangely. "You came here, and were granted a place for appearing to have performed a major magic. Yet...you don't seem to me to understand the rudiments of magic. It can't be wrong, young woman. The very rules of sympathetic magic are scalar relationships. They are very precise. One grain of weight becomes seven or seventy-seven or seven hundred and seventy-seven. One hair width is multiplied by precisely the same measurements. Not somehow some arbitrary number! Magic would be chaos then!"

His eyes narrowed. "You've claimed to be a worker of magic, but yet you do not appear to know the very most basic principles. What is the law of contagion?"

"If you get sick it spreads?" said Meb, who honestly had no idea.

The prince rolled his eyes. "How were we ever fooled by you, woman? I was shaken, I suppose, by Alois. But even the newest of adepts learns the principles of 'once together, always together.' You claim to be a summonser and do not understand how the basis of it works. Lady Cardun was right: you are simply a fraud."

"I never claimed to be anything," said Meb. "You all said I was. And anyway that's not how summonsing works. If I need it and want it badly enough, and can imagine it clearly... it comes."

That provoked scornful laughter from the prince. "Yes, that is how the commons think it works. Well, you've had a good time imagining you can live as your betters do. And I'll be first to admit, you were a quick imitator. Well, you seem to have a taste for the neyfs and kitchen trulls, by all reports. You will make an excellent one. But first you can have some time at the posts and a good whipping. Afterwards I will be back to ask some questions and finally get some straight answers." He gestured to one of his bodyguards. "Methgin. Take the two of them to the posts. And you, Captain, get them to open that gate so we can go and try to establish just what sort of mess we have to deal with this time."

The gate swung open and the press of horses rode out. For a mad moment, Meb thought of trying to run with them.

But Methgin was in the way and she still had Neve with her, and besides, they would have to cross the causeway single file... there was no point in even trying to run.

Methgin grabbed Neve roughly with one hand and then reached to twitch Meb's "stick" from her with the other, plainly thinking two women no match for his burly frame.

"Haaaa!" he screamed. Fortunately there was still a lot of noise outside. He let go of Neve and clutched his partially severed finger. And found himself staring at the bloody edge of the spatha-axe he had just grabbed. "I think," hissed Meb, "that I am going to cut you in half right now. I forgot I had my axe with me or I would have cut your prince in half. Neve. Take that sword of his, and his knife. We're going to walk out of that gate. And if you try anything, Methgin, I'll kill you."

He was a braver man than many. "Where . . . where did the axe come from?"

"Magic. Real magic," said Meb. "Not your feeble magic. It's an alvar axe. It'll cut through that armor of yours like thin parchment. You've felt how sharp it is."

The three of them walked out past the gate . . . which swung closed behind them. The last of the troop of horses was still about thirty yards away, waiting their turn to ride the narrow causeway path over to the main cape.

Meb was wondering just what to do, and what to do with the prisoner when Neve solved part of her problem for her. She hit him really hard, two-handed, with the back of his own sword on the back of his head, just below the helmet. Neve was not a large woman, and she'd been sick and was weakened by that. She made up for it in fury. The big man fell like a poleaxed steer. Neve kicked him. "And that's for trying to kill my lady. He was about to call out, or try something, m'lady. I could see his shoulders tense. What do we do now?"

They were just outside the gate, with two baskets, an unconscious bodyguard and an axe. There were guards on the gate towers, but presumably, as no one had yelled out, they were watching the horsemen on the causeway. There was no way that Meb and Neve could get across that causeway unseen, though. "Let's just walk along the wall. There might be somewhere we can sit down until dark or something."

"There's the cave . . ." said Neve, doubtfully, "but surely they'd look there?"

"It's better than standing here."

So they walked slowly and calmly along the narrow track directly below the castle wall, along to the seaward side, where the peninsula sloped into the water. Then down over some rough ground and a few scraps of half-rotten shale and down onto the sea shelf. As they walked along this, Meb was trying hard to project "you can't see us" thoughts at the ramparts above.

The sea raced and fumed into the dark, steep-sided zawn. Above was just cliff, now, and above that . . .

"That's the queen's window up there," said Neve. "Poor dear. They were some who said he pushed her rather than that she jumped. I don't believe it myself, because they say he was a broken man afterwards. Never went to bed anything but dead drunk ever again for the rest of his days. He had lost both his son and heir and her."

"We'd better get down in the gully before someone spots us from it," said Meb. It was a long fall from that window.

And the water looked deep and cold, and laced with rocks.

"There are bats in the cave, m'lady," said Neve, wrinkling her nose in distaste, as they advanced towards the point where the cliff on both this and the foreland overhung, to join in a dark hole where the water surged and gurgled inward. They must be under the edge of the causeway now. Someday the hungry sea would eat through here and make an arch, and then collapse the causeway. Right now it offered a dark refuge, if a smelly one. But part of Meb's apprenticeship with the gleeman-dragon didn't like it. "It's the place anyone would hide. They'll look there."

Neve shook her head. "They say there are knockers down there. It's a place that the haerthmen, let alone neyfs, won't venture, not without ten of them, and then if they hear a squeak, they'll run. I wouldn't go down there myself, except with you!"

Meb wasn't sure what a knocker was, but it was a heavy load to bear. "What's a knocker?" she asked as they walked forward into the ammoniacal gloom.

"They live underground..."

Her voice died as they came face to face with the current occupants of the sea-grotto.

Not all of the Fomoire had escaped or been drowned. A few of them had been left behind. The five broad, huge, shaggy men with their long iron swords came running, whooping, for the bounty that had suddenly walked into their hiding place.

Meb swung the axe, trying to defend herself, as one of the others was throwing Neve down and tearing at her skirt. Meb had plainly forgotten to tell it not to look like a stick. The lead Fomoire warrior batted it away with his round whale-hide shield as he tried to both grab her and hold a sword.

The axe cut through the shield, through the arm and through the hide-coated body behind it, nearly jarring itself out of her hands. She wrenched it free of his body as the other Fomoire—the slower ones—turned and ran. The one who had been about to rape Neve rolled frantically away, as Meb's next clumsy axe stroke took the horn off his helmet and a slice off his buttocks. He rolled on and screamed and somehow rolled into a staggering run, diving into the churn of the water after his fellows.

Something behind them cheered and clapped. Meb turned to deal with whatever this new menace was.

High on the rock next to a fissure in the wall were a new crowd. They were not tall and aggressive...the biggest was only about two cubits high. There were half a dozen of them, though.

But the worst thing they were doing was to clap. So why was Neve clinging to her, gibbering in fright, seeming even more terrified than when she was going to be raped?

"Nnn Na..." was all Neve managed to get out, pointing a quivering finger. Meb patted her, and tightened her grip on the axe.

The tallest of the shaggy-haired, bright-eyed dwarfish gang bounced down. Bowed. "Ah. The Royal House of Lyonesse has decided to pay us a visit," he said sardonically. "To what do we owe this unexpected pleasure?"

Meb knew and had liked and got on with the dvergar back on Tasmarin. These looked similar. "I had heard of the hospitality of the knockers," she said, for that, she decided, was what they had to be, "so we thought we'd find some refuge with them. Seeing as we're being hunted."

"No orders? No commands? No demands for jewels?" asked the hairy little man. He carried, Meb noted, a mattock rather than a sword or axe.

"No. I have all the treasure I could desire," said Meb. "And most people don't seem to listen when I give them orders."

The knocker chief grinned, teeth white in a dark

face. "Eh. I see the treasure. Dvergar work. Worth a good few kingdoms."

So he could see the necklace. No point in denying it then. She nodded. "It's made of dragon gold, and has eyes of wood-opal, made with the cunning and virtue of the dvergar. It was made for me by Breshy, also sometimes called Dvalinn, at the order of his father Motsognir."

The knocker nodded. "Names of powerful cousins. Not us. We're just miners for silver and tin. And how did you make them give you such a talisman? Or did you steal it from them?"

Meb looked at him crossly. "Breshy is nice, not like you. Anyway, only a fool steals from the dvergar. It was a gift. I wished for him some fish when he needed them. Finn said he would get them."

"Finn?"

"He . . . he's a dragon. Called Fionn sometimes." They were non-humans themselves.

"A black dragon. We've not seen him for many centuries," said the knocker. "Nor any other dragons, mind you. Not a bad thing. Fionn was something of a joker, but he usually paid for what he took."

Meb's heart leapt just at a mention of the dragon. "He always paid, just not always in the coin you expected," she said defensively.

That actually got a snort of laughter. "Sometimes in mayhem."

"That's . . . fair enough," admitted Meb. "What is your name, knocker?."

"Names are tricky things. But you can call me Jack."

The others seemed to find that funny. "And we're all Jack, too."

"I am called Meb," said Meb, thinking to not even start the Anghared business. "Now we need to hide or get away from here. Could you show us where to go?"

"Getting away from here at your size, by our ways, that could be a bit tricky," said the chief Jack, tugging his beard. "You'd be like a stopper in most of our tunnels. We could widen them, but it would take time. And the only human audits would not be taking you away from the castle. Mind you, the human tunnel would be a fair place to hide for now, at least in the entry to it. It's hidden from human eyes, it seems."

"That'll do. Thank you."

"Polite too," said the chief Jack. "Well, well. Come along then."

It was near low water, and they walked along a splashing path, part of which must be underwater at high tide. The knocker Jacks lit their lanterns and led them deeper into the grotto, to where the sea and the back wall came to join each other in a gurgling corner.

"Just to the side there," said the chief Jack.

Meb saw a small door, and beside it, a coracle.

"Where does it lead?" she asked.

"Where does what lead?" asked Neve, still clinging to her.

"The door," said Meb.

"What door?"

"That one," said Meb, pointing.

"But . . . that's just a rock."

"It's bespelled," said the chief Jack, chuckling. "Leads to the tide caves for the great machine above."

"Can we go in?" asked Meb.

"It's locked," said the knocker, shaking his head. "We can break it open, but that'd tell the mage. And we're banished from in there. It's part of the castle and we can't go there anymore. Will you set that to rights? It was ours before it was theirs."

"Um. How?" asked Meb.

"Now if we knew that, we'd be doing it ourselves," said the chief Jack. His smaller fellows bobbed their heads in agreement. "But you could sit on the doorstep with the little round boat and be hidden with it."

"I still don't see the door," said Neve.

So Meb led her up to it.

"I can feel it...but not see it. It looks like you pushed my hand into a damp rock," said Neve, incredulously.

"There's a cockle shell of a coracle there too," said Meb. "Here. Come closer."

"Oh. I can see it now," said Neve, puzzled.

"'Tis because you're inside the illusion," said the chief Jack. "Anyone coming down here would not see you."

It was chilly, clammy and dark. And, Meb thought, quite difficult for anyone but Aberinn to find. This must be his bolt-hole. She looked at the coracle. "Could we use that to get across the gully?"

"At low water, probably," said the knocker.

"Well. Our thanks, again." Meb wished she had some kind of payment, some small gift to give them. Her time with the dvergar had taught her that that could pay handsome dividends. Well, the dvergar had loved to watch her juggle. And it would help to pass the time and keep her warm. "Would you like me to juggle for you? A small entertainment in thanks for your help?"

There was a moment's silence. Almost breathless. Then the chief Jack said: "Indeed," followed by a chorus of "Yes," and "Yes, yes!"

So Meb dug out her precious tasseled balls and lost herself in their rhythms. She made her strange audience gasp and she made them laugh and clap.

And then the chief Jack held up his hand. "They come."

In the silence Meb caught the sound of men's shuffling feet. "I swear I heard something down here," said a nervous voice.

"Maybe the rest of the Fomoire," said another, sounding no less nervous. "That one was barely cold. Not more than two hours dead, I'd reckon."

=== Chapter 15 ===

FIONN WAS BACK TO FOLLOWING THE DOG. IT WAS
something he was used to doing by now. The trouble,
in a way, was that the dog was intent on the straightest
line to his goal. Fionn had a slightly wider world view,
which included being able to see obstacles which they
could not simply go through. Where it might be faster
and easier to go around. Unfortunately, all he could
work out about "where" was somewhere more or less
directly in front of the dog, because the dog would
follow a path or road . . . if it didn't deviate too much.
Díleas was bright enough to know that straight was
not always fast.

Obstacles, like meals and drinks, were Fionn's
responsibility to deal with.

"I think we're going to need to try some flying,
young dog. At night, perhaps. This country is as stirred
up as a hornet's nest," said Fionn as they emerged
from the ditch where they had just watched a troop
of soldiers—and a troop of new-pressed recruits—pass.
"If they'd been less noisy calling step, we might have

walked into them and they'd probably have wanted me to join the army, which seems odd, because I have never wanted the army to join me. Also, I don't think they take dogs, and they were going the wrong way, and they'd object to my not going the wrong way with them. Sometimes it would be very convenient not have this inbuilt prohibition on taking intelligent life. Unfortunately, that is the way I am made."

Díleas nosed him behind the knee. He'd come to understand that by now. It meant "get a move on, that direction," in basic overintelligent sheepdog language.

So Fionn did. It involved some trespass in various fields, including one with a bull who felt quite strongly about trespassers. "Next time," said Fionn to Díleas, surveying the bull, who was now convinced the far corner of his paddock was very interesting and that if he ever saw a trespasser again, he would rapidly retreat to it, "Try not to run behind me when you've made the bull mad."

At length they spotted a huddle of buildings, and as the day was drawing to a close, Fionn informed Díleas that they had the prospects of supper and a basket. "If I can find a suitable one, we will try you on being a flying dog. I hope you do that better than you herd sheep."

The cluster of buildings proved to be a farmhouse, with a farmer's wife, three small children and another due all too soon, and a sheepdog. The sheepdog was less than pleased to see them. The farmer's wife was more than pleased to see a man, of any sort.

"My man's been taken for the army and I've yet to get the hay in," she said, "and there's two dozen sheep to be crutched and sheared still, and I've got the children to cope with. I see you have an eye dog there." Díleas was staring intently at the other sheep-dog. Who was staring just as intently back.

"He's young yet," said Fionn. "I'll help with the hay, ma'am. You can get on with what needs be done here, if you'll feed me and the dog tonight. He'll only take food from my hand, and if I am taken for the army, as my lord wanted, well, he'll starve." It was too good a story not to reuse.

The woman nodded. "It's the paddock just behind the hedge. Tom had it scythed and drying. But do you think they'd give him another day to get in?" she spat. "Damn them and Lyonesse too. Now it'll rain for sure before I can get half of it stacked. What we'll do in winter for feed, I have no idea."

The field had a high surrounding hedge. And days of work, forking the hay into a handcart and gathering it to stack. Days for a man, anyway. Not quite that long for a dragon with talons that did a fair job as four outsize hayforks, and a tail that could wield the actual hayfork. "It'll ruin my reputation if this gets out," said Fionn to Díleas. "Why don't you watch to see if the farmer's wife—or anyone else likely to be alarmed by a dragon doing farm chores—is coming, and give me warning. It's that or collect hay in your mouth."

Díleas seemed to prefer keeping watch.

The job still took a good three hours. Fionn then thatched the rick in the only manner he knew, which was centuries old and cultures away. But it was a fair method for keeping the water off.

He then walked back to the house, with the hayfork, having thoughtfully thrust a few haystalks in his hair.

"You're not much of a sticker," said the farmer's wife. "Three hours' work and you'll be looking for me to feed you. There's still a good bit of daylight left."

"Well, I've done the hay, and I came to see what else you could use a hand with. Looks like the wood-pile could use a bit of splitting."

"You've never raked up all the hay!" she said incredulously.

Fionn shrugged. "Come and have a look."

She did... obviously ready to exercise a shrewish tongue. And gaped at the field and the neat stacks with their plaited caps. "And stacked! Well... well, I'll be..."

Looking at her, Fionn was fairly sure she had been.

"I've never seen stacks like that," she said.

"Old custom in my parts. Holds the stack together and keeps the rain out as well."

"You've earned a good feed, shepherd. That lord of yours was daft to let them take you," she said.

"I'll split a cord or so of wood for you. That green wood needs to dry or those babies will get cold this winter."

Fionn enjoyed splitting wood, so it was not a chore for him. Also, he'd been aware of the fear, bordering on desperation, in her eyes, for all her brash talk. His Scrap had had something of the same feeling about her when he'd first met her, trying to rob him and nearly getting drowned. Perhaps it was a human thing.

The farmer's wife had plainly been feeling the isolation as well as the fear. She talked almost nonstop. Partially about the farm, but more about the war.

"I'd like to know," she said belligerently—a tired woman who had had a little more cider with supper than usual, seeing as she was feeling just a little better about winter and surviving—"just how this Mage Spathos knows when the Ways will open. You ask me... he's in with them. Letting our men be taken for slaves."

Fionn subtly found out a little more about Mage Spathos, who it appeared was driving war preparations and recruitment to fever pitch. He was based in Goteng, and lived very well.

Later that evening the farmer's wife indicated that there was other work the farmer wasn't doing.

Fionn had to wonder at his desire to get too closely involved with this species. Fortunately they weren't interfertile, even if other dragons had mixed with them. The thought of dragon-human crosses with the proclivities and abilities of both was quite alarming.

He left early the next morning, before cockcrow, with the deep hop-picking basket he had bought from her the night before. He left a little extra silver on the table, because winter would probably be harder and longer than she guessed, and having a baby seemed to be something humans found harder than dragons found laying fertile eggs.

A few miles down the road he came upon a placard nailed to a tree. Obviously they had some sort of rudimentary printing press now in Annvn. Fionn was all in favor of cultures learning to print. It meant more books, which he found entertaining, and it tended to make for a broader, more entertaining society in time.

He didn't approve of it being used to reproduce pictures of himself and Díleas, and offering a reward.

The farmer's wife could have earned a lot more than the paltry amount of silver he'd left her.

Paid by one Mage Spathos.

"It's time," said Fionn, removing it, "for us to experiment with flight and dogs. I suggest you climb into the basket, and I will try a short, low hop. Try to stay in the basket. Climbing out while we're flying will probably kill you, and I am trying to avoid that. Your mistress would get upset with me, and against all logic I am becoming fond of you myself."

They did a very short few hundred yards of quite hard work—wing muscles and magic and no thermals, keeping very low and slow, in which Díleas decided that sitting up in the basket was a bad idea and curling uncomfortably into the bottom was a better one.

The landing, where the basket touched ground first, spilled Díleas out into a somersault or three. The sheepdog did appear unhurt, but very unimpressed.

"Yes. All right. A slower landing and keeping the basket up. And stop looking at me like that. I've seen you do somersaults when chasing your own tail. I'm sorry, right? It's just going to be faster and safer. And I think putting some distance between here and us is called for. Now, exactly which direction are we going?"

Díleas showed him with his nose.

"Well, it wants a half hour to sunrise. It'll be hard work, but fast. Into the basket again, young dog. We'll go a fair bit higher this time. And I'll take great care setting you down."

They took to the wing again. Fionn noticed a poacher fleeing the woods, dropping his pheasants. Too bad. He probably would talk and wouldn't be believed. And it was good to be above the world again, where a dragon belonged, watching the sun lip the far horizon.

They flew for less than half an hour, as Fionn

wanted to set down in a good spot, where they could land unseen. And there was a town not half a league ahead, so Fionn picked a field and actually slowed to a hover before setting down the basket as light as thistledown.

Díleas did not emerge from the basket. Fionn peered anxiously into it. Had he dropped the dog without knowing?

Díleas was there. Shivering. Uncoiling from his tight ball slowly. "By the First . . . I had forgotten how sensitive to cold you mammals are. I was generating lots of heat, flying."

Fionn took the basket and the dog at a run to the edge of the woods. Dragon breath kindled a fire. He could even make rocks burn, if need be. He cradled Díleas against his still-flight-hot body and in front of the fire. Gradually the dog emerged from his tight ball and stretched.

"I am sorry. It was more complicated than I realized. It's cold up there, and the basket lets the wind through. And you couldn't exactly tell me you were freezing."

Díleas stuck out his tongue and licked Fionn on the dragon nose. They sat there. Then Díleas got up, stretched, shook himself and did a little tentative bounce.

Never had a dragon been so glad to see a dog bark at him. "Yes. All right. We'll walk though. And I will change my appearance, which is harder work, as I am used to the Finn visage. Blond and a beard, and a little shorter and broader, I think."

Díleas watched intently as Fionn's visage and appearance changed. "I know you're an eye dog, but this staring is quite disconcerting," said the new Fionn, tousling the dog's fur. It was a good thing, he thought, that it was so thick. It had probably stopped him from actually freezing up in the cool, thin air. Fionn would never have forgiven himself for that.

They walked on to a minor road, heading towards the town. A pair of bored soldiers were checking papers as people crossed a bridge, but as Fionn had heard them well before, he and Díleas were able to go around and swim the river. It was deep and fast, and fairly cold. Not, as Díleas's look informed him, anything like as cold as flying.

They dried off and then walked on. The town offered a chance to relieve a thief of some loot—a merchant who had thought to doctor his scales—and to use some of it to purchase some black hair dye, and a loaf of good bread, a sheepskin with the wool still on and a couple of fine blankets. It was amazing how easy it was to spend other people's money. And there were plenty of posters and several agents of the local military in plain clothes, looking for draft dodgers. They were rather obvious and inept at it, to someone of Fionn's experience, and so it was his pleasure to pick their pockets and acquire their papers.

Fionn was quite skilled at altering documents subtly.

He left the walled town cheerfully just after curfew, by means of a little private door from the house of ill repute. Some things are very predictable.

Díleas was very impressed with the sheepskin basket liner and the warm, thick blankets for sleeping on that night. Less so with the idea that they might be used to keep warm in flight. But he braved that again, somewhere the wrong side of midnight. They did not fly so long or so high, and Díleas was actually panting a little from heat when they landed, gently, to have another snooze before dawn. And walked on again...

There were more wanted posters.

These showed a blond man with a beard, and a black-and-white sheepdog. And a reward, payable by Mage Spathos.

Dead or alive.

═ Chapter 16 ═

THE KNOCKERS HAD ALL SLIPPED AWAY INTO A
fissure in the rock, far too narrow for humans. Meb
gripped the axe, and they waited. There was nowhere
to run.

The search party from Dun Tagoll was twelve
strong—and by the way they pressed together, swords
out, lanterns held high, they felt they were still twenty
too few.

They came on cautiously. Soon they were shining
their lights onto Meb and Neve, sitting huddled, holding their breath...

And were not seeing them. "Well, we can get out
of here," said their leader, relieved. "It wasn't to be
thought they'd really still be here."

"But by the dead Fomoire and the blood trail to
the sea, she must have come that far."

"Did you see what she did to that one? I'm glad
we didn't find them. I don't care what anyone says,
the prince made a mistake."

"Shut your face, Hwell," said another warningly as
they began to walk away.

209

"I reckon that the Fomoire must have had a boat and taken them. It's a pity. She was a good lass, and that Neve was a gamesome little kitty. I fancied her."

Neve snorted, but they did not hear.

A little later the knocker Jacks came back. "Ahem. Lady Meb," said the chief Jack. "We . . . we was wondering . . . if you'd mind doing a few more tricks for us? A couple of the younger ones will fetch the little ones. It would be something for them to see, I reckon. It's not entertainment that has come our way before."

Meb had seen Fionn work the crowd before. She smiled. "I'd love to. But look at poor Neve. She's so cold and hungry. I'll have to hold her to keep her warm. And I am so famished I might fall over if I tried. Besides, they might come looking for us again."

"We'll post a watch, and give plenty of warning. Anyway, the tide is coming in. They won't be able to get here without getting their feet wet, soon enough. Besides, we'll pelt them with rocks. Drop a piece of the roof on them. And we'll bring hot soup and hot food and hot apple wine and honey for you. And a good blanket of mink fur for the young lady."

Meb smiled. "Bring them."

She really enjoyed the next hour or so. She stretched herself a little too, performing a trick Fionn had done—but she'd no idea how he'd done. She cheated and did it magically—making the juggling balls glow as if lit internally by different-colored lanterns. The knockers—at her order—put out their lanterns, and watched, spellbound, the dance of the lights, as she made patterns in the darkness with them. She noticed, in the light of the balls, that Neve's face was every bit as delighted and rapt as the smallest knocker child.

"Ach, it's better than a piskie dance!" said the chief Jack, when she had finally stopped, lanterns had been lit again, and the clapping had stopped. "You'd best not tell them I said that, though. They're inclined to be spiteful."

A smaller Jack popped his head out of a fissure. "There are men coming along the sea trail. They got dogs a-smelling."

"Illusions won't hide us from dogs," said Meb, worried.

The chief Jack laughed. "But the water will. Tide's in enough. And so will we. Lend us your shoes... and we'll lead them there. If the dogs smell us and try and climb into our holes, it'll be the worse for them." The expression on his face said that the dog that tried to eat a knocker was going to regret it for the rest of his life.

"Try not to hurt their noses too much," said Meb.

"It's their ears we hurt. The little 'uns can let out a squeal that no man can hear, but it surely upsets the dogs."

They sat and waited in the darkness. Faintly they could hear the mournful baying of the dogs. And a yelping.

A little later the knockers came back, cheerful. "They're thinking you went into the water. And they're fair afraid because the dogs won't go more than under the first overhang."

"Still," said Meb, finding a very small knocker tugging at her skirts and looking hopefully up at her, and picking it up and putting it on her lap, "I think we'd better leave when we can."

The chief Jack shook his head, looking at the littlest knocker babe happily sitting on her lap. "Now they'll all be wanting to do it."

"One at a time they shall," said Meb, doing a single-handed toss for the small one. They had hours to darkness, and longer still to the low tide.

The chief Jack looked at her with what could only be respect. "You've the gift, to turn what is yours to command into a pleasure for us to give. We're long-lived and we don't have that many young ones."

"When I was very little, a gleeman sat me on his knee and did a few tricks. I never forgot it. How could I not do the same?" she paused. "And it was another gleeman who saved my life, who taught me to juggle. That gleeman was your black dragon."

"Aha. Well, he did a fine job," said the chief Jack. "Although, like most of the things he did, we'll be cursing for months as these young cloth-heads all make the tunnels and shafts echo with dropped pebbles and rocks that they'll be trying to juggle with."

By the time darkness and the low tide came, Meb was very tired of small knockers. She noticed Neve had gone from terror of them to cuddling and rocking the smaller ones to sleep. The coracle, never the largest of vessels, now had sufficient food for a few days: oatcakes, a small crock of honey, some dried meat, some dried apples, a metal flask of apple wine, a blanket sewed of mink strips and a knocker lantern, with a magical flame that came when you tapped three times on the metal, a couple of small bags—to knockers they would have been very big bags—and a very good supply of good will. They paddled out cautiously, edging between the rocks.

"Can you swim?" asked Meb.

"No, m'lady."

"Well, that's two of us then. We'd better not tip this up or our drowned bodies will wash up with the Fomoire after all."

"No, m'lady. The current will bring the bodies into Degin bay. Always does with those that drown around here," said Neve.

"That's so cheerful. Let's just paddle carefully."

"Yes, m'lady," said Neve, dutiful as ever. "The knockers are quite different from the stories, aren't they?"

"Some things are," said Meb, paddling. "But at least we know we can get food and shelter if I can find an audience who don't just decide to kill us first. And the knockers will help us and hide us if they can."

"So where are we going to go and what are we going to do, m'lady?" asked Neve.

"Well, I'd thought getting away from where they were trying to kill me—where they all hated me, spied on me and were willing to make you murder me—was a good start," said Meb, yawning. "We'll need someplace to rest later tonight, hide for the day, and then get a bit further away. Then we need to find some breeches, because it'll be hard enough for men traveling in these times. Then I thought we might go north, just because Prince Medraut's demesnes are east, and the South is where that earl who tried to kill me came from, the sea is to the west, and I know nothing about the north. Vivien said there are other Duns. We can find ourselves a better place than Dun Tagoll, even if it isn't as magically protected and fed."

"The north parts . . . it's wild, m'lady. Forest and mountain and forgotten people up there," said Neve warily. "I've never been there, of course."

"Wild and forgotten sound good to me right now. Mind that rock."

Despite their inept paddling of the loaded little vessel, they got across to the shingle on the far side of the narrow inlet without any mishap. They pulled it up, and at Meb's insistence, carried it to under the cliff, tripping over rocks in the darkness. They left it between two boulders and covered it in dried seaweed. It took time, but there was no point in telling some sharp-eyed guard, first thing in the morning, just where the prince's men should start looking with the dogs. It took more time to move around the cliff edge in the darkness, lit by a bare sliver of moonlight. They found a gully that took them up to the top. Then they made their way away from the coast, where the salt wind kept down the trees, to look for forest and shelter. At first they walked through the dew-wet grass, and then, with wet shoes, and wet clinging skirts and cold legs, through heather and gorse. Finally they came to a little V-shaped valley with a thick stand of trees and the gurgle of a stream.

"Enough," said Meb. "We're probably not more than a mile from Dun Tagoll, but I am so tired that I don't care if they catch us. Let's light the light, make a fire and try and dry our shoes a bit and eat something."

So they did. Meb had had her experience of living rough with Fionn to turn to . . . and poor Neve fell asleep, wet feet and all. The axe was better, Meb thought, for carving up anyone that tried to molest them than for cutting firewood. It didn't have much bevel on it. But there was some dry deadwood, and using the knocker lantern, and splinter to take flame from it, she managed a respectable fire. She ate some of the dried meat the knockers had provided—she had no idea whether it was dried miner or rabbit, and couldn't care right then—put their shoes to toast a safe distance from the fire and snuggled in next to Neve, blessing the knockers for the fur. Their skirts, however, were too cold and damp. She managed to remove Neve's and hers, and hung them on a branch near the fire. And tried lying down again, wrapping the fur around numb, cold legs and toes that she'd tried warming at the fire. The axe she kept in her hand.

And then sleep came.

She awoke to the sound of a rather nasty snigger. There was something up the tree . . . with their skirts. A tiny blue-green-skinned man with a little tuft beard and narrow eyes all dancing with mischief. He was wearing nothing more than a hat of new leaves pinned with a hawthorn spike and a ragged cloak, so perhaps he didn't consider skirts as necessary.

Meb leapt up, axe in hand. "You drop those! Or I'll . . . I'll chop your tree down!"

"Ach. Mean and spiteful. Then I'll toss them in the stream. You'll be lucky to find them at all, and they'll be even wetter!" said the little green fellow, sticking his tongue out at them.

Bribery might work better. "You just woke me up suddenly. Come down and have some breakfast. We've got oatcakes and some honey."

"Oh, changing our tune, are we, fine ladies. Fine ladies without skirts," he said, wrinkling his pointy little nose at them, but coming down.

"It's a piskie...just like in Gamma stories," said Neve warily.

"Aye, and she had her skirts up or right off often enough, too," said the piskie. "Now you promised oatcakes and honey. We're fond of honey. Doesn't come our way too often, because bees are not fond of us."

"It's only a very little jar of honey," said Meb.

And in the distance—but not too great a distance—a horn sounded.

"What's that?" said Meb, relieving the piskie of her damp skirts. He wasn't worried by his nakedness, so she didn't see why she should be, although Neve stuck under the fur and struggled with hers.

"Just the soldiers from the Dun. They probably saw the smoke of your fire," said the piskie disinterestedly.

"We must find somewhere to hide," said Meb, looking around.

"But you offered me oatcakes and honey," said the piskie, sticking out his lower jaw, plainly angry, his little tuft of a beard wobbling, his cheeks flushing green.

"No time to find them now." said Meb, grabbing the little knocker bag. "If they don't catch us, you can have the whole jar as far as I am concerned."

"Now that's a bargain. Just you wait right here!" said the piskie, and let out a shrill whistle. Other whistles answered, and he bounded off, up into the tree.

"What do we do?" asked Neve nervously.

"Move. I haven't been through all of this to get caught without at least trying to get away," said Meb, pulling her to her feet.

"Ouch. Blisters," said Neve, hobbling.

Meb's own feet were not in a much better state. They'd been cold and numb the night before. Now the sun was up and it was looking to be a glorious spring day. "As far as those rocks. Let me see if I can manage some sort of glamor to hide us there." If she could look like Hallgerd, and make the axe look like a stick, surely she could make herself look like a rock.

And it seemed she could. There was a little niche and, with Neve inside it, Meb sat against her legs and thought rock thoughts. The axe she made into a flying holly sapling. So they sat, Meb wondering if this could possibly work, and thinking "don't see me" thoughts.

No riders came. She heard them in the distance, several times. What did come was a little naked blue-green man, in a green hat and a ragged cloak—with half a dozen of his kind, some male, some female, and all wearing little more than leaves or acorn-cap outfits.

"Ach, tricksie humans. Cheated me," said the piskie crossly. "She promised me a whole jar of honey."

"I don't cheat," said Meb.

Piskies vanished in the twinkling of an eye.

And then the little leaf hat reappeared, followed by the piskie wearing it. "You gave us a fright," he said crossly. "We trick humans. Not you trick us. Not unless you want us to curse you."

"I can hide better than you. Maybe I can curse better than you, too," said Meb.

That took a moment to sink in. "Ah. Well now, no offense, but if you can hide better than we can, why did the horsemen worry you?"

Meb did not say "because I didn't know I could, and I am not sure it would work on Neve." She had a feeling telling the piskies that would only lead to more trouble, and a fair amount of mischief directed at her companion. "Because I knew you could lead them astray better than I can. And last time the castle people came hunting...let's put it this way: I should have hidden from them the first time, because ever since Earl Alois tried to kill me, they've tried."

"Aye," said tufty beard proudly. "That we can. We're the best. They're so mazed they'll never be home before nightfall. Earl Alois, eh? He went through our woods a while back. We didn't know or we'd have made him so lost he never got home."

"A pity you didn't," said Meb as she dug through the bag and came up with the little crock of honey. "Here you are. As promised. We'll have our oatcakes without it."

"Ach," said the piskie generously. "I daresay we'll spare you a little."

So they broke their fast on little knocker oatcakes with a circle of largely naked—bar leaf and wood scraps—piskies. Meb reflected their food would last far less time than she'd thought, at this rate. On the other hand, not only had any form of pursuit failed to find them, the men of the troop would probably be blaming her, and far less keen to try again. For once, being blamed for something she hadn't done was going to work in her favor. That made a change.

After they'd eaten, lighter by some oatcakes and their honey, Meb and Neve took their leave and hobbled on. After a little while, Meb stopped and took her shoes off. "I'll try barefoot for a bit, Neve. My heels and toes are raw."

"We'll look like poor peasants then, m'lady."

"Well, that'll be a good thing," said Meb.

And it was easier walking. Yes, it still hurt when the grass touched raw flesh, but they came on a path quickly enough. All of these lands must have been farmed—and probably still would be, if Lyonesse stayed free of invaders for any time. The path must have been a cart track once, between fields and hedges and forest patches, all overgrown and beginning to show spring signs. It was too early in the season for most food plants, but they gathered asparagus shoots from the banks as they walked, and ate some of them raw. It was a long day, and warm. "Oatcakes and asparagus are not as fine as castle food, but they taste fresher," said Neve.

"That's because the castle food was mostly stale bread, bespelled and stretched," said Meb. "And this might be simple, but it's real. But by the look of the sky, food and shelter are going to be real issues, and soon, too, not to mention piskies."

"You should never mention them," said the ugly pile of misshapen rock fallen from the lichen-cloaked drystone wall on the corner. It stood up, and Neve tried to pull Meb into joining her in running away.

"It's a spriggan! Run!" shrieked Neve.

The spriggan was growing before their eyes and was now considerably bigger than they were. It still looked like it had been badly carved out of granite. "You run. I'll hold it back," Meb said, swinging the axe.

"I can run faster than you," said the spriggan, showing square teeth. "And your axe is not cold iron, but some faerie metal. 'Tis sharp. Magic sharp, I'd grant."

"If you want to try it out, I'll help you," said Meb, looking it in the eye. She couldn't think of what else to do, really.

"I thought I was going to help you," said the spriggan, shrinking and changing before their eyes. Meb knew where she'd seen that sort of triangular alvish grey face before—when she'd been riding with the hunting party. They'd been watching her then.

"What are you planning to help us with?" asked Meb.

"Food and shelter were what you sought, I thought," said the spriggan. "Shelter is easy enough. Food is a bit more difficult. Not food for the likes of you, anyway. Simple fare is easy enough. But the noble ladies of Lyonesse wouldn't want to eat that."

"Given a choice, I would," said Meb. "I've had enough of fancy food that tasted of stale bread for my lifetime. Give me stale bread that tastes like stale bread and I'll be happy."

"Ah. Stale bread is a challenge. We've got fresh, but it'd take a few days to make it stale. But if that's what you want..."

"No, fresh is even better."

"Well, it'll make you sick, I shouldn't wonder," said the spriggan.

"They're dangerous, m'lady," said Neve timidly. "Spirits of old giants, so they do say."

"Spirits of the rocks and tors actually," said the spriggan. "And we're dangerous all right, but not to you. Sadly."

"The knockers and piskies did us no harm, Neve," said Meb reasonably. "You even had knocker babies on your lap."

"Probably piddled on you," said the spriggan with a kind of gloomy satisfaction. "They do."

"They were good little things," said Neve defensively. "Nice to me and m'lady."

"Ah, should have been suspicious then," said the spriggan. "I daresay they gave you food which turned your insides to wax or something."

"You're a grumpy so-and-so," said Meb.

"We have that reputation, yes. Now if you'll follow me, I think we've got a few rabbits and some wild onions in the pot. Won't agree with you, of course."

Meb shouldered the axe, stepped forward and took the rather surprised-looking spriggan by the arm. Grey-skinned and touched with lichens, he was still warm, she noticed. "Lead on. Come on, Neve. He won't eat us, or he would have, because there is another one at the start of the lane. We're between them."

The spriggan blinked. "My brother will give you a hand with the bags, if you like," he said, escorting her in as courtly a manner as any of the haerthmen of the prince's retinue.

They walked up the hill, to where the abandoned walled fields gave way to grazing lands and to the rocky tor at the top. Meb recognized it from her day's hunting, and realized just how close to Dun Tagoll they still were. "It was you that I saw, watching me, wasn't it?"

The spriggan nodded. "We weren't too sure how to talk to you in all that press around you. Too much cold iron. It won't kill us straight off, but we don't like it."

He tapped a rock and it slid aside to reveal a passage down. "An old tomb," he said cheerfully. "Gloomy, but clean and dry."

Meb suppressed a shudder. "Just don't mention the tomb part to Neve. She's . . . she's lived a bit of a sheltered life, compared to me. Can we leave it open?"

"It'll let the spiders in, I daresay."

"For now." A glance showed Neve was almost white with terror. Meb winked at her to tell her it would be all right. And Neve managed a smile, and appeared to relax slightly.

They walked down stone steps and into what should have been the cold of the tomb. The spriggans plainly didn't have much regard for these ideas, as it was pleasantly warm, and scented with ... not dust and decay, but the smell of onions, garlic, wild thyme, and cooking meat. It might once have been a tomb, but the current occupants had scant respect for funerary furniture or the dead that might have lain there, having used the central sarcophagus to make a table, on which they had laid a cloth, and around which they'd placed several three-legged stools. A fire burned in a grate in the corner, with a pot hanging from a hob, from which the smells were plainly coming.

"Welcome to our lair," said the spriggan, rather formally.

Meb wasn't sure how one answered that, but she had a feeling that formally would be best. "Our thanks to you. May it remain dry and warm and safe," she said.

"What ... what are you cooking?" asked Neve, warily.

"Rabbits. We have to make do. We can't get enough unwary travelers these days," said the spriggan tending the pot.

"Stop teasing her," said Meb sternly, hoping she was the one not being naive. But they were just enough like Finn, when he was being outrageous, for her to recognize it. "The fay here seem to delight in mocking people."

"But there is so much to mock," said the spriggan who had escorted her. "I suppose it is that you humans are more numerous, more powerful than us in many ways. It's that or kowtow to you. And we'd rather mock."

The cook looked thoughtful. "The muryans are

hard-working, serious and not given to practical jokes, if they understand jokes at all."

"Yes, but there are more of them than humans. And look where it has gotten them."

Meb looked at the stone-coffin table. Five places laid, trenchers ready. Three spriggans and the two of them. "Either you were expecting us, or you're expecting some more spriggans."

"Ah. It's what they said. She's so sharp it's a wonder she doesn't cut herself. Probably will, with that axe. Or her brain will overheat with all that thinking," said the spriggan cook.

"Don't you say nasty things about m'lady," said Neve, straightening up. "She's had enough of that."

That seemed to amuse the spriggans. "Wouldn't dare, your majesty, wouldn't dare. Now, if you want to put your things down and take a seat, the food has been ready awhile, but you're slow."

"Who told you to expect us?" asked Meb.

"The knockyan—what you call knockers. Very full of it they were. But their tunnels are a bit tight for your kind."

That was reassuring. Meb knew the knockers had liked them, and if they were willing to trust the spriggans, then presumably the rabbit stew wasn't a first course to fatten up two women as the main roast. The stew was very good indeed, so good that it didn't worry either of them that one of their hosts got up to close the front door to keep the rain out.

"To think," said Meb, stomach full, warm, and sore feet up on what could easily be the treasure chest of a dead king, "that I worried about food and shelter on our journeying."

"Tonight is well enough," said the spriggan, "but they'll be looking for you. The mage has tools in his tower and he'll have traces of you. Best to go further off, and to keep moving a while."

"The piskies seemed to think they could stop us being followed."

"Ah, but that's piskies for you," said the spriggan. "They're not great on the understanding of things. We can't really shelter you indefinitely, any more than the piskies can mislead the prince's troops indefinitely. Neither we nor they can stand cold iron, and their misleading and mazing can be dealt with by turning your clothes. Once the prince's men realize that they're being piskie-led, they'll counter it. Our kind are weak and small here, for all we seem frightening. There are places where it is otherwise, where our kin rule. We are kin to those you call alvar, just as the knockyan are distant cousins to the dvergar."

"Um. You're nicer than a lot of the alvar I've met," said Meb, thinking of the faintly supercilious attitude of even Finn's friends Leilin and her sister. Finn had told her that the alvar were of many different groups, but this degree of difference had not occurred to her.

It amused them, and seemed to please them.

"It's not a reputation we need among humans. We've changed too, with being here. The underlying magic of the worlds shapes us."

Meb juggled for them. It seemed the least payment she could offer for shelter and food. The spriggans enjoyed it. Not with the childlike delight of the knockers, but with an appreciation of craft. They slept on a bed of heather in the corner of the tomb that night, and Meb slept better and longer than she had since she'd lost Finn and Díleas. Tiredly, just before she slept, she wondered if there was some kind of magic that would at least allow her to see them. It would make such a difference to know they were safe and happy and that all was well back in Tasmarin.

The next day brought a gruel breakfast, salve and leaf plasters for their feet, and a quiet, friendly but firm escort further from Dun Tagoll. "We are tied to the tor. We cannot go more than half a league from it. You'll find that's true of all of the spriggans and piskies here. They have their place, and they're quite strong in it," said the spriggan walking along with them. "The knockyan can travel but don't like to. The muryans, well, they do move, but it's war when one tribe meets another."

Neve coughed. "I didn't ever believe in the muryans either." She turned to Meb. "Do the magic creatures come to see you, m'lady? I mean . . . I lived all my life in the village and people talked of these things . . . it was stories. Some you believed and some, well, you mostly didn't. Never saw any myself, never saw one in Dun Tagoll either . . . until with you. Now, it is as if they're everywhere. Even," she colored, "when I went to relieve myself, without you. There was this little blue-green man looking at me."

"I hope you were very rude to him!"

"I was," admitted Neve.

"The piskie have no sense of privacy," said the spriggan. "Now if it had been one of us, you could have known it was to laugh at you. But they barely understand clothes. They wear them for pretty, when they feel like it. And of course we come to see you. We've always been here, but many were in a kind of hibernation. Like bears in winter. Now the fay of the land are waking as the magic pours back in. Like the equinox flood tide it's been, after so many years."

Tasmarin. Magic and energy confined there for so long must be flowing back here. Suddenly Meb knew exactly what the problem with their Changer was. In a way, she was really the right one for the mage to blame. It was her, her and Fionn, back in Tasmarin, that had started this. Mind you, it could have been worse, had Fionn succeeded in his original aim of destroying the place and returning all its parts and people to where they came from.

"And, of course," said the spriggan, "we can't go to the Old Place on the headland, where the castle now stands. It's been bespelled against us for many a year. But even that weakens."

"Fleeing certainly confirms her treachery," said Lady Cardun.

"It may, but how was she able to do so?" asked Prince Medraut. "My man should easily have been able to deal with two women. And yet they disarmed him, cost him a finger, and frightened him into gibbering superstitious nonsense at half of the men-at-arms in the Dun. And the troop that was out this morning managed to get lost. Lost! A good half of them were born around here. They couldn't get lost in a thick fog. But they claim they blundered around country they've never even seen. And I've been shown it myself—they're black and blue from something. They're claiming it was bewitchment or a curse. And half of them are blaming Shadow Hall and the other half are saying it was Lady Anghared punishing them. If it wasn't for Aberinn and the fact that he keeps the Dun safe and provisioned, they'd desert."

Earl Alois had been relieved to see the moon full, hoping the Changer would bring some respite. Perhaps he'd been wrong about that girl being the Defender. But no. He'd seen it with his own eyes. It had been grim fighting the Fomoire, but the earl and his men had dealt them some doughty blows. More by luck than judgement, some of them. A sheep carcass landing in one of the chariots of the evil-eye men had been one such. It had caused a fight among them. There had only been nine by the time they got ashore. And the men of Carfon had laid traps that didn't involve looking, had the archers drop shots in a valley, had fired from ambush once the chariots had passed. The evil eye was terrifying, but there were few of them, and they had to look at you for a good few moments.

If Dun Tagoll and the North had held them off too, and there were no more coming south . . . they'd won.

And of course . . . if there was no next army. But there would be, and a next. And a next.

=== Chapter 17 ===

FIONN WAS BOTH WORRIED BY THIS PLACARD, AND
seriously quite put out by it. So he was a spy from
Lyonesse, now. How had this human mage—they were
fairly inept generally—found out this quickly and not
only found out but also got more posters out?

And the dead or alive part was . . . interesting.

It was quite a generous sum. In gold, too.

That had to be very tempting.

"I think you're going to get your fur dyed, and I
am going to have to change yet again," he said to
Díleas. "This is getting tiresome."

A little work and he and Díleas had different
appearances and, according to the documents he carried, Fionn was an agent of Prince Maric, the local
panjandrum. He and his agents plainly commanded a
great deal of respect and fear, by the way that they
passed through the checkpoints. Fionn was able to
glean a fair bit of information about himself in the
process. He'd been seen in an amazing number of
places. Fionn could imagine there were any number

of very upset shepherds. Well, as the city of Goteng seemed to lie directly in their path, Fionn thought he'd do some reparation. Fionn and Díleas made their way through the streets peacefully, with a brief contretemps with some butcher's dogs who thought they owned the streets of Goteng, and not this black upstart who was passing through. The smell of dragon gave them pause, and Díleas delusions of grandeur.

Mage Spathos lived in a sumptuous tower within the grounds of the military barracks—where even the parade ground was now full of tents.

It was near evening anyway, so Fionn found a tavern, fed himself and Díleas, avoided trouble with some bored conscripts on a pass out of their camp, before he went to the military barracks. As was usual with taverns near military camps, this one was something of a freelance brothel too—except that the women were very wary. Spathos's guards had apparently taken to collecting fresh meat for him every night, and payment was not part of his equation. Fionn decided that the man was due a call. Besides putting a price on the head of a dragon, such conduct deserved it.

As with most military establishments of the kind, the barracks were designed, really, to keep bored soldiers in, rather than determined dragons out. Seeing as dogs did not climb as well as dragons, they used the forged documents to enter the barracks and Spathos's tower, and to pass all the guards, except for the last two. With those ones he used the documents to distract, before cracking their heads together with calculated force—calculated not to kill, but to stun. After which he tied and gagged them and put them into a storeroom.

He did lock and bar the mage's door for them, but
it was probable that they had been supposed to do
this...with him on the outside.

He then stopped and examined the passage quite
carefully. It was likely that any self-respecting magic
worker would have a few other defenses, besides
guards. Fionn's vision helped him to spot such dis-
turbances of natural energy. He was not disappointed.
They were there.

They were also inept rent-from-a-grimoire-I-don't-
understand-properly spells. Spells written into that
grimoire in the first place by someone who barely understood effects and had no real grasp of the causes. Not
quite what he'd expected after the wanted posters. He
was able to erase a little of the pattern and proceed to
the wizard's workshop, where Mage Spathos was hard
at work...eating supper. Most of the paraphernalia,
Fionn judged at a glance, had no purpose and had not
actually been used. It looked good though.

"I thought that I had given orders I was not to be
disturbed. Or have you brought the girl here early?
Take her to my bedroom. It had better be a younger
one this time."

"I am so sorry to disturb your meal," said Fionn,
who had taken the liberty of changing his appearance
in the antechamber. He was blond and bearded now.

"Not as sorry as you will be," said Spathos.

Díleas growled and that finally got the man's attention. "I've come to claim the reward," said Fionn.

Spathos's face would really have looked far more
entertaining on those posters, decided Fionn. It was
an interesting shade of white almost tinged with
green. "The food obviously hasn't agreed with you,"

said Fionn with mock sympathy. "Now you promised fifty golden pounds, or twelve thousand silver pennies for me, dead or alive. I am here, alive. I want the reward. And the gold will be easier to carry."

His dragonish senses said that there was in fact a considerable amount of gold in the desk at which Spathos now quivered. "And it's not much use calling your guards, as they will not be able to help. And screams from your tower are what the soldiers regard as quite normal, I gather."

Spathos opened the upper drawer and reached inside. Something about the way he did it cried warning to Fionn. "Slowly," said Fionn. "Very slowly bring your hand out. Otherwise you may...regret it. Or worse, not live to regret it. I am not planning to kill you, you know. But I could change my mind."

That was a lie, but Fionn could lie quite cheerfully. It was just often more entertaining to tell the truth in ways that would not be believed. He couldn't intentionally kill.

The hand came out with a single gold coin. "Here!" shrieked Spathos, and flung it at Fionn.

Dragons will instinctively catch gold. Even bespelled gold.

Unless of course a sheepdog jumps up and catches the coin...and deliberately swallows it.

Díleas had seen that trap used before. It wasn't going to happen again.

Fionn had Spathos by the throat and hauled across his dinner before Díleas even burped. "This will need some very good explanation," he said in a quiet hiss. That act implied that the man had known that Fionn was a dragon merely passing as a man. And that in turn carried many other implications, none of which Fionn liked. And all of which he intended to get answers to. "Just what was on that coin? If the dog suffers any ill effects, I'll sit you on your own flagpole. After I sharpen it."

"A spell...just a spell. He said it would knock you out. I swear, nothing else. I made him hold it in case it was poisoned. He said...he said I should have it ready. In case you came. He said it was the kind of thing you might well do."

So whoever this foe was, he not only knew enough to try what seemed likely to be dragon-trapping magic, but also knew enough about Fionn to predict the course he might follow. "So who is this 'he'?" asked Fionn.

"I don't know! Truly I don't. I thought he came from the witch of the Shadow Hall."

Fionn was very good at detecting the change of inflection in human speech. It was not infallible, but it did help to split the liars out. This "mage" was little more than a hedge-magician. But it appeared that Annvn had very little magic or practitioners of the art, these days. It had once been quite a rich place for the magical arts. Fionn had had to come and fix things here. Not as often as Brocéliande, or some of the others, but often enough.

Before the eyes of the horrified "mage" he changed into his dragon form. He went on asking questions... now there was such naked fear in Spathos's voice that Fionn was fairly sure he was getting straight answers. He learned of the hedge-magician's source of information on Lyonesse—a crone in a house that moved.

"You won't find it unless she wishes you to," the terrified Spathos assured him.

Fionn was not some hedge-wizard, so he doubted that. However, it soon became apparent that Spathos's power had been built on the drip feed of information about Lyonesse raids from this source. And it told him when the next "Way" would open to that land, and where.

Yet he earnestly believed that the order—and money—to kill Fionn had not come from her, but from someone else. He'd lied when he thought he'd had just a man to deal with.

The questioning was interrupted by a pounding on the outer door. "Doubtless your entertainment for the evening arriving," said Fionn.

For a moment hope bloomed in Spathos's cheeks. Then he looked at the dragon and it died.

"Yes," said Fionn. "You guessed right. It won't help to save you from a dragon. And I wouldn't call to them because that could be worse right now." He wrapped Spathos in his tail. It wouldn't kill to be that constricted, but Spathos would not scream much either. He rifled the desk where his senses said that there was a substantial amount of gold. There was quite a lot. Quite a lot of silver too. Too much to carry... along with this Spathos. It would take the soldiery some time to brave breaking in here, depending on how soon someone got to asking about whether the agent who had come in had left. It was a good, solid, iron-reinforced door, too. Fionn gave Spathos the sort of squeeze that would probably crack a rib or two and certainly render him malleable. It would not be wise to leave him here. He knew too much and, what was more, dragons—including Fionn—had no tolerance for those who could bespell dragons, or even knew it was possible. At the very least, a salutatory lesson was called for.

Fionn stripped him, tied him up thoroughly. Blind-folded him and gagged him with his own clothing. Fionn then took fifty pieces of gold, and a handful of silver, and added it to his pouch. The dragon then moved himself, the victim and the remaining four bags—two of gold and two large ones of silver—onto the balcony. Tied them onto the other end of the rope. "Watch him. I'll be back in a few minutes," he said to Díleas. Because it was easier, he used human form to haul himself up onto the roof. Pulled up the bags of loot. He poured gold in a nice flat layer into the gutter, enjoying touching the gold, however briefly. He picked up the silver bags. Selected his targets—a handsome statue of one of the local robber barons in the town square two hundred yards away, neatly lit by two oil lamps; and a harder one, a flagpole on the parade ground a mere eight-five yards off. They were also some five stories down. The tower doubtless gave the so-called mage status, as well as giving Fionn good throwing practice. He pitched at the flagpole first. It snapped, but not before the bag ripped and showered coins onto the tents of the conscripts.

Fionn tossed the other at the statue. The stone copy of the local robber baron was so excited by the money that he completely lost his head, and coins sprayed far and wide, splattering against buildings and even in through windows.

By the sounds of it, the conscripts had discovered their pay had come from above, thought Fionn, as he dropped onto the balcony.

The guards were trying to pound down the door. He wondered how long it would take before the mayhem in camp got to them, but thought it might be fun to watch . . . "Time to fly, Díleas."

Díleas climbed into his basket. Fionn carefully put the blankets around him, took a firm hold of the basket and the end of the rope, cut the blindfold and gag away with a talon, and launched into the night sky. The weight of the screaming mage strained his wing muscles and they dropped before the dragon began to gain height.

The fighting and looting and destruction happening in the army encampment was briefly stilled by a near miss of the tent canvas by a hurtling, screaming wizard.

Fionn flapped on, having checked that Díleas was secure. The gold revived him a great deal, and his target was near enough. The slave vessels berthed on the river just outside the city opened their hold lids to allow a little air to their pitiful cargo.

Fionn considered the possibilities of dropping the man into the hole from the air . . . but decided that he might hurt Díleas, with yards and spars and ropes to crash into. So he landed on the quayside. Spathos got a little dragged and bounced, but he was beyond complaining and screaming, and merely at the whimpering stage. The slaver vessel was showing signs of readying itself for sea, with men on the foredeck. Fionn could quite see why the city appeared to be in something of an uproar.

The only watch on the hold was looking at the city. Fionn dropped him—and Spathos—into the hold, before jumping ashore. Once he and Díleas were back in the shadows, Fionn yelled. "There's a rebellion! They're coming to free the slaves!" and the two of them walked off into the night.

A little later they took to wing again. From the air Fionn could see that there were several fires in the city of Goteng, and there appeared to be some burning vessels on the river. Tch. Humans did get carried away. He hoped that Spathos's tower survived. He had gold to collect from that gutter. It was too heavy and flat to easily wash out.

In the meanwhile, traveling by day, as a man and a dog on their own, could become difficult, no matter just what the man or dog looked like.

Fionn looked for an alternative. And found it in a small group of carts, going in more or less the right direction. Travelers. Mostly they had a very poor relationship with authority. It could be worth looking into.

The ancient energy beings pondered the situation. Annvn had seemed an ideal trap. The planomancer dragons were incredibly rare, and had been constructed far more robustly than the messenger-errand-beast kind. They were neither easily nor lightly killed. Merely putting him into some form of suspended animation in a slower time plane would have been preferable, but Annvn had good pawns and he was there...and now, it was likely he would deduce the role of a conspirator of greater reach than mere local humans. Possibly realize that it stretched as far as the Tasmarin pseudoplane. Possibly even deduce the existence of their hand in this.

That was most undesirable.

Worse than letting him interbreed with their creations. Those were—at least in major forms—not interfertile. Quite a lot of them simply physically could not do it, and even those that could tended to produce offspring that were either less fertile or sterile mules.

But shape-shifting dragons...

❖   ❖   ❖

Fionn studied the carts from a safe distance. He was almost sure that they were the same brightly colored ones he'd encountered back in the lands of the creatures of smokeless fire.

There was a chance they'd be less than pleased with him, he had to admit. But on the other hand he knew things about them that might make life awkward with the local authorities. If they had papers of any sort, they were almost certainly forgeries or bought for a backhanded payment.

And, in a pinch, he could pay them. That, of course, would be a last resort. He had a feeling that if he was ever going to get to the bottom of these pathways between worlds that he had known nothing about, he was going to have to get the information out of the travelers, as Díleas was limited to yes-and-no barks. Besides, he had a feeling that Díleas did not know where, or understand how, the Ways between worked; he just was following his mistress, by the shortest possible route.

"I think," said Fionn, "that I'll have to alter my appearance and yours a little, my dog. I can change shape, but the best I can do for you now is to hide that flame bauble of yours. We're less likely to meet creatures of smokeless flame here than in Tasmarin, but protection is still a good idea. They don't have to be seen to work, though."

He sat and fashioned a tube of cloth and put it around the collar of silver and crystal. Funny, people assumed it was a cheap chain with a bauble on it. People saw what they wanted to see. The chain was of alvar manufacture and probably valuable. And the glowing little crystal bead, probably priceless. The creatures of smokeless flame would certainly give their entire stock of gold for it, rather than have it in the possession of another.

He walked closer to the carts. The travelers were lighting a fire and busying themselves with morning chores. It was indeed the same group of travelers, but somewhat less wary in Annvn than they had been traversing the flame-creature lands of Gylve.

Their dogs let them know he was coming. Díleas ran straight up to the cart of their leader and was wagging his tail very fast at Avram's Mitzi. She wasn't barking at him...

"Better call him off, mister," said Avram. "I don't want puppies this trip."

"Here, dog." He should have arranged a pseudonym for Díleas. He slapped his leg and whistled.

Díleas paid absolutely no attention.

Fionn hauled him off by the hair. "Sit! Or else!" and he took ahold of the collar.

The traveler laughed. "I reckon you'll have to tie him up. Our lot are. What do you want, stranger?"

"A place to hide," said Fionn. "To be something other than a single man and a dog. The authorities are looking for one of those."

Avram's eyes narrowed slightly. "We've seen the poster. Didn't look much like you." There was definite suspicion in his voice.

"Fortunately, yes. But they're still giving men on their own trouble. I've got some good papers and a little silver to pay for being one of the band for a few days. I'm going the same way as you are."

"Papers? What excuse do you have to travel? We've got war materiel."

"I'm supposed to be an agent of Prince Maric. I'm

not, but it looks good," said Fionn. "And I can tell you Mage Spathos had a tragic accident and isn't paying any rewards right now. I'll give you ten silver pennies to travel along with you for the next three days."

"Let's see the color of your money," said the traveler.

So Fionn produced and counted out the silver.

Avram tested and smelled the coins. Pocketed them. A couple of the others had wandered over from their chores and were watching. Fionn scented something that could be trouble. But there was cover nearby and not a bow in sight. "You can travel with Nikos. He lost his dog, but you'll have to tie yours up," said Avram. "You still got that rope we sold you, Finn?" he asked, grinning.

"How did you know?" asked Fionn.

"Heh. It was the first poster. Dravko took one look and said he had no idea having a sense of balance could make you so valuable. He was quite proud of having been gulled by a man that could make himself that unpopular. And it's the way you speak and the way you stand. In our trade it pays to notice those things. What did you do to them?" There was serious admiration in that tone.

"The annoying thing," said Fionn, "is that I don't know, and I want to know. I know exactly what I've done to Mage Spathos since. He's not going be paying any rewards, but he could only tell me someone was offering to pay him a great deal for me—dead. I have a description, but not a name. And I have been told who he thinks it isn't . . . but that leaves a lot of people—and things which are not people—that I could possibly have made very angry over the years."

The travelers laughed. "We're making breakfast,"

said Avram. "Come and eat. We can swap lies easier over bread and salt."

"I'll need to tie this dog up," said Fionn, as Díleas was sniffing the air hungrily and just about turning his neck all the way around to admire the come-hither look in Mitzi's eyes.

"Let him go and get friendly with Mitzi," said Avram. "He's a smart dog."

"You have no idea just how smart," said Fionn, letting go. Díleas charged off, and leapt up on the seat of the wagon, to indulge in some more stiff-tailed fast wagging and some very personal sniffing.

Avram led Fionn to the fire, where bacon was being sliced into the long-handled skillet. "Ah, but when that starts thinking," he said, pointing at his groin, "the brains stop."

"Never a truer thing was said," said Fionn, thinking that it might almost apply to him. But there was heart there too, which he had noticed actually made it less logical and more intense.

They ate rosemary-scented pot bread and salt, and drank ale. When the bacon was done, they all speared pieces of it on their knives and rubbed their bread in the grease as they passed the iron skillet around. Fionn was aware he was being watched carefully. They were friendly, but watching. When he handed the skillet on, Avram asked, "What are you, Finn? You're not one of the Beng. You're too at ease with iron to be one of the alv, although I thought so because of the glamor. You're too big to be one of the Dueregar. And the water-people don't like rosemary."

"I could be a giant," said Fionn, trying to weigh this up, "that's washed himself too often and shrunk."

"Bit sharp-witted for one of those. But men don't handle hot iron that easily either. And that's not glamor. Simon has a special bespelled mirror for spotting that. He checked when he was fetching the salt."

"I would have thought it was pretty obvious," said Fionn, reading posture, preparing himself, trying to work out just how he would get Díleas, who was far too busy to even notice possible trouble. They had just shared bread and salt with him . . . that was not usually a precursor to treachery. "I'm a dragon."

He was surprised to see them smile and relax.

"Welcome," said Avram. "You are the kind that works the balances, I think? The others don't change shape happily and don't think as fast from what I have heard."

"You don't seem very surprised," said Fionn guardedly.

Avram shrugged. "You said you came from a plane of dragons. And we have met your kind of dragon before."

"Oh? There were never that many of us. I thought I might be the last. It's been a long time since I met another one. We each had our planes and subplanes. I was trapped in Tasmarin for a long time. Like you, I used to travel around. Which is what I need to ask you about. These paths between planes . . ."

"The Tolmen Ways, yes."

"How do you find them? I didn't know they existed, and I think I need to know, to . . . do what I have to do. To go on with the balancing. I am not going to close them. They seem well made, very convenient, and magically near neutral."

"The dragon Corran made them and showed us. He helped us with the protections against the Beng and alv, and the tree-people too. We regard ourselves as his people."

"Oh?" This was possibly dangerous territory. Some dragons could be quite possessive. The last thing he needed was a fight with another planomancer. That could be ugly. And he should have guessed that the Ways between planes were planomancer work. No wonder they were stable and hard to find.

"Yes, the legends said he was very rude about the idea," said Dravko, "which we like too. We don't do very well with overlords. But we are the friends of the dragon."

Fionn bit his knuckle. "Take my advice on this. Don't be. Most of them are not our kind of dragon and would eat you and steal your gold."

"Not just trick us out of it?" said Avram cheerfully.

"That was a fee, for teaching you a valuable lesson, and organizing water and a safe spot in future in Gylve," said Fionn. "And as a lesson to not sell other travelers into slavery."

"We only talked about it," said Mirko. "We might have changed our minds."

"You might have ended up being sold instead," said Fionn.

═ Chapter 18 ═

EARL ALOIS WAS GRATEFUL FOR HIS OWN MAGICAL skills, which included the ability to divine a way home. That was how they finally got back to the Dun—the troop had blundered through places he would swear were not in Lyonesse, let alone his familiar Southern Marches. He'd been aware that his people had been encountering the various non-humans more and more frequently. But suddenly they seemed to have turned inimical, to him in particular.

And now, thanks to rude piskies who had misled them, and pelted them with pine cones, he knew why. Somehow they'd heard that he'd tried to kill the Defender. And the fay—at least the piskies—were taking it out on him and his. He needed help. Allies. Not this.

The spriggan escort handed Meb and Neve on to a fair of piskies. "They're flighty and troublesome," said the spriggan as the piskies stuck their tongues out at them. "But they'll see you further north."

"Thank you. I'd like to be further from Dun Tagoll, but north was a direction chosen for no good reason. I'm really not too sure where we should go," admitted Meb.

The spriggan smiled wryly. "So now you're asking me for advice, and my thoughts, beyond that it will all end in tears, I shouldn't wonder. And if I know humans, you want more than that. Go north. We don't really believe in chance or coincidence. There are forces pushing you north. Powers in the land itself. The humans believe the King is the Land and Land is the King, and it's been without one for too long. Humans, of course, have a poor understanding of it, but that's no surprise. Anyway: the forest people in the deep woods are closest to the Land, of all those in it. They could give you refuge. And they have a freedom of movement across the country that we don't."

Meb thought of her brush with the sprites—Lyr—for they were all, effectively, the same vegetative intelligence. They hadn't liked people much. "Oh. You also have sprites here?"

"Sprites?" asked the spriggan.

"Tree people . . . sort of like trees but people too," explained Meb.

"Ah," said the spriggan, nodding. "The dryads. This is far from their realms. We've had a few once, long ago. No, I speak of the Wudewasa, the wild people of the deep forest. Lyonesse was once all theirs when it was also almost all forest. They're touchy and dangerous."

"And that was supposed to cheer me up, was it, as well as help?" said Meb.

The spriggan smiled. "Can't have you getting too enthusiastic. May the Land stay with you." And he turned and left.

So they were left to travel on with the piskies. They were flighty travel companions, needing to be reminded that they weren't actually here just to play little practical jokes on the two humans with them. The idea that humans might not like their hair tweaked, and that it was a bad idea to do, took a while to get into their heads too. Neve finally did it, catching one shrieking with laughter in her ear as he did so, and holding him up in front of her. "It's being put over my knee for a good spanking that you'll get if you do that again. Go and tweak the squirrels' tails instead."

"They bite," said the piskie, looking sulkily at her. "It was no harm we were doing. Just a bit of fun."

"And it's no harm I'll do to your tail end. No worse than you did to my hair."

"Then you wait and see what I'll do to you next," said the piskie crossly.

Meb thought it was wise to try for a distraction. She'd started to try and learn the cartwheels and tumbling and flick-flacks that Fionn used as part of his gleeman showmanship. She wasn't particularly good at them, in skirts... but then the piskies seemed totally unaware of clothing's purpose being to cover nakedness. "Can you do this?" she asked, managing a credible cartwheel... and resolving never ever to do it in a skirt again.

They didn't seem to notice that part at all, and next thing they were all cartwheeling and tumbling and spinning. From there it was natural enough for Meb and Neve to start singing. And the piskies found that a good reason to weave dances around them, and between their legs, rather like cats. It was noisy, but it beat having your hair tweaked and ears pulled by bored piskies. It was a relief to come to the point where the fair said: "Thus far and no further," and left them with capers and cartwheels and a raspberry or two.

"You know, m'lady," said Neve tiredly, when they were out of sight of the little people. "They're like little children. There's never been anything quite like piskies to make even spriggans look very nice."

"I had always wondered what they were good for," said the spriggan, who had been doing a good job of looking like an old milestone. "But they're not always or all quite such flighty fellows. They're fast workers, when it takes their fancy. Of course they'll usually leave you in the lurch just when you needed them most."

"And spriggans do a good job of frightening me out of a year's growth, and you can rely on them to come up with the next glum prediction," said Meb.

"Yes. Those are the things we do best," agreed the spriggan. "I'll tell you there is a group of Angevins prowling the lanes in the next few miles, along this way. They're best avoided, I would say. They're hungry and mean. If you detour a bit west, that trail has got nothing particularly nasty that we can't discourage."

That night was their first full night beneath the stars, sleeping rough. Meb had the feeling they were being watched but no piskies or spriggans or knockers or even Angevin mercenaries disturbed their rest. It was cold, but survivable, thanks to the fur blanket, and a layer of bracken to keep them off the ground, fire and a bit of shelter from the wind with an old stone wall and a tree. Food, however, was getting sparse. They had some of the dried meat they'd got from the knockers, and some fiddlehead fern shoots that they boiled in a bark bowl, and a last oatcake

divided between them and washed down with what
the knockers probably considered quite a lot of apple
wine. It didn't really go very far. Meb was seriously
thinking magic was going to have to be employed to
find them food, soon.

Except that morning brought food. Food laid out
neatly in precise rows next to their bed . . . nuts—some
squirrel had plainly not eaten his winter store—and
a pile of sulphur-yellow bracket fungus neatly laid
out on some young leaves. Meb recognized that from
her time with Fionn, mushroom hunting. "Chicken-of-
the-woods! And there are two small bird's eggs. We
have breakfast."

"But who brought it?" asked Neve. "The grass—look,
it's full of dew, but there isn't a sign of a footprint
in it."

There wasn't.

"Maybe piskies?" suggested Meb, yawning, looking
around.

"I don't see them laying out the food precisely. It'd
be tossed in a heap and probably tumbled in the grass.
And look how neatly the fungus is cut," said Neve,
pointing. "My ma is . . . was a fussy housekeeper. And
she was never that picky."

"Well, let's make a little fire and cook the chicken-
of-the-woods. I'm just grateful for it. We should have
got a cooking pot from the knockers," said Meb, suddenly thinking of mushrooms and bacon. "Finn always
had a little iron skillet."

"He must have had a pack horse to carry everything he had . . . I am sorry, m'lady. Didn't mean to
make you cry."

"You didn't," said Meb, sniffing determinedly and

rubbing her eyes. "Something just got in my eyes, that's all." And out of my memory box, she thought. It was the mushroom smell and the mention of that skillet. Determinedly, she thought of where the food could have come from rather than dwelling on happier times. It was good to have food, at least. It seemed they'd better hang on to it, because a determined team of ants were rolling one of the walnuts away...

And then she looked again. They weren't rolling the nut away. They were bringing it to add to the rows. She peered closely. The ants all had remarkably human faces. And they stared back at her.

"Neve," she said quietly, as the young maid picked up twigs from the leaf litter to start the fire, "I think I found out who brought us the food. Look."

Neve followed her pointing finger. Clung to her arm.

"Muryans. As I live and breathe, muryans!" said Neve, incredulously. "Whatever you do, m'lady, don't make them angry. They're small but there be millions and millions of them."

Meb looked at the tiny creatures positioning the nut, which was far bigger than they were, with meticulous precision. "Right now I'd rather work out how to thank them. The spriggans said they were very serious and hard workers. I don't think juggling or tumbling will have much appeal."

"They say they are ruled by a queen," said Neve, "and she looks just like a person, only tiny. They say if she's your captive, they'll serve you."

It brought to mind the doll's house stuff that Meb had seen in Aberinn's workshop. Well, why not? She'd been fascinated enough to study it, to remember it in detail. The queen's chamber with its little mirrors and brushes and combs... She called them. Wanted them. It produced a very strange feeling... and an entire little room in her hands. Meb put it in the basket, but picked out the tiny silver comb, which was smaller than her pinkie fingernail. It was perfect and must have taken some artificer many hours of painstaking labor to make... or some form of magic. She knelt down and looked at the laboring muryans. They stopped, little ant antennae twitching at her. She held out the comb, balanced on a finger. "A small gift. For your lady, with thanks for your breakfast."

One, and then a second of the muryans approached her finger. They had antlike, sharp-biting jaws—doubtless what had cut the tough bracket fungus. They took the comb—it was still big enough to need two of them to handle it—and ant-handled it back to the wall, and down between the stones.

A little later, just as they'd got the fire lit, a small sea of muryans came pouring out from between the rocks. Then came several hundred larger muryans, with jaws like scimitars, nearly an inch long. And then, carried on a litter made of grass stalks with highly polished seed handles... their queen. The soldiers arrayed themselves watchfully. Meb was sure that if either of them made the slightest move toward the muryan queen they would attack with suicidal ferocity.

The little queen was human-looking. Her clothes— probably woven from something like spider web—were remarkably fine, and bright colored. She was perhaps six inches tall—big compared to her subjects. And she had the comb in her hands.

Meb and Neve stared at the perfect, doll-like little woman. Her skin was porcelain white and her hair long and dark and intricately braided. There were little sparkling lights set in it. "My subjects are very worried about me being aboveground," she said in a piping little voice. "But I wished to thank you for the gift, Land Queen." She admired the comb, delight written on tiny features. "You did not have to do that."

"It seemed only polite to say thank you for breakfast," said Meb. "Fionn said that only a fool takes without giving something in exchange. Even if it is only his gratitude making the giver feel good."

"That is wisdom. We struggle to fashion metals. And the knockyan work is not so fine as this. They are miners, not artificers. Thank you," said the muryan queen.

"It is our pleasure. We appreciate breakfast."

The queen nodded regally. "My workers want to know if you can spare them an ember on a stick. They struggle to kindle fire, and it has been damp and cold and we lost ours."

"Nothing easier," said Meb, taking a smouldering stick from the fire. Was Lyonesse full of such obliging fay? It was very different from Tasmarin, then. "All of the non-human people here seem so... helpful. Generous. Thank you."

"It is our duty to serve. We have waited a long time for you," said the queen muryan.

Meb blinked. What? Then it struck her. It must be this prophecy. She did *not* want to be their "Defender." Although, she admitted to herself, it was easier to have to defend the knockers, spriggans, muryans and even the annoying piskies than the nobles of Dun Tagoll. "I don't know what I am supposed to do," she admitted.

The muryan queen toyed with the comb. "The Land

knows. And you do it in a better fashion than the last one. He took it as his right. Never gave anything or thanked anyone for anything."

One of the soldier muryans clicked his mandibles.

The queen nodded. "He says there are large birds coming. I must go back to my palace."

The bearers literally whisked her away just as she was finishing speaking, carrying her back down into the mound.

"Large birds?" said Meb looking around. They were under a tree, and the un-farmed countryside was returning to woodland. A bird, she supposed, especially a bird of prey, could be a grave danger to the muryans, to their queen.

"You can see them over there," said Neve in an odd voice, pointing. "I think we need to hide, m'lady."

They gleamed golden as they caught the sun. It was a reflection off metal, but they flew and tumbled through the sky like a murder of crows. Even from here you could hear their harsh cawing cry.

"Aberinn's crow." She'd seen it, in his tower, in the gilded cage.

"Yes, m'lady. One is the same as many. And what they sees, he sees," said Neve, fearfully.

"Let's put that fire out, and think hidden thoughts," said Meb.

So they did, sitting tight, staying under the tree and cracking nuts.

The golden birds scattered across the sky. Hunting.

On the ground the piskies could maze and mislead, and the spriggans could give warning. Meb had a feeling that up close the muryan could deal with any attacker, just by sheer numbers. But the metallic crows stayed above, in the sky, and Meb honestly could not think what to do about them, except to wait them out.

They had to sit for a good hour, as the day grew warmer, before they could start walking again. It had given Meb a chance to think about what the various fay had said, and she'd perhaps not really understood. She had no desire to be some kind of savior. She'd just wanted . . . well, she knew what she'd just wanted, but as she couldn't have that, she'd just wanted somewhere quiet to be relatively miserable and peaceful about it all. Then she'd said she would help . . . and found that she'd promised a spy. Vivien had been kind to her. She'd been grateful. The castle's "little people" had been good to her. The non-human denizens of Lyonesse had been helpful . . . and in their ways, generous. Well, the piskies had helped rather than just generating mayhem, their most frequent habit. The spriggans had as much said they thought the whole process was using her. If it had to be that way, and she wasn't sure why it should, she'd shape it to her, not the other way around. And why her? Neve said only those of Lyonesse's noble ruling house had magic—but that just meant one of her parents had to have been. And she was a realist enough to know that could have been on the wrong side of wedlock. She was no lost princess: the last king had been dead more than fifty years, and the queen nearly sixty years. No one else at Dun Tagoll had been leaping up and claiming a child lost eighteen years ago. Or no one who was willing to admit to it, which put her as likely to be the love child of a servant. It would have been some small consolation for losing Fionn and Díleas to have loving parents waiting for her. She had never had a father. Hallgerd had at least been a kind of mother.

And then her type of magic was simply so different from the way they seemed to do things here. Did it really mark her as from their royal house at all? They knew precisely what and how they were doing what they were doing, and followed precise methods, but were quite weak in their degree of success. She had no real idea how she did what she did, had no real clear method, except that of a clear image and real desire or need, and a sort of daydreaming focus seemed to help. But she was far more successful than most, she gathered, excluding the likes of Aberinn.

She was still deep in thought as they began their walk. Eventually she asked Neve, "What would fix Lyonesse? If you could, I mean, just could...wave your hand and it happened."

Neve blinked. Meb had decided a while back that it wasn't that Neve was stupid. She just hadn't ever done much thinking and wasn't too eager to start. Meb understood that too. In a village, being smart or daydreaming weren't things that helped you to fit in, and it was easier to fit in than not to. "I'd stop the fighting. Stop the armies coming along the Ways. Never mind the Changes. Just leave us alone."

"But Vivien said it was needed to keep magic going in Lyonesse."

"Aye. It is," agreed Neve. "But no good that's been to burned villages and burned fishing boats, and killed people."

Meb suspected that the nobility of Lyonesse, whose power rested on that magic, would not see it that way. Well, she had no reason to care how they felt. But she did have reason to care for the spriggans and knockers, and the muryans and even the piskies. They needed magic. They were "wakening" because of the magic...then it dawned on her. They were wakening because the flows of magical energy had been restored because of the reintegration of Tasmarin, not because of the device in the tower. "So all we need is a bit of peace."

Neve nodded. "Mind you, stopping fighting usually takes some fighting." She swallowed. "I had...two little brothers. Only way to stop them fighting was to spank both of them, my mother said."

Meb suddenly felt overwhelmingly guilty. She'd never really found out much about Neve's family, beyond stories of her grandmother. "What happened to your family? Your village? Could I take you back there?"

"It isn't there anymore. No one along the coast near Dun Tagoll after the Vanar's last raids. M'mother and the boys...they were killed. Later, in Dun Telas, my Gamma...Well, she had money and my uncles, they moved to Dun Telas. I am not going back there." There was a terseness in her voice that said "don't ask me any more."

But Meb wouldn't have anyway, because just then a javelin spiked the trail in front of them.

Chapter 19

"SO, FINN. HOW FAR DO YOU TRAVEL WITH US?" asked Avram, as the carts made their way along the track. Fionn was sitting up on the box with him, and Díleas was fast asleep just behind him. He'd growled at Mitzi a little earlier, and she was still bright-eyed and eyeing him with interest. Fionn had been keeping an eye on Díleas for an entirely different reason. He was aware of gold, and had known just where in the dog's digestive tract the bespelled gold coin was. The spell probably wouldn't survive stomach acid, but the coin might do Díleas some harm, Fionn feared. He was relieved to know the coin wasn't in the dog anymore, but had been deposited somewhere. Díleas had obviously made sure it was a long way from Fionn, and that was one piece of gold Fionn had no interest in finding.

"Until the dog tells me it's time to go elsewhere. And right now he's too tired and his mind seems elsewhere."

"You're following the dog?" said Avram, incredulously.

Fionn nodded. "I told you he was smarter than you realized. He's following his mistress. He's taken me straight across four planes and back across a fifth. He takes me to these Tolmen Ways of yours, which are shorter, straighter, and less dangerous than the planar intersections that I know. Right now I believe you're going in the right direction."

"What are you seeking?" asked Avram.

"I said: the dog's mistress. She is very important and special to me."

Avram nodded. "She is a very desirable dragon, then?"

"She's a human," said Fionn.

Avram nearly dropped the reins. "There are some very fair young women among our people," he said cautiously.

"She's rather special, and to be honest with you, given all the time rates out here, I am not too sure if she'll be a young woman by the time I find her. The planes are extensive, although her magic use tends to make her stand out like a bonfire on a dark night," said Fionn.

"She's a mage?"

"Of sorts, yes," replied Fionn, smiling, thinking about it. "More like an accidental mage with more innate power than most dedicated and trained practitioners."

"Has she enchanted you, Dragon?" asked Avram. "We've got a few back home who are good at undoing those things..."

Fionn shook his head, knowing it wasn't entirely true, but preferring matters the way they were. "In theory, anyway, it is very hard for one human to use magic on our type of dragon. We are mostly proofed against magic for good reason. I think I love her in the same way and for the same reason the dog does. Because she is what she is, and she loves us."

"So...how did you lose her?" asked Avram, in the fashion of someone who knows this a bad question to ask, but is going to ask it anyway.

Fionn shrugged. "She used her power to go, and we don't know exactly where. I believe she was misled by...by something. And I intend to find out, and I intend to find out why."

"We have a saying that if there is one thing more determined than a man led by his testicles, it's one led by his emotions."

"It's true of dogs and dragons too," admitted Fionn.

Now that he was accepted as a dragon, there were no major secrets, and Fionn had built up something of a picture of the travelers. Their base was on the Blessed Isles, and there were ten carts in this venture, making it a small one. There had been eleven but one had had to be cannibalized to make a bridge. Twenty-two men, no women or children this trip; Annvn was considered too dangerous, as were the shifting gateways or Tolmen. There were several that the travelers never quite knew where they would come out. Some outcomes, like Brocéliande and Finvarra's kingdom, were merely dangerous, and places they visited in the normal course of business anyway. But Annvn, despite being profitable, was so full of regulation—and corruption—that travelers had had major problems, entire parties being sold into slavery, and needing expensive rescues.

"We're officially going to the assembly point to the way to Lyonesse, with supplies for the army," explained

Avram. "Actually, in two days we slip off the pike road for a mile or two and there's a Tolmen Way to Alba, and then about two weeks' travel and back to the Blessed Isles. Alba's none too bad. We're not going to Lyonesse. Not with or without an army. It's a bad spot, even if it didn't have the habit of raiding its neighbors. The land is unfriendly."

They showed Fionn several maps, indicating the Tolmen Ways, which he faithfully copied. He was pleased to add some extra points to their maps, too, with notes. Díleas had taken him places they either didn't know or didn't go to. Some could be awkward with a cart. Horses probably wouldn't enjoy being driven over a cliff.

He was still musing ways to get around this when they came to one of the inevitable checkpoints. Mind you, Fionn thought, this one was in more chaos than check. The soldiers were busy dismantling their camp. Avram waved his papers at them.

"Oh hell, check them," said one of the sergeants busy packing his kit. "You, soldier."

So the soldier came over and looked. Snorted. "You might want to turn back. They'll probably not pay you," he said as he returned them and took Fionn's papers.

"Not pay us?" said Avram, looking suitably horrified.

"We're not even sure if they'll pay us." He looked at Fionn's papers and began laughing. "You're out of a job, scumbag. They hung Maric last night."

"I can't tell you how pleased I am," said Fionn, beaming at him. "Finally. Tell me what happened."

The soldier, who, in Fionn's judgement, had been about to haul off and punch the supposed agent in the mouth, paused. "What?"

"I bought the papers from a pickpocket," said Fionn cheerfully. "Do I look like an agent? What happened to Maric? I can go home now!"

"I'll have to arrest you..."

"For what and for who?" asked Fionn, grinning and slapping his back. "If Maric's dead, who is paying you and who is giving you orders? So who is the new prince going to be?"

"Who knows? Sounds like there is a civil war going on. Slaves broke out, half the town in flames, looting, rebellion..."

"I think," said Avram, "that we'll keep going a bit, and let it all settle down."

He flicked his whip and the horses began to trot. They didn't stop and the soldiers didn't bother to try and stop them.

They slowed up about a mile further on. "That, Finn, could have been ugly," said Avram.

"The law of unintended consequences," said Fionn, "and how all things are interconnected and balanced always amazes me. I tossed a spark in there, I suppose. Didn't expect a wildfire. Yet, I couldn't have made as big a one if I tried."

"Still, it makes getting ourselves and our goods on the trail to Alba ever more important. Civil wars are bad for trade and bad for travelers. I'll be glad to get there."

"I'll be glad to be going with you if I am," said Fionn. "Let's see what Díleas says."

Díleas informed Fionn by leaping off the cart—and away from Mitzi—that he was going straight on, on foot toward the staging post of the army, not on by cart towards a stone arch—a Tolmen which opened a

Way to Alba—but to one which intermittently led to
Lyonesse. There were a couple of other possibilities
beyond that, but that was the closest. And what could
be more likely than that his Scrap of humanity would
be in the middle of a war, in a place which everyone
seemed to detest?

The countryside became hillier and intermittently
wooded as they walked on. Fionn had rather expected
it to be full of troops heading back to their homes or
to the city, but it wasn't. In fact the road was deserted,
as were most of the farms. He did see smoke coming
from the two chimneys of an odd, shadowy, angular
building on a hilltop that had some magic-use problems
which he would have gone to deal with normally, but
that was the only sign of human life he saw. There
were signs of devastation, though. Reading the map,
late that afternoon, Fionn decided they had barely a
mile or two to go, and was about to press on, when
he realized they were being approached. By a tall,
graceful tree-woman.

"Fionn. The black dragon?" She asked as if she were
some messenger, checking she had the right person.

"Yes," said Fionn. There seemed little point in
denying it.

"You move fast and far. My sisters have sent me
news for you," she said. "The trees pass word slowly
from tree to tree, plant to plant, growing thing to
growing thing. The planes are not a divider to them,
because they do not understand them or comprehend
them, and thus are not limited by them. They bring
us word, in time. The woman you seek," said the tall
tree-sprite, "is in the land humans know as Lyonesse.

She walks among the new-leaf oaks there. And at her side and following behind her are the myriads."

Fionn took a deep breath. He'd found her, and his secret, never-voiced fear had not been realized. The wilder worlds out there had not killed his precious Scrap of humanity. "I owe you . . . your kind . . . a debt. And I never forget," he said, his voice thick. "Hear that, Díleas? We know where we're going now. It sounds like she has a big army."

"It is not a big army. Just very numerous," said the sprite. "Or that is how the trees see it."

She gave him a swaying bow, and turned away. Fionn knew her kind better than to waste his time running after her and asking for clarification.

At least he knew she was alive and where she was.

"Come on, Díleas. Let's go."

So they went.

But their way was blocked by an army that was both numerous and big. And which had rather effectively blocked the gate, even for a dragon in a hurry.

The gate looked rather like a castle gatehouse, and was—unlike the ancient triliths—an obviously recent construction . . . so much so that there were still construction materials piled near them. It was quite different too in that it smelled of oil and human magic to Fionn's senses. Quite unlike the other Ways.

The gatehouse still looked imposing. Complete with solid gates, and a portcullis. And an army camped outside, and a formation of pikemen at the ready.

"The Annvn invasion force might not be going through at the moment," said Fionn to Díleas, inspecting it from a nearby hill with a convenient forested gully for cover, "but nothing is coming out, either."

Fortunately, it appeared that the army was looking for trouble not from within Annvn but from elsewhere.

He inspected the gate as carefully as he could at this distance. Breaking into places was, after all, very much his stock in trade.

Normally over, rather than through, would have been his chosen method.

Only he doubted that would help here. "Over" would merely get him to the other side of the gate, not to another plane. The same probably applied to "around" or even to "under."

It would have to be "through." And while dragon fire would deal with their gate, and even with the portcullis... That rather depended on no humans being in the way to get incinerated.

Fionn scratched his head in irritation. "The answer might be to frighten them off. But every now and then, they can be very hard to frighten. Their unpredictability makes planning interesting. Normally I enjoy that."

He fished out the maps while Díleas stared curiously. "On the other hand... It's late afternoon now. How about if we try a two-pronged strategy here. Come dusk, a dragon will drop on the army with as much tumult and hair-searing flame as I can muster. If they run, the dragon's dog guide will be sitting ready on this hillside in his flying basket for me to pick up. Are you with me? Two barks for yes."

"Hrf, hrf."

"Then a bit more dragon fire and we're into Lyonesse, and we go hunting for your mistress's magical pyrotechnics."

"Hrf hrf!"

Fionn held up a hand. "But if they stand... well,

the Tolmen Way to Vanaheim is close, and then from that, it's a flight out to sea, and we come to this islet, from which we can get to Lyonesse."

Never had a wait seemed quite so long to Fionn. He was used to exercising patience. Energy was about alignment and flow, all in their proper times... Right now he would have moved the sun itself, if he could.

At last the sun touched the far horizon in a crimson blaze of dying glory. Fionn readied the basket for Díleas, made sure it stood securely. The dog was pacing, plainly impatient too. The moment it was ready he jumped in, but he didn't lie down. Instead, he sat, looking at the gate.

"I can understand you wanting to do that, I suppose," said Fionn. "If we get through, we can stop. If we don't... we can stop in a mile or two." He took on his dragon form, spread and stretched his wings. Warmed them up with a few flaps. All good things for a dragon to do, but seldom done. He was putting this off, he knew. He leapt upwards into the purple sky spattered with the first stars and still with the memory of red on the western horizon. He flapped his way upwards, and then dived, spreading wing tendrils and talons to make the loudest possible air-shriek.

As pale faces turned upwards, he gave their wagons and mess tents a brief wash of flame. And then began to climb again, to arc around, letting his claws rip canvas down one row of tents, sending men diving into the mud. Then he climbed again, looking down at the chaos he'd stirred.

The camp was scattering. Parts of it were burning. But, to his annoyance, the pikemen assembled before the gate had not joined the chaos. They'd turned their formation to defend the gate. Their officers must be made of stern stuff, and the pikemen, hard men.

Normally, with dragons, that would have meant crisp men. Fionn climbed higher, and dived again, this time coming from behind the gate that they had just turned away from.

Dragon fire seared over them, melting pike points, causing considerable blistering.

But they held. Fionn flapped upward. Someone even managed to loft an arrow at him. He burned it midair, to discourage that.

"Hold hard, the forty-fifth!" bellowed a voice that would have done a bull mammoth proud. "About... turn! Face the gate. They must be planning to break through!"

Fionn sighed. It was cook them or give up and go around. So he flew back and picked up Díleas, and flapped off into the night.

The glorious forty-fifth would remember their night of triumph. By the looks of it, half of the rest of the army wouldn't. From a bit of altitude and in the infrared spectrum, Fionn could see them scattering. He dropped down and encouraged a few to keep running, and then flew onward, to the gate into Vanaheim.

He stopped a few miles down the road, to tuck Díleas in, and apologized. "I can't just cook them, Díl. It'd be easier if I could."

"Hrf." A resigned sort of "Hrf."

"There is no point in your getting out of the basket. You'll get killed back there. We'll just go around them. It won't take any longer than your walking would."

They flew on. Fionn had the feeling that his status

was a little dented. But when they landed at the little stone Tolmen, Díleas gave Fionn a lick. On the nose.

They walked through together. Into sunlight and a crackling breeze.

The queen of Shadow Hall was tempted to spit into her seeing pool. She knew it would not make her vision any better or sweeter, and they would not feel it on the other side, but it might make her feel better.

She'd worked so hard on Annvn. And now, when an army twenty times the size of anything Lyonesse could possibly manage, with siege engines and good maps and wagonloads of provisions, and more and more reserves pouring in...

A revolution. A slave uprising too. The army dispersed and their stores demolished, and half their war machines burned. And the survivors were all very pleased with themselves for holding off the dragon. Why had the fools not let it through to ravage Lyonesse?

With an exasperated sigh she turned her attention to the next place the Changer would link Lyonesse to. Or should. She looked to Vanaheim. She'd kept them from their normal happy pastime of butchering each other for the last few years and goaded them into building a vast fleet to attack Lyonesse instead.

It seemed, on looking at the empty harbors in West Vanaheim, that the fleets were at sea.

Sweeping her gaze around, she found them to the southeast, heading for shelter...

Loaded for war and conquest.

Only the wind wasn't helping.

Where did they think they were going! She'd prepared them for her use against Lyonesse, not their own petty wars. She had her cauldron-men among them, of course. She would find out.

And she did. They had their own seers and seid-women, the völva. Ones who were as capable of finding the Ways and when they were open.

They were sailing to attack Lyonesse. Just as soon as the wind cooperated.

The queen set her muryan slaves to work, moving Shadow Hall to Vanaheim.

It was late that evening that it occurred to her to check on the gate in Annvn. She might as well start the slow process of reorganizing against the next cycle.

Out of habit, she checked the Way.

And it was open too.

Then she began feverishly checking the others, cackling with glee. Rubbing her bony hands in delight. How had he botched so? Ha ha ha.

At last. At long, long last! She began sending out messengers to her cauldron-men, to those she had implanted as counselors and advisors to the kings, queens, princes and chieftains of the nineteen worlds.

Someone was at her outer door.

How dare they interrupt her triumph? And how could they? Shadow Hall was moving steadily. It was not easy to see. And it had its defenders. She used the seeing bowl to look.

The creature of smokeless flame, which the locals would probably call a demon, had no trouble keeping up with Shadow Hall, or with seeing it. And it could probably devour her cauldron-men, if they succeeded in attacking it.

She'd done business with them before, so she went to see what it wanted. She had some defenses on hand, but theirs was a mutually beneficent arrangement. She could kill this one, if she needed to, but she would rather hear what it had to say.

The hooded creature bowed respectfully. That, of course, was something it would do, and she was not fooled. They had scant respect for any other life-form, except where that was reenforced by fear. Among their own, of course, they were hierarchical to the extreme. Other life-forms were theirs to use ... if they could. If vanity was the key, they'd use it. She did not bow back. "Well. Why do you interrupt my work?"

"My apologies, great queen of Magic Workers. My master's masters ... offer great rewards for a simple service."

They paid. They paid in whatever form she asked and without any form of haggling—no matter how ridiculous her asking price. The entire funding of that Spathos had come for the hire of one cauldron-giant. Giants were hard to make, being so large, and needing thus to be assembled in sections, but still ... "What do you need?" She had a list of raw materials for the cauldron needed from other planes. She'd had difficulty getting them before.

"My master's masters require the disposal of two beings. One is in Lyonesse, and one is proceeding there. We think he is in Vanaheim now. We believe you will be in the best position, with your seeing device, to find them and destroy them. I have images of both." He handed her a crystal into which a three-dimensional image of a young woman with an axe sprang into existence, sitting in a little coracle.

"A little warrior princess," said the queen of Shadow Hall, faintly amused. The child had a determined chin. But, as she had found out when she had tried her own hand at armed combat, those many, many years ago, men were physically stronger. You had to defeat them more subtly.

"She goes by the name of Meb. We believe she fled Dun Tagoll. Briefly she was on the water but she has returned to land."

"If she fled Dun Tagoll she is hardly an enemy of mine."

"She is one girl-child," said the flame creature dismissively. "There are many such, but my master's masters have concerns about her associate. She must die, to control him. Name your price."

"Tell me about the other one," said the queen.

The flame creature produced a second crystal. In it was the image of a black dragon.

"The dragon that thwarted me in Annvn," said the queen.

"He's a shape-changer. Turn the crystal over, and more images will show. We had a very good visual trace on him, but it has been obscured. He is both clever and a great deal harder to kill than most dragons, and dragons are not easy to kill. This one can only be bespelled with gold, and only confined in adamantine."

She had quite a bit of that. The Shadow Hall relied on adamantine hardness, as well as the ductility of its joints, to survive the inevitable strain of moving all the time. Her first three attempts had jolted apart. "I have been wanting a dragon for my cauldron."

"That can be provided. But you are no match for him in physical contest."

"What are his weak points?" asked the queen. There was no point in telling the demon she'd kill this one for nothing. Merely as repayment for what he'd done to her many years of work. And the girl . . . well, most of those in Lyonesse would die. They might as well pay her for the killing. The cauldron took certain rare materials, and of course raising a war took gold and silver, a great deal of it.

"He does not kill intelligent life-forms."

She turned the crystal over, and a tall, dark-skinned, foxy-faced man appeared. Ah. They'd had Spathos hunting him. Cutting out the middleman, as it were. But, she admitted, it was possible they had not known that he was her lackey.

It appeared Spathos had vanished in the rebellion against Prince Maric.

It would seem that brushing up against this dragon could be unhealthy even if he did not kill.

"Is this what you pitted my other cauldron-creatures against?" she said, suddenly suspicious.

"Yes," said the creature of smokeless flame. "Or rather, his guide."

It did not even try to lie. Interesting. And it spoke of its master's master. Very high. Very powerful. "This will be very, very expensive," said the queen.

"Name your price."

Vanaheim was a place where dragons felt at home. Someone had to. Dragons liked volcanoes and jagged new mountains, and a vast blue sky feathered with thin cloud. The land, where it wasn't edging into sea cliffs, was mostly fells full of sheep. Fionn knew the other coast had a gentler slope, a warmer current and forests for Vanar's fleets. This piece of the Celtic was colored by their Nordic conquerors—a gift the islanders liked to spread around. Fionn was convinced it was the long, cold, dark winters that made them so homicidal—that or their beer. Or it could be eating slow-fermented basking sharks. Fionn had sampled this "delicacy" once.

From up here, where the Tolmen Way had brought them, they could see the fleet was on the water—every longship the islanders could find, by the look of it.

And also by the look of it, most of them were returning to the fiords of Vanaheim, because there really was a stiff onshore breeze blowing. A few determined ships were trying to row their way into it, but most had turned for home.

Besides their taste for mayhem and loot, fermented basking shark and too many salt herring dishes, the other flaw that Fionn felt the Vanar culture had was their desire to shoot dragons, and they had strong muscles, good composite bows and strong nerves that made it possible. Fionn understood fully that the desire was fueled by conflict over who would eat the coarse-haired fell sheep. But it made flying low any-where near the coast—where the Vanar lived—quite a dangerous pastime for dragons. It took a lucky shot to kill or even seriously injure a dragon, but it could damage their wings. And killing the dog would be easy too. The air here was cold. At altitude it was winter-arctic cold. It added a layer of complications to flying to the next Tolmen Way. One forgot the flexing in time between worlds. He'd expected to fly on in the night, not to waste another day!

Díleas was already heading across the meadow, down toward the fiord below. "Where are you going, you fool dog?" asked Fionn.

"A dragon!" came a sudden shout. The Vanar warrior charged, swinging his double-bladed axe and blond plaits.

Fionn knocked him down with a swipe of the tail. Just because he wasn't supposed to kill them didn't mean that he had to put up with someone swinging an axe at him. Fionn rolled him over and sat on the warrior, as Díleas came charging to the rescue. Fionn changed his form as the stunned seat groaned. "Have you been eating those mushrooms again?" demanded Fionn. Agaric tended to make for berserker warriors... and some strange visions. And this one smelled of the mushroom. Fionn got up and rolled him over, kicking the axe away. "You just called me a dragon, tried to chop me up, and fell over my dog," he said accusingly. "What's wrong with you?"

"There was a dragon..."

"No, there wasn't. If there was, do you think either I, or the sheepdog, would be here?"

The large warrior sat up. Groaned. "I gotta go. I promised Thor Red-Axe I'd join his war band."

"Where are you going?" asked Fionn, although he suspected he already knew.

"Vleidhama, to find a ship. The völva say that the way is open to Lyonesse! We must go aviking!"

Which translated as "loot, rape and pillage and maybe even stay in a place where it isn't dark for half of the year." Fionn clipped him, hard, behind the head. He fell over again. "You were right, Díleas. Just let me relieve him of these fashion accessories, and we can walk down and join a boat."

The Vanar warrior was relieved of his mail shirt, helmet, axe and woolly breeches. Fionn looked into his travel bag. A side of salted smoked salmon, a loaf of rye bread, a bag of coarsely ground oatmeal, and yes, dried red-and-white-spotted mushrooms... a leather bag with a little money—the clumsy coinage of Vanar: iron, copper and a little gold. Díleas growled at him. "Another one of these mushrooms and he wouldn't know I relieved him of it. But you're right. I'll leave him with some of Spathos's silver. I'm not that fond of silver, but it's valued here. And his cloak. But to make you my partner in crime, I'll give you some of the salmon. It's mostly salt and smoke with a bit of fish. Consistency of leather. Keeps well and exercises the jaw. We'll leave him the bread and that flask which I think might make him see more than dragons, by the smell of it."

Disguised as a Vanar warrior—a not very rich or bright one—who came down from the sheep in the mountains, Fionn walked into the nearest crowded fishing village. Finding a place for himself and Díleas on one of the good *Skei* was not likely, but some of the bigger *Busse* were struggling to find oarsmen. Anyone who thought they were anyone wanted a place on one of the faster ships, so a slightly slow-witted shepherd who wasn't prepared to leave his smart dog behind could find a place, and be away for the shores of Lyonesse just as soon as the wind turned again. That, according to the weather-wise, would be sometime after midday, and the captains were trying to keep the oarsmen sober until then... or at least not quite paralytic.

Fionn found it amusing, seeing as his multiple livers meant he could drink their Branntwein and barley beer until it ran out of his ears without any effect.

The Hákarl they were eating with it was a different matter. He'd need more than multiple livers for that. It was considered a manly thing to eat.

Fionn was glad he was a dragon, and not in need of eating ammonia-scented, fermented shark meat to prove this. Díleas, however, had embraced local behavior with gusto, eaten far too much salty smoked salmon, and was now throwing up, and needing water, along with Vanar's finest warriors. Perhaps this was why men and dogs had such a natural affinity, reflected Fionn, noting that the wind was dropping.

═ Chapter 20 ═

MEB LOOKED AT THE JAVELIN, AND AT THE GROUP of ... possibly people, all with more throwing spears at the ready, in the forest shadows on either side. She could see the weapons clearly enough, and their sharp stone points. The wielders ... were a mat of hair and twigs and vine. Rather like bears that had rolled in honey and then down a steep brush slope, thought that dispassionate part of her mind. She wondered in a panic if it would do any good at all to try and "hide" Neve and herself. Probably not, thought the pragmatic part of her mind. They would throw their spears the moment she and Neve disappeared.

And then she realized that she and Neve had not walked alone into the deep woods after all. And if anyone was in trouble it would certainly also be the spearmen. Not that she and Neve would be any the better off for the fact that the muryan bit the attackers to death.

The odd spear-wielders plainly spotted the tide of muryan. They lowered their spear points warily. But how do you point a spear at thousands of foes, each smaller than a thumbnail? Quite a few spear-wielders backed off completely, vanishing into the shadows. "Are you the Wudewasa?" said Meb. "Because we were told to look for you."

"Who sent you?" said one of the hairy, twiggy people stepping out of the dense leaf-mottled shade, away from the muryan. "We have no dealing with incomers. Even ones served by the muryan." He sounded a lot more doubtful about that part.

"One of the spriggans," said Meb. "They said the Land wanted us to come to you."

"Just who are you, and where are you from?" asked the hairy man with the added leaves and twigs.

Why did they all want to know that? Did it really matter?

"She's the Defender," said Neve, proudly touching Meb, who still stood holding her axe. "Prince Medraut and Mage Aberinn didn't believe her, but she made the sea-wall window come back. And it was her, not Aberinn, that defeated the Fomoire's evil eye! The fay come to her. They look after her. Have you ever seen the muryan before? They feed us, and protect us."

"We see muryan from time to time in the woods. We leave them alone, maybe leave them some scraps of food, and they leave us alone." He looked at the ground, and at the warrior muryan there. "I'll grant I have never seen them seeming to defend anyone before. But the prince and the mage and all the rest: they mean nothing to us. We stay in our deep woods and they do nothing for us and we owe nothing to them. This is our land. Our forest."

"Yes, but we've knockers and spriggans and even the piskies helping her."

"Even the piskies! Now that would be something to see," said the hairy man, sounding faintly amused. Looking closer now, Meb could see that not all of it was growing on him, but that some of it was woven into a kind of cloth. Hairy cloth. "But it seems your friend has lost her tongue. Maybe she can talk for herself?"

Meb shrugged. "I am just me. That's all. I call myself Meb. I have been told my birth name was Anghared. I came from a place called Tasmarin, where the dragons rule. They told me here that I had magic and I must be of the House of Lyonesse. And then they decided I didn't and wasn't. They do their magic by patterns and diagrams and models and calculations and rituals. I don't even know how to start that. It comes to me sometimes, because I need it, and because I dream it. And now you see me." She concentrated hard on not being seen and walked away. He stared, blinked, rubbed his eyes. Reached out to where she'd been. Just behind him she tapped him on his shoulder, willing herself to be seen again. "And now you don't."

He turned and stared. She dug out her juggling balls, simply because they helped her think. Began tossing them one-handed, the other hand holding the axe. "If," she said, "we just wanted to go through your woods, we could. You wouldn't have even known we were there. And if I was interested in conquering and killing, I could have come unseen and sent the muryan to deal with you in your sleep."

She passed the axe to the other hand, and caught the balls with it. "But we were looking for you, because I was told you were the right people to look for. That you were, of all the humans, closest to the Land."

The hairy man nodded. "I will take you to the wisewoman and the shamans. They said . . . disaster had come. They said all the Ways were open and invaders who have no respect for our forest will be coming soon. We watched for that. Not two women."

"M'lady," said Neve, timidly. "Do you mind if I carry the axe? It's really scary when you toss it up and catch the balls. I've seen how sharp it is."

The Wudewasa man smiled and nodded. "But a woman with a big axe and balls . . . makes men nervous."

They were led through the forest, carefully skirting around several places where the trail seemed to go. Someone had plainly gone ahead, because the wisewoman who seemed to lead the tribe, as much as they had a leader, was waiting with the two shamans in their equivalent of a reception room—a huge, hollow tree set at the end of a double row of mossy rocks, with a wooden chair carved into the wood itself. It was occupied by the Wudewasa's wisewoman, with the two shamans with their drums and bones having to settle for logs.

The wisewoman's hair was white. There was a vast amount of it, and barring the addition of a willow catkin, she didn't have any twigs or leaves in it. She was tiny and frail, and attended by a young girl, because moving was obviously painful for her. Her brown eyes, peering out of a mass of wrinkles, were rheumy, and she blinked a lot. But her wits and tongue were still sharp. "I thought you said it was a woman carrying the weight of the Land. I'm seeing two girls, who couldn't carry more than a peck of dirt."

"That shows that you need look a lot more carefully, Mortha," said one of the mossy stones, unwinding itself into a spriggan. "We know, the muryan know, the knockyan know, the piskies know, and, if you look properly, you'll find you do, too. Did you think it comes with a fine horse and a coronet and troops of soldiers? You're in for a sad disappointment."

The silver-haired woman didn't move. "Those are holy rocks."

The spriggan snorted: "Then maybe you should count them more often. To not notice there was an extra one might be seen as disrespect," he said tartly, showing no deference at all for her age or the rocks. "A few minutes ago you were twittering in fear because the Vanar were coming. Wondering how best to keep them from cutting your trees for charcoal or ship timbers, like last time. Now you're fussing about the size of the help."

The wisewoman kept her dignity...barely. "We were hoping...for what is asked, that we'd get something in return. Some troops of fighting men with iron swords, against their iron axes."

"She seems to have odd ideas," said the spriggan, jerking a thumb at Meb. "Believes in giving something back in exchange for what she is given. The old kings of Lyonesse would be very shocked." He seemed to enjoy that idea.

Meb sighed. "Do you mind stopping this talking over my head? I don't know what is going on, and I think if I am going to help I will need to."

"All the Ways are open," said the wisewoman, Mortha. "All our enemies will come. And while many pass through the forest without much searching or effect, the first here, the soothsayers say, will be the Vanar. They've cut out most of their own forest. Now they want ours."

"It was the Vanar who burned my village and our boats," said Neve. "Please, m'lady. You've got to stop them."

"They burn what they can't carry away," said Mortha. "The soothsayers say the sea will be black with their dragon ships this time."

"Dragon ships?" The dragons Meb knew would make poor boats. Or even poor pullers of boats, if this was something like a donkey cart.

"Their ship's prows are carved to look like dragons or great monstrous serpents. They come from Vana-heim, where it is cold and the trees don't grow well. So they come for ours. And anything else they can find," said Neve, quite used to explaining by now. "They're not quite as big as the Fomoire, and they don't have much magic, but there are lots of them and they go berserk when they fight. You have to kill them to stop them."

"They chew mushrooms that make them mad," said Mortha.

"Where will they beach?" asked Meb. "Can we stop them getting to the land at all?"

"My Gamma Elis said that in King Angbord's day they had watchtowers along the coast and warning bonfires. The troops would ride out from Dun Tagoll, Dun Argol, Dun Telas, Dun Carfon, and fight them on the beaches. There was talk of having catapults to sink their ships while they were still at sea. But the people of Lyonesse never did it, and then the towers fell or were burned after King Geoph died."

The wisewoman sighed. "The only thing that'll hold them on land is horsemen, horsemen who fight to order, with long lances, and good massed bowmen. Our forest people . . . We can ambush and fight in the dark, but we cannot hold them back. And we've seen what Medraut does: fight a quick skirmish and run for Dun Tagoll, and leave those outside to feel their wrath."

The spriggan looked thoughtful. "They fear magic, though. Especially women's magic. They'd be more afraid of a woman mage than a male one. And, the truth be told, they treat us with fear and respect. That'll not keep them from the forests, and they have too much iron for us. It's a slow poison to our kind, and even being close to it in concentrated or purified form for too long weakens us. If the Lady Land asks it, tribes of piskies can mislead them for a while. And we can look very large. The muryan . . . well, if they slow down enough, the muryan can and will overwhelm anything. And neither iron nor anything else holds much threat to them. The knockyan, well, let's be honest, they don't really fight or do more than play jokes on those who wander underground. They have tunnels everywhere, of course."

"And they will all stand against the invaders?" asked Meb.

"If you tell them to, yes." The spriggan pulled a face. "Of course . . . it's not quite as easy as that."

"No," said Meb, "that would all be too simple, wouldn't it?"

"Exactly, and if life were simple, we'd all have warm palaces to live in and strawberries to eat every day, in winter too. But it isn't. See, we're yours to command, but you must command us."

"I'm telling you to resist the invaders," said Meb obligingly.

"And I will," said the spriggan. "But I'm bound to

a certain area. Bound within seven miles of my place. And you've told me. But you'll have to tell each of the spriggans. We tend to live three or four together. The knockyan, well, they talk and pass it on. By now I'd guess stories about you and your juggling, and having knockyan babies on your lap, will have spread from one end of Lyonesse to the other, and are being told to others. Other spriggans, some human miners too. The muryan will defend you if they are where you are, and will attack if you tell them to. But there are tens of thousands of queens. Each only controls their own nest. As for the piskies ... well, they're family groups. And they don't keep their mind on the task very easily. They'll enjoy misleading and mazing the Vanar. But sooner or later the Vanar will find out how to counter that. It's best saved for when you need it. And by then it'll be too late, I shouldn't wonder."

Meb sighed. "The real wonder is how cheerful you are. Tell me. Do I command anyone else? Merrows? Do you have them here?"

"Well, there are merpeople, but they live in the sea, and are no part of the land. And they're not good to deal with."

"Even so," said Meb, "I think that's what we're going to have to try and do, and quickly because I'd rather not have more mad people here. Most of the ones here seem quite mad enough already."

The gilded crows gave Aberinn a wide view of Lyonesse, and a headache. Too many images to process. He had as yet not found any sign of the two women. They probably had not gotten very far before falling prey to what young women roaming Lyonesse without protectors would fall prey to. He felt Medraut's reaction to them simply too extreme. But then Medraut alternated between believing in the prophecy and believing, somehow, that it was all a plot against him. Either by the mage or one of the factions of nobles who still squabbled over Lyonesse like real crows over a corpse. Well, he'd had his own suspicions about the girl. It appeared at most she was adept with a knife and a few magic tricks—probably prepared by some adept for her, to be displayed suitably.

Anyway, they were dead and gone and Lyonesse faced an influx as she had never suffered before. As yet, the gilded crows reported no major invasions. But they would come soon. The land would suffer, fortresses would fall. And somehow he must work out just what had happened to the Changer.

Meb traveled with an escort of forest people, down a wooded valley, to the coast. They had provided her with a jacket of coarse brown cloth, set with fresh twigs and branches, but it could not come close to their camouflage. They could freeze and look like trees or shrubs or just the branches of one. They were experts at not moving suddenly, and at sticking to places where the light was broken with shadows. And for most of the journey down to the coast, that was adequate. Neither Aberinn's gilded crows nor anything else could possibly have seen them. Meb was surprised at how many other people—peasants mostly—they did see. Here a nervous group of ex-soldiers from some foreign place eking out a living, there a solitary fisherman working a stream. Lyonesse was a rich country for those needing to live off the land. It made her realize that the various fay had probably worked quite hard to get her and Neve that far without meeting anyone. She was realistic enough to realize that such a meeting would only have been an ugly experience, needing the axe and luck to survive. They crossed several open patches during the night, but the problem came the next day, when they were close enough to smell the sea, and cover was sparse.

And the gilded crow was circling.

It was probably just trying to gain height. From here in the tree shadows, Meb could see that it didn't fly as well as a real crow might.

She wished it would go away. Wished it with real urgency and irritation. Wondered if she could simply "hide" them all, and whether this would work to deceive Aberinn's magical-mechanical creatures. Just wished it would hurry up and go away, that flying should be for real birds.

And, as they watched and waited, a real bird buzzed the contrivance. And then another. Smaller than the gilded crow, of course, but far more agile. She'd seen blackbirds pack a hawk like this. And now there were more birds, mobbing the crow. The gilded crow tried to flee them, but even the sparrows were as fast as it was. And it was as if they'd realized that although the interloper might be bigger, it was fairly helpless and far from as agile as they were. Then more birds came and they mobbed it down.

It crash-landed awkwardly. The birds all flew off about their business.

The crow plainly tried to fly again. And the birds drove it down. "Good," said Meb. "It can *walk* back to Dun Tagoll, and tell Aberinn what sore feet it has."

"You're a very powerful mage," said one of her escort, fearfully.

Meb swallowed. "Birds do that to foreign interlopers from time to time." Silently, to herself, she said, "but if I made it happen... I wish you all lots of worms, or seeds or fruit, and a safe nest for your help. I don't want them spying."

They took her to the water's edge. And she had absolutely no idea what to do. She'd had the idea that the merpeople would come to her, the way the others had.

And the waves remained...waves.

"Is anyone listening?"

No mermaids appeared dancing on the water.

The sea just sighed against the rocks.

She reached down to it, picking up a handful and letting it dribble through her fingers, sighing back at it. She wondered how the spirit of the sea was doing with the lord of the mountains. Groblek had had no limitation to planes and places...

"And neither does the sea," whispered a voice. "It is many seas, but it is all aspects of one Sea." The face in the foam tracery looked...like that of someone who had forgotten to do their hair. "Forgive me. I am a little...busy," said the sea.

"Oh dear. Groblek?"

"No, you were quite right. We've found ways...it has been some years. But we have a child, and he is never still unless he is asleep."

Years? Fionn had said that time ran differently in some places. How was he after...years? Was Díleas old? She swallowed. "I was hoping to negotiate for some help. We're expecting to be attacked from the sea."

"The Vanar. Good seamen. Quite respectful," said the Spirit of the Sea.

"Oh. But we can't have them here, lady. Please."

"No. They don't belong here. A few are relatively harmless. But many would upset your dragon's balance."

"He . . . he still works on that?"

Lady Skay seemed amused. "Sometimes."

"Is he . . . well?"

"He's a dragon. They don't usually get sick. But he, and that black-and-white dog, seemed well last time they went paddling in my water."

"Thank you. Thank you so much," said Meb, smiling tremulously.

"It seems a fair repayment. You carried similar information for me. And I will deal with the Vanar fleet. Have no fear of them. Or any further troubles with mermen. Call on me again . . . I must go."

Meb could swear she heard a crash somewhere. It could have been a wave breaking.

Meb turned away from the sea, to the Wudewasa and the spriggan waiting on the shore behind her.

"They're not usually interested in talking to people," said the spriggan. "I don't know why, but they're a nasty bunch, this lot of sea-people. We'll just have to fight the Vanar on land."

"Um. Didn't you see her?" asked Meb.

"Was there a mermaid?" asked the spriggan.

If the Spirit of the Sea did not want them to see her . . . well, who was Meb to tell anyone about it. "We can stop worrying about the Vanar," said Meb. "Now we just need to deal with any other invaders."

"Oh. All it needed was for you to splash your hand

in the water," said the Wudewasa warrior. "We could have done that."

"But you didn't," said Meb, with a sweet smile. "So it's a good thing that I did. And you never know, it might not have worked for you. Actually, I am certain it wouldn't. Now, I think we need to work out where the next threat is, and deal with that. Those soothsayers are supposed to predict these things, aren't they? Because if I have to go and ask the muryan and others for help in person, I will have to get there in time to do it. And in between I'd like to try and fit in some sleeping and some eating, which I have found make me think better, and be better tempered, too. I daresay Wudewasa and spriggans don't work like that, but we spoiled fishing village royalty do."

She'd made them laugh, which Finn had said was half the battle won. She had a feeling it might be the easy half.

═ Chapter 21 ═

FIONN HAD FLOWN WILD RIDES THROUGH STORM and chaos on far too many worlds. He'd been at sea and shipwrecked in more tempests than most people have days to their lives. Never had he been on such an angry sea. It was not just an angry sea, with waterspouts and waves taller than the *Busse* itself... but it was also a beautiful day, with the sun shining and not much more than a breath of wind.

They were rowing, as fast as possible, toward the fiords of Vanar. The sea was pushing them, them and all the other surviving vessels, back toward the land. Fionn was seriously weighing the possibilities of taking to the air, along with Díleas, and never mind those who saw the sailor turn into a dragon. Their chances of living to tell the story were scant. But it did seem that so far, anyway, this particular vessel had been spared the worst. Even the waterspouts had sheared away and gone to sink other, less fortunate ships. The sea did not stop its wildness inside the fiord. It seemed to be trying to spit out, or wreck, as many

Vanar ships as possible. The steersman of this vessel, very sensibly, beached it on the first bit of land that wasn't cliff. It made a few holes in the ship but the fury of the waves had driven her bow well up onto the steep, rocky, grassy slope. They all scrambled off her anyway, all wanting to be away from the angry water.

"It's as if the Goddess Rán has taken against us. And we give her thralls and branntwein every year. Ai, she's a capricious one," said the steersman, looking glumly at the ship. "Come on, lads. Let's see if we can haul her up a bit. Or the sea'll have her tail off, and we'll not be getting more timber to build another like her. Not from Lyonesse anyway."

Fionn agreed with the last part, even if he called to Díleas and then sneaked off among the boulders that had fallen from the cliffs above, rather than help with the hauling.

He was also sure that it hadn't been all Rán's—as she was called locally—idea. This was his Scrap. It had her mark of total overkill about it, he thought ruefully. She'd got on with Lady Skay of the sea, and with Groblek of the mountains.

He started walking uphill. Below, in the fiord, the water, having disgorged or sunk the fleet of Vanar, was settling back to its normal mirror-calm.

"We'll do it by flying to the island with the Tolmen Way, boy. Let's get a little distance from the shipwrecks first. I'm tired after that row, and wouldn't mind a nice easy launch. We'll need to get a fair bit of altitude, because shipwreck or no, some of these Vanar will shoot arrows at us. And your basket won't stop those."

Díleas seemed quite happy to be back on dry land,

and not frantic to set off for his mistress just yet. They were both wet through and it was fairly cold this late in the afternoon. Fionn was just wondering if he ought to try drying the contents of Díleas's basket with a fire, or just take a chance on getting to the Skerry island that was their target, wet and cold, when he spotted the building.

He had excellent recall. He'd seen this angular building with its two chimneys before.

Only that had been in Annvn, not on a steep slope above a fiord in Vanaheim. And...now that he looked carefully, it was attempting to meld with the shadows of the cliffs, to look like a trick of the light. A powerful piece of spellwork, that. And it was clearly and definitely moving.

And now that he tasted the air, it smelled faintly of dead things.

It was time, Fionn decided, to go and ask some questions.

He began running up the slope. The shadowy, hard-to-see house moved faster, almost as if it knew it were being chased.

"I think we'll have to try and work it as if between two sheepdogs," he said to Díleas, who plainly did not think a building should be able to move, and probably deserved to be bitten for it. They split and Díleas raced ahead, and Fionn, in dragon form, angled away to flank it. It was a bit steep for houses here, let alone ones that were trying to run away. They cornered it in a corrie and jumped up onto the portico.

"It occurs to me that owners of moving houses may have some nasty surprises waiting inside," said Fionn to Díleas. "So behind me, dog. Dragons are a lot harder to hurt, or kill, than dogs, and I have not got this close to our human to lose you. Besides, I've become fond of you. It's probably the way you share your fleas. Very generous of you, but they can't eat me, they just irritate me."

Fionn looked carefully at the door, at its patterns of energy, and the diagram used to hold it there. The human mage who had done this was no Spathos. This was art and power. The dangerous one-every-ten-generations level of human magecraft.

So naturally Fionn scratched a break in the pattern, and added another symbol or two. The mage had thought himself clever to use an invisible ink for this. Well, invisible to human eyes... now he would have a little surprise as the energy in that door accumulated and spread. The break allowed Finn to push the door open.

The inside was even stranger. It was quite a bit larger inside than it appeared outside. That was a neat piece of dimensional folding. Fionn looked for traps. Found none, bar the smell of decay and various exotic chemicals, rare materials and unusual compounds for the apparent vintage of the building. They advanced cautiously along the shadowy passage. Fionn detected symbolic magic at fairly high levels behind one of the doors. He cracked it. Peered inside. It contained a planar orrery, from which a bright light shone patterns onto the floor area. That showed Vanaheim—spiky and ripped with fiords. And yes, there was a shadowy hall in miniature on it, moving slowly across the landscape on tiny muryan legs. "Hmm. 'As within, so without,' rather the classic 'as above, so below' formulation," said Fionn quietly. So that was how it moved. Dangerous, clever and tricky.

Going any further into the room, Fionn realized, would
be even more dangerous. He'd find himself part of the
symbolism. And he was too big to survive it.

They moved on. The next door was too heavily
spell-guarded to get through quickly. But his nose told
him: that was where the smell of decay and exotic
chemicals came from. Also there was a fire in there.

"Keep a good few paces back, Díleas. This is no
hedge-wizard. This is a great adept. And there is
almost bound to be a trap," he said, sotto voce, in
a pitch the dog could hear, but humans would not.

He looked carefully ahead, looking for magic, looking for betraying energy patterns. They'd come to a
ramp, and there was an anomaly at the bottom. He
could see part of the scripts of it...

And then, as he stepped onto the ramp, he was
caught by a purely mechanical trap. The floor—obviously a circular sheet of segments—was on some kind
of castors. He barely had time to yell "BACK!" before
it had cascaded him into the spell-trap. There was a
sharp discharge of magic. And Fionn tumbled into
the trap—a sort of box at least twenty cubits deep.
There was an opening at the top...but it hummed
with energies. Examining it, Fionn could see that it
was nothing more than an illusion of an opening. The
box was actually solid—barring a fingernail-width gap
along the lid, and a small grating in the lowest corner.
Too small a grating for a mouse.

He was aware that he was being watched, from the
"gap" he'd fallen through. She was, by all appearances,
a beautiful woman with flawless skin. She regarded him
with a sort of clinical interest. That wouldn't help him
get out, of course. He was also aware that Díleas was

behind her. "I wouldn't come any closer," said Fionn, hoping sound at least carried out of here. "This is a trap."

It appeared sound did. "I know. I built it. It is a one-way portal. The walls are adamantine, and the roof is fitted to a device which magically multiplies pressure manyfold. It will shortly crush you and your tissues will flow into the holding vats for the cauldron. It appears the creatures of smokeless flame overrated your cunning and prowess."

Fionn shrugged. "I took one step further than you are standing, because of the rolling floor. It could happen to you."

"The floor is now frozen until I reset it. As you are going to die...Agh!! No! Dog..."

She tried to turn and grab, but tumbled over the edge, and into the magical discharge. Fionn caught her to stop her landing on her head.

Díleas looked down at him. "Good dog!" said Fionn, surprised himself at the pride he felt in Díl's intelligence and ability to take initiative. "Don't come any closer."

The woman struggled. Lashed out at him. He caught her hand. She was bleeding where Díleas had bitten her. "Hitting me might make me angry," said Fionn, "and I think that is all that it could achieve. So stop it. Behave yourself."

If he'd hit her he could hardly have had more effect. "Don't you dare talk to me like that!"

"Why not?" asked Fionn sardonically. "Oh, I know. You might put me in an adamantine trap and crush me to death."

She opened her mouth to scream. And then thought better of it. "You have killed me. But I will die like a queen!"

"Actually, I haven't killed anyone deliberately, yet. And we're not dead yet."

"There is no way out of here," she said with a gloomy satisfaction.

"Seems very clean for something that has no exit," said Fionn mildly.

She pointed at the grid in the lowest corner. "The remains flush through there. The muryan come up it and clean out anything that is left."

"So how long before the roof comes down?" asked Fionn. He hoped that it would not be impossible for Díleas to stop. He could of course resist considerable pressure. But it depended on how much it was.

"It won't. I did not speak the words to activate it. We will starve or die of thirst in here."

Fionn hoped not. She smelled faintly ripe already. He objected to eating carrion, and he would live a lot longer than a human, "Surely your faithful henchmen, slaves, retainers . . ." best to know of those to keep Díleas informed.

"There are only the muryan in this part of the house. The cauldron-men I keep confined elsewhere. And the muryan will only come here to clean every two weeks unless ordered," she said dully. "So this is how it ends, so close, but yet so far."

"So close to what?" asked Fionn. "Seeing we are both doomed, you may as well tell me, and tell me why the creatures of smokeless flame have been telling you about me."

"Baelzeboul's master said that his master wanted you dead," she said. "Running the Cauldron of Gwalar takes a lot of resources, and they were willing to pay."

Fionn explored the trap with his vision, noting the

energy flux points, thinking about the shape. "You are aware, Queen—I presume you are a queen of some sort—that the flame creature's middle name is treachery. Actually, even if it called itself Baelzeboul, its first name is treachery, middle name is treachery and all the rest are treachery too."

·She raised herself up. "I am Queen Gwenhwyfach. It matters not who knows that now. And I know more about treachery than you can dream. That is why I have labored these fifty years. Lyonesse crumbles... and I am here."

"I am several thousand years old," said Fionn calmly, "and the flame creatures have tricked me a few times. They did you, this time. Baelzeboul—if it was the one who calls himself Baelzeboul—stands one below their great master. His master has no master, barring the First themselves. So they wanted me dead, did they? How did you know it was me?"

She drew two little crystal cubes from a pocket. Fionn looked at them, at his own visage, and that of Meb.

"Stranger and stranger," said Fionn. He hadn't seen one of those for millennia. "Me. And my Scrap of humanity. I wouldn't have thought they hated us enough, or that we mattered enough. Or that they still had First-cubes."

"Your Scrap of humanity? Dragons are now keeping people as slaves and she escaped?"

"I think I was more her babysitter," said Fionn, smiling at the thought. "But she is a human, yes. A very nice child, growing into a young woman of character and courage. The dog and I are exceptionally fond of her. I would strongly advise you against even thinking about as much as harming a hair on her head. Or you may find being trapped in an adamantine cage with a dragon is a very pleasant thing."

Something about his voice made her edge away. She caught herself doing so, and steadied her spine. "She is in Lyonesse. She will die. She is just a girl-child."

"That's what the flame creature said, was it?" said Fionn. "I suppose to flame creatures any human is fairly unimportant. But this one has the happy knack of making friends, and we don't think her unimportant. I think one of her friends smashed the fleet today. So, seeing as I am going to die of starvation, how about you tell me, Queen Gwenhwyfach, why you wish to destroy Lyonesse, and just who you are. Someone may as well hear the story." He yawned. "Sorry, it has been a long day. It's not that I find you boring."

"Lyonesse is mine. Mine to destroy for what they did to me."

"They all did something to you?" asked Fionn. "Every last one of its people, and they're all still alive, are they? You did say fifty years. Mind you, you are very well preserved."

"I am as I was seventy years ago, thanks to the Cauldron of Gwalar. And almost all of the ones who conspired against me are dust, dust or grist for the cauldron."

"So why bother then?" said Fionn, tracing patterns on the adamantine with his claws. "What did they do to you?"

"They stole my child. And that cost me my throne."

"I see," said Fionn. "Just a human girl-child, probably."

"She was a princess. My daughter! Even if she wasn't the son the king hoped for."

Fionn nodded. "A grave disappointment to kings, I have been told. No heir."

She laughed harshly. "He could have no heir. I made sure of that, but he didn't realize it. He didn't even know she was a girl."

"And her name was Anghared," said Fionn.

"How did you know?" she demanded, darkly suspicious. "No one knew. No one but the midwife. And she would never tell."

"The knowing of names is a gift of mine. I am afraid I knew your name too. I merely led you on, Gwenhwyfach. And you should never underestimate the treachery of the creatures of smokeless flame, and certainly not their masters. You see, the name of the human girl child in the crystal...is Anghared. I would guess by your posture that she is your daughter. There is something in the jawline that is similar, but you are otherwise not alike."

The queen of Shadow Hall shook her head. "Impossible. My daughter would be fifty-three years old, if she was still alive. And while I denied it for years, the conspirators must have killed her. I searched for her. And searched for her. I hunted for years with all my art and with all my skill. Every noble house, every hamlet. I decided they must have taken her over the Ways to hide her. I searched Annvn, Vanaheim...the Blessed Isles and onward."

"She was a lot further away. In a place where time moves slower," said Fionn.

"I can't believe you, dragon." said the queen, eyes narrowed.

Fionn shrugged. "Why should I lie to you? I am trapped here, too. We're both doomed. You may as well tell me the whole sad story."

She looked at him intently. He said nothing. She

would talk or she wouldn't. "It may be better for the telling," she said eventually. "I was walking back with my women. I drove them out while the babe was born, and only the midwife was in the room. But there I was, with the babe in swaddling clothes, going out of my chamber for the first time, and suddenly this great drawing magic sucked at her. As if a myriad arms, wrapped around her, pulling, pulling. I clung as hard as I could . . . I fell out of the window, trying to hold her. But I must have been stunned or . . ."

She sat in silence for a bit before obviously deciding to continue. "I woke in corpse bay, cold as death and without her. And she was not on the sand. I searched and searched. We do not drown. I couldn't go back without the child. I knew she'd been taken from me by enchantment, by my enemies from the northern parts, I thought. There was a faction that hated me. And they would claim I killed the child. I . . . I almost did when the midwife told me it was a girl. But she put the babe on my breast."

Slowly it came out. Fionn listened. Pieced parts together. She had been a powerful woman, and not afraid to make enemies. Deep in her pride and power.

Broken.

Convinced finally that it had been her husband's doing, when she had exhausted all the other foes.

"And why would that have been?" asked Fionn, keeping her talking.

"Because he was a fool. But he was the king." snapped Gwenhwyfach.

She said no more, and Fionn did not press it. But he had an inkling. The woman went on, talking of her capture of a muryan queen, and the gaining of her cauldron—which appeared to be an evasion of "murdered its guardian and stole it," and the gradual building of her forces with the device. Talking of how hard it was, as the ever-moving Ways to Lyonesse bled magic from the worlds she sought to raise against it.

She didn't explain how Lyonesse did this. But it helped Fionn to understand Díleas's changing of direction . . . and the smell of her and her creations now. And just how she administered to her own vanity in keeping herself flawless, in spite of the side effect of the smell. She herself only had the faintest taint. "Of course if they're fresher, they smell less," she said, in reply to his question. "But the cauldron merely requires the patterns of their being. I had to experiment to get the mixtures I wanted, as well as mere copies, to stir the war."

"Ah," he said. "Giants. It was very hard to kill. I presume the werewolves are yours too. Anyway, thank you for telling me so much. She is your daughter, and the magic that took her had nothing to do with Lyonesse or with politics at all. It was merely choosing the most powerful mage possible to balance out the absence of humans with that ability in Tasmarin. Tasmarin now achieves its own balance, and she has returned to where she came from. And now, I think I must leave."

"You can't. I built this trap to be inescapable."

Fionn felt that her pride and absolute self-assurance had cost many others their lives. She was Meb's mother, and he didn't kill. But she was due some retribution. "If only you were always right, then it would be. I assume the muryan will come to clean eventually. Here is a bottle of water I keep for the dog that will probably keep you alive until then. You can get them to bring you food and drink, and probably will eventually get out, at which point, if you care to, you can verify what I say. Now, I need to get on to Lyonesse. There is someone I need to find, and puzzles I still need to solve."

Fionn finished pulling back the long tendril he had transformed his tail into from the drainhole. They referred to dragons as great wyrms sometimes. The device which would press the lid of the trap down, no longer could. "Stand back, Díleas." He altered his form completely to that of the ancestral wyrm form... which was very well structured for pushing and was a great deal longer than twenty cubits. He used the walls to balance himself and heaved. The lid moved. And moved more, and then popped off, and like a great snake Fionn slid out, shaking the queen off as she tried to cling to him.

"I think, Díleas," said Fionn, petting the dancing dog, while down in the pit the woman screamed and cursed at him, "that we should leave this place. I understand a lot more about why some humans live in dread of their mothers-in-law."

$=$ Chapter 22 $=$

VIVIEN LOOKED LANDWARDS FROM THE WALL OF the castle. Maybe that child and her maid were still alive out there. She'd seen Anghared's spatha-axe. Seen and understood just how deadly it could be. And she knew, although she was not believed, that Anghared had some powerful magical skills. Maybe she'd been taken by the Fomoire where they'd found the dead one and the blood trail. She hoped and prayed to all the Gods, not. They should never have been able to leave the castle, let alone deal with Medraut's bodyguard and nasty errand boy. And a Fomoire warrior was bigger and worse yet. And yet . . . they had.

She hugged herself, not daring to let herself hope again.

Meanwhile, there was a thin, broken stream of gold heading for Dun Tagoll. They'd been trickling in all day now. A stream of slightly dented gilt crows, walking slowly along the causeway, cawing at the gate to be let in. Looking as sorry for themselves as any magical-mechanical contrivance could.

Vivien could not find it in herself to feel sorry for them, just afraid. Mage Aberinn would blame it on the enchantress of Shadow Hall, no doubt. But whoever it was, it had deprived Dun Tagoll's mage of his ability to see enemies coming.

That was worrying enough.

The soothsayers had rounded it down to two immediate threats: the Angevins in the South and, closer at hand, the forces of Ys marching on Dun Calathar in the Cal valley to the north.

"It's not forest land," said the Wudewasa in a not-our-problem tone. "The settlers live there. Let them defend it."

"When they have finished with Dun Calathar, where will they go next? What happens to all the people living there? Those who do not stay and fight?" asked Neve in her quiet voice.

"They flee into the forests. And the men of Ys chase them. Then they and the men of Ys are our problem," said the Wudewasa gloomily. "But you don't understand, lady. We are not warriors. We have no armor, and we cannot stand against their iron swords and long spears. It's open moorland there. They would massacre us. And the Vanar. You say they will not come, but we cannot know."

A panting Wudewasa runner appeared. "News! News from . . . coast." he gasped out.

Meb's heart fell.

"Vanar . . . Vanar landed."

"We must go . . ."

The messenger held up his hand. "W . . . wait." He was smiling, trying to catch his breath. Finally he got it out. Holding up a finger. "One ship. One ship...and they were bailing...as fast as they...paddled. They, they lie on the beach, half-dead. Forty-three men!"

"No more?" asked the wisewoman, plainly delighted.

The scout runner shook his twiggy head. "No. We crept close. Could have killed them. They are too tired to even set guards. They talk, hard to understand, but a storm, I think. Many, many pieces of ship wash up. Maybe more ships, elsewhere. But not more than hundreds. Not thousands."

Meb let them celebrate for a bit. Then she held up her hands. And gradually, they were hushed. "We don't have to worry about the Vanar...as I promised. But if your soothsayers are right, nearly ten thousand men threaten Dun Calathar. They'll come marching and burning their way down the Cal to the fort, they will destroy the new-planted fields, chase off anyone who isn't inside the fort."

"We can't fight them until they come to the forest, so we'll have to take the forest to them," said Meb. She could steal ideas from this prophecy, too, if they had decided it applied to her anyway, no matter how she tried to tell them otherwise. One couldn't argue with ideas that people had fixed in their heads. It was better just to work around them sometimes.

"Earl Simon will try to meet and weaken them here," said the man who had once been a man-at-arms, before he had stabbed his sergeant in a fight and fled to the forests, pointing at the rough map of the Cal valley. "He always does. Look, the road goes next to the river, and goes through the narrows here. He'll have his archers up on the rocks above it and his men here on the slope so they can charge downhill. He's too dumb to figure that means they'll have to retreat uphill, but it does mean they can get away over the neck and run for the Dun while the bowmen on the rocks slow them down."

"And what would you do?" asked Meb, having no idea that you shouldn't ask common men-at-arms these sorts of questions.

He wrinkled his forehead. "Make them come to me, if I could."

"How big is the river?"

"At this time of year? It's just a lot of braided streams on the gravel."

"And the other side of the river?"

"Well, it goes up to the cliff on the narrows. So the earl can't run back to the Dun from there."

"And what does it look like?"

"Dunno. Stony. Got a few scrubby trees I think."

"It might just have a small forest. I really need to see it. To see what can be done."

"It's half a day's run, and the men of Ys are through the Way and into Lyonesse. They'll be there within the day, I reckon."

Meb got up and paced. "I need a horse. I can't run like the Wudewasa. And we need to move as many spearmen as possible closer, but still in the woods. Are there any fay folk up there?" she asked the spriggan.

"They're everywhere. More waking everyday. But the Cal valley is famous for my kind. There are some choice residences in the rocks. There'll be a grundylow in the river, not that you'd want to have anything to do with it, such a big wet. And of course the muryan are everywhere, and piskies are usually where you don't want them to be."

"I really need a horse!" She visualized the lovely dun mare...hoping to translate her need into a summonsing.

She got a horse.

Just not the right horse. Instead, a furious blue-black stallion with a wild silken mane so long it almost could have reached the ground...and grass-green eyes as angry as the beautiful dun mare's had been placid. A horse that was yelling at her in what could only be swear words in mixed neighs, while gnashing its teeth and stamping.

The spriggan appeared to be choking until she realized she'd never seen a spriggan actually laugh. If this one was laughing, whatever horse she'd summonsed must be a particularly awful fate. The Wudewasa had backed away, spears ready, as the horse faced her. He reared up, flailing hooves. She held the axe in front of her and tried speaking to him. It had worked on the mare that was supposed to be a killer...Only you had use the right words for the right horse, and for this one, her step-brother's choicest fishing vocabulary definitely was right. It seemed there was a time and a place for whispering to a horse and a time and a place for yelling obscenities, because the horse stopped rearing, lashing out and stood. She finished it off by waving the axe under his nose. "See this! See this? Kick me and I'll turn you into a gelding. The grooms told me that made wild horses gentler."

The horse snorted. But not very loudly. His eyes were still wild. But whereas before there had been naked aggression in them, now it was a horse looking for a good way out.

Meb had never seen a horse quite like him.

"Do you know what you have there, Lyon lady?" said the spriggan.

"I think it's a horse. But not quite like any other horse I have ever met."

"It's a water-horse. A fay creature. They live in the waterfalls, and pools sometimes. Like to trick people up onto their backs and drown them."

The spriggan looked at the horse. "Her kind can't drown, so I wouldn't try it, water-horse." And then he turned to Meb: "They're water creatures so I am surprised it obeys you. But the river water is drawn from the land."

"Besides," said Meb to the horse, holding the gleaming axe up, "if I can call you, I can call this axe. And I am telling the axe what to do to you if you give me a moment's trouble. It'll follow you, even if I am dead, see." This was pure invention. She had no idea if she could do that, or how to even try. But the water-horse obviously believed her.

She got a leg up, up onto the horse. Then she realized that there were no stirrups, and this was bareback . . . with no reins either. She'd surely gone mad. "I don't want to fall off," she said, a sudden dose of common sense coming to her head.

"Oh, you can't," said the spriggan. "Not unless he wants you to."

"Right." She tapped the horse's neck. "Unless you want to be tacked up, saddle, bridle, the lot, I hate the idea of falling off. Now, I need to go to the Cal valley. Pass me the axe, will you, goodman. I don't think I can manage the bags or a basket, but the axe is coming with me." She took it from one of the Wudewasa.

"The other thing about water-horses," said the spriggan, as this one turned, bunched its hindquarters, and
took off, "is that they can fly."

If Meb hadn't been magically glued to the glossy
back, she would have fallen off right then.

The Cal valley was divided by Dun Calathar. The
fort stood at the top of the hill where the steep upland
valley spread out into a broader, fertile dale. The point
at which the earl usually attempted to hold the invasions
was about two miles higher up the valley. The reason was
twofold. Firstly, although the gap cut by the river was
too wide and river-scoured to be blocked easily, the road
could be blocked, and had been, with heavy logs, well
staked in. Going past that point on a horse required that
the riders get down into the hundred-yard-wide riverbed,
and pick their way over the boulders, and through the
deep pools and small rapids that marked the constric-
tion, because the riverbed was wider above. Secondly,
by holding the south bank and charging down—and
retreating back up that—the earl's riders had a flatter
upper tier to race back to the Dun, whereas the road
along the river valley meandered and crisscrossed the
river through various fords.

Meb was no strategist, but she could see the logic.
She could also see several spriggans, a fair of piskies
and a strange, squat, green, shell-coated, toadlike
creature. Those were the ones curious enough to come
and look when she stopped the water-horse. There was
a sentry, with a horn, too, at the top of the rocky
outcrop. He probably was more frightened than curious. He was still blowing his horn. It sounded rather
like a sick cow, echoing down the valley.

Meb dismounted. "I suppose you'd be offended by an apple. What would you like?

The water-horse blew out through its nostrils. "Watercress," said a spriggan, behind her. "But you can't get it at this time of year up here."

Meb hoped her real desire for peppery salad leaves didn't end up with a piece of salt cod. But this time the summonsing seemed to work well . . . except she hadn't really meant a bushel. However, it seemed that the water-horse had. And it was very fond of watercress. "I'll need you later. You are very beautiful, you know."

He rolled an eye at her. But continued to eat.

The other fay had come closer. Even the grundylow, pond-scum green and wearing a coat spattered with freshwater mussels, was eyeing her from the undercut edge of the river bank.

"There's an army coming. I need you to help," said Meb.

"You're the juggler, aren't you?" said the biggest spriggan. "The knockyan told us about the axe."

"Not about the water-horse," said the spriggan. "And where is the second noble Lyon lady they were bragging about? We see you for what you are, but what happened to the other?"

"Neve's coming. The water-horse is new . . . I didn't know they flew."

That caused a snigger. She felt something nudge her elbow. It was the water-horse. He had a certain look in his eye. She had been quite good at reading Díleas. This was not dissimilar. "You can kick them if any more show you any disrespect, or I'll sort them out," said Meb, patting the nose absently. He belched watercress at her, and . . . went back to the bushel.

"You have a way about you," said the biggest sprig-gan grudgingly. "You could have taught the last Land something. He got kicked. So what do you want of us?"

"Your help in giving the army the kicking instead. A lesson. We can defeat the men of Ys. Kill every man there. The muryan can come and stick them with poison as they sleep. And next year, or the year after, they'll come back."

"That is usually what happens," said the local sprig-gan family head, happy in this dour wisdom.

"Which is why I don't want to do that. Finn said a frightened man is a lot more dangerous than a dead one to an army."

"Oh, that is generally true," said the spriggan. "It works for us. Humans could destroy us utterly, if we didn't frighten them witless. Which means you do have to let some survive to frighten the others still more by stretching the story. Which in turn means that they leave us alone."

"That is more or less what I had in mind."

"We could like you," said the spriggan. "Even if you didn't have the right to command. Who is this Finn?"

There seemed no harm in telling them. "A dragon. A black dragon. A . . . a friend of mine. He taught me nearly everything I know."

"Cleverer than most dragons then. Mind you, they're not all alike. Well, what do you plan?"

"I hope it includes drowning a few," said the grun-dylow. "My larder is nearly empty."

"I have a few ideas. Possibly involving drowning. But I was hoping for tips from the experts at fright-ening people witless. I want a bit of time to prepare though. Could you piskies maze them?"

"There's a lot of them, and a lot of cold iron," said a little piskie matron, dressed with decorum in two acorn caps.

"I assume they have scouts. Could you maze them? Slow them down. Panic a few."

The piskie grinned. "We can do panic. And misleading a bit. But their horses won't let us lead them over cliffs."

"We'd like them to get here in the dawn, or better, the evening. Bad light is good."

"This Finn is a fine teacher," said the biggest spriggan.

"I know you spriggans can look like giants. And I know you can look like rocks. But can you do giant rocks? Look like you fill the gap?"

"That would be easy enough," said the spriggan, thoughtfully.

"Good. We will give them talking rocks and moving forests and maybe something nasty in the river."

The pond-slime green, flattened, wide-lipped mouth of the grundylow grinned. It had lots of sharp teeth.

The forest—or at least large tree limbs and Wudewasa in their usual mix of hair and twigs, which made them look like shrubs with spears—moved past Dun Calathar in the early morning, before the gates opened. It certainly did not pass unobserved. They were only just over two thousand strong but, spread along the road, they covered a lot of road. The men-at-arms of the Dun saw them, despite the hour, and as a result, so did most of the people.

The valley of the Cal, beyond the gap, had been transformed by knockyan and muryan. The slope below where the "forest" would stand was not possible to ride. It was steeper than it used to be and carpeted with millions of small, round rocks from the riverbed, held in place by terrace after terrace of twig stakes, and woven-grass-stalk lines. A man, walking carefully, might get up. A horse on the slope would not. Every five rows was a stouter stake line to stop the entire slope cascading. And in knocker tunnels below that, ready to be pulled down, lines to remove those stakes. Piles more rocks waited at the top of the slope, ready to be pushed. The flatter "forest" area itself was a zigzag of broad trenches and narrow ridges that would channel any who rode in from further up to the valley between the trees.

And that was just the start to the preparations that had been made to meet the men of Ys. Meb had neither thought of all of them, nor had very much to do with organizing them. But the fay and the Wudewasa of Lyonesse had taken having the full cooperation of the knockers and the muryan as a chance to exercise their imagination.

They had the better part of the day to set up and prepare. The earl of Calathar did come riding up the valley at the head of his men, around midday. It had obviously taken him a lot of time, and every other ability from threat to cajolement, to get the men-at-arms to ride out from the Dun. The spriggans had not been very kind to the sentries at the gap, Meb gathered. She'd have to have words with them.

She rode up to speak to the Calathar men on the water-horse.

She hadn't really anticipated the effect of the water-horse on their nags. The stallions and geldings wanted to get back to their stables. A few of them decided to go with or without their riders. The mares had other ideas entirely.

The earl had control of his horse. Barely. Its behavior didn't sweeten him. "What are you doing on my lands?" he demanded.

Meb had expected thanks or an offer of help. Or both. "Are your wits as fat as your behind?" she demanded, entirely forgetting that she was alone and he was a noble of the realm. "The men of Ys will be here by dusk if not sooner. We're getting ready to send them home if we can. To defend the land."

"It's my right..."

At this point his horse reared, turned suddenly and tossed him out of the saddle, and headed home as fast as it could go. The haerthman who had placed the sharp point of his lance just exactly where the horse would think it a very cheeky horsefly indeed, saluted her. "Hail, Defender. We are here to fight for you. At least, I am. Who is with me?"

Most of the men raised their lances in salute, and shouted, "Defender!"

For a brief moment it was quite heady. But then the reality of it all came back to her.

The earl sat up, groaning. "Have you rebelled against your liege? Where is your respect? I'll have you all tossed out to be landless, masterless men! Take her back to the Dun!"

The haerthman who had assisted him out of the saddle pointed his lance at him. "It's you, Earl Simon, who have not shown respect to your liege. She is the Defender. The sea-window returned, the forest walked."

"And she spoke to the sea and it destroyed the

Vanar fleet for her," said the spriggan neither Meb nor the earl's men had known was there.

The men of Dun Calathar were wide-eyed. But they stood, respectful.

Earl Simon flapped his mouth, but no words came out.

"The giant should be fun," said the spriggan with morbid satisfaction.

"Giant? What giant?" asked Meb, with a sinking feeling. The spriggan looked pleased. It had been looking quite put out, and had found nothing to think of that could go wrong with the trenchwork at the forest, a sure sign that it was well prepared—and probably would go wrong. But she had no preparations for giants.

"Ach, he'll be one of the half-dead ones. They always have some half-dead marching along with them."

"Half-dead ones?" Meb was beginning to feel like one of those birds trained to repeat what was said. "What are they?"

"People, or various creatures, monsters mostly, that are not alive but aren't dead. They come with the invaders. They're often quite hard to kill," explained the spriggan.

"If they're not alive, how do you kill them?"

"They're dead but have been reanimated magically. Rebuilt, as it were," explained the spriggan. "Sometimes they have been mixed with things that are harder to kill, and they're generally not too sensitive to pain. Or very clever. A clever man knows when to be afraid and to run away. The half-dead just keep coming."

And Meb remembered Vivien speaking of her husband Cormac being seen among the forces of various other places. She understood, now, how that could be. It still made her shudder, and got her no closer to how to deal with the giant.

"Just how big is this giant?" she asked in a fading voice.

"Oh, not so big. The last one had three heads, and was terrible. This one isn't more than eighteen cubits tall. Living stone too, though, so not much use firing arrows into him. You'll deal with him, though."

"You could have told me earlier," said Meb.

"Why?" asked the spriggan.

"I could have got a better head start, running away," said Meb, bitterly. "I need to talk to the muryan."

"There is nothing like ants to bring down giants," agreed the spriggan.

"I hope you're right," said Meb. "Because that's all I can think of right now.

They came, with the sound of drums, and the tramp of the giant. It was just before sundown and a curling mist was falling over the top edge of the valley, making the upper rock walls hazy and indistinct, muting colors.

The men of Ys, in their fish-scalelike armor, each troop of horse behind its brave standard, were plainly expecting the usual trouble at the gap. They halted, just below the "forest," to tighten their formations and ready themselves. Oddly, in this light, Meb thought it really did look like a vast forest, far bigger than a mere couple of thousand branches and Wudewasa. The noise that came from it was more alarming than the drum or tread of the giant. It was a strange, deep roaring sound, pulsing, rising and falling. Meb knew the Wudewasa

made the noise by whirling flat-bladed pieces of wood.
Knowing full well what it was, it still made the hair on
the nape of her neck want to stand on end.

Some scouts had ridden along the upper part of the
valley and into the wood. None had given warning.

But now the gap was closed.

And the sound of the bullroarers in the valley was
suddenly made faint by her own yell. It was supposed
to be done in unison. Supposed to echo. Somehow,
with the nerves of the moment or maybe the water-
horse deciding to rear and charge—which was anything
but what Meb had had in mind—"Go home!" should
have been a lost squeak, only fit for annoying children.
Instead, it reverberated from the rocks and echoed
up and down the valley—as Meb, on the runaway
water-horse that wanted nothing more than to fight,
charged down at them, followed by the men of Dun
Calathar. The water-horse, merely walking, had had
a bad effect on the normal horses. Galloping full tilt,
dashing its wild mane about and somehow managing
to scream horse defiance, and show itself as the biggest, most attractive, toughest stallion in existence,
its effect on a horse-mounted army was . . . interesting.

The cavalry might largely have disintegrated, crash-
ing through the foot soldiers, but the giant advanced.
About three steps . . . before toppling.

Meb rode—flying—over its back. Other cavalry
spilled around, driving men into the river—which was
rising and full of something that pulled men under—or
to scramble to the woods or just turn and run for the
gateway back to Ys as if pursued by more than just
nasty piskies. The giants that chased them were mere
glamor, but no one stopped to check. They just ran.

As a battle it proved to be a complete rout, and fairly short.

Meb actually found herself feeling mildly guilty that she'd had the piskies dose the Ys men's water with buckthorn when they'd stopped at midday. They really didn't need stomach cramps and bowels that turned to water as well. She was glad, though, that they'd dosed the giant with arsenic and now had it tied down with cables of spider silk. It would take hammering hard steel spikes through it to kill it.

And Meb knew the heady sound of cheering.

It didn't improve the sight of dead men or horses much.

But Ys's soldiery would not be in a hurry to come back to this haunted, accursed and protected land.

Now the other armies had to get that message.

═ Chapter 23 ═

OUT ON THE OPEN MOUNTAINSIDE, FIONN SAT LOOK-
ing down on the tranquil blue sea, far below. He patted
Díleas, sitting next to him. "It's good to breathe clean
air again, air that has none of that scent of decay and
intrigue. It's helping me to think, and we have a lot
to think about. It appears our Scrap must have called
in help from the Spirit of the Sea. So I thought we
might try Groblek, the Lord of the Mountains, instead.
He's not very fond of dogs. Do you think you could
pretend to be a cat?"

Díleas turned his head away and studiously ignored
Fionn.

Fionn got up. "Groblek!" he yelled. "GROBLEK!"
The echo repeated it, fainter and fainter.

"I've no idea if that'll work. In the meanwhile, we
may as well walk up the mountain a little further, get
a good line out to the Skerries, and fly out and see
if we can find that Tolmen Way."

Díleas barked. The "big trouble" bark. Fionn was
getting better at telling them apart by now. Walking
toward them was the reason.

A bear.

Not just any bear, but an enormous beast who must have weighed at least a thousand pounds.

And his growl was like slow thunder.

"Greetings, Groblek," said Fionn, with a wave.

"I should have guessed it would be you," rumbled the bear. "Waking the child, just when we had got it to sleep. And I do not like dogs."

"Congratulations! I hadn't heard," said Fionn. "You're quick about it. And that's not a dog. It's a cat."

"Time moves differently for us. And it barks like a dog, and smells like a dog. Therefore, it is a dog."

"Appearances can be deceptive," said Fionn mildly. "When did you last hear of a dog having anything to do with a dragon? Cats do. And it is very good with children. Besides, it's her cat. I am just looking after it. I wouldn't dare let it get hurt."

"You're incorrigible," said Groblek. "Very well. I suppose you can come in, you and her 'cat.' What do you want this time?"

"To talk. The last time we spoke you said she had been drawn back to where she came from."

"She told us that looking into the flame she'd seen that Tasmarin must lose either her or you. I thought her heart would break. But she was a brave little human."

"More courage than common sense," said Fionn, gruffly. "Might-be futures can be circumvented."

"Would you have taken the chance, had things been the other way around?" asked Groblek as he led them toward a cave mouth.

"I thought I asked the trick questions. No."

"So your choices are right, and hers wrong?"

Fionn sighed as they entered a vast hall. A noisy,

vast hall. Groblek had not been joking about having woken someone. "You ask awkward questions. And I apologize for waking him. I really do."

"I love him dearly, nearly more dearly than anything else, but sometimes he is his mother's child. Noisy, tumultuous and restless, just like the sea," said Groblek.

Fionn was amused. "Lady Skay, of course, sees it otherwise."

"How right you are, dragon. Somehow he reminds her of avalanches, which is not inaccurate at times, I will admit."

"Well, as I imagine you have tried remedying all the usual real reasons for unhappiness, let us see if he can be distracted by juggling or by...cats," said Fionn.

"Is the...cat safe with children?" asked Groblek, to whom sheepdogs were barely a bite.

Fionn smiled reassuringly. "Children are quite dangerous to them, yes, but they're very tolerant despite that. And this one will not bite a child. Not for any provocation. Will you bite, Díleas? One bark for yes, two for no."

"Hrf hrf."

"Those are of course 'meows' in his breed," said Fionn. "My Scrap raised his intelligence somewhat, Groblek, and he's of a bright breed. Your child is safe with him."

The babe was, luckily for Díleas, not as large as his father suggested he might become. And he was distracted, almost hypnotized, by the bright balls being thrown in patterns. And Díleas's bouncing and his soft fur. "Not so tight, little one. You'll squeeze the life out of him," said Groblek. Fortunately Díleas discovered he could tickle by licking.

Between them they settled a small restless, tumultuous avalanche back to sleep.

"I had no idea," said Fionn, "just how tiring they could be. Anyway, now that you have given me a great deal to think about, can you let us out? We need to go on our way. Whatever else I do...she needs her cat."

"I will let you out in the mountains of Lyonesse. And I will give you your apprentice's advice to us. Talk about it."

"Your kindness wouldn't run to dinner, would it? For the cat, of course. I wouldn't trespass on your hospitality," said Fionn.

"You nearly made me laugh and wake him up again. You are a perpetual trespasser. And I am sure I could find a bowl of milk and some fish...I do believe the cat is baring its teeth at me," said Groblek.

"He's a very intelligent animal. And you shouldn't tease him after your child has had such pleasure trying to catch his tail and tasting his ear. Díleas thinks it may be teething causing the unrest."

So it was, well fed and without having to travel any further, that Fionn and Díleas came out into the mountains on the borders of Southern Lyonesse.

It was late afternoon here, and from the mountainside, Fionn and Díleas got a fair prospect of the land of Lyonesse stretching out to a distant sea. If they'd been conquerors, it would be the kind of view they'd have wanted to plan their campaign. From here Fionn could see a number of towns—really forts that settlements had grown up around—roads, forests, plains, and brown rivers winding their way to the coast. There in the distance was a flash of armor. It had been many centuries since Fionn was last here. The chief settlement was further north and west. Their kings lived in a sea-girt castle with only a narrow peninsula to access it. Very defensible, and a sacred site too. That would be where he'd hope to find his Scrap. She must have got to the sea to talk to it, and yes, the First-crystal image had showed her in a coracle. Well, she was safer on the sea than almost anyone else would be.

And Díleas was already starting to walk northwards. "It'll be quicker to fly," said Fionn.

Díleas turned around and pawed at the basket. And as Fionn knew he did not love flying, that said a great deal. "Let me just organize it properly. Even if she's in the very furthest corner of this place—it can't take us more than another day, as long as you know where to go. Do you?"

"Hrf." Díleas lifted a paw, and pointed. It was a little inland of where Fionn had expected. But perhaps the coast curved. He tucked the blankets in around the dog, and took to the wing. It was still warm enough to find some thermals...

They hadn't flown more than twenty yards, when something pecked at his tail tendrils as he flapped up. It was a thrush, attacking a dragon.

Then an eagle dive-bombed him—talons missing Fionn's eyes by a few hairbreadths, wings actually hitting the basket.

And that was just the start. With Díleas sitting up in the basket barking and snapping, and, it seemed, every bird from half a mile around came to peck or claw or beat at them with their wings, Fionn struggled to land a quarter of mile away from where he had taken to the air.

Díleas was not impressed by the landing. Or the flight, or the fact that he had feathers in his mouth.

But Fionn was very, very happy.

It was one thing to be told she was here. To follow the faithful dog, faithfully.

It was however much much sweeter to feel and recognize her magic.

"She's gotten even more powerful. And even more prone to cause chaos," said Fionn. "The dvergar would be proud of their work and proud of her! I am. We've walked before, Díleas. We can walk again. We're here and so is she. And it feels like she has the wherewithal to look after herself."

The air, now free of flying dragons—or any other thing that did not belong there—the birds resumed their singing, and Fionn and Díleas began picking their way down the mountain towards those forts and their towns, with Fionn choosing to appear in his normal human guise, in case they met any of the locals. The mountains were relatively bare of the things Fionn expected of mountains—sheep and bandits. There was a bear, but not even Díleas's "let's you and him fight" barking could get either Fionn or the bear, busy with fishing, interested. "It's not the same bear," said Fionn. "This one did not call you a cat, and I am not going to pick on it just because you want me to. And bears like fish. He's not catching them for you."

They walked on down, until met by a rock that turned into a spriggan. The spriggan was not expecting a dragon, not even one doing a very good shape-shift impression of a human. He didn't realize Fionn could see him, until Fionn sat down next to him and took a firm hold of his ear. "Glamor has never worked very well on me," he said, calmly but firmly. Spriggans could be decidedly nasty. In fact they usually were, unless they had reason for respect or had decided they liked you as someone trickier and nastier than themselves, or preferably, both. "Generally speaking, I find spriggans give me indigestion," said Fionn, conversationally. "But one of my fellow dragons said that if you roast them slowly enough, they become crisp and quite tasty."

"Dragons blowing in here, too, now. What is the place coming to?" said the spriggan. "I didn't recognize you. I thought dragons were more on the spiky tails and bat wings and flame-out-the-nostrils side."

"I can do that if you like," said Fionn, "but I find this so much better for nasty surprises."

"I think you might get one, coming here," said the spriggan. "We have a new Defender. I saw her birds chase you out of the sky."

"Defender, eh? I'm looking for her. She's . . . you might say a friend of mine. I want to return the dog that she left in my care. He's about to mark you as his territory, so I would lose the glamor hastily, my spriggan friend, and tell me where to find Meb. Díleas and I have searched long and far for her. And yes, we're friends of hers. I swear it on my hoard. That's a very serious oath for dragonkind."

"Your name wouldn't happen to be Finn, would it?" said the spriggan, hastily becoming less than rock in appearance. "Or something like that . . . I got it from the knockyan, and they do mangle names. And it was supposed to be a black dragon, now that I recall."

"Fionn is my name and, yes, I am called Finn among humans," said Fionn. He remembered the knockyan.

Miner cousins to the dvergar. Not great artisans like the dvergar, but good miners.

"Then you could let go of my ear," said the spriggan. "I believe it's due to your ideas that the men of Ys are now back in Ys, scrubbing the insides of their armor. She frightened them near witless and sent them home with their tails firmly between their legs. Said it was your idea, I've been told."

"Can you take me to her?" asked Fionn.

The spriggan shook his head. "I'd like to, but I can't, no. We're bound to our rocks. Half a league is what I can wander."

"It seems you're quite informed for all that."

"The knockyan. They love to gossip. And now that Earl Alois has pulled nearly everyone out of the mountains and into Dun Carfon, it's quite quiet here."

"Hmm. Why don't you tell me some of the gossip. It might make travel easier. I've always preferred knowing what is happening to blundering in blindly. And if my Scrap needs help, well, best I know what help to bring."

"There's a knockyan mine a little down the hill. If you want their gossip, it might be best to get it from them," said the spriggan.

"What do they mine?" He knew he shouldn't ask, but some things were too ingrained in dragonish nature to avoid.

The spriggan grinned nastily. "You don't think I'd be stupid enough to take you to a gold mine, do you? Lead, tin and antimony as far as I know. Ask them."

"Of course they would tell me," said Fionn. "Lead on. I'll do my best not to eat you, or too many of them—as long as they're also friends of my Scrap of humanity."

"They, and we, are hers to command. But she has a way of winning loyalty, it seems."

"My dvergar friends and their little contrivances. I wonder if they had any idea what they wrought when they gave her that one," said Fionn, thoughtfully, to himself. They had accentuated certain aspects of her nature. Convinced the dvergar those powerful aspects were hers to command...which could go to her head.

From the little knockers Fionn learned much more, although Díleas would not have agreed. The little miners were not comfortable with the dog, and all Díleas wanted was to go north. Now. But their tunnels were such tiny, narrow passages, spread across the land like some vast spiderweb. It took a week or two for the stories to travel, but if it happened in Lyonesse, the knockers got to hear about it. There were several armies still abroad in Lyonesse, and Meb had defeated two of them. And here in the south, they hoped for her. But the earl of the Southern Marches did not, because he'd tried to kill her, or so the story went.

"Where is this earl?" asked Fionn, grimly.

"Well, if he's not out with his troops, he'll be in Dun Carfon. He's much loved here in the south, dragon. He alone has managed to really keep his Marches more or less safe."

"Choosing to try and kill my Scrap is not going to help to keep him safe," said Fionn. "Is this Dun Carfon on or near to my way north?"

"It would be hard not to go past it, dragon. It lies at the end of this valley, where the river flows into the lakes."

Fionn remembered the lakes—a chain of shallow, marshy lakes just inside the foreshore dune lands.

The dunes would be a good defense in themselves from seaborne attackers, and the marshes were good sources of fish and mosquitos. It was easier and faster traveling along the rolling lowlands just above the lakes than climbing up the steep montane countryside and then through the forest up to the bleak moorlands that they would cross going that way. "My thanks," he said, getting to his feet. "I'll relieve you of an impatient dog's presence. We'll stop and talk to an earl along the way."

"Be careful, dragon."

"That's difficult for me, but I'll do my best," said Fionn, with a wave, as they set off.

═ Chapter 24 ═

IT TOOK THEM ANOTHER TWO DAYS' HARD WALKING to get to Dun Carfon. It was enough time and distance for Fionn to see the ravages of war on the land of Lyonesse, and that this corner at least was doing its best to hold and somehow even to prosper. It must have been an irritation to Queen Gwenhwyfach.

Dun Carfon itself was plainly preparing for war. The abatis on the steep earth slope up to the wall was being repaired, a few burned trees being pulled away. People, some with carts full of fodder and livestock, were all heading into the Dun. Fionn joined them.

The gateway had signs of human mage-craft on it. Fionn regarded that as hardly surprising, and besides, to turn around now—from the one-way press of traffic—was to label himself as someone who had something to fear.

He felt the surge of energy as he walked through. And a squad of men-at-arms and an officer moved in very quickly to surround him, spears at the ready, but at a respectful distance.

"We must ask you to come with us, sir. Earl Alois assures you that no harm will come to you, and he will not attempt to stop you leaving. He just wants to talk."

Fionn said, sotto voce in a pitch they could not hear, to Díleas: "Stay in sight but not too close." To the officer he said: "And where do you want to take me?"

"To see the earl, fay creature."

Fionn knew what the spell was now. Some form of working to identify non-humans. If he'd known, he could have disguised himself as a very big sheep and made Díleas feel important. Well, they had something that looked like a man, but wasn't. They just didn't know what they had. And Fionn was not ready to give this Earl Alois the same assurances. Some very real harm might come to him.

They found the earl in the final stages of preparing to ride out with his troops. When the officer told him what he had brought, that was put into immediate abeyance. Except that the woman he was talking to, with a girl child clinging to her knees, another baby on her hip and a sturdy young boy with far too worried an expression on his face for his age, came along. Fionn was politely taken into a large, comfortable chamber that opened onto the courtyard that, obviously by the maps and drinking horns, had served as a planning room for his staff.

"I need to talk to you about the Defender," said the earl. "Branwen. Can I ask you to leave us, my dearest?"

She looked him straight in the eye, a tear already forming on her cheek, and shook her head. "No. This concerns me and Owain," she patted the boy's shoulder, "as much too."

"Well," said Fionn, "that's why I came here. To talk to you about her."

"I had no idea who she was," said the earl. "I know now. I will pay the penalty for my error. No, Bran. Owain. It is my duty and my right."

Fionn grinned. Not an encouraging grin at all. And then there was a barking at the door. "Ah. Díleas. I'll be right back."

He moved fast. That had been quite an urgent bark.

Outside the room, a man-at-arms was attempting to spear Díleas.

Fionn snatched the spear, and snapped it like a carrot. Tossed the guard forty yards across the courtyard. Picked up Díleas, and turned on Earl Alois as other men-at-arms came running. "First you try to kill my lady, then your men try and kill her dog," he said. "Can you give me three good reasons why I shouldn't pull both your arms off and beat you with them?" Something about the way he said it told the earl and the running men-at-arms that he was not joking—that, perhaps, and the snapped spear in one hand, and the groaning man-at-arms trying to sit up on the far side of the courtyard.

"Don't you dare hurt my father." The boy had himself between Fionn and the earl. Fists up.

"That's one good reason," said Fionn.

"He's a good earl, he rules well," said his wife.

"That's a good reason for someone else." There were men with weapons in hand surrounding the doorway.

"Hold," said the earl to his haerthmen.

Fionn dropped the broken spear and reached out and calmly plucked the sword from the nearest man, without letting go of Díleas. It was not hard steel—these cultures hadn't developed that yet, so, only cheating a little, Fionn bent it double... and handed it back to the man-at-arms. He was showing off and knew it. But he was also hammering home the fact that his Scrap had powerful friends. "Hold that up so that your comrades can see exactly what I am going to make them sit on if I see one outside its scabbard in either my presence or my mistress's presence. Ever."

"Hrf!" said Díleas.

"Or the dog," said Fionn, his sense of humor reasserting itself. "Now go away. We're talking at the moment. I will call you if I want to fight."

It said a great deal for the earl and his men that most of them did not melt away. Not more than half had their swords back in their scabbards.

"Sheathe your weapons," the earl shouted. "Owain. Go to the kitchens and see if you can find a mutton bone for the dog."

The boy stood, hands on his hips. "You won't hurt my father." It was an ultimatum rather than a question.

"Certainly not while you're fetching a bone for Díleas," said Fionn. "And it'll improve things for him if you bring back a bowl of water for the dog, too."

"Owain," said his mother, in a tone that plainly brooked no argument. "Go. And tell Osric I said to bring food and beer, too."

"A woman of good sense," said Fionn. "A lot more sense than you, Earl Alois."

"I made a mistake. I am willing to pay for it. But not at the expense of my family. My wife and son and daughters had no part in it. I didn't know who she was. If I had, I would have been the first to bend my knee."

"The second part of that will do as the second acceptable reason," said Fionn.

The woman holding onto him said: "And I love him and I...don't want him to sacrifice himself for me or our children. I want Owain to have a father, spriggan lord."

Spriggan? They thought he was a spriggan. That was almost enough to make Fionn start laughing aloud. But he was not yet ready to consider letting them off the hook.

"Hmm. That's a fairly good reason, too. Meb values loyalty and love. Now, why don't you tell me the story from your point of view, and I'll see if they're good enough reasons."

The boy returned, spilling water on the flagstones, with a shoulder of lamb, still with the meat on. "My father is worth more than a mutton bone," he said defiantly, partly to Fionn and partly to his parents.

Fionn set Díleas down and the dog walked over to the boy, waving his tail and looking hopeful. Meat was a powerful attractant. "Díleas is worth more than all the sheep in Lyonesse to his mistress. I am not joking. And one of your fool men tried to stick a spear into him."

"I was in too much of a hurry to use my sword too," said Earl Alois quietly. He told how he had conspired with some of the court to remove the regent.

"Why?" asked Fionn.

"Because the constant Changes were destroying us here in South Lyonesse," said the earl. "We'd deal with one foe by force of arms...and they'd get rid of their problem by changing the Ways. We can't... couldn't go on like that. Medraut wanted to keep the regency. He wanted the power for power's sake.

We'd come so close. Lord Isadore had been killed when we dealt with the door warden. It was just me left, and nothing between me and Prince Medraut. And then... there she was. I couldn't risk her waking the castle... one woman's life against the future of Lyonesse. To be honest with you, Sir Spriggan, she looked like some... drab."

"Appearances can be deceptive," said Fionn. "He looks just like a black sheepdog. But he isn't."

"Is he also something magic?" asked the boy.

"No. Well, only in a manner of speaking. But he's black and white. I had to dye his hair."

At this point someone knocked on the door. "Food and ale, my lady," said a voice from outside.

"Good," said Fionn. "Listening to people tell me how noble their motives are always makes me hungry. It's that or be queasy."

Díleas growled at the man bearing the large tray. A nasty, deep, throbbing growl.

"Yes, Díleas. I see he's got an axe under the tray. No doubt to cut the cheese."

The man nearly dropped the tray.

"You fool, Gwalach!" said the earl, in the voice of a man much tried. "Put it down. We are trying to negotiate a peace here, help for the Southern Marches. And all my men seem to be doing is repeating my errors. My apologies, Sir Spriggan. My second-in-command. He's loyal."

"I thought I might help, Earl Alois," said the man.

"We need their help, not yours! Abalach knights and the troops of Cantre'r Gwaelod both approach. And so far we seem to be doing everything wrong. Yes, Sir Spriggan. There is a time to be honest. I had hoped to seize the regency. I hoped that my son might be king one day, if we found the anointing bowl. I have always suspected that it was the Mage Aberinn who stole it, not this imaginary enchantress of Shadow Hall who he blamed."

"Oh, she's real enough," said Fionn. "And behind many of the troubles you've had, too. She is Queen Gwenhwyfach, your last queen, I believe. But hopefully we put a stop to her meddling."

"Queen Gwenhwyfach?" The earl shook his head. "No, Sir Spriggan, she fell from the sea-window with the son and heir and was drowned."

"They never found the body of either, Alois," said his wife.

"But . . . but she was from Clan Carfon. She would have been my great-aunt," said Alois.

"I bet she never sent you birthday presents," said Fionn wryly. "This may be a bit too complicated for you, Earl Alois, but the young woman you nearly killed would be your cousin, the queen's daughter, out of that murky past. And now to the matter of these problems you have with the various invaders . . ."

The earl's eyes were half closed, as he interrupted:

> *Till from the dark past, Defender comes,*
> *and forests walk, the rocks talk,*
> *till the mountain bows to the sea,*
> *Till the window returns to the sea-wall*
> *of great Dun Tagoll,*
> *beware, prince, beware, Mage Aberinn,*
> *mage need.*
> *For only she can hold the sons of*
> *Dragon,*

> *Or Lyonesse will be shredded and*
> *broken and burned.*
> *Only she can banish the shades,*
> *and find the bowl of kings.*
> *Mage need, mage need.*

"If it's supposed to be poetry, it doesn't scan or rhyme properly," said Fionn, disapprovingly. He had strong ideas on poetry. It was powerful stuff, not wise left unshackled by verse.

"It is the prophecy Mage Aberinn made," said the earl. "Is it not known among the fay? She does come from the dark past! I saw her restore the window to Dun Tagoll. And they say the forests walked to Dun Calathar, and the rocks shouted, and the army and the giant of Ys were destroyed."

"For what it's worth," said Fionn, "she got the sea to destroy the fleet from Vanar. And you might say it's thanks to her the mountain has bowed to the sea."

"We walk in the new age of magics. When the fay return and the land is restored," said Alois wonderingly.

"And you nearly killed your new age," said Fionn, "in which case, I would have killed you, but over several millennia. Fortunately for you, you failed."

"She is the Defender. She will return our true king to us. And we need her, to fend off the sons of the dragon."

"Yes," said Fionn, dryly. "Only she can hold them."

"I . . . we, the South, need to make our submission. We need her help now, and it seems we will need her even more," said the earl. "So. Do your worst, Sir Spriggan. My head if need be. But the South and my family need her."

"I think we can spare you your head. For now," said Fionn, taking a horn of ale. "I think the right answer is a suitable hostage to your ambitions. To stop you acting quickly and then telling us you regret it later."

The earl was a quick thinker. "No! Not my son!"

"I'll offer the same guarantees you offered me," said Fionn. "Your men assured me that no harm would come to me. Even if some of them carry axes under trays."

"Alois," said his wife. "I'll go. I'll go with Owain if need be. We have to trust him. We have to make her trust us."

"But he's my son. I can't."

"Alois, look how he looks after the dog. He's . . . not evil. And you know . . . you said to me yourself, the Southern Marches can't hold. Not against both of those armies. Not even one of them. Then Owain, Elana, and little Selene will die or be enslaved. We need her. And there is worse to come, the prophecy says. Only she can hold the sons of the Dragon."

The dragon said nothing. His experience with prophecies is that they were generally very profitable for the prophets, and only accidentally accurate. But he was withholding judgement on this one.

"But . . . but it's dangerous. She's somewhere in the north. There are bandits, deserters, pieces of armies."

"Did you notice what the spriggan did to your men's weapons?" she said, tartly. "Do you think it will be safe here? You were telling us we'd have to hide in the marshes or flee north only yesterday."

"I planned to send my bodyguards with you," said the earl.

"And who will guard you while you try to fight the

men of Abalach and Cantre'r Gwaelod?" she demanded. "You will need every man."

"Oh, you can send a few along with the boy, if you're worried about bandits," said Fionn. "I won't guarantee they won't come to any harm if they carry axes under trays though. I don't know about your wife. I find traveling with other people's wives leads to trouble, and there are the little ones, and I need to move far and fast."

The earl took a deep breath. "Gwalach. Go and prepare my bodyguard to ride. The best of my horses, and spare steeds. The Lady Branwen and my family go north. Sir Spriggan. Do I have your word that you will guarantee their safety?"

"No," said Fionn. "It's dangerous out there. I will swear that I will do them no harm, and that they're safe from my lady's wrath, until you come to make your submission and she decides what is to happen to you. I know her well enough to say she will not punish your family for what you have done. You, I don't know about. But she is kinder than I am."

The earl bowed his head. Nodded. "I am content with that. I had no idea you spriggans were so strong." He gathered his family around him, holding them. "Sir Spriggan . . . I have never established your name."

"Spriggans don't give out their names," said Fionn, truthfully. "You can call me Finn. Some humans do."

"Sir Finn . . .

"Just Finn. Nobility is supposed to come with noblesse oblige and I don't have much."

"Can we provide you with a horse? You are welcome to the pick of my stables."

"Horses don't like my kind, unfortunately. But I can run as far and as fast as anyone can ride."

"How soon do you wish to go?" asked Branwen.

"How soon can you get the horses saddled?" said Fionn, helping himself to a piece of cheese.

It was rather more than an hour later that Fionn and Díleas left, complete with an escort of twenty— just enough to get into trouble and not quite enough to get out of it, in Fionn's opinion. Still, they'd eaten, and at least where Earl Alois's writ ran, would have no opposition.

Well, mostly. Fionn very soon found out why Earl Alois had been so eager to make his peace with his Scrap, besides mere invasion and fear for his family and lands. The country was alive with various fay creatures, and the piskies seemed rather prone to play nasty tricks on the earl and his people. At the first mazing, Fionn strode ahead and found the three piskies doing it. They'd already separated out Alois's son and were leading him off to a stinking bog.

Díleas ran after the piskies. Rounded them up a lot more effectively than he had done the sheep, perhaps because they were a little brighter than sheep, and perhaps because he'd been studying sheepdog tactics now, with every chance he got. It left the boy on his pony blinking at the bog, at the rest of the party, and at the little, largely naked blue-green piskies, running around in a tight circle in front of Díleas.

"Just what do you think you're doing?" asked Fionn.

One of the piskies sniffed at him, sulkily. "It's of Earl Alois's blood. He nearly killed the lady of Land. She told us."

That was the trouble with piskies. They were all too good at forgetting most of what they were told. But if they fixated on a point, well, they fixated on it. "And I am dealing with that. Do you see me for what I am?" And he let a tongue of fire lick at their underprotected nether quarters. Not enough to burn, but enough to frighten them with the smell of dragon fire. They squealed, and Díleas barked at them. Short, snappy barks. Fionn did not have to have a large imagination to hear "shut up" in that bark. The piskies obviously got it. "You tell your friends, and get them to tell their friends, or I'll send Díleas back to fetch you. And them. He's a demon dog, see," said Fionn. "Now scram. Leave them and Alois alone until she tells you otherwise."

When he thought about it logically, Fionn could understand why Earl Alois hadn't told him about it. It was one of the dubious fruits of deception: the earl assumed he knew, and that all the fay were doing it in an orchestrated fashion, and not that it was merely piskies. It hadn't seemed to him that the spriggans held this view, or the knockyan. So it was probably just the piskies. They were numerous, and so annoying that most of the others avoided them. But while Fionn knew that, most humans would not.

"Thank you, Finn," said the boy, as the piskies disappeared, leaping into the brambles that trailed over the green duckweed-covered pond.

"Think nothing of it. And thank Díleas," said Fionn. "He's the one to stay close to the boy. He's smarter than piskies and he can smell them out. They're not fond of bathing. Neither is he, but he'll tell you that's different."

Fionn noticed the boy glued himself to Díleas and spoiled him where possible, and was soon playing various games with Díleas.

"He's a very clever dog. You can't pretend to throw something. And he was throwing sticks," Owain told Fionn the next day.

"Ah. He's trying to train you to fetch them and give them back," said Fionn. "Some humans can manage that. His mistress juggles. He's fascinated by that. Watch." And he juggled as Díleas followed the balls. Fionn was amused to notice the young human and Díleas looking rather like marionettes on the same string. As they traveled, Fionn learned a great deal about Lyonesse, its ruling class and just what they'd been up to since he'd been trapped on Tasmarin. This Changer device had to go. It allowed them to leech the magic of other places into Lyonesse, but unbalanced everything—besides the socio-political effects, causing war and destruction.

Their transit across the heart of Lyonesse was relatively uneventful. Fionn was glad. It gave him a chance to think. He had an eye out for the various fay creatures, and the knockyan. A few questions kept him informed of where they'd last heard of his Scrap. She was being, as usual, a busy little lass. There were traces of her magic abroad.

She was busy fixing things. Fionn undid a few workings that were fixing things best left broken, or that hadn't been broken in the first place.

═ Chapter 25 ═

"YES," SAID THE SPRIGGAN, EVEN BEFORE FIONN had to do something like twist his ear. "She and the Lady Neve are up ahead. Half a mile or so. They're moving across to the east to deal with a mob from Finvarra's land. They've stopped at the stream to water men and beasts."

All morning Díleas had simply wanted to run on, and had been doing little forays of a few hundred yards and then running back to chivvy them on.

Now Fionn came back to the small party of Southerners. "Let me go ahead. We're just about there, and I'd rather there be no misunderstandings."

Such was the extent that they'd got used to Fionn that no one even questioned this.

So he and Díleas ran. He could run steady as a horse at a trot all day if need be. Díleas had no such systematic method. He ran too fast, panted back, and then kept just ahead.

Fionn saw her in the distance, hair flared as she turned, a face he knew every line of, and his two hearts beat faster.

Díleas must have got the scent at that point, because he deserted Fionn and sprinted.

Díleas ran up to her with little crying whimpering noises. Danced up at Meb on his hind feet, and leapt up at her, making squeaking, yipping noises and literally quivering, his fan tail threatening to beat his head to death.

"Boy, you seem pleased to see me. You look just like my Díleas, only bigger and black."

"Hrf AWHRFFF!" Díleas pawed at his neck.

"What's wrong, boy? You got something around your neck?" She knelt down on the soft green turf next to the stream and pulled away some of the rolled cloth Fionn had covered the chain with. Looked at it. And with shaking hands she uncovered the bauble on his neck while Díleas attempted to cover her face with adoring doggy kisses. She saw the red glow of it and hugged him fiercely. "Oh, Díleas. It is you. It is! Oh, my dog. Oh, my baby." Díleas sprawled himself against her, tongue hanging out, panting happiness.

She pushed him away a little bit, to look at him sternly. Still holding him with the other hand, of course. "But, Díleas, I told you to look after him. You didn't leave him, did you?"

"No," said Fionn. "He brought me along."

She looked up from where she had her arms buried in Díleas's fur. Looked at Fionn. He'd been nervous about this. Nervous about the passage of, possibly, years. He'd arranged his gleeman cloak—colors out—around himself, as he stood there.

"Finn!" she screamed and ran into his arms while an overexcited sheepdog danced and bounced and barked around them.

And for a long time, that was all, and that was enough. They stood with the dog leaning against their legs, holding each other.

Fionn was aware first of the humming. And then, looking down at Díleas, who had just decided he needed to stop for a drink at the stream, the energy flow.

He dived at the dog, grabbing for its throat, snatching the now white-hot piece of crystal there, burning hair. It seared into his hand as he ripped it away, flinging it as hard as he could. It was still not hard or far or fast enough.

It exploded midair, perhaps seventy yards away, in a column of violet and incarnadine fire. The explosion shockwave was enough to knock people down and send horses fleeing. Fionn pushed his burning hand into the stream. It steamed and the pain was savage. Díleas, shivering with fright, was in the water too.

"Finn!" screamed his Scrap, holding him. "What can I do!? Are you all right? Oh, Finn!"

"Need to keep it cold," said Finn, through gritted teeth.

The stream began to crackle with ice growing in it. "Enough, Scrap. Enough." She was a very powerful mage. And she was very frightened. He was lucky not to have the forelimb frozen off. Díleas scrambled out of the ice-sparred water. "Get a piece of ice and put it on the burn on Díl. I think I got it away from him in time, but check his throat and chest, ugh, worse than a hand."

Fionn looked into the clear icy stream water at the damage. He was going to lose part of that limb. At least two talons' worth.

But another two seconds and they would have been dead.

"What happened?" said Meb, shakily fending off the panicky ministration of another round-faced young woman. "I'm fine, Neve. Just frizzled my hair and lashes a bit. Fionn's burned. And so is Díleas. Just tell everyone I am fine. Just helping the injured."

"The tiny piece of primal fire that should have burned for several millennia was made to give up all its energy at once. Someone made it die in order to try and kill us. But the energy was limited and constrained by the crystal and the magic on it. So that had to grow hot enough to shatter before it could incandesce. Someone wanted to kill us."

"Who?"

Fionn shrugged. It sent a wave of pain up from his hand. "In my case, there is quite a list. But there are very few powerful enough to do it this way. I thought the First had gone. I did not think the creatures of smokeless flame were able to do that, and I thought it would be too holy to them."

"I'll find them, burn their homes and plow their fields with salt," said his Scrap grimly.

He could see her mother in her now. "They'd like that," he said, with as much cheerfulness as he could muster above the pain.

"What . . . ? Oh. Yes. I suppose they would. What would they fear and hate most?"

"Having known them, failure. It hurts worse than anything we could do to them."

"Won't they just try again?" she asked.

"Possibly. But doing so means admitting they've failed. Humans are quite used to failure. You admire people who keep trying. The First do not fail in their endeavors, so, gradually, they did less and less, just in case they did fail."

He could read her expressions by now. That one translated as "It's not enough." But all she said was: "What about your hand?"

He shrugged again. Regretted it again. "I'm going to have to lose part of it."

"Do you need a chirurgeon?" she asked, worriedly.

Fionn thought of the local bonesetters and what passed for medicine in Lyonesse, and how they'd deal with dragon skin and flesh. "No," he said, wincing, pulling the injured hand out. The effects of that kind of heat were grave even on dragon skin and flesh. But dragon tissue did not transmit heat well. That was how they survived brushes with dragon fire. Two fingers and part of his palm to just below the knuckle were largely carbonized. So he bit it off. That was painful. But compared to the pain from the burn damage, not so awful. He squeezed the wound closed.

"You . . . just bit off half your hand," said his Scrap, incredulously.

Fionn nodded. "Less damaging than the burn. My kind of dragon cells are toti-potent. It'll grow again eventually. Dig into my pouch and give me a piece of gold to put on it."

She did. Fionn noticed how the party with her had rapidly shifted from "with her" to "guarding her." That was good, even if it would not have stopped this. With the gold there, and some mind control exercises, the bleeding slowed, and the pain eased. "That's a bit better."

Díleas licked him. Someone had shaved away the fur on his neck and upper chest. He had a blistering of the skin there, but it did not appear to be any worse. Fionn was still worried.

"How about we bandage the hand tightly with some pieces of gold against it," said his Scrap.

"That sounds better than this," said Fionn.

So they did. "How long have you been here?" asked Fionn as she wrapped torn linen around the hand. "Time can move quite differently in different planes, and I knew that it was possible that you'd be old, or even dead, before I found you. You've grown. Well, yes, the hair, but as a person."

"I think four or five months. I missed you so badly, Finn. I really didn't keep track too well at first."

"I thought it could have been years."

"Excuse me, m'lady. But there's a party of Southerners approaching," said the little round-faced girl. "What do you want us to do?"

Meb looked up from her bandaging at Neve. Neve had proved surprisingly good at telling other people what to do, that privies were needed, to fetch water, organize fires . . . on her mistress's behalf, without her mistress having a clue what needed doing. But there were times when she felt it was politics, and insisted on leaving it to Meb . . . who felt that she knew more about privies. The Southerners were led by a sturdy, worried-looking boy, a girl on a smaller pony, supremely unconcerned about everything, and a woman, quite beautiful, with a young child sitting in front of her. Behind them were what could only be men-at-arms.

"Ah, Branwen and the children. That's Owain, Elana on the horse, and little Selene with her mother. I brought them along."

Meb knew a moment of terrible jealousy. Tried to stifle it. He'd just explained it could have been years. Probably was for them. And Díleas went running up, and dancing up at the boy. She would understand. She wouldn't hate them.

"That's quite tight enough, Scrap," said Finn. "It's Earl Alois's wife and children. Officially, they're hostages. Unofficially, I brought them along to teach him a lesson about attempting to kill my favorite human."

"Oh. Um," she colored. "I thought..."

He was always quick on the uptake. He gave a shout of laughter. "No, I haven't decided to start collecting humans. Mind you, there was a farmer's wife in Annvn who wanted to collect me. And besides, I think it's been weeks rather than years, Scrap. It just felt like years, while Díleas led me to you."

"He did? He's so clever. Even though I wanted you to stay away."

"You should see him herd sheep," said Fionn. "We can talk about staying away in a while. Meanwhile, I am afraid I did give my word that they'd be as safe as I could make them."

"I don't trust Alois."

"I wouldn't too far. He is ambitious. But the boy is his life. They're very patrilineal here. That's what caused all the mess with the queen. Your mother."

"What?"

"I'll explain. But for now, maybe we need to be nice to Alois's wife. She's solid and sensible. If you get her on your side, she'll keep him there. And Díleas likes the boy."

So Meb graciously met the wife and children of the first man in Lyonesse to try and kill her. "I am sorry. We just had an attempt at assassination," said Meb. "Finn saved us, though."

"The spriggan Finn is a great warrior," said Branwen. "Defender. I . . . I come to ask clemency for my husband, and help for the South. Alois wants to make his submission, but we face two great armies. And the fay seem to have risen against him."

"I think I may have dealt with that," said Finn. "But you may have to tell the piskies to stop harassing him, and to harass the invaders instead, Anghared."

Spriggan? Anghared? thought Meb.

"It's what you are, here," said Finn, winking at her.

That was enough to make her smile. He was up to his Finn tricks again! "Lady Branwen, you and your retainers are welcome here," said Meb. "This is our war band, and we are dealing with those who come in by the Ways. But that is a fair number of armies. I'll discuss it with Finn and see what we can do for the South."

"It is a part of Lyonesse, and very loyal to your mother," said the woman, looking relieved.

Her mother. They all seemed to know a great deal more about her than Meb ever had. "I will see what can be done," she repeated. "Now if you will forgive us, I'd like to finish dealing with Finn's injury."

The woman curtseyed, as did the little girl. The boy bowed. "Is Díleas all right?" he blurted, having not said a word earlier.

"We hope so," said Finn.

"You'll deal with whoever hurt him?" asked the boy, hand on his dagger. Plain that he would, if she wasn't going to.

"Oh yes," said Meb, "of that you may be sure. Even if it takes the rest of my life."

❖   ❖   ❖

"Tell me," said Meb, once they had privacy and space again. "What brought you here, Finn? I mean, I love you..."

"Oh, mostly my feet," said Fionn, trying for insouciance. Scared of saying the wrong thing. "But then I got Díleas to stay in a basket while I flew. He knew precisely where to go, and took me to Ways between planes that I did not know of."

"You know perfectly well what I mean," said Meb, sternly. "You knew—because I asked the Sea and Groblek to tell you—what I had seen in the fireball of the creatures of smokeless flame. You knew I did this for you, Finn. To keep you alive. I saw what I saw. And I love you, and one of us will have to go away."

Fionn took her in his arms. Held her for a bit, and said, carefully, and as calmly as he could, "The being of energy probably did not lie. But the truth is complex, and they leave things out to suit themselves. Or they tell the truth in ways so that we can deceive ourselves. It seems probable that my being with you will result in my death..."

"Then, Finn, I must go. Or you must."

"Wait," said the dragon. "Let me say what I must say, and then you can decide what we must do. You made a great and loving brave choice last time. But you did not ask me what I would choose. And this is my choice: I would rather die loving and loved, than live forever without you."

She held him very tight.

"It's very hard...knowing someone you love is going to die," she said quietly.

"But my dearest," said Fionn, lifting her chin and

kissing her, "I have always known that you will. In the normal course of things, dragons live far longer than humans. And humans cope with humans dying before they do, all the time. You ... we love Díleas even though we will outlive him. And, there is an anchor of hope. The First have been trying to kill both of us. They just tried again, in a way that must have hurt them."

"That's ... hope?" said Meb doubtfully.

"Yes. Great hope. Because if our meeting was going to cause instant death, why bother? They'd simply facilitate our getting together."

"Oh. Um, that's true enough," she said, brightening.

"And besides, there is this prophecy of yours."

"I don't think I am this marvelous Defender of theirs. I just have some dvergar help with my magic. I've been playing along a bit, Finn. They needed to believe or they'd never have had the courage."

"Maybe. But it did say that only you could hold the sons of the Dragon."

She looked at him with very wide eyes. "How is your hand?" she asked.

"Healing slowly. Not as painful as it was. Gold is good for dragons."

"Maybe we need to go for a very long, private walk," she said, with a look that was love, mischief, magic and desire all in one. "There are things that Hallgerd warned me about, that I need to find out about, firsthand."

"It looks like we have visitors," said Fionn, simply because Díleas was barking, which distracted him from kissing her and planning an immediate departure.

"Noisy cat," said Groblek.

"But our son likes him," said the Sea.

And they bowed to each other.

"We thought we would fulfil your prophecy and wish you very happy."

"And if you have a need of a quiet place in the mountains..."

"Or a noisy one by the sea..." said the two of them.

Fionn looked at his Scrap, and she at him, blushing. "Um. Tonight?"

There is a place somewhere under a warm sun where the jagged mountains meet the limpid turquoise sea in perfect scalloped bays of white sand. A week there is a day in Lyonesse. It is a place of exceptional beauty. But the two transported thence really didn't notice.

The girl kissed the dragon, and the dragon, considerably more nervous than any dragon had a right to be, carried her out of the water to the huge golden cushion that their generous host had provided. It was real cloth-of-gold, and more comfortable than a bed of coin and other treasures might have been to the girl.

The dragon would have shared even that with her. No. He would have given it all to her.

"Finn," she said, looking up at him.

"What, my dearest Scrap?"

"Nothing," she said contentedly, trailing her fingers down his chest. "Nothing more. Just Finn."

The dog, being more intelligent than most dogs, found it a good time and place to chase seagulls.

The Mountain and the Sea gave them some time— they were never sure just how long—in their secret place, which is beautiful, but not beautiful beyond human conception.

✧　　✧　　✧

"The tricky part is not dealing with the invasions, or frightening them off. It's getting to them. Knowing where they are," said Meb, still touching him. She just liked to have a hand on him. "We head east towards Dun Telas, and they pop up in the northwest on the coast—we had ships of Blessed Isles beach themselves there. It's too many enemies at once."

"You need better communications at least," said Fionn thoughtfully. "And to pass the word among the muryan and piskies that harassment is good. Have you tried asking the knockers to pass the word along? They have extensive tunnels and a system of using their little crowdicrawn drums to talk across the length of them. They need it for the spreading of gossip and warnings and calling for help when they have ground-falls."

"No. No one tells me. They all assume I know everything," said Meb. "And what I wanted to ask, that you and half of the country seems to know, is just who my mother was?"

"Queen Gwenhywfach, the last queen of Lyonesse."

"Who was supposed to have fallen or dived or been pushed out of the sea-window at Dun Tagoll with her son."

"Yes. But she fell trying to hold you. And as for the son: she hadn't quite got around to admitting to the king or to anyone else, that the longed-for heir... was a girl. They're patrilineal here. Girl-children don't count much, except as trading counters in dynastic marriages. Only you've proved them wrong."

Meb pursued her line of thought relentlessly though. "So: is my mother some kind of ghost? Is this what Shadow Hall is? A place of ghosts?"

"No, she's very much alive. Has been waging and orchestrating war on the House of Lyon and every other imagined enemy in Lyonesse who stole and killed her baby. She seems to have a particular hate for Mage Aberinn."

As Meb stared at him, he said: "I hope Díleas and I put a stop to it. But I couldn't actually kill her. And she is the kind that it would take death to really stop. Shadow Hall is a real place, though. She just uses her art to hide in shadow illusions and moves it with her muryan slaves."

"You have to tell me the whole story," said Meb, snuggling up to him.

Fionn did, using his precise recall to fill in as much as he could.

At the end of it Meb sighed. "I always wanted my real mother. Dreamed she'd be everything Hallgerd wasn't when I was being lectured. Being told to concentrate, work harder, find a nice fisherman who could support me. I think...when I had to leave you, I dreamed that my mother would be here waiting. I never thought she might be...like that."

"Environment and our society shapes us. Some more than others, I suppose. You're my Scrap. The person you chose to be, that I love. Who, if I have daughters by, I would love as much as sons. You would be Scrap, not your mother."

"So my father was King Geoph, who thought I was his son."

"It's possible," said Fionn warily.

She didn't notice. "I don't feel like a princess. I'm just me."

Fionn shrugged. "What's the difference between

a princess and someone else, beside politics? And sometimes money?"

"But I thought only their nobility had magical power," said Meb, puzzled.

Fionn laughed. And laughed. And eventually stopped laughing to explain. "It's a myth, Meb, to justify them being 'nobles.' At one time it must have been a rare genetic condition. That means, before you ask me, something like the color of your eyes or the tilt of your nose, that you get from your mother or father's bloodline. It gave those who had it an advantage, so they ended up as the nobility. And it might have stayed that way, if the nobility had only bedded nobility. But the nobility spread it around by exercising droit du seigneur. By now I doubt if there is a single human in Lyonesse without some of the ability. Unfortunately most of it is weak, and needs ritual and training to use. Your maid, Neve, for example, has some. I can tell. She's even managed occasional small workings. But she's never been taught, and thus doesn't know she's as much one of the overlords by blood as they are."

The First knew fear. And worse, knew uncertainty. They retreated into their councils. It would take some time to decide just what they would . . . or could do next. There were plenty of pawns . . . But their source of fears had allied themselves with powerful allies, and were hard to find or harm. And the future was uncertain.

= Chapter 26 =

IT HAD TAKEN QUEEN GWENHWYFACH A DAY TO get out of the now lidless adamantine box. The black dragon had left it open, and she had at least some of the tools for symbolic magic with her. True, if it failed, she would be out of water. But she hadn't. She had flooded the trap instead and swum to the lip.

It had taken her a while to think of this, and she'd also had a period of reflection on what the black dragon had said about her daughter.

So her first reaction was not in fact to pursue revenge, but to use her seeing-basin to scan across Lyonesse. She still could not see inside Dun Tagoll, but the rest of the country was hers to overlook.

She had expected a fair proportion of it in flames by now. It did not take her long to find that this was not so. It took her a great deal longer to find the "girl-child" that Baelzeboul had tried to pass off as an irrelevant someone they wanted killed.

Gwenhwyfach followed and studied her with great care for nearly an entire day, although it had taken the queen seconds to decide the dragon was probably right and, moreover, that the child was a many-times-more-powerful magic worker than she was.

The Cauldron of Gwalar had almost finished producing the new crop with the material she had been provided with by the creatures of smokeless flame. As soon as they were ready, she set them to work. There were eight of them, and she'd made them so large that, once they emerged from the cauldron, she had to assemble them with her muryan slaves.

While this was underway, she sent orders to all of her other minions.

"What I don't understand," said Meb, "is why you came on foot through the Southern Marches at all. I mean, why didn't you fly? You were telling me you flew with Díleas in the basket."

"Because, my dearest Scrap, we couldn't. Someone," he said, kissing the top of her head, "has bespelled all the birds of the air to attack dragons. I wanted to fly to you as fast as I possibly could, but it was still wonderful to be attacked, because your magic has a distinct signature to it. I finally knew I had found you. Still, now I think it would be useful if you took it off."

"Of course," she gave him a squeeze. "I just did it for Aberinn's mechanical gilded crows. I made them walk back to him. I suppose they would be able to fly again."

"Possibly. But even if this mage wishes to find you, what he sees with the crows will probably discourage him," said Fionn. "I plan to discourage him. Permanently. Him and this Medraut. I think I already put any ideas of killing you firmly out of Alois's head.

Not, to be fair, that he wanted to kill you once he had decided you were this promised Defender. But it would be nice if I could fly again at need."

"Yes. How do you think I undo something I don't even know how I did?" asked Meb, seriously.

"I'd start with calling a bird and telling it. And telling it to tell others."

So she did.

They moved against the men of Erith that afternoon—to get news that they were already fleeing. So Meb's army set up camp in a gentle valley just outside the fortress of Dun Telas.

Neve, blushing and wringing her hands, came to Meb. "M'lady, I'd like to ask leave . . . to go into the town. I've got family here."

Meb seemed to recall a "better not ask" zone around this. "Of course."

Neve smiled a tight little smile. "They said I'd end up a castle slut. They, they were very . . . unpleasant. I'm . . . I'm going back to rub a few noses in things."

Fionn smiled. Dug in his pouch. Handed her some silver—by the look on her face, more coined money than she'd ever seen in her life before, let alone held. "I'll bet she's never paid you either. Go and be generous. Nothing hurts more. My dearest, can you spare Neve an escort of men-at-arms? Say half a dozen of those stout fellows from Dun Calathar. Show them how important she is to you."

"Oh, Finn. You make me feel so guilty. I should have paid you, Neve . . . only I forget you aren't just my friend. And, uh, I didn't have any money. Never thought of getting any."

Little tears started on Neve's cheeks. "That is the greatest thing you could have done for me. But...I couldn't take your money, my lady. I want to serve you."

"It's not hers, it's mine," said Fionn. "And I have lots more, and your being lady bountiful to your kin is a small thank-you from me for looking after my lady."

"And you'll have an honor guard and a fine horse to ride. I can escort you myself."

Neve shook her head. "I'd rather you didn't see me doing this, m'lady. It's...its not very nice. But they need to learn."

Neve had not been gone for more than an hour when Fionn wished Scrap had gone with her.

He could defend her and the camp against one dragon easily enough. Two, possibly.

But the eight—flying in a rigid formation, and thus very undragonlike—were six too many. And they were carrying something beneath them in a spiderweb of lines. Had the creatures of smokeless flame gone into alliance with some of the dragons who were less than pleased about the opening up of Tasmarin?

"I think this may call for your magic, Scrap. And quite quickly. No, Díleas. You cannot see them off, or herd them."

"They're carrying white flags, Finn. And...they seem to be settling. Putting down whatever it is they're carrying."

Fionn could work out what it was, now. And that didn't make him much happier than the dragons had. Actually the dragons might be less trouble, but he did understand why they behaved so undragonishly now.

Shadow Hall began to trundle slowly toward them. It was as hard as ever to see. But the white flag was easy enough to spot. It stopped a hundred yards away, and a party of men came out escorting someone.

"Queen Gwenhwyfach," said Fionn. "And that is Shadow Hall. And the ones escorting her I would guess are some of her cauldron-men. She makes them, as I told you, from dead tissue."

"Do you think she's come to surrender? They have a white flag."

"Let me go and find out," said Fionn.

"Not without me. And by the looks of the way Díleas is bristling, not without him, either. I don't... really think I want to meet her, Finn."

"I think you'll have to, nonetheless."

They walked forward to meet the queen of Shadow Hall. She was, Fionn noted, much better at playing the traditional part of being nobility than his Scrap could ever be. Gwenhwyfach was being carried on a palanquin of golden silk, dressed in velvet and ermine, with a crown. Meb was wearing an old skirt, a shirt that had blood on it, and her only "dressing" was an alvar comb in her hair. There was quite a lot of glamor on that ancient alvar piece, and it did make her hair exceptionally bright and flowing. Like that spatha-axe she carried... she didn't seem to realize that she called the most powerful magical artifacts to herself. The axe had been buried a long time. As Fionn recalled, it was supposed to be sharp enough to cleave stone, and she'd magically sharpened it further.

Still, his Scrap looked very ordinary compared to Gwenhwyfach's pomp. That was good in Fionn's opinion. He wasn't sure how it sat with humans. "She did plan to kill us both," he said quietly. "This may be a relatively unwise thing to do."

"Good thing that it's us doing it then," said Meb, squeezing his good hand.

The bearers set the palanquin down and a flunky gave her his arm to stand up. The queen did not appear to need it.

"It smells a bit," said Meb quietly as the queen approached.

"My darling daughter! Anghared, how I have longed to hold you! Come to your mother's arms!"

"I hear you were trying to kill me," said Meb, not moving. "I also hear you tried to kill Finn. And that you've been sending your half-dead creatures to stir up war. That stops."

Fionn wondered if his Scrap even knew that she was projecting her voice so that the entire camp, and probably the town and fortress, could hear it.

It must have got to the queen too, because she took one more step, and stood, arms outstretched. Or perhaps it was Díleas, growling with deep menace. "I never tried to kill you, child. As the dragon told me, it was the flame creatures and their masters and their treachery. I have been working on some traps for them. And Lyonesse...I merely repaid them for their treason."

"There was no treason. You were wrong, you blamed the wrong people," said Meb flatly.

The queen drew herself up. "There was much treason, even if I was wrong about who had stolen you and where you were taken to. But now you will be queen after me. Together we'll take Dun Tagoll and put that traitor Aberinn and his hireling regent onto sharpened pikes. We will find you a suitable noble from the House of Lyon to be your king. And your sons will rule. It is what I thought I would do, but I will celebrate your ascension to the throne..."

"No, thank you," said Meb. Fionn had heard that tone from her before. And he and Díleas knew it meant trouble. "I don't want you, or need you, or your dreams. I defend Lyonesse. I do not attack it, nor will I let anyone else do so. Not you, not anyone." And with that, Meb turned and began walking back to the camp.

For a moment Fionn thought the old queen would have apoplexy on the spot. She did take one angry step forward...and sank up to the knees into the earth.

"Hee hee hee," chortled the spriggan who had been doing a passable imitation of a rock. "She's the Land, old Lyon. It won't let you harm her, even if you could."

"That...that is not possible," said Queen Gwenhwyfach. "The King is the Land, and the Land is the King. It only serves the anointed king!"

Fionn could see deep energy patterns. "I'd go," he said quietly to the queen, as his Scrap turned her back and walked away. "Go and do your best to make reparations. Stop the invasions, make peace. Don't do anything else. In time she may come around, but not if you make things worse."

And then he turned and followed his human.

She had a dog and dragon for comfort, and needed them.

Fionn had been glad to see Shadow Hall—and the dragons—leave. His Scrap now of course wanted to know all about it, about the Cauldron of Gwalar, about how it moved. She could have had a guided tour, Fionn was sure. But perhaps better not.

"The cauldron appears to be a magical artifact that

takes the patterns of the living creatures from dead
matter and makes more, and reanimates them. She
had her muryan slaves collecting corpses, and then she
puts them back together and to work for her. It seems
they have no free will and fairly limited intelligence."

"Slaves and prisoners should be set free," said Meb
firmly.

"In the case of the muryan," said Fionn, "it raises
an interesting question. The workers and soldiers are
slaves to the queen, to the death, by their very nature.
They are imprinted on her and cannot do anything
but what she wants them to do. They adore her, and
in that you might say it is a willing bondage that they
would never swap. The queen, on the other hand, is
their prisoner, watched and guarded every second.
The soldiers assess danger to her; they will not permit
her to expose herself to anything they consider even
faintly risky. She will never touch the ground nor eat
food that has not been tasted and waited upon for an
adverse response on the health of the taster. She will
never be alone. They would do anything for her but
leave her to her own devices. And she would never
choose otherwise. To be served, to be their prisoner,
is as much part of her as being her slave is to them."

"Yes, but she is the prisoner of this woman. And
that isn't right. I'm not sure about the rest, but that
isn't right."

"We'll liberate the muryan queen from her somehow," said Fionn, not adding that the muryan queen
would then be indebted to Meb.

Earl Alois and his troops had been hiding in ambush
for the knights of Abalach when the dragons came. He

thought it was the end, after their success against the troops of Cantre'r Gwaelod, who had been in disarray and piskie-led already. It had seemed that the Gods above and below might grant them victory. And now defeat, and disaster, and death.

It was . . . for many of the knights of Abalach.

Afterwards, one of his men stood up from where they'd cowered in the forest brake. "Do we chase after them, my liege?"

"No." He took a deep breath. "No. We go north to meet the Defender."

There was a cheer from his men.

"How far north?" asked one of the officers. The man on whom provisioning rested, Alois realized.

"At least as far as Dun Tagoll. I think," said Alois.

For the second time in her life Gwenhwyfach found herself in the pit of despair. It was worse than being in an adamantine cage with a dragon.

She had begun to dream great things of her daughter. And also realized that she was eclipsed in power by her. That was enough to make her both proud and afraid.

At first she had been inclined to blame the dragon.

But, stripped of her illusions, she realized that the dragon had firstly spared her life. Even though he could not kill, to put the lid back on the trap was not beyond him, and he had left her water, and told her she'd eventually get out, and secondly he had told her the truth. There were almost shreds of sympathy there. His kind were long-lived. And what did she have to fight for anymore? She'd hoped her daughter's son might eventually rule. She'd thought, once, that she might be the power behind the throne, but, whatever, her bloodline would rule Lyonesse. She'd never dreamed of ruling it herself. That was for men.

And now her daughter did, although she seemed unaware of it.

So Queen Gwenhwyfach took the dragon's advice and sent out her dragons, and word to any of her minions that had not already been told: stop the invaders, at any cost.

The Shadow Hall settled on a high hill in her native South while she was doing these things.

When she came to notice it, she realized that the muryan slaves were gone, and Shadow Hall would not be moving.

The Land did not like slaves, and its magic was far more powerful than hers.

So she sat in her high room and looked via the basin at Dun Tagoll.

Anghared would turn her attention there, eventually.

And that, at least, would be sweet.

Maybe she could get used to being old, and contemplating grandchildren and not plotting revenge. Then she thought of the creatures of smokeless flame and thought: maybe not.

═ Chapter 27 ═

DUN TAGOLL BASKED IN THE SPRING. THE PRINCE and his troop rode out on local patrols, but there had been none of the deluge of foes they'd expected.

No messengers came from the other Duns. Not from the north, the center, the prince's own lands in the east, and of course not from the south.

Eventually, Prince Medraut sent out a strong party to Dun Telas. To get a message back that the men of Telas had marched south with the Defender. They were full of stories about how the Lady Anghared had dealt with the men of Ys, the Vanar, and soldiers from Erith. Even driven off the dragons of Shadow Hall.

The prince sent a message for the royal mage.

Aberinn appeared in a good mood. "I have discovered what the problem in my spells is. It appears there is now considerably more magic in Lyonesse, which has meant all our workings were miscalibrated. That's why the Changer overshot. That's why we had sufficient power so much sooner. Anyway, I have run a number of calibration spells. I can adjust the Changer so that it operates as normal."

"Why bother?" asked Prince Medraut sourly.

"Have your wits gone begging, Medraut? To allow us access to fresh magical energy. To allow us to escape our enemies." said the elderly mage.

Medraut shrugged, insolently. "You've just said there is considerably more magical energy in Lyonesse. And that young woman, it appears, is not dead. She is this Defender that you prophesied."

"Don't be stupider than you have to be, Prince Medraut."

"I've just had my messengers return from Dun Telas. She's defeated Ys, Vanar, Erith and your Shadow Hall. And she will want my head. Yours, too, I would think."

The mage rolled his eyes and said in a voice of severely tried patience, "She is not this legendary Defender, whoever she is. If she has defeated Shadow Hall, my crows can fly. I will test that, but I doubt it. Shadow Hall merely waits. The enchantress has that kind of patience, that long view. The Vanar were destroyed by a storm. We saw wreckage. As for the rest, Ys under Dahut is dissolute..."

"How do you know that she's not this Defender? It was prophesied..."

Aberinn drew himself up. Shook his head. "Because I made it up, Medraut. I made it up so it would be easy enough for me to arrange if my son returns. I did it so it would be easy to get rid of the likes of you."

And he turned on his heel and walked out, leaving Medraut without a word to say. He was still standing staring at the door when Lady Cardun came bustling in. "Those crows fly again from Aberinn's tower. What's this story we're getting via the men-at-arms, Prince?"

"How is your scrubbing, Cardun?" he asked. "Kitchen floors, I would say, would be the best you can hope for."

She looked at him as if he'd gone mad. "What are you talking about, Prince Medraut?"

"The news from Dun Telas is that that girl Anghared has been hailed as the Defender. She's defeated our worst foes, even Shadow Hall. Aberinn says it is impossible, but that he'd test it with his gilded crows. You say they fly out. So, therefore, that at least is true."

The chatelaine's face went white under the face paint. "It can't be."

"That's what Aberinn said. He said the entire prophecy was a fraud set up so that he could claim the throne for his son," said Prince Medraut.

"But . . . he doesn't even like women. He has no son . . . Let me go and speak to Vivien. There was gossip. But it can't be true."

"You'll be scrubbing and I'll be at the whipping posts before I lose my head," said Prince Medraut, glumly. But his aunt had not stayed. She'd gone in search of Vivien.

Lady Vivien was out on the battlements, looking at the distant golden flashes. "It seems you were wrong, and I should have been braver. I was afraid of Aberinn and afraid for my boys."

"Hmph. What do you mean, Vivien?" demand Lady Cardun, unable to leave go of her hectoring tone, even now.

Vivien shrugged. "Just what I say. She was the Defender. And I was too weak to go with her when she asked me for help, to leave. I told her to fit in here. She went, with just a maid to support her. Now, Lyonesse itself is changing, and we are not part of it."

"Not while Prince Medraut holds Dun Tagoll, it is not. Is it true that Aberinn has a son?"

"Not that I know of. He uses women sometimes, so he could have, I suppose." The younger woman turned. "I see that some of the golden crows are coming back already. Why don't you ask him yourself?"

And she walked away.

Vivien had taken herself to the wizard's tower, a little later, unable to not know. It was possible to do this in a way which did not make it easy to overlook, as she knew all too well.

The inner door was open. It was never open. She tip-toed in. She could hear them now—Aberinn, Medraut, Cardun. Voices raised. Aberinn: "The neyfs are even plowing again."

"Where is she?" asked Medraut.

"South of Dun Telas, dealing with a handful of knights under the banners of Brocéliande. The crows show that they've made a peace with them and the knights are being taken back to the Way, under escort."

"Is it definitely this Anghared?" asked Cardun.

The sarcasm in Aberinn's voice was thick. "It was a woman who looks as like her as two peas in a pod, mounted on a warhorse, with that silver axe Vivien told me of. She is accompanied by that maid of hers or someone who looks exactly like her, but other than that, no, I am not certain."

"Can we . . . you, kill her?" Medraut asked. "With your art, perhaps."

"You tried and failed. I used my art to shoot at her with the model-bow. And somehow . . . that failed. I made two other attempts. She is defended in some way. She is now accompanied by what I take to be her master. He must be a mage of considerable power."

"So what are we going to do?" asked Cardun.

"We hold Dun Tagoll. If she could act against it, she would have while she was here," said Medraut.

"It is defended and provisioned," said Aberinn. "And we control the Changer."

"What good will that do?" asked the chatelaine.

Vivien tiptoed away, not waiting, going back to the women's quarters. For a long time she stood in the passage outside the bower. She went in. It was empty. She took a deep breath and looked among the embroidery frames. Found the one she was looking for. Marveled at the stitches. And got up and did what no castle lady would do: she went down to the barracks. It was in a ferment, a cheerful happy hubbub. It also hushed the moment she walked in. She had two sons here. Likely lads, good squires, walking in a famous father's footsteps. It could have been worse, because they assumed she'd come to see them.

They were desperately embarrassed to see her there. "Mother, you shouldn't be here," said the older, Cadoc. Melehan just stared at his mother, as if he could make her go away by eyes alone.

"I need to speak to you," she said.

"Come, we'll escort you back to the bower," said Cadoc, taking her elbow.

She found her courage. "No. What I need to say

to you may as well be heard by everyone. We need
to leave Dun Tagoll. The mage's gilded crows bring
word that our foes are banished. The Defender has
won, Lyonesse is at peace. Prince Medraut and Mage
Aberinn have decided to keep the gate of Dun Tagoll
closed on the Defender. To keep things as they are.
I should have taken you and gone with her the first
time, when she wanted to leave. I will not make that
mistake again. We leave now."

There was a silence.

Then one of the grizzled veterans spoke. "How do
you know this, Lady Vivien?"

"I have just heard it with my own ears. Do you
doubt me? The gilded crows brought the mage news
and sight of the land. You saw them fly and you've
seen some return. Our foes are gone. Out there the
peasants plow again. They've come out of the woods.
Left the shelter of Telas and the other forts. They
know it's over. Do you think I would risk my sons'
lives for nothing? It's over. The Defender has come.
There will be a new king. But those who rule here
do not wish it to be over."

"It's true enough," said one of the men-at-arms who
had ridden to Dun Telas. "I saw some of the neyfs
on the ride. No beast so they'd yoked two of them
to the plow."

He stood up. "I'm not one to stand against my
sworn liege. But I'll not hold Dun Tagoll against her.
She's a good lass, that one. I saw her at the queen's
window, and I saw her put that axe in front of her
face and face down the Fomoire. I'm for leaving."

"Aye," said the veteran. "Me too." And then another...
A little later they spilled out of the barracks. Some went

to the kitchens, to their peculiars, and others to the stables to get horses, Vivien among them. The grooms had liked Anghared, it seemed. They provided horses, and were mounting themselves. The men-at-arms had gone to the gate guard, and the gate was opened.

A few minutes later the entire courtyard was full. The gate was wide and people had already begun to walk and ride out.

The noise brought Prince Medraut and the Mage Aberinn and Lady Cardun out of the wizard's tower.

"What is happening here?" demanded Prince Medraut.

On the causeway, Vivien could hear his voice.

"Keep riding," she said to her sons. The causeway was no place to gallop, or she would have told them to do that.

"We're going to join the Defender, Prince Medraut," shouted someone.

"Close those gates! Get within, all of you! I command here! You will follow my orders."

"Ach. We'll take orders from her instead," shouted someone else. "You cannot stop us, Medraut."

"Go then. Be masterless, landless men. When the next invasions come, Dun Tagoll will be closed to those who leave. There will be no fortress whose walls cannot be breached to shelter you. There will be no magical multiplication of scant rations. You will starve or be killed."

"I can stop you," said Aberinn's cold voice, carrying above the noise.

Vivien knew how dangerous the narrow causeway was. "Run," she yelled.

They did, the press of people all scrambling for the headland.

And behind them the gates of Dun Tagoll swung closed, crushing the last few who tried to force their way out of the gates.

But they'd won free to the headland. "We will gallop now," said Vivien.

Then felt the blow and then, as she fell from the horse, the pain.

Someone yelled: "Run. They're firing the scorpios at us."

The next Vivien knew, she was surfacing as someone bathed her face. She looked up into the tear-filled face of her younger son. "Don't die, Mother, please don't die."

She was not sure she would be able to do that for him. "In the...little bag...on the saddle. Tapestry. With black dragon. Give it to her. Ask kindness to you...my sake. Cormac..." she whispered. Maybe she would be with him now.

"It would seem," said Finn, "that the last of Lyonesse's foes has retreated in some disarray. Now all that remains is Dun Tagoll itself."

"Do we have to do anything about it?" asked Meb. "I've seen Aberinn's crows. He knows what has happened."

"I think it is necessary to deal with this Changer device. The levels of magical energy it has caused to flow into Lyonesse...are not good. Some of it must run back to where it came from, Scrap. And then I think things can return to normal here."

Meb sighed. "I don't really want to go back. But let us go down there and see what we can do."

"Let's not use more magic than you have to, Scrap.

It's quite unstable as it is. And every time you summons something... it has knock-ons. They use magic too freely here anyway."

"My magic is quite different from theirs, though."

"Part of it is. The part with fertility and life, yes. The rest is very human magic. They just draw and chant to achieve their visualization of the symbols. They complete things they have a little of, physically. You do the same, but the entire image is within you, and that part of the the thing—its essence, as it were—is also within you. But it should be used with caution, because it draws from within you, and, of course, makes work for me."

"Lady Anghared," said a respectful man-at-arms. "There are people here from Dun Tagoll. Shall I bring them?"

She smiled at him. Nodded. All she really had to give was a smile, but they seemed happy with that. She felt faintly guilty. By virtue of fighting the invaders, she had somehow ended up largely running the country and had absolutely no idea how to do so. Fortunately, she had Finn, and, oddly, Neve, who was proving very good at telling others what to do. "Maybe it has all resolved itself," she said hopefully.

A few minutes later she realized it hadn't. And that it would have to be dealt with, right now.

They were Vivien's sons. She recognized them although they were white-faced and plainly had been crying. The older one bowed and handed her a piece of tapestry. It was her own work. A black dragon... and it had blood on it. "My mother asked that we give this to you. Just before she died," said the older boy, his voice tight. "It has her blood on it. They shot her in the back from the walls as we fled." He started crying. Tried to control himself. "She brought most... of Dun Tagoll to your banner, Defender. She asked a kindness... for my brother and me, for her sake."

Meb found it hard to talk past the lump in her throat. She nodded. "What I can do, I will. She was good to me."

"I just ask that I..."

"*We!*" interrupted the younger boy.

"We can have a part in bringing down Dun Tagoll, in the downfall of Medraut and Aberinn."

"We go to achieve that end," said Meb. "And... I know your mother worried about you being provided for. Having a place was important to her. I will see that you have one. I promise."

So by afternoon the greater part of Meb's raggle-taggle army was heading west. And Meb had put a stop to the flying of the gilded crows again.

"There is no point in going to the headland. Dun Tagoll will stand any siege and its walls repair themselves," said Meb. "They have scorpios and catapults, and hot pitch. But there is a little hidden door at the back of the zawn to the south. The knockers said that leads to the tide engines and up to the wizard's tower. If Neve's count of those who left is right, then there can't be more than seventy people still inside Dun Tagoll, and very few of those are soldiers. Courtiers, a few servants. Medraut and his inner circle of haerthmen."

"I'll go and scout it then," said Finn. "Before you, or Díleas, argue or try and come with me, I can swim across, transformed into a seal at high tide. The knockers will tell us if there are any guards outside the cave, and I can swim right in and have a look at the spellcraft. I promise I will go no further. And you can think about crossing the gully in the meanwhile. I'd suggest making a pontoon-way of small boats and planks. I'll interfere with the weather a little. A bit of energy adjustment and we'll have a sea mist tonight."

By dark Fionn was back, pleased with himself. "It was a bolt-hole, I think. A neat piece of spellwork, but rubbed out now. I had words with the knockers to stop them going in before us, in case there are other alarms and defenses. How is the pontoon-bridge?"

"We've had some of the Lyonesse nobility exercise their magic," said Meb. "We took the coracle apart, gave a fragment to each of them and had them apply their magic. We've got planks to put across the top. Now all we need is low tide."

"That comes, as does the mist," said Fionn.

And it did. At dusk a column of men came down. A few paddled across in a coracle with the ropes and soon the floating bridge was in place. There were a good two thousand men there.

"They'll have to be deaf up there if they don't realize something is going on," said Fionn, grumpily.

The little door proved no match for Fionn. But the narrow passage beyond was going to be something of an impediment to the invaders. Getting thousands up was going to take time. Fionn went ahead. He knew better than to tell Meb—or Díleas—to stay back more than a few paces. The narrow passage brought them out into huge caverns. The knockers provided light, showing the great iron chains and sluices and a waterwheel that drove the engines far above.

The stairwell led upwards and upwards. Fionn looked and listened intently and, when he got to a certain point, called a knocker miner out from the crowd following. "There's a hollow just behind this wall."

"That'll be the wine cellar. We used to visit it. There are a few of our passages into it," said the chief Jack, with a toothy smile.

"Send a few of your lads in there to see if it is empty. Not of wine. Of people. And if it is, we'll have this wall down and send some men that way."

About a minute later the knocker was back. "Just the chief steward. Drunk. He's locked himself in. By what he's muttering, the murdering bastards upstairs will have no more wine even if he can't get out. The wine is dreadful. My lads will have that little wall down in no time at all. And quietly too."

"Good. We'll go on up while you do that."

They did. Another two flights of stairs and Díleas growled.

Fionn could hear him now, too. The dog had keen ears and a keener sense of smell. They advanced slowly on the human they could hear snoring on the other side of the door.

Then there were shouts and yells and the sound of swordplay in the distance. Fionn pulled the door open. The men coming in through the cellars must have encountered some resistance.

The door opened onto the courtyard, at the foot of Aberinn's tower. The guard who had been asleep at the tower door was still trying to wake up when a sheepdog bit him, and rough hands grabbed him and threw him down as more men spilled up out into the moonlight.

Fionn and Meb had not waited. The key here was not the castle. It was the mage's tower. And the iron-studded door was locked. Meb swung her axe at it, the magical blade cut through the bolts, and they were into Aberinn's tower.

There were signs that the mage had left in haste. Part of a machine was scattered onto the floor, in contrast to the neatness of the other tables.

Outside there was screaming and shouting.

Here, only a gilded crow looked at them from its cage. "Upstairs!"

So they ran up towards them. "Stop!" shouted Fionn. They did and he disarmed the little cross-bow miniature set to fire across the passage. Disarmed two other trap-spells.

They advanced cautiously. There was a great creaking sound. The next room was a mass of cogs and interlocking wheels—a great driver for the planar orrery above.

And that was where they found Aberinn. Behind a phalanx of forty-nine armed and fully armored men that advanced as one.

Meb looked at the small army that faced them. "They're not real! It's a broomstick and some tin."

"Curse you," screamed Aberinn, pulling a lever down. Machinery began to clank, and he took the long lever and ran to the stair up to the roof, Díleas tearing his robe.

And there on the roof, they cornered him, standing on the edge of the parapet.

"Come any closer and I will throw the key to the Changer. I may get it into the sea from here."

"Give up, Mage. The Defender has come," said one of the men who had come up with them. Everyone wanted to be there with her.

"Defender!" spat Aberinn. "You fools! I made that prophecy up. I invented it. I did it so that when my son returns I could use some stupid woman to get rid of the regent easily. So I could avoid the silly plots in the meantime. Lyonesse needed me. I preserved it. And my son still lives and only he, because he is my blood, will be able to find the ancient font. Without it Lyonesse will never have a king who is the Land. It will never be able to defeat the invaders."

When the black dragon had opened the castle, he had broken Aberinn's circle of protection. Queen Gwenhwyfach, sitting peering into her basin, had at last been able to see into Dun Tagoll. She'd seen how Medraut fled to the women's quarters and was dragged out by two young squires.

She'd seen surrender and the bloodshed she'd dreamed of.

She was quite empty of emotion now, as her daughter and the black dragon faced her former lover across the roof of the tower.

And now she understood what had driven him.

He'd never known that she'd given birth to a daughter.

When she'd found out about King Geoph's little pleasures with her chambermaid Elis, when Gwenhwyfach herself could not fall pregnant . . . She'd gone to Aberinn, and the magics they'd worked had made sure the king would sire no more bastards.

Then she'd needed a lover to see to that herself.

His spells on cord-blood told him their child lived.
It did not tell Aberinn the sex of that child.

Fionn could feel the build of energies. It worried
him. These humans had no idea what forces they dealt
with messing about as they did with the planes and
subplanes. "Let us stop your Changer. I think I may
be able to solve the mystery of this son you wait for.
I saw the workings you had below. They're centered
on your blood."

"All is made for my blood and my son. And I will
destroy you now, woman!" screamed Aberinn. "It's too
late. The Changer is set so it will try to change . . .
when there are no Ways to open! All that energy will
pour in here, and the tower will burn. I just had to
hold you for a few more minutes. I have the key."
And he threw it, out into the darkness. "And now no
one does! You will all die with me."

"You fool," said Fionn. "You've probably destroyed
Lyonesse, let alone this tower. And it should have
been obvious to you who your child was. Díleas, NO!"

The sheepdog had been edging forward quietly.
He took a nip at a skinny calf. Just as he might have
worried a recalcitrant sheep into moving.

The sheep would have pulled away too.

But it probably would not have been standing on
a narrow parapet eighty cubits above a stone-flagged
courtyard.

And from below them in the tower, there was a
horrible scream and a grating noise.

Silence. And another scream from inside the tower.
They ran down.

It was Alois's son, Owain, his hand trapped in the

cogs. Whatever he'd done, the Changer would not change anything anymore. Pieces of spring and little brass cogs lay scattered about.

"Axe," said Fionn grimly, holding out his hand for the ancient and magical alvar blade.

It would cut steel.

It cut brass.

The alternative would have been to cut the arm off.

"I . . . heard what the mage said," said the boy. "I squirmed between the legs, back down here. Stabbed it. It . . . drew my hand in," he said through gritted teeth. "Mother . . . said I wasn't to come. But I wanted to do something for the Lady Anghared. So . . . so she would pardon my father. Not have his head . . . I was too scared already when I thought he was dead last time."

"Whatever else you've done by this deed," said Meb, "I promise that I am not going to have your father's head. I was never planning to."

"Tell my mother I am sorry . . . I disobeyed," he said faintly and slumped in Fionn's arms.

There was cheering and shouting down the stairs.

But Fionn only had space for the small sorrow in his arms. "He's a brave lad. We must see if we can save the arm. But he saved all of us. I think the castle has been taken. You'd better send for his mother, Scrap."

It was only a few hours until morning. When the sun came up that day, the gates of Dun Tagoll were open. The bodies had been dragged away. People came and went. Messengers rode north and south.

And the dragon, dog, and the daughter of Queen Gwenhwyfach and Mage Aberinn stood together in a little oasis of quiet by the outer wall, where the water trickled through the now luxuriant ferns and tiny star lilies and into the stone basin.

"This is my favorite place here. About the only place I like here, actually. I didn't like this castle when I came to it. And now I like it even less," said Meb. "I always wondered just who my parents were. Daydreamed I might be a princess or the daughter of a great magician. Did I make that happen?" she said, touching the dragon pendant at her throat.

"No," said the dragon. "It's common enough, I gather, for humans to dream such things, especially when they know little of them, or the price of them. Would you have dreamed them as they were?"

Meb shook her head. "No. I . . . I didn't like either of them. I should have loved them. They were my parents."

"If you had, Scrap, I would be worried about you," said the dragon. "They had their strengths. Even, oddly, good points. But they were not strong enough to rise above their upbringing and society."

"It's not a society I want. Not for the sons of the Dragon," she said, twisting her fingers in his. "So what do we do now?"

"Eat breakfast, I would think. Ruling is what they expect of you, though."

"Me?"

"It seems you have found their holy puddle. Díleas is drinking from it, which probably makes him the king dog. I wouldn't tell him, because he gets insufferable enough anyway."

Meb looked at the rock-bowl. "This is the font? I thought it was a horse trough. No one ever comes near it."

Fionn shrugged. "Because they can't see it. It looks like a rock to them. Aberinn hid it so only his bloodline could see it, the same as his other illusions. The question now is what you are going to do with it."

"But I thought it was for kings. I drank from it. Washed my face in it."

"Some of the best kings have clean faces, at least once in a lifetime," said Fionn.

"So what do you think I should do?"

"That you must decide. I can't decide for you," said Fionn, hoping he hid his nervousness.

"I'd make a slightly worse king than Neve."

"In the way they see matters, in terms of bloodlines anyway, she has a better claim," said Fionn. "She's the king's granddaughter; you are not actually more than the queen's daughter. And of course there are any number of others. Getting this society to accept that may be difficult, though. They have gotten used to the idea of you."

"I think I would make the worst possible queen or king or..."

"Dragon partner? Troublemaker? Provider of breakfast to faithful sheepdogs?"

She smiled and kissed him. "I think those sound more like what I wish to be good at."

And, thought Fionn, will be, even possibly without help from a dragon pendant. "I hear Earl Alois has arrived. I think we need to go and give him greeting."

Meb winced. "We'd better."

They found the earl with his son.

He knelt when he saw Meb. "Lady Anghared. Defender of Lyonesse."

Meb looked at him. Looked at the boy, pale and

drugged by Fionn. Looked at his wife, holding him by the shoulder. "He's a very fine son, Earl Alois. He did this for you. And even if I had wanted your head as much as I wanted Medraut's or Aberinn's, I would have forgiven you, for his sake."

"I failed you, too, Alois," said Fionn. "I did not keep him safe."

The earl stood. "My son has taught me honor. And they tell me that he would have lost his arm completely if it were not for you, Sir Spriggan. That you were the one who set the bones and sewed the skin. I cannot blame you for his actions."

"Then you'd blame me for his courage too. And that, I think he learned from his father," said Fionn. "And actually, I'm a dragon, not a spriggan."

"Oh, I'd say his mother, too," said his Scrap, as Alois stared at him.

Fionn could see it in her face. She reached her decision. "Earl Alois. Pick him up. I know he is sore, but this is important. Lady Branwen, please bring your daughters. I've learned that the land doesn't care what sex its kings are. They might have to find a better word than 'king.'"

They walked out into the courtyard, to the outer wall, with, by now, a large following.

Meb came to what everyone else there perceived as a protruding piece of rock.

She told it to be what she could see. Then she made Earl Alois come forward and took a handful of water from the stone bowl. Bathed Owain's forehead in it. "And your daughters. The land is a heavy burden, best shared. One guardian for the South, one for the North, one for the East."

So she bathed their foreheads too.

"But you are the Defender. You are the Land," said Earl Alois.

"The Land does not belong to any one person," said Meb. "Lyonesse belongs to the people of Lyonesse, and they belong to it. But you will be the regent for it."

"But you . . ."

"I came to change it, not rule it. I am going to hold the sons of the Dragon, not Lyonesse. However, I do need two favors of you."

"You will always command whatever I or mine can do, Lady Anghared," he said earnestly.

"My Neve is to be chatelaine of Dun Tagoll. And a place of honor and lands must go to Vivien's sons."

Earl Alois nodded. "My word on it."

Meb smiled at them. Patted Owain's head. Took a firm hold of Finn and called Díleas to her.

It was easy to vanish.

And it was also easier to vanish from their sight, to leave them with an event that would grow in song and story, than to try and leave in any normal manner.

"Where now?" asked Fionn, enjoying sitting watching the confusion.

"We can still see you," said the spriggan. "And they'll make a mess of it. Just you wait."

"Probably," said Meb, smiling at the grey-faced fay. "But that'll make you happy. Anyway, this is not our place. And Finn would make a worse ruler than I would."

Fionn nodded. "I can't think of anything I'd like less. My work still needs doing, and if the First are going to meddle . . . it may need more. There are some travelers out there we can quietly fit in with. We can come back from time to time. When they least expect us. I will make you and Díleas a home somewhere, but this is not it.

She put her arms around them, dog and dragon. "Home is not one place. It's where we are together."

"So let's go home," said the dragon.

— Appendix —

Afanc   A monster with a tail like a
                   beaver and a crocodile head.

Cauldron of   A magical artifact in which the
Gwalar   enchantress of Shadow Hall cooks
                   apart dead tissue and then grows
                   her reanimated creatures.

Dun   A fortress. The principal
                   fortresses in Lyonesse are Dun
                   Tagoll (center West Coast), Dun
                   Argol (Northwest), Dun Telas
                   (East), Dun Carfon (South), Dun
                   Calathar (North).

Haerthmen   Knights directly loyal to the earl
                   of the Dun.

Muryan   Fay creatures rather like ants and
                   ruled by a tiny human-looking
                   queen.

Neyfs   Serfs.

Knockers/   Dwarflike miners.
knockyan

Piskies   Field and woodland fay,
                       mischievious, not too bright, about
                       ten to twelve inches high. Live in
                       family clans or tribes.

Spriggans   Larger, generally malevolent (by
                       repute) fay, masters of glamor, and
                       bound to rocky outcrops.

Shadow Hall   Queen Gwenhywfach's moving home.

Water-horse   Kelpie.

Wudewasa   Forest people.

Soul traps   made of human hair with the
                       souls of drowned sailors inside.

Yenfar   large island ruled by Zuamar that
                       Meb lives on.

CELTIC CYCLE SUBPLANES:

Cantre'r   The land below.
Gwaelod

Ys   Ruled by Queen Dahut.

Mag Mell   Fomoire land beneath the waves.

Finvarra's kingdom — A wild Irish place.

Vanaheim — A mythical Iceland/Shetlands.

The Blessed Isles

Brocéliande — A forested land with a large population of magical beasts.

Annvn — One of the least magical, where things are very regimented.

Albar

Carmarthen — Great for sheep.

Abalach — Good for apples.

The Angevin Empire — Unmagical, but technologically advanced.

The following is an excerpt from:

PORTAL

ERIC FLINT
RYK E. SPOOR

Available from Baen Books
May 2013
hardcover

Chapter 1

I still have no answers.

That was the thing that kept him here now in an office lit mostly by the ruddy glow of Mars swinging regularly by. Nicholas Glendale was *used* to having answers, to knowing what he wanted to do and how to achieve it. By the time he'd been five, he'd known he wanted to be a paleontologist, and he'd succeeded—beyond his expectations, even.

Then when one of his best students, Helen Sutter, had discovered something impossible and the impossible had turned out to be true—a fossil of an alien creature whose species had built bases across the Solar System in the days of the dinosaurs—he had wanted to become a part of that, follow the dream into space. And he'd succeeded in that, too, and again beyond his wildest dreams.

But now that brilliant student, and her friends—*his* friends as well—now all of them were gone, and a hundred other people with them. The faces refused to leave, the crew of the half-alien vessel *Nebula Storm* kept coming and going like phantoms in his mind: Helen, with her blond hair tied back, looking at a dessicated *Bemmius Secordii* mummy sixty-five million years old; A.J. Baker, irreverent and irrepressible sensor expert whose blond hair, cocky smile, and not-too-well hidden vulnerability had eventually led to his marriage to Helen; dark-haired, dark-skinned Jackie Secord, who'd found the first trace of Bemmie on her family's ranch and later become a rocket engineer for the first manned interplanetary vessel, *Nike*; Joe Buckley, brown hair above a face whose lines showed patience and acceptance of whatever the universe threw at him—good or bad. Madeline Fathom, golden-blonde, delicately built, the single most dangerous—and most reliable—person Nicholas had ever met, one-time agent for the least-known American intelligence agency, later Nicholas' own right hand and married to Joe; Larry Conley, tall and always somehow stooped over as though to apologize for his height, slow-talking but with encyclopedic knowledge of astrophysics.

But *Nebula Storm* was lost with its crew, as were over a hundred others on the ship she had been pursuing, the immense mass-beam drive vessel *Odin*, both vessels lost with all hands in what was in all likelihood an act of corporate greed gone utterly insane, or—possibly—a terrible accident triggered by misunderstanding.

And now he had to decide what to do. The others at Ares Corporation—Glenn Friedet, Reynolds Jones, and the rest of their Board—were waiting on his decision as "Director Nicholas Glendale of the Interplanetary Research Institute of the United Nations."

He snorted at the pomposity of the title and stood angrily, the rotation of Phobos Station keeping him as firmly planted on the floor as if he'd been on

Earth. Out of habit he began pacing again. *If I keep this up, I'll wear a hole in the exceedingly expensive imported carpet.*

It had all started so simply—as most disasters do. With the discovery of the first two alien bases, one on Mars and one on Mars' moon Phobos, it had become a virtual certainty that there must be other alien installations, possibly with incalculably valuable artifacts within, waiting for salvage elsewhere in the Solar System. The Buckley Accords gave the first discoverer to, literally, set foot on any other system body long-term rights to exploit resources on that body, within a certain range of that first footstep. That was the starter's gun on the greatest race in history—a race to discover these new locations and reach them first, claiming those resources for the country—or the corporation—that first placed a human being upon the planet, moon, or asteroid on which the alien base was located.

Larry Conley had made it three-for-three discoveries for the Ares Corporation; his co-worker, A.J. Baker, had made the first earthshaking discovery within Phobos, and later found the pieces of the puzzle that led to a huge installation in Mars' Melas Chasma region, and now Larry had found unmistakable clues indicating that the minor planet or giant asteroid, Ceres, was the site of another alien base.

Keeping the discovery a secret, Ares and the Interplanetary Research Institute (usually just called the IRI) had prepared and finally launched an expedition to Ceres, locating and setting foot directly above the base—which turned out to be at least as extensive as the one on Mars.

And that, Nicholas thought sadly, *was probably the last straw*.

The European Union's flagship vessel, the *Odin*, had visited Ceres and remained there for some months. Cooperation had seemed to have been established, and many wonderful results had come of it—ranging from the commercialization of room-temperature superconductors found on Phobos to the discovery of structures which might hold the key, finally, to successful commercial fusion, and a completely intact alien vessel whose drive system and purpose was a mystery.

But the *Odin* had a secret agenda, and within the mass of scientific data one of their people—astronomer Anthony LaPointe—found indications of *another* alien installation on Enceladus, a moon of Saturn known to have many strange characteristics indeed. Keeping their discovery secret, the *Odin* prepared for departure, even as a meteor impacted the IRI-Ares base and took out her main reactor.

Except that it *hadn't* been a meteor, and A.J. Baker had been able to show that it was almost certainly a projectile from a coilgun, a magnetic acceleration cannon concealed—against all international and established space travel law—within the mass-driver elements of *Odin*. There was no *proof* of this, and neither the IRI nor Ares could afford to accuse the European Union of such things without ironclad evidence. The action showed that their worst fears had been true; the security officer of *Odin*, Richard Fitzgerald, was an old adversary of Madeline Fathom's and was just as willing to use extreme methods to assure the completion of his mission.

Ares and the IRI had, in the meantime, discovered

the principle behind the alien vessel's drive system—something called a "dusty plasma" drive which acted like a solar sail combined with a magnetosail, requiring no physical "sail" to capture much of the sun's incident energy to propel it—and using the most advanced nanotech sensor and effector motes had restructured the key elements to work again. For various reasons the Ares personnel decided to attempt to beat the *Odin* to the now-known base on Enceladus, and revived the sixty-five million year old vessel, launching it as the IRI vessel *Nebula Storm*.

The modified alien vessel had performed well and the *Nebula Storm* caught up with *Odin* near Jupiter, where both vessels were expected to perform an "Oberth Maneuver" to increase their speed and change their course to send them on a rendezvous with Saturn and Enceladus. The situation had been tense but Nicholas had felt that it was under control. Madeline's terse but informative final report had indicated that they had preliminary evidence that the *Odin* was indeed armed with up to four coilgun-based cannons concealed as part of the main mass-beam drive system, and thus was virtually certainly the cause of the apparent meteor strike that had temporarily disabled the Ceres base and almost killed Joe Buckley.

She had also stated that they were going to be able to obtain proof during the Oberth maneuver. From the specific way the former secret agent phrased her report, he suspected they were planning some actions which he, as Director, would be better of not being aware of since he would be then required to advise against it, but he couldn't be sure. Still, he trusted...*had* trusted...Madeline Fathom (Buckley) to take no unnecessary risks four hundred million miles from home.

And in the normal course of things, he *still* would have at least known what *happened*. While professional astronomical instruments, both land and space-based, had more important things to do, WASTA would have been focused on the most exciting space travel event in history. The World Amateur Space Telescope Array had been a project started shortly after *Meru*, the Indian space elevator, had become fully operational, to deploy an inexpensive array of optical telescopes which would be able to be synchronized and controlled from the ground for amateur astronomers to use. It had been an ambitious and ultimately surprisingly successful project, with its multiplicity of smaller aperture space telescopes sometimes nearly matching the performance of some of the professional telescope arrays.

Unfortunately, only minutes before *Odin* and *Nebula Storm* had passed out of sight around Jupiter, WASTA's control system had crashed due to an adaptive virus infection which had taken a day and a half to eradicate, and another twelve hours had elapsed before the multiple elements of WASTA could be realigned properly; even a very small element of uncertainty in the positioning of the several dozen WASTA telescopes would eliminate their tremendous light-gathering capacity and resolution.

So instead of pictures of the ships down to less than a meter resolution—almost enough to read the Odin's *name on the hull—we lost them entirely for a few days.* Odin's *a shattered hulk, front half severed from the rear and most of two of its drive spines shattered, and* Nebula Storm . . . *is nowhere to be seen.*

Even radar had been misled, because whatever had happened, the two vessels had completely changed their courses. Instead of charging forward out of the Jovian system, both had for reasons unknown *decelerated* and emerged—or *not* emerged, he corrected himself, since *Nebula Storm* was nowhere to be seen— on utterly unexpected vectors. It had actually fallen to the Infra-Red Survey Telescope (IRST) to detect the wreckage of *Odin* and allow the others to home in on it and try to start making sense of the disaster.

As no trace of *Nebula Storm* had yet been found, the theory that made the most sense—a terrible sort of sense—was that she had for some reason slowed enough to drop orbit, scrape the atmosphere of Jupiter itself and be drawn ever closer until the friction melted even her alien hull and Jove pulled the remains down into the crushing blackness of its deadly atmosphere.

Nicholas shook his head and felt the ache not just in his head but in his joints, seeming buried in his bones. *I'm getting too old for this,* he thought.

It dawned on him with a faint chill that, in fact, he *was* getting old. *I'm past seventy now. It's been nearly fifteen years since Helen, Joe, and Jackie first dug up Bemmie. Ten years since I stood on Earth and watched* Nike *blaze its way out of orbit. Almost five years since we discovered a base on Ceres.*

These days seventy wasn't *that* old, true. When he was born—when personal computers were new and the web not yet worldwide—seventy was nearing the end of a man's life. People lived longer now and the last great medical advances had pushed active, healthy lifestyles even farther, so that he was physically more as his father had been at forty or forty-five.

But right now he felt more like twice that.

He sat back down and called up the almost blank document which was supposed to be a press release—one he simply couldn't put off much longer. Oh, there'd been a quick one expressing everyone's shock and loss, with some hope that perhaps *Nebula Storm* would be located soon—but this was different. He would have to decide what direction he would take, both in public and behind closed doors, in placing—or not placing—blame for the disaster.

The European Union itself certainly wouldn't have resorted to such tactics . . . but the European Space Development Corporation might have; according to Walter Keldering, who was still the United States' representative here at Phobos Base, the ESDC's Chief of Operations Osterhoudt had some rather dark-gray, not to say black, operations history.

"Not *directly*, of course," Keldering had said, some weeks ago, "but he's connected. We're sure of it back at the Agency. And with the political pressure and having seen the benefits coming out of the discovered bases thus far . . . no, I wouldn't put it past him." He'd made a very expressive face. "And picking—rather forcefully—*FITZGERALD* for this? Sorry, Nick, but that pretty much screams 'dirty tricks.'"

He'd appreciated Keldering's honest input—the more so since he could *get* it now. The President who'd tried to screw Madeline over and, when Maddie foiled him by resigning and signing on with the IRI, sent out Keldering as a replacement was gone now, his final term marred by a completely home-grown scandal that put the opposite party in power. The new President was much more interested in cooperation, the more since he could then rely on others to do a lot of the work while he showed a focus on domestic issues. With those pressures gone, Agent Walter Keldering had become more an associate who simply had to be treated with respect and the same caution over proprietary information as any other, not a specifically-assigned spy.

He sighed again and started dictating. "The IRI apologizes for the delay in this announcement, but we have all been in a state of shock, and mourning, ever since we received the news that the *Nebula Storm* and the *Odin* had both been lost or suffered terrible damage, presumably resulting in the deaths of all aboard. We have lost friends and even family on those vessels, as have those in the European Union, and we extend our own sympathies to our brethren in the EU over this terrible accident . . ."

This was, naturally, the obvious and wisest course, to say nothing to anyone. Treat it as a terrible tragedy whose cause would likely never be known and perhaps arrange a true joint mission to Enceladus with the EU.

But he had to stop the dictation again, because the very idea made his gut rebel. *They killed my friends. How can I allow anyone to get away with that?*

He knew he couldn't really live with himself if he did. That was the reason Madeline, Helen, A.J., Joe, and even Jackie and Larry had gone out on that half-mad venture, chasing down the *Odin* in a vessel sixty-five million years old: because that kind of action, that sort of robber-baron treachery, could not be tolerated, *must* not be tolerated in the greater reaches of the solar system.

But at the same time he couldn't afford to lose the support of the European Union.

I really should have stayed a paleontologist. I had no trouble dealing with the petty politics there.

A light blinked on his desktop and he touched the icon. *A message from Ceres. Encrypted.*

Perhaps they'd found some evidence, at least. If he could *prove* what had happened on Ceres . . .

He was startled to find it was *heavily* encrypted. The standard decrypt key in the desktop wasn't sufficient; it was demanding a personal one-time key and biometric verification. *It must be something important.*

The screen lit up and his heart seemed to stop for a moment.

Then it gave a great leap and he felt a laugh of joy and relief rising as the golden-haired (if somewhat bedraggled) woman on the screen smiled at him.

"Hello, Nicholas," said Madeline Fathom. "I'm using the secure Ceres relay for this because I'm *sure* you'll want to decide what to do—and what you want *us* to do—very much in private.

"A warm hello from all of us here on sunny Europa."

—end excerpt—

from *Portal*
available in hardcover,
May 2013, from Baen Books

THESE BOOTS WERE MADE FOR WALKING

"Díleas, come here!"

The dog did turn and look at him, with a "what do you think you're wasting time at?" look.

"This muck will cut your feet to ribbons. And then you won't be able to walk to her." Fionn had to smile wryly at himself. Talking to the dog. Just like his Scrap of humanity had.

The dog turned around and came back to him. Lifted a foot.

Fionn's eye's widened. He'd have to do some serious reevaluation. The dog was substantially magically... enhanced. Curse the dvergar and their tricksy magics. He was supposed to be the practical joker, not them.

He took the section of dragon leather from his pouch and rent it into four pieces, and then made a neat row of talon punctures around the edge, before transforming his own shape. He was far too heavy and too strong for a human—but hands were easier to sew with than clawed talons. A piece of thong threaded through the holes and Díleas had four baggy boots.

Díleas looked critically at the things on his feet. Sniffed them.

"Dragon hide," said Fionn. "I wouldn't show them to any dragons you happen to meet, but otherwise they'll do. And really, scarlet boots match the bauble on your collar."

Díleas cocked an ear at him. Fionn wasn't ready to bet the dog didn't grasp sarcasm, so he merely said, "Well, let's go. The only thing we're likely to meet are demondim, and they like red anyway."

BAEN BOOKS by DAVE FREER

Dragon's Ring
Dog and Dragon

A Mankind Witch

The Forlorn

WITH ERIC FLINT
Rats, Bats & Vats
The Rats, the Bats & the Ugly

Pyramid Scheme
Pyramid Power

Slow Train to Arcturus

The Sorceress of Karres

WITH ERIC FLINT & MERCEDES LACKEY
The Shadow of the Lion
This Rough Magic
Much Fall of Blood
Burdens of the Dead (forthcoming)

The Wizard of Karres

To purchase these and all Baen Book titles in
e-book format, please go to www.baen.com.

THE WORLD'S CLASSICS

===

GEORGE MEREDITH

The Egoist
A Comedy in Narrative

===

Edited with an Introduction by
MARGARET HARRIS

Oxford   New York
OXFORD UNIVERSITY PRESS
1992

Oxford University Press, Walton Street, Oxford OX2 6DP

Oxford New York Toronto
Delhi Bombay Calcutta Madras Karachi
Petaling Jaya Singapore Hong Kong Tokyo
Nairobi Dar es Salaam Cape Town
Melbourne Auckland

and associated companies in
Berlin Ibadan

Oxford is a trade mark of Oxford University Press

Introduction, Select Bibliography, Chronology, and Notes
© Margaret Harris 1992

First published as a World's Classics paperback 1992

British Library Cataloguing in Publication Data
Data available

Library of Congress Cataloging in Publication Data
Meredith, George, 1828–1909.
The egoist: a comedy in narrative/George Meredith: edited with
an introduction by Margaret Harris.
p. cm.—(The World's classics)
Includes bibliographical references.
I. Harris, Margaret. II. Title. III. Series.
PR5006.E3 1992 823'.8—dc20 91–14084
ISBN 0–19–281817–1

Printed in Great Britain by
BPCC Hazells Ltd.
Aylesbury, Bucks

CONTENTS

INTRODUCTION

THIS World's Classics edition of George Meredith's ninth and best-known novel succeeds one published in 1947, with an introduction by Lord Dunsany. Edward John Morton Drax Plunkett, eighteenth Baron Dunsany, was by then almost 90, and it is not surprising that he should evoke a version of the Meredith renowned forty or so years earlier.[1] Dunsany extols Meredith as a philosopher and observer whose virtues are those of affinity with a timeless pre-industrial natural world. Functional necessities of prose fiction such as plot are secondary in Dunsany's reading of *The Egoist* to its poetic qualities, which he sees as deriving particularly from Meredith's power to fashion fresh metaphors in the interests of vivid characterization and of sympathetic description of the beauties of the earth.

Dunsany's reading is a distillation of the essence of the Meredith E. M. Forster recalls as a 'spiritual power . . . about the year 1900'[2] especially in Cambridge. By 1927 when Forster was delivering his Clark Lectures at that same University, however, the elder novelist was seen differently: 'What with the faking [of social values], what with the preaching, which was never agreeable and is now said to be hollow, and what with the home counties posing as the universe, it is no wonder Meredith now lies in the trough.'[3] Forster's is a reaction against the Meredith who was the object of attention and adulation in the last decades of his long life, and for a decade or so after his death in 1909. John Lucas has shown how Meredith was taken up particularly after the publication of *Diana of the Crossways* in 1885, and constructed according to the needs and ambitions of younger writers and critics: 'whatever marked a rejection of high-Victorianism could be attributed to Meredith. He became the figure who embodied modernity, a man for the

---

[1] Born in 1858, Dunsany lived until 1957. His literary reputation derives principally from his association with Yeats, Gogarty, and Lady Gregory in the Irish revival of the late 19th and early 20th centuries. In addition, he published extensively: Maeterlinck-like fantasies, verse, a series of popular stories beginning with *The Travel Tales of Mr Joseph Jorkens* in 1931, novels, essays, autobiographies.

[2] *Aspects of the Novel* (London, 1927), 85.   [3] Ibid. 86.

times.'[4] But times change, so that Forster came to articulate an inevitable disenchantment with Meredith.

Forster in his dismissal does admit an important qualification: 'He is the finest contriver that English fiction has ever produced, and any lecture on plot must do homage to him.'[5] Contrivance has always been recognized, and mostly regretted, as a feature of Meredith's writing, though as John Lucas reminds us, Meredith's artificiality and obscurity at times have been offered as a guarantee of his importance.[6] The contemporary reviews of *The Egoist* were mainly favourable, though even his great supporters W. E. Henley (spreading himself through the *Pall Mall Gazette*, *Athenaeum*, *Academy*, and *Teacher*) and James Thomson (in *Cope's Tobacco Plant*) had to acknowledge the preciosity which was forthrightly condemned as 'cranky, obscure, and hieroglyphical' by Margaret Oliphant, writing in *Blackwood's Edinburgh Magazine*.[7] Henley, while conceding that Meredith can be his own worst enemy ('tediously amusing; . . . brilliant to the point of being obscure'[8]), maintains that the contrivances of language and action in *The Egoist* are appropriate to its genre. Meredith's 'intention is not naturalistic, it is comic; his work is not a novel nor even a romance, it is a comedy in chapters.'[9]

At the time he was working on *The Egoist*, Meredith was thinking in a formal way about the properties of comedy for a lecture entitled 'On the Idea of Comedy, and of the Uses of the Comic Spirit', which he delivered to the London Institution on 1 February 1877.[10] This *Essay on Comedy* (the short version of the title under which it was published in book form in 1897) has received a good deal of attention in its own right: thus

---

[4] 'Meredith's Reputation', in Ian Fletcher (ed.), *Meredith Now: Some Critical Essays* (London, 1971), 7. See also Ioan Williams (ed.), *Meredith: The Critical Heritage* (London, 1971).

[5] *Aspects of the Novel*, 86. [6] 'Meredith's Reputation', 3.

[7] Williams, *Meredith: The Critical Heritage*, 240. The other reviews of the novel mentioned are included in this volume.

[8] *Meredith: The Critical Heritage*, 207.

[9] Ibid. 216–17.

[10] Gillian Beer observes that 'In the late eighteen-seventies Meredith explored the idea of comedy in a variety of works—short stories ("The House on the Beach" and "The Case of General Ople and Lady Camper"), an unpublished drama, "The Satirist", the *Essay* and two novels, *The Egoist* and *The Tragic Comedians*' (*Meredith: A Change of Masks*, London, 1970, 114).

Robert Bernard Martin proposes that 'Rather than a piece of original speculation, the *Essay* may be seen as the culmination of the attempt to rid Victorian comic writing of the incubus of sentimental humour',[11] while Roger B. Henkle claims that it is 'the most extended statement of comic theory in the nineteenth century—by a major comic artist'.[12] Henkle goes further, arguing that the *Essay* can be considered in a line of descent from Matthew Arnold's *Culture and Anarchy* (1869) as 'a document of the "high culture" movement of the 1870s and 1880s, a concerted attempt to define "culture" as a set of ideals of judgment, taste, and action that surmount the crass, materialistic, mundane processes of ordinary life'.[13] This association of Meredith with Arnold's project of countering Philistinism locates the *Essay*, and *The Egoist*, in a particular Victorian cultural context. Indeed, *The Egoist* engages closely with a number of live issues of its time—concepts of evolution, together with ideas in psychology and ethics, and political questions to do with authority—in ways that are belied by an emphasis on the timeless universality of its comedy.[14]

The essential proposition that Meredith argues in his lecture is that good comedy is rare, since for the comic poet to exercise his skill:

A society of cultivated men and women is required, wherein ideas are current and the perceptions quick, that he may be supplied with matter and an audience. The semi-barbarism of merely giddy communities, and feverish emotional periods, repel him; and also a state of marked social inequality of the sexes; nor can he whose business is to

---

[11] *The Triumph of Wit: A Study of Victorian Comic Theory* (Oxford, 1974), 90.

[12] *Comedy and Culture: England 1820–1900* (Princeton, NJ, 1980), 259.

[13] *Comedy and Culture*, 261. In connection with Henkle's discussion of the *Essay on Comedy* in relation to the ideas of Arnold and Pater, compare Martin's comment that in the *Essay* Meredith is concerned with 'what occupied him so often: the meaning of real aristocracy' (p. 90).

[14] John Goode makes important observations about the intellectual contexts of the novel in '*The Egoist*: Anatomy or Striptease?', in Fletcher, *Meredith Now*, 205–30; and see Explanatory Notes, especially notes to pp. 1 and 4. On Darwinism, see Carolyn Williams's penetrating discussion, 'Natural Selection and Narrative Form in *The Egoist*', *Victorian Studies*, 27 (1983), 53–79. On topical political issues, see James S. Stone, *George Meredith's Politics as seen in his Life, Friendships, and Works* (Port Credit, Ont., 1986), 76–88. The action of the novel takes place in the 1870s: the evidence is internal (e.g. references to Irish affairs, p. 191; to women's rights, p. 309; to papal infallibility, p. 329).

address the mind be understood where there is not a moderate degree of intellectual activity.[15]

Indeed, 'One excellent test of the civilization of a country, as I have said, I take to be the flourishing of the Comic idea and Comedy; and the test of true Comedy is that it shall awaken thoughtful laughter' (p. 46). The *Essay* ranges through comedy from the time of the ancients to the present, with the highest praise—higher even than for Aristophanes—being accorded to Molière, who had the inestimable advantage of working in the court of Louis XIV. Meredith's comments bear directly on *The Egoist*:

Politically it is accounted a misfortune for France that her nobles thronged to the Court of Louis Quatorze. It was a boon to the comic poet. He had that lively quicksilver world of the animalcule passions, the huge pretensions, the placid absurdities, under his eyes in full activity . . . A simply bourgeois circle will not furnish it, for the middle class must have the brilliant, flippant, independent upper for a spur and a pattern; otherwise it is likely to be inwardly dull as well as outwardly correct. (p. 12)

In the world of his novel, Meredith reproduces a microcosm which gives him the advantages he sees to have been enjoyed by comic writers under the *ancien régime*. In *The Egoist*, the court of the Sun King offers the model according to which Sir Willoughby Patterne of Patterne Hall provides 'a spur and a pattern', not only to the upper class assembled in his domain, but to the bourgeois circle of presumed and implied readers of the novel. The absolutism of the royal power is the particular attraction for Willoughby, and the anachronism of that principle one of which the reader is made keenly aware.

To restrict consideration of comedy in *The Egoist* to reading the novel as a demonstration of the propositions advanced in the *Essay* is limiting, for in various ways this novel actively engages with the conventions of dramatic comedy. For instance, Molière's *Le Misanthrope* (1666) stands as the type of

[15] 'Essay: On the Idea of Comedy and of the Uses of the Comic Spirit', in *Miscellaneous Prose* (The Works of George Meredith, Memorial Edition, xxiii: London, 1910), 3. All subsequent references are to this edition, and use the familiar title *Essay on Comedy*. See also Explanatory Notes to pp. 1, 5, etc.

classical dramatic comedy from which *The Egoist* takes its bearings; while English Restoration comedy of manners, with its obsession with sexual intrigue and sexual humiliation, is another precedent. But such genres, innovatory in their own day, are by implication outmoded in relation to the novel, now the dominant genre. Meredith none the less grafts the artifice of comedy of manners on to the classic realist text. The declaration of the subtitle is supported explicitly in the body of the text by chapter headings which are often in effect stage directions. For the most part, the book works through dialogue, both voiced and unvoiced. The fifty chapters of the novel divide readily into a five-act structure, and traditional comic types and devices are used, for example in the chorus of county gossips, and situations like that in Chapter XL, in which Crossjay is the hidden listener. Moreover, there are gestures towards the classic unities: after an overture which runs from the 'Prelude' to Chapter IV, the action proper, beginning with the betrothal of Clara Middleton and Sir Willoughby Patterne, is continuous and in one place.

The Egoist plays variations on that staple of romantic comedy, the courtship plot, as the narrative follows through the turns by which the order Sir Willoughby Patterne attempts to perpetuate at Patterne Hall is destabilized. But the old order is no longer viable, as is demonstrated in various ways in the course of the novel, and eventually a dubious order is reinscribed in the obligatory marriages. Meredith modulates this variant of a standard comic plot by adopting a particular paradigm, taken from the visual arts and drawn from a culture remote in time and distance from England in the last quarter of the nineteenth century. The story of the Willow Pattern is retold in the novel. The designation of Sir Willoughby Patterne himself gives a·clue to the dependence of the plot on the Chinese legend depicted on the blue-and-white Willow Pattern china which became popular in England in the eighteenth century.[16] The

---

[16] R. D. Mayo, in '*The Egoist* and the Willow Pattern', *ELH: A Journal of English Literary History*, 9 (1942), 71–8, first pointed out the relevance of the Willow Pattern to the novel. See also R. D. Mayo, 'Sir Willoughby's Pattern', *Notes and Queries*, 183 (1942), 362–3; Daniel R. Schwartz, 'The Porcelain-Pattern Leitmotif in Meredith's *The Egoist*', *Victorian Newsletter* (Spring 1968), 26–8; and Gillian Beer, *Meredith: A Change of Masks*, pp. 131–2. It is significant, given the various kinds of play on china

story goes that the rich widowed mandarin who lives in the mansion on the right of the image intended to marry his daughter to a wealthy suitor of high degree. But the maiden loved a poor man, her father's secretary, whom she met in secret under the blossoming tree. The father's suspicions were aroused, and he imprisoned her, extracting from her the promise that she would marry the man of his choice. The lovers escaped over the bridge, pursued by the father and the rejected suitor. Not only does *The Egoist* redeploy the elements of the legend, but images drawn from china and porcelain are worked throughout the novel in ways which suggest Meredith's cognizance of a literary tradition of sexual innuendo exemplified by the 'viewing the china' scene in Wycherley's *The Country Wife* (1675).

While images to do with china are in play from the point at which Mrs Mountstuart Jenkinson coins her phrase for Clara, 'a dainty rogue in porcelain' (p. 41), the premonitory power of the Willow Pattern story for Sir Willoughby Patterne does not emerge explicitly until well on in the book. Mrs Mountstuart Jenkinson, in conversation with him concerning the behaviour of the guests at her dinner-party the previous evening, opens the question of her wedding present to him and Clara:

I mean to consult her; I have come determined upon a chat with her. I think I understand. But she produces false impressions on those who don't know you both. 'I shall have that porcelain back,' says Lady Busshe to me, when we were shaking hands last night: 'I think,' says she, 'it should have been the Willow Pattern.' And she really said: 'he's in for being jilted a second time!' (pp. 364–5)

Mrs Mountstuart Jenkinson explicitly translates to Willoughby what Lady Busshe has said, and becomes quite blatant about the real object of her visit, which is to find out where matters stand between the engaged couple. It is noticeable that she deflects part of the thrust of the Willow Pattern analogy, namely that Vernon, the secretary, will be the preferred suitor, as she dwells on the particular import of her rival's sally. Willoughby

that occur in the novel, that the name of Sir Willoughby Patterne should be reminiscent of earthenware in domestic use. Nevertheless Willoughby is a name common among heroes of eighteenth-century romances of sentiment.

is terrified, for Lady Busshe 'had spoken the hideous English of his fate' (p. 397; see also p. 367): yet her actual formulation proceeds within the allusive, veiled discursive practice of their social class and set.

The process of translation undertaken by Mrs Mountstuart Jenkinson exemplifies in a relatively straightforward instance the way meanings are generated and circulated in this text, most often by responses to what is ambiguous or latent in direct speech. *The Egoist* frequently works through internal dialogue (a fine extended instance is Chapter XXXIX, 'In the Heart of the Egoist', where Willoughby runs through various punitive scenarios). In other cases there is orchestration of a play of voices which are never individualized, but whose identity is implicit. A notorious instance is the 'Prelude', scored for elaborate and elevated discourses remote from ordinary language, which are tacitly—and mockingly—attributed to men of culture in the process of speculating about the potential of comic correction.

The pleasure of the text of *The Egoist* derives not only from exposing euphemism, but from apprehending the full extent of dialogue and its various processes in the novel. I am using the term 'dialogue' here with the inflection proposed by Mikhail Bakhtin, whose concept of dialogism is particularly apposite to reading this novel. The meaning of any utterance, Bakhtin stresses, is determined by the multiplicity of conditions operating in the particular circumstances in which that utterance is made, so that 'there is a constant interaction between meanings, all of which have the potential of conditioning others. Which will affect the other, how it will do so and in what degree is what is actually settled at the moment of utterance.'[17] It is part of the distinction of *The Egoist* that so much of the competition of potential meaning inheres in the text.

A good deal of the novel is occupied with demonstration of the production of meaning, and one of its principal concerns is

[17] *The Dialogic Imagination: Four Essays*, ed. Michael Holquist (Austin, Tex., 1981), p. 426. This introduction does not provide scope to apply Bakhtin's formulations in a more thorough way to Meredith's text. Donald David Stone's 'Meredith and Bakhtin: Polyphony and Bildung', *Studies in English Literature*, 28 (1988), 693–712, takes *Diana of the Crossways* as a test-case for Bakhtin's 'stimulating and usable' concept of novelistic polyphony.

with the reading of texts, most evidently in the processes of interpretation of the epithets that are circulated by the characters.[18] These epithets express perceptions which are not fully articulated, sometimes because suggestion is of the essence of a witty conceit, sometimes because they convey implications that cannot with propriety be explicit, or because they signify uncertainty or an enigma. The novel itself uses the metaphor of coinage as phrases are minted and assayed, and then pass current within the economy, occasionally tested to see if they ring true.

The first new coinage is Mrs Mountstuart Jenkinson's '*You see he has a leg*' (p. 10). This widow is the acknowledged leader of county society, a cabal of mature women like Lady Busshe and Lady Culmer who have usurped the power of language traditionally vested in the males and exercise considerable power through gossip. Mrs Mountstuart is particularly notable for minting phrases, but her pronouncements are given qualified endorsement: 'Mrs Mountstuart was a lady certain to say the remembered, if not the right, thing' (p. 9).[19] What is soon evident in this instance is that her 'quiet little touch of nature' (p. 10) is essentially concupiscent, providing a decorous form for an allusion to another male member than the leg. Willoughby's potency is dubiously expressed, though, in the image which summons up both the sophistication and the decadence of the Restoration court of Charles II. This regal style has been superseded in the two centuries of revolution

18 See Garry J. Handwerk, 'Linguistic Blindness and Ironic Vision in *The Egoist*', *Nineteenth-Century Fiction*, 39 (1984), 172–9, for an interesting account of the functioning of epithets in this novel. J. Hillis Miller emphasizes the particular potency of the metaphor of 'reading' character for *The Egoist* in ' "Herself Against Herself": The Clarification of Clara Middleton', in Carolyn G. Heilbrun and Margaret R. Higonnet (eds.), *The Representation of Women in Fiction* (Baltimore and London, 1983), 99–100.

19 There are reservations expressed elsewhere about Mrs Mountstuart's epithets: see e.g. pp. 45 and 324. In some readings, Mrs Mountstuart's word is given almost divine authority, with her assuming some of the condensing function of the Comic Spirit. Carolyn Williams argues a discriminating version of this position: 'Natural Selection', 70, and 'Unbroken Patterns: Gender, Culture, and Voice in *The Egoist*', *Browning Institute Studies*, 13 (1985), 45–70, see especially 56–8. Various of the characters—Vernon, Clara, Laetitia—have been identified with the Comic Spirit: see Maaja A. Stewart and Elvira Casal, 'Clara Middleton: Wit and Pattern in *The Egoist*', *Studies in the Novel*, 12 (1980), 210–27, for an argument rejecting the identification of any one character with the Comic Spirit.

and reform intervening. Perhaps inadvertently, Mrs Mount-stuart does here say at once the remembered and the right thing, as the drive for sexual pre-eminence comes more and more to be seen as powering the egoist.

The epithet which is most puzzled over in the novel, especially by Sir Willoughby, is the phrase in which Mrs Mount-stuart describes Clara, 'a dainty rogue in porcelain' (p. 41). Because his egoism is active in the interests not only of maintaining but also of repeating the Patterne, his requirements of his consort are basic: 'Clara was young, healthy, handsome; she was therefore fitted to be his wife, the mother of his children, his companion picture' (p. 42). Mrs Mountstuart yields a little to Willoughby's anxiety, and glosses her epithet: 'prize the porcelain and play with the rogue' (p. 43). It is not difficult for him to 'prize the porcelain', to reify Clara as a figurine, valuable but static and brittle (a quality of fine china that is dwelt on in its physical existence in the novel—thus De Craye's vase is smashed, an ill omen for the union it is intended to celebrate, while Lady Busshe's dinner-service provides an occasion, already quoted, for bringing the literal and the figurative into alignment).

It is considerably more difficult for Sir Willoughby to conceive of ways to 'play with the rogue'. The insubordinate in 'rogue' bothers him, and he worries away at the term until he is able ultimately to defuse it by constructing an image of Laetitia's fidelity as its opposite: 'There was an end to his tortures. He sailed on a tranquil sea, the husband of a stedfast woman—no rogue. The exceeding beauty of stedfastness in women clothed Laetitia in graces Clara could not match. A tried stedfast woman is the one jewel of her sex. She points to her husband like the sunflower . . . she justifies him in his own esteem' (p. 405; see e.g. pp. 91 and 168–9 for his fretting at the phrase). The chapter from which this passage is drawn (XXXVII, 'Contains clever Fencing and Intimations of the need for it') shows Willoughby's egotistical capacities at full stretch, and the final quarter of the book will indeed see him achieve the union he envisages, but in circumstances and on terms quite other than those he has in mind at this stage. Here he represents himself as having learned through suffering, .

whereas the text represents him as more profoundly than ever the prisoner of his egoism. Rather, it is the women who learn to recognize, acknowledge, and transcend their egotistical tendencies (see Clara's speech at p. 525, and Laetitia's at p. 540). Clara has to reconcile imposed male expectations with the qualities of energy and independence pointed out by Mrs Mountstuart in 'rogue'.

Willoughby's reactions to Mrs Mountstuart's description of Clara show how women are impeded by if not imprisoned in traditional constructions of femininity. A prime instance of the degree to which women are in thrall to such assumptions occurs in the chapter of 'Clara's Meditations' (XXI), particularly in ruminations on the paradoxes of female knowledge: 'Total ignorance being their pledge of purity to men, they have to expunge the writing of their perceptives on the tablets of the brain: they have to know not when they do now' (p. 214). That is, Clara has not only to work through to a knowledge of her own needs, but must find a way to restrain or suppress her knowledge. Such complex demonstration of the pressures of the culture is distinctive of Meredith's fiction, in more situations than those showing the processes of gender formation.

Mrs Mountstuart's is the most celebrated of the epithets coined for Clara: Vernon Whitford's 'She gives you an idea of the Mountain Echo' (p. 32) is the first. The significance of mountains, and particularly the Alps, in the novel is signalled in the 'Prelude', where we are told of 'the broad Alpine survey of the spirit born of our united social intelligence, which is the Comic Spirit' (p. 2); augmented throughout, as both Clara and Vernon demonstrate their affinity with the purity and sublimity of the Alps; and culminates as the novel is brought to an end, 'upon the season when two lovers met between the Swiss and Tyrol Alps over the Lake of Constance' (p. 547).

While Vernon presumably intends to elevate Clara by association with the sublimity of the mountains, there is a way in which the epithet is a dubious compliment. An echo returns sound, perhaps resonating and enriched, but essentially in response to a stimulus. In Willoughby's frequent thoughts of women as providing reflections and echoes, the male by definition is the active force. Though Vernon is regarded as a friend to women, his phrase betrays a degree of complicity in this masculinist assumption—and it is notable that his poetic description of Miss Middleton is in conjunction with comment on her father.

For all that Vernon's phrase for Clara has ambiguities, casting her into an idealized stereotype which aligns the female with nature, he is nevertheless able to recognize dimensions of Clara's character which others do not perceive—her wit, for example (pp. 41–2). Clara similarly registers affinities with Vernon which are not at once articulated. She is to liberate the Phoebus Apollo from the fasting friar in him, in a process which reaches a climax though not a consummation in the famous episode where she comes upon him asleep under the double-blossom wild cherry-tree. This is a passage frequently discussed, or adduced—for instance by Dunsany—as 'sheer description, mere pictures of the beauty of the earth lying about us, a beauty to which poets are always dwelling near'. The play of language that is central to *The Egoist*, and well demonstrated in this episode, entails more than essentially descriptive poetical effects. For instance, Clara's slip of the tongue, in which she 'put another name for Oxford' (p. 106), betrays her perception of an analogy between her situation and that of Constantia Durham; that is, at the point of the encounter under the cherry-tree, she has already unconsciously registered a particular attraction to Vernon. There are other word-games: Willoughby and Clara have met at Cherriton Grange (p. 37), De Craye describes Constantia and Harry Oxford as 'a pair as happy as blackbirds in a cherry-tree, in a summer sunrise, with the owner of the garden asleep' (p. 460).

The cherry-tree episode is orchestrated in three phases. The first, in the closing pages of Chapter XI, has Clara directed by young Crossjay to Vernon, asleep under the tree whose profusion of blossom has been achieved at the expense of its capacity to bear fruit. There is a reversal of the more usual situation, in which the sleeping female is the object of a male gaze, as Clara stoops to try to see what Vernon has been reading. To avoid a fall, as she thinks, she looks up into the thick clusters of blossom, and experiences a chaste ectasy. This ethereal vision of the beauty and purity of the natural world cannot be sustained in interpretation: Clara's verbal reaction to what she sees is in terms of a trite morality ('He must be good who loves to lie and sleep beneath the branches of this tree!' (p. 118)). Her physical response is differently mediated. As Vernon stirs, she launches into a game of chase with Crossjay, pre-pubescent and hence both a safe lover and a surrogate child.

The second phase is the complement of Clara's experience, giving Vernon's waking reactions. Unlike Clara, he is able explicitly to identify awareness of sexual arousal and threat as a component of his response, but proposes to deal with 'his brief drama of fantasy' (pp. 119–20) by a brisk walk. The transcendent experience each has had separately is followed in the third phase by lively communication in a dialogue marked by *double entendre* that takes the Alps as a metaphoric ground in which they imagine themselves climbing freely, and moves to a specific discussion of challenges to authority in talk of Constantia Durham and the breaking of engagements. Crossjay falls from a tree to bring their tête-à-tête and Chapter XII to a close, with Clara and Vernon united in their ministrations to the boy.

This three-way alliance is an important one in terms of resistance to the authority and dominion of Willoughby. All three have a capacity to revel and thrive in the natural world which is denied to him. He misguidedly seeks in Science a form of authority by which to contain the anarchy of Nature, and his sexual vanity causes him to misread evolutionary theory after a fashion which is particularly ironic given his difficulty in finding and keeping a mate (pp. 37–8). Not only is his attempt to dominate nature doomed, but other significant manifestations of his authority also take obsolete forms (patriarchal, aristocratic, and chauvinist). Thus he is disappointed by the plebeian Lieutenant Patterne, defied by the inconstant Constantia Durham, offended by 'our democratic cousins' (p. 24) in America (and foreigners generally), outraged and gratified by Flitch's petitioning to be allowed to return to his employ. The politics of the novel are clear though covert.

Nowhere is the impotence of that patriarchal authority more emphatically evident than in Willoughby's union with Laetitia Dale. For one thing, it is unlikely to have issue, as Dr Corney explains (p. 519). For another, the conclusion of the compact empowers Laetitia. Marriage is still her fate—the time when women of her class can find vocation outside or without marriage has not yet come—but since Willoughby has been forced to seek terms, she does hold a definite advantage.

The ending of *The Egoist* is equivocal. Meredith's comedy has mischievously put into question male assumptions of superiority, yet the arch-egoist retains a semblance of authority. Some readers express disappointment, even hostility, at this outcome: Kate Millett, for example, takes Meredith to be retreating from 'the liberating turmoil of the sexual revolution' to 'the mundane activities of a matchmaking bureau'.[20] The kind of position articulated by Millett is interrogated and refined by Carolyn Williams, who argues that the resolution of the novel is achieved by a transaction among men, in which Clara is passed from her father to Willoughby over the port, and then, with Dr Middleton's express sanction, from cousin to cousin:

Clara's transfer from Willoughby to Vernon is made to look like her choice, like her movement. . . . For what really happens in this novel is that the male power has been shifted from Willoughby to Vernon through Clara. . . . Evolution is still registered in the line of Patternes, the male line from Willoughby to Vernon, from Dr. Middleton to Vernon. Clara herself has been an accessory after the fact, a conduit, a place of exchange, the location of a transaction between men, the mid-point, the 'middleton'.[21]

Williams's reading commands assent but admits of qualification. Despite her convincing demonstration of an affirmative answer to the question, 'are the same old Patternes simply re-inscribed at closure?',[22] I do not read the union of Clara and Vernon as wholly compromised, but rather as a significant step towards redefinition of gender roles. It is true that female energies are channelled towards advancing a social order whose values remain male, but the process does require major male adaptation. Consider Clara's influence on Vernon: she enables him to moderate the excesses of asceticism and to take more evident pleasure in social activity, for instance by

[20] *Sexual Politics* (New York, 1970), 139.
[21] 'Unbroken Patternes', 65.   [22] Ibid. 48.

schooling him to dance. Their attunement is not only physical (though that dimension is important): Clara's education has included a grounding in the classics, so that she can to some degree speak the language of men.

There are important ways in which Vernon is a kind of 'New Man'. He is feminized by his financial dependence on Willoughby, and mocked by his cousin, but it is Vernon who really ensures the Patterne succession by taking responsibility for Crossjay who will be the heir. His identification with women is principled, if at times misguided, as in his first marriage; and in consort with his egalitarian tendencies. The union of Clara and Vernon has a reciprocity whose value as a harbinger of an approach to equality of the sexes is significant. *The Egoist*, in a manner consonant with Meredith's practice elsewhere in his fiction (*Beauchamp's Career*, *Diana of the Crossways*, *One of Our Conquerors*), is concerned rather to expose shortcomings in the present than to delineate a utopian future. Any development must be plotted against the extended scale of evolutionary time.

Clara's voice may not resonate as fully in its own right as some readers might wish. There is a sense, however, in which she does issue in a powerful female voice. Though Meredith was falling from critical favour in the early part of the century, his fictional practice was not without effect among the next generation of writers. Gillian Beer speaks of their reactions to Meredith: 'The responses of Wilde, of James, of Lawrence, of Forster and of Virginia Woolf all betray admiration and a sense of creative kinship . . . Meredith's closest kinship is with James Joyce.'[23] Of practitioners in the generation following Meredith, it is Virginia Woolf who is most forthright in admiration of his achievement.

Virginia Woolf had a profound though troubled relationship with her Victorian forefathers, among whom she counted Meredith. Furthermore, her relationship to *The Egoist* in particular has a peculiar intimacy, since the central action concerns a character drawn from her father Leslie Stephen.[24]

---

[23] *Meredith: A Change of Masks*, 193.
[24] See note to p. 10. Gillian Beer, in 'The Victorians in Virginia Woolf: 1832–1941', in *Arguing with the Past: Essays in Narrative from Woolf to Sidney* (London and New

She addressed herself explicitly to Forster's judgement on
Meredith in 1928, in an essay written for the hundredth
anniversary of Meredith's birth. While she allows Forster's
verdict on the shallow stridency of Meredith's teaching, she
does not dismiss his work as obsolete and pernicious. Rather,
she insists that 'Meredith deserves our gratitude and excites
our interest as a great innovator.'[25] She credits him with
having struck out new directions for English fiction 'after those
two perfect novels, *Pride and Prejudice* and *The Small House at
Allington*' (p. 231), setting aside 'the sober reality of Trollope
and Jane Austen ... to prepare the way for a new and an
original sense of the human scene' (p. 226). Woolf locates
Meredith's innovation in his capacity to produce splendid and
memorable scenes which illuminate characters and their
actions. She speaks of his narrative self-consciousness and
sophistication recognizing that he represents at times in-
coherent, discontinuous subjectivity rather than providing
'rounded' characters, and does not observe accustomed
notions of identity, causality, and sequence. 'But', she
concludes, 'if English fiction continues to be read, the novels of
Meredith must inevitably rise from time to time into view; his
work must inevitably be disputed and discussed' (p. 232). It is
in keeping with the evolutionary progression represented in
and by *The Egoist* that the daughter of Clara Middleton and
Vernon Whitford should have the last word.

York, 1989), 138–58, acutely discerns the intricacy of Woolf's dialogue with her
Victorian forebears.

[25] 'The Novels of George Meredith', in *Collected Essays*, ed. Leonard Woolf, i
(London, 1966), 231. Subsequent references are to this edition.

NOTE ON THE TEXT

The Egoist was first published in three volumes by Kegan Paul in London in October 1879. A serial version under the title *Sir Willoughby Patterne, the Egoist* appeared in the *Glasgow Weekly Herald* from 21 June 1879 to 10 January 1880, much to the chagrin of Meredith who had not authorized it. There was a second edition in three volumes in 1880. Meredith complained that the first edition had 'Errata innumerable, incredible, a printer's carnival' (inscription in a copy of *The Egoist* in the Widener Collection at Harvard, quoted in Michael Collie, *George Meredith: A Bibliography*, Toronto, 1974, 42. Collie comments that Meredith's handwritten emendations were all in the first volume.)

Meredith revised the novel lightly for the Chapman and Hall collected edition of his fiction, in which *The Egoist* was published in one volume in 1886. This edition was distributed and subsequently published in the United States by Roberts Brothers of Boston. In 1895 Meredith's long association with Chapman and Hall came to an end, and he revised his novels again for the De Luxe edition prepared by Constable, his new publisher (36 vols., 1896–8, and 1910–11; *The Egoist* came out in 1897). Again, the revision was light (including seven deletions of the phrase 'anything but obtuse'—referring to Willoughby—in addition to the two deletions of the same phrase in the revision for the Collected Edition). All subsequent editions in Meredith's lifetime, and the Memorial Edition (27 vols., London: Constable; New York: Scribner, 1909–11) essentially follow the De Luxe text.

The present edition reproduces the earlier World's Classic of 1947, which gives the De Luxe text. A few errors have been silently corrected: e.g. the reference on p. 10 to a 'Louis XIV perruquier' is amended from 'Louis IV.', an evident slip in the manuscript repeated in printed versions. The manuscript of the novel from which the first edition was set is in the Beinecke Rare Book and Manuscript Library, Yale University. I have not attempted a collation of manuscript and printed versions, though the Explanatory Notes include some references to the manuscript.

Lorie Roth, in 'Meredith's Revisions of *The Egoist*' (Ph.D. diss., Kent State University, 1983), has made an intensive study of the composition, revision, and publication of *The Egoist*. She pays particular attention to amplification and expansion within the manuscript, and concludes that 'The final version of *The Egoist* is more lucid and trenchant than the original fair copy' (p. 248).

SELECT BIBLIOGRAPHY

THE most recent bibliography of Meredith's works is Michael Collie, *George Meredith: A Bibliography* (Toronto, 1974). J. C. Olmsted has produced *George Meredith: An Annotated Bibliography of Criticism 1925–1975* (New York, 1978). Commentary on Meredith studies down to the late 1970s is to be found in Gillian Beer, 'George Meredith', in George H. Ford (ed.), *Victorian Fiction: A Second Guide to Research* (New York, 1978), which follows on from C. L. Cline, 'George Meredith', in Lionel Stevenson (ed.), *Victorian Fiction: A Guide to Research* (Cambridge, Mass., 1966).

The Letters of George Meredith, ed. C. L. Cline (3 vols., Oxford, 1970), is the major source for an understanding of Meredith's career. Diane Johnson's *Lesser Lives: The True History of the First Mrs Meredith and Other Lesser Lives* (New York, 1972) offers an effective challenge to the assumptions of received biographical accounts, such as Lionel Stevenson's *The Ordeal of George Meredith* (New York, 1953). Meredith's working notebooks have been edited by Gillian Beer and Margaret Harris (*The Notebooks of George Meredith*, Salzburg, 1983).

The reactions of Meredith's contemporaries to *The Egoist* are documented in Ioan Williams (ed.), *George Meredith: The Critical Heritage* (London, 1971). See also L. T. Hergenhan, 'Meredith Achieves Recognition: The Reception of *Beauchamp's Career* and *The Egoist*', *Texas Studies in Literature and Language*, 11 (1969), 1247–68.

The following is a highly selective list of discussions of *The Egoist*: Robert S. Baker, 'Faun and Satyr: Meredith's Theory of Comedy and *The Egoist*', *Mosaic*, 9 (1976), 173–93; Gillian Beer, *Meredith: A Change of Masks* (London, 1970); Rachel M. Brownstein, *Becoming a Heroine: Reading about Women in Novels* (New York, 1982); Randall Craig, 'Promising Marriage: *The Egoist*, Don Juan, and Language', *ELH: A Journal of English Literary History*, 56 (1989), 897–921; John Goode, '*The Egoist*: Anatomy or Striptease?', in Ian Fletcher (ed.), *Meredith Now: Some Critical Essays* (London, 1971); Gary J. Handwerk,

'Linguistic Blindness and Ironic Vision in *The Egoist*', *Nineteenth-Century Fiction*, 39 (1984), 163–85; J. Hillis Miller, ' "Herself Against Herself": The Clarification of Clara Middleton', in Carolyn G. Heilbrun and Margaret R. Higonnet, eds., *The Representation of Women in Fiction* (Baltimore and London, 1983); Robert M. Polhemus, *Comic Faith: The Great Comic Tradition from Austen to Joyce* (Chicago, 1980); Daniel Smirlock, 'Rough Truth: Synecdoche and Interpretation in *The Egoist*', *Nineteenth-Century Fiction*, 31 (1976), 313–28; Donald David Stone, *Novelists in a Changing World: Meredith, James, and the Transformation of English Fiction in the 1880s* (Cambridge, Mass., 1972); Dorothy van Ghent, *The English Novel: Form and Function* (New York, 1953); Michael Wheeler, *The Art of Allusion in Victorian Fiction* (London, 1979); Carolyn Williams, 'Natural Selection and Narrative Form in *The Egoist*', *Victorian Studies*, 27 (1983), 53–79, and 'Unbroken Patternes: Gender, Culture, and Voice in *The Egoist*', *Browning Institute Studies*, 13 (1985), 45–70; Judith Wilt, *The Readable People of George Meredith* (Princeton, NJ, 1975); Walter H. Wright, *Art and Substance in George Meredith: A Study in Narrative* (Lincoln, Nebr., 1953).

A CHRONOLOGY OF
GEORGE MEREDITH

1828   Born in Portsmouth on 12 February.

1842–4 Schooling at the Moravian School at Neuwied, on the Rhine.

1845   Articled to Richard Charnock, a London solicitor.

1849   First published poem, 'Chillianwallah', *Chambers' Edinburgh Journal*, 7 July. Marriage to Mary Ellen Peacock Nicolls (August).

1851   *Poems* (1 vol., J. W. Parker).

1853   Birth of son, Arthur Gryffydh (June).

1856 [1855] First novel, *The Shaving of Shagpat: An Arabian Entertainment* (1 vol., Chapman & Hall).

1857   *Farina: A Legend of Cologne* (1 vol., Smith, Elder).

1858   Elopement of Mary Ellen Meredith with Henry Wallis.

1859   *The Ordeal of Richard Feverel* (3 vols., Chapman & Hall).

1860–95 Reading for Chapman & Hall.

1860   *Evan Harrington; or, He would be a Gentleman* serialized in *Once a Week*, February–October; published in America by Harper, 1 vol.

1861   *Evan Harrington* (3 vols., Bradbury & Evans). First tour of the Tyrol and Italy (July–August). Death of Mary Ellen Meredith (October).

1862   *Modern Love and Poems of the English Roadside, with Poems and Ballads* (1 vol., Chapman & Hall).

1864   Marriage to Marie Vulliamy (September). A condensed version of *Emilia in England* serialized in *Revue des deux Mondes*, November–December; published by Chapman & Hall, 3 vols. (renamed *Sandra Belloni* when published in 1 vol. in Collected Edition, 1886).

1865   Birth of son, William Maxse (July). *Rhoda Fleming, A Story* (3 vols., Tinsley).

1866   Correspondent on the Italian war for the *Morning Post* (summer). *Vittoria* serialized in the *Fortnightly Review*, January–December.

1867 [1866]　*Vittoria* (3 vols., Chapman & Hall). Moved to Flint House, Box Hill, Dorking: his home for the rest of his life.

1870–1　*The Adventures of Harry Richmond*, serialized in the *Cornhill Magazine*, September 1870–November 1871.

1871　Birth of daughter, Marie Eveleen (June). *The Adventures of Harry Richmond* (3 vols., Smith, Elder).

1874–5　*Beauchamp's Career* serialized in the *Fortnightly Review*, August 1874–December 1875.

1876　*Beauchamp's Career* (3 vols., Chapman & Hall).

1877　*The House on the Beach* in the *New Quarterly Magazine*, January; published in 1 vol. by Harper in America, and in *The Tale of Chloe and other stories* by Ward, Lock, and Bowden, 1894. Lecture 'On the Idea of Comedy, and of the Uses of the Comic Spirit' delivered 1 February; published in the *New Quarterly Magazine*, April; published in 1 vol. by Constable in England and Charles Scribner's Sons in America, 1897. *The Case of General Ople and Lady Camper* in the *New Quarterly Magazine*, July; published in 1 vol. by John W. Lovell in America in 1890, and in *The Tale of Chloe and other stories* by Ward, Lock, and Bowden, 1894.

1879–80　*The Egoist* serialized under the title 'Sir Willoughby Patterne, the Egoist', in the *Glasgow Weekly Herald*, June 1879–January 1880.

1879　*The Egoist: A Comedy in Narrative* (3 vols., Kegan Paul). *The Tale of Chloe* in the *New Quarterly Magazine*, July; published in 1 vol. by John W. Lovell in America in 1890, and by Ward, Lock, and Bowden in 1894.

1880–1　*The Tragic Comedians* serialized in the *Fortnightly Review*, October 1880–February 1881.

1880　*The Tragic Comedians: A Study in a well-known Story* (2 vols., Chapman & Hall).

1883　*Poems and Lyrics of the Joy of Earth* (1 vol., Macmillan; Roberts in America).

1884　*Diana of the Crossways* serialized in an abbreviated version in the *Fortnightly Review*, June–December.

1885　*Diana of the Crossways* (3 vols., Chapman & Hall). The first titles of Chapman & Hall's Collected Edition of Meredith's fiction issued. Death of Marie Vulliamy Meredith (September).

1887   *Ballads and Poems of Tragic Life* (1 vol., Macmillan; Roberts in America).

1888   *A Reading of Earth* (1 vol., Macmillan; Roberts in America).

1890   Death of Arthur Meredith (September).

1890–1 *One of Our Conquerors* serialized October 1890–May 1891 simultaneously in the *Fortnightly Review*, *The Sun* (New York), and *The Australasian*.

1891   *One of Our Conquerors* (3 vols., Chapman & Hall).

1892   *Poems: The Empty Purse with Odes to the Comic Spirit: To Youth in Memory and Verses* (1 vol., Macmillan; Roberts in America).

1893–4 *Lord Ormont and His Aminta*, serialized in the *Pall Mall Magazine*, December 1893–July 1894.

1894   *Lord Ormont and His Aminta* (3 vols., Chapman & Hall).

1895   *The Amazing Marriage*, serialized in *Scribner's Magazine*, January–December; published in 2 vols. by Constable; Scribner in America.

1896   The first volumes of Constable's De Luxe Edition of Meredith's work issued (eventually 36 vols., 1896–8 and 1910–11).

1898   *Odes in Contribution to the Song of French History*, in *Cosmopolis*, March–May; published in 1 vol. by Constable; Scribner in America.

1901   *A Reading of life, with Other Poems* (1 vol., Constable; Scribner in America).

1905   Order of Merit conferred.

1909   Died on 18 May. *Last Poems* (1 vol., Constable; Scribner in America). The first volumes of the Memorial Edition of Meredith's work issued (Constable, 27 vols., 1909–11; Scribner in America).

1910   *Celt and Saxon* (unfinished novel) serialized in the *Fortnightly Review*, January–August, and in *The Forum* (New York), January–June. *Celt and Saxon* (1 vol., Constable).

CONTENTS

CONTENTS

PRELUDE

A Chapter of which the Last Page only is of any Importance

COMEDY is a game played to throw reflections upon social life, and it deals with human nature in the drawing-room of civilized men and women, where we have no dust of the struggling outer world, no mire, no violent crashes, to make the correctness of the representation convincing.* Credulity is not wooed through the impressionable senses; nor have we recourse to the small circular glow of the watchmaker's eye* to raise in bright relief minutest grains of evidence for the routing of incredulity. The Comic Spirit conceives a definite situation for a number of characters, and rejects all accessories in the exclusive pursuit of them and their speech.* For, being a spirit, he hunts the spirit in men; vision and ardour constitute his merit: he has not a thought of persuading you to believe in him. Follow and you will see. But there is a question of the value of a run at his heels.

Now the world is possessed of a certain big book, the biggest book on earth; that might indeed be called the Book of Earth; whose title is the Book of Egoism,* and it is a book full of the world's wisdom. So full of it, and of such dimensions is this book, in which the generations have written ever since they took to writing, that to be profitable to us the Book needs a powerful compression.

Who, says the notable humourist, in allusion to this Book, who can studiously travel through sheets of leaves now capable of a stretch from the Lizard*to the last few poor pulmonary snips and shreds of leagues dancing on their toes for cold, explorers tell us, and catching breath by good luck, like dogs at bones about a table, on the edge of the Pole? Inordinate unvaried length, sheer longinquity, staggers the heart, ages the very heart of us at a view. And how if we manage finally to print one of our pages on the crow-scalp of that solitary majestic

outsider?* We may with effort get even him into the
Book; yet the knowledge we want will not be more present
with us than it was when the chapters hung their end over
the cliff you ken of at Dover,* where sits our great lord
and master contemplating the seas without upon the reflex
of that within!

In other words, as I venture to translate him (humour-
ists are difficult: it is a piece of their humour to puzzle
our wits), the inward mirror, the embracing and condensing spirit, is required to give us those interminable
milepost piles of matter (extending well-nigh to the very
Pole) in essence, in chosen samples, digestibly. I conceive
him to indicate that the realistic method of a conscientious transcription of all the visible, and a repetition of
all the audible, is mainly accountable for our present
branfulness, and for that prolongation of the vasty and
the noisy, out of which, as from an undrained fen, steams
the malady of sameness, our modern malady. We have
the malady, whatever may be the cure or the cause. We
drove in a body to Science the other day for an antidote;
which was as if tired pedestrians should mount the
engine-box of headlong trains; and Science introduced
us to our o'er-hoary ancestry—them in the Oriental
posture: whereupon we set up a primaeval chattering to
rival the Amazon forest nigh nightfall, cured, we fancied.
And before daybreak our disease was hanging on to us
again, with the extension of a tail. We had it fore and
aft. We were the same, and animals into the bargain.
That is all we got from Science.*

Art is the specific. We have little to learn of apes,
and they may be left. The chief consideration for us is,
what particular practice of Art in letters is the best for
the perusal of the Book of our common wisdom; so that
with clearer minds and livelier manners we may escape,
as it were, into daylight and song from a land of fog-
horns. Shall we read it by the watchmaker's eye in
luminous rings eruptive of the infinitesimal, or pointed
with examples and types under the broad Alpine survey
of the spirit born of our united social intelligence, which
is the Comic Spirit?* Wise men say the latter. They tell

us that there is a constant tendency in the Book to accumulate excess of substance, and such repleteness, obscuring the glass it holds to mankind, renders us inexact in the recognition of our individual countenances: a perilous thing for civilization. And these wise men are strong in their opinion that we should encourage the Comic Spirit, who is, after all, our own offspring, to relieve the Book. Comedy, they say, is the true diversion, as it is likewise the key of the great Book, the music of the Book. They tell us how it condenses whole sections of the Book in a sentence, volumes in a character; so that a fair part of a book outstripping thousands of leagues when unrolled, may be compassed in one comic sitting.

For verily, say they, we must read what we can of it, at least the page before us, if we would be men. One, with an index on the Book cries out, in a style pardonable to his fervency: The remedy of your frightful affliction is here, through the stillatory* of Comedy, and not in Science, nor yet in Speed, whose name is but another for voracity. Why, to be alive, to be quick in the soul, there should be diversity in the companion-throbs of your pulses. Interrogate them. They lump along like the old lob-legs of Dobbin the horse; or do their business like cudgels of carpet-thwackers expelling dust, or the cottage-clock pendulum teaching the infant hour over midnight simple arithmetic. This too in spite of Bacchus.* And let them gallop; let them gallop with the God bestriding them, gallop to Hymen, gallop to Hades,* they strike the same note. Monstrous monotonousness has enfolded us as with the arms of Amphitrite!* We hear a shout of war for a diversion.—Comedy he pronounces to be our means of reading swiftly and comprehensively. She it is who proposes the correcting of pretentiousness, of inflation, of dulness, and of the vestiges of rawness and grossness to be found among us. She is the ultimate civilizer, the polisher, a sweet cook.* If, he says, she watches over sentimentalism with a birch-rod, she is not opposed to romance. You may love, and warmly love, so long as you are honest. Do not offend reason. A lover pretending too much by one foot's length of pretence, will have

that foot caught in her trap. In Comedy is the singular
scene of charity issuing of disdain under the stroke of
honourable laughter: an Ariel released by Prospero's
wand from the fetters of the damned witch Sycorax.*
And this laughter of reason refreshed is floriferous, like
the magical great gale of the shifty Spring deciding for
Summer. You hear it giving the delicate spirit his
liberty. Listen, for comparison, to an unleavened
society: a low as of the udderful cow past milking hour!
O for a titled ecclesiastic to curse to excommunication
that unholy thing!—So far an enthusiast perhaps; but
he should have a hearing.

Concerning pathos, no ship can now set sail without
pathos; and we are not totally deficient of pathos;
which is, I do not accurately know what, if not the
ballast, reducible to moisture by patent process, on
board our modern vessel; for it can hardly be the cargo,
and the general water-supply has other uses; and ships
well charged with it seem to sail the stiffest:—there is a
touch of pathos. The Egoist*surely inspires pity. He who
would desire to clothe himself at everybody's expense,
and is of that desire condemned to strip himself stark
naked,* he, if pathos ever had a form, might be taken for
the actual person. Only he is not allowed to rush at you,
roll you over and squeeze your body for the briny drops.
There is the innovation.

You may as well know him out of hand, as a gentleman
of our time and country, of wealth and station; a not
flexile figure, do what we may with him; the humour of
whom scarcely dimples the surface and is distinguishable
but by very penetrative, very wicked imps, whose fits of
roaring below at some generally imperceptible stroke of
his quality, have first made the mild literary angels aware
of something comic in him, when they were one and all
about to describe the gentleman on the heading of the
records baldly (where brevity is most complimentary)
as a gentleman of family and property, an idol of a
decorous island that admires the concrete. Imps have
their freakish wickedness in them to kindle detective
vision: malignly do they love to uncover ridiculousness

in imposing figures. Wherever they catch sight of Egoism they pitch their camps, they circle and squat, and forthwith they trim their lanterns, confident of the ludicrous to come. So confident that their grip of an English gentleman, in whom they have spied their game, never relaxes until he begins insensibly to frolic and antic, unknown to himself, and comes out in the native steam which is their scent of the chase. Instantly off they scour, Egoist and imps. They will, it is known of them, dog a great House for centuries, and be at the birth of all the new heirs in succession, diligently taking confirmatory notes, to join hands and chime their chorus in one of their merry rings round the tottering pillar of the House, when his turn arrives; as if they had (possibly they had) smelt of old date a doomed colossus of Egoism in that unborn, unconceived inheritor of the stuff of the family. They dare not be chuckling while Egoism is valiant, while sober, while socially valuable, nationally serviceable. They wait.

Aforetime a grand old Egoism built the House. It would appear that ever finer essences of it are demanded to sustain the structure: but especially would it appear that a reversion to the gross original, beneath a mask and in a vein of fineness, is an earthquake at the foundations of the House. Better that it should not have consented to motion, and have held stubbornly to all ancestral ways, than have bred that anachronic spectre. The sight, however, is one to make our squatting imps in circle grow restless on their haunches, as they bend eyes instantly, ears at full cock, for the commencement of the comic drama of the suicide. If this line of verse be not yet in our literature:

> Through very love of self himself he slew,

let it be admitted for his epitaph.

CHAPTER I

A Minor Incident, showing an Hereditary Aptitude in the Use of the Knife

THERE was an ominously anxious watch of eyes visible and invisible over the infancy of Willoughby, fifth in descent from Simon Patterne,* of Patterne Hall, premier of this family, a lawyer, a man of solid acquirements and stout ambition, who well understood the foundation-work of a House, and was endowed with the power of saying No to those first agents of destruction, besieging relatives. He said it with the resonant emphasis of death to younger sons.* For if the oak is to become a stately tree, we must provide against the crowding of timber. Also the tree beset with parasites prospers not. A great House in its beginning, lives, we may truly say, by the knife. Soil is easily got, and so are bricks, and a wife, and children come of wishing for them, but the vigorous use of the knife is a natural gift and points to growth. Pauper Patternes were numerous when the fifth head of the race was the hope of his county. A Patterne was in the Marines.*

The country and the chief of this family were simultaneously informed of the existence of one Lieutenant Crossjay Patterne, of the corps of the famous hard fighters, through an act of heroism of the unpretending cool sort which kindles British blood, on the part of the modest young officer, in the storming of some eastern riverain stronghold, somewhere about the coast of China.* The officer's youth was assumed on the strength of his rank, perhaps likewise from the tale of his modesty: 'he had only done his duty.' Our Willoughby was then at College, emulous of the generous enthusiasm of his years, and strangely impressed by the report, and the printing of his name in the newspapers. He thought over it for several months, when, coming to his title and heritage, he sent Lieutenant Crossjay Patterne a cheque for a sum of money amounting to the gallant fellow's pay per annum, at the same time showing his acquaintance with the first, or chemical, principles of generosity, in the remark to friends at home, that 'blood is thicker than water.' The man is a Marine, but he is a Patterne. How any Patterne should have drifted into the Marines, is of the order of questions which are senselessly asked of the great dispensary.* In the complimentary letter accompanying his cheque, the lieutenant was invited to present himself at the ancestral Hall, when convenient to him, and he was assured that he had given his relative and friend a taste for a soldier's life. Young Sir Willoughby was fond of talking of his 'military namesake and distant cousin, young Patterne—the Marine.' It was funny; and not less laughable was the description of his namesake's deed of valour: with the rescued British sailor inebriate, and the hauling off to captivity of the three braves of the black dragon on a yellow ground,* and the tying of them together back to back by their pigtails, and driving of them into our lines upon a newly devised dying-top style of march that inclined to the oblique, like the astonished six eyes of the celestial prisoners,* for straight they could not go. The humour of gentlemen at home is always highly excited by such cool feats. We are a small island, but you see what we do. The ladies at the Hall, Sir Willoughby's mother, and his aunts Eleanor and Isabel, were more affected than he by the circumstance of their having a Patterne in the Marines. But how then! We English have ducal blood in business: we have, genealogists tell us, royal blood in common trades. For all our pride we are a queer people; and you may be ordering butcher's meat of a Tudor, sitting on the cane-bottom chairs of a Plantagenet.* By and by you may . . . but cherish your reverence. Young Willoughby made a kind of shock-head or football hero of his gallant distant cousin, and wondered occasionally that the fellow had been content to despatch a letter of effusive thanks without availing himself of the invitation to partake of the hospitalities of Patterne.

He was one afternoon parading between showers on the stately garden terrace of the Hall, in company with his affianced, the beautiful and dashing Constantia

Durham, followed by knots of ladies and gentlemen vowed to fresh air before dinner, while it was to be had. Chancing with his usual happy fortune (we call these things dealt to us out of the great hidden dispensary, chance) to glance up the avenue of limes, as he was in the act of turning on his heel at the end of the terrace, and it should be added, discoursing with passion's privilege of the passion of love to Miss Durham, Sir Willoughby, who was anything but obtuse, experienced a presentiment upon espying a thick-set stumpy man crossing the gravel space from the avenue to the front steps of the Hall, decidedly *not* bearing the stamp of the gentleman 'on his hat, his coat, his feet, or anything that was his,'* Willoughby subsequently observed to the ladies of his family in the Scriptural style of gentlemen who do bear the stamp. His brief sketch of the creature was repulsive. The visitor carried a bag, and his coat-collar was up, his hat was melancholy; he had the appearance of a bankrupt tradesman absconding; no gloves, no umbrella.

As to the incident we have to note, it was very slight. The card of Lieutenant Patterne was handed to Sir Willoughby, who laid it on the salver, saying to the footman: 'Not at home.'

He had been disappointed in the age, grossly deceived in the appearance of the man claiming to be his relative in this unseasonable fashion; and his acute instinct advised him swiftly of the absurdity of introducing to his friends a heavy unpresentable senior as the celebrated gallant Lieutenant of Marines, and the same as a member of his family! He had talked of the man too much, too enthusiastically, to be able to do so. A young subaltern, even if passably vulgar in figure, can be shuffled through by the aid of the heroical story humourously exaggerated in apology for his aspect. Nothing can be done with a mature and stumpy Marine of that rank. Considerateness dismisses him on the spot, without parley. It was performed by a gentleman supremely advanced at a very early age in the art of cutting.

Young Sir Willoughby spoke a word of the rejected visitor to Miss Durham, in response to her startled look:

'I shall drop him a cheque,' he said, for she seemed personally wounded, and had a face of crimson.

The young lady did not reply.

Dating from the humble departure of Lieutenant Crossjay Patterne up the limes-avenue under a gathering rain-cloud, the ring of imps in attendance on Sir Willoughby maintained their station with strict observation of his movements at all hours; and were comparisons in quest, the sympathetic eagerness of the eyes of caged monkeys for the hand about to feed them, would supply one. They perceived in him a fresh development and very subtle manifestation of the very old thing from which he had sprung.

CHAPTER II

The Young Sir Willoughby

THESE little scoundrel imps, who have attained to some respectability as the dogs and pets of the Comic Spirit, had been curiously attentive three years earlier, long before the public announcement of his engagement to the beautiful Miss Durham, on the day of Sir Willoughby's majority,* when Mrs. Mountstuart Jenkinson said her word of him. Mrs. Mountstuart was a lady certain to say the remembered, if not the right, thing.* Again and again was it confirmed on days of high celebration, days of birth or bridal, how sure she was to hit the mark that rang the bell; and away her word went over the county: and had she been an uncharitable woman she could have ruled the county with an iron rod of caricature, so sharp was her touch. A grain of malice would have sent county faces and characters awry into the currency. She was wealthy and kindly, and resembled our mother Nature in her reasonable antipathies to one or two things which none can defend, and her decided preference of persons that shone in the sun. Her word sprang out of her. She looked at you, and forth it came: and it stuck to you, as nothing laboured or literary could have adhered. Her saying of Laetitia Dale:*

'Here she comes, with a romantic tale on her eyelashes,'
was a portrait of Laetitia. And that of Vernon Whitford:
'He is a Phoebus Apollo turned fasting friar,'*painted the
sunken brilliancy of the lean long-walker and scholar at
a stroke.

Of the young Sir Willoughby, her word was brief; and
there was the merit of it on a day when he was hearing
from sunrise to the setting of the moon salutes in his
honour, songs of praise and Ciceronian eulogy.* Rich,
handsome, courteous, generous, lord of the Hall, the
feast, and the dance, he excited his guests of both sexes
to a holiday of flattery. And, says Mrs. Mountstuart,
while grand phrases were mouthing round about him:
'*You see he has a leg.*'

That you saw, of course. But after she had spoken
you saw much more. Mrs. Mountstuart said it just as
others utter empty nothings, with never a hint of a stress.
Her word was taken up, and very soon, from the extreme
end of the long drawing-room, the circulation of something of Mrs. Mountstuart's was distinctly perceptible.
Lady Patterne sent a little Hebe* down, skirting the
dancers, for an accurate report of it; and even the in-
appreciative lips of a very young lady transmitting the
word could not damp the impression of its weighty truthfulness. It was perfect! Adulation of the young Sir
Willoughby's beauty and wit, and aristocratic bearing
and mien, and of his moral virtues, was common: welcome if you like, as a form of homage; but common,
almost vulgar, beside Mrs. Mountstuart's quiet little
touch of nature.* In seeming to say infinitely less than
others, as Miss Isabel Patterne pointed out to Lady
Busshe, Mrs. Mountstuart comprised all that the others
had said, by showing the needlessness of allusions to the
saliently evident. She was the aristocrat reproving the
provincial. 'He is everything you have had the goodness to remark, ladies and dear sirs, he talks charmingly,
dances divinely, rides with the air of a commander-in-
chief, has the most natural grand pose possible without
ceasing for a moment to be the young English gentleman
he is. Alcibiades,* fresh from a Louis xiv perruquier,*

could not surpass him: whatever you please; I could outdo you in sublime comparisons, were I minded to pelt him. Have you noticed that he has a leg?'

So might it be amplified. A simple-seeming word of this import is the triumph of the spiritual, and where it passes for coin of value, the society has reached a high refinement: Arcadian* by the aesthetic route. Observation of Willoughby was not, as Miss Eleanor Patterne pointed out to Lady Culmer, drawn down to the leg, but directed to estimate him from the leg upward. That, however, is prosaic. Dwell a short space on Mrs. Mountstuart's word; and whither, into what fair region, and with how decorously voluptuous a sensation, do not we fly, who have, through mournful veneration of the Martyr Charles, a coy attachment to the Court of his Merrie Son, where the leg was ribanded with love-knots and reigned.* Oh! it was a naughty Court. Yet have we dreamed of it as the period when an English cavalier*was grace incarnate; far from the boor now hustling us in another sphere; beautifully mannered, every gesture dulcet. And if the ladies were . . . we will hope they have been traduced. But if they were, if they were too tender, ah! gentlemen were gentlemen then—worth perishing for! There is this dream in the English country; and it must be an aspiration after some form of melodious gentlemanliness which is imagined to have inhabited the island at one time; as among our poets the dream of the period of a circle of chivalry here is encouraged for the pleasure of the imagination.

Mrs. Mountstuart touched a thrilling chord. 'In spite of men's hateful modern costume, you see he has a leg.'

That is, the leg of the born cavalier is before you: and obscure it as you will, dress degenerately, there it is for ladies who have eyes. You *see* it: or, you see *he* has it. Miss Isabel and Miss Eleanor disputed the incidence of the emphasis, but surely, though a slight difference of meaning may be heard, either will do: many, with a good show of reason, throw the accent upon *leg*. And the ladies knew for a fact that Willoughby's leg was exquisite; he had a cavalier court-suit in his wardrobe. Mrs.

Mountstuart signified that the leg was to be seen because it was a burning leg. There it is, and it *will* shine through! He has the leg of Rochester, Buckingham, Dorset, Suckling;* the leg that smiles, that winks, is obsequious to you, yet perforce of beauty self-satisfied; that twinkles to a tender midway between imperiousness and seductiveness, audacity and discretion; between 'you shall worship me,' and 'I am devoted to you'; is your lord, your slave, alternately and in one. It is a leg of ebb and flow and high-tide ripples. Such a leg, when it has done with pretending to retire, will walk straight into the hearts of women. Nothing so fatal to them.

Self-satisfied it must be. Humbleness does not win multitudes or the sex. It must be vain to have a sheen. Captivating melodies (to prove to you the unavoidableness of self-satisfaction when you know that you have hit perfection), listen to them closely, have an inner pipe of that conceit almost ludicrous when you detect the chirp.

And you need not be reminded that he has the leg without the naughtiness. You see eminent in him what we would fain have brought about in a nation that has lost its leg in gaining a possibly cleaner morality. And that is often contested; but there is no doubt of the loss of the leg.

Well, footmen and courtiers and Scottish highlanders, and the corps de ballet, draymen too, have legs, and staring legs, shapely enough. But what are they? not the modulated instrument we mean—simply legs for legwork, dumb as the brutes. Our cavalier's is the poetic leg, a portent, a valiance.* He has it as Cicero had a tongue. It is a lute to scatter songs to his mistress; a rapier, is she obdurate. In sooth a leg with brains in it, soul.

And its shadows are an ambush, its lights a surprise. It blushes, it pales, can whisper, exclaim. It is a peep, a part revelation, just sufferable, of the Olympian god—Jove playing carpet-knight.*

For the young Sir Willoughby's family and this thoughtful admirers, it is not too much to say that Mrs. Mountstuart's little word fetched an epoch of our history to colour the evening of his arrival at man's estate. He was all that Merrie Charles's Court should have been, subtracting not a sparkle from what it was. Under this light he danced, and you may consider the effect of it on his company.

He had received the domestic education of a prince. Little princes abound in a land of heaped riches. Where they have not to yield military service to an Imperial master, they are necessarily here and there dainty during youth, sometimes unmanageable, and as they are bound in no personal duty to the State, each is for himself, with full present, and what is more, luxurious prospective leisure for the practice of that allegiance. They are sometimes enervated by it: that must be in continental countries. Happily our climate and our brave blood precipitate the greater number upon the hunting-field, to do the public service of heading the chase of the fox, with benefit to their constitutions. Hence a manly as well as useful race of little princes, and Willoughby was as manly as any. He cultivated himself, he would not be outdone in popular accomplishments. Had the standard of the public taste been set in philosophy, and the national enthusiasm centred in philosophers, he would at least have worked at books. He did work at science, and had a laboratory. His admirable passion to excel, however, was chiefly directed in his youth upon sport; and so great was the passion in him, that it was commonly the presence of rivals which led him to the declaration of love.

He knew himself nevertheless to be the most constant of men in his attachment to the sex. He had never discouraged Laetitia Dale's devotion to him, and even when he followed in the sweeping tide of the beautiful Constantia Durham (whom Mrs. Mountstuart called 'The Racing Cutter'),* he thought of Laetitia, and looked at her. She was a shy violet.

Willoughby's comportment while the showers of adulation drenched him might be likened to the composure of Indian Gods* undergoing worship, but unlike them he reposed upon no seat of amplitude to preserve him from a betrayal of intoxication; he had to continue tripping, dancing, exactly balancing himself, head to right, head to left, addressing his idolaters in phrases of perfect choiceness. This is only to say, that it is easier to be a wooden idol than one in the flesh; yet Willoughby was equal to his task. The little prince's education teaches him that he is other than you, and by virtue of the instruction he receives, and also something, we know not what, within, he is enabled to maintain his posture where you would be tottering. Urchins upon whose curly pates grey seniors lay their hands with conventional encomium and speculation, look older than they are immediately, and Willoughby looked older than his years, not for want of freshness, but because he felt that he had to stand eminently and correctly poised.

Hearing of Mrs. Mountstuart's word on him, he smiled and said: 'It is at her service.'

The speech was communicated to her, and she proposed to attach a dedicatory strip of silk. And then they came together, and there was wit and repartee suitable to the electrical atmosphere of the dancing-room, on the march to a magical hall of supper. Willoughby conducted Mrs. Mountstuart to the supper-table.

'Were I,' said she, 'twenty years younger, I think I would marry you, to cure my infatuation.'

'Then let me tell you in advance, madam,' said he, 'that I will do everything to obtain a new lease of it, except divorce you.'

They were infinitely wittier, but so much was heard and may be reported.

'It makes the business of choosing a wife for him superhumanly difficult!' Mrs. Mountstuart observed, after listening to the praises she had set going again when the ladies were weeded of us, in Lady Patterne's Indian room, and could converse unhampered upon their own ethereal themes.

'Willoughby will choose a wife for himself,' said his mother.

CHAPTER III

Constantia Durham

THE great question for the county was debated in many
households, daughter-thronged and daughterless, long
subsequent to the memorable day of Willoughby's coming of age. Lady Busshe was for Constantia Durham.
She laughed at Mrs. Mountstuart Jenkinson's notion of
Laetitia Dale. She was a little older than Mrs. Mountstuart, and had known Willoughby's father, whose
marriage into the wealthiest branch of the Whitford
family had been strictly sagacious. 'Patternes marry
money: they are not romantic people,' she said. Miss
Durham had money, and she had health and beauty:
three mighty qualifications for a Patterne bride. Her
father, Sir John Durham, was a large landowner in the
western division of the county; a pompous gentleman,
the picture of a father-in-law for Willoughby. The
father of Miss Dale was a battered army surgeon from
India, tenant of one of Sir Willoughby's cottages bordering Patterne Park. His girl was portionless and a poetess.
Her writing of the song in celebration of the young
baronet's birthday was thought a clever venture, bold
as only your timid creatures can be bold. She let the cat
out of her bag of verse before the multitude; she almost
proposed to her hero in her rhymes. She was pretty,
her eyelashes were long and dark, her eyes dark blue,
and her soul was ready to shoot like a rocket out of them
at a look from Willoughby. And he looked, he certainly
looked, though he did not dance with her once that
night, and danced repeatedly with Miss Durham. He
gave Laetitia to Vernon Whitford for the final dance of
the night, and he may have looked at her so much in
pity of an elegant girl allied to such a partner. The
'Phoebus Apollo turned fasting friar' had entirely forgotten his musical gifts in motion. He crossed himself
and crossed his bewildered lady, and crossed everybody
in the figure, extorting shouts of cordial laughter from
his cousin Willoughby. Be it said that the hour was four

in the morning, when dancers must laugh at somebody, if only to refresh their feet, and the wit of the hour administers to the wildest laughter. Vernon was likened to Theseus in the maze, entirely dependent upon his Ariadne; to a fly released from a jam-pot; to a 'salvage,' or green, man caught in a web of nymphs and made to go the paces. Willoughby was inexhaustible in the happy similes he poured out to Miss Durham across the lines of Sir Roger de Coverley, and they were not forgotten, they procured him a reputation as a convivial sparkler. Rumour went the round that he intended to give Laetitia to Vernon for good, when he could decide to take Miss Durham to himself; his generosity was famous; but that decision, though the rope was in the form of a knot, seemed reluctant for the conclusive close haul; it preferred the state of slackness; and if he courted Laetitia on behalf of his cousin, his cousinly love must have been greater than his passion, one had to suppose. He was generous enough for it, or for marrying the portionless girl himself.

There was a story of a brilliant young widow of our aristocracy who had very nearly snared him. Why should he object to marry into our aristocracy? Mrs. Mountstuart asked him, and he replied, that the girls of that class have no money, and he doubted the quality of their blood. He had his eyes awake. His duty to his House was a foremost thought with him, and for such a reason he may have been more anxious to give the slim and not robust Laetitia to Vernon than accede to his personal inclination. The mention of the widow singularly offended him, notwithstanding the high rank of the lady named. 'A widow?' he said. 'I!' He spoke to a widow; an oldish one truly; but his wrath at the suggestion of his union with a widow, led him to be for the moment oblivious of the minor shades of good taste. He desired Mrs. Mountstuart to contradict the story in positive terms. He repeated his desire; he was urgent to have it contradicted, and said again: 'A widow!' straightening his whole figure to the erectness of the letter I. She was a widow unmarried a second time; and it has been known of the stedfast women who retain the name of their first husband, or do not hamper his title with a little new squire at their skirts, that they can partially approve the objections indicated by Sir Willoughby. They are thinking of themselves when they do so, and they will rarely say, 'I might have married'; rarely within them will they avow that, with their permission, it might have been. They can catch an idea of a gentleman's view of the the widow's cap. But a niceness that could feel sharply wounded by the simple rumour of his alliance with the young relict of an earl, was mystifying. Sir Willoughby unbent. His military letter I took a careless glance at itself lounging idly and proudly at ease in the glass of his mind, decked with a wanton wreath, as he dropped a hint, generously vague, just to show the origin of the rumour, and the excellent basis it had for not being credited. He was chidden. Mrs. Mountstuart read him a lecture. She was however able to contradict the tale of the young countess. 'There is no fear of his marrying her, my dears.'

Meanwhile there was a fear that he would lose his chance of marrying the beautiful Miss Durham.

The dilemmas of little princes are often grave. They should be dwelt on now and then for an example to poor struggling commoners of the slings and arrows* assailing fortune's most favoured men, that we may preach contentment to the wretch who cannot muster wherewithal to marry a wife, or has done it and trots the streets, packladen, to maintain the dame and troops of children painfully reared to fill subordinate stations. According to our reading, a moral is always welcome in a moral country, and especially so when silly envy is to be chastised by it, the restless craving for change rebuked. Young Sir Willoughby, then, stood in this dilemma:—a lady was at either hand of him; the only two that had ever, apart from metropolitan conquests, not to be recited,* touched his emotions. Susceptible to beauty, he had never seen so beautiful a girl as Constantia Durham. Equally susceptible to admiration of himself, he considered Laetitia Dale a paragon of cleverness. He stood between

the queenly rose and the modest violet. One he bowed
to; the other bowed to him. He could not have both;
it is the law governing princes and pedestrians alike.
But which could he forfeit? His growing acquaintance
with the world taught him to put an increasing price on
the sentiments of Miss Dale. Still Constantia's beauty
was of a kind to send away beholders aching. She had
the glory of the racing cutter full sail on a winning
breeze; and she did not court to win him, she flew. In
his more reflective hour the attractiveness of that lady
which held the mirror to his features was paramount.
But he had passionate snatches when the magnetism of
the flyer drew him in her wake. Further to add to the
complexity, he loved his liberty; he was princelier free;
he had more subjects, more slaves; he ruled arrogantly
in the world of women; he was more himself. His
metropolitan experiences did not answer to his liking the
particular question, Do we bind the woman down to us
idolatrously by making a wife of her?

In the midst of his deliberations, a report of the hot
pursuit of Miss Durham, casually mentioned to him by
Lady Busshe, drew an immediate proposal from Sir
Willoughby. She accepted him, and they were engaged.
She had been nibbled at, all but eaten up, while he hung
dubitative; and though that was the cause of his winning
her, it offended his niceness. She had not come to him
out of cloistral purity, out of perfect radiancy. Spiritually, likewise, was he a little prince, a despotic prince.
He wished for her to have come to him out of an egg-
shell, somewhat more astonished at things than a chicken,
but as completely enclosed before he tapped the shell,
and seeing him with her sex's eyes first of all men. She
talked frankly of her cousins and friends, young males.
She could have replied to his bitter wish: 'Had you
asked me on the night of your twenty-first birthday,
Willoughby!' Since then she had been in the dust of the
world, and he conceived his peculiar antipathy, destined
to be so fatal to him, from the earlier hours of his engagement. He was quaintly incapable of a jealousy of indi-
viduals. A young Captain Oxford*had been foremost in

the swarm pursuing Constantia. Willoughby thought as little of Captain Oxford as he did of Vernon Whitford. His enemy was the world, the mass, which confounds us in a lump, which has breathed on her whom we have selected, whom we cannot, can never, rub quite clear of her contact with the abominated crowd. The pleasure of the world is to bowl down our soldierly letter I; to encroach on our identity, soil our niceness. To begin to think is the beginning of disgust of the world.

As soon as the engagement was published, all the county said that there had not been a chance for Laetitia, and Mrs. Mountstuart Jenkinson humbly remarked, in an attitude of penitence: 'I'm not a witch.' Lady Busshe could claim to be one; she had foretold the event. Laetitia was of the same opinion as the county. She had looked up, but not hopefully. She had only looked up to the brightest, and, as he was the highest, how could she have hoped? She was the solitary companion of a sick father, whose inveterate prognostic of her, that she would live to rule at Patterne Hall, tortured the poor girl in proportion as he seemed to derive comfort from it. The noise of the engagement merely silenced him; recluse invalids cling obstinately to their ideas. He had observed Sir Willoughby in the society of his daughter, when the young baronet revived to a sprightly boyishness immediately. Indeed, as a big boy and little girl, they had played together of old. Willoughby had been a handsome fair boy. The portrait of him at the Hall, in a hat, leaning on his pony, with crossed legs and long flaxen curls over his shoulders, was the image of her soul's most present angel; and, as a man, he had—she did not suppose intentionally—subjected her nature to bow to him; so submissive was she, that it was fuller happiness for her to think him right in all his actions than to imagine the circumstances different. This may appear to resemble the ecstasy of the devotee of Juggernaut.* It is a form of the passion inspired by little princes, and we need not marvel that a conservative sex should assist to keep them in their lofty places. What were there otherwise to look up to? We should have no dazzling beacon-lights if they

were levelled and treated as clod earth; and it is worth
while for here and there a woman to be burnt,* so long as
women's general adoration of an ideal young man shall
be preserved. Purity is our demand of them. They may
justly cry for attraction. They cannot have it brighter
than in the universal bearing of the eyes of their sisters
upon a little prince, one who has the ostensible virtues in
his pay, and can practise them without injuring himself
to make himself unsightly. Let the races of men be by-
and-by astonished at their Gods, if they please. Meantime they had better continue to worship.

Laetitia did continue. She saw Miss Durham at Patterne on several occasions. She admired the pair. She
had a wish to witness the bridal ceremony. She was
looking forward to the day with that mixture of eagerness
and withholding which we have as we draw nigh the dis-
enchanting termination of an enchanting romance, when
Sir Willoughby met her on a Sunday morning, as she
crossed his park solitarily to church. They were within
ten days of the appointed ceremony. He should have
been away at Miss Durham's end of the county. He had,
Laetitia knew, ridden over to her the day before; but
here he was; and very unwontedly, quite surprisingly, he
presented his arm to conduct Laetitia to the church-door,
and talked and laughed in a way that reminded her of a
hunting gentleman she had seen once rising to his feet,
staggering from an ugly fall across hedge and fence into
one of the lanes of her short winter walks: 'All's well,
all sound, never better, only a scratch!' the gentleman
had said, as he reeled and pressed a bleeding head. Sir
Willoughby chattered of his felicity in meeting her. 'I
am really wonderfully lucky,' he said, and he said that
and other things over and over, incessantly talking, and
telling an anecdote of county occurrences, and laughing
at it with a mouth that would not widen. He went on
talking in the church porch, and murmuring softly some
steps up the aisle, passing the pews of Mrs. Mountstuart
Jenkinson and Lady Busshe. Of course he was entertaining, but what a strangeness it was to Laetitia! His
face would have been half under an antique bonnet. It

came very close to hers, and the scrutiny he bent on her was most solicitous.

After the service, he avoided the great ladies by sauntering up to within a yard or two of where she sat; he craved her hand on his arm to lead her forth by the park entrance to the church, all the while bending to her, discoursing rapidly, appearing radiantly interested in her quiet replies, with fits of intentness that stared itself out into dim abstraction. She hazarded the briefest replies for fear of not having understood him.

One question she asked: 'Miss Durham is well, I trust?'

And he answered: 'Durham?' and said: 'There is no Miss Durham to my knowledge.'

The impression he left with her was, that he might yesterday during his ride have had an accident and fallen on his head.

She would have asked that, if she had not known him for so thorough an Englishman, in his dislike to have it thought that accidents could hurt even when they happened to him.

He called the next day to claim her for a walk. He assured her she had promised it, and he appealed to her father, who could not testify to a promise he had not heard, but begged her to leave him to have her walk. So once more she was in the park with Sir Willoughby, listening to his raptures over old days. A word of assent from her sufficed him. 'I am now myself,' was one of the remarks he repeated this day. She dilated on the beauty of the Park and the Hall to gratify him.

He did not speak of Miss Durham, and Laetitia became afraid to mention her name.

At their parting, Willoughby promised Laetitia that he would call on the morrow. He did not come; and she could well excuse him, after her hearing of the tale.

It was a lamentable tale. He had ridden to Sir John Durham's mansion, a distance of thirty miles, to hear, on his arrival, that Constantia had quitted her father's house two days previously on a visit to an aunt in London, and had just sent word that she was the wife of Captain

Oxford, hussar,* and messmate of one of her brothers. A letter from the bride awaited Willoughby at the Hall. He had ridden back at night, not caring how he used his horse in order to get swiftly home, so forgetful of himself was he under the terrible blow. That was the night of Saturday. On the day following, being Sunday, he met Laetitia in his park, led her to church, led her out of it, and the day after that, previous to his disappearance for some weeks, was walking with her in full view of the carriages along the road.

He had indeed, you see, been very fortunately, if not considerately, liberated by Miss Durham. He, as a man of honour, could not have taken the initiative, but the frenzy of a jealous girl might urge her to such a course; and how little he suffered from it had been shown to the world. Miss Durham, the story went, was his mother's choice for him, against his heart's inclinations; which had finally subdued Lady Patterne. Consequently, there was no longer an obstacle between Sir Willoughby and Miss Dale. It was a pleasant and romantic story, and it put most people in good humour with the county's favourite, as his choice of a portionless girl of no position would not have done without the shock of astonishment at the conduct of Miss Durham, and the desire to feel that so prevailing a gentleman was not in any degree pitiable. Constantia was called 'that mad thing.' Laetitia broke forth in novel and abundant merits; and one of the chief points of requisition in relation to Patterne—a Lady Willoughby who would entertain well and animate the deadness of the Hall, became a certainty when her gentleness and liveliness and exceeding cleverness were considered. She was often a visitor at the Hall by Lady Patterne's express invitation, and sometimes on these occasions Willoughby was there too, superintending the fitting up of his laboratory, though he was not at home to the county; it was not expected that he should be yet. He had taken heartily to the pursuit of science, and spoke of little else. Science, he said, was in our days the sole object worth a devoted pursuit. But the sweeping remark could hardly apply to Laetitia, of whom he was the courteous quiet wooer you behold when a man has broken loose from an unhappy tangle to return to the lady of his first and strongest affections.

Some months of homely courtship ensued, and then, the decent interval prescribed by the situation having elapsed, Sir Willoughby Patterne left his native land on a tour of the globe.

CHAPTER IV

Laetitia Dale

THAT was another surprise to the county.

Let us not inquire into the feelings of patiently starving women: they must obtain some sustenance of their own, since, as you perceive, they live; evidently they are not in need of a great amount of nourishment; and we may set them down for creatures with a rushlight of animal fire to warm them. They cannot have much vitality who are so little exclamatory. A corresponding sentiment of patient compassion, akin to scorn, is provoked by persons having the opportunity for pathos and declining to use it. The public bosom was open to Laetitia for several weeks, and had she run to it to bewail herself, she would have been cherished in thankfulness for a country drama. There would have been a party against her, cold people, critical of her pretensions to rise from an unrecognized sphere to be mistress of Patterne Hall; but there would also have been a party against Sir Willoughby, composed of the two or three revolutionists, tired of the yoke, which are to be found in England when there is a stir; a larger number of born sympathetics, ever ready to yield the tear for the tear; and here and there a Samaritan soul*prompt to succour poor humanity in distress. The opportunity passed undramatized. Laetitia presented herself at church with a face mildly devout, according to her custom, and she accepted invitations to the Hall, she assisted at the read-ing of Willoughby's letters to his family, and fed on dry husks of him wherein her name was not mentioned; never one note of the summoning call for pathos did this young lady blow.

So, very soon the public bosom closed. She had, under the fresh interpretation of affairs, too small a spirit to be Lady Willoughby of Patterne; she could not have entertained becomingly; he must have seen that the girl was not the match for him in station, and off he went to conquer the remainder of a troublesome first attachment, no longer extremely disturbing, to judge from the tenour of his letters: really incomparable letters! Lady Busshe and Mrs. Mountstuart Jenkinson enjoyed a perusal of them. Sir Willoughby appeared as a splendid young representative island lord in these letters to his family, despatched from the principal cities of the United States of America. He would give them a sketch of 'our democratic cousins,' he said. Such cousins! They might all have been in the Marines. He carried his English standard over that Continent, and by simply jotting down facts, he left an idea of the results of the measurement to his family and friends at home. He was an adept in the irony of incongruously grouping. The nature of the Equality under the stars and stripes was presented in this manner. Equality! Reflections came occasionally:— 'These cousins of ours are highly amusing. I am among the descendants of the Roundheads. Now and then an allusion to old domestic differences, in perfect good temper. We go on in our way; they theirs, in the apparent belief that Republicanism operates remarkable changes in human nature. Vernon tries hard to think it does. The upper ten of our cousins are the Infernal of Paris.* The rest of them is Radical England, as far as I am acquainted with that section of my country.'—Where we compared, they were absurd; where we contrasted, they were monstrous. The contrast of Vernon's letters with Willoughby's was just as extreme. You could hardly have taken them for relatives travelling together, or Vernon Whitford for a born and bred Englishman. The same scenes furnished by these two pens might have been sketched in different hemispheres. Vernon had no irony.

He had nothing of Willoughby's epistolary creative power, which, causing his family and friends to exclaim, 'How like him that is!' conjured them across the broad Atlantic to behold and clap hands at his lordliness.

They saw him distinctly, as with the naked eye: a word, a turn of the pen, or a word unsaid, offered the picture of him in America, Japan, China, Australia, nay, the Continent of Europe, holding an English review of his Maker's grotesques. Vernon seemed a sheepish fellow, without stature abroad, glad of a compliment, grateful for a dinner, endeavouring sadly to digest all he saw and heard. But one was a Patterne; the other a Whitford. One had genius; the other pottered after him with the title of student. One was the English gentleman wherever he went; the other was a new kind of thing, nondescript, produced in England of late, and not likely to come to much good himself, or do much good to the country.

Vernon's dancing in America was capitally described by Willoughby. 'Adieu to our cousins!' the latter wrote on his voyage to Japan. 'I may possibly have had some vogue in their ball-rooms, and in showing them an English seat on horseback: I must resign myself if I have not been popular among them. I could not sing their national song—if a congery of States be a nation—and I must confess I listened with frigid politeness to their singing of it. A great people, no doubt. Adieu to them. I have had to tear old Vernon away. He had serious thoughts of settling, means to correspond with some of them.' On the whole, forgetting two or more 'traits of insolence' on the part of his hosts, which he cited, Willoughby escaped pretty comfortably. The President* had been, consciously or not, uncivil, but one knew his origin! Upon these interjections, placable flicks of the lionly tail addressed to Britannia the Ruler, who expected him in some mildish way to lash terga cauda* in retiring, Sir Willoughby Patterne passed from a land of alien manners; and ever after he spoke of America respectfully and pensively, with a tail tucked in, as it were. His travels were profitable to himself. The fact is, that there are cousins who come to greatness and must be pacified, or they will prove annoying. Heaven forefend a collision between cousins!

Willoughby returned to his England after an absence of three years. On a fair April morning, the last of the month, he drove along his park palings, and by the luck of things, Laetitia was the first of his friends whom he met. She was crossing from field to field with a band of school-children, gathering wild flowers for the morrow May-day. He sprang to the ground and seized her hand. 'Laetitia Dale!' he said. He panted. 'Your name is sweet English music! And you are well?' The anxious question permitted him to read deeply in her eyes. He found the man he sought there, squeezed him passionately,* and let her go, saying, 'I could not have prayed for a lovelier home-scene to welcome me than you and these children flower-gathering. I don't believe in chance. It was decreed that we should meet. Do not you think so?'

Laetitia breathed faintly of her gladness.

He begged her to distribute a gold coin among the little ones; asked for the names of some of them, and repeated, 'Mary, Susan, Charlotte—only the Christian names, pray! Well, my dears, you will bring your garlands to the Hall to-morrow morning; and mind, early! no slugabeds to-morrow; I suppose I am browned, Laetitia?' He smiled in apology for the foreign sun, and murmured with rapture, 'The green of this English country is unsurpassed. It is wonderful. Leave England and be baked, if you would appreciate it. You can't, unless you taste exile as I have done—for how many years? How many?'

'Three,' said Laetitia.

'Thirty!' said he. 'It seems to me that length. At least, I am immensely older. But looking at you, I could think it less than three. You have not changed. You are absolutely unchanged. I am bound to hope so. I shall see you soon. I have much to talk of, much to tell you. I shall hasten to call on your father. I have specially to speak with him. I—what happiness this is, Laetitia!

But I must not forget I have a mother. Adieu; for some hours—not for many!'

He pressed her hand again. He was gone.

She dismissed the children to their homes. Plucking primroses was hard labour now—a dusty business. She could have wished that her planet had not descended to earth, his presence agitated her so; but his enthusiastic patriotism was like a shower that in the Spring season of the year sweeps against the hard-binding East and melts the air, and brings out new colours, makes life flow; and her thoughts recurred in wonderment to the behaviour of Constantia Durham. That was Laetitia's manner of taking up her weakness once more. She could almost have reviled the woman who had given this beneficent magician, this pathetic exile, of the aristocratic sunburnt visage and deeply-scrutinizing eyes, cause for grief. How deeply his eyes could read! The starveling of patience awoke to the idea of a feast. The sense of hunger came with it, and hope came, and patience fled. She would have rejected hope to keep patience nigh her; but surely it cannot always be Winter! said her reasoning blood, and we must excuse her as best we can if she was assured by her restored warmth that Willoughby came in the order of the revolving seasons, marking a long Winter past. He had specially to speak with her father, he had said. What could that mean? What but—! She dared not phrase it or view it.

At their next meeting she was 'Miss Dale.'

A week later he was closeted with her father.

Mr. Dale, in the evening of that pregnant day, eulogized Sir Willoughby as a landlord. A new lease of the cottage was to be granted him on the old terms, he said. Except that Sir Willoughby had congratulated him in the possession of an excellent daughter, their inter-view was one of landlord and tenant, it appeared; and Laetitia said, 'So we shall not have to leave the cottage?' in a tone of satisfaction, while she quietly gave a wrench to the neck of the young hope in her breast. At night her diary received the line: 'This day I was a fool. To-morrow?'

To-morrow and many days after there were dashes instead of words.

Patience travelled back to her sullenly. As we must have some kind of food, and she had nothing else, she took to that and found it dryer than of yore. It is a composing but a lean dietary. The dead are patient, and we get a certain likeness to them in feeding on it unintermittingly overlong. Her hollowed cheeks with the fallen leaf in them pleaded against herself to justify her idol for not looking down on one like her. She saw him when he was at the Hall. He did not notice any change. He was exceedingly gentle and courteous. More than once she discovered his eyes dwelling on her, and then he looked hurriedly at his mother, and Laetitia had to shut her mind from thinking lest thinking should be a sin and hope a guilty spectre. But had his mother objected to her? She could not avoid asking herself. His tour of the globe had been undertaken at his mother's desire; she was an ambitious lady, in failing health; and she wished to have him living with her at Patterne, yet seemed to agree that he did wisely to reside in London.

One day Sir Willoughby, in the quiet manner which was his humour, informed her that he had become a country gentleman; he had abandoned London, he loathed it as the burial-place of the individual man. He intended to sit down on his estates and have his cousin Vernon Whitford to assist him in managing them, he said; and very amusing was his description of his cousin's shifts to live by literature, and add enough to a beggarly income to get his usual two months of the year in the Alps. Previous to his great tour, Willoughby had spoken of Vernon's judgement with derision; nor was it entirely unknown that Vernon had offended his family pride by some extravagant act. But after their return he acknowledged Vernon's talents, and seemed unable to do without him.

The new arrangement gave Laetitia a companion for her walks. Pedestrianism was a sour business to Willoughby, whose exclamation of the word indicated a willingness for any amount of exercise on horseback;

but she had no horse, and so, while he hunted, Laetitia and Vernon walked, and the neighbourhood speculated on the circumstances, until the ladies Eleanor and Isabel Patterne engaged her more frequently for carriage exercise, and Sir Willoughby was observed riding beside them.

A real and sunny pleasure befell Laetitia, in the establishment of young Crossjay Patterne under her roof; the son of the lieutenant, now captain, of Marines; a boy of twelve, with the sprights of twelve boys in him, for whose board and lodgement Vernon provided by arrangement with her father. Vernon was one of your men that have no occupation for their money, no bills to pay for repair of their property, and are insane to spend. He had heard of Captain Patterne's large family, and proposed to have his eldest boy at the Hall, to teach him; but Willoughby declined to house the son of such a father, predicting that the boy's hair would be red, his skin eruptive, and his practices detestable. So Vernon, having obtained Mr. Dale's consent to accommodate this youth, stalked off to Devonport, and brought back a rosy-cheeked, round-bodied rogue of a boy, who fell upon meats and puddings, and defeated them, with a captivating simplicity in his confession that he had never had enough to eat in his life. He had gone through a training for a plentiful table. At first, after a number of helps, young Crossjay would sit and sigh heavily, in contemplation of the unfinished dish. Subsequently, he told his host and hostess that he had two sisters above his own age, and three brothers and two sisters younger than he: 'All hungry!' said the boy.

His pathos was most comical. It was a good month before he could see pudding taken away from table without a sigh of regret that he could not finish it as deputy for the Devonport household. The pranks of the little fellow, and his revel in a country life, and muddy wildness in it, amused Laetitia from morning to night. She, when she had caught him, taught him in the morning; Vernon, favoured by the chase, in the afternoon. Young Crossjay would have enlivened any household.

He was not only indolent, he was opposed to the acquisition of knowledge through the medium of books, and
would say: 'But I don't want to!' in a tone to make a
logician thoughtful. Nature was very strong in him. He
had, on each return of the hour for instruction, to be
plucked out of the earth, rank of the soil, like a root, for
the exercise of his big round headpiece on those tyran-
nous puzzles. But the habits of birds, and the place for
their eggs, and the management of rabbits, and the tickling
of fish, and poaching joys with combative boys of the district, and how to wheedle a cook for a luncheon for a
whole day in the rain, he soon knew of his great nature.
His passion for our naval service was a means of screwing
his attention to lessons after he had begun to understand
that the desert had to be traversed to attain midship-
man's rank. He boasted ardently of his fighting father,
and, chancing to be near the Hall as he was talking to
Vernon and Laetitia of his father, he propounded a question close to his heart; and he put it in these words, following: 'My father's the one to lead an army!' when he
paused: 'I say, Mr. Whitford, Sir Willoughby's kind to
me, and gives me crown-pieces, why wouldn't he see my
father, and my father came here ten miles in the rain
to see him, and had to walk ten miles back, and sleep
at an inn?'

The only answer to be given was, that Sir Willoughby
could not have been at home. 'Oh! my father saw him,
and Sir Willoughby said he was not at home,' the boy
replied, producing an odd ring in the ear by his repetition of 'not at home' in the same voice as the apology,
plainly innocent of malice. Vernon told Laetitia, however, that the boy never asked an explanation of Sir
Willoughby.

Unlike the horse of the adage, it was easier to compel
young Crossjay to drink of the waters of instruction than
to get him to the brink. His heart was not so antagonistic
as his nature, and by degrees, owing to a proper mixture
of discipline and cajolery, he imbibed. He was whistling
at the cook's windows after a day of wicked truancy, on
an April night, and reported adventures over the supper

supplied to him. Laetitia entered the kitchen with a reproving forefinger. He jumped to kiss her, and went on
chattering of a place fifteen miles distant, where he had
seen Sir Willoughby riding with a young lady. The
impossibility that the boy should have got so far on foot
made Laetitia doubtful of his veracity, until she heard that
a gentleman had taken him up on the road in a gig, and
had driven him to a farm to show him strings of birds'
eggs and stuffed birds of every English kind, kingfishers,
yaffles,* black woodpeckers, goat-sucker owls, more mouth
than head, with dusty, dark-spotted wings, like moths;
all very circumstantial. Still, in spite of his tea at the
farm, and ride back by rail at the gentleman's expense,
the tale seemed fictitious to Laetitia until Crossjay related how that he had stood to salute on the road to the
railway, and taken off his cap to Sir Willoughby, and
Sir Willoughby had passed him, not noticing him, though
the young lady did, and looked back and nodded. The
hue of truth was in that picture.

Strange eclipse, when the hue of truth comes shadowing over our bright ideal planet. It will not seem the
planet's fault, but truth's. Reality is the offender; delusion our treasure that we are robbed of. Then begins
with us the term of wilful delusion, and its necessary
accompaniment of the disgust of reality; exhausting the
heart much more than patient endurance of starvation.

Hints were dropping about the neighbourhood; the
hedgeways twittered, the tree-tops cawed. Mrs. Mountstuart Jenkinson was loud on the subject: 'Patterne is to
have a mistress at last, you say? But there never was a
doubt of his marrying—he must marry; and, so long as
he does not marry a foreign woman, we have no cause to
complain. He met her at Cherriton. Both were struck
at the same moment. Her father is, I hear, some sort
of learned man; money; no land. No house either, I
believe. People who spend half their time on the Continent. They are now for a year at Upton Park. The very
girl to settle down and entertain when she does think of
settling. Eighteen, perfect manners; you need not ask
if a beauty. Sir Willoughby will have his dues. We must

teach her to make amends to him—but don't listen to
Lady Busshe! He was too young at twenty-three or
twenty-four. No young man is ever jilted; he is allowed
to escape. A young man married is a fire-eater bound
over to keep the peace; if he keeps it he worries it. At
thirty-one or thirty-two he is ripe for his command,
because he knows how to bend. And Sir Willoughby is
a splendid creature, only wanting a wife to complete
him. For a man like that to go on running about would
never do. Soberly—no! It would soon be getting ridiculous. He has been no worse than other men, probably
better—infinitely more excuseable; but now we have
him, and it was time we should. I shall see her and study
her, sharply, you may be sure; though I fancy I can rely
on his judgement.'

In confirmation of the swelling buzz, the Rev. Dr.
Middleton and his daughter paid a flying visit to the
Hall, where they were seen only by the members of the
Patterne family. Young Crossjay had a short conversation with Miss Middleton, and ran to the cottage full of
her—she loved the navy and had a merry face. She had
a smile of very pleasant humour, according to Vernon.
The young lady was outlined to Laetitia as tall, elegant,
lively; and painted as carrying youth like a flag. With
her smile of 'very pleasant humour,' she could not but
be winning.

Vernon spoke more of her father, a scholar of high
repute; happily, a scholar of an independent fortune.
His maturer recollection of Miss Middleton grew poetic,
or he described her in an image to suit a poetic ear:
'She gives you an idea of the Mountain Echo. Dr.
Middleton has one of the grandest heads in England.'

'What is her Christian name?' said Laetitia.

He thought her Christian name was Clara.*

Laetitia went to bed and walked through the day conceiving the Mountain Echo, the swift wild spirit, Clara by
name, sent fleeting on a far half-circle by the voice it is
roused to subserve; sweeter than beautiful, high above
drawing-room beauties as the colours of the sky; and if,
at the same time, elegant and of loveable smiling, could a

man resist her? To inspire the title of Mountain Echo
in any mind, a young lady must be singularly spiritualized. Her father doated on her, Vernon said. Who
would not? It seemed an additional cruelty that the
grace of a poetical attractiveness should be round her,
for this was robbing Laetitia of some of her own little
fortune, mystical though that might be. But a man like
Sir Willoughby had claims on poetry, possessing as he
did every manly grace; and to think that Miss Middleton
had won him by virtue of something native to her likewise, though mystically, touched Laetitia with a faint
sense of relationship to the chosen girl. 'What is in me,
he sees on her.' It decked her pride to think so, as a
wreath on the gravestone. She encouraged her imagination to brood over Clara, and invested her designedly
with romantic charms, in spite of pain: the ascetic zealot
hugs his share of heaven—most bitter, most blessed—in
his hair shirt and scourge, and Laetitia's happiness was
to glorify Clara. Through that chosen rival, through her
comprehension of the spirit of Sir Willoughby's choice of
one such as Clara, she was linked to him yet.

Her mood of ecstatic fidelity was a dangerous exalta-
tion: one that in a desert will distort the brain, and in the
world where the idol dwells will put him, should he come
nigh, to its own furnace-test, and get a clear brain out of
a burnt heart. She was frequently at the Hall, helping
to nurse Lady Patterne. Sir Willoughby had hitherto
treated her as a dear insignificant friend, to whom it was
unnecessary that he should mention the object of his
rides to Upton Park.

He had, however, in the contemplation of what he was
gaining, fallen into anxiety about what he might be
losing. She belonged to his brilliant youth; her devotion
was the bride of his youth; he was a man who lived backwards almost as intensely as in the present; and, notwithstanding Laetitia's praiseworthy zeal in attending on
his mother, he suspected some unfaithfulness: hardly
without cause: she had not looked paler of late, her eyes
had not reproached him; the secret of the old days between them had been as little concealed as it was exposed.

She might have buried it, after the way of women, whose bosoms can be tombs, if we and the world allow them to be; absolutely sepulchres, where you lie dead, ghastly. Even if not dead and horrible to think of, you may be lying cold, somewhere in a corner. Even if embalmed, you may not be much visited. And how is the world to know you are embalmed? You are no better than a rotting wretch to the world that does not have peeps of you in the woman's breast, and see lights burning and an occasional exhibition of the services of worship. There are women—tell us not of her of Ephesus!*—that have embalmed you, and have quitted the world to keep the tapers alight, and a stranger comes, and they, who have your image before them, will suddenly blow out the vestal flames and treat you as dust to fatten the garden of their bosoms for a fresh flower of love. Sir Willoughby knew it; he had experience of it in the form of the stranger; and he knew the stranger's feelings towards his predecessor and the lady.

He waylaid Laetitia, to talk of himself and his plans: the project of a run to Italy. Enviable? Yes, but in England you live the higher moral life. Italy boasts of sensual beauty; the spiritual is yours. 'I know Italy well; I have often wished to act as cicerone to you there. As it is, I suppose I shall be with those who know the land as well as I do, and will not be particularly enthusiastic: . . . if you are what you were?' He was guilty of this perplexing twist from one person to another in a sentence more than once. While he talked exclusively of himself, it seemed to her a condescension. In time he talked principally of her, beginning with her admirable care of his mother; and he wished to introduce 'a Miss Middleton' to her; he wanted her opinion of Miss Middleton; he relied on her intuition of character, had never known it err.

'If I supposed it could err, Miss Dale, I should not be so certain of myself. I am bound up in my good opinion of you, you see; and you must continue the same, or where shall I be?' Thus he was led to dwell upon friendship, and the charm of the friendship of men and women, 'Platonism,'*as it was called. 'I have laughed at it in the world, but not in the depth of my heart. The world's platonic attachments are laughable enough. You have taught me that the ideal of friendship *is* possible—when we find two who are capable of a disinterested esteem. The rest of life is duty; duty to parents, duty to country. But friendship is the holiday of those who can be friends. Wives are plentiful, friends are rare. I know *how* rare!'

Laetitia swallowed her thoughts as they sprang up. Why was he torturing her?—to give himself a holiday? She could bear to lose him—she was used to it—and bear his indifference, but not that he should disfigure himself; it made her poor. It was as if he required an oath of her when he said: 'Italy! But I shall never see a day in Italy to compare with the day of my return to England, or know a pleasure so exquisite as your welcome of me! Will you be true to that? May I look forward to just another such meeting?'

He pressed her for an answer. She gave the best she could. He was dissatisfied, and to her hearing it was hardly in the tone of manliness that he entreated her to reassure him; he womanized his language. She had to say: 'I am afraid I cannot undertake to make it an appointment, Sir Willoughby,' before he recovered his alertness, which he did, for he was anything but obtuse, with the reply, 'You would keep it if you promised, and freeze at your post. So, as accidents happen, we must leave it to fate. The will's the thing. You know my detestation of changes. At least I have you for my tenant, and wherever I am, I see your light at the end of my park.'

'Neither my father nor I would willingly quit Ivy Cottage,' said Laetitia.

'So far, then'; he murmured. 'You will give me a long notice, and it must be with my consent if you think of quitting?'

'I could almost engage to do that,' she said.

'You love the place?'

'Yes; I am the most contented of cottagers.'

'I believe, Miss Dale, it would be well for my happiness were I a cottager.'

'That is the dream of the palace. But to be one, and not to wish to be other, is quiet sleep in comparison.'

'You paint a cottage in colours that tempt one to run from big houses and households.'

'You would run back to them faster, Sir Willoughby.'

'You may know me,' said he, bowing and passing on contentedly. He stopped: 'But I am not ambitious.'

'Perhaps you are too proud for ambition, Sir Willoughby.'

'You hit me to the life!'

He passed on regretfully. Clara Middleton did not study and know him like Laetitia Dale.

Laetitia was left to think it pleased him to play at cat and mouse. She had not 'hit him to the life,' or she would have marvelled in acknowledging how sincere he was.

At her next sitting by the bedside of Lady Patterne, she received a certain measure of insight that might have helped her to fathom him, if only she could have kept her feelings down. The old lady was affectionately confidential in talking of her one subject, her son. 'And here is another dashing girl, my dear; she has money and health and beauty; and so has he; and it appears a fortunate union; I hope and pray it may be; but we begin to read the world when our eyes grow dim, because we read the plain lines, and I ask myself whether money and health and beauty on both sides, have not been the mutual attraction. We tried it before; and that girl Durham was honest, whatever we may call her. I should have desired an appreciative, thoughtful partner for him, a woman of mind, with another sort of wealth and beauty. She was honest, she ran away in time; there was a worse thing possible than that. And now we have the same chapter, and the same kind of person, who may not be quite as honest; and I shall not see the end of it. Promise me you will always be good to him; be my son's friend; his Egeria,* he names you. Be what you were to him when that girl broke his heart, and no one, not even his mother, was allowed to see that he suffered anything. Comfort him in his sensitiveness. Willoughby has the most entire faith in you. Were that destroyed—I shudder! You are, he says, and he has often said, his image of the constant woman. . . .'

Laetitia's hearing took in no more. She repeated to herself for days: 'His image of the constant woman!' Now, when he was a second time forsaking her, his praise of her constancy wore the painful ludicrousness of the look of a whimper on the face.

CHAPTER V

Clara Middleton

THE great meeting of Sir Willoughby Patterne and Miss Middleton had taken place at Cherriton Grange, the seat of a county grandee, where this young lady of eighteen was first seen rising above the horizon. She had money and health and beauty, the triune of perfect starriness, which makes all men astronomers. He looked on her, expecting her to look at him. But as soon as he looked he found that he must be in motion to win a look in return. He was one of a pack; many were ahead of him, the whole of them were eager. He had to debate within himself how best to communicate to her that he was Willoughby Patterne, before her gloves were too much soiled to flatter his niceness, for here and there, all around, she was yielding her hand to partners—obscurant males whose touch leaves a stain. Far too generally gracious was Her Starriness to please him. The effect of it, nevertheless, was to hurry him with all his might into the heat of the chase, while yet he knew no more of her than that he was competing for a prize and Willoughby Patterne only one of dozens to the young lady.

A deeper student of Science*than his rivals, he appreciated Nature's compliment in the fair one's choice of you. We now scientifically know that in this department of the universal struggle, success is awarded to the bettermost. You spread a handsomer tail than your fellows, you dress a finer top-knot, you pipe a newer note, have a longer stride; she reviews you in competition, and selects you.

The superlative is magnetic to her. She may be looking elsewhere, and you will see—the superlative will simply have to beckon, away she glides. She cannot help herself; it is her nature, and her nature is the guarantee for the noblest race of men to come of her. In complimenting you, she is a promise of superior offspring. Science thus—or it is better to say, an acquaintance with science facilitates the cultivation of aristocracy. Consequently a successful pursuit and a wresting of her from a body of competitors, tells you that you are the best man. What is more, it tells the world so.

Willoughby aired his amiable superlatives in the eye of Miss Middleton; he had a leg. He was the heir of successful competitors. He had a style, a tone, an artist tailor, an authority of manner: he had in the hopeful ardour of the chase among a multitude a freshness that gave him advantage; and together with his undeviating energy when there was a prize to be won and possessed, these were scarcely resistible. He spared no pains, for he was adust and athirst for the winning-post. He courted her father, aware that men likewise, and parents preeminently, have their preference for the larger offer, the deeper pocket, the broader lands, the respectfuller consideration. Men, after their fashion, as well as women, distinguish the bettermost, and aid him to succeed, as Dr. Middleton certainly did in the crisis of the memorable question proposed to his daughter within a month of Willoughby's reception at Upton Park. The young lady was astonished at his whirlwind wooing of her, and bent to it like a sapling. She begged for time; Willoughby could barely wait. She unhesitatingly owned that she liked no one better, and he consented. A calm examination of his position told him that it was unfair so long as he stood engaged and she did not. She pleaded a desire to see a little of the world before she plighted herself. She alarmed him; he assumed the amazing God of Love under the subtlest guise of the divinity. Willingly would he obey her behests, resignedly languish, were it not for his mother's desire to see the future lady of Patterne established there before she died. Love shone cunningly through the mask of filial duty, but the plea of urgency was reasonable. Dr. Middleton thought it reasonable, supposing his daughter to have an inclination. She had no disinclination, though she had a maidenly desire to see a little of the world—grace for one year, she said. Willoughby reduced the year to six months, and granted that term, for which, in gratitude, she submitted to stand engaged; and that was no light whispering of a word. She was implored to enter the state of captivity by the pronunciation of vows—a private but a binding ceremonial. She had health and beauty, and money to gild these gifts: not that he stipulated for money with his bride, but it adds a lustre to dazzle the world; and, moreover, the pack of rival pursuers hung close behind, yelping and raising their dolorous throats to the moon. Captive she must be.

He made her engagement no light whispering matter. It was a solemn plighting of a troth. Why not? Having said, I am yours, she could say, I am wholly yours, I am yours for ever, I swear it, I will never swerve from it, I am your wife in heart, yours utterly; our engagement is written above. To this she considerately appended, 'as far as I am concerned'; a piece of somewhat chilling generosity, and he forced her to pass him through love's catechism in turn, and came out with fervent answers that bound him to her too indissolubly to let her doubt of her being loved. And I am loved! she exclaimed to her heart's echoes, in simple faith and wonderment. Hardly had she begun to think of love ere the apparition arose in her path. She had not thought of love with any warmth, and here it was. She had only dreamed of love as one of the distant blessings of the mighty world, lying somewhere in the world's forests, across wild seas, veiled, encompassed with beautiful perils, a throbbing secrecy, but too remote to quicken her bosom's throbs. Her chief idea of it was, the enrichment of the world by love.

Thus did Miss Middleton acquiesce in the principle of selection.

And then did the best man of a host blow his triumphant horn, and loudly.

He looked the fittest; he justified the dictum of Science. The survival of the Patternes was assured. 'I would,' he said to his admirer, Mrs. Mountstuart Jenkinson, 'have bargained for health above everything, but she has everything besides—lineage, beauty, breeding: is what they call an heiress, and is the most accomplished of her sex.' With a delicate art he conveyed to the lady's understanding that Miss Middleton had been snatched from a crowd, without a breath of the crowd having offended his niceness. He did it through sarcasm at your modern young women, who run about the world nibbling and nibbled at, until they know one sex as well as the other, and are not a whit less cognizant of the market than men: pure, possibly; it is not so easy to say innocent; decidedly not our feminine ideal. Miss Middleton was different: she was the true ideal, fresh-gathered morning fruit in a basket, warranted by her bloom.

Women do not defend their younger sisters for doing what they perhaps have done—lifting a veil to be seen, and peeping at a world where innocence is as poor a guarantee as a babe's caul against shipwreck.* Women of the world never think of attacking the sensual stipulation for perfect bloom, silver purity, which is redolent of the Oriental origin of the love-passion of their lords. Mrs. Mountstuart congratulated Sir Willoughby on the prize he had won in the fair western-eastern.*

'Let me see her,' she said; and Miss Middleton was introduced and critically observed.

She had the mouth that smiles in repose. The lips met full on the centre of the bow and thinned along to a lifting dimple; the eyelids also lifted slightly at the outer corners and seemed, like the lip into the limpid cheek, quickening up the temples, as with a run of light, or the ascension indicated off a shoot of colour. Her features were play-fellows of one another, none of them pretending to rigid correctness, nor the nose to the ordinary dignity of governess among merry girls, despite which the nose was of a fair design, not acutely interrogative or inviting to gambols. Aspens imaged in water, waiting for the breeze, would offer a susceptible lover some suggestion of

her face: a pure smooth-white face, tenderly flushed in
the cheeks, where the gentle dints were faintly intermelting
even during quietness. Her eyes were brown, set well between mild lids, often shadowed, not unwakeful. Her hair
of lighter brown, swelling above her temples on the sweep
to the knot, imposed the triangle of the fabulous wild
woodland visage from brow to mouth and chin, evidently
in agreement with her taste; and the triangle suited her;
but her face was not significant of a tameless wildness or
of weakness; her equable shut mouth threw its long
curve to guard the small round chin from that effect;
her eyes wavered only in humour, they were steady
when thoughtfulness was awakened; and at such seasons
the build of her winter-beechwood hair lost the touch of
nymph-like and whimsical, and strangely, by mere outline, added to her appearance of studious concentration.
Observe the hawk on stretched wings over the prey he
spies, for an idea of this change in the look of a young
lady whom Vernon Whitford could liken to the Mountain Echo, and Mrs. Mountstuart Jenkinson pronounced
to be 'a dainty rogue in porcelain.'*

Vernon's fancy of her must have sprung from her
prompt and most musical responsiveness. He preferred
the society of her learned father to that of a girl under
twenty engaged to his cousin, but the charm of her ready
tongue and her voice was to his intelligent understanding
wit, natural wit, crystal wit, as opposed to the paste-
sparkle of the wit of the town. In his encomiums he did
not quote Miss Middleton's wit; nevertheless he ventured
to speak of it to Mrs. Mountstuart, causing that lady to
say: 'Ah, well, I have not noticed the wit. You may
have the art of drawing it out.'

No one had noticed the wit. The corrupted hearing of
people required a collision of sounds, Vernon supposed.
For his part, to prove their excellence, he recollected a
great many of Miss Middleton's remarks; they came flying to him; and as long as he forbore to speak them
aloud, they had a curious wealth of meaning. It could
not be all her manner, however much his own manner
might spoil them. It might be, to a certain degree, her

quickness at catching the hue and shade of evanescent conversation. Possibly by remembering the whole of a conversation wherein she had her place, the wit was to be tested; only how could any one retain the heavy portion? As there was no use in being argumentative on a subject affording him personally, and apparently solitarily, refreshment and enjoyment, Vernon resolved to keep it to himself. The eulogies of her beauty, a possession in which he did not consider her so very conspicuous, irritated him in consequence. To flatter Sir Willoughby, it was the fashion to exalt her as one of the types of beauty: the one providentially selected to set off his masculine type. She was compared to those delicate flowers, the ladies of the Court of China, on rice-paper. A little French dressing would make her at home on the sward by the fountain among the lutes and whisperers of the bewitching silken shepherdesses, who live though they never were. Lady Busshe was reminded of the favourite lineaments of the women of Leonardo, the angels of Luini.* Lady Culmer had seen crayon sketches of demoiselles of the French aristocracy resembling her. Some one mentioned an antique statue of a figure breathing into a flute: and the mouth at the flute-stop might have a distant semblance of the bend of her mouth, but this comparison was repelled as grotesque.

For once Mrs. Mountstuart Jenkinson was unsuccessful. Her 'dainty rogue in porcelain' displeased Sir Willoughby. 'Why rogue?' he said. The lady's fame for hitting the mark fretted him, and the grace of his bride's fine bearing stood to support him in his objection. Clara was young, healthy, handsome; she was therefore fitted to be his wife, the mother of his children, his companion picture. Certainly they looked well side by side. In walking with her, in drooping to her, the whole man was made conscious of the female image of himself by her exquisite unlikeness. She completed him, added the softer lines wanting to his portrait before the world. He had wooed her rageingly; he courted her becomingly; with the manly self-possession enlivened by watchful tact which is pleasing to girls. He never seemed to undervalue himself in valuing her: a secret priceless in the courtship of young women that have heads; the lover doubles their sense of personal worth through not forfeiting his own. Those were proud and happy days when he rode Black Norman over to Upton Park, and his lady looked forth for him and knew him coming by the faster beating of her heart.

Her mind, too, was receptive. She took impressions of his characteristics, and supplied him a feast. She remembered his chance phrases; noted his ways, his peculiarities, as no one of her sex had done. He thanked his cousin Vernon for saying she had wit. She had it, and of so high a flavour that the more he thought of the epigram launched at her, the more he grew displeased. With the wit to understand him, and the heart to worship, she had a dignity rarely seen in young ladies.

'Why rogue?' he insisted with Mrs. Mountstuart.

'I said—in porcelain,' she replied.

'Rogue perplexes me.'

'Porcelain explains it.'

'She has the keenest sense of honour.'

'I am sure she is a paragon of rectitude.'

'She has a beautiful bearing.'

'The carriage of a young princess!'

'I find her perfect.'

'And still she may be a dainty rogue in porcelain.'

'Are you judging by the mind or the person, ma'am?'

'Both.'

'And which is which?'

'There's no distinction.'

'Rogue and mistress of Patterne do not go together.'

'Why not? She will be a novelty to our neighbourhood and an animation of the Hall.'

'To be frank, rogue does not rightly match with *me*.'

'Take her for a supplement.'

'You like her?'

'In love with her! I can imagine life-long amusement in her company. Attend to my advice: prize the porcelain and play with the rogue.'

Sir Willoughby nodded unilluminated. There was

nothing of rogue in himself, so there could be nothing of it in his bride. Elfishness, tricksiness, freakishness, were antipathetic to his nature; and he argued that it was impossible he should have chosen for his complement a person deserving the title. It would not have been sanctioned by his guardian genius. His closer acquaintance with Miss Middleton squared with his first impressions; you know that this is convincing; the common jury justifies the presentation of the case to them by the grand jury; and his original conclusion, that she was essentially feminine, in other words, a parasite and a chalice, Clara's conduct confirmed from day to day. He began to instruct her in the knowledge of himself without reserve, and she, as she grew less timid with him, became more reflective.

'I judge by character,' he said to Mrs. Mountstuart.

'If you have caught the character of a girl,' said she.

'I think I am not far off it.'

'So it was thought by the man who dived for the moon in a well.'

'How women despise their sex!'

'Not a bit. She has no character yet. You are forming it, and pray be advised and be merry; the solid is your safest guide; physiognomy and manners will give you more of a girl's character than all the divings you can do. She is a charming young woman, only she is one of that sort.'

'Of what sort?' Sir Willoughby asked impatiently.

'Rogues in porcelain.'

'I am persuaded I shall never comprehend it!'

'I cannot help you one bit further.'

'The word rogue!'

'It was dainty rogue.'

'Brittle, would you say?'

'I am quite unable to say.'

'An innocent naughtiness?'

'Prettily moulded in a delicate substance.'

'You are thinking of some piece of Dresden you suppose her to resemble.'

'I daresay.'

'Artificial?'

'You would not have her natural?'

'I am heartily satisfied with her from head to foot, my dear Mrs. Mountstuart.'

'Nothing could be better. And sometimes she will lead, and generally you will lead, and everything will go well, my dear Sir Willoughby.'

Like all rapid phrasers, Mrs. Mountstuart detested the analysis of her sentence. It had an outline in vagueness, and was flung out to be apprehended, not dissected. Her directions for the reading of Miss Middleton's character were the same that she practised in reading Sir Willoughby's, whose physiognomy and manners bespoke him what she presumed him to be, a splendidly proud gentleman, with good reason.

Mrs. Mountstuart's advice was wiser than her procedure, for she stopped short where he declined to begin. He dived below the surface without studying that index-page. He had won Miss Middleton's hand; he believed he had captured her heart; but he was not so certain of his possession of her soul, and he went after it. Our enamoured gentleman had therefore no tally of Nature's writing above to set beside his discoveries in the deeps. Now it is a dangerous accompaniment of this habit of diving, that where we do not light on the discoveries we anticipate, we fall to work sowing and planting; which becomes a disturbance of the gentle bosom. Miss Middleton's features were legible as to the mainspring of her character. He could have seen that she had a spirit with a natural love of liberty, and required the next thing to liberty, spaciousness, if she was to own allegiance. Those features, unhappily, instead of serving for an introduction to the within, were treated as the mirror of himself. They were indeed of an amiable sweetness to tempt an accepted lover to angle for the first person in the second. But he had made the discovery that their minds differed on one or two points, and a difference of view in his bride was obnoxious to his repose. He struck at it recurringly to show her error under various aspects. He desired to shape her character to the feminine of his own, and betrayed the surprise of a slight disappointment at her advocacy of her ideas. She said immediately: 'It is not too late, Willoughby,' and wounded him, for he wanted her simply to be material in his hands for him to mould her; he had no other thought. He lectured her on the theme of the infinity of love. How was it not too late? They were plighted; they were one eternally; they could not be parted. She listened gravely, conceiving the infinity as a narrow dwelling where a voice droned and ceased not. However, she listened. She became an attentive listener.

CHAPTER VI

His Courtship

THE world was the principal topic of dissension between these lovers. His opinion of the world affected her like a creature threatened with a deprivation of air. He explained to his darling that lovers of necessity do loathe the world. They live in the world, they accept its benefits, and assist it as well as they can. In their hearts they must despise it, shut it out, that their love for one another may pour in a clear channel, and with all the force they have. They cannot enjoy the sense of security for their love unless they fence away the world. It is, you will allow, gross; it is a beast. Formally we thank it for the good we get of it; only we two have an inner temple where the worship we conduct is actually, if you would but see it, an excommunication of the world. We abhor that beast to adore that divinity. This gives us our oneness, our isolation, our happiness. This is to love with the soul. Do you see, darling?

She shook her head; she could not see it. She would admit none of the notorious errors of the world; its backbiting, selfishness, coarseness, intrusiveness, infectiousness. She was young. She might, Willoughby thought, have let herself be led: she was not docile. She must be up in arms as a champion of the world: and one saw she was hugging her dream of a romantic world, nothing else. She spoilt the secret bower-song he delighted to tell over to her. And how, Powers of Love! is love-making to be pursued if we may not kick the world out of our bower and wash our hands of it? Love that does not spurn the world when lovers curtain themselves is a love—is it not so?—that seems to the unwhipped scoffing world to go slinking into basiation's obscurity,* instead of on a glorious march behind the screen. Our hero had a strong sentiment as to the policy of scorning the world for the sake of defending his personal pride and (to his honour, be it said) his lady's delicacy.

The act of scorning put them both above the world, said, retro Sathanas!* So much, as a piece of tactics: he was highly civilized: in the second instance, he knew it to be the world which must furnish the dry sticks for the bonfire of a woman's worship. He knew, too, that he was prescribing poetry to his betrothed, practicable poetry. She had a liking for poetry, and sometimes quoted the stuff in defiance of his pursed mouth and pained murmur: 'I am no poet'; but his poetry of the enclosed and fortified bower, without nonsensical rhymes to catch the ears of women, appeared incomprehensible to her, if not adverse. She would not burn the world for him; she would not, though a purer poetry is little imaginable, reduce herself to ashes, or incense, or essence, in honour of him, and so, by love's transmutation, literally be the man she was to marry. She preferred to be herself, with the egoism of women! She said it: she said: 'I must be myself to be of any value to you, Willoughby.' He was indefatigable in his lectures on the aesthetics of love. Frequently, for an indemnification to her (he had no desire that she should be a loser by ceasing to admire the world), he dwelt on his own youthful ideas; and his original fancies about the world were presented to her as a substitute for the theme.

Miss Middleton bore it well, for she was sure that he meant well. Bearing so well what was distasteful to her, she became less well able to bear what she had merely noted in observation before: his view of scholarship; his manner toward Mr. Vernon Whitford, of whom her father spoke warmly; the rumour concerning his treatment

of a Miss Dale. And the country tale of Constantia
Durham sang itself to her in a new key. He had no contempt for the world's praises. Mr. Whitford wrote the
letters to the county paper which gained him applause
at various great houses, and he accepted it, and betrayed
a tingling fright lest he should be the victim of a sneer of
the world he contemned. Recollecting his remarks, her
mind was afflicted by the 'something illogical' in him
that we readily discover when our natures are no longer
running free, and then at once we yearn for a disputation.
She resolved that she would one day, one distant day,
provoke it—upon what? The special point eluded her.
The world is too huge a client, and too pervious, too
spotty, for a girl to defend against a man. That 'something illogical' had stirred her feelings more than her
intellect to revolt. She could not constitute herself the
advocate of Mr. Whitford. Still she marked the disputation for an event to come.

Meditating on it, she fell to picturing Sir Willoughby's
face at the first accents of his bride's decided disagreement with him. The picture once conjured up would
not be laid. He was handsome; so correctly handsome,
that a slight unfriendly touch precipitated him into caricature. His habitual air of happy pride, of indignant
contentment rather, could easily be overdone. Surprise,
when he threw emphasis on it, stretched him with the
tall eyebrows of a mask—limitless under the spell of
caricature; and in time, whenever she was not pleased
by her thoughts, she had that, and not his likeness, for
the vision of him. And it was unjust, contrary to her
deeper feelings; she rebuked herself, and as much as her
naughty spirit permitted, she tried to look on him as
the world did; an effort inducing reflections upon the
blessings of ignorance. She seemed to herself beset by a
circle of imps, hardly responsible for her thoughts.

He outshone Mr. Whitford in his behaviour to young
Crossjay. She had seen him with the boy, and he was
amused, indulgent, almost frolicsome, in contradistinc-
tion to Mr. Whitford's tutorly sharpness. He had the
English father's tone of a liberal allowance for boy's

tastes and pranks, and he ministered to the partiality of the genus for pocket-money. He did not play the schoolmaster, like bookworms who get poor little lads in their grasp.

Mr. Whitford avoided her very much. He came to Upton Park on a visit to her father, and she was not particularly sorry that she saw him only at table. He treated her by fits to a level scrutiny of deep-set eyes unpleasantly penetrating. She had liked his eyes. They became unbearable; they dwelt in the memory as if they had left a phosphorescent line. She had been taken by playmate boys in her infancy to peep into hedge-leaves, where the mother-bird brooded on the nest; and the eyes of the bird in that marvellous dark thickset home, had sent her away with worlds of fancy. Mr. Whitford's gaze revived her susceptibility, but not the old happy wondering. She was glad of his absence, after a certain hour that she passed with Willoughby, a wretched hour to remember. Mr. Whitford had left, and Willoughby came, bringing bad news of his mother's health. Lady Patterne was fast failing. Her son spoke of the loss she would be to him; he spoke of the dreadfulness of death. He alluded to his own death to come, carelessly, with a philosophical air.

'All of us must go! our time is short.'

'Very,' she assented.

It sounded like want of feeling.

'If you lose me, Clara!'

'But you are strong, Willoughby.'

'I may be cut off to-morrow.'

'Do not talk in such a manner.'

'It is as well that it should be faced.'

'I cannot see what purpose it serves.'

'Should you lose me, my love!'

'Willoughby!'

'Oh, the bitter pang of leaving you!'

'Dear Willoughby, you are distressed; your mother may recover; let us hope she will; I will help to nurse her; I have offered, you know; I am ready, most anxious. I believe I am a good nurse.'

'It is this belief—that one does not die with death!'

'That is our comfort.'

'When we love?'

'Does it not promise that we meet again?'

'To walk the world and see you perhaps . . . with another!'

'See me?—Where? Here?'

'Wedded . . . to another. You! my bride; whom I call mine; and you are! You would be still—in that horror! But all things are possible; women are women; they swim in infidelity, from wave to wave! I know them.'

'Willoughby, do not torment yourself and me, I beg you.'

He meditated profoundly, and asked her: 'Could you be such a saint among women?'

'I think I am a more than usually childish girl.'

'Not to forget me?'

'Oh! no.'

'Still to be mine?'

'I am yours.'

'To plight yourself?'

'It is done.'

'Be mine beyond death?'

'Married is married, I think.'

'Clara! to dedicate your life to our love! Never one touch! not one whisper! not a thought, not a dream! Could you?—it agonizes me to imagine . . . be inviolate? mine above?—mine before all men, though I am gone:— true to my dust? Tell me. Give me that assurance. True to my name!—Oh! I hear them. "His relict." Buzzings about Lady Patterne. "The widow." If you knew their talk of widows! Shut your ears, my angel! But if she holds them off and keeps her path, they are forced to respect her. The dead husband is not the dishonoured wretch they fancied him, because he was out of their way. He lives in the heart of his wife. Clara! my Clara! as I live in yours, whether here or away; whether you are a wife or widow, there is no distinction for love—I am your husband—say it—eternally. I must have peace; I cannot endure the pain. Depressed, yes;

I have cause to be. But it has haunted me ever since we joined hands. To have you—to lose you!'

'Is it not possible that I may be the first to die?' said Miss Middleton.

'And lose you, with the thought that you, lovely as you are, and the dogs of the world barking round you, might . . . . Is it any wonder that I have my feeling for the world? This hand!—the thought is horrible. You would be surrounded; men are brutes; the scent of unfaithfulness excites them, overjoys them. And I helpless! The thought is maddening. I see a ring of monkeys grinning. There is your beauty, and man's delight in desecrating. You would be worried night and day to quit my name, to . . . I feel the blow now. You would have no rest for them, nothing to cling to without your oath.'

'An oath!' said Miss Middleton.

'It is no delusion, my love, when I tell you that with this thought upon me I see a ring of monkey-faces grinning at me: they haunt me. But you do swear it! Once, and I will never trouble you on the subject again. My weakness! if you like. You will learn that it is love, a man's love, stronger than death.'

'An oath?' she said, and moved her lips to recall what she might have said and forgotten. 'To what? what oath?'

'That you will be true to me dead as well as living! Whisper it.'

'Willoughby, I shall be true to my vows at the altar.'

'To me! me!'

'It will be to you.'

'To my soul. No heaven can be for me—I see none, only torture, unless I have your word, Clara. I trust it. I will trust it implicitly. My confidence in you is absolute.'

'Then you need not be troubled.'

'It is for *you*, my love; that you may be armed and strong when I am not by to protect you.'

'Our views of the world are opposed, Willoughby.'

'Consent; gratify me; swear it. Say, "Beyond death."'

Whisper it. I ask for nothing more. Women think the husband's grave breaks the bond, cuts the tie, sets them loose. They wed the flesh—pah! What I call on you for is nobility: the transcendant nobility of faithfulness beyond death. "*His* widow!" let them say; a saint in widowhood.'

'My vows at the altar must suffice.'

'You will not? Clara!'

'I am plighted to you.'

'Not a word?—a simple promise? But you love me?'

'I have given you the best proof of it that I can.'

'Consider how utterly I place confidence in you.'

'I hope it is well placed.'

'I could kneel to you, to worship you, if you would, Clara!'

'Kneel to heaven, not to me, Willoughby. I am ... I wish I were able to tell what I am. I may be inconstant: I do not know myself. Think; question yourself whether I am really the person you should marry. Your wife should have great qualities of mind and soul. I will consent to hear that I do not possess them, and abide by the verdict.'

'You do; you do possess them!' Willoughby cried. 'When you know better what the world is, you will understand my anxiety. Alive, I am strong to shield you from it; dead, helpless—that is all. You would be clad in mail, steel-proof, inviolable, if you would ... But try to enter into my mind; think with me, feel with me. When you have once comprehended the intensity of the love of a man like me, you will not require asking. It is the difference of the elect and the vulgar; of the ideal of love from the coupling of the herds. We will let it drop. At least, I have your hand. As long as I live I have your hand. Ought I not to be satisfied? I am; only, I see farther than most men, and feel more deeply. And now I must ride to my mother's bedside. She dies Lady Patterne! It might have been that she ... but she is a woman of women! With a father-in-law!* Just heaven! Could I have stood by her then with the same feelings of reverence? A very little, my love, and everything gained for us by civilization crumbles; we fall back to the first mortar-bowl we were bruised and stirred in. My thoughts, when I take my stand to watch by her, come to this conclusion, that, especially in women, distinction is the thing to be aimed at. Otherwise we are a weltering human mass. Women must teach us to venerate them, or we may as well be bleating and barking and bellowing. So, now enough. You have but to think a little. I must be off. It may have happened during my absence. I will write. I shall hear from you? Come and see me mount Black Norman. My respects to your father. I have no time to pay them in person. One!'

He took the one—love's mystical number—from which commonly spring multitudes; but, on the present occasion, it was a single one, and cold. She watched him riding away on his gallant horse, as handsome a cavalier as the world could show, and the contrast of his recent language and his fine figure was a riddle that froze her blood. Speech so foreign to her ears, unnatural in tone, unmanlike even for a lover (who is allowed a softer dialect) set her vainly sounding for the source and drift of it. She was glad of not having to encounter eyes like Mr. Vernon Whitford's.

On behalf of Sir Willoughby, it is to be said that his mother, without infringing on the degree of respect for his decisions and sentiments exacted by him, had talked to him of Miss Middleton, suggesting a volatility of temperament in the young lady, that struck him as consentaneous with Mrs. Mountstuart's 'rogue in porcelain,' and alarmed him as the independent observations of two world-wise women. Nor was it incumbent upon him personally to credit the volatility in order, as far as he could, to effect the soul-insurance of his bride, that he might hold the security of the policy. The desire for it was in him; his mother had merely tolled a warning-bell that he had put in motion before. Clara was not a Constantia. But she was a woman, and he had been deceived by women, as a man fostering his high ideal of them will surely be. The strain he adopted was quite

natural to his passion and his theme. The language of
the primitive sentiments of men is of the same expression
at all times, minus the primitive colours when a modern
gentleman addresses his lady.

Lady Patterne died in the Winter season of the new
year. In April Dr. Middleton had to quit Upton Park,
and he had not found a place of residence, nor did he
quite know what to do with himself in the prospect of
his daughter's marriage and desertion of him. Sir Willoughby proposed to find him a house within a circuit
of the neighbourhood of Patterne. Moreover, he invited
the Rev. Doctor and his daughter to come to Patterne
from Upton for a month, and make acquaintance with
his aunts, the ladies Eleanor and Isabel Patterne, so that
it might not be so strange to Clara to have them as her
housemates after her marriage. Dr. Middleton omitted
to consult his daughter before accepting the invitation,
and it appeared, when he did speak to her, that it should
have been done. But she said mildly: 'Very well,
papa.'

Sir Willoughby had to visit the metropolis and an
estate in another county, whence he wrote to his betrothed daily. He returned to Patterne in time to arrange
for the welcome of his guests; too late, however, to ride
over to them; and, meanwhile, during his absence, Miss
Middleton had bethought herself that she ought to have
given her last days of freedom to her friends. After the
weeks to be passed at Patterne, very few weeks were left
to her, and she had a wish to run to Switzerland or Tyrol
and see the Alps;* a quaint idea, her father thought.
She repeated it seriously, and Dr. Middleton perceived
a feminine shuttle of indecision at work in her head,
frightful to him, considering that they signified hesitation
between the excellent library and capital wine-cellar of
Patterne Hall, together with the society of that promising young scholar Mr. Vernon Whitford, on the one side,
and a career of hotels—equivalent to being rammed into
monster artillery with a crowd every night, and shot off
on a day's journey through space every morning—on the
other.

'You will have your travelling and your Alps after the ceremony,' he said.

'I think I would rather stay at home,' said she.

Dr. Middleton rejoined: '*I* would.'

'But I am not married yet, papa.'

'As good, my dear.'

'A little change of scene, I thought . . .'

'We have accepted Willoughby's invitation. And he helps me to a house near you.'

'You wish to be near me, papa?'

'Proximate—at a remove: communicable.'

'Why should we separate?'

'For the reason, my dear, that you exchange a father for a husband.'

'If I do not want to exchange?'

'To purchase, you must pay, my child. Husbands are not given for nothing.'

'No. But I should have you, papa!'

'Should?'

'They have not yet parted us, dear papa.'

'What does that mean?' he asked fussily. He was in a gentle stew already, apprehensive of a disturbance of the serenity precious to scholars by postponements of the ceremony, and a prolongation of a father's worries.

'Oh, the common meaning, papa,' she said, seeing how it was with him.

'Ah,' said he, nodding and blinking gradually back to a state of composure, glad to be appeased on any terms; for mutability is but another name for the sex, and it is the enemy of the scholar.

She suggested that two weeks at Patterne would offer plenty of time to inspect the empty houses of the district, and should be sufficient, considering the claims of friends, and the necessity for going the round of London shops.

'Two or three weeks,' he agreed hurriedly, by way of compromise with that fearful prospect.

CHAPTER VII

The Betrothed

DURING the drive from Upton to Patterne, Miss Middleton hoped, she partly believed, that there was to be a change in Sir Willoughby's manner of courtship. He had been so different a wooer. She remembered with some half-conscious desperation of fervour what she had thought of him at his first approaches, and in accepting him. Had she seen him with the eyes of the world, thinking they were her own? That look of his, the look of 'indignant contentment,' had then been a most noble conquering look, splendid as a general's plume at the gallop. It could not have altered. Was it that her eyes had altered?

The spirit of those days rose up within her to reproach her and whisper of their renewal: she remembered her rosy dreams and the image she had of him, her throbbing pride in him, her choking richness of happiness: and also her vain attempting to be very humble, usually ending in a carol, quaint to think of, not without charm, but quaint, puzzling.

Now men whose incomes have been restricted to the extent that they must live on their capital, soon grow relieved of the forethoughtful anguish wasting them by the hilarious comforts of the lap upon which they have sunk back, insomuch that they are apt to solace themselves for their intolerable anticipations of famine in the household by giving loose to one fit or more of reckless lavishness. Lovers in like manner live on their capital from failure of income: they, too, for the sake of stifling apprehension and piping to the present hour, are lavish of their stock, so as rapidly to attenuate it: they have their fits of intoxication in view of coming famine: they force memory into play, love retrospectively, enter the old house of the past and ravage the larder, and would gladly, even resolutely, continue in illusion if it were possible for the broadest honey-store of reminiscences to hold out for a length of time against a mortal appetite:

which in good sooth stands on the alternative of a con-
sumption of the hive or of the creature it is for nourishing.
Here do lovers show that they are perishable. More
than the poor clay world they need fresh supplies, right
wholesome juices; as it were, life in the burst of the bud,
fruits yet on the tree, rather than potted provender. The
latter is excellent for by-and-by, when there will be a
vast deal more to remember, and appetite shall have but
one tooth remaining. Should their minds perchance have
been saturated by their first impressions and have retained them, loving by the accountable light of reason,
they may have fair harvests, as in the early time; but
that case is rare. In other words, love is an affair of two,
and is only for two that can be as quick, as constant in
intercommunication as are sun and earth, through the
cloud or face to face. They take their breath of life from
one another in signs of affection, proofs of faithfulness,
incentives to admiration. Thus it is with men and women
in love's good season. But a solitary soul dragging a log,
must make the log a God to rejoice in the burden. That
is not love.

Clara was the least fitted of all women to drag a log.
Few girls would be so rapid in exhausting capital. She
was feminine indeed, but she wanted comradeship, a
living and frank exchange of the best in both, with the
deeper feelings untroubled. To be fixed at the mouth of
a mine, and to have to descend it daily, and not to discover great opulence below; on the contrary, to be
chilled in subterranean sunlessness, without any substantial quality that she could grasp, only the mystery of
inefficient tallow-light in those caverns of the complacent
talking man: this appeared to her too extreme a probation for two or three weeks. How of a lifetime of it!

She was compelled by her nature to hope, expect, and
believe that Sir Willoughby would again be the man she
had known when she accepted him. Very singularly,
to show her simple spirit at the time, she was unaware of
any physical coldness to him; she knew of nothing but
her mind at work, objecting to this and that, desiring
changes. She did not dream of being on the giddy ridge

of the passive or negative sentiment of love, where one step to the wrong side precipitates us into the state of repulsion.

Her eyes were lively at their meeting—so were his. She liked to see him on the steps, with young Crossjay under his arm. Sir Willoughby told her in his pleasantest humour of the boy's having got into the laboratory that morning to escape his taskmaster, and blown out the windows. She administered a chiding to the delinquent in the same spirit, while Sir Willoughby led her on his arm across the threshold, whispering, 'Soon for good!' In reply to the whisper, she begged for more of the story of young Crossjay. 'Come into the laboratory,' said he, a little less laughingly than softly; and Clara begged her father to come and see young Crossjay's latest pranks. Sir Willoughby whispered to her of the length of their separation and his joy to welcome her to the house where she would reign as mistress *very* soon. He numbered the weeks. He whispered, 'Come.' In the hurry of the moment she did not examine a lightning terror that shot through her. It passed, and was no more than the shadow which bends the summer grasses, leaving a ruffle of her ideas, in wonder of her having feared herself for something. Her father was with them. She and Willoughby were not yet alone.

Young Crossjay had not accomplished so fine a piece of destruction as Sir Willoughby's humour proclaimed of him. He had connected a battery with a train of gunpowder, shattering a window-frame and unsettling some bricks. Dr. Middleton asked if the youth was excluded from the library, and rejoiced to hear that it was a sealed door to him. Thither they went. Vernon Whitford was away on one of his long walks.

'There, papa, you see he is not so very faithful to you,' said Clara.

Dr. Middleton stood frowning over MS. notes on the table, in Vernon's handwriting. He flung up the hair from his forehead and dropped into a seat to inspect them closely. He was now immoveable. Clara was obliged to leave him there. She was led to think that Willoughby

had drawn them to the library with the design to be rid
of her protector, and she began to fear him. She proposed to pay her respects to the ladies Eleanor and Isabel.
They were not seen, and a footman reported in the
drawing-room that they were out driving. She grasped
young Crossjay's hand. Sir Willoughby despatched him
to Mrs. Montague, the housekeeper, for a tea of cakes
and jam.

'Off!' he said, and the boy had to run.

Clara saw herself without a shield.

'And the garden!' she cried. 'I love the garden; I
must go and see what flowers are up with you. In Spring
I care most for wild flowers, and if you will show me
daffodils, and crocuses, and anemones . . .'

'My dearest Clara! my bride!' said he.

'Because they are vulgar flowers?' she asked him
artlessly, to account for his detaining her.

Why would he not wait to deserve her!—no, not deserve—to reconcile her with her real position; not reconcile, but to repair the image of him in her mind, before
he claimed his apparent right!

He did not wait. He pressed her to his bosom.

'You are mine, my Clara—utterly mine; every
thought, every feeling. We are one: the world may do
its worst. I have been longing for you, looking forward.
You save me from a thousand vexations. One is perpetually crossed. That is all outside us. We two! With
you I am secure! Soon! I could not tell you whether
the world's alive or dead. My dearest!'

She came out of it with the sensations of the frightened
child that has had its dip in sea-water, sharpened to think
that after all it was not so severe a trial. Such was her
idea; and she said to herself immediately: What am I
that I should complain? Two minutes earlier she would
not have thought it; but humiliated pride falls lower
than humbleness.

She did not blame him; she fell in her own esteem;
less because she was the betrothed Clara Middleton,
which was now palpable as a shot in the breast of a
bird, than that she was a captured woman, of whom it is

absolutely expected that she must submit, and when she would rather be gazing at flowers. Clara had shame of her sex. They cannot take a step without becoming bondwomen; into what a slavery! For herself, her trial was over, she thought. As for herself, she merely complained of a prematureness and crudity best unanalysed. In truth, she could hardly be said to complain. She did but criticize him and wonder that a man was unable to perceive, or was not arrested by perceiving, unwillingness, discordance, dull compliance; the bondwoman's due instead of the bride's consent. Oh, sharp distinction, as between two spheres!

She meted him justice; she admitted that he had spoken in a lover-like tone. Had it not been for the iteration of 'the world,' she would not have objected critically to his words, though they were words of downright appropriation. He had the right to use them, since she was to be married to him. But if he had only waited before playing the privileged lover!

Sir Willoughby was enraptured with her. Even so purely, coldly, statue-like, Dian-like,* would he have prescribed his bride's reception of his caress. The suffusion of crimson coming over her subsequently, showing her divinely feminine in reflective bashfulness, agreed with his highest definitions of female character.

'Let me conduct you to the garden, my love,' he said.

She replied, 'I think I would rather go to my room.'

'I will send you a wild-flower posy.'

'Flowers, no; I do not like them to be gathered.'

'I will wait for you on the lawn.'

'My head is rather heavy.'

His deep concern and tenderness brought him close.

She assured him sparklingly that she was well: she was ready to accompany him to the garden and stroll over the park.

'Head*ache* it is not,' she said.

But she had to pay the fee for inviting a solicitous accepted gentleman's proximity.

This time she blamed herself and him, and the world he abused, and destiny into the bargain. And she cared

less about the probation; but she craved for liberty.
With a frigidity that astonished her, she marvelled at the
act of kissing, and at the obligation it forced upon an
inanimate person to be an accomplice. Why was she
not free? By what strange right was it that she was
treated as a possession?

'I will try to walk off the heaviness,' she said.

'My own girl must not fatigue herself.'

'Oh, no; I shall not.'

'Sit with me. Your Willoughby is your devoted
attendant.'

'I have a desire for the air.'

'Then we will walk out.'

She was horrified to think how far she had drawn away
from him, and now placed her hand on his arm to appease her self-accusations and propitiate duty. He spoke
as she had wished; his manner was what she had wished;
she was his bride, almost his wife; her conduct was a kind
of madness; she could not understand it.

Good sense and duty counselled her to control her
wayward spirit.

He fondled her hand, and to that she grew accustomed; her hand was at a distance. And what is a hand?
Leaving it where it was, she treated it as a link between
herself and dutiful goodness. Two months hence she was
a bondwoman for life! She regretted that she had not
gone to her room to strengthen herself with a review of
her situation, and meet him thoroughly resigned to her
fate. She fancied she would have come down to him
amicably. It was his present respectfulness and easy
conversation that tricked her burning nerves with the
fancy. Five weeks of perfect liberty in the mountains,
she thought, would have prepared her for the day of bells.
All that she required was a separation offering new
scenes, where she might reflect undisturbed, feel clear
again.

He led her about the flower-beds; too much as if he
were giving a convalescent an airing. She chafed at it,
and pricked herself with remorse. In contrition she
expatiated on the beauty of the garden.

'All is yours, my Clara.'

An oppressive load it seemed to her! She passively yielded to the man in his form of attentive courtier; his mansion, estates, and wealth overwhelmed her. They suggested the price to be paid. Yet she recollected that on her last departure through the park she had been proud of the rolling green and spreading trees. Poison of some sort must be operating in her. She had not come to him to-day with this feeling of sullen antagonism; she had caught it here.

'You have been well, my Clara?'

'Quite.'

'Not a hint of illness?'

'None.'

'My bride must have her health if all the doctors in the kingdom die for it! My darling!'

'And tell me: the dogs?'

'Dogs and horses are in very good condition.'

'I am glad. Do you know, I love those ancient French châteaux and farms in one, where salon windows look on poultry-yard and stalls. I like that homeliness with beasts and peasants.'

He bowed indulgently.

'I am afraid we can't do it for you in England, my Clara.'

'No.'

'And I like the farm,' said he. 'But I think our drawing-rooms have a better atmosphere off the garden. As to our peasantry, we cannot, I apprehend, modify our class demarcations without risk of disintegrating the social structure.'

'Perhaps. I proposed nothing.'

'My love, I would entreat you to propose, if I were convinced that I could obey.'

'You are very good.'

'I find my merit nowhere but in your satisfaction.'

Although she was not thirsting for dulcet sayings, the peacefulness of other than invitations to the exposition of his mysteries and of their isolation in oneness, inspired her with such calm that she beat about in her brain, as if it were in the brain, for the specific injury he had committed. Sweeping from sensation to sensation, the young, whom sensations impel and distract, can rarely date their disturbance from a particular one; unless it be some great villain injury that has been done: and Clara had not felt an individual shame in his caress; the shame of her sex was but a passing protest that left no stamp. So she conceived she had been behaving cruelly, and said: 'Willoughby'; because she was aware of the omission of his name in her previous remarks.

His whole attention was given to her.

She had to invent the sequel: 'I was going to beg you, Willoughby, do not seek to spoil me. You compliment me. Compliments are not suited to me. You think too highly of me. It is nearly as bad as to be slighted. I am ... I am a ...' But she could not follow his example: even as far as she had gone, her prim little sketch of herself, set beside her real, ugly, earnest feelings, rang of a mincing simplicity, and was a step in falseness. How could she display what she was?

'Do I not know you?' he said.

The melodious bass notes, expressive of conviction on that point, signified as well as the words, that no answer was the right answer. She could not dissent without turning his music to discord, his complacency to amazement. She held her tongue, knowing that he did not know her, and speculating on the division made bare by their degrees of the knowledge; a deep cleft.

He alluded to friends in her neighbourhood and his own. The bridesmaids were mentioned.

'Miss Dale, you will hear from my aunt Eleanor, declines, on the plea of indifferent health. She is rather a morbid person, with all her really estimable qualities. It will do no harm to have none but young ladies of your own age; a bouquet of young buds: though one blowing flower among them ... However, she has decided. My principal annoyance has been Vernon's refusal to act as my best man.'

'Mr. Whitford refuses?'

'He half refuses. I do not take no from him. His pretext is a dislike to the ceremony.'

'I share it with him.'

'I sympathize with you. If we might say the words and pass from sight! There is a way of cutting off the world: I have it at times completely: I lose it again, as if it were a cabalistic phrase one had to utter. But with you! You give it me for good. It will be for ever, eternally, my Clara. Nothing can harm, nothing touch us; we are one another's. Let the world fight it out: we have nothing to do with it.'

'If Mr. Whitford should persist in refusing?'

'So entirely one, that there never can be question of external influences. I am, we will say, riding home from the hunt: I see you awaiting me: I read your heart as though you were beside me. And I know that I am coming to the one who reads mine! You have me, you have me like an open book, you, and only you!'

'I am to be always at home?' Clara said, unheeded, and relieved by his not hearing.

'Have you realized it?—that we are invulnerable! The world cannot hurt us: it cannot touch us. Felicity is ours, and we are impervious in the enjoyment of it. Something divine! surely something divine on earth? Clara!—being to one another that between which the world can never interpose! What I do is right: what you do is right. Perfect to one another! Each new day we rise to study and delight in new secrets. Away with the crowd! We have not even to say it; we are in an atmosphere where the world cannot breathe.'

'O the world!' Clara partly carolled on a sigh that sank deep.

Hearing him talk as one exulting on the mountain top, when she knew him to be in the abyss, was very strange, provocative of scorn.

'My letters?' he said incitingly.

'I read them.'

'Circumstances have imposed a long courtship on us, my Clara: and I, perhaps lamenting the laws of decorum —I have done so!—still felt the benefit of the gradual initiation. It is not good for women to be surprised by a sudden revelation of man's character. We also have

things to learn:—there is matter for learning everywhere. Some day you will tell me the difference of what
you think of me now, from what you thought when we
first . . . ?'

An impulse of double-minded acquiescence caused
Clara to stammer as on a sob:

'I—I daresay I shall.'

She added: 'If it is necessary.'

Then she cried out. 'Why do you attack the world?
You always make me pity it.'

He smiled at her youthfulness. 'I have passed through
that stage. It leads to my sentiment. Pity it, by all
means.'

'No,' said she, 'but pity it, side with it, not consider it
so bad. The world has faults; glaciers have crevasses,
mountains have chasms; but is not the effect of the
whole sublime? not to admire the mountain and the
glacier because they can be cruel, seems to me . . . And
the world is beautiful.'

'The world of nature, yes. The world of men?'

'Yes.'

'My love, I suspect you to be thinking of the world of
ball-rooms.'

'I am thinking of the world that contains real and
great generosity, true heroism. We see it round us.'

'We read of it. The world of the romance-writer!'

'No: the living world. I am sure it is our duty to love
it. I am sure we weaken ourselves if we do not. If I did
not, I should be looking on mist, hearing a perpetual
boom instead of music. I remember hearing Mr. Whitford say that cynicism is intellectual dandyism without
the coxcomb's feathers; and it seems to me that cynics
are only happy in making the world as barren to others
as they have made it for themselves.'

'Old Vernon!' ejaculated Sir Willoughby, with a countenance rather uneasy, as if it had been flicked with a
glove. 'He strings his phrases by the dozen.'

'Papa contradicts that, and says he is very clever and
very simple.'

'As to cynics, my dear Clara, oh! certainly, certainly:

you are right. They are laughable, contemptible. But understand me, I mean, we cannot feel, or if we feel we cannot so intensely feel, our oneness, except by dividing ourselves from the world.'

'Is it an art?'

'If you like. It is our poetry! But does not love shun the world? Two that love must have their substance in isolation.'

'No: they will be eating themselves up.'

'The purer the beauty, the more it will be out of the world.'

'But not opposed.'

'Put it in this way,' Willoughby condescended. 'Has experience the same opinion of the world as ignorance?'

'It should have more charity.'

'Does virtue feel at home in the world?'

'Where it should be an example, to my idea.'

'Is the world agreeable to holiness?'

'Then, are you in favour of monasteries?'

He poured a little runlet of half-laughter over her head, of the sound assumed by genial compassion.

It is irritating to hear that when we imagine we have spoken to the point.

'Now in my letters, Clara . . .'

'I have no memory, Willoughby!'

'You will however have observed that I am not completely myself in my letters . . .'

'In your letters to men, you may be.'

The remark threw a pause across his thoughts. He was of a sensitiveness terribly tender. A single stroke on it reverberated swellingly within the man, and most, and infuriately searching, at the spots where he had been wounded, especially where he feared the world might have guessed the wound. Did she imply that he had no hand for love-letters? Was it her meaning that women would not have much taste for his epistolary correspondence? She had spoken in the plural, with an accent on 'men.' Had she heard of Constantia? Had she formed her own judgement about the creature? The supernatural sensitiveness of Sir Willoughby shrieked a peal

of affirmatives. He had often meditated on the moral
obligation of his unfolding to Clara the whole truth
of his conduct to Constantia; for whom, as for other
suicides, there were excuses. He at least was bound to
supply them. She had behaved badly; but had he not
given her some cause? If so, manliness was bound to
confess it.

Supposing Clara heard the world's version first! Men
whose pride is their backbone suffer convulsions where
other men are barely aware of a shock, and Sir Willoughby was taken with galvanic jumpings of the spirit
within him, at the idea of the world whispering to Clara
that he had been jilted.

'My letters to men, you say, my love?'

'Your letters of business.'

'Completely myself in my letters of business?' He
stared indeed.

She relaxed the tension of his figure by remarking:

'You are able to express yourself to men as your meaning dictates. In writing to . . . to us it is, I suppose, more
difficult.'

'True, my love. I will not exactly say difficult. I
can acknowledge no difficulty. Language, I should say,
is not fitted to express emotion. Passion rejects it.'

'For dumb-show and pantomime?'

'No: but the writing of it coldly.'

'Ah, coldly!'

'My letters disappoint you?'

'I have not implied that they do.'

'My feelings, dearest, are too strong for transcription.
I feel, pen in hand, like the mythological Titan at war
with Jove,* strong enough to hurl mountains, and finding
nothing but pebbles. The simile is a good one. You
must not judge of me by my letters.'

'I do not; I like them,' said Clara.

She blushed, eyed him hurriedly, and seeing him complacent, resumed: 'I prefer the pebble to the mountain;
but if you read poetry you would not think human speech
incapable of . . . '

'My love, I detest artifice. Poetry is a profession.'

'Our poets would prove to you . . .'

'As I have often observed, Clara, I am no poet.'

'I have not accused you, Willoughby.'

'No poet, and with no wish to be a poet. Were I one, my life would supply material, I can assure you, my love. My conscience is not entirely at rest. Perhaps the heaviest matter troubling it is that in which I was least wilfully guilty. You have heard of a Miss Durham?'

'I have heard—yes—of her.'

'She may be happy. I trust she is. If she is not, I cannot escape some blame. An instance of the difference between myself and the world, now. The world charges it upon her. I have interceded to exonerate her.'

'That was generous, Willoughby.'

'Stay. I fear I was the primary offender. But I, Clara, I, under a sense of honour, acting under a sense of honour, would have carried my engagement through.'

'What had you done?'

'The story is long, dating from an early day, in the "downy antiquity of my youth," as Vernon says.'

'Mr. Whitford says that?'

'One of old Vernon's odd sayings. It's a story of an early fascination.'

'Papa tells me Mr. Whitford speaks at times with wise humour.'

'Family considerations—the lady's health among other things; her position in the calculations of relatives—intervened. Still there was the fascination. I have to own it. Grounds for feminine jealousy.'

'Is it at an end?'

'Now? with you? my darling Clara! indeed at an end, or could I have opened my inmost heart to you! Could I have spoken of myself so unreservedly that in part you know me as I know myself! Oh! but would it have been possible to enclose you with myself in that intimate union? so secret, unassailable!'

'You did not speak to her as you speak to me?'

'In no degree.'

'What *could* have . . . !' Clara checked the murmured exclamation.

Sir Willoughby's expoundings on his latest of texts would have poured forth, had not a footman stepped across the lawn to inform him that his builder was in the laboratory and requested permission to consult with him.

Clara's plea of a horror of a talk of bricks and joists excused her from accompanying him. He had hardly been satisfied by her manner, he knew not why. He left her, convinced that he must do and say more to reach down to her female intelligence.

She saw young Crossjay, springing with pots of jam in him, join his patron at a bound, and taking a lift of arms, fly aloft, clapping heels. Her reflections were confused. Sir Willoughby was admirable with the lad. 'Is he two men?' she thought: and the thought ensued: 'Am I unjust?' She headed a run with young Crossjay to divert her mind.

CHAPTER VIII

A Run with the Truant: A Walk with the Master

THE sight of Miss Middleton running inflamed young Crossjay with the passion of the game of hare and hounds. He shouted a view-halloo, and flung up his legs. She was fleet; she ran as though a hundred little feet were bearing her onward smooth as water over the lawn and the sweeps of grass of the park, so swiftly did the hidden pair multiply one another to speed her. So sweet was she in her flowing pace, that the boy, as became his age, translated admiration into a dogged frenzy of pursuit, and continued pounding along, when far outstripped, determined to run her down or die. Suddenly her flight wound to an end in a dozen twittering steps, and she sank. Young Crossjay attained her, with just breath enough to say: 'You are a runner!'

'I forgot you had been having your tea, my poor boy,' said she.

'And you don't pant a bit!' was his encomium.

'Dear me, no; not more than a bird. You might as well try to catch a bird.'

Young Crossjay gave a knowing nod. 'Wait till I get my second wind.'

'Now you must confess that girls run faster than boys.'

'They may at the start.'

'They do everything better.'

'They're flash-in-the-pans.'

'They learn their lessons.'

'You can't make soldiers or sailors of them, though.'

'And that is untrue. Have you never read of Mary Ambree? and Mistress Hannah Snell of Pondicherry? And there was the bride of the celebrated William Taylor. And what do you say to Joan of Arc? What do you say to Boadicea? I suppose you have never heard of the Amazons.'*

'They weren't English.'

'Then, it is your own countrywomen you decry, sir!'

Young Crossjay betrayed anxiety about his false position, and begged for the stories of Mary Ambree and the others who were English.

'See, you will not read for yourself, you hide and play truant with Mr. Whitford, and the consequence is you are ignorant of your country's history!' Miss Middleton rebuked him, enjoying his wriggle between a perception of her fun and an acknowledgement of his peccancy. She commanded him to tell her which was the glorious Valentine's day of our naval annals;* the name of the hero of the day, and the name of his ship. To these questions his answers were as ready as the guns of the good ship *Captain* for the Spanish four-decker.

'And that you owe to Mr. Whitford,' said Miss Middleton.

'He bought me the books,' young Crossjay growled, and plucked at grass-blades and bit them, foreseeing dimly but certainly the termination of all this.

Miss Middleton lay back on the grass, and said: 'Are you going to be fond of me, Crossjay?'

The boy sat blinking. His desire was to prove to her that he was immoderately fond of her already; and he might have flown at her neck had she been sitting up, but her recumbency and eyelids half closed excited wonder in him and awe. His young heart beat fast.

'Because, my dear boy,' she said, leaning on her elbow, 'you are a very nice boy, but an ungrateful boy, and there is no telling whether you will not punish any one who cares for you. Come along with me; pluck me some of these cowslips, and the speedwells near them; I think we both love wild-flowers.' She rose and took his arm. 'You shall row me on the lake while I talk to you seriously.'

It was she, however, who took the sculls at the boat-house, for she had been a playfellow with boys, and knew that one of them engaged in a manly exercise is not likely to listen to a woman.

'Now, Crossjay,' she said. Dense gloom overcame him like a cowl. She bent across her hands to laugh. 'As if I were going to lecture you, you silly boy!' He began to brighten dubiously. 'I used to be as fond of birdsnesting as you are. I like brave boys, and I like you for wanting to enter the Royal Navy. Only, how can you if you do not learn? You must get the captains to pass you, you know. Somebody spoils you: Miss Dale or Mr. Whitford.'

'Do they!' sang out young Crossjay.

'Sir Willoughby does?'

'I don't know about spoil. I can come round him.'

'I am sure he is very kind to you. I daresay you think Mr. Whitford rather severe. You should remember he has to teach you, so that you may pass for the navy. You must not dislike him because he makes you work. Supposing you had blown yourself up to-day! You would have thought it better to have been working with Mr. Whitford.'

'Sir Willoughby says, when he's married, you won't let me hide.'

'Ah! It is wrong to pet a big boy like you. Does not he what you call tip you, Crossjay?'

'Generally half-crown pieces. I've had a crown-piece. I've had sovereigns.'*

'And for that you do as he bids you? and he indulges you because you . . . Well, but though Mr. Whitford does not give you money, he gives you his time, he tries to get you into the navy.'

'He pays for me.'

'What do you say?'

'My keep. And, as for liking him, if he were at the bottom of the water here, I'd go down after him. I mean to learn. We're both of us here at six o'clock in the morning, when it's light, and have a swim. He taught me. Only, I never cared for school-books.'

'Are you quite certain that Mr. Whitford pays for you?'

'My father told me he did, and I must obey him. He heard my father was poor, with a family. He went down to see my father. My father came here once, and Sir Willoughby wouldn't see him. I know Mr. Whitford does. And Miss Dale told me he did. My mother says she thinks he does it to make up to us for my father's long walk in the rain and the cold he caught coming here to Patterne.'

'So you see you should not vex him, Crossjay. He is a good friend to your father and to you. You ought to love him.'

'I like him, and I like his face.'

'Why his face?'

'It's not like those faces! Miss Dale and I talk about him. She thinks that Sir Willoughby is the best-looking man ever born.'

'Were you not speaking of Mr. Whitford?'

'Yes; old Vernon. That's what Sir Willoughby calls him,' young Crossjay excused himself to her look of surprise. 'Do you know what he makes me think of?—his eyes, I mean. He makes me think of Robinson Crusoe's old goat in the cavern.* I like him because he's always the same, and you're not positive about some people. Miss Middleton, if you look on at cricket, in comes a safe man for ten runs. He may get more, and he never gets less; and you should hear the old farmers talk of him in the booth. That's just my feeling.'

Miss Middleton understood that some illustration from

the cricketing-field was intended to throw light on the boy's feeling for Mr. Whitford. Young Crossjay was evidently warming to speak from his heart. But the sun was low, she had to dress for the dinner-table, and she landed him with regret, as at a holiday over. Before they parted, he offered to swim across the lake in his clothes, or dive to the bed for anything she pleased to throw, declaring solemnly that it should not be lost.

She walked back at a slow pace, and sang to herself above her darker-flowing thoughts, like the reed-warbler on the branch beside the night-stream; a simple song of a light-hearted sound, independent of the shifting black and grey of the flood underneath.

A step was at her heels.

'I see you have been petting my scapegrace.'

'Mr. Whitford! Yes; not petting, I hope. I tried to give him a lecture. He's a dear lad, but, I fancy, trying.'

She was in fine sunset colour, unable to arrest the mounting tide. She had been rowing, she said; and, as he directed his eyes, according to his wont, penetratingly, she defended herself by fixing her mind on Robinson Crusoe's old goat in the recess of the cavern.

'I must have him away from here very soon,' said Vernon. 'Here he's quite spoilt. Speak of him to Willoughby. I can't guess at his ideas of the boy's future, but the chance of passing for the navy won't bear trifling with, and if ever there was a lad made for the navy, it's Crossjay.'

The incident of the explosion in the laboratory was new to Vernon.

'And Willoughby laughed?' he said. 'There are seaport crammers who stuff young fellows for examination, and we shall have to pack off the boy at once to the best one of the lot we can find. I would rather have had him under me up to the last three months, and have made sure of some roots to what is knocked into his head. But he's ruined here. And I am going. So I shall not trouble him for many weeks longer. Dr. Middleton is well?'

'My father is well, yes. He pounced like a falcon on your notes in the library.'

Vernon came out with a chuckle.

'They were left to attract him. I am in for a controversy.'

'Papa will not spare you, to judge from his look.'

'I know the look.'

'Have you walked far to-day?'

'Nine and a half hours. My Flibbertigibbet* is too much for me at times, and I had to walk off my temper.'

She cast her eyes on him, thinking of the pleasure of dealing with a temper honestly coltish, and manfully open to a specific.

'All those hours were required?'

'Not quite so long.'

'You are training for your Alpine tour.'

'It's doubtful whether I shall get to the Alps this year. I leave the Hall, and shall probably be in London with a pen to sell.'

'Willoughby knows that you leave him?'

'As much as Mont Blanc* knows that he is going to be climbed by a party below. He sees a speck or two in the valley.'

'He has not spoken of it.'

'He would attribute it to changes . . .'

Vernon did not conclude the sentence.

She became breathless, without emotion, but checked by the barrier confronting an impulse to ask, what changes? She stooped to pluck a cowslip.

'I saw daffodils lower down the park,' she said. 'One or two; they're nearly over.'

'We are well-off for wild-flowers here,' he answered.

'Do not leave him, Mr. Whitford.'

'He will not want me.'

'You are devoted to him.'

'I can't pretend that.'

'Then it is the changes you imagine you foresee . . .? If any occur, why should they drive you away?'

'Well, I'm two and thirty, and have never been in the fray: a kind of nondescript, half-scholar, and by nature half billman* or bowman or musketeer; if I'm worth any-

thing, London's the field for me. But that's what I have
to try.'

'Papa will not like your serving with your pen in
London: he will say you are worth too much for that.'

'Good men are at it; I should not care to be ranked
above them.'

'They are wasted, he says.'

'Error! If they have their private ambition, they may
suppose they are wasted. But the value to the world of
a private ambition I do not clearly understand.'

'You have not an evil opinion of the world?' said
Miss Middleton, sick at heart as she spoke, with the
sensation of having invited herself to take a drop of
poison.

He replied: 'One might as well have an evil opinion of
a river: here it's muddy, there it's clear; one day
troubled, another at rest. We have to treat it with common sense.'

'Love it?'

'In the sense of serving it.'

'Not think it beautiful?'

'Part of it is, part of it the reverse.'

'Papa would quote the "mulier formosa."'

'Except that "fish" is too good for the black extremity. "Woman" is excellent for the upper.'

'How do you say that?—not cynically, I believe.
Your view commends itself to my reason.'

She was grateful to him for not stating it in ideal contrast with Sir Willoughby's view. If he had, so intensely
did her youthful blood desire to be enamoured of the
world, that she felt he would have lifted her off her feet.
For a moment a gulf beneath had been threatening.
When she said, 'Love it?' a little enthusiasm would have
wafted her into space fierily as wine; but the sober, 'In
the sense of serving it,' entered her brain, and was matter for reflection upon it and him.

She could think of him in pleasant liberty, uncorrected
by her woman's instinct of peril. He had neither arts
nor graces; nothing of his cousin's easy social front-
face. She had once witnessed the military precision of his

dancing, and had to learn to like him before she ceased to pray that she might never be the victim of it as his partner. He walked heroically, his pedestrian vigour being famous, but that means one who walks away from the sex, not excelling in the recreations where men and women join hands. He was not much of a horseman either. Sir Willoughby enjoyed seeing him on horseback. And he could scarcely be said to shine in a drawing-room, unless when seated beside a person ready for real talk. Even more than his merits, his demerits pointed him out as a man to be a friend to a young woman who wanted one. His way of life pictured to her troubled spirit an enviable smoothness: and his having achieved that smooth way she considered a sign of strength; and she wished to lean in idea upon some friendly strength. His reputation for indifference to the frivolous charms of girls clothed him with a noble coldness, and gave him the distinction of a far-seen solitary iceberg in Southern waters. The popular notion of hereditary titled aristocracy resembles her sentiment for a man that would not flatter and could not be flattered by her sex: he appeared superior almost to awfulness. She was young, but she had received much flattery in her ears, and by it she had been snared; and he, disdaining to practise the fowler's arts or to cast a thought on small fowls, appeared to her to have a pride founded on natural loftiness.

They had not spoken for a while, when Vernon said abruptly: 'The boy's future rather depends on you, Miss Middleton. I mean to leave as soon as possible, and I do not like his being here without me, though you will look after him, I have no doubt. But you may not at first see where the spoiling hurts him. He should be packed off at once to the crammer, before you are Lady Patterne. Use your influence. Willoughby will support the lad at your request. The cost cannot be great. There are strong grounds against my having him in London, even if I could manage it. May I count on you?'

'I will mention it: I will do my best,' said Miss Middleton, strangely dejected.

They were now on the lawn, where Sir Willoughby

was walking with the ladies Eleanor and Isabel, his maiden aunts.

'You seem to have coursed the hare and captured the hart': he said to his bride.

'Started the truant and run down the paedagogue,' said Vernon.

'Ay, you won't listen to me about the management of that boy,' Sir Willoughby retorted.

The ladies embraced Miss Middleton. One offered up an ejaculation in eulogy of her looks, the other of her healthfulness: then both remarked that with indulgence young Crossjay could be induced to do anything. Clara wondered whether inclination or Sir Willoughby had disciplined their individuality out of them and made them his shadows, his echoes. She gazed from them to him, and feared him. But as yet she had not experienced the power in him which could threaten and wrestle to subject the members of his household to the state of satellites. Though she had in fact been giving battle to it for several months, she had held her own too well to perceive definitely the character of the spirit opposing her.

She said to the ladies: 'Ah, no! Mr. Whitford has chosen the only method for teaching a boy like Crossjay.'

'I propose to make a man of him,' said Sir Willoughby.

'What is to become of him if he learns nothing?'

'If he pleases me, he will be provided for. I have never abandoned a dependant.'

Clara let her eyes rest on his, and without turning or dropping, shut them.

The effect was discomforting to him. He was very sensitive to the intentions of eyes and tones; which was one secret of his rigid grasp of the dwellers in his household. They were taught that they had to render agreement under sharp scrutiny. Studious eyes, devoid of warmth, devoid of the shyness of sex, that suddenly closed on their look, signified a want of comprehension of some kind, it might be hostility of understanding. Was it possible he did not possess her utterly? He frowned up.

Clara saw the lift of his brows, and thought: 'My mind is my own, married or not.'

It was the point in dispute.

CHAPTER IX

Clara and Laetitia meet: they are Compared

An hour before the time for lessons next morning young Crossjay was on the lawn with a big bunch of wild-flowers. He left them at the Hall-door for Miss Middleton, and vanished into bushes.

These vulgar weeds were about to be dismissed to the dust-heap by the great officials of the household; but as it happened that Miss Middleton had seen them from the window in Crossjay's hands, the discovery was made that they were indeed his presentation-bouquet, and a foot-man received orders to place them before her. She was very pleased. The arrangement of the flowers bore wit-ness to fairer fingers than the boy's own in the disposition of the rings of colour, red campion and anemone, cowslip and speedwell, primroses and wood-hyacinths; and rising out of the blue was a branch bearing thick white blos-som, so thick, and of so pure a whiteness, that Miss Middleton, while praising Crossjay for soliciting the aid of Miss Dale, was at a loss to name the tree.

'It is a gardener's improvement on the Vestal*of the forest, the wild cherry,' said Dr. Middleton, 'and in this case we may admit the gardener's claim to be valid, though I believe that, with his gift of double-blossom, he has improved away the fruit. Call this the Vestal of civilization, then; he has at least done something to vindicate the beauty of the office as well as the justness of the title.'

'It is Vernon's Holy Tree the young rascal has been despoiling,' said Sir Willoughby merrily.

Miss Middleton was informed that this double-blossom wild cherry-tree was worshipped by Mr. Whitford.

Sir Willoughby promised he would conduct her to it. 'You,' he said to her, 'can bear the trial; few complexions

can; it is to most ladies a crueller test than snow. Miss
Dale, for example, becomes old lace within a dozen
yards of it. I should like to place her under the tree
beside you.'

'Dear me, though; but that is investing the hama-
dryad with novel and terrible functions,' exclaimed Dr.
Middleton.

Clara said, 'Miss Dale could drag me into a superior
Court to show me fading beside her in gifts more valuable
than a complexion.'

'She has a fine ability,' said Vernon.

All the world knew, so Clara knew of Miss Dale's
romantic admiration of Sir Willoughby; she was curious
to see Miss Dale and study the nature of a devotion that
might be, within reason, imitable—for a man who could
speak with such steely coldness of the poor lady he had
fascinated? Well, perhaps it was good for the hearts of
women to be beneath a frost; to be schooled, restrained,
turned inward on their dreams. Yes, then, his coldness
was desireable; it encouraged an ideal of him. It suggested and seemed to propose to Clara's mind the divine-
ness of separation instead of the deadly accuracy of an
intimate perusal. She tried to look on him as Miss Dale
might look, and while partly despising her for the dupery
she envied, and more than criticizing him for the inhuman
numbness of sentiment which offered up his worshipper
to point a complimentary comparison, she was able to
imagine a distance whence it would be possible to observe
him uncritically, kindly, admiringly; as the moon a
handsome mortal, for example.

In the midst of her thoughts, she surprised herself by
saying, 'I certainly was difficult to instruct. I might see
things clearer if I had a fine ability. I never remember
to have been perfectly pleased with my immediate
lesson . . .'

She stopped, wondering whither her tongue was leading her; then added, to save herself, 'And that may be
why I feel for poor Crossjay.'

Mr. Whitford apparently did not think it remarkable
that she should have been set off gabbling of a 'fine

ability,' though the eulogistic phrase had been pronounced by him with an impressiveness to make his ear
aware of an echo.

Sir Willoughby dispersed her vapourish confusion.
'Exactly,' he said. 'I have insisted with Vernon, I don't
know how often, that you must have the lad by his affections. He won't bear driving. It had no effect on me.
Boys of spirit kick at it. I think I know boys, Clara.'

He found himself addressing eyes that regarded him as
though he were a small speck, a pin's head, in the circle
of their remote contemplation. They were wide; they
closed.

She opened them to gaze elsewhere.

He was very sensitive.

Even then, when knowingly wounding him, or because
of it, she was trying to climb back to that altitude of the
thin division of neutral ground, from which we see a
lover's faults and are above them, pure surveyors. She
climbed unsuccessfully, it is true; soon despairing and
using the effort as a pretext to fall back lower.

Dr. Middleton withdrew Sir Willoughby's attention
from the imperceptible annoyance:

'No, sir, no; the birch! the birch! Boys of spirit commonly turn into solid men, and the solider the men the
more surely do they vote for Busby.* For me, I pray he
may be immortal in Great Britain. Sea-air nor moun-
tain-air is half so bracing. I venture to say that the power
to take a licking is better worth having than the power to
administer one. Horse him and birch him* if Crossjay
runs from his books.'

'It is your opinion, sir?' his host bowed to him affably,
shocked on behalf of the ladies.

'So positively so, sir, that I will undertake without
knowledge of their antecedents, to lay my finger on the
men in public life who have not had early Busby. They
are ill-balanced men. Their seat of reason is not a concrete. They won't take rough and smooth as they come.
They make bad blood, can't forgive, sniff right and left
for approbation, and are excited to anger if an East wind
does not flatter them. Why, sir, when they have grown

to be seniors, you find these men mixed up with the nonsense of their youth; you see they are unthreshed. We English beat the world because we take a licking well. I hold it for a surety of a proper sweetness of blood.'

The smile of Sir Willoughby waxed ever softer as the shakes of his head increased in contradictoriness. 'And yet,' said he, with the air of conceding a little after having answered the Rev. Doctor and convicted him of error, 'Jack requires it to keep him in order. On board ship your argument may apply. Not, I suspect, among gentlemen. No.'

'Good night to your gentlemen!' said Dr. Middleton.

Clara heard Miss Eleanor and Miss Isabel interchange remarks:

'Willoughby would not have suffered it!'

'It would entirely have altered him!'

She sighed and put a tooth on her underlip. The gift of humourous fancy is in women fenced round with forbidding placards; they have to choke it; if they perceive a piece of humour, for instance, the young Willoughby grasped by his master, and his horrified relatives rigid at the sight of preparations for the deed of sacrilege, they have to blindfold the mind's eye. They are society's hard-drilled soldiery, Prussians that must both march and think in step.* It is for the advantage of the civilized world, if you like, since men have decreed it, or matrons have so read the decree; but here and there a younger woman, haply an uncorrected insurgent of the sex matured here and there, feels that her lot was cast with her head in a narrower pit than her limbs.

Clara speculated as to whether Miss Dale might be perchance a person of a certain liberty of mind. She asked for some little, only some little, free play of mind in a house that seemed to wear, as it were, a cap of iron. Sir Willoughby not merely ruled, he throned, he inspired: and how? She had noticed an irascible sensitiveness in him alert against a shadow of disagreement; and as he was kind when perfectly appeased, the sop was offered by him for submission. She noticed that even Mr. Whitford forebore to alarm the sentiment of authority

in his cousin. If he did not breathe Sir Willoughby,
like the ladies Eleanor and Isabel, he would either
acquiesce in a syllable, or be silent. He never strongly
dissented. The habit of the house, with its iron cap, was
on him; as it was on the servants, and would be, Oh,
shudders of the shipwrecked that see their end in drowning! on the wife.

'When do I meet Miss Dale?' she inquired.

'This very evening, at dinner,' replied Sir Willoughby.
Then, thought she, there is that to look forward to!

She indulged her morbid fit, and shut up her senses
that she might live in the anticipation of meeting Miss
Dale; and, long before the approach of the hour, her
hope of encountering any other than another dull ad-
herent of Sir Willoughby had fled. So she was languid
for two of the three minutes when she sat alone with
Laetitia in the drawing-room before the ladies had assembled.

'It is Miss Middleton?' Laetitia said, advancing to her.
'My jealousy tells me; for you have won my boy Crossjay's heart, and done more to bring him to obedience in
a few minutes than we have been able to do in months.'

'His wild-flowers were so welcome to me,' said Clara.

'He was very modest over them. And I mention it
because boys of his age usually thrust their gifts in our
faces fresh as they pluck them, and you were to be
treated quite differently.'

'We saw his good fairy's hand.'

'She resigns her office; but I pray you not to love him
too well in return; for he ought to be away reading with
one of those men who get boys through their examina-
tions. He is, we all think, a born sailor, and his place is
in the navy.'

'But, Miss Dale, I love him so well that I shall consult
his interests and not my own selfishness. And, if I have
influence, he will not be a week with you longer. It
should have been spoken of to-day; I must have been in
some dream; I thought of it, I know. I will not forget to
do what may be in my power.'

Clara's heart sank at the renewed engagement and

plighting of herself involved in her asking a favour, urging any sort of petition. The cause was good. Besides, she was plighted already.

'Sir Willoughby is really fond of the boy,' she said.

'He is fond of exciting fondness in the boy,' said Miss Dale. 'He has not dealt much with children. I am sure he likes Crossjay; he could not otherwise be so forbearing; it is wonderful what he endures and laughs at.'

Sir Willoughby entered. The presence of Miss Dale illuminated him as the burning taper lights up consecrated plate. Deeply respecting her for her constancy, esteeming her for a model of taste, he was never in her society without that happy consciousness of shining which calls forth the treasures of the man; and these it is no exaggeration to term unbounded, when all that comes from him is taken for gold.

The effect of the evening on Clara was to render her distrustful of her later antagonism. She had unknowingly passed into the spirit of Miss Dale, Sir Willoughby aiding; for she could sympathize with the view of his constant admirer on seeing him so cordially and smoothly gay; as one may say, domestically witty, the most agreeable form of wit. Mrs. Mountstuart Jenkinson discerned that he had a leg of physical perfection; Miss Dale distinguished it in him in the vital essence; and before either of these ladies he was not simply a radiant, he was a productive creature, so true it is that praise is our fructifying sun. He had even a touch of the romantic air which Clara remembered as her first impression of the favourite of the county: and strange she found it to observe this resuscitated idea confronting her experience. What if she had been captious, inconsiderate? O blissful revival of the sense of peace! The happiness of pain departing was all that she looked for, and her conception of liberty was to learn to love her chains, provided that he would spare her the caress. In this mood she sternly condemned Constantia. 'We must try to do good; we must not be thinking of ourselves; we must make the best of our path in life.' She revolved these infantile precepts with humble earnestness; and not to be tardy in her

striving to do good, with a remote but pleasurable
glimpse of Mr. Whitford hearing of it, she took the opportunity to speak to Sir Willoughby on the subject of young
Crossjay, at a moment when, alighting from horseback,
he had shown himself to advantage among a gallant
cantering company. He showed to great advantage on
horseback among men, being invariably the best mounted, and he had a cavalierly style, possibly cultivated,
but effective. On foot his raised head and half-dropped
eyelids too palpably assumed superiority. 'Willoughby,
I want to speak,' she said, and shrank as she spoke,
lest he should immediately grant everything in the mood
of courtship, and invade her respite; 'I want to speak
of that dear boy Crossjay. You are fond of him. He is
rather an idle boy here, and wasting time . . .'

'Now you are here, and when you are here for good,
my love, for good . . .' he fluted away in loverliness,
forgetful of Crossjay, whom he presently took up. 'The
boy recognizes his most sovereign lady, and will do your
bidding, though you should order him to learn his lessons! Who would not obey? Your beauty alone commands. But what is there beyond?—a grace, a hue
divine, that sets you not so much above as apart, severed
from the world.'

Clara produced an active smile in duty, and pursued:
'If Crossjay were sent at once to some house where men
prepare boys to pass for the navy, he would have his
chance, and the navy is distinctly his profession. His
father is a brave man, and he inherits bravery, and he has
a passion for a sailor's life; only he must be able to pass
his examination, and he has not much time.'

Sir Willoughby gave a slight laugh in sad amusement.
'My dear Clara, you adore the world; and I suppose
you have to learn that there is not a question in this
wrangling world about which we have not disputes and
contests ad nauseam.* I have my notions concerning
Crossjay, Vernon has his. I should wish to make a
gentleman of him. Vernon marks him for a sailor. But
Vernon is the lad's protector, I am not. Vernon took
him from his father to instruct him, and he has a right to

say what shall be done with him. I do not interfere.
Only I can't prevent the lad from liking me. Old Vernon
seems to feel it. I assure you I hold entirely aloof. If I
am asked, in spite of my disapproval of Vernon's plans
for the boy, to subscribe to his departure, I can but shrug,
because, as you see, I have never opposed. Old Vernon
pays for him, he is the master, he decides, and if Crossjay is blown from the mast-head in a gale, the blame
does not fall on me. These, my dear, are matters of
reason.'

'I would not venture to intrude on them,' said Clara,
'if I had not suspected that money . . .'

'Yes,' cried Willoughby; 'and it is a part. And let old
Vernon surrender the boy to me, I will immediately
relieve him of the burden on his purse. Can I do that,
my dear, for the furtherance of a scheme I condemn?
The point is this: latterly I have invited Captain Patterne
to visit me: just previous to his departure for the African
Coast, where Government despatches Marines when
there is no other way of killing them, I sent him a special
invitation. He thanked me and curtly declined. The
man, I may almost say, is my pensioner. Well, he calls
himself a Patterne, he is undoubtedly a man of courage,
he has elements of our blood, and the name. I think I
am to be approved for desiring to make a better gentleman of the son than I behold in the father: and seeing
that life from an early age on board ship has anything
but made a gentleman of the father, I hold that I am
right in shaping another course for the son.'

'Naval officers . . .' Clara suggested.

'Some,' said Willoughby. 'But they must be men of
birth, coming out of homes of good breeding. Strip
them of the halo of the title of naval officers, and I fear
you would not often say gentlemen when they step into
a drawing-room. I went so far as to fancy I had some
claim to make young Crossjay something different. It
can be done: the Patterne comes out in his behaviour
to you, my love: it can be done. But if I take him, I
claim undisputed sway over him. I cannot make a
gentleman of the fellow if I am to compete with this

person and that. In fine, he must look up to me, he must have one model.'

'Would you, then, provide for him subsequently?'

'According to his behaviour.'

'Would not that be precarious for him?'

'More so than the profession you appear inclined to choose for him?'

'But there he would be under clear regulations.'

'With me he would have to respond to affection.'

'Would you secure to him a settled income? For an idle gentleman is bad enough; a penniless gentleman . . .!'

'He has only to please me, my dear, and he will be launched and protected.'

'But if he does not succeed in pleasing you!'

'Is it so difficult?'

'Oh!' Clara fretted.

'You see, my love, I answer you,' said Sir Willoughby. He resumed: 'But let old Vernon have his trial with the lad. He has his own ideas. Let him carry them out. I shall watch the experiment.'

Clara was for abandoning her task in sheer faintness.

'Is not the question one of money?' she said shyly, knowing Mr. Whitford to be poor.

'Old Vernon chooses to spend his money that way,' replied Sir Willoughby. 'If it saves him from breaking his shins and risking his neck on his Alps, we may consider it well employed.'

'Yes,' Clara's voice occupied a pause.

She seized her langour as it were a curling snake and cast it off. 'But I understand that Mr. Whitford wants your assistance. Is he not——not rich? When he leaves the Hall to try his fortune in literature in London, he may not be so well able to support Crossjay and obtain the instruction necessary for the boy: and it would be generous to help him.'

'Leaves the Hall!' exclaimed Willoughby. 'I have not heard a word of it. He made a bad start at the beginning, and I should have thought that would have tamed him: had to throw over his Fellowship; ahem. Then he received a small legacy some time back, and wanted to be off to push his luck in Literature: rank gambling, as I told him. Londonizing can do him no good. I thought that nonsense of his was over years ago. What is it he has from me?—about a hundred and fifty a year: and it might be doubled for the asking: and all the books he requires: and these writers and scholars no sooner think of a book than they must have it. And do not suppose me to complain. I am a man who will not have a single shilling expended by those who serve immediately about my person. I confess to exacting that kind of dependancy. Feudalism is not an objectionable thing if you can be sure of the lord. You know, Clara, and you should know me in my weakness too, I do not claim servitude, I stipulate for affection. I claim to be surrounded by persons loving me. And with one? . . . dearest! So that we two can shut out the world: we live what is the dream of others. Nothing imaginable can be sweeter. It is a veritable heaven on earth. To be the possessor of the whole of you! Your thoughts, hopes, all.'

Sir Willoughby intensified his imagination to conceive more: he could not, or could not express it, and pursued: 'But what is this talk of Vernon's leaving me? He cannot leave. He has barely a hundred a year of his own. You see, I consider him. I do not speak of the ingratitude of the wish to leave. You know, my dear, I have a deadly abhorrence of partings and such like. As far as I can, I surround myself with healthy people specially to guard myself from having my feelings wrung; and excepting Miss Dale, whom you like—my darling does like her?'—the answer satisfied him; 'with that one exception, I am not aware of a case that threatens to torment me. And here is a man, under no compulsion, talking of leaving the Hall! In the name of goodness, why? But why? Am I to imagine that the sight of perfect felicity distresses him? We are told that the world is "desperately wicked." I do not like to think it of my friends; yet otherwise their conduct is often hard to account for.'

'If it were true, you would not punish Crossjay?' Clara feebly interposed.

'I should certainly take Crossjay and make a man of him after my own model, my dear. But who spoke to you of this?'

'Mr. Whitford himself. And let me give you my opinion, Willoughby, that he will take Crossjay with him rather than leave him, if there is a fear of the boy's missing his chance of the navy.'

'Marines appear to be in the ascendant,' said Sir Willoughby, astonished at the locution and pleading in the interests of a son of one. 'Then Crossjay he must take. I cannot accept half the boy. I am,' he laughed, 'the legitimate claimant in the application for judgement before the wise King.* Besides, the boy has a dose of my blood in him; he has none of Vernon's, not one drop.'

'Ah!'

'You see, my love.'

'Oh! I do see; yes.'

'I put forth no pretensions to perfection,' Sir Willoughby continued. 'I can bear a considerable amount of provocation; still I can be offended, and I am unforgiving when I have been offended. Speak to Vernon, if a natural occasion should spring up. I shall, of course, have to speak to him. You may, Clara, have observed a man who passed me on the road as we were cantering home, without a hint of a touch to his hat. That man is a tenant of mine, farming six hundred acres, Hoppner by name: a man bound to remember that I have, independently of my position, obliged him frequently. His lease of my ground has five years to run. I must say I detest the churlishness of our country population, and where it comes across me I chastise it. Vernon is a different matter: he will only require to be spoken to. One would fancy the old fellow laboured now and then under a magnetic attraction to beggary. My love,' he bent to her and checked their pacing up and down, 'you are tired?'

'I am very tired to-day,' said Clara.

His arm was offered. She laid two fingers on it, and

they dropped when he attempted to press them to his rib.

He did not insist. To walk beside her was to share in the stateliness of her walking.

He placed himself at a corner of the doorway for her to pass him into the house, and doated on her cheek, her ear, and the softly dusky nape of her neck, where this way and that the little lighter-coloured irreclaimable curls running truant from the comb and the knot—curls, half-curls, root-curls, vine-ringlets, wedding-rings, fledgeling feathers, tufts of down, blown wisps—waved or fell, waved over or up or involutedly, or strayed, loose and downward, in the form of small silken paws, hardly any of them much thicker than a crayon shading, cunninger than long round locks of gold to trick the heart.

Laetitia had nothing to show resembling such beauty.

CHAPTER X

In Which Sir Willoughby chances to supply the Title for Himself

Now Vernon was useful to his cousin; he was the accomplished secretary of a man who governed his estates shrewdly and diligently, but had been once or twice unlucky in his judgements pronounced from the magisterial bench as a Justice of the Peace, on which occasions a half-column of trenchant English supported by an apposite classical quotation impressed Sir Willoughby with the value of such a secretary in a controversy. He had no fear of that fiery dragon of scorching breath—the newspaper Press—while Vernon was his right-hand man; and as he intended to enter Parliament, he foresaw the greater need of him. Furthermore, he liked his cousin to date his own controversial writings, on classical subjects, from Patterne Hall. It caused his house to shine in a foreign field; proved the service of scholarship by giving it a flavour of a bookish aristocracy that, though not so well worth having, and indeed in

itself contemptible, is above the material and titular; one
cannot quite say how. There, however, is the flavour.
Dainty sauces are the life, the nobility, of famous dishes;
taken alone, the former would be nauseating, the latter
plebeian. It is thus, or somewhat so, when you have a
poet, still better a scholar, attached to your household.
Sir Willoughby deserved to have him, for he was above
his county friends in his apprehension of the flavour bestowed by the man; and having him, he had made them
conscious of their deficiency. His cook, M. Dehors, pupil
of the great Godefroy, was not the only French cook in
the county; but his cousin and secretary, the rising
scholar, the elegant essayist, was an unparalleled decora-
tion; of his kind, of course. Personally, we laugh at him;
you had better not, unless you are fain to show that the
higher world of polite literature is unknown to you. Sir
Willoughby could create an abject silence at a county
dinner-table by an allusion to Vernon 'at work at home
upon his Etruscans or his Dorians';* and he paused a
moment to let the allusion sink, laughed audibly to himself over his eccentric cousin, and let him rest.

In addition, Sir Willoughby abhorred the loss of a
familiar face in his domestic circle. He thought ill of
servants who could accept their dismissal without petitioning to stay with him. A servant that gave warning
partook of a certain fiendishness. Vernon's project of
leaving the Hall offended and alarmed the sensitive
gentleman. 'I shall have to hand Letty Dale to him at
last!' he thought, yielding in bitter generosity to the
conditions imposed on him by the ungenerousness of
another. For, since his engagement to Miss Middleton,
his electrically forethoughtful mind had seen in Miss
Dale, if she stayed in the neighbourhood, and remained
unmarried, the governess of his infant children, often
consulting with him. But here was a prospect dashed
out. The two, then, may marry, and live in a cottage on
the borders of his park; and Vernon can retain his post,
and Laetitia her devotion. The risk of her casting it off
had to be faced. Marriage has been known to have such
an effect on the most faithful of women, that a great

passion fades to naught in their volatile bosoms when
they have taken a husband. We see in women especially
the triumph of the animal over the spiritual. Nevertheless, risks must be run for a purpose in view.

Having no taste for a discussion with Vernon, whom it
was his habit to confound by breaking away from him
abruptly when he had delivered his opinion, he left it to
both the persons interesting themselves in young Crossjay
to imagine that he was meditating on the question of the
lad, and to imagine that it would be wise to leave him to
meditate; for he could be preternaturally acute in reading any of his fellow-creatures if they crossed the current
of his feelings. And, meanwhile, he instructed the ladies
Eleanor and Isabel to bring Laetitia Dale on a visit to the
Hall, where dinner-parties were soon to be given and a
pleasing talker would be wanted; where also a woman
of intellect, steeped in a splendid sentiment, hitherto a
miracle of female constancy, might stir a younger woman
to some emulation. Definitely to resolve to bestow Laetitia upon Vernon, was more than he could do; enough
that he held the card.

Regarding Clara, his genius for perusing the heart
which was not in perfect harmony with him through the
series of responsive movements to his own, informed
him of a something in her character that might have suggested to Mrs. Mountstuart Jenkinson her indefensible,
absurd 'rogue in porcelain.' Idea there was none in that
phrase; yet, if you looked on Clara as a delicately inimitable porcelain beauty, the suspicion of a delicately
inimitable ripple over her features touched a thought of
innocent roguery, wildwood roguery; the likeness to the
costly and lovely substance appeared to admit a fitness
in the dubious epithet. He detested but was haunted by
the phrase.

She certainly had at times the look of the nymph that
has gazed too long on the faun, and has unwittingly
copied his lurking lip and long sliding eye. Her play
with young Crossjay resembled a return of the lady to
the cat; she flung herself into it as if her real vitality had
been in suspense till she saw the boy. Sir Willoughby by

no means disapproved of a physical liveliness that promised him health in his mate; but he began to feel in their conversations that she did not sufficiently think of making herself a nest for him. Steely points were opposed to him when he, figuratively, bared his bosom to be taken to the softest and fairest. She reasoned: in other words, armed her ignorance. She reasoned against him publicly, and lured Vernon to support her. Influence is to be counted for power, and her influence over Vernon was displayed in her persuading him to dance one evening at Lady Culmer's, after his melancholy exhibitions of himself in the art; and not only did she persuade him to stand up fronting her, she manoeuvred him through the dance like a clever boy cajoling a top to come to him without reeling, both to Vernon's contentment and to Sir Willoughby's; for he was the last man to object to a manifestation of power in his bride. Considering her influence with Vernon, he renewed the discourse upon young Crossjay; and, as he was addicted to system, he took her into his confidence, that she might be taught to look to him and act for him.

'Old Vernon has not spoken to you again of that lad?' he said.

'Yes, Mr. Whitford has asked me.'

'He does not ask me, my dear!'

'He may fancy me of greater aid than I am.'

'You see, my love, if he puts Crossjay on me, he will be off. He has this craze for "enlisting" his pen in London, as he calls it; and I am accustomed to him; I don't like to think of him as a hack scribe, writing nonsense from dictation to earn a pitiful subsistence; I want him here; and, supposing he goes, he offends me; he loses a friend; and it will not be the first time that a friend has tried me too far; but, if he offends me, he is extinct.'

'Is what?' cried Clara, with a look of fright.

'He becomes to me at once as if he had never been. He is extinct.'

'In spite of your affection?'

'On account of it, I might say. Our nature is mysterious, and mine as much so as any. Whatever my regrets, he goes out. This is not a language I talk to the world. I do the man no harm; I am not to be named unchristian. But . . .!'

Sir Willoughby mildly shrugged, and indicated a spreading out of the arms.

'But do, do talk to me as you talk to the world, Willoughby; give me some relief!'

'My own Clara, we are one. You should know me, at my worst, we will say, if you like, as well as at my best.'

'Should I speak too?'

'What could you have to confess?'

She hung silent: the wave of an insane resolution swelled in her bosom and subsided before she said: 'Cowardice, incapacity to speak.'

'Women!' said he.

We do not expect so much of women; the heroic virtues as little as the vices. They have not to unfold the scroll of character.

He resumed, and by his tone she understood that she was now in the inner temple of him: 'I tell you these things; I quite acknowledge they do not elevate me. They help to constitute my character. I tell you most humbly that I have in me much too much of the fallen archangel's pride.'

Clara bowed her head over a sustained indrawn breath.

'It must be pride,' he said, in reverie superinduced by her thoughtfulness over the revelation, and glorying in the black flames demoniacal wherewith he crowned himself.

'Can you not correct it?' said she.

He replied, profoundly vexed by disappointment: 'I am what I am. It might be demonstrated to you mathematically that it is corrected by equivalents or substitutions in my character. If it be a failing—assuming that.'

'It seems one to me: so cruelly to punish Mr. Whitford for seeking to improve his fortunes.'

'He reflects on my share in his fortunes. He has had but to apply to me, for his honorarium to be doubled.'

'He wishes for independence.'

'Independence of *me*!'

'Liberty!'

'At my expense!'

'Oh! Willoughby.'

'Ay, but this is the world, and I know it, my love; and beautiful as your incredulity may be, you will find it more comforting to confide in my knowledge of the self-ishness of the world. My sweetest, you will?—you do! For a breath of difference between us is intolerable. Do you not feel how it breaks our magic ring? One small fissure, and we have the world with its muddy deluge!—But my subject was old Vernon. Yes, I pay for Crossjay, if Vernon consents to stay. I waive my own scheme for the lad, though I think it the better one. Now, then, to induce Vernon to stay. He has his ideas about staying under a mistress of the household; and therefore, not to contest it—he is a man of no argument; a sort of lunatic determination takes the place of it with old Vernon!—let him settle close by me, in one of my cottages; very well, and to settle him we must marry him.'

'Who is there?' said Clara, beating for the lady in her mind.

'Women,' said Willoughby, 'are born match-makers, and the most persuasive is a young bride. With a man—and a man like old Vernon!—she is irresistible. It is my wish, and that arms you. It is your wish, that subjugates him. If he goes, he goes for good. If he stays, he is my friend. I deal simply with him, as with every one. It is the secret of authority. Now Miss Dale will soon lose her father. He exists on a pension; she has the prospect of having to leave the neighbourhood of the Hall, unless she is established near us. Her whole heart is in this region; it is the poor soul's passion. Count on her agreeing. But she will require a litttle wooing: and old Vernon wooing! Picture the scene to yourself, my love. His notion of wooing, I suspect, will be to treat the lady like a lexicon, and turn over the leaves for the word, and fly through the leaves for another word, and so get a sentence. Don't frown at the poor old fellow, my Clara; some have the language on their tongues, and some have not. Some are very dry sticks; manly men, honest fellows, but so cut away, so polished away from the sex, that they are in absolute want of outsiders to supply the silken filaments to attach them. Actually!' Sir Willoughby laughed in Clara's face to relax the dreamy stoniness of her look. 'But I can assure you, my dearest, I have seen it. Vernon does not know how to speak—as *we* speak. He has, or he had, what is called a sneaking affection for Miss Dale. It was the most amusing thing possible: his courtship!—the air of a dog with an uneasy conscience, trying to reconcile himself with his master! We were all in fits of laughter. Of course it came to nothing.'

'Will Mr. Whitford,' said Clara, 'offend you to extinction if he declines?'

Willoughby breathed an affectionate 'Tush,' to her silliness.

'We bring them together, as we best can. You see, Clara, I desire, and I will make some sacrifices to detain him.'

'But what do you sacrifice?—a cottage?' said Clara, combative at all points.

'An ideal, perhaps. I lay no stress on sacrifice. I strongly object to separations. And therefore, you will say, I prepare the ground for unions? Put your influence to good service, my love. I believe you could persuade him to give us the Highland fling on the drawing-room table.'

'There is nothing to say to him of Crossjay?'

'We hold Crossjay in reserve.'

'It is urgent.'

'Trust me. I have my ideas. I am not idle. That boy bids fair for a capital horseman. Eventualities might . . .' Sir Willoughby murmured to himself, and addressing his bride; 'The cavalry? If we put him into the cavalry, we might make a gentleman of him—not be ashamed of him. Or, under certain eventualities, the Guards. Think it over, my love. De Craye, who will, I assume, act best man for me, supposing old Vernon to pull at the collar, is a Lieutenant-Colonel in the Guards, a thorough gentleman

—of the brainless class, if you like, but an elegant fellow; an Irishman; you will see him, and I should like to set a naval lieutenant beside him in a drawing-room, for you to compare them and consider the model you would choose for a boy you are interested in. Horace is grace and gallantry incarnate; fatuous, probably; I have always been too friendly with him to examine closely. He made himself one of my dogs, though my elder, and seemed to like to be at my heels. One of the few men's faces I can call admirably handsome;—with nothing behind it, perhaps. As Vernon says, "a nothing picked by the vultures and bleached by the desert." Not a bad talker, if you are satisfied with keeping up the ball. He will amuse you. Old Horace does not know how amusing he is!'

'Did Mr. Whitford say that of Colonel De Craye?'

'I forget the person of whom he said it. So you have noticed old Vernon's foible? Quote him one of his epigrams, and he is in motion head and heels! It is an infallible receipt for tuneing him. If I want to have him in good temper, I have only to remark, "as you said." I straighten his back instantly.'

'I,' said Clara, 'have noticed chiefly his anxiety concerning the boy; for which I admire him.'

'Creditable, if not particularly far-sighted and sagacious. Well, then, my dear, attack him at once: lead him to the subject of our fair neighbour. She is to be our guest for a week or so, and the whole affair might be concluded far enough to fix him before she leaves. She is at present awaiting the arrival of a cousin to attend on her father. A little gentle pushing will precipitate old Vernon on his knees as far as he ever can unbend them; but when a lady is made ready to expect a declaration, you know, why, she does not—does she?—demand the entire formula?—though some beautiful fortresses . . .'

He enfolded her. Clara was growing hardened to it. To this she was fated; and not seeing any way of escape, she invoked a friendly frost to strike her blood, and passed through the minute unfeelingly. Having passed it, she reproached herself for making so much of it, thinking it a lesser endurance than to listen to him. What could she do?—she was caged; by her word of honour, as she at one time thought; by her cowardice, at another; and dimly sensible that the latter was a stronger lock than the former, she mused on the abstract question whether a woman's cowardice can be so absolute as to cast her into the jaws of her aversion. Is it to be conceived? Is there not a moment when it stands at bay? But haggard-visaged Honour then starts up claiming to be dealt with in turn; for having courage restored to her, she must have the courage to break with honour, she must dare to be faithless, and not merely say, I will be brave, but be brave enough to be dishonourable. The cage of a plighted woman hungering for her disengagement has two keepers, a noble and a vile; where on earth is creature so dreadfully enclosed? It lies with her to overcome what degrades her, that she may win to liberty by over-coming what exalts.

Contemplating her situation, this idea (or vapour of youth taking the godlike semblance of an idea) sprang, born of her present sickness, in Clara's mind; that it must be an ill-constructed tumbling world where the hour of ignorance is made the creator of our destiny by being forced to the decisive elections upon which life's main issues hang. Her teacher had brought her to con-template his view of the world.

She thought likewise: how must a man despise women, who can expose himself as he does to me!

Miss Middleton owed it to Sir Willoughby Patterne that she ceased to think like a girl. When had the great change begun? Glancing back, she could imagine that it was near the period we call, in love, the first—almost from the first. And she was led to imagine it through having become barred from imagining her own emotions of that season. They were so dead as not to arise even under the forms of shadows in fancy. Without imputing blame to him, for she was reasonable so far, she deemed herself a person entrapped. In a dream somehow she had committed herself to a life-long imprisonment; and, oh terror! not in a quiet dungeon; the barren walls closed round her, talked, called for ardour, expected admiration.

She was unable to say why she could not give it; why she retreated more and more inwardly; why she invoked the frost to kill her tenderest feelings. She was in revolt, until a whisper of the day of bells reduced her to blank submission; out of which a breath of peace drew her to revolt again in gradual rapid stages, and once more the aspect of that singular day of merry blackness felled her to earth. It was alive, it advanced, it had a mouth, it had a song. She received letters of bridesmaids writing of it, and felt them as waves that hurl a log of wreck to shore. Following which afflicting sense of antagonism to the whole circle sweeping on with her, she considered the possibility of her being in a commencement of madness. Otherwise might she not be accused of a capriciousness quite as deplorable to consider? She had written to certain of those young ladies not very long since of this gentleman—how?—in what tone? And was it her madness then?—her recovery now? It seemed to her that to have written of him enthusiastically resembled madness more than to shudder away from the union; but standing alone, opposing all she has consented to set in motion, is too strange to a girl for perfect justification to be found in reason when she seeks it.

Sir Willoughby was destined himself to supply her with that key of special insight which revealed and stamped him in a title to fortify her spirit of revolt, consecrate it almost.

The popular physician of the county and famous anecdotal wit, Dr. Corney, had been a guest at dinner overnight, and the next day there was talk of him, and of the resources of his art displayed by Armand Dehors on his hearing that he was to minister to the tastes of a gathering of hommes d'esprit.* Sir Willoughby glanced at Dehors with his customary benevolent irony in speaking of the persons, great in their way, who served him. 'Why he cannot give us daily so good a dinner, one must, I suppose, go to French nature to learn. The French are in the habit of making up for all their deficiencies with enthusiasm. They have no reverence; if I had said to him,

"I want something particularly excellent, Dehors," I should have had a commonplace dinner. But they have enthusiasm on draught, and that is what we must pull at. Know one Frenchman and you know France. I have had Dehors under my eye two years, and I can mount his enthusiasm at a word. He took hommes d'esprit to denote men of letters. Frenchmen have destroyed their nobility, so, for the sake of excitement, they put up the literary man—not to worship him; that they can't do; it's to put themselves in a state of effervescence. They will not have real greatness above them, so they have sham. That they may justly call it equality, perhaps! Ay, for all your shake of the head, my good Vernon! You see, human nature comes round again, try as we may to upset it, and the French only differ from us in wading through blood to discover that they are at their old trick once more: "I am your equal, sir, your born equal. Oh! you are a man of letters? Allow me to be in a bubble about you." Yes, Vernon, and I believe the fellow looks up to you as the head of the establishment. I am not jealous. Provided he attends to his functions! There's a French philosopher who's for naming the days of the year after the birthdays of French men of letters, Voltaire-day, Rousseau-day, Racine-day, so on. Perhaps Vernon will inform us who takes April 1st.'*

'A few trifling errors are of no consequence when you are in the vein of satire,' said Vernon. 'Be satisfied with knowing a nation in the person of a cook.'

'They may be reading us English off in a jockey!' said Dr. Middleton. 'I believe that jockeys are the exchange we make for cooks; and our neighbours do not get the best of the bargain.'

'No, but, my dear good Vernon, it's nonsensical,' said Sir Willoughby; 'why be bawling every day the names of men of letters?'

'Philosophers.'

'Well, philosophers.'

'Of all countries and times. And they are the benefactors of humanity.'

'Bene . . .!' Sir Willoughby's derisive laugh broke the

word. 'There's a pretension in all that, irreconcilable with English sound sense. Surely you see it?'

'We might,' said Vernon, 'if you like, give alternative titles to the days, or have alternating days, devoted to our great families that performed meritorious deeds upon such a day.'

The rebel Clara, delighting in his banter, was heard; 'Can we furnish sufficient?'

'A poet or two could help us.'

'Perhaps a statesman,' she suggested.

'A pugilist, if wanted.'

'For blowy days,' observed Dr. Middleton, and hastily in penitence picked up the conversation he had unintentionally prostrated, with a general remark on new-fangled notions, and a word aside to Vernon; which created the blissful suspicion in Clara, that her father was indisposed to second Sir Willoughby's opinions even when sharing them.

Sir Willoughby had led the conversation. Displeased that the lead should be withdrawn from him, he turned to Clara and related one of the after-dinner anecdotes of Dr. Corney; and another, with a vast deal of human nature in it, concerning a valetudinarian gentleman, whose wife chanced to be desperately ill, and he went to the physicians assembled in consultation outside the sickroom, imploring them by all he valued, and in tears, to save the poor patient for him, saying: 'She is everything to me, everything, and if she dies I am compelled to run the risks of marrying again; I must marry again; for she has accustomed me so to the little attentions of a wife, that in truth I can't, I can't lose her! She must be saved!' And the loving husband of any devoted wife wrung his hands.

'Now, there, Clara, there you have the Egoist,' added Sir Willoughby. 'That is the perfect Egoist. You see what he comes to—and his wife! The man was utterly unconscious of giving vent to the grossest selfishness.'

'An Egoist!' said Clara.

'Beware of marrying an Egoist, my dear!' He bowed gallantly; and so blindly fatuous did he appear to her that she could hardly believe him guilty of uttering the words she had heard from him, and kept her eyes on him vacantly till she came to a sudden full stop in the thoughts directing her gaze. She looked at Vernon, she looked at her father, and at the ladies Eleanor and Isabel. None of them saw the man in the word, none noticed the word; yet this word was her medical herb, her illuminating lamp, the key of him (and, alas, but she thought it by feeling her need of one), the advocate pleading in apology for her. Egoist! She beheld him—unfortunate, self-designated man that he was!—in his good qualities as well as bad under the implacable lamp, and his good were drenched in his first person singular. His generosity roared of *I* louder than the rest. Conceive him at the age of Dr. Corney's hero: 'Pray, save my wife for me. I shall positively have to get another if I lose her, and one who may not love me half so well, or understand the peculiarities of my character and appreciate my attitudes.' He was in his thirty-second year, therefore a young man, strong and healthy, yet his garrulous return to his principal theme, his emphasis on I and me, lent him the seeming of an old man spotted with decaying youth.

'Beware of marrying an Egoist.'

Would he help her to escape? The idea of the scene ensuing upon her petition for release, and the being dragged round the walls of his egoism, and having her head knocked against the corners, alarmed her with sensations of sickness.

There was the example of Constantia. But that desperate young lady had been assisted by a gallant, loving gentleman; she had met a Captain Oxford.

Clara brooded on those two until they seemed heroic. She questioned herself: Could she . . .? were one to come? She shut her eyes in languor, leaning the wrong way of her wishes, yet unable to say No.

Sir Willoughby had positively said beware! Marrying him would be a deed committed in spite of his express warning. She went so far as to conceive him subsequently saying: 'I warned you.' She conceived the state of marriage with him as that of a woman tied not to a man of heart, but to an obelisk lettered all over with hieroglyphics, and everlastingly hearing him expound them, relishingly renewing his lectures on them.

Full surely this immoveable stone-man would not release her. This petrifaction of egoism would from amazedly to austerely refuse the petition. His pride would debar him from understanding her desire to be released. And if she resolved on it, without doing it straightway in Constantia's manner, the miserable bewilderment of her father, for whom such a complication would be a tragic dilemma, had to be thought of. Her father, with all his tenderness for his child, would make a stand on a point of honour; though certain to yield to her, he would be distressed, in a tempest of worry; and Dr. Middleton thus afflicted threw up his arms, he shunned books, shunned speech, and resembled a castaway on the ocean, with nothing between himself and his calamity. As for the world, it would be barking at her heels. She might call the man she wrenched her hand from, Egoist; jilt, the world would call her. She dwelt bitterly on her agreement with Sir Willoughby regarding the world, laying it to his charge that her garden had become a place of nettles, her horizon an unlighted fourth side of a square.

Clara passed from person to person visiting the Hall. There was universal, and as she was compelled to see, honest admiration of the host. Not a soul had a suspicion of his cloaked nature. Her agony of hypocrisy in accepting their compliments as the bride of Sir Willoughby Patterne was poorly moderated by contempt of them for their infatuation. She tried to cheat herself with the thought that they were right and that she was the foolish and wicked inconstant. In her anxiety to strangle the rebelliousness which had been communicated from her mind to her blood, and was present with her whether her mind was in action or not, she encouraged the ladies Eleanor and Isabel to magnify the fictitious man of their idolatry, hoping that she might enter into them imaginatively, that she might to some degree subdue herself to the necessity of her position.

If she partly succeeded in stupefying her antagonism, five minutes of him undid the work.

He requested her to wear the Patterne Pearls for a dinner-party of grand ladies, telling her that he would commission Miss Isabel to take them to her. Clara begged leave to decline them, on the plea of having no right to wear them. He laughed at her modish modesty. 'But really it might almost be classed with affectation,' said he. 'I give you the right. Virtually you are my wife.'

'No.'

'Before heaven?'

'No. We are not married.'

'As my betrothed, will you wear them, to please me?'

'I would rather not. I cannot wear borrowed jewels. These I cannot wear. Forgive me, I cannot. And Willoughby,' she said, scorning herself for want of fortitude in not keeping to the simply blunt provocative refusal, 'does one not look like a victim decked for the sacrifice? —the garlanded heifer you see on Greek vases, in that array of jewelry?'

'My dear Clara!' exclaimed the astonished lover, 'how can you term them borrowed, when they are the Patterne jewels, our family heirloom pearls, unmatched, I venture to affirm, decidedly in my county and many others, and passing to the use of the mistress of the house in the natural course of things?'

'They are yours, they are not mine.'

'Prospectively they are yours.'

'It would be to anticipate the fact to wear them.'

'With my consent, my approval? at my request?'

'I am not yet . . . I never may be . . .'

'My wife?' He laughed triumphantly, and silenced her by manly smothering.

Her scruple was perhaps an honourable one, he said. Perhaps the jewels were safer in their iron box. He had merely intended a surprise and gratification to her.

Courage was coming to enable her to speak more plainly, when his discontinuing to insist on her wearing the jewels, under an appearance of deference to her wishes, disarmed her by touching her sympathies.

She said, however: 'I fear we do not often agree, Willoughby.'

'When you are a little older!' was the irritating answer.

'It would then be too late to make the discovery.'

'The discovery, I apprehend, is not imperative, my love.'

'It seems to me that our minds are opposed.'

'I should,' said he, 'have been awake to it at a single indication, be sure.'

'But I know,' she pursued, 'I have learnt, that the ideal of conduct for women, is to subject their minds to the part of an accompaniment.'

'For women, my love? my wife will be in natural harmony with me.'

'Ah!' She compressed her lips. The yawn would come. 'I am sleepier here than anywhere.'

'Ours, my Clara, is the finest air of the kingdom. It has the effect of sea-air.'

'But if I am always asleep here?'

'We shall have to make a public exhibition of the Beauty.'

This dash of his liveliness defeated her.

She left him, feeling the contempt of the brain feverishly quickened and fine-pointed, for the brain chewing the cud in the happy pastures of unawakenedness. So violent was the fever, so keen her introspection, that she spared few, and Vernon was not among them. Young Crossjay, whom she considered the least able of all to act as an ally, was the only one she courted with a real desire to please him; he was the one she affectionately envied; he was the youngest, the freest, he had the world before him, and he did not know how horrible the world was, or could be made to look. She loved the boy from expecting nothing of him. Others, Vernon Whitford, for instance, could help, and moved no hand. He read her case. A scrutiny so penetrating under its air of abstract thoughtfulness, though his eyes did but rest on her a second or two, signified that he read her line by line, and to the end—excepting what she thought of him for probing her with that sharp steel of insight without a purpose.

She knew her mind's injustice. It was her case, her
lamentable case—the impatient panic-stricken nerves of
a captured wild creature, which cried for help. She
exaggerated her sufferings to get strength to throw them
off, and lost it in the recognition that they were exaggerated: and out of the conflict issued recklessness, with a
cry as wild as any coming of madness; for she did not
blush in saying to herself; 'If some one loved me!' Before
hearing of Constantia, she had mused upon liberty as a
virgin Goddess,—men were out of her thoughts; even
the figure of a rescuer, if one dawned in her mind,
was more angel than hero. That fair childish maidenliness had ceased. With her body straining in her dragon's
grasp, with the savour of loathing, unable to contend,
unable to speak aloud, she began to speak to herself, and
all the health of her nature made her outcry womanly:—
'If I were loved!'—not for the sake of love, but for free
breathing; and her utterance of it was to ensure life and
enduringness to the wish, as the yearning of a mother on
a drowning ship is to get her infant to shore. 'If some
noble gentleman could see me as I am and not disdain
to aid me! Oh! to be caught up out of this prison of
thorns and brambles. I cannot tear my own way out.
I am a coward. My cry for help confesses that. A
beckoning of a finger would change me, I believe. I
could fly bleeding and through hootings to a comrade.
Oh! a comrade. I do not want a lover. I should find
another Egoist, not so bad, but enough to make me take
a breath like death. I could follow a soldier, like poor
Sally or Molly. He stakes his life for his country, and a
woman may be proud of the worst of men who do that.
Constantia met a soldier. Perhaps she prayed and her
prayer was altered. She did ill. But, oh, how I love her
for it! His name was Harry Oxford. Papa would call
him her Perseus.* She must have felt that there was no
explaining what she suffered. She had only to act, to
plunge. First she fixed her mind on Harry Oxford. To
be able to speak his name and see him awaiting her,
must have been relief, a reprieve. She did not waver,
she cut the links, she signed herself over. O brave girl!

what do you think of me? But I have no Harry Whitford, I am alone. Let anything be said against women;
we must be very bad to have such bad things written of
us: only, say this, that to ask them to sign themselves
over by oath and ceremony, because of an ignorant
promise, to the man they have been mistaken in, is . . . it
is——' the sudden consciousness that she had put another
name for Oxford,* struck her a buffet, drowning her in
crimson.

CHAPTER XI

The Double-Blossom Wild Cherry-Tree

Sir Willoughby chose a moment when Clara was with
him and he had a good retreat through folding-win-
dows to the lawn, in case of cogency on the enemy's part,
to attack his cousin regarding the preposterous plot to
upset the family by a scamper to London: 'By the way,
Vernon, what is this you've been mumbling to everybody save me, about leaving us to pitch yourself into the
stew-pot and be made broth of?—London is no better,
and you are fit for considerably better. Don't, I beg you,
continue to annoy me. Take a run abroad, if you are
restless. Take two or three months, and join us as we
are travelling home; and then think of settling, pray.
Follow my example, if you like. You can have one of my
cottages, or a place built for you. Anything to keep a
man from destroying the sense of stability about one. In
London, my dear old fellow, you lose your identity.
What are you there? I ask you, what? One has the
feeling of the house crumbling when a man is perpetually
for shifting and cannot fix himself. Here you are known,
you can study at your ease; up in London you are nobody; I tell you honestly, I feel it myself; a week of London literally drives me home to discover the individual
where I left him. Be advised. You don't mean to go.'

'I have the intention,' said Vernon.

'Why?'

'I've mentioned it to you.'

'To my face?'

'Over your shoulder, is generally the only chance you give me.'

'You have not mentioned it to me, to my knowledge. As to the reason, I might hear a dozen of your reasons, and I should not understand one. It's against your interests and against my wishes. Come, friend, I am not the only one you distress. Why, Vernon, you yourself have said that the English would be very perfect Jews if they could manage to live on the patriarchal system. You said it, yes, you said it!—but I recollect it clearly. Oh! as for your double-meanings, you said the thing, and you jeered at the incapacity of English families to live together, on account of bad temper; and now you are the first to break up our union! I decidedly do not profess to be perfect Jew, but I do . . .'

Sir Willoughby caught signs of a probably smiling commerce between his bride and his cousin. He raised his face, appeared to be consulting his eyelids, and resolved to laugh: 'Well, I own it, I do like the idea of living patriarchally.' He turned to Clara. 'The Rev. Doctor one of us!'

'My father?' she said.

'Why not?'

'Papa's habits are those of a scholar.'

'That you might not be separated from him, my dear.'

Clara thanked Sir Willoughby for the kindness of thinking of her father, mentally analyzing the kindness, in which at least she found no unkindness, scarcely egoism, though she knew it to be there.

'We might propose it,' said he.

'As a compliment?'

'If he would condescend to accept it as a compliment. These great scholars! . . . And if Vernon goes, our inducement for Dr. Middleton to stay . . . But it is too absurd for discussion. Oh, Vernon, about Master Crossjay; I will see to it.'

He was about to give Vernon his shoulder and step into the garden, when Clara said, 'You will have Crossjay trained for the navy, Willoughby? There is not a day to lose.'

'Yes, yes; I will see to it. Depend on me for holding the young rascal in view.'

He presented his hand to her to lead her over the step to the gravel, surprised to behold how flushed she was.

She responded to the invitation by putting her hand forth from a bent elbow, with hesitating fingers. 'It should not be postponed, Willoughby.'

Her attitude suggested a stipulation before she touched him.

'It's an affair of money, as you know, Willoughby,' said Vernon. 'If I'm in London, I can't well provide for the boy for some time to come, or it's not certain that I can.'

'Why on earth should you go!'

'That's another matter. I want you to take my place with him.'

'In which case the circumstances are changed. I am responsible for him, and I have a right to bring him up according to my own prescription.'

'We are likely to have one idle lout the more.'

'I guarantee to make a gentleman of him.'

'We have too many of your gentlemen already.'

'You can't have enough, my good Vernon.'

'They're the national apology for indolence. Training a penniless boy to be one of them is nearly as bad as an education in a thieves' den; he will be just as much at war with society, if not game for the police.'

'Vernon, have you seen Crossjay's father, the now Captain of Marines? I think you have.'

'He's a good man and a very gallant officer.'

'And in spite of his qualities he's a cub, and an old cub. He is a captain now, but he takes that rank very late, you will own. There you have what you call a good man, undoubtedly a gallant officer, neutralized by the fact that he is not a gentleman. Holding intercourse with him is out of the question. No wonder Government declines to advance him rapidly. Young Crossjay does not bear your name. He bears mine, and on that point alone I should have a voice in the settlement of his career. And I say emphatically that a drawing-room approval of a young man is the best certificate for his general chances in life. I know of a City of London merchant of some sort, and I know a firm of lawyers, who will have none but University men in their office; at least, they have the preference.'

'Crossjay has a bullet head, fit neither for the University nor the drawing-room,' said Vernon; 'equal to fighting and dying for you, and that's all.'

Sir Willoughby contented himself with replying, 'The lad is a favourite of mine.'

His anxiety to escape a rejoinder caused him to step into the garden, leaving Clara behind him. 'My love!' said he, in apology as he turned to her. She could not look stern, but she had a look without a dimple to soften it, and her eyes shone. For she had wagered in her heart that the dialogue she provoked upon Crossjay would expose the Egoist. And there were other motives, wrapped up and intertwisted, unrecognizable, sufficient to strike her with worse than the flush of her self-knowledge of wickedness when she detained him to speak of Crossjay before Vernon.

At last it had been seen that she was conscious of suffering in her association with this Egoist! Vernon stood for the world taken into her confidence. The world, then, would not think so ill of her, she thought hopefully, at the same time that she thought most evilly of herself. But self-accusations were for the day of reckoning; she would and must have the world with her, or the belief that it was coming to her, in the terrible struggle she foresaw within her horizon of self, now her utter boundary. She needed it for the inevitable conflict. Little sacrifices of her honesty might be made. Considering how weak she was, how solitary, how dismally entangled, daily disgraced beyond the power of any veiling to conceal from her fiery sensations, a little hypocrisy was a poor girl's natural weapon. She crushed her conscientious mind with the assurance that it was magnifying trifles: not entirely unaware that she was magnifying trifles: not entirely unaware that she was thereby preparing it for a convenient blindness in the presence of dread

alternatives; but the pride of laying such stress on small
sins gave her purity a blush of pleasure and overcame the
inner warning. In truth she dared not think evilly of
herself for long, sailing into battle as she was. Nuns and
anchorites may; they have leisure. She regretted the
forfeits she had to pay for self-assistance and, if it might
be won, the world's; regretted, felt the peril of the loss,
and took them up and flung them.

'You see, old Vernon has no argument,' Willoughby
said to her.

He drew her hand more securely on his arm, to make
her sensible that she leaned on a pillar of strength.

'Whenever the little brain is in doubt, perplexed, undecided which course to adopt, she will come to me, will
she not? I shall always listen,' he resumed soothingly.
'My own! and I to you when the world vexes me. So
we round our completeness. You will know me; you
will know me in good time. I am not a mystery to those
to whom I unfold myself. I do not pretend to mystery:
yet, I will confess, your home—your heart's—Willoughby
is not exactly identical with the Willoughby before
the world. One must be armed against that rough
beast.'

Certain is the vengeance of the young upon monotony;
nothing more certain. They do not scheme it, but sameness is a poison to their systems; and vengeance is their
heartier breathing, their stretch of the limbs, run in the
fields; nature avenges them.

'When does Colonel De Craye arrive?' said Clara.

'Horace? In two or three days. You wish him to be
on the spot to learn his part, my love?'

She had not flown forward to the thought of Colonel
De Craye's arrival; she knew not why she had mentioned
him; but now she flew back, shocked, first into shadowy
subterfuge, and then into the criminal's dock.

'I do not wish him to be here. I do not know that he
has a part to learn. I have no wish. Willoughby, did
you not say I should come to you and you would listen?
—will you listen? I am so commonplace that I shall not
be understood by you unless you take my words for the

very meaning of the words. I am unworthy. I am volatile. I love my liberty. I want to be free . . .'

'Flitch!' he called.

It sounded necromantic.

'Pardon me, my love,' he said. 'The man you see
yonder violates my express injunction that he is not to
come on my grounds, and here I find him on the borders
of my garden!'

Sir Willoughby waved his hand to the abject figure of
a man standing to intercept him.

'Volatile, unworthy, liberty—my dearest!' he bent to
her when the man had appeased him by departing, 'You
are at liberty within the law, like all good women; I shall
control and direct your volatility; and your sense of
worthiness must be re-established when we are more
intimate; it is timidity. The sense of unworthiness is a
guarantee of worthiness ensuing. I believe I am in the
vein of a sermon! Whose the fault? The sight of that
man was annoying. Flitch was a stable-boy, groom, and
coachman, like his father before him, at the Hall thirty
years; his father died in our service. Mr. Flitch had not
a single grievance here; only one day the demon seizes
him with the notion of bettering himself, he wants his
independence, and he presents himself to me with a story
of a shop in our county town.—Flitch! remember, if you
go you go for good.—Oh! he quite comprehended.—
Very well; good-bye, Flitch;—The man was respectful:
he looked the fool he was very soon to turn out to be.
Since then, within a period of several years, I have had
him, against my express injunctions, ten times on my
grounds. It's curious to calculate. Of course the shop
failed, and Flitch's independence consists in walking
about with his hands in his empty pockets, and looking
at the Hall from some elevation near.'

'Is he married? Has he children?' said Clara.

'Nine; and a wife that cannot cook or sew or wash linen.'

'You could not give him employment?'

'After his having dismissed himself?'

'It might be overlooked.'

'Here he was happy. He decided to go elsewhere, to

be free—of course, of my yoke. He quitted my service
against my warning. Flitch, we will say, emigrated with
his wife and nine children, and the ship foundered. He
returns, but his place is filled; he is a ghost here, and I
object to ghosts.'

'Some work might be found for him.'

'It will be the same with old Vernon, my dear. If he
goes, he goes for good. It is the vital principle of my
authority to insist on that. A dead leaf might as reasonably demand to return to the tree. Once off, off for all
eternity! I am sorry, but such was your decision, my
friend. I have, you see, Clara, elements in me——'

'Dreadful!'

'Exert your persuasive powers with Vernon. You can
do well-nigh what you will with the old fellow. We have
Miss Dale this evening for a week or two. Lead him to
some ideas of her.—Elements in me, I was remarking,
which will no more bear to be handled carelessly than
gunpowder. At the same time, there is no reason why
they should not be respected, managed with some degree
of regard for me and attention to consequences. Those
who have not done so have repented.'

'You do not speak to others of the elements in you,'
said Clara.

'I certainly do not: I have but one bride,' was his
handsome reply.

'Is it fair to me that you should show me the worst of
you?'

'All myself, my own?'

His ingratiating droop and familiar smile rendered
'All myself' so affectionately meaningful in its happy
reliance upon her excess of love, that at last she understood she was expected to worship him and uphold him
for whatsoever he might be, without any estimation of
qualities: as indeed love does, or young love does: as
she perhaps did once, before he chilled her senses. That
was before her 'little brain' had become active and had
turned her senses to revolt.

It was on the full river of love that Sir Willoughby
supposed the whole floating bulk of his personality to be

securely sustained; and therefore it was that, believing himself swimming at his ease, he discoursed of himself.

She went straight away from that idea with her mental exclamation: 'Why does he not paint himself in brighter colours to me!' and the question: 'Has he no ideal of generosity and chivalry?'

But the unfortunate gentleman imagined himself to be loved, on Love's very bosom. He fancied that everything relating to himself excited maidenly curiosity, womanly reverence, ardours to know more of him, which he was ever willing to satisfy by repeating the same things. His notion of women was the primitive black and white: there are good women, bad women; and he possessed a good one. His high opinion of himself fortified the belief that Providence, as a matter of justice and fitness, must necessarily select a good one for him—or what are we to think of Providence? And this female, shaped by that informing hand, would naturally be in harmony with him, from the centre of his profound identity to the raying circle of his variations. Know the centre, you know the circle, and you discover that the variations are simply characteristics, but you must travel on the rays from the circle to get to the centre. Consequently Sir Willoughby put Miss Middleton on one or other of these converging lines from time to time. Us, too, he drags into the deeps, but when we have harpooned a whale and are attached to the rope, down we must go; the miracle is to see us rise again.

Women of mixed essences shading off the divine to the considerably lower, were outside his vision of woman. His mind could as little admit an angel in pottery as a rogue in porcelain. For him they were what they were when fashioned at the beginning; many cracked, many stained, here and there a perfect specimen designed for the elect of men. At a whisper of the world he shut the prude's door on them with a slam; himself would have branded them with the letters in the hue of fire. Privately he did so: and he was constituted by his extreme sensitiveness and taste for ultra-feminine refinement to be a severe critic of them during the carnival of egoism, the love-season. Constantia . . . can it be told? She had been, be it said, a fair and frank young merchant with him in that season; she was of a nature to be a mother of heroes; she met the salute, almost half-way, ingenuously unlike the coming mothers of the regiments of marionettes, who retire in vapours, downcast, as by convention; ladies most flattering to the egoistical gentleman, for they proclaim him the 'first.' Constantia's offence had been no greater, but it was not that dramatic performance of purity which he desired of an affianced lady, and so the offence was great.

The love-season is the carnival of egoism, and it brings the touchstone to our natures. I speak of love, not the mask, and not of the flutings upon the theme of love, but of the passion; a flame having, like our mortality, death in it as well as life, that may or may not be lasting. Applied to Sir Willoughby, as to thousands of civilized males, the touchstone found him requiring to be dealt with by his betrothed as an original savage. She was required to play incessantly on the first reclaiming chord which led our ancestral satyr to the measures of the dance, the threading of the maze, and the setting conformably to his partner before it was accorded to him to spin her with both hands and a chirrup of his frisky heels. To keep him in awe and hold him enchained, there are things she must never do, dare never say, must not think. She must be cloistral. Now, strange and awful though it be to hear, women perceive this requirement of them in the spirit of the man; they perceive, too, and it may be gratefully, that they address their performances less to the taming of the green and prankish monsieur of the forest than to the pacification of a voracious aesthetic gluttony, craving them insatiably, through all the tenses, with shrieks of the lamentable letter 'I' for their purity. Whether they see that it has its foundation in the sensual, and distinguish the ultra-refined but lineally greatgrandson of the Hoof in this vast and dainty exacting appetite is uncertain. They probably do not; the more the damage; for in the appeasement of the glutton they have to practise much simulation; they are in their way losers

like their ancient mothers. It is the palpable and
material of them still which they are tempted to flourish,
wherewith to invite and allay pursuit: a condition under
which the spiritual, wherein their hope lies, languishes.
The capaciously strong in soul among women will ultimately detect an infinite grossness in the demand for
purity infinite, spotless bloom. Earlier or later they see
they have been victims of the singular Egoist, have worn
a mask of ignorance to be named innocent, have turned
themselves into market produce for his delight, and have
really abandoned the commodity in ministering to the
lust for it, suffered themselves to be dragged ages back
in playing upon the fleshly innocence of happy accident
to gratify his jealous greed of possession, when it should
have been their task to set the soul above the fairest
fortune, and the gift of strength in women beyond ornamental whiteness. Are they not of a nature warriors,
like men?—men's mates to bear them heroes instead of
puppets? But the devouring male Egoist prefers them
as inanimate overwrought polished pure-metal precious
vessels, fresh from the hands of the artificer, for him to
walk away with hugging, call all his own, drink of, and
fill and drink of, and forget that he stole them.

This running off on a by-road is no deviation from Sir
Willoughby Patterne and Miss Clara Middleton. He, a
fairly intelligent man, and very sensitive, was blinded to
what was going on within her visibly enough, by her production of the article he demanded of her sex. He had
to leave the fair young lady to ride to his county-town,
and his design was to conduct her through the covert of
a group of laurels, there to revel in her soft confusion.
She resisted; nay, resolutely returned to the lawn-sward.
He contrasted her with Constantia in the amorous time,
and rejoiced in his disappointment. He saw the Goddess
Modesty guarding Purity; and one would be bold to say
that he did not hear the Precepts, Purity's aged grannams
maternal and paternal, cawing approval of her over their
munching gums. And if you ask whether a man, sensitive
and a lover, can be so blinded, you are condemned to
re-peruse the foregoing paragraph.

Miss Middleton was not sufficiently instructed in the position of her sex to know that she had plunged herself in the thick of the strife of one of their great battles. Her personal position, however, was instilling knowledge rapidly, as a disease in the frame teaches us what we are and have to contend with. Could she marry this man? He was evidently manageable. Could she condescend to the use of arts in managing him to obtain a placable life?—a horror of swampy flatness! So vividly did the sight of that dead heaven over an unvarying level earth, swim on her fancy, that she shut her eyes in angry exclusion of it as if it were outside, assailing her: and she nearly stumbled upon young Crossjay.

'Oh! have I hurt you?' he cried.

'No,' said she, 'it was my fault. Lead me somewhere, away from everybody.'

The boy took her hand, and she resumed her thoughts; and, pressing his fingers and feeling warm to him both for his presence and silence, so does the blood in youth lead the mind, even cool and innocent blood, even with a touch, that she said to herself: 'And if I marry, and then . . . Where will honour be then? I marry him to be true to my word of honour, and if then . . .!' An intolerable languor caused her to sigh profoundly. It is written as she thought it; she thought in blanks, as girls do, and some women. A shadow of the male Egoist is in the chamber of their brains overawing them.

'Were I to marry, and to run!' There is the thought; she is offered up to your mercy. We are dealing with a girl feeling herself desperately situated, and not a fool.

'I'm sure you're dead tired, though,' said Crossjay.

'No, I am not; what makes you think so?' said Clara.

'I do think so.'

'But why do you think so?'

'You're so hot.'

'What makes you think that?'

'You're so red.'

'So are you, Crossjay.'

'I'm only red in the middle of the cheeks, except when

I've been running. And then you talk to yourself, just as boys do when they are blown.'

'Do they?'

'They say, "I know I could have kept up longer," or, "my buckle broke," all to themselves, when they break down running.'

'And you have noticed that?'

'And, Miss Middleton, I don't wish you were a boy, but I should like to live near you all my life and be a gentleman. I'm coming with Miss Dale this evening to stay at the Hall and be looked after, instead of stopping with her cousin, who takes care of her father. Perhaps you and I'll play chess at night.'

'At night you will go to bed, Crossjay.'

'Not if I have Sir Willoughby to catch hold of. He says I'm an authority on birds' eggs. I can manage rabbits and poultry. Isn't a farmer a happy man? But he doesn't marry ladies. A cavalry officer has the best chance.'

'But you are going to be a naval officer.'

'I don't know. It's not positive. I shall bring my two dormice, and make them perform gymnastics on the dinner-table. They're such dear little things. Naval officers are not like Sir Willoughby.'

'No, they are not,' said Clara; 'they give their lives to their country.'

'And then they're dead,' said Crossjay.

Clara wished Sir Willoughby were confronting her: she could have spoken.

She asked the boy where Mr. Whitford was. Crossjay pointed very secretly in the direction of the double-blossom wild-cherry. Coming within gaze of the stem she beheld Vernon stretched at length, reading, she supposed; asleep, she discovered: his finger in the leaves of a book; and what book? She had a curiosity to know the title of the book he would read beneath these boughs, and grasping Crossjay's hand fast she craned her neck, as one timorous of a fall in peeping over chasms, for a glimpse of the page; but immediately, and still with a bent head, she turned her face to where the load of virginal blossom, whiter than summer-cloud on the sky, showered and drooped and clustered so thick as to claim colour and seem, like higher Alpine snows in noon-sun-light, a flush of white. From deep to deeper heavens of white, her eyes perched and soared. Wonder lived in her. Happiness in the beauty of the tree pressed to sup-plant it, and was more mortal and narrower. Reflection came, contracting her vision and weighing her to earth. Her reflection was: 'He must be good who loves to lie and sleep beneath the branches of this tree!' She would rather have clung to her first impression: wonder so divine, so unbounded, was like soaring into homes of angel-crowded space, sweeping through folded and on to folded white fountain-bow of wings, in innumerable columns: but the thought of it was no recovery of it; she might as well have striven to be a child. The sensation of happiness promised to be less short-lived in memory, and would have been, had not her present disease of the longing for happiness ravaged every corner of it for the secret of its existence. The reflection took root. 'He must be good . . .!' That reflection vowed to endure. Poor by comparison with what it displaced, it presented itself to her as conferring something on him, and she would not have had it absent though it robbed her.

She looked down. Vernon was dreamily looking up.

She plucked Crossjay hurriedly away, whispering that he had better not wake Mr. Whitford, and then she pro-posed to reverse their previous chase, and she be the hound and he the hare. Crossjay fetched a magnificent start. On his glancing behind he saw Miss Middleton walking listlessly, with a hand at her side.

'There's a regular girl!' said he, in some disgust; for his theory was, that girls always have something the matter with them to spoil a game.

CHAPTER XII

Miss Middleton and Mr. Vernon Whitford

Looking upward, not quite awakened out of a transient doze, at a fair head circled in dazzling blossom, one may temporize awhile with common sense, and take it for a vision after the eyes have regained direction of the mind. Vernon did so until the plastic vision interwound with reality alarmingly. This is the embrace of a Melusine who will soon have the brain if she is encouraged. Slight dalliance with her makes the very diminutive seem as big as life. He jumped to his feet, rattled his throat, planted firmness on his brows and mouth, and attacked the dream-giving earth with tremendous long strides, that his blood might be lively at the throne of understanding. Miss Middleton and young Crossjay were within hail: it was her face he had seen, and still the idea of a vision, chased from his reasonable wits, knocked hard and again for readmission. There was little for a man of humble mind toward the sex to think of in the fact of a young lady's bending rather low to peep at him asleep, except that the poise of her slender figure, between an air of spying and of listening, vividly recalled his likening of her to the Mountain Echo. Man or maid sleeping in the open air provokes your tip-toe curiosity. Men, it is known, have in that state cruelly been kissed; and no rights are bestowed on them, they are teased by a vapourish rapture; what has happened to them the poor fellows barely divine: they have a crazy step from that day. But a vision is not so distracting; it is our own, we can put it aside and return to it, play at rich and poor with it, and are not to be summoned before your laws and rules for secreting it in our treasury. Besides, it is the golden key of all the possible: new worlds expand beneath the dawn it brings us. Just outside reality, it illumines, enriches and softens real things;—and to desire it in preference to the simple fact, is a damning proof of enervation.

Such was Vernon's winding up of his brief drama of

fantasy. He was aware of the fantastical element in him and soon had it under. Which of us who is of any worth is without it? He had not much vanity to trouble him, and passion was quiet, so his task was not gigantic. Especially be it remarked, that he was a man of quick pace, the sovereign remedy for the dispersing of the mental fen-mist. He had tried it and knew that nonsense is to be walked off.

Near the end of the park young Crossjay overtook him, and after acting the pumped one a trifle more than needful, cried: 'I say, Mr. Whitford, there's Miss Middleton with her handkerchief out.'

'What for, my lad?' said Vernon.

'I'm sure I don't know. All of a sudden she bumped down. And, look what fellows girls are!—here she comes as if nothing had happened, and I saw her feel at her side.'

Clara was shaking her head to express a denial. 'I am not at all unwell,' she said when she came near. 'I guessed Crossjay's business in running up to you; he's a good-for-nothing, officious boy. I was tired, and rested for a moment.'

Crossjay peered at her eyelids. Vernon looked away and said: 'Are you too tired for a stroll?'

'Not now.'

'Shall it be brisk?'

'You have the lead.'

He led at a swing of the legs that accelerated young Crossjay's to the double, but she with her short swift equal steps glided along easily on a line by his shoulder, and he groaned to think that of all the girls of earth this one should have been chosen for the position of fine lady.

'You won't tire me,' said she, in answer to his look.

'You remind me of the little Piedmontese Bersaglieri* on the march.'

'I have seen them trotting into Como from Milan.'

'They cover a quantity of ground in a day, if the ground's flat. You want another sort of step for the mountains.'

'I should not attempt to dance up.'

'They soon tame romantic notions of them.'

'The mountains tame luxurious dreams, you mean. I see how they are conquered. I can plod. Anything to be high up!'

'Well, there you have the secret of good work: to plod on and still keep the passion fresh.'

'Yes, when we have an aim in view.'

'We always have one.'

'Captives have?'

'More than the rest of us.'

Ignorant man! What of wives miserably wedded? What aim in view have these most woeful captives? Horror shrouds it, and shame reddens through the folds to tell of innermost horror.

'Take me back to the mountains, if you please, Mr. Whitford,' Miss Middleton said, fallen out of sympathy with him. 'Captives have death in view, but that is not an aim.'

'Why may not captives expect a release?'

'Hardly from a tyrant.'

'If you are thinking of tyrants, it may be so. Say the tyrant dies?'

'The prison-gates are unlocked and out comes a skeleton. But why will you talk of skeletons! The very name of mountain seems life in comparison with any other subject.'

'I assure you,' said Vernon, with the fervour of a man lighting on an actual truth in his conversation with a young lady, 'it's not the first time I have thought you would be at home in the Alps. You would walk and climb as well as you dance.'

She liked to hear Clara Middleton talked of, and of her having been thought of: and giving him friendly eyes, barely noticing that he was in a glow, she said, 'If you speak so encouragingly I shall fancy we are near an ascent.'

'I wish we were,' said he.

'We can realize it by dwelling on it, don't you think?'

'We can begin climbing.'

'Oh!' she squeezed herself shadowily.

'Which mountain shall it be?' said Vernon in the right real earnest tone.

Miss Middleton suggested a lady's mountain first, for a trial. 'And then, if you think well enough of me—if I have not stumbled more than twice, or asked more than ten times how far it is from the top, I should like to be promoted to scale a giant.'

They went up some of the lesser heights of Switzerland and Styria,* and settled in South Tyrol, the young lady preferring this district for the strenuous exercise of her climbing powers because she loved Italian colour; and it seemed an exceedingly good reason to the genial imagination she had awakened in Mr. Whitford: 'Though,' said he abruptly, 'you are not so much Italian as French.'

She hoped she was English, she remarked.

'Of course you are English; . . . yes.' He moderated his assent with the halting affirmative.

She inquired wonderingly why he spoke in apparent hesitation.

'Well, you have French feet, for example: French wits; French impatience,' he lowered his voice, 'and charm.'

'And love of compliments.'

'Possibly. I was not conscious of paying them.'

'And a disposition to rebel?'

'To challenge authority, at least.'

'That is a dreadful character.'

'At all events it is a character.'

'Fit for an Alpine comrade?'

'For the best of comrades anywhere.'

'It is not a piece of drawing-room sculpture: that is the most one can say for it!' she dropped a dramatic sigh.

Had he been willing she would have continued the theme, for the pleasure a poor creature long gnawing her sensations finds in seeing herself from the outside. It fell away. After a silence, she could not renew it: and he was evidently indifferent, having to his own satisfaction dissected and stamped her a foreigner. With it passed her holiday. She had forgotten Sir Willoughby: she remembered him and said: 'You knew Miss Durham, Mr. Whitford.'

He answered briefly: 'I did.'

'Was she . . .?' some hot-faced inquiry peered forth and withdrew.

'Very handsome,' said Vernon.

'English?'

'Yes: the dashing style of English.'

'Very courageous.'

'I daresay she had a kind of courage.'

'She did very wrong.'

'I won't say no. She discovered a man more of a match with herself; luckily not too late. We're at the mercy . . .'

'Was she not unpardonable?'

'I should be sorry to think that of any one.'

'But you agree that she did wrong.'

'I suppose I do. She made a mistake and she corrected it. If she had not, she would have made a greater mistake.'

'The manner . . .'

'That was bad—as far as we know. The world has not much right to judge. A false start must now and then be made. It's better not to take notice of it, I think.'

'What is it we are at the mercy of?'

'Currents of feeling, our natures. I am the last man to preach on the subject: young ladies are enigmas to me; I fancy they must have a natural perception of the husband suitable to them, and the reverse; and if they have a certain degree of courage, it follows that they please themselves.'

'They are not to reflect on the harm they do?' said Miss Middleton.

'By all means let them reflect; they hurt nobody by doing that.'

'But a breach of faith!'

'If the faith can be kept through life, all's well.'

'And then there is the cruelty, the injury!'

'I really think that if a young lady came to me to inform me she must break our engagement—I have never been put to proof, but to suppose it:—I should not think her cruel.'

'Then she would not be much of a loss.'

'And I should not think so for this reason, that it is impossible for a girl to come to such a resolution without previously showing signs of it to her . . . the man she is engaged to. I think it unfair to engage a girl for longer than a week or two, just time enough for her preparations and publications.'

'If he is always intent on himself, signs are likely to be unheeded by him,' said Miss Middleton.

He did not answer, and she said quickly:

'It must always be a cruelty. The world will think so. It is an act of inconstancy.'

'If they knew one another well before they were engaged.'

'Are you not singularly tolerant?' said she.

To which Vernon replied with airy cordiality:

'In some cases it is right to judge by results; we'll leave severity to the historian, who is bound to be a professional moralist and put pleas of human nature out of the scales. The lady in question may have been to blame, but no hearts were broken, and here we have four happy instead of two miserable.'

His persecuting geniality of countenance appealed to her to confirm this judgement by results, and she nodded and said, 'Four,' as the awe-stricken speak.

From that moment until young Crossjay fell into the green-rutted lane from a tree, and was got on his legs half-stunned, with a hanging lip and a face like the inside of a flayed eel-skin, she might have been walking in the desert, and alone, for the pleasure she had in society.

They led the fated lad home between them, singularly drawn together by their joint ministrations to him, in which her delicacy had to stand fire, and sweet good nature made naught of any trial. They were hand in hand with the little fellow as physician and professional nurse.

CHAPTER XIII

The First Effort after Freedom

CROSSJAY'S accident was only another proof, as Vernon told Miss Dale, that the boy was but half monkey.

'Something fresh?' she exclaimed on seeing him brought into the Hall, where she had just arrived.

'Simply a continuation,' said Vernon. 'He is not so prehensile as he should be. He probably in extremity relies on the tail that has been docked. Are you a man, Crossjay?'

'I should think I was!' Crossjay replied with an old man's voice, and a ghastly twitch for a smile overwhelmed the compassionate ladies.

Miss Dale took possession of him. 'You err in the other direction,' she remarked to Vernon.

'But a little bracing roughness is better than spoiling him,' said Miss Middleton.

She did not receive an answer, and she thought, 'Whatever Willoughby does is right, to this lady!'

Clara's impression was renewed when Sir Willoughby sat beside Miss Dale in the evening; and certainly she had never seen him shine so picturesquely as in his bearing with Miss Dale. The sprightly sallies of the two, their rallyings, their laughter, and her fine eyes, and his handsome gestures, won attention like a fencing match of a couple keen with the foils to display the mutual skill. And it was his design that she should admire the display; he was anything but obtuse; enjoying the match as he did and necessarily did to act so excellent a part in it, he meant the observer to see the man he was with a lady not of raw understanding. So it went on from day to day for three days.

She fancied once that she detected the agreeable stirring of the brood of jealousy, and found it neither in her heart nor in her mind, but in the book of wishes, well known to the young, where they write matter which may sometimes be independent of both those volcanic albums. Jealousy would have been a relief to her, a dear devil's aid. She studied the complexion of jealousy to delude herself with the sense of the spirit being in her, and all the while she laughed, as at a vile theatre whereof the imperfection of the stage machinery rather than the performance is the wretched source of amusement.

Vernon had deeply depressed her. She was hunted by the figure 4. *Four happy instead of two miserable.* He had said it, involving her among the four; and so it must be, she considered, and she must be as happy as she could; for not only was he incapable of perceiving her state, he was unable to imagine other circumstances to surround her. How, to be just to him, were they imaginable by him or any one?

Her horrible isolation of secrecy in a world amiable in unsuspectingness, frightened her. To fling away her secret, to conform, to be unrebellious, uncritical, submissive, became an impatient desire; and the task did not appear so difficult since Miss Dale's arrival. Endearments had been rarer, more formal; living bodily untroubled and unashamed, and, as she phrased it, having no one to care for her, she turned insensibly in the direction where she was due; she slightly imitated Miss Dale's colloquial responsiveness. To tell truth, she felt vivacious in a moderate way with Willoughby after seeing him with Miss Dale. Liberty wore the aspect of a towering prison-wall; the desperate undertaking of climbing one side and dropping to the other was more than she, unaided, could resolve on; consequently, as no one cared for her, a worthless creature might as well cease dreaming and stipulating for the fulfilment of her dreams; she might as well yield to her fate: nay, make the best of it.

Sir Willoughby was flattered and satisfied. Clara's adopted vivacity proved his thorough knowledge of feminine nature; nor did her feebleness in sustaining it displease him. A steady look of hers had of late perplexed the man, and he was comforted by signs of her inefficiency where he excelled. The effort and the failure were both of good omen.

But she could not continue the effort. He had overweighted her too much for the mimicry of a sentiment to harden and have an apparently natural place among her impulses; and now an idea came to her that he might, it might be hoped, possibly see in Miss Dale, by present contrast, the mate he sought; by contrast with an unanswering creature like herself, he might perhaps realize in Miss Dale's greater accomplishments and her devotion to him the merit of suitability; he might be induced to do her justice. Dim as the loophole was, Clara fixed her mind on it till it gathered light. And as a prelude to action, she plunged herself into a state of such profound humility, that to accuse it of being simulated would be venturesome, though it was not positive. The tempers of the young are liquid fires in isles of quicksand; the precious metals not yet cooled in a solid earth. Her compassion for Laetitia was less forced; but really she was almost as earnest in her self-abasement, for she had not latterly been brilliant, not even adequate to the ordinary requirements of conversation. She had no courage, no wit, no diligence, nothing that she could distinguish save discontentment like a corroding acid, and she went so far in sincerity as with a curious shift of feeling to pity the man plighted to her. If it suited her purpose to pity Sir Willoughby, she was not moved by policy, be assured; her needs were her nature, her moods her mind; she had the capacity to make anything serve her by passing into it with the glance which discerned its usefulness; and this is how it is that the young, when they are in trouble, without approaching the elevation of scientific hypocrites, can teach that able class lessons in hypocrisy.

'Why should not Willoughby be happy,' she said; and the explanation was pushed forth by the second thought: 'Then I shall be free!' Still that thought came second.

The desire for the happiness of Willoughby was fervent on his behalf, and wafted her far from friends and letters to a narrow Tyrolean valley, where a shallow river ran, with the indentations of a remotely-seen army of winding ranks in column, topaz over the pebbles, to hollows of ravishing emerald. There sat Liberty, after her fearful leap over the prison-wall, at peace to watch the water and the falls of sunshine on the mountain above, between descending pine-stem shadows. Clara's wish for his happiness, as soon as she had housed herself in the imagination of her freedom, was of a purity that made it seem exceedingly easy for her to speak to him.

The opportunity was offered by Sir Willoughby. Every morning after breakfast, Miss Dale walked across the park to see her father, and on this occasion Sir Willoughby and Miss Middleton went with her as far as the lake, all three discoursing of the beauty of various trees, birches, aspens, poplars, beeches, then in their new green. Miss Dale loved the aspen, Miss Middleton the beech, Sir Willoughby the birch, and pretty things were said by each in praise of the favoured object, particularly by Miss Dale. So much so that when she had gone on he recalled one of her remarks, and said: 'I believe, if the whole place were swept away to-morrow, Laetitia Dale could reconstruct it, and put those aspens on the north of the lake in number and situation correctly where you have them now. I would guarantee her description of it in absence correct.'

'Why should she be absent?' said Clara, palpitating.

'Well, why!' returned Sir Willoughby. 'As you say, there is no reason why. The art of life, and mine will be principally a country life—town is not life, but a tornado whirling atoms—the art is to associate a group of sympathetic friends in our neighbourhood; and it is a fact worth noting that if ever I feel tired of the place, a short talk with Laetitia Dale refreshes it more than a month or two on the Continent. She has the well of enthusiasm. And there is a great advantage in having a cultivated person at command, with whom one can chat of any topic under the sun. I repeat, you have no need of town if you have friends like Laetitia Dale within call. My mother esteemed her highly.'

'Willoughby, she is not obliged to go.'

'I hope not. And, my love, I rejoice that you have taken to her. Her father's health is poor. She would be a young spinster to live alone in a country cottage.'

'What of your scheme?'

'Old Vernon is a very foolish fellow.'

'He has declined?'

'Not a word on the subject! I have only to propose it to be snubbed, I know.'

'You may not be aware how you throw him into the shade with her.'

'Nothing seems to teach him the art of dialogue with ladies.'

'Are not gentlemen shy when they see themselves out-shone?'

'He hasn't it, my love: Vernon is deficient in the lady's tongue.'

'I respect him for that.'

'Outshone, you say? I do not know of any shining— save to one, who lights me, path and person!'

The identity of the one was conveyed to her in a bow and a soft pressure.

'Not only has he not the lady's tongue, which I hold to be a man's proper accomplishment,' continued Sir Willoughby, 'he cannot turn his advantages to account. Here has Miss Dale been with him now four days in the house. They are exactly on the same footing as when she entered it. You ask? I will tell you. It is this: it is want of warmth. Old Vernon is a scholar—and a fish. Well, perhaps he has cause to be shy of matrimony: but he is a fish.'

'You are reconciled to his leaving you?'

'False alarm! The resolution to do anything unaccus-tomed is quite beyond old Vernon.'

'But if Mr. Oxford—Whitford . . . your swans coming sailing up the lake, how beautiful they look when they are indignant! I was going to ask you, surely men witnessing a marked admiration for some one else will naturally be discouraged?'

Sir Willoughby stiffened with sudden enlightenment. Though the word jealousy had not been spoken, the drift of her observations was clear. Smiling inwardly, he said: and the sentences were not enigmas to her: 'Surely, too, young ladies . . . a little?—Too far? But an old friend-ship! About the same as the fitting of an old glove to a hand. Hand and glove have only to meet. Where there is natural harmony you would not have discord. Ay, but you have it if you check the harmony. My dear girl! You child!'

He had actually, in this parabolic and commendable obscureness, for which she thanked him in her soul, struck the very point she had not named and did not wish to hear named, but wished him to strike. His exultation, of the compressed sort, was extreme, on hearing her cry out:

'Young ladies may be. Oh! not I, not I. I can convince you. Not that. Believe me, Willoughby. I do not know what it is to feel that, or anything like it. I cannot conceive a claim on any one's life—as a claim: or the continuation of an engagement not founded on perfect, *perfect* sympathy. How should I feel it, then? It is, as you say of Mr. Ox—Whitford, beyond me.'

Sir Willoughby caught up the Ox—Whitford.

Bursting with laughter in his joyful pride, he called it a portrait of old Vernon in society. For she thought a trifle too highly of Vernon, as here and there a raw young lady does think of the friends of her plighted man: which is waste of substance properly belonging to him: as it were, in the loftier sense, an expenditure in genuflexions to wayside idols of the reverence she should bring intact to the temple. Derision instructs her.

Of the other subject—her jealousy—he had no desire to hear more. She had winced: the woman had been touched to smarting in the girl: enough. She attempted the subject once, but faintly, and his careless parrying threw her out. Clara could have bitten her tongue for that reiterated stupid slip on the name of Whitford; and because she was innocent at heart she persisted in asking herself how she could be guilty of it.

'You both know the botanic titles of these wild-flowers,' she said.

'Who?' he inquired.

'You and Miss Dale.'

Sir Willoughby shrugged. He was amused.

'No woman on earth will grace a barouche* so exquisitely as my Clara!'

'Where?' said she.

'During our annual two months in London. I drive a barouche there, and venture to prophecy that my equipage will create the greatest excitement of any in London. I see old Horace De Craye gazing!'

She sighed. She could not drag him to the word, or a hint of it necessary to her subject.

But there it was; she saw it. She had nearly let it go, and blushed at being obliged to name it.

'Jealousy, do you mean, Willoughby? the people in London would be jealous?—Colonel De Craye? How strange! That is a sentiment I cannot understand.'

Sir Willoughby gesticulated the 'Of course not' of an established assurance to the contrary.

'Indeed, Willoughby, I do not.'

'Certainly not.'

He was now in her trap. And he was imagining himself to be anatomizing her feminine nature.

'Can I give you a proof, Willoughby? I am so utterly incapable of it that—listen to me—were you to come to me to tell me, as you might, how much better suited to you Miss Dale has appeared than I am—and I fear I am not; it should be spoken plainly; unsuited altogether, perhaps—I would, I beseech you to believe—you must believe me—give you . . . give you your freedom instantly; most truly; and engage to speak of you as I should think of you. Willoughby, you would have no one to praise you in public and in private as I should, for you would be to me the most honest, truthful, chivalrous gentleman alive. And in that case I would undertake to declare that she would not admire you more than I: Miss Dale would not; she would not admire you more than I; not even Miss Dale!'

This, her first direct leap for liberty, set Clara panting, and so much had she to say that the nervous and the intellectual halves of her clashed like cymbals, dazing and stunning her with the appositeness of things to be said, and dividing her in indecision as to the cunningest to move him, of the many pressing.

The condition of feminine jealousy stood revealed.

He had driven her farther than he intended.

'Come, let me allay these . . .' he soothed her with hand and voice while seeking for his phrase; 'these magnified pin-points. Now, my Clara! on my honour! and when I put it forward in attestation, my honour has the most serious meaning speech can have; ordinarily my word has to suffice for bonds, promises or asseverations: on my honour! not merely is there, my poor child! no ground of suspicion, I assure you, I declare to you, the fact of the case is the very reverse. Now, mark me; of her sentiments I cannot pretend to speak; I did not, to my knowledge, originate, I am not responsible for them, and I am, before the law, as we will say, ignorant of them: that is, I have never heard a declaration of them, and I am, therefore, under pain of the stigma of excessive fatuity, bound to be non-cognizant. But as to myself, I can speak for myself, and, on my honour! Clara—to be as direct as possible, even to baldness, and you know I loathe it—I could not, I repeat, *I could not marry Laetitia Dale!* Let me impress it on you. No flatteries—we are all susceptible more or less—no conceivable condition could bring it about; no amount of admiration. She and I are excellent friends; we cannot be more. When you see us together, the natural concord of our minds is of course misleading. She is a woman of genius. I do not conceal, I profess my admiration of her. There are times when, I confess, I require a Laetitia Dale to bring me out, give and take. I am indebted to her for the enjoyment of the duet few know, few can accord with, fewer still are allowed the privilege of playing with a human being. I am indebted, I own, and I feel deep gratitude; I own to a lively friendship for Miss Dale, but if she is displeasing in the sight of my bride by . . . by the breadth of an eye-lash, then . . .'

Sir Willoughby's arm waved Miss Dale off away into outer darkness in the wilderness.

Clara shut her eyes and rolled her eyeballs in a frenzy of unuttered revolt.

But she was not engaged in the colloquy to be an advocate of Miss Dale or of common humanity.

'Ah!' she said, simply determining that the subject should not drop.

'And, ah!' he mocked her tenderly. 'True, though! And who knows better than my Clara that I require youth, health, beauty, and the other undefinable attributes fitting with mine and beseeming the station of the lady called to preside over my household and represent me? What says my other self? my fairer? But you are! my love, you are! Understand my nature rightly, and you . . .'

'I do! I do!' interposed Clara: 'if I did not by this time I should be idiotic. Let me assure you, I understand it. Oh! listen to me: one moment. Miss Dale regards me as the happiest woman on earth. Willoughby, if I possessed her good qualities, her heart and mind, no doubt I should be. It is my wish—you must hear me, hear me out—my wish, my earnest wish, my burning prayer, my wish to make way for her. She appreciates you: I do not—to my shame, I do not. She worships you: I do not, I cannot. You are the rising sun to her. It has been so for years. No one can account for love: I daresay not for the impossibility of loving . . . loving where we should; all love bewilders me. I was not created to understand it. But she loves you, she has pined. I believe it has destroyed the health you demand as one item in your list. But you, Willoughby, can restore that. Travelling, and . . . and your society, the pleasure of your society would certainly restore it. You look so handsome together! She has unbounded devotion: as for me I cannot idolize. I see faults; I see them daily. They astonish and wound me. Your pride would not bear to hear them spoken of, least of all by your wife. You warned me to beware—that is, you said, you said something.'

Her busy brain missed the subterfuge to cover her slip of the tongue.

Sir Willoughby struck in: 'And when I say that the entire concatenation is based on an erroneous observation of facts, and an erroneous deduction from that erroneous observation!—? No, no. Have confidence in me. I propose it to you in this instance, purely to save you from deception. You are cold, my love? you shivered.'

'I am not cold,' said Clara. 'Some one, I suppose, was walking over my grave.'

The gulf of a caress hove in view like an enormous billow hollowing under the curled ridge.

She stooped to a buttercup; the monster swept by.

'Your grave!' he exclaimed over her head; 'my own girl!'

'Is not the orchis naturally a stranger in ground so far away from the chalk, Willoughby?'

'I am incompetent to pronounce an opinion on such important matters. My mother had a passion for every description of flower. I fancy I have some recollection of her scattering the flower you mention over the park.'

'If she were living now!'

'We should be happy in the blessing of the most estimable of women, my Clara.'

'She would have listened to me. She would have realized what I mean.'

'Indeed, Clara—poor soul!' he murmured to himself aloud: 'indeed you are absolutely in error. If I have seemed—but I repeat, you are deceived. The idea of "fitness" is a total hallucination. Supposing you—I do it even in play painfully—entirely out of the way, unthought of . . .'

'Extinct,' Clara said low.

'Non-existent for me,' he selected a preferable term. 'Suppose it; I should still, in spite of an admiration I have never thought it incumbent on me to conceal, still be—I speak emphatically—*utterly incapable of the offer of my hand to Miss Dale*. It may be that she is embedded in my mind as a friend, and nothing but a friend. I received the stamp in early youth. People have noticed it—we do, it seems, bring one another out, reflecting, counterreflecting.'

She glanced up at him with a shrewd satisfaction to see that her wicked shaft had stuck.

'You do: it is a common remark,' she said. 'The instantaneous difference when she comes near, any one might notice.'

'My love,' he opened the iron gate into the garden, 'you encourage the naughty little suspicion.'

'But it is a beautiful sight, Willoughby. I like to see you together. I like it as I like to see colours match.'

'Very well. There is no harm, then. We shall often be together. I like my fair friend. But the instant!—you have only to express a sentiment of disapprobation.'

'And you dismiss her.'

'I dismiss her. That is, as to the word, I constitute myself your echo, to clear any vestige of suspicion. She goes.'

'That is a case of a person doomed to extinction without offending.'

'Not without: for whoever offends my bride, my wife, my sovereign lady, offends me: very deeply offends me.'

'Then the caprices of your wife . . .' Clara stamped her foot imperceptibly on the lawn-sward, which was irresponsibly soft to her fretfulness. She broke from the inconsequent meaningless mild tone of irony, and said: 'Willoughby, women have their honour to swear by equally with men:—girls have: they have to swear an oath at the altar: may I to you now? Take it for uttered when I tell you that nothing would make me happier than your union with Miss Dale. I have spoken as much as I can. Tell me you release me.'

With the well-known screw-smile of duty upholding weariness worn to inanition, he rejoined: 'Allow me once more to reiterate, that it is repulsive, inconceivable, that I should *ever, under any mortal conditions, bring myself to the point of taking Miss Dale for my wife.* You reduce me to this perfectly childish protestation—pitiably childish! But, my love, have I to remind you that you and I are plighted, and that I am an honourable man?'

'I know it, I feel it, release me!' cried Clara.

Sir Willoughby severely reprehended his shortsightedness for seeing but the one proximate object in the particular attention he had bestowed on Miss Dale. He could not disavow that they had been marked, and with an object, and he was distressed by the unwonted want of wisdom through which he had been drawn to overshoot his object. His design to excite a touch of the insane emotion in Clara's bosom was too successful, and, 'I was not thinking of her,' he said to himself in his candour, contrite.

She cried again: 'Will you not, Willoughby?—release me?'

He begged her to take his arm.

To consent to touch him while petitioning for a detachment, appeared discordant to Clara, but, if she expected him to accede, it was right that she should do as much as she could, and she surrendered her hand at arm's length, disdaining the imprisoned fingers. He pressed them and said: 'Dr. Middleton is in the library. I see Vernon is at work with Crossjay in the West-room —the boy has had sufficient for the day. Now, is it not like old Vernon to drive his books at a cracked head before it's half mended?'

He signalled to young Crossjay, who was up and out through the folding windows in a twinkling.

'And you will go in, and talk to Vernon of the lady in question,' Sir Willoughby whispered to Clara. 'Use your best persuasions in our joint names. You have my warrant for saying that money is no consideration; house and income are assured. You can hardly have taken me seriously when I requested you to undertake Vernon before. I was quite in earnest then as now. I prepare Miss Dale. I will not have a wedding on *our* wedding-day: but either before or after it, I gladly speed their alliance. I think now I give you the best proof possible; and though I know that with women a delusion may be seen to be groundless and still be cherished, I rely on your good sense.'

Vernon was at the window and stood aside for her to enter. Sir Willoughby used a gentle insistence with her. She bent her head as if she were stepping into a cave. So frigid was she, that a ridiculous dread of calling Mr. Whitford Mr. Oxford was her only present anxiety when Sir Willoughby had closed the window on them.

CHAPTER XIV

Sir Willoughby and Laetitia

'I PREPARE Miss Dale.'

Sir Willoughby thought of his promise to Clara. He trifled awhile with young Crossjay, and then sent the boy flying, and wrapped himself in meditation. So shall you see standing many a statue of statesmen who have died in harness for their country.

In the hundred and fourth chapter of the thirteenth volume of the BOOK OF EGOISM, it is written: *Possession without obligation to the object possessed approaches felicity.*

It is the rarest condition of ownership. For example: the possession of land is not without obligation both to the soil and the tax-collector; the possession of fine clothing is oppressed by obligation: gold, jewelry, works of art, enviable household furniture, are positive fetters: the possession of a wife we find surcharged with obligation. In all these cases, possession is a gentle term for enslavement, bestowing the sort of felicity attained to by the helot drunk. You can have the joy, the pride, the intoxication of possession: you can have no free soul.

But there is one instance of possession, and that the most perfect, which leaves us free, under not a shadow of obligation, receiving ever, never giving, or if giving, giving only of our waste; as it were (sauf votre respect), by form of perspiration, radiation, if you like; unconscious poral bountifulness; and it is a beneficial process for the system. Our possession of an adoring female's worship, is this instance.

The soft cherishable Parsee* is hardly at any season other than prostrate. She craves nothing save that you continue in being—her sun: which is your firm constitutional endeavour: and thus you have a most exact alliance; she supplying spirit to your matter, while at the same time presenting matter to your spirit, verily a comfortable apposition. The Gods do bless it.

That they do so indeed is evident in the men they select for such a felicitous crown and aureole. Weak men would be rendered nervous by the flattery of a woman's worship; or they would be for returning it, at least partially, as though it could be bandied to and fro without emulgence* of the poetry; or they would be pitiful, and quite spoil the thing. Some would be for transforming the beautiful solitary vestal flame by the first effort of the multiplication-table into your hearth-fire of slippered affection. So these men are not they whom the Gods have ever selected, but rather men of a pattern with themselves, very high and very solid men, who maintain the crown by holding divinely independent of the great emotion they have sown.

Even for them a pass of danger is ahead, as we shall see in our sample of one among the highest of them.

A clear approach to felicity had long been the portion of Sir Willoughby Patterne in his relations with Laetitia Dale. She belonged to him; he was quite unshackled by her. She was everything that is good in a parasite, nothing that is bad. His dedicated critic she was, reviewing him with a favour equal to perfect efficiency in her office; and whatever the world might say of him, to her the happy gentleman could constantly turn for his refreshing balsamic bath. She flew to the soul in him, pleasingly arousing sensations of that inhabitant; and he allowed her the right to fly, in the manner of kings, as we have heard, consenting to the privileges acted on by cats. These may not address their Majesties, but they may stare; nor will it be contested that the attentive circular eyes of the humble domestic creatures are an embellishment to Royal pomp and grandeur, such truly as should one day gain for them an inweaving and figurement—in the place of bees, ermine tufts, and their various present decorations—upon the august great robes back-flowing and foaming over the gaspy page-boys.

Further to quote from the same volume of THE BOOK: *There is pain in the surrendering of that we are fain to relinquish.*

The idea is too exquisitely attenuate, as are those of the whole body-guard of the heart of Egoism, and will slip through you unless you shall have made a study of the gross of volumes of the first and second sections of THE

BOOK, and that will take you up to senility; or you must make a personal entry into the pages, perchance; or an escape out of them. There was once a venerable gentleman for whom a white hair grew on the cop of his nose, laughing at removals. He resigned himself to it in the end, and lastingly contemplated the apparition. It does not concern us what effect was produced on his countenance and his mind; enough that he saw a fine thing, but not so fine as the idea cited above; which has been between the two eyes of humanity ever since women were sought in marriage. With yonder old gentleman it may have been a ghostly hair or a disease of the optic nerves; but for us it is a real growth, and humanity might profitably imitate him in his patient speculation upon it.

Sir Willoughby Patterne, though ready in the pursuit of duty and policy (an oft-united couple) to cast Miss Dale away, had to consider that he was not simply, so to speak, casting her over a hedge, he was casting her for a man to catch her; and this was a much greater trial than it had been on the previous occasion, when she went over bump to the ground. In the arms of a husband, there was no knowing how soon she might forget her soul's fidelity. It had not hurt him to sketch the project of the conjunction; benevolence assisted him; but he winced and smarted on seeing it take shape. It sullied his idea of Laetitia.

Still, if, in spite of so great a change in her fortune, her spirit could be guaranteed changeless, he, for the sake of pacifying his bride, and to keep two serviceable persons near him at command, might resolve to join them. The vision of his resolution brought with it a certain pallid contempt of the physically faithless woman; no wonder he betook himself to THE BOOK, and opened it on the scorching chapters treating of the sex, and the execrable wiles of that foremost creature of the chase, who runs for life. She is not spared in the Biggest of Books. But close it.

The writing in it having been done chiefly by men, men naturally receive their fortification from its wisdom, and half a dozen of the popular sentences for the confusion of women (cut in brass worn to a polish like sombre gold), refreshed Sir Willoughby for his undertaking.

An examination of Laetitia's faded complexion braced him very cordially.

His Clara jealous of this poor leaf!

He could have desired the transfusion of a quality or two from Laetitia to his bride; but you cannot, as in cookery, obtain a mixture of the essences of these creatures; and if, as it is possible to do, and as he had been doing recently with the pair of them at the Hall, you stew them in one pot, you are far likelier to intensify their little birth-marks of individuality. Had they a tendency to excellence, it might be otherwise; they might then make the exchanges we wish for; or scientifically concocted in a harem for a sufficient length of time by a sultan anything but obtuse, they might. It is however fruitless to dwell on what was only a glimpse of a wild regret, like the crossing of two express trains along the rails in Sir Willoughby's head.

The ladies Eleanor and Isabel were sitting with Miss Dale, all three at work on embroideries. He had merely to look at Miss Eleanor. She rose. She looked at Miss Isabel, and rattled her châtelaine to account for her departure. After a decent interval Miss Isabel glided out. Such was the perfect discipline of the household.

Sir Willoughby played an air on the knee of his crossed leg.

Laetitia grew conscious of a meaning in the silence. She said, 'You have not been vexed by affairs to-day?'

'Affairs,' he replied, 'must be peculiarly vexatious to trouble me. Concerning the country or my personal affairs?'

'I fancy I was alluding to the country.'

'I trust I am as good a patriot as any man living,' said he; 'but I am used to the follies of my countrymen, and we are on board a stout ship. At the worst it's no worse than a rise in rates and taxes; soup at the Hall-gates, perhaps; licence to fell timber in one of the outer copses, or some dozen loads of coal. You hit my feudalism.'

'The knight in armour has gone,' said Laetitia, 'and

the castle with the drawbridge. Immunity for our island has gone too since we took to commerce.'

'We bartered independence for commerce. You hit our old controversy. Ay, but we do not want this over-grown population! However, we will put politics and sociology and the pack of their modern barbarous words aside. You read me intuitively. I have been, I will not say annoyed, but ruffled. I have much to do, and going into Parliament would make me almost helpless if I lose Vernon. You know of some absurd notion he has?—literary fame, and bachelor's chambers, and a chop-house, and the rest of it.'

She knew; and thinking differently in the matter of literary fame, she flushed, and ashamed of the flush, frowned.

He bent over to her with the perusing earnestness of a gentleman about to trifle.

'You cannot intend that frown?'

'Did I frown?'

'You do.'

'Now?'

'Fiercely.'

'Oh!'

'Will you smile to reassure me?'

'Willingly, as well as I can.'

A gloom overcame him. With no woman on earth did he shine so as to recall to himself seigneur and dame of the old French Court, as he did with Laetitia Dale. He did not wish the period revived, but reserved it as a garden to stray into when he was in the mood for displaying elegance and brightness in the society of a lady; and in speech Laetitia helped him to the nice delusion. She was not devoid of grace of bearing either.

Would she preserve her beautiful responsiveness to his ascendancy? Hitherto she had, and for years, and quite fresh. But how of her as a married woman? Our souls are hideously subject to the conditions of our animal nature! A wife, possibly mother, it was within sober calculation that there would be great changes in her. And the hint of any change appeared a total change to one of the lofty order who, when they are called on to relinquish possession instead of aspiring to it, say, All or nothing!

Well, but if there was danger of the marriage-tie effecting the slightest alteration of her character or habit of mind, wherefore press it upon a tolerably hardened spinster!

Besides, though he did once put her hand in Vernon's for the dance, he remembered acutely that the injury then done by his generosity to his tender sensitiveness had sickened and tarnished the effulgence of two or three successive anniversaries of his coming of age. Nor had he altogether yet got over the passion of greed for the whole group of the well-favoured of the fair sex, which in his early youth had made it bitter for him to submit to the fickleness, not to say immodest fickleness, of any handsome one of them in yielding her hand to a man and suffering herself to be led away. Ladies whom he had only heard of as ladies of some beauty, incurred his wrath for having lovers or taking husbands. He was of a vast embrace; and do not exclaim, in covetousness;—for well he knew that even under Moslem law*he could not have them all;—but as the enamoured custodian of the sex's purity, that blushes at such big spots as lovers and husbands; and it was unbearable to see it sacrificed for others. Without their purity what are they!—what are fruiterer's plums?—unsaleable. O for the bloom on them!

'As I said, I lose my right hand in Vernon,' he resumed, 'and I am, it seems, inevitably to lose him, unless we contrive to fasten him down here. I think, my dear Miss Dale, you have my character. At least, I should recommend my future biographer to you—with a caution, of course. You would have to write selfishness with a dash under it. I cannot endure to lose a member of my household—not under any circumstances; and a change of feeling to me on the part of any of my friends because of marriage, I think hard. I would ask you, how can it be for Vernon's good to quit an easy pleasant home for the wretched profession of Literature?—wretchedly paying, I mean,' he bowed to the authoress. 'Let him leave the house, if he imagines he will not harmonize with its young mistress. He is queer, though a good fellow. But he ought, in that event, to have an establishment. And my scheme for Vernon—men, Miss Dale, do not change to their old friends when they marry—my scheme, which would cause the alteration in his system of life to be barely perceptible, is to build him a poetical little cottage, large enough for a couple, on the borders of my park. I have the spot in my eye. The point is, can he live alone there? Men, I say, do not change. How is it that we cannot say the same of women?'

Laetitia remarked: 'The generic woman appears to have an extraordinary faculty for swallowing the individual.'

'As to the individual, as to a particular person, I may be wrong. Precisely because it is her case I think of, my strong friendship inspires the fear: unworthy of both, no doubt, but trace it to the source. Even pure friendship, such is the taint in us, knows a kind of jealousy; though I would gladly see her established, and near me, happy and contributing to my happiness with her incomparable social charm. Her I do not estimate generically, be sure.'

'If you do me the honour to allude to me, Sir Willoughby,' said Laetitia, 'I am my father's housemate.'

'What wooer would take that for a refusal? He would beg to be a third in the house and a sharer of your affectionate burden. Honestly, why not? And I may be arguing against my own happiness: it may be the end of me!'

'The end?'

'Old friends are captious, exacting. No, not the end. Yet if my friend is not the same to me, it is the end to that form of friendship: not to the degree possibly. But when one is used to the form! And do you, in its application to friendship, scorn the word "use"? We are creatures of custom. I am, I confess, a poltroon in my affections; I dread changes. The shadow of the tenth of an inch in the customary elevation of an eyelid!—to give you an idea of my susceptibility. And, my dear

Miss Dale, I throw myself on your charity, with all my weakness bare, let me add, as I could do to none but you. Consider, then, if I lose you! The fear is due to my pusillanimity entirely. High-souled women may be wives, mothers, and still reserve that home for their friend. They can and will conquer the viler conditions of human life. Our states, I have always contended, our various phases have to be passed through, and there is no disgrace in it so long as they do not levy toll on the quintessential, the spiritual element. You understand me? I am no adept in these abstract elucidations.'

'You explain yourself clearly,' said Laetitia.

'I have never pretended that psychology was my forte,' said he, feeling overshadowed by her cold commendation: he was not less acutely sensitive to the fractional divisions of tones than of eyelids, being, as it were, a melody with which everything was out of tune that did not modestly or mutely accord; and to bear about a melody in your person is incomparably more searching than the best of touchstones and talismans ever invented. 'Your father's health has improved latterly?'

'He did not complain of his health when I saw him this morning. My cousin Amelia is with him, and she is an excellent nurse.'

'He has a liking for Vernon.'

'He has a great respect for Mr. Whitford.'

'You have?'

'Oh! yes; I have it equally.'

'For a foundation, that is the surest. I would have the friends dearest to me begin on that. The headlong match is!—how can we describe it? By its finale, I am afraid. Vernon's abilities are really to be respected. His shyness is his malady. I suppose he reflected that he was not a capitalist. He might, one would think, have addressed himself to me; my purse is not locked.'

'No, Sir Willoughby!' Laetitia said warmly, for his donations in charity were famous.

Her eyes gave him the food he enjoyed, and basking in them, he continued:

'Vernon's income would at once have been regulated

commensurately with a new position requiring an increase. This money, money, money! But the world will have it so. Happily I have inherited habits of business and personal economy. Vernon is a man who would do fifty times more with a companion appreciating his abilities and making light of his little deficiencies. They are palpable, small enough. He has always been aware of my wishes:—when perhaps the fulfilment might have sent me off on another tour of the world, home-bird though I am! When was it that our friendship commenced? In my boyhood, I know. Very many years back.'

'I am in my thirtieth year,' said Laetitia.

Surprised and pained by a baldness resembling the deeds of ladies (they have been known, either through absence of mind, or mania, to displace a wig) in the deadly intimacy which slaughters poetic admiration, Sir Willoughby punished her by deliberately reckoning that she did not look less.

'Genius,' he observed, 'is unacquainted with wrinkles': hardly one of his prettiest speeches; but he had been wounded, and he never could recover immediately. Coming on him in a mood of sentiment, the wound was sharp. He could very well have calculated the lady's age. It was the jarring clash of her brazen declaration of it upon his low rich flute-notes that shocked him.

He glanced at the gold cathedral-clock on the mantelpiece, and proposed a stroll on the lawn before dinner. Laetitia gathered up her embroidery work.

'As a rule,' he said, 'authoresses are not needle-women.'

'I shall resign the needle or the pen if it stamps me an exception,' she replied.

He attempted a compliment on her truly exceptional character. As when the player's finger rests in distraction on the organ, it was without measure and disgusted his own hearing. Nevertheless she had been so good as to diminish his apprehension that the marriage of a lady in her thirtieth year with his cousin Vernon would be so much of a loss to him; hence, while parading the lawn, now and then casting an eye at the window of the room

where his Clara and Vernon were in council, the schemes
he indulged for his prospective comfort and his feelings
of the moment were in such striving harmony as that
to which we hear orchestral musicians bringing their
instruments under the process called tuneing. It is not
perfect, but it promises to be soon. We are not angels,
which have their dulcimers ever on the choral pitch. We
are mortals, attaining the celestial accord with effort,
through a stage of pain. Some degree of pain was necessary to Sir Willoughby, otherwise he would not have
seen his generosity confronting him. He grew, therefore,
tenderly inclined to Laetitia once more, so far as to say
within himself, 'For conversation she would be a valuable
wife.' And this valuable wife he was presenting to his
cousin.

Apparently, considering the duration of the conference
of his Clara and Vernon, his cousin required strong persuasion to accept the present.

CHAPTER XV

The Petition for a Release

NEITHER Clara nor Vernon appeared at the mid-day
table. Dr. Middleton talked with Miss Dale on classical
matters, like a good-natured giant giving a child the
jump from stone.to stone across a brawling mountain
ford, so that an unedified audience might really suppose,
upon seeing her over the difficulty, she had done something for herself. Sir Willoughby was proud of her, and
therefore anxious to settle her business while he was in the
humour to lose her. He hoped to finish it by shooting a
word or two at Vernon before dinner. Clara's petition to
be set free, released from *him*, had vaguely frightened
even more than it offended his pride.

Miss Isabel quitted the room.

She came back, saying, 'They decline to lunch.'

'Then we may rise,' remarked Sir Willoughby.

'She was weeping,' Miss Isabel murmured to him.

'Girlish enough,' he said.

The two elderly ladies went away together. Miss Dale, pursuing her theme with the Rev. Doctor, was invited by him to a course in the library. Sir Willoughby walked up and down the lawn, taking a glance at the West-room as he swung round on the turn of his leg. Growing impatient, he looked in at the window and found the room vacant.

Nothing was to be seen of Clara and Vernon during the afternoon. Near the dinner-hour the ladies were informed by Miss Middleton's maid that her mistress was lying down on her bed, too unwell with headache to be present. Young Crossjay brought a message from Vernon (delayed by birds' eggs in the delivery), to say that he was off over the hills, and thought of dining with Dr. Corney.

Sir Willoughby despatched condolences to his bride. He was not well able to employ his mind on its customary topic, being, like the dome of a bell, a man of so pervading a ring within himself concerning himself, that the recollection of a doubtful speech or unpleasant circumstance touching him closely, deranged his inward peace; and as dubious and unpleasant things will often occur, he had great need of a worshipper, and was often compelled to appeal to her for signs of antidotal idolatry. In this instance, when the need of a worshipper was sharply felt, he obtained no signs at all. The Rev. Doctor had fascinated Miss Dale; so that, both within and without, Sir Willoughby was uncomforted. His themes in public were those of an English gentleman; horses, dogs, game, sport, intrigue, scandal, politics, wines, the manly themes; with a condescension to ladies' tattle, and approbation of a racy anecdote. What interest could he possibly take in the Athenian Theatre and the girl whose flute-playing behind the scenes, imitating the nightingale, enraptured a Greek audience! He would have suspected a motive in Miss Dale's eager attentiveness, if the motive could have been conceived. Besides, the ancients were not decorous; they did not, as we make our moderns do, write for ladies. He ventured at the dinner-table to interrupt Dr. Middleton once;

'Miss Dale will do wisely, I think, sir, by confining herself to your present edition of the classics.'

'That,' replied Dr. Middleton, 'is the observation of a student of the dictionary of classical mythology in the English tongue.'

'The Theatre is a matter of climate, sir. You will grant me that.'

'If quick wits come of climate, it is as you say, sir.'

'With us it seems a matter of painful fostering, or the need of it,' said Miss Dale, with a question to Dr. Middleton, excluding Sir Willoughby, as though he had been a temporary disturbance of the flow of their dialogue.

The ladies Eleanor and Isabel, previously excellent listeners to the learned talk, saw the necessity of coming to his rescue; but you cannot converse with your aunts, inmates of your house, on general subjects at table; the attempt increased his discomposure; he considered that he had ill-chosen his father-in-law; that scholars are an impolite race; that young or youngish women are devotees of power in any form, and will be absorbed by a scholar for a variation of a man; concluding that he must have a round of dinner-parties to friends, especially ladies, appreciating him, during the Doctor's visit. Clara's headache above, and Dr. Middleton's unmannerliness below, affected his instincts in a way to make him apprehend that a stroke of misfortune was impending; thunder was in the air. Still he learnt something, by which he was to profit subsequently. The topic of Wine withdrew the Doctor from his classics; it was magical on him. A strong fraternity of taste was discovered in the sentiments of host and guest upon particular wines and vintages; they kindled one another by naming great years of the grape, and if Sir Willoughby had to sacrifice the ladies to the topic, he much regretted a condition of things that compelled him to sin against his habit, for the sake of being in the conversation and probing an elderly gentleman's foible.

Late at night he heard the house-bell, and meeting Vernon in the hall, invited him to enter the laboratory and tell him Dr. Corney's last. Vernon was brief; Corney had not let fly a single anecdote, he said, and lighted his candle.

'By the way, Vernon, you had a talk with Miss Middleton?'

'She will speak to you to-morrow at twelve.'

'To-morrow at twelve?'

'It gives her four and twenty hours.'

Sir Willoughby determined that his perplexity should be seen; but Vernon said good-night to him, and was shooting up the stairs before the dramatic exhibition of surprise had yielded to speech.

Thunder was in the air and a blow coming. Sir Willoughby's instincts were awake to the many signs, nor, though silenced, were they hushed by his harping on the frantic excesses to which women are driven by the passion of jealousy. He believed in Clara's jealousy because he really had intended to rouse it; under the form of emulation, feebly. He could not suppose she had spoken of it to Vernon. But as for the seriousness of her desire to be released from her engagement, that was little credible. Still the fixing of an hour for her to speak to him after an interval of four and twenty hours, left an opening for the incredible to add its weight to the suspicious mass: and who would have fancied Clara Middleton so wild a victim of the intemperate passion! He muttered to himself several assuageing observations to excuse a young lady half-demented, and rejected them in a lump for their nonsensical inapplicability to Clara. In order to obtain some sleep, he consented to blame himself slightly, in the style of the enamoured historian of erring Beauties alluding to their peccadilloes. He had done it to edify her. Sleep, however, failed him. That an inordinate jealousy argued an overpowering love, solved his problem until he tried to fit the proposition to Clara's character. He had discerned nothing southern in her. Latterly, with the blushing Day in prospect, she had contracted and frozen. There was no reading either of her or the mystery.

In the morning, at the breakfast-table, a confession of sleeplessness was general. Excepting Miss Dale and Dr. Middleton, none had slept a wink. 'I, sir,' the Doctor replied to Sir Willoughby, 'slept like a lexicon in your library when Mr. Whitford and I are out of it.'

Vernon incidentally mentioned that he had been writing through the night.

'You fellows kill yourselves,' Sir Willoughby reproved him. 'For my part, I make it a principle to get through my work without self-slaughter.'

Clara watched her father for a symptom of ridicule. He gazed mildly on the systematic worker. She was unable to guess whether she would have in him an ally or a judge. The latter, she feared. Now that she had embraced the strife, she saw the division of the line where she stood from that one where the world places girls who are affianced wives: her father could hardly be with her; it had gone too far. He loved her, but he would certainly take her to be moved by a maddish whim; he would not try to understand her case. The scholar's detestation of a disarrangement of human affairs that had been by miracle contrived to run smoothly, would of itself rank him against her; and with the world to back his view of her, he might behave like a despotic father. How could she defend herself before him? At one thought of Sir Willoughby, her tongue made ready, and feminine craft was alert to prompt it; but to her father she could imagine herself opposing only dumbness and obstinacy.

'It is not exactly the same kind of work,' she said.

Dr. Middleton rewarded her with a bushy eyebrow's beam of his revolving humour at the baronet's notion of work.

So little was needed to quicken her that she sunned herself in the beam, coaxing her father's eyes to stay with hers as long as she could, and beginning to hope he might be won to her side, if she confessed she had been more in the wrong than she felt; owned to him, that is, her error in not earlier disturbing his peace.

'I do not say it is the same,' observed Sir Willoughby, bowing to their alliance of opinion. 'My poor work is for the day, and Vernon's, no doubt, for the day to come. I contend, nevertheless, for the preservation of health, as the chief implement of work.'

'Of continued work: there I agree with you,' said Dr. Middleton cordially.

Clara's heart sank; so little was needed to deaden her.

Accuse her of an overweening antagonism to her be-trothed; yet remember that though the words had not been uttered to give her good reason for it, nature reads nature; captives may be stript of everything save that power to read their tyrant; remember also that she was not, as she well knew, blameless; her rage at him was partly against herself.

The rising from table left her to Sir Willoughby. She swam away after Miss Dale, exclaiming, 'The laboratory! Will you have me for a companion on your walk to see your father? One breathes earth and heaven to-day out of doors. Isn't it Summer with a Spring-breeze? I will wander about your garden and not hurry your visit, I promise.'

'I shall be very happy indeed. But I am going im-mediately,' said Laetitia, seeing Sir Willoughby hovering to snap up his bride.

'Yes; and a garden-hat and I am on the march.'

'I will wait for you on the terrace.'

'You will not have to wait.'

'Five minutes at the most,' Sir Willoughby said to Laetitia, and she passed out, leaving them alone together.

'Well, and my love!' he addressed his bride almost huggingly; 'and what is the story? and how did you succeed with old Vernon yesterday? He will and he won't? He's a very woman in these affairs. I can't forgive him for giving you a headache. You were found weeping.'

'Yes, I cried,' said Clara.

'And now tell me about it. You know, my dear girl, whether he does or doesn't, our keeping him somewhere in the neighbourhood—perhaps not in the house—that is the material point. It can hardly be necessary in these days to urge marriages on. I'm sure the country is over . . . Most marriages ought to be celebrated with the funeral knell!'

'I think so,' said Clara.

'It will come to this, that marriages of consequence, and none but those, will be hailed with joyful peals.'

'Do not say such things in public, Willoughby.'

'Only to you, to you! Don't think me likely to expose myself to the world. Well, and I sounded Miss Dale, and there will be no violent obstacle. And now about Vernon?'

'I will speak to you, Willoughby, when I return from my walk with Miss Dale, soon after twelve.'

'Twelve!' said he.

'I name an hour. It seems childish. I can explain it. But it is named, I cannot deny, because I am a rather childish person perhaps, and have it prescribed to me to delay my speaking for a certain length of time. I may tell you at once that Mr. Whitford is not to be persuaded by me, and the breaking of our engagement would not induce him to remain.'

'Vernon used those words?'

'It was I.'

' "The breaking of our engagement!" Come into the laboratory, my love.'

'I shall not have time.'

'Time shall stop rather than interfere with our conversation! "The breaking . . .!" but it's a sort of sacrilege to speak of it.'

'That I feel; yet it has to be spoken of.'

'Sometimes? Why? I can't conceive the occasion. You know, to me, Clara, plighted faith, the affiancing of two lovers, is a piece of religion. I rank it as holy as marriage; nay, to me it is holier; I really cannot tell you how; I can only appeal to you in your bosom to understand me. We read of divorces with comparative indifference. They occur between couples who have rubbed off all romance.'

She could have asked him in her fit of ironic iciness, on hearing him thus blindly challenge her to speak out, whether the romance might be his piece of religion.

He propitiated the more unwarlike sentiments in her by ejaculating: 'Poor souls! let them go their several ways. Married people no longer lovers are in the category of the unnameable. But the hint of the breaking of an engagement—our engagement!—between *us*? Oh!'

'Oh!' Clara came out with a swan's note swelling
over mechanical imitation of him to dolorousness illimit-
able. 'Oh!' she breathed short, 'let it be now. Do not
speak till you have heard me. My head may not be
clear by-and-by. And two scenes—twice will be beyond
my endurance. I am penitent for the wrong I have done
you. I grieve for you. All the blame is mine. Willoughby,
you must release me. Do not let me hear a word of
that word; jealousy is unknown to me. . . . Happy if I
could call you friend and see you with a worthier than
I, who might by-and-by call me friend! You have my
plighted troth . . . given in ignorance of my feelings.
Reprobate a weak and foolish girl's ignorance. I have
thought of it, and I cannot see wickedness, though the
blame is great, shameful. You have none. You are
without any blame. You will not suffer as I do. You will
be generous to me? I have no respect for myself when I
beg you to be generous and release me.'

'But this was the . . .' Willoughby preserved his calmness,
'this, then, the subject of your interview with Vernon?'

'I have spoken to him. I did my commission, and I
spoke to him.'

'Of me?'

'Of myself. I see how I hurt you; I could not avoid it.
Yes, of you, as far as we are related. I said I believed
you would release me. I said I could be true to my
plighted word, but that you would not insist. Could a
gentleman insist? But not a step beyond; not love; I
have none. And, Willoughby, treat me as one perfectly
worthless; I am. I should have known it a year back.
I was deceived in myself. There should be love.'

'Should be!' Willoughby's tone was a pungent comment on her.

'Love, then, I find I have not. I think I am antagonistic to it. What people say of it I have not experienced
I find I was mistaken. It is lightly said, but very painful.
You understand me, that my prayer is for liberty, that I
may not be tied. If you can release and pardon me, or
promise ultimately to pardon me, or say some kind word,
I shall know it is because I am beneath you utterly that I

have been unable to give you the love you should have with a wife. Only say to me, go! It is you who break the match, discovering my want of a heart. What people think of me matters little. My anxiety will be to save you annoyance.'

She waited for him: he seemed on the verge of speaking.

He perceived her expectation; he had nothing but clownish tumult within, and his dignity counselled him to disappoint her.

Swaying his head, like the oriental palm whose shade is a blessing to the perfervid wanderer below, smiling gravely, he was indirectly asking his dignity what he could say to maintain it and deal this mad young woman a bitterly compassionate rebuke. What to think, hung remoter. The thing to do struck him first.

He squeezed both her hands, threw the door wide open, and said, with countless blinkings: 'In the laboratory we are uninterrupted. I was at a loss to guess where that most unpleasant effect on the senses came from. They are always "guessing" through the nose. I mean, the remainder of breakfast here. Perhaps I satirized them too smartly—if you know the letters. When they are not "calculating." More offensive than débris of a midnight banquet! An American tour is instructive, though not so romantic. Not so romantic as Italy, I mean. Let us escape.'

She held back from his arm. She had scattered his brains; it was pitiable: but she was in the torrent and could not suffer a pause or a change of place.

'It must be here; one minute more—I cannot go elsewhere to begin again. Speak to me here; answer my request. Once; one word. If you forgive me, it will be superhuman. But, release me.'

'Seriously,' he rejoined, 'tea-cups and coffee-cups, bread-crumbs, egg-shells, caviare, butter, beef, bacon! Can we? The room reeks.'

'Then I will go for my walk with Miss Dale. And you will speak to me when I return?'

'At all seasons. You shall go with Miss Dale. But, my dear! my love! Seriously, where are we? One hears of lover's quarrels. Now, I never quarrel. It is a characteristic of mine. And you speak of me to my cousin Vernon! Seriously, plighted faith signifies plighted faith, as much as an iron-cable is iron to hold by. Some little twist of the mind? To Vernon, of all men! Tush! she has been dreaming of a hero of perfection, and the comparison is unfavourable to her Willoughby. But, my Clara, when I say to you, that bride is bride, and you are mine, mine!'

'Willoughby, you mentioned them,—those separations of two married. You said, if they do not love . . . Oh! say, is it not better . . . instead of later?'

He took advantage of her modesty in speaking to exclaim: 'Where are we now? Bride is bride, and wife is wife, and *affianced* is, in honour, *wedded*. You cannot be released. We are united. Recognize it: united. There is no possibility of releasing a wife!'

'Not if she ran . . . ?'

This was too direct to be histrionically misunderstood. He had driven her to the extremity of more distinctly imagining the circumstance she had cited, and with that cleared view the desperate creature gloried in launching such a bolt at the man's real or assumed insensibility as must, by shivering it, waken him.

But in a moment she stood in burning rose, with dimmed eyesight. She saw his horror, and seeing shared it; shared just then only by seeing it; which led her to rejoice with the deepest of sighs that some shame was left in her.

'Ran? ran? ran?' he said as rapidly as he blinked. 'How? where? what idea . . . ?'

Close was he upon an explosion that would have sullied his conception of the purity of the younger members of the sex hauntingly.

That she, a young lady, maiden, of strictest education, should, and without his teaching, know that wives ran!— know that by running they compelled their husbands to abandon pursuit, surrender possession!—and that she should suggest it of herself as a wife!—that she should speak of running!—

His ideal, the common male Egoist ideal of a waxwork sex would have been shocked to fragments had she spoken further to fill in the outlines of these awful interjections.

She was tempted: for during the last few minutes the fire of her situation had enlightened her understanding upon a subject far from her as the ice-fields of the North a short while before; and the prospect offered to her courage if she would only outstare shame and seem at home in the doings of wickedness, was his loathing and dreading so vile a young woman. She restrained herself; chiefly, after the first bridling of maidenly timidity, because she could not bear to lower the idea of her sex even in his esteem.

The door was open. She had thoughts of flying out to breathe in an interval of truce.

She reflected on her situation hurriedly askance:

'If one must go through this, to be disentangled from an engagement, what must it be to poor women seeking to be free of a marriage?'

Had she spoken it, Sir Willoughby might have learnt that she was not so iniquitously wise of the things of this world as her mere sex's instinct, roused to the intemperateness of a creature struggling with fetters, had made her appear in her dash to seize a weapon, indicated moreover by him.

Clara took up the old broken vow of women to vow it afresh: 'Never to any man will I give my hand.'

She replied to Sir Willoughby: 'I have said all. I cannot explain what I have said.'

She had heard a step in the passage. Vernon entered. Perceiving them, he stated his mission in apology: 'Dr. Middleton left a book in this room. I see it; it's a Heinsius.'*

'Ha! by the way, a book; books would not be left here if they were not brought here, with my compliments to Dr. Middleton, who may do as he pleases, though seriously order is order,' said Sir Willoughby. 'Come away to the laboratory, Clara. It's a comment on human beings that wherever they have been there's a mess, and you admirers of them,' he divided a sickly nod between Vernon and the stale breakfast-table, 'must make what you can of it. Come, Clara.'

Clara protested that she was engaged to walk with Miss Dale.

'Miss Dale is waiting in the hall,' said Vernon.

'Miss Dale is waiting,' said Clara.

'Walk with Miss Dale; walk with Miss Dale,' Sir Willoughby remarked pressingly. 'I will beg her to wait another two minutes. You shall find her in the hall when you come down.'

He rang the bell and went out.

'Take Miss Dale into your confidence; she is quite trustworthy,' Vernon said to Clara.

'I have not advanced one step,' she replied.

'Recollect that you are in a position of your own choosing; and if, after thinking over it, you mean to escape, you must make up your mind to pitched battles, and not be dejected if you are beaten in all of them; there is your only chance.'

'Not my choosing; do not say choosing, Mr. Whitford. I did not choose. I was incapable of really choosing. I consented.'

'It's the same in fact. But be sure of what you wish.'

'Yes,' she assented, taking it for her just punishment that she should be supposed not quite to know her wishes. 'Your advice has helped me to-day.'

'Did I advise?'

'Do you regret advising?'

'I should certainly regret a word that intruded between you and him.'

'But you will not leave the Hall yet? You will not leave me without a friend? If papa and I were to leave to-morrow, I foresee endless correspondence. I have to stay at least some days, and wear through it, and then, if I have to speak to my poor father you can imagine the effect on him.'

Sir Willoughby came striding in, to correct the error of his going out.

'Miss Dale awaits you, my dear. You have bonnet,

hat?—No? Have you forgotten your appointment to walk with her?'

'I am ready,' said Clara, departing.

The two gentlemen behind her separated in the passage. They had not spoken.

She had read of the reproach upon women, that they divide the friendships of men. She reproached herself, but she was in action, driven by necessity, between sea and rock. Dreadful to think of! she was one of the creatures who are written about.

CHAPTER XVI

Clara and Laetitia

In spite of his honourable caution, Vernon had said things to render Miss Middleton more angrily determined than she had been in the scene with Sir Willoughby. His counting on pitched battles and a defeat for her in all of them, made her previous feelings appear slack in comparison with the energy of combat now animating her. And she could vehemently declare that she had not chosen; she was too young, too ignorant to choose. He had wrongly used that word; it sounded malicious; and to call consenting the same in fact as choosing, was wilfully unjust. Mr. Whitford meant well; he was conscientious, very conscientious. But he was not the hero descending from heaven bright-sworded to smite a woman's fetters off her limbs and deliver her from the yawning mouth-abyss.*

His logical coolness of expostulation with her when she cast aside the silly mission entrusted to her by Sir Willoughby and wept for herself, was unheroic in proportion to its praiseworthiness. He had left it to her to do everything she wished done, stipulating simply that there should be a pause of four and twenty hours for her to consider of it before she proceeded in the attempt to extricate herself. Of consolation there had not been a word. Said he, 'I am the last man to give advice in such a case.' Yet she had by no means astonished him when her confession came out. It came out, she knew not how. It was led up to by his declining the idea of marriage, and her congratulating him on his exemption from the prospect of the yoke, but memory was too dull to revive the one or two fiery minutes of broken language when she had been guilty of her dire misconduct.

This gentleman was no flatterer, scarcely a friend. He could look on her grief without soothing her. Supposing he had soothed her warmly? All her sentiments collected in her bosom to dash in reprobation of him at the thought. She nevertheless condemned him for his excessive coolness; his transparent anxiety not to be compromised by a syllable; his air of saying, 'I guessed as much, but why plead your case to me?' And his recommendation to her to be quite sure she did know what she meant, was a little insulting. She exonerated him from the intention; he treated her as a girl. By what he said of Miss Dale, he proposed that lady for imitation.

'I must be myself or I shall be playing hypocrite to dig my own pitfall,' she said to herself, while taking counsel with Laetitia as to the route for their walk, and admiring a becoming curve in her companion's hat.

Sir Willoughby, with many protestations of regret that letters of business debarred him from the pleasure of accompanying them, remarked upon the path proposed by Miss Dale: 'In that case you must have a footman.'

'Then we adopt the other,' said Clara, and they set forth.

'Sir Willoughby,' Miss Dale said to her, 'is always in alarm about our unprotectedness.'

Clara glanced up at the clouds and closed her parasol. She replied, 'It inspires timidity.'

There was that in the accent and character of the answer which warned Laetitia to expect the reverse of a quiet chatter with Miss Middleton.

'You are fond of walking?' She chose a peaceful topic.

'Walking or riding; yes, of walking,' said Clara. 'The difficulty is to find companions.'

'We shall lose Mr. Whitford next week.'

'He goes?'

'He will be a great loss to me, for I do not ride,' Laetitia replied to the off-hand inquiry.

'Ah!'

Miss Middleton did not fan conversation when she simply breathed her voice.

Laetitia tried another neutral theme.

'The weather to-day suits our country,' she said.

'England, or Patterne Park? I am so devoted to mountains that I have no enthusiasm for flat land.'

'Do you call our country flat, Miss Middleton? We have undulations, hills, and we have sufficient diversity, meadows, rivers, copses, brooks, and good roads, and pretty by-paths.'

'The prettiness is overwhelming. It is very pretty to see; but to live with, I think I prefer ugliness. I can imagine learning to love ugliness. It's honest. However young you are, you cannot be deceived by it. These parks of rich people are a part of the prettiness. I would rather have fields, commons.'

'The parks give us delightful green walks, paths through beautiful woods.'

'If there is a right of way for the public.'

'There should be,' said Miss Dale, wondering; and Clara cried, 'I chafe at restraint; hedges and palings everywhere! I should have to travel ten years to sit down contented among these fortifications. Of course I can read of this rich kind of English country with pleasure in poetry. But it seems to me to require poetry. What would you say of human beings requiring it?'

'That they are not so companionable but that the haze of distance improves the view.'

'Then you do know that you are the wisest!'

Laetitia raised her dark eyelashes; she sought to understand. She could only fancy she did; and if she did, it meant that Miss Middleton thought her wise in remaining single.

Clara was full of a sombre preconception that her 'jealousy' had been hinted to Miss Dale.

'You knew Miss Durham?' she said.

'Not intimately.'

'As well as you know me?'

'Not so well.'

'But you saw more of her?'

'She was more reserved with me.'

'Oh! Miss Dale, I would not be reserved with you.'

The thrill of the voice caused Laetitia to steal a look. Clara's eyes were bright, and she had the readiness to run to volubility of the feverstricken; otherwise she did not betray excitement.

'You will never allow any of these noble trees to be felled, Miss Middleton.'

'The axe is better than decay, do you not think?'

'I think your influence will be great and always used to good purpose.'

'My influence, Miss Dale? I have begged a favour this morning and cannot obtain the grant.'

It was lightly said, but Clara's face was more significant, and 'What?' leapt from Laetitia's lips.

Before she could excuse herself, Clara had answered: 'My liberty.'

In another and higher tone Laetitia said: 'What?' and she looked round on her companion; she looked in doubt that is open to conviction by a narrow aperture, and slowly and painfully yields access. Clara saw the vacancy of her expression gradually filling with woefulness.

'I have begged him to release me from my engagement, Miss Dale.'

'Sir Willoughby?'

'It is incredible to you. He refuses. You see I have no influence.'

'Miss Middleton, it is terrible!'

'To be dragged to the marriage service against one's will? Yes.'

'Oh! Miss Middleton.'

'Do you not think so?'

'That cannot be your meaning.'

'You do not suspect me of trifling? You know I would not. I am as much in earnest as a mouse in a trap.'

'No, you will not misunderstand me! Miss Middleton,

such a blow to Sir Willoughby would be shocking, most cruel! He is devoted to you.'

'He was devoted to Miss Durham.'

'Not so deeply: differently.'

'Was he not very much courted at that time? He is now; not so much: he is not so young. But my reason for speaking of Miss Durham was to exclaim at the strangeness of a girl winning her freedom to plunge into wedlock. Is it comprehensible to you? She flies from one dungeon into another. These are the acts which astonish men at our conduct, and cause them to ridicule and, I daresay, despise us.'

'But, Miss Middleton, for Sir Willoughby to grant such a request, if it was made . . .'

'It was made, and by me, and will be made again. I throw it all on my unworthiness, Miss Dale. So the county will think of me, and quite justly. I would rather defend him than myself. He requires a different wife from anything I can be. That is my discovery; unhappily a late one. The blame is all mine. The world cannot be too hard on me. But I must be free if I am to be kind in my judgements even of the gentleman I have injured.'

'So noble a gentleman!' Laetitia sighed.

'I will subscribe to any eulogy of him,' said Clara, with a penetrating thought as to the possibility of a lady experienced in him like Laetitia taking him for noble. 'He has a noble air. I say it sincerely, that your appreciation of him proves his nobility.' Her feeling of opposition to Sir Willoughby pushed her to this extravagance, gravely perplexing Laetitia. 'And it is,' added Clara, as if to support what she had said, 'a withering rebuke to me; I know him less, at least have not had so long an experience of him.'

Laetitia pondered on an obscurity in these words which would have accused her thick intelligence but for a glimmer it threw on another most obscure communication. She feared it might be, strange though it seemed, jealousy, a shade of jealousy affecting Miss Middleton, as had been vaguely intimated by Sir Willoughby when they were waiting in the hall. 'A little feminine ailment,

a want of comprehension of a perfect friendship'; those
were his words to her: and he suggested vaguely that
care must be taken in the eulogy of her friend.

She resolved to be explicit.

'I have not said that I think him beyond criticism,
Miss Middleton.'

'Noble?'

'He has faults. When we have known a person for
years the faults come out, but custom makes light of
them; and I suppose we feel flattered by seeing what it
would be difficult to be blind to! A very little flatters
us!—Now, do you not admire that view? It is my
favourite.'

Clara gazed over rolling richness of foliage, wood and
water, and church spire, a town and horizon hills. There
sang a skylark.

'Not even the bird that does not fly away!' she said;
meaning, she had no heart for the bird satisfied to rise and
descend in this place.

Laetitia travelled to some notion, dim and immense, of
Miss Middleton's fever of distaste. She shrank from it in
a kind of dread lest it might be contagious and rob her of
her one ever-fresh possession of the homely picturesque;
but Clara melted her by saying: 'For your sake I could
love it . . . in time: or some dear old English scene.
Since . . . since this . . . this change in me, I find I
cannot separate landscape from associations. Now I
learn how youth goes. I have grown years older in a
week.—Miss Dale, if he were to give me my freedom? if
he were to cast me off? if he stood alone?'

'I should pity him.'

'Him—not me! Oh! right. I hoped you would; I
knew you would.'

Laetitia's attempt to shift Miss Middleton's shiftiness
was vain; for now she seemed really listening to the
language of jealousy:—jealous of the ancient Letty
Dale!—and immediately before, the tone was quite void
of it.

'Yes,' she said, 'but you make me feel myself in the
dark, and when I do I have the habit of throwing myself

for guidance upon such light as I have within. You shall
know me, if you will, as well as I know myself. And do
not think me far from the point when I say I have a
feeble health. I am what the doctors call anaemic; a
rather bloodless creature. The blood is life, so I have not
much life. Ten years back—eleven, if I must be precise,
I thought of conquering the world with a pen! The
result is that I am glad of a fireside, and not sure of always
having one: and that is my achievement. My days are
monotonous, but if I have a dread, it is that there will be
an alteration in them. My father has very little money.
We subsist on what private income he has, and his
pension: he was an army doctor. I may by-and-by have
to live in a town for pupils. I could be grateful to any
one who would save me from that. I should be astonished
at his choosing to have me burden his household as well.—
Have I now explained the nature of my pity? It would
be the pity of common sympathy, pure lymph of pity,
as nearly disembodied as can be. Last year's sheddings
from the tree do not form an attractive garland. Their
merit is, that they have not the ambition. I am like
them. Now, Miss Middleton, I cannot make myself more
bare to you. I hope you see my sincerity.'

'I do see it,' Clara said.

With the second heaving of her heart, she cried: 'See
it, and envy you that humility! proud if I could ape it!
Oh! how proud if I could speak so truthfully true!—You
would not have spoken so to me without some good
feeling out of which friends are made. That I am sure
of. To be very truthful to a person, one must have a
liking. So I judge by myself. Do I presume too much?'

Kindness was on Laetitia's face.

'But now,' said Clara, swimming on the wave in her
bosom, 'I tax you with the silliest suspicion ever entertained by one of your rank. Lady, you have deemed me
capable of the meanest of our vices!—Hold this hand,
Laetitia, my friend, will you? Something is going on in
me.'

Laetitia took her hand, and saw and felt that something was going on.

Clara said: 'You are a woman.'

It was her effort to account for the something.

She swam for a brilliant instant on tears, and yielded to the overflow.

When they had fallen, she remarked upon her first long breath quite coolly; 'An encouraging picture of a rebel, is it not?'

Her companion murmured to soothe her.

'It's little, it's nothing,' said Clara, pained to keep her lips in line.

They walked forward, holding hands, deep-hearted to one another.

'I like this country better now,' the shaken girl resumed. 'I could lie down in it and ask only for sleep. I should like to think of you here. How nobly self-respecting you must be, to speak as you did! Our dreams of heroes and heroines are cold glitter beside the reality. I have been lately thinking of myself as an outcast of my sex, and to have a good woman liking me a little . . . loving? Oh! Laetitia, my friend, I should have kissed you, and not made this exhibition of myself —and if you call it hysterics, woe to you! for I bit my tongue to keep it off when I had hardly strength to bring my teeth together—if that idea of jealousy had not been in your head. You had it from him.'

'I have not alluded to it in any word that I can recollect.'

'He can imagine no other cause for my wish to be released. I have noticed, it is his instinct to reckon on women as constant by their nature. They are the needles, and he the magnet. Jealousy of you, Miss Dale! Laetitia, may I speak?'

'Say everything you please.'

'I could wish:—Do you know my baptismal name?'

'Clara.'

'At last! I could wish . . . that is, if it were your wish. Yes, I could wish that. Next to independence, my wish would be that. I risk offending you. Do not let your delicacy take arms against me. I wish him happy in the only way that he can be made happy. There is my jealousy.'

'Was it what you were going to say just now?'

'No.'

'I thought not.'

'I was going to say—and I believe the rack would not make me truthful like you, Laetitia—well, has it ever struck you: remember, I do see his merits; I speak to his faithfullest friend, and I acknowledge he is attractive, he has manly tastes and habits; but has it never struck you . . . I have no right to ask; I know that men must have faults, I do not expect them to be saints; I am not one; I wish I were.'

'Has it never struck me . . . ?' Laetitia prompted her.

'That very few women are able to be straightforwardly sincere in their speech, however much they may desire to be?'

'They are differently educated. Great misfortune brings it to them.'

'I am sure your answer is correct. Have you ever known a woman who was entirely an Egoist?'

'Personally known one? We are not better than men.'

'I do not pretend that we are. I have latterly become an Egoist, thinking of no one but myself, scheming to make use of every soul I meet. But then, women are in the position of inferiors. They are hardly out of the nursery when a lasso is round their necks; and if they have beauty, no wonder they turn it to a weapon and make as many captives as they can. I do not wonder! My sense of shame at my natural weakness and the arrogance of men would urge me to make hundreds captive, if that is being a coquette. I should not have compassion for those lofty birds, the hawks. To see them with their wings clipped would amuse me. Is there any other way of punishing them?'

'Consider what you lose in punishing them.'

'I consider what they gain if we do not.'

Laetitia supposed she was listening to discursive observations upon the inequality in the relations of the sexes. A suspicion of a drift to a closer meaning had been lulled, and the colour flooded her swiftly when Clara said:

'Here is the difference I see; I see it; I am certain of it: women who are called coquettes make their conquests not of the best of men; but men who are Egoists have *good* women for their victims; women on whose devoted constancy they feed; they drink it like blood. I am sure I am not taking the merely feminine view. They punish themselves too by passing over the one suitable to them, who could really give them what they crave to have, and they go where they . . . ' Clara stopped. 'I have not your power to express ideas,' she said.

'Miss Middleton, you have a dreadful power,' said Laetitia.

Clara smiled affectionately: 'I am not aware of any. Whose cottage is this?'

'My father's. Will you not come in? into the garden?'

Clara took note of ivied windows and roses in the porch. She thanked Laetitia and said: 'I will call for you in an hour.'

'Are you walking on the road alone?' said Laetitia incredulously, with an eye to Sir Willoughby's dismay.

'I put my trust in the highroad,' Clara replied, and turned away, but turned back to Laetitia and offered her face to be kissed.

The 'dreadful power' of this young lady had fervently impressed Laetitia, and in kissing her she marvelled at her gentleness and girlishness.

Clara walked on, unconscious of her possession of power of any kind.

CHAPTER XVII

The Porcelain Vase

DURING the term of Clara's walk with Laetitia, Sir Willoughby's shrunken self-esteem, like a garment hung to the fire after exposure to tempestuous weather, recovered some of the sleekness of its velvet pile in the society of Mrs. Mountstuart Jenkinson, who represented to him the world he feared and tried to keep sunny for himself by all the arts he could exercise. She expected him to be the gay Sir Willoughby, and her look being as good as an incantation-summons, he produced the accustomed sprite, giving her sally for sally. Queens govern the polite. Popularity with men, serviceable as it is for winning favouritism with women, is of poor value to a sensitive gentleman, anxious even to prognostic apprehension on behalf of his pride, his comfort and his prevalence. And men are grossly purchaseable; good wines have them, good cigars, a goodfellow air: they are never quite worth their salt even then; you can make head against their ill looks. But the looks of women will at one blow work on you the downright difference which is between the cock of lordly plume and the moulting. Happily they may be gained: a clever tongue will gain them, a leg. They are with you to a certainty if Nature is with you; if you are elegant and discreet: if the sun is on you, and they see you shining in it; or if they have seen you well-stationed and handsome in the sun. And once gained they are your mirrors for life, and far more constant than the glass. That tale of their caprice is absurd. Hit their imaginations once, they are your slaves, only demanding common courtier service of you. They will deny that you are ageing, they will cover you from scandal, they will refuse to see you ridiculous. Sir Willoughby's instinct, or skin, or outfloating feelers, told him of these mysteries of the influence of the sex; he had as little need to study them as a lady breathed on.

He had some need to know them, in fact; and with him the need of a protection for himself called it forth; he was intuitively a conjuror in self-defence, long-sighted, wanting no directions to the herb he was to suck at when fighting a serpent. His dulness of vision into the heart of his enemy was compensated by the agile sensitiveness obscuring but rendering him miraculously active, and without supposing his need immediate, he deemed it politic to fascinate Mrs. Mountstuart and anticipate ghastly possibilities in the future by dropping a hint; not of Clara's fickleness, you may be sure; of his own, rather; or more justly, of an altered view of Clara's character. He touched on the *rogue in porcelain*.

Set gently laughing by his relishing humour: 'I get nearer to it,' he said.

'Remember, I'm in love with her,' said Mrs. Mountstuart.

'That is our penalty.'

'A pleasant one for you.'

He assented. 'Is the "rogue" to be eliminated?'

'Ask, when she's a mother, my dear Sir Willoughby.'

'This is how I read you:—'

'I shall accept any interpretation that is complimentary.'

'Not one will satisfy me of being sufficiently so, and so I leave it to the character to fill out the epigram.'

'Do. What hurry is there? And don't be misled by your objection to rogue; which would be reasonable if you had not secured her.'

The door of a hollow chamber of horrible reverberation was opened within him by this remark.

He tried to say in jest, that it was not always a passionate admiration that held the rogue fast; but he muddled it in the thick of his conscious thunder, and Mrs. Mountstuart smiled to see him shot from the smooth-flowing dialogue into the cataracts by one simple reminder to the lover of his luck. Necessarily after a fall, the pitch of their conversation relaxed.

'Miss Dale is looking well,' he said.

'Fairly: she ought to marry,' said Mrs. Mountstuart.

He shook his head. 'Persuade her.'

She nodded: 'Example may have some effect.'

He looked extremely abstracted. 'Yes, it is time. Where is the man you could recommend for her complement? She has now what was missing before, a ripe intelligence in addition to her happy disposition—romantic, you would say. I can't think women the worse for that.'

'A dash of it.'

'She calls it "leafage."'

'Very pretty. And have you relented about your horse Achmet?'

'I don't sell him under four hundred.'

'Poor Johnny Busshe! You forget that his wife doles him out his money. You're a hard bargainer, Sir Willoughby.'

'I mean the price to be prohibitive.'

'Very well; and "leafage" is good for hide and seek; especially when there is no rogue in ambush. And that's the worst I can say of Laetitia Dale. An exaggerated devotion is the scandal of our sex. They say you're the hardest man of business in the county too, and I can believe it; for at home and abroad your aim is to get the best of everybody. You see I've no leafage, I am perfectly matter-of-fact, bald.'

'Nevertheless, my dear Mrs. Mountstuart, I can assure you that conversing with you has much the same exhilarating effect on me as conversing with Miss Dale.'

'But, leafage! leafage! You hard bargainers have no compassion for devoted spinsters.'

'I tell you my sentiments absolutely.'

'And you have mine moderately expressed.'

She recollected the purpose of her morning's visit, which was to engage Dr. Middleton to dine with her, and Sir Willoughby conducted her to the library door. 'Insist,' he said.

Awaiting her reappearance, the refreshment of the talk he had sustained, not without point, assisted him to distinguish in its complete abhorrent orb the offence committed against him by his bride. And this he did through projecting it more and more away from him, so that in the outer distance it involved his personal emotions less, while observation was enabled to compass its vastness, and, as it were, perceive the whole spherical mass of the wretched girl's guilt impudently turning on its axis.

Thus to detach an injury done to us, and plant it in space, for mathematical measurement of its weight and bulk, is an art; it may also be an instinct of self-preservation; otherwise, as when mountains crumble adjacent villages are crushed, men of feeling may at any moment be killed outright by the iniquitous and the callous. But, as an art, it should be known to those who are for practising an art so beneficent, that circumstances must lend their aid. Sir Willoughby's instinct even had sat dull and crushed before his conversation with Mrs. Mountstuart. She lifted him to one of his ideals of himself. Among gentlemen he was the English gentleman; with ladies his aim was the Gallican courtier of any period from Louis Treize to Louis Quinze.* He could doat on those who led him to talk in that character—backed by English solidity, you understand. Roast beef stood eminent behind the soufflé and champagne. An English squire excelling his fellows at hazardous leaps in public, he was additionally a polished whisperer, a lively dialoguer, one for witty bouts, with something in him—capacity for a drive and dig or two—beyond mere wit, as they soon learnt who called up his reserves, and had a bosom for pinking. So much for his ideal of himself. Now, Clara not only never evoked, never responded to it, she repelled it; there was no flourishing of it near her. He considerately overlooked these facts in his ordinary calculations; he was a man of honour and she was a girl of beauty; but the accidental blossoming of his ideal, with Mrs. Mountstuart, on the very heels of Clara's offence, restored him to full command of his art of detachment, and he thrust her out, quite apart from himself, to contemplate her disgraceful revolutions.

Deeply read in the Book of Egoism that he was, he knew the wisdom of the sentence: *An injured pride that strikes not out will strike home.* What was he to strike with? Ten years younger, Laetitia might have been the instrument. To think of her now was preposterous. Beside Clara she had the hue of Winter under the springing bough. He tossed her away, vexed to the very soul by an ostentatious decay that shrank from comparison with the blooming creature he had to scourge in self-defence, by some agency or other.

Mrs. Mountstuart was on the step of her carriage when the silken parasols of the young ladies were descried on a slope of the park, where the yellow green of May-clothed beeches flowed over the brown ground of last year's leaves.

'Who's the cavalier?' she inquired.

A gentleman escorted them.

'Vernon? No! he's pegging at Crossjay,' quoth Willoughby.

Vernon and Crossjay came out for the boy's half-hour's run before his dinner. Crossjay spied Miss Middleton and was off to meet her at a bound. Vernon followed him leisurely.

'The rogue has no cousin, has she?' said Mrs. Mountstuart.

'It's a family of one son or one daughter for generations,' replied Willoughby.

'And Letty Dale?'

'Cousin!' he exclaimed, as if wealth had been imputed to Miss Dale; adding: 'No male cousin.'

A railway-station fly drove out of the avenue on the circle to the hall-entrance. Flitch was driver. He had no right to be there, he was doing wrong, but he was doing it under cover of an office, to support his wife and young ones, and his deprecating touches of the hat spoke of these apologies to his former master with dog-like pathos.

Sir Willoughby beckoned to him to approach.

'So you are here,' he said. 'You have luggage.'

Flitch jumped from the box and read one of the labels aloud: 'Lieut.-Colonel H. De Craye.'

'And the colonel met the ladies? Overtook them?'

Here seemed to come dismal matter for Flitch to relate.

He began upon the abstract origin of it: he had lost his place in Sir Willoughby's establishment, and was obliged to look about for work where it was to be got, and though he knew he had no right to be where he was, he hoped to be forgiven because of the mouths he had to feed as a flyman attached to the railway station, where this gentleman, the colonel, hired him, and he believed Sir Willoughby would excuse him for driving a friend, which the colonel was, he recollected well, and the colonel recollected him, and he said, not noticing how he was rigged: 'What! Flitch! back in your old place?—Am I expected?' and he told the colonel his unfortunate situation; 'Not back, colonel; no such luck for me': and

Colonel De Craye was a very kind-hearted gentleman, as
he always had been, and asked kindly after his family.
And it might be that such poor work as he was doing
now he might be deprived of, such is misfortune when
it once harpoons a man; you may dive, and you may fly,
but it sticks in you, once do a foolish thing. 'May I
humbly beg of you, if you'll be so good, Sir Willoughby,'
said Flitch, passing to evidence of the sad mishap. He
opened the door of the fly, displaying fragments of
broken porcelain.

'But, what, what! what's the story of this?' cried Sir
Willoughby.

'What is it?' said Mrs. Mountstuart, pricking up her
ears.

'It was a vaws,' Flitch replied in elegy.

'A porcelain vase!' interpreted Sir Willoughby.

'China!' Mrs. Mountstuart faintly shrieked.

One of the pieces was handed to her inspection.

She held it close, she held it distant. She sighed
horribly.

'The man had better have hanged himself,' said she.

Flitch bestirred his misfortune-sodden features and
members for a continuation of the doleful narrative.

'How did this occur?' Sir Willoughby peremptorily
asked him.

Flitch appealed to his former master for testimony that
he was a good and careful driver.

Sir Willoughby thundered: 'I tell you to tell me how
this occurred.'

'Not a drop, my lady! not since my supper last night,
if there's any truth in me'; Flitch implored succour of
Mrs. Mountstuart.

'Drive straight,' she said, and braced him.

His narrative was then direct.

Near Piper's mill, where the Wicker brook crossed the
Rebdon road, one of Hoppner's waggons, overloaded as
usual, was forcing the horses uphill, when Flitch drove
down at an easy pace, and saw himself between Hoppner's cart come to a stand, and a young lady advancing:
and just then the carter smacks his whip, the horses pull

half mad. The young lady starts behind the cart, and up jumps the colonel, and to save the young lady, Flitch dashed ahead and did save her, he thanked heaven for it, and more when he came to see who the young lady was.

'She was alone?' said Sir Willoughby, in tragic amazement, staring at Flitch.

'Very well, you saved her, and you upset the fly,' Mrs. Mountstuart jogged him on.

'Bartlett, our old head-keeper, was a witness, my lady; I had to drive half up the bank, and it's true—over the fly did go; and the vaws it shoots out against the twelfth milestone, just as though *there* was the chance for it! for nobody else was injured, and knocked against anything else, it never would have flown all to pieces, so that it took Bartlett and me ten minutes to collect every one, down to the smallest piece there was; and he said, and I can't help thinking myself, there was a Providence in it, for we all come together so as you might say we was made to do as we did.'

'So then Horace adopted the prudent course of walking on with the ladies instead of trusting his limbs again to this capsizing fly,' Sir Willoughby said to Mrs. Mountstuart; and she rejoined: 'Lucky that no one was hurt.'

Both of them eyed the nose of poor Flitch, and simultaneously they delivered a verdict of 'Humph.'

Mrs. Mountstuart handed the wretch a half-crown from her purse. Sir Willoughby directed the footman in attendance to unload the fly and gather up the fragments of porcelain carefully, bidding Flitch be quick in his departing.

'The colonel's wedding-present! I shall call tomorrow,' Mrs. Mountstuart waved her adieu.

'Come every day!—Yes, I suppose we may guess the destination of the vase.' He bowed her off: and she cried:

'Well, now the gift can be shared, if you're either of you for a division.' In the crash of the carriage-wheels he heard: 'At any rate there was a rogue in *that* porcelain.'

These are the slaps we get from a heedless world.

As for the vase, it was Horace De Craye's loss. Wedding-present he would have to produce, and decidedly not in chips. It had the look of a costly vase, but that was no question for the moment:—What was meant by Clara being seen walking on the highroad alone?—What snare, traceable ad inferas,* had ever induced Willoughby Patterne to make her the repository and fortress of his honour!

CHAPTER XVIII

Colonel De Craye

CLARA came along chatting and laughing with Colonel De Craye, young Crossjay's hand under one of her arms, and her parasol flashing; a dazzling offender; as if she wished to compel the spectator to recognize the dainty rogue in porcelain; really insufferably fair: perfect in height and grace of movement; exquisitely-tressed; red-lipped, the colour striking out to a distance from her ivory skin: a sight to set the woodland dancing, and turn the heads of the town; though beautiful, a jury of art-critics might pronounce her not to be. Irregular features are condemned in beauty. Beautiful figure, they could say. A description of her figure and her walking would have won her any praises: and she wore a dress cunning to embrace the shape and flutter loose about it, in the spirit of a Summer's day. Calypso-clad,* Dr. Middleton would have called her. See the silver birch in a breeze: here it swells, there it scatters, and it is puffed to a round and it streams like a pennon, and now gives the glimpse and shine of the white stem's line within, now hurries over it, denying that it was visible, with a chatter along the sweeping folds, while still the white peeps through. She had the wonderful art of dressing to suit the season and the sky. To-day the art was ravishingly companionable with her sweet-lighted face: too sweet, too vividly-meaningful for pretty, if not of the strict severity for beautiful. Millinery would tell us that she wore a fichu of thin white muslin crossed in front on a dress of the same light stuff, trimmed with deep rose. She carried a grey-silk parasol, traced at the borders with green creepers, and across the arm devoted to Crossjay, a length of trailing ivy, and in that hand a bunch of the first long grasses. These hues of red rose and green and pale green, ruffled and pouted in the billowy white of the dress ballooning and valleying softly, like a yacht before the sail bends low; but she walked not like one blown against; resembling rather the day of the South-west driving the clouds, gallantly firm in commotion; interfusing colour and varying in her features from laugh to smile and look of settled pleasure, like the heavens above the breeze.*

Sir Willoughby, as he frequently had occasion to protest to Clara, was no poet: he was a more than commonly candid English gentleman in his avowed dislike of the poet's nonsense, verbiage, verse; not one of those latterly terrorized by the noise made about the fellow into silent contempt; a sentiment that may sleep, and has not to be defended. He loathed the fellow, fought the fellow. But he was one with the poet upon that prevailing theme of verse, the charms of women. He was, to his ill-luck, intensely susceptible, and where he led men after him to admire, his admiration became a fury. He could see at a glance that Horace De Craye admired Miss Middleton. Horace was a man of taste, could hardly, could not, do other than admire; but how curious that in the setting forth of Clara and Miss Dale, in his own contemplation and comparison of them, Sir Willoughby had given but a nodding approbation of his bride's appearance! He had not attached weight to it recently.

Her conduct, and foremost, if not chiefly, her having been discovered, positively met by his friend Horace, walking on the highroad without companion or attendant, increased a sense of pain so very unusual with him that he had cause to be indignant. Coming on this condition, his admiration of the girl who wounded him was as bitter a thing as a man could feel. Resentment, fed from the main springs of his nature, turned it to wormwood, and not a whit the less was it admiration when he resolved to chastise her with a formal indication of his disdain. Her present gaiety sounded to him like laughter heard in the shadow of the pulpit.

'You have escaped!' he said to her, while shaking the hand of his friend Horace and cordially welcoming him: 'My dear fellow! and by the way, you had a squeak for it, I hear from Flitch.'

'I, Willoughby? not a bit,' said the colonel; 'we get into a fly to get out of it; and Flitch helped me out as well as in, good fellow; just dusting my coat as he did it. The only bit of bad management was that Miss Middleton had to step aside a trifle hurriedly.'

'You knew Miss Middleton at once?'

'Flitch did me the favour to introduce me. He first precipitated me at Miss Middleton's feet, and then he introduced me, in old oriental fashion, to my sovereign.'

Sir Willoughby's countenance was enough for his friend Horace. Quarter-wheeling to Clara, he said: ' 'Tis the place I'm to occupy for life, Miss Middleton, though one is not always fortunate to have a bright excuse for taking it at the commencement.'

Clara said: 'Happily you were not hurt, Colonel De Craye.'

'I was in the hands of the Loves. Not the Graces;* I'm afraid; I've an image of myself. Dear, no! My dear Willoughby, you never made such a headlong declaration as that. It would have looked like a magnificent impulse, if the posture had only been choicer. And Miss Middleton didn't laugh. At least I saw nothing but pity.'

'You did not write,' said Willoughby.

'Because it was a toss-up of a run to Ireland or here, and I came here not to go there; and by the way, fetched a jug with me to offer up to the Gods of ill-luck; and they accepted the propitiation.'

'Wasn't it packed in a box?'

'No, it was wrapped in paper, to show its elegant form. I caught sight of it in the shop yesterday, and carried it off this morning, and presented it to Miss Middleton at noon, without any form at all.'

Willoughby knew his friend Horace's mood when the Irish tongue in him threatened to wag.

'You see what may happen,' he said to Clara.

'As far as I am in fault I regret it,' she answered.

'Flitch says the accident occurred through his driving up the bank to save you from the wheels.'

'Flitch may go and whisper that down the neck of his empty whisky flask,' said Horace De Craye. 'And then let him cork it.'

'The consequence is that we have a porcelain vase broken. You should not walk on the road alone, Clara. You ought to have a companion, always. It is the rule here.'

'I had left Miss Dale at the cottage.'

'You ought to have had the dogs.'

'Would they have been any protection to the vase?' Horace De Craye crowed cordially.

'I'm afraid not, Miss Middleton. One must go to the witches for protection to vases; and they're all in the air now, having their own way with us, which accounts for the confusion in politics and society, and the rise in the price of broomsticks, to prove it true, as they tell us, that every nook and corner wants a mighty sweeping. Miss Dale looks beaming,' said De Craye, wishing to divert Willoughby from his anger with sense as well as nonsense.

'You have not been visiting Ireland recently,' said Sir Willoughby.

'No, nor making acquaintance with an actor in an Irish part in a drama cast in the green island. 'Tis Flitch, my dear Willoughby, has been and stirred the native in me, and we'll present him to you for the like good office when we hear after a number of years that you've not wrinkled your forehead once at your liege lady. Take the poor old dog back home, will you? He's crazed to be at the Hall. I say, Willoughby, it would be a good bit of work to take him back. Think of it; you'll do the popular thing, I'm sure. I've a superstition that Flitch ought to drive you from the church-door. If I were in luck, I'd have him drive me.'

'The man's a drunkard, Horace.'

'He fuddles his poor nose. 'Tis merely unction to the exile. Sober struggles below. He drinks to rock his heart, because he has one. Now let me intercede for poor Flitch.'

'Not a word of him. He threw up his place.'

'To try his fortune in the world, as the best of us do, though livery runs after us to tell us there's no being an independent gentleman, and comes a cold day we haul on the metal-button coat again, with a good ha! of satisfaction. You'll do the popular thing. Miss Middleton joins in the pleading.'

'No pleading!'

'When I've vowed upon my eloquence, Willoughby, I'd bring you to pardon the poor dog?'

'Not a word of him!'

'Just one!'

Sir Willoughby battled with himself to repress a state of temper that put him to marked disadvantage beside his friend Horace in high spirits. Ordinarily he enjoyed these fits of Irish* of him, which were Horace's fun and play, at times involuntary, and then they indicated a recklessness that might embrace mischief. De Craye, as Willoughby had often reminded him, was properly Norman. The blood of two or three Irish mothers in his line, however, was enough to dance him, and if his fine profile spoke of the stiffer race, his eyes and the quick run of the lip in the cheek, and a number of his qualities, were evidence of the maternal legacy.

'My word has been said about the man,' Willoughby replied.

'But I've wagered on your heart against your word, and can't afford to lose; and there's a double reason for revoking for you!'

'I don't see either of them. Here are the ladies.'

'You'll think of the poor beast, Willoughby.'

'I hope for better occupation.'

'If he drives a wheelbarrow at the Hall he'll be happier than on board a chariot at large. He's broken-hearted.'

'He's too much in the way of breakages, my dear Horace.'

'Oh! the vase! the bit of porcelain!' sang De Craye. 'Well, we'll talk him over by-and-by.'

'If it pleases you; but my rules are never amended.'

'Inalterable, are they?—like those of an ancient people who might as well have worn a jacket of lead for the comfort they had of their boast. The beauty of laws for human creatures is their adaptability to new stitchings.'

Colonel De Craye walked at the heels of his leader to make his bow to the ladies Eleanor and Isabel.

Sir Willoughby had guessed the person who inspired his friend Horace to plead so pertinaciously and inopportunely for the man Flitch; and it had not improved his temper or the pose of his rejoinders; he had winced under the contrast of his friend Horace's easy, laughing, sparkling, musical air and manner with his own stiffness; and he had seen Clara's face, too, scanning the contrast—he was fatally driven to exaggerate his discontentment, which did not restore him to serenity. He would have learnt more from what his abrupt swing round of the shoulder precluded his beholding. There was an interchange between Colonel De Craye and Miss Middleton; spontaneous on both sides. His was a look that said; 'You were right'; hers: 'I knew it.' Her look was calmer, and after the first instant clouded as by wearifulness of sameness; his was brilliant, astonished, speculative, and admiring, pitiful: a look that poised over a revelation, called up the hosts of wonder to question strange fact.

It had passed unseen by Sir Willoughby. The observer was the one who could also supply the key of the secret. Miss Dale had found Colonel De Craye in company with Miss Middleton at her gateway. They were laughing and talking together like friends of old standing, De Craye as Irish as he could be: and the Irish tongue and gentlemanly manner are an irresistible challenge to the opening steps of familiarity when accident has broken the ice. Flitch was their theme; and: 'Oh! but if we go up to Willoughby hand in hand, and bob a curtsey to 'm and beg his pardon for Mister Flitch, won't he melt to such a pair of suppliants? of course he will!' Miss Middleton said he would not. Colonel De Craye wagered he would; he knew Willoughby best. Miss Middleton looked simply grave; a way of asserting the contrary opinion that tells of rueful experience. 'We'll see,' said the colonel. They chatted like a couple unexpectedly discovering in one another a common dialect among strangers. Can there be an end to it when those two meet? They prattle, they fill the minutes, as though they were violently to be torn asunder at a coming signal, and must have it out while they can; it is a meeting of mountain brooks; not a colloquy but a chasing, impossible to say which flies, which follows, or what the topic, so interlinguistic are they and rapidly counterchanging. After their conversation of an hour before, Laetitia watched Miss Middleton in surprise at her lightness of mind. Clara bathed in mirth. A boy in a Summer stream shows not heartier refreshment of his whole being. Laetitia could now understand Vernon's idea of her wit. And seemed that she also had Irish blood. Speaking of Ireland, Miss Middleton said she had cousins there, her only relatives. 'The laugh told me that,' said Colonel De Craye.

Laetitia and Vernon paced up and down the lawn. Colonel De Craye was talking with English sedateness to the ladies Eleanor and Isabel. Clara and young Crossjay strayed.

'If I might advise, I would say, do not leave the Hall immediately, not yet,' Laetitia said to Vernon.

'You know, then?'

'I cannot understand why it was that I was taken into her confidence.'

'I counselled it.'

'But it was done without an object that I can see.'

'The speaking did her good.'

'But how capricious! how changeful!'

'Better now than later.'

'Surely she has only to ask to be released?—to ask earnestly: if it is her wish.'

'You are mistaken.'

'Why does she not make a confidant of her father?'

'That she will have to do. She wished to spare him.'

'He cannot be spared if she is to break the engagement.'

'She thought of sparing him the annoyance. Now there's to be a tussle he must share in it.'

'Or she thought he might not side with her?'

'She has not a single instinct of cunning. You judge her harshly.'

'She moved me on the walk out. Coming home I felt differently.'

Vernon glanced at Colonel De Craye.

'She wants *good* guidance,' continued Laetitia.

'She has not an idea of treachery.'

'You think so? It may be true. But she seems one born devoid of patience, easily made reckless. There is a wildness . . . I judge by her way of speaking; that at least appeared sincere. She does not practise concealment. He will naturally find it almost incredible. The change in her, so sudden, so wayward, is unintelligible to me. To me it is the conduct of a creature untamed. He may hold her to her word and be justified.'

'Let him look out if he does!'

'Is not that harsher than anything I have said of her?'

'I'm not appointed to praise her. I fancy I read the case; and it's a case of opposition of temperaments. We never can tell the person quite suited to us; it strikes us in a flash.'

'That they are *not* suited to us? Oh, no; that comes by degrees.'

'Yes, but the accumulation of evidence, or sentience, if you like, is combustible; we don't command the spark: it may be late in falling. And you argue in her favour. Consider her as a generous and impulsive girl, outwearied at last.'

'By what?'

'By anything; by his loftiness, if you like. He flies too high for her, we will say.'

'Sir Willoughby an eagle?'

'She may be tired of his eyrie.'

The sound of the word in Vernon's mouth smote on a consciousness she had of his full grasp of Sir Willoughby,

and her own timid knowledge, though he was not a man
who played on words.

If he had eased his heart in stressing the first syllable, it
was only temporary relief. He was heavy-browed enough.

'But I cannot conceive what she expects me to do by
confiding her sense of her position to me,' said Laetitia.

'We none of us know what will be done. We hang on
Willoughby, who hangs on whatever it is that supports
him: and there we are in a swarm.'

'You see the wisdom of staying, Mr. Whitford.'

'It must be over in a day or two. Yes, I stay.'

'She inclines to obey you.'

'I should be sorry to stake my authority on her obedience. We must decide something about Crossjay, and
get the money for his crammer, if it is to be got. If not,
I may get a man to trust me. I mean to drag the boy
away. Willoughby has been at him with the tune of
gentleman, and has laid hold of him by one ear. When
I say "her obedience," she is not in a situation, nor in a
condition, to be led blindly by anybody. She must rely
on herself, do everything herself. It's a knot that won't
bear touching by any hand save hers.'

'I fear . . .' said Laetitia.

'Have no such fear.'

'If it should come to his positively refusing.'

'He faces the consequences.'

'You do not think of her.'

Vernon looked at his companion.

CHAPTER XIX

Colonel De Craye and Clara Middleton

Miss Middleton finished her stroll with Crossjay by
winding her trailer of ivy in a wreath round his hat and
sticking her bunch of grasses in the wreath. She then
commanded him to sit on the ground beside a big rhododendron, there to await her return. Crossjay had informed her of a design he entertained to be off with a
horde of boys nesting in high trees, and marking spots

where wasps and hornets were to be attacked in Autumn:
she thought it a dangerous business, and as the boy's
dinner-bell had very little restraint over him when he was
in the flush of a scheme of this description, she wished to
make tolerably sure of him through the charm she not
unreadily believed she could fling on lads of his age.
'Promise me you will not move from here until I come
back, and when I come I will give you a kiss.' Crossjay
promised. She left him and forgot him.

Seeing by her watch fifteen minutes to the ringing of
the bell, a sudden resolve that she would speak to her
father without another minute's delay, had prompted her
like a superstitious impulse to abandon her aimless course
and be direct. She knew what was good for her; she
knew it now more clearly than in the morning. To be
taken away instantly! was her cry. There could be no
further doubt. Had there been any before? But she
would not in the morning have suspected herself of a
capacity for evil, and of a pressing need to be saved from
herself. She was not pure of nature: it may be that we
breed saintly souls which are: she was pure of will: fire
rather than ice. And in beginning to see the elements
she was made of, she did not shuffle them to a heap with
her sweet looks to front her. She put to her account
some strength, much weakness; she almost dared to
gaze unblinking at a perilous evil tendency. The glimpse
of it drove her to her father.

'He must take me away at once; to-morrow!'

She wished to spare her father. So unsparing of herself was she, that in her hesitation to speak to him of her
change of feeling for Sir Willoughby, she would not suffer
it to be attributed in her own mind to a daughter's
anxious consideration about her father's loneliness; an
idea she had indulged formerly. Acknowledging that it
was imperative she should speak, she understood that she
had refrained, even to the inflicting upon herself of such
humiliation as to run dilating on her woes to others,
because of the silliest of human desires to preserve her
reputation for consistency. She had heard women abused
for shallowness and flightiness: she had heard her father

denounce them as veering weather-vanes, and his oft-repeated quid femina possit:*for her sex's sake, and also to appear an exception to her sex, this reasoning creature desired to be thought consistent.

Just on the instant of her addressing him, saying: 'Father': a note of seriousness in his ear; it struck her that the occasion for saying all had not yet arrived, and she quickly interposed: 'Papa'; and helped him to look lighter. The petition to be taken away was uttered.

'To London?' said Dr. Middleton. 'I don't know who'll take us in.'

'To France, papa?'

'That means hotel-life.'

'Only for two or three weeks.'

'Weeks! I am under an engagement to dine with Mrs. Mountstuart Jenkinson five days hence: that is, on Thursday.'

'Could we not find an excuse?'

'Break an engagement? No, my dear, not even to escape drinking a widow's wine.'

'Does a word bind us?'

'Why, what else should?'

'I think I am not very well.'

'We'll call in that man we met at dinner here: Corney: a capital doctor; an old-fashioned anecdotal doctor. How is it you are not well, my love? You look well. I cannot conceive your not being well.'

'It is only that I want a change of air, papa.'

'There we are—a change! semper eadem!* Women will be wanting a change of air in Paradise; a change of angels too, I might surmise. A change from quarters like these to a French hotel, would be a descent!—"this the seat, this mournful gloom for that celestial light?"** I am perfectly at home in the library here. That excellent fellow Whitford and I have real days: and I like him for showing fight to his elder and better.'

'He is going to leave.'

'I know nothing of it, and I shall append no credit to the tale until I do know. He is headstrong, but he answers to a rap.'

Clara's bosom heaved. The speechless insurrection threatened her eyes.

A South-west shower lashed the window-panes and suggested to Dr. Middleton shuddering visions of the channel-passage on board a steamer.

'Corney shall see you: he is a sparkling draught in person; probably illiterate, if I may judge from one interruption of my discourse when he sat opposite me, but lettered enough to respect Learning and write out his prescription: I do not ask more of men or of physicians.' Dr. Middleton said this rising, glancing at the clock and at the back of his hands. ' "Quod autem secundum litteras difficillimum esse artificium?" But what after letters is the most difficult practice? "Ego puto medicum."* The medicus next to the scholar: though I have not to my recollection required him next me, nor ever expected child of mine to be crying for that milk. Daughter she is—of the unexplained sex: we will send a messenger for Corney. Change, my dear, you will speedily have, to satisfy the most craving of women, if Willoughby, as I suppose, is in the neoteric fashion of spending a honeymoon on a railway: apt image, exposition and perpetuation of the state of mania conducting to the institution! In my time we lay by to brood on happiness; we had no thought of chasing it over a Continent, mistaking hurly-burly clothed in dust for the divinity we sought. A smaller generation sacrifices to excitement. Dust and hurly-burly must perforce be the issue. And that is your modern world. Now, my dear, let us go and wash our hands. Mid-day bells expect immediate attention. They know of no ante-room of assembly.'

Clara stood gathered up, despairing at opportunity lost. He had noticed her contracted shape and her eyes, and had talked magisterially to smother and overbear the something disagreeable prefigured in her appearance.

'You do not despise your girl, father?'

'I do not; I could not; I love her; I love my girl. But you need not sing to me like a gnat to propound that question, my dear.'

'Then, father, tell Sir Willoughby to-day we have to

leave to-morrow. You shall return in time for Mrs. Mountstuart's dinner. Friends will take us in, the Darletons, the Erpinghams. We can go to Oxford, where you are sure of welcome. A little will recover me. Do not mention doctors. But you see I am nervous. I am quite ashamed of it; I am well enough to laugh at it, only I cannot overcome it; and I feel that a day or two will restore me. Say you will. Say it in First-Lesson-Book language; anything above a primer splits my foolish head to-day.'

Dr. Middleton shrugged, spreading out his arms.

'The office of ambassador from you to Willoughby, Clara? You decree me to the part of ball between two bats. The Play being assured, the prologue is a bladder of wind. I seem to be instructed in one of the mysteries of erotic esotery, yet on my word I am no wiser. If Willoughby is to hear anything from you, he will hear it from your lips.'

'Yes, father, yes. We have differences. I am not fit for contests at present; my head is giddy. I wish to avoid an illness. He and I . . . I accuse myself.'

'There is the bell!' ejaculated Dr. Middleton. 'I'll debate on it with Willoughby.'

'This afternoon?'

'Somewhen, before the dinner-bell. I cannot tie myself to the minute-hand of the clock, my dear child. And let me direct you, for the next occasion when you shall bring the vowels I and A, in verbally detached letters, into collision, that you do not fill the hiatus with so pronounced a Y. It is the vulgarization of our tongue of which I y-accuse you. I do not like my girl to be guilty of it.'

He smiled to moderate the severity of the correction, and kissed her forehead.

She declared her inability to sit and eat; she went to her room, after begging him very earnestly to send her the assurance that he had spoken. She had not shed a tear, and she rejoiced in her self-control; it whispered to her of true courage when she had given herself such evidence of the reverse.

Shower and sunshine alternated through the half-hours of the afternoon, like a procession of dark and fair holding hands and passing. The shadow came, and she was chill; the light yellow in moisture, and she buried her face not to be caught up by cheerfulness. Believing that her head ached, she afflicted herself with all the heavy symptoms and oppressed her mind so thoroughly that its occupation was to speculate on Laetitia Dale's modest enthusiasm for rural pleasures, for this place especially, with its rich foliage and peeps of scenic peace. The prospect of an escape from it inspired thoughts of a loveable round of life where the sun was not a naked ball of fire but a friend clothed in woodland; where park and meadow swept to well-known features East and West; and distantly circling hills, and the hearts of poor cottagers too—sympathy with whom assured her of goodness—were familiar, homely to the dweller in the place, morning and night. And she had the love of wild flowers, the watchful happiness in the seasons; poets thrilled her, books absorbed. She dwelt strongly on that sincerity of feeling; it gave root in our earth; she needed it as she pressed a hand on her eyeballs, conscious of acting the invalid, though the reasons she had for languishing under headache were so convincing that her brain refused to disbelieve in it and went some way to produce positive throbs. Otherwise she had no excuse for shutting herself in her room. Vernon Whitford would be sceptical. Headache or none, Colonel De Craye must be thinking strangely of her; she had not shown him any signs of illness. His laughter and his talk sang about her and dispersed the fiction; he was the very sea-wind for bracing unstrung nerves. Her ideas reverted to Sir Willoughby, and at once they had no more cohesion than the foam on a torrent-water.

But soon she was undergoing a variation of sentiment. Her maid Barclay brought her this pencilled line from her father:

'Factum est; laetus est; amantium irae, etc.'*

That it was done, that Willoughby had put on an air of glad acquiescence, and that her father assumed the exist-

ence of a lover's quarrel, was wonderful to her at first
sight, simple the succeeding minute. Willoughby indeed
must be tired of her, glad of her going. He would know
that it was not to return. She was grateful to him for
perhaps hinting at the amantium irae, though she rejected the folly of the verse. And she gazed over dear
homely country through her windows now. Happy the
lady of the place, if happy she can be in her choice!
Clara Middleton envied her the double-blossom wild
cherry-tree, nothing else. One sprig of it, if it had not
faded and gone to dust-colour like crusty Alpine snow in
the lower hollows, and then she could depart, bearing
away a memory of the best here! Her fiction of the
headache pained her no longer. She changed her muslin
dress for silk; she was contented with the first bonnet
Barclay presented. Amicable toward every one in the
house, Willoughby included, she threw up her window,
breathed, blessed mankind: and she thought: 'If Willoughby would open his heart to nature, he would be
relieved of his wretched opinion of the world.' Nature
was then sparkling refreshed in the last drops of a sweeping rain-curtain, favourably disposed for a background to
her joyful optimism. A little nibble of hunger within,
real hunger, unknown to her of late, added to this
healthy view, without precipitating her to appease it;
she was more inclined to foster it, for the sake of the
sinewy activity of limb it gave her; and in the style of
young ladies very light of heart, she went downstairs like
a cascade; and like the meteor observed in its vanishing
trace she alighted close to Colonel De Craye and
entered one of the rooms off the hall.

He cocked an eye at the half-shut door.

Now, you have only to be reminded that it is the habit
of the sportive gentleman of easy life, bewildered as he
would otherwise be by the tricks, twists and windings of
the hunted sex, to parcel out fair women into classes;
and some are flyers and some are runners; these birds
are wild on the wing, those expose their bosoms to the
shot. For him there is no individual woman. He grants
her a characteristic only to enrol her in a class. He is

our immortal dunce at learning to distinguish her as a personal variety, of a separate growth.

Colonel De Craye's cock of the eye at the door said that he had seen a rageing coquette go behind it. He had his excuse for forming the judgement. She had spoken strangely of the fall of his wedding present, strangely of Willoughby; or there was a sound of strangeness in an allusion to her appointed husband; and she had treated Willoughby strangely when they met. Above all, her word about Flitch was curious. And then that look of hers! And subsequently she transferred her polite attentions to Willoughby's friend. After a charming colloquy, the sweetest give and take rattle he had ever enjoyed with a girl, she developed headache to avoid him; and next she developed blindness, for the same purpose.

He was feeling hurt, but considered it preferable to feel challenged.

Miss Middleton came out of another door. She had seen him when she had passed him and when it was too late to convey her recognition; and now she addressed him with an air of having bowed as she went by.

'No one?' she said. 'Am I alone in the house?'

'There is a figure naught,' said he, 'but it's as good as annihilated, and no figure at all, if you put yourself on the wrong side of it, and wish to be alone in the house.'

'Where is Willoughby?'

'Away on business.'

'Riding?'

'Achmet is the horse, and pray don't let him be sold, Miss Middleton. I am deputed to attend on you.'

'I should like a stroll.'

'Are you perfectly restored?'

'Perfectly.'

'Strong?'

'I was never better.'

'It was the answer of the ghost of the wicked old man's wife when she came to persuade him he had one chance remaining. Then, says he, I'll believe in heaven if ye'll stop that bottle, and hurls it; and the bottle broke and he committed suicide, not without suspicion of her laying

a trap for him. These showers curling away and leaving
sweet scents, are divine, Miss Middleton. I have the
privilege of the Christian name on the nuptial-day. This
park of Willoughby's is one of the best things in England.
There's a glimpse over the lake that smokes of a corner
of Killarney; tempts the eye to dream, I mean.' De
Craye wound his finger spirally upward like a smoke
wreath. 'Are you for Irish scenery?'

'Irish, English, Scottish.'

'All's one so long as it's beautiful: yes; you speak for
me. Cosmopolitanism of races is a different affair. I beg
leave to doubt the true union of some; Irish and Saxon,
for example, let Cupid be master of the ceremonies and
the dwelling-place of the happy couple at the mouth of
a Cornucopia. Yet I have seen a flower of Erin worn by a
Saxon gentleman proudly; and the Hibernian courting
a Rowena!* So we'll undo what I said, and consider it
cancelled.'

'Are you of the rebel party, Colonel De Craye?'*

'I am Protestant and Conservative, Miss Middleton.'

'I have not a head for politics.'

'The political heads I have seen would tempt me to
that opinion.'

'Did Willoughby say when he would be back?'

'He named no particular time. Dr. Middleton and
Mr. Whitford are in the library upon a battle of the
books.'

'Happy battle!'

'You are accustomed to scholars. They are rather
intolerant of us poor fellows.'

'Of ignorance perhaps; not of persons.'

'Your father educated you himself, I presume.'

'He gave me as much Latin as I could take. The
fault is mine that it is little.'

'Greek?'

'A little Greek.'

'Ah! And you carry it like a feather.'

'Because it is so light.'

'Miss Middleton, I could sit down to be instructed,
old as I am. When women beat us, I verily believe we

are the most beaten dogs in existence. You like the theatre?'

'Ours?'

'Acting, then.'

'Good acting, of course.'

'May I venture to say you would act admirably?'

'The venture is bold, for I have never tried.'

'Let me see; there is Miss Dale and Mr. Whitford: you and I; sufficient for a two-act piece.* THE IRISHMAN IN SPAIN would do.' He bent to touch the grass as she stepped on it. 'The lawn is wet.'

She signified that she had no dread of wet, and said: 'English women afraid of the weather might as well be shut up.'

De Craye proceeded: 'Patrick O'Neill passes over from Hibernia to Iberia, a disinherited son of a father in the claws of the lawyers, with a letter of introduction to Don Beltran d'Arragon, a Grandee of the First Class, who has a daughter, Doña Serafina (Miss Middleton), the proudest beauty of her day, in the custody of a dueña (Miss Dale), and plighted to Don Fernan, of the Guzman family (Mr. Whitford). There you have our dramatis personae.'

'You are Patrick?'

'Patrick himself. And I lose my letter, and stand on the Prado*of Madrid with the last portrait of Britannia*in the palm of my hand, and crying in the purest brogue of my native land: "It's all through dropping a letter I'm here in Iberia instead of Hibernia, worse luck to the spelling!"'

'But Patrick will be sure to aspirate the initial letter of Hibernia.'

'That is clever criticism, upon my word, Miss Middleton! So he would. And there we have two letters dropped. But he'd do it in a groan, so that it wouldn't count for more than a ghost of one; and everything goes on the stage, since it's only the laugh we want on the brink of the action. Besides you are to suppose the performance before a London audience, who have a native opposition to the aspirate and wouldn't bear to hear him spoil a joke, as if he were a lord or a constable. It's an instinct of the English democracy. So with my bit of coin turning over and over in an undecided way, whether it shall commit suicide to supply me a supper, I behold a pair of Spanish eyes like violet lightnings in the black heavens of that favoured clime. Won't you have violet?'

'Violet forbids my impersonation.'

'But the lustre on black is dark violet blue.'

'You remind me that I have no pretension to black.'

Colonel De Craye permitted himself to take a flitting gaze at Miss Middleton's eyes. 'Chestnut,' he said. 'Well, and Spain is the land of chestnuts.'

'Then it follows that I am a daughter of Spain.'

'Clearly.'

'Logically!'

'By positive deduction.'

'And how do I behold Patrick?'

'As one looks upon a beast of burden.'

'Oh!'

Miss Middleton's exclamation was louder than the matter of the dialogue seemed to require. She caught her hands up.

In the line of the outer extremity of the rhododendron, screened from the house windows, young Crossjay lay at his length, with his head resting on a doubled arm, and his ivy-wreathed hat on his cheek, just where she had left him, commanding him to stay. Half-way toward him up the lawn, she saw the poor boy, and the spur of that pitiful sight set her gliding swiftly. Colonel De Craye followed, pulling an end of his moustache.

Crossjay jumped to his feet.

'My dear, dear Crossjay!' she addressed him and reproached him. 'And how hungry you must be! And you must be drenched! This is really too bad.'

'You told me to wait here,' said Crossjay, in shy self-defence.

'I did, and you should not have done it, foolish boy! I told him to wait for me here before luncheon, Colonel De Craye, and the foolish foolish boy!—he has had nothing to eat and he must have been wet through two or three times:—because I did not come to him!'

'Quite right. And the lava might overflow him and take the mould of him, like the sentinel at Pompeii,* if he's of the true stuff.'

'He may have caught cold, he may have a fever.'

'He was under your orders to stay.'

'I know, and I cannot forgive myself. Run in, Crossjay, and change your clothes. Oh! run, run to Mrs. Montague, and get her to give you a warm bath, and tell her from me to prepare some dinner for you. And change every garment you have. This is unpardonable of me. I said—"not for politics"!—I begin to think I have not a head for anything. But could it be imagined that Crossjay would not move for the dinner-bell! through all that rain! I forgot you, Crossjay. I am so sorry; so sorry! You shall make me pay any forfeit you like. Remember I am deep deep in your debt. And now let me see you run fast. You shall come in to dessert this evening.'

Crossjay did not run. He touched her hand.

'You said something?'

'What did I say, Crossjay?'

'You promised.'

'What did I promise?'

'Something.'

'Name it, dear boy.'

He mumbled '. . . kiss me.'

Clara plumped down on him, enveloped him and kissed him.

The affectionately remorseful impulse was too quick for a conventional note of admonition to arrest her from paying that portion of her debt. When she had sped him off to Mrs. Montague, she was in a blush.

'Dear, dear Crossjay!' she said, sighing.

'Yes, he's a good lad,' remarked the colonel. 'The fellow may well be a faithful soldier and stick to his post, if he receives promise of such a solde.* He is a great favourite with you.'

'He is. You will do him a service by persuading Wil-

loughby to send him to one of those men who get boys
through their naval examination. And, Colonel De
Craye, will you be kind enough to ask at the dinner-table
that Crossjay may come in to dessert?'

'Certainly,' said he, wondering.

'And will you look after him while you are here?
See that no one spoils him. If you could get him away
before you leave, it would be much to his advantage. He
is born for the navy and should be preparing to enter it
now.'

'Certainly, certainly,' said De Craye, wondering more.

'I thank you in advance.'

'Shall I not be usurping . . . ?'

'No, we leave to-morrow.'

'For a day?'

'For longer.'

'Two?'

'It will be longer.'

'A week? I shall not see you again?'

'I fear, not.'

Colonel De Craye controlled his astonishment; he
smothered a sensation of veritable pain, and amiably
said: 'I feel a blow, but I am sure you would not willingly
strike. We are all involved in the regrets.'

Miss Middleton spoke of having to see Mrs. Montague,
the housekeeper, with reference to the bath for Crossjay,
and stepped off the grass. He bowed, watched her a
moment, and for parallel reasons, running close enough
to hit one mark, he commiserated his friend Willoughby.
The winning or the losing of that young lady struck him
as equally lamentable for Willoughby.

CHAPTER XX

An Aged and a Great Wine

THE leisurely promenade up and down the lawn with
ladies and deferential gentlemen, in anticipation of the
dinner-bell, was Dr. Middleton's evening pleasure. He
walked as one who had formerly danced (in Apollo's time

and the young God Cupid's), elastic on the muscles of the calf and foot, bearing his broad iron-grey head in grand elevation. The hard labour of the day approved the cooling exercise and the crowning refreshments of French cookery and wines of known vintages. He was happy at that hour in dispensing wisdom or nugae*to his hearers, like the Western sun, whose habit it is, when he is fairly treated, to break out in quiet splendours, which by no means exhaust his treasury. Blest indeed above his fellows, by the height of the bow-winged bird in a fair weather sunset sky above the pecking sparrow, is he that ever in the recurrent evening of his day sees the best of it ahead and soon to come. He has the rich reward of a youth and manhood of virtuous living. Dr. Middleton misdoubted the future as well as the past of the man who did not, in becoming gravity, exult to dine. That man he deemed unfit for this world and the next.

An example of the good fruit of temperance, he had a comfortable pride in his digestion,* and his political sentiments were attuned by his veneration of the Powers rewarding virtue. We must have a stable world where this is to be done.

The Rev. Doctor was a fine old picture; a specimen of art peculiarly English; combining in himself piety and epicurism, learning and gentlemanliness, with good room for each and a seat at one another's table: for the rest, a strong man, an athlete in his youth, a keen reader of facts and no reader of persons, genial, a giant at a task, a steady worker besides, but easily discomposed. He loved his daughter and he feared her. However much he liked her character, the dread of her sex and age was constantly present to warn him that he was not tied to perfect sanity while the damsel Clara remained unmarried. Her mother had been an amiable woman, of the poetical temperament nevertheless, too enthusiastic, imaginative, impulsive, for the repose of a sober scholar; an admirable woman, still, as you see, a woman, a firework. The girl resembled her. Why should she wish to run away from Patterne Hall for a single hour? Simply because she was of the sex born mutable and explosive. A husband was her proper custodian, justly relieving a father. With demagogues abroad and daughters at home, philosophy is needed for us to keep erect. Let the girl be Cicero's Tullia: well, she dies! The choicest of them will furnish us examples of a strange perversity.

Miss Dale was beside Dr. Middleton. Clara came to them and took the other side.

'I was telling Miss Dale that the signal for your subjection is my enfranchisement,' he said to her, sighing and smiling. 'We know the date. The date of an event to come certifies to it as a fact to be counted on.'

'Are you anxious to lose me?' Clara faltered.

'My dear, you have planted me on a field where I am to expect the trumpet, and when it blows I shall be quit of my nerves, no more.'

Clara found nothing to seize on for a reply in these words. She thought upon the silence of Laetitia.

Sir Willoughby advanced, appearing in a cordial mood.

'I need not ask you whether you are better,' he said to Clara, sparkled to Laetitia, and raised a key to the level of Dr. Middleton's breast, remarking: 'I am going down to my inner cellar.'

'An inner cellar!' exclaimed the Doctor.

'Sacred from the butler. It is interdicted to Stoneman. Shall I offer myself as guide to you? My cellars are worth a visit.'

'Cellars are not catacombs. They are, if rightly constructed, rightly considered, cloisters, where the bottle meditates on joys to bestow, not on dust misused! Have you anything great?'

'A wine aged ninety.'

'Is it associated with your pedigree, that you pronounce the age with such assurance?'

'My grandfather inherited it.'

'Your grandfather, Sir Willoughby, had meritorious offspring, not to speak of generous progenitors. What would have happened, had it fallen into the female line! I shall be glad to accompany you. Port? Hermitage?'

'Port.'

'Ah! We are in England!'

'There will just be time,' said Sir Willoughby, inducing Dr. Middleton to step out.

A chirrup was in the Rev. Doctor's tone: 'Hocks, too, have compassed age. I have tasted senior Hocks.* Their flavours are as a brook of many voices; they have depth also. Senatorial Port! we say. We cannot say that of any other wine. Port is deep-sea deep. It is in its flavour deep; mark the difference. It is like a classic tragedy, organic in conception. An ancient Hermitage has the light of the antique; the merit that it can grow to an extreme old age; a merit. Neither of Hermitage nor of Hock can you say that it is the blood of those long years, retaining the strength of youth with the wisdom of age. To Port for that! Port is our noblest legacy! Observe, I do not compare the wines; I distinguish the qualities. Let them live together for our enrichment; they are not rivals like the Idaean Three.* Were they rivals, a fourth would challenge them. Burgundy has great genius. It does wonders within its period; it does all except to keep up in the race; it is short-lived. An aged Burgundy runs with a beardless Port. I cherish the fancy that Port speaks the sentences of wisdom, Burgundy sings the inspired Ode. Or put it, that Port is the Homeric hexameter, Burgundy the Pindaric dithyramb.* What do you say?'

'The comparison is excellent, sir.'

'The distinction, you would remark. Pindar astounds. But his elder brings us the more sustaining cup. One is a fountain of prodigious ascent. One is the unsounded purple sea of marching billows.'

'A very fine distinction.'

'I conceive you to be now commending the similes. They pertain to the time of the first critics of those poets. Touch the Greeks, and you can nothing new: all has been said: "Graiis, . . . praeter laudem, nullius avaris."* Genius dedicated to Fame is immortal. We, sir, dedicate genius to the cloacaline floods. We do not address the unforgetting Gods, but the popular stomach.'

Sir Willoughby was patient. He was about as accord-

antly coupled with Dr. Middleton in discourse as a drum
duetting with a bass-viol; and when he struck in he
received correction from the paedagogue-instrument.
If he thumped affirmative or negative, he was wrong.
However, he knew scholars to be an unmannered species;
and the Doctor's learnedness would be a subject to
dilate on.

In the cellar, it was the turn for the drum. Dr. Middleton was tongue-tied there. Sir Willoughby gave the
history of his wine in heads of chapters; whence it came
to the family originally, and how it had come down to
him in the quantity to be seen. 'Curiously, my grandfather, who inherited it, was a water-drinker. My father
died early.'

'Indeed! Dear me!' the Doctor ejaculated in astonishment and condolence. The former glanced at the
contrariety of man, the latter embraced his melancholy
destiny.

He was impressed with respect for the family. This
cool vaulted cellar, and the central square block, or
enceinte, where the thick darkness was not penetrated by
the intruding lamp, but rather took it as an eye, bore
witness to forethoughtful practical solidity in the man
who had built the house on such foundations. A house
having a great wine stored below, lives in our imaginations as a joyful house fast and splendidly rooted in the
soil. And imagination has a place for the heir of the
house. His grandfather a water-drinker, his father
dying early, present circumstances to us arguing predestination to an illustrious heirship and career. Dr.
Middleton's musings were coloured by the friendly vision
of glasses of the great wine; his mind was festive; it
pleased him, and he chose to indulge in his whimsical-
robustious, grandiose-airy style of thinking: from which
the festive mind will sometimes take a certain print
that we cannot obliterate immediately. Expectation is
grateful, you know; in the mood of gratitude we are
waxen. And he was a self-humouring gentleman.

He liked Sir Willoughby's tone in ordering the servant
at his heels to take up 'those two bottles': it prescribed,

without overdoing it, a proper amount of caution, and it named an agreeable number.

Watching the man's hand keenly, he said:

'But here is the misfortune of a thing super-excellent: —not more than one in twenty will do it justice.'

Sir Willoughby replied: 'Very true, sir, and I think we may pass over the nineteen.'

'Women, for example: and most men.'

'This wine would be a sealed book to them.'

'I believe it would. It would be a grievous waste.'

'Vernon is a claret-man: and so is Horace De Craye. They are both below the mark of this wine. They will join the ladies. Perhaps you and I, sir, might remain together.'

'With the utmost good will on my part.'

'I am anxious for your verdict, sir.'

'You shall have it, sir, and not out of harmony with the chorus preceding me, I can predict. Cool, not frigid.' Dr. Middleton summed the attributes of the cellar on quitting it: 'North side and South. No musty damp. A pure air! Everything requisite. One might lie down oneself and keep sweet here.'

Of all our venerable British of the two Isles professing a suckling attachment to an ancient port-wine, lawyer, doctor, squire, rosy admiral, city merchant, the classic scholar is he whose blood is most nuptial to the webbed bottle. The reason must be, that he is full of the old poets. He has their spirit to sing with, and the best that Time has done on earth to feed it. He may also perceive a resemblance in the wine to the studious mind, which is the obverse of our mortality, and throws off acids and crusty particles in the piling of the years, until it is fulgent by clarity. Port hymns to his conservatism. It is magical: at one sip he is off swimming in the purple flood of the ever-youthful antique.

By comparison, then, the enjoyment of others is brutish; they have not the soul for it; but he is worthy of the wine, as are poets of Beauty. In truth, these should be severally apportioned to them, scholar and poet, as his own good thing. Let it be so.

Meanwhile Dr. Middleton sipped.

After the departure of the ladies, Sir Willoughby had practised a studied curtness upon Vernon and Horace.

'You drink claret,' he remarked to them, passing it round. 'Port, I think, Dr. Middleton? The wine before you may serve for a preface. We shall have *your* wine in five minutes.'

The claret jug empty, Sir Willoughby offered to send for more. De Craye was languid over the question. Vernon rose from the table.

'We have a bottle of Dr. Middleton's Port coming in,' Willoughby said to him.

'Mine, you call it?' cried the Rev. Doctor.

'It's a royal wine, that won't suffer sharing,' said Vernon.

'We'll be with you, if you go into the billiard-room, Vernon.'

'I shall hurry my drinking of good wine for no man,' said the Rev. Doctor.

'Horace?'

'I'm beneath it, ephemeral, Willoughby. I am going to the ladies.'

Vernon and De Craye retired upon the arrival of the wine; and Dr. Middleton sipped. He sipped and looked at the owner of it.

'Some thirty dozen?' he said.

'Fifty.'

The Doctor nodded humbly.

'I shall remember, sir,' his host addressed him, 'whenever I have the honour of entertaining you, I am cellarer of that wine.'

The Rev. Doctor set down his glass. 'You have, sir, in some sense, an enviable post. It is a responsible one, if that be a blessing. On you it devolves to retard the day of the last dozen.'

'Your opinion of the wine is favourable, sir?'

'I will say this:—shallow souls run to rhapsody:—I will say, that I am consoled for not having lived ninety years back, or at any period but the present, by this one glass of your ancestral wine.'

'I am careful of it,' Sir Willoughby said modestly; 'still its natural destination is to those who can appreciate it. You do, sir.'

'Still, my good friend, still! It is a charge: it is a possession, but part in trusteeship. Though we cannot declare it an entailed estate, our consciences are in some sort pledged that it shall be a succession not too considerably diminished.'

'You will not object to drink it, sir, to the health of your grandchildren. And may you live to toast them in it on their marriage-day!'

'You colour the idea of a prolonged existence in seductive hues. Ha! It is a wine for Tithonus.* This wine would speed him to the rosy Morning—aha!'

'I will undertake to sit you through it up to morning,' said Sir Willoughby, innocent of the Bacchic nuptiality of the allusion.

Dr. Middleton eyed the decanter. There is a grief in gladness, for a premonition of our mortal state. The amount of wine in the decanter did not promise to sustain the starry roof of night and greet the dawn. 'Old wine, my friend, denies us the full bottle!'

'Another bottle is to follow.'

'No!'

'It is ordered.'

'I protest.'

'It is uncorked.'

'I entreat.'

'It is decanted.'

'I submit. But, mark, it must be honest partnership. You are my worthy host, sir, on that stipulation. Note the superiority of wine over Venus!—I may say, the magnanimity of wine; our jealousy turns on him that will not share! But the corks, Willoughby. The corks excite my amazement.'

'The corking is examined at regular intervals. I remember the occurrence in my father's time. I have seen to it once.'

'It must be perilous as an operation for tracheotomy; which I should assume it to resemble in surgical skill

and firmness of hand, not to mention the imminent gasp
of the patient.'

A fresh decanter was placed before the doctor.

He said: 'I have but a girl to give!' He was melted.

Sir Willoughby replied: 'I take her for the highest
prize this world affords.'

'I have beaten some small stock of Latin into her head,
and a note of Greek. She contains a savour of the
classics. I hoped once . . . but she is a girl. The
nymph of the woods is in her. Still she will bring you
her flower-cup of Hippocrene.* She has that aristocracy
—the noblest. She is fair; a Beauty, some have said,
who judge not by lines. Fair to me, Willoughby! She
is my sky. There were applicants. In Italy she was
besought of me. She has no history. You are the first
heading of the chapter. With you she will have her one
tale, as it should be. "Mulier tum bene olet,"*you know.
Most fragrant she that smells of naught. She goes to
you from me, from me alone, from her father to her
husband. "Ut flos in septis secretus nascitur hortis."
. . . He murmured on the lines to, "Sic virgo, dum . . ."*I
shall feel the parting. She goes to one who will have my
pride in her, and more. I will add, who will be envied.
Mr. Whitford must write you a Carmen Nuptiale.'

The heart of the unfortunate gentleman listening to
Dr. Middleton set in for irregular leaps. His offended
temper broke away from the image of Clara, revealing
her as he had seen her in the morning beside Horace De
Craye, distressingly sweet; sweet with the breezy radiance of an English soft-breathing day; sweet with sharpness of young sap. Her eyes, her lips, her fluttering
dress that played happy mother across her bosom, giving
peeps of the veiled twins; and her laughter, her slim
figure, peerless carriage, all her terrible sweetness touched
his wound to the smarting quick.

Her wish to be free of him was his anguish. In his
pain he thought sincerely. When the pain was easier he
muffled himself in the idea of her jealousy of Laetitia Dale,
and deemed the wish a fiction. But she had expressed
it. That was the wound he sought to comfort; for the

double reason, that he could love her better after punishing her, and that to meditate on doing so masked the fear of losing her—the dread abyss she had succeeded in forcing his nature to shudder at as a giddy edge possibly near, in spite of his arts of self-defence.

'What I shall do to-morrow evening!' he exclaimed. 'I do not care to fling a bottle to Colonel De Craye and Vernon. I cannot open one for myself. To sit with the ladies will be sitting in the cold for me. When do you bring me back my bride, sir?'

'My dear Willoughby!' The Rev. Doctor puffed, composed himself, and sipped. 'The expedition is an absurdity. I am unable to see the aim of it. She had a headache, vapours. They are over, and she will show a return of good sense. I have ever maintained that nonsense is not to be encouraged in girls. *I* can put my foot on it. My arrangements are for staying here a further ten days, in the terms of your hospitable invitation. And I stay.'

'I applaud your resolution, sir. Will you prove firm?'

'I am never false to my engagement, Willoughby.'

'Not under pressure?'

'Under no pressure.'

'Persuasion, I should have said.'

'Certainly not. The weakness is in the yielding, either to persuasion or to pressure. The latter brings weight to bear on us; the former blows at our want of it.'

'You gratify me, Dr. Middleton, and relieve me.'

'I cordially dislike a breach in good habits, Willoughby. But I do remember—was I wrong?—informing Clara that you appeared light-hearted in regard to a departure, or gap in a visit, that was not, I must confess, to my liking.'

'Simply, my dear Doctor, your pleasure was my pleasure; but make my pleasure yours, and you remain to crack many a bottle with your son-in-law.'

'Excellently said. You have a courtly speech, Willoughby. I can imagine you to conduct a lover's quarrel with a politeness to read a lesson to well-bred damsels. Aha?'

'Spare me the futility of the quarrel.'

'All's well?'

'Clara,' replied Sir Willoughby, in dramatic epigram, 'is perfection.'

'I rejoice,' the Rev. Doctor responded; taught thus to understand that the lover's quarrel between his daughter and his host was at an end.

He left the table a little after eleven o'clock. A short dialogue ensued upon the subject of the ladies. They must have gone to bed? Why yes; of course they must. It is good that they should go to bed early to preserve their complexions for us. Ladies are creation's glory, but they are anti-climax, following a wine of a century old. They are anti-climax, recoil, cross-current; morally, they are repentance, penance; imagerially, the frozen North on the young brown buds bursting to green. What know they of a critic in the palate, and a frame all revelry! And mark you, revelry in sobriety, containment in exultation: classic revelry. Can they, dear though they be to us, light up candelabras in the brain, to illuminate all history and solve the secret of the destiny of man? They cannot; they cannot sympathize with them that can. So therefore this division is between us; yet are we not turbaned Orientals, nor are they inmates of the harem. We are not Moslem.* Be assured of it, in the contemplation of the table's decanter.

Dr. Middleton said: 'Then I go straight to bed.'

'I will conduct you to your door, sir,' said his host.

The piano was heard. Dr. Middleton laid his hand on the banisters, and remarked: 'The ladies must have gone to bed?'

Vernon came out of the library and was hailed: 'Fellow-student!'

He waved a good-night to the Doctor and said to Willoughby: 'The ladies are in the drawing-room.'

'I am on my way upstairs,' was the reply.

'Solitude and sleep, after such a wine as that; and forefend us human society!' the Doctor shouted. 'But, Willoughby!'

'Sir.'

'*One* to-morrow!'

'You dispose of the cellar, sir.'

'I am fitter to drive the horses of the sun.* I would rigidly counsel, one, and no more. We have made a breach in the fiftieth dozen. Daily one, will preserve us from having to name the fortieth quite so unseasonably. The couple of bottles per diem prognosticates disintegration, with its accompanying recklessness. Constitutionally, let me add, I bear three. I speak for posterity.'

During Dr. Middleton's allocution the ladies issued from the drawing-room, Clara foremost, for she had heard her father's voice, and desired to ask him this in reference to their departure: 'Papa, will you tell me the hour to-morrow?'

She ran up the stairs to kiss him, saying again: 'When will you be ready to-morrow morning?'

Dr. Middleton announced a stoutly deliberative mind in the bugle-notes of a repeated ahem. He bethought him of replying in his doctorial tongue. Clara's eager face admonished him to brevity: it began to look starved. Intruding on his vision of the houris couched in the inner cellar to be the reward of valiant men, it annoyed him. His brows joined. He said: 'I shall not be ready tomorrow morning.'

'In the afternoon?'

'Nor in the afternoon.'

'When?'

'My dear, I am ready for bed at this moment, and know of no other readiness. Ladies,' he bowed to the group in the hall below him, 'may fair dreams pay court to you this night!'

Sir Willoughby had hastily descended and shaken the hands of the ladies, directed Horace De Craye to the laboratory for a smoking-room, and returned to Dr. Middleton. Vexed by the scene, uncertain of his temper if he stayed with Clara, for whom he had arranged that her disappointment should take place on the morrow, in his absence, he said, 'Good night, good night,' to her, with due fervour, bending over her flaccid finger-tips; then offered his arm to the Rev. Doctor.

'Ay, son Willoughby, in friendliness, if you will, though I am a man to bear my load,' the father of the stupefied girl addressed him. 'Candles, I believe, are on the first landing. Good night, my love. Clara!'

'Papa!'

'Good night.'

'Oh!' she lifted her breast with the interjection, stand· ing in shame of the curtained conspiracy and herself, 'good night.'

Her father wound up the stairs. She stepped down.

'There was an understanding that papa and I should go to London to-morrow early,' she said unconcernedly to the ladies, and her voice was clear, but her face too legible. De Craye was heartily unhappy at the sight.

CHAPTER XXI

Clara's Meditations

Two were sleepless that night: Miss Middleton and Colonel De Craye.

She was in a fever, lying like stone, with her brain burning. Quick natures run out to calamity in any little shadow of it flung before. Terrors of apprehension drive them. They stop not short of the uttermost when they are on the wings of dread. A frown means tempest, a wind wreck; to see fire is to be seized by it. When it is the approach of their loathing that they fear, they are in the tragedy of the embrace at a breath; and then is the wrestle between themselves and horror; between themselves and evil, which promises aid; themselves and weakness, which calls on evil; themselves and the better part of them, which whispers no beguilement.

The false course she had taken through sophistical cowardice appalled the girl; she was lost. The advantage taken of it by Willoughby put on the form of strength, and made her feel abject, reptilious; she was lost, carried away on the flood of the cataract. He had won her father for an ally. Strangely, she knew not how, he had succeeded in swaying her father, who had previously not more than tolerated him. 'Son Willoughby' on her father's lips meant something that scenes and scenes would have to struggle with, to the out-wearying of her father and herself. She revolved the 'Son Willoughby' through moods of stupefaction, contempt, revolt, subjection. It meant that she was vanquished. It meant that her father's esteem for her was forfeited. She saw him a gigantic image of discomposure.

Her recognition of her cowardly feebleness brought the brood of fatalism. What was the right of so miserable a creature as she to excite disturbance, let her fortunes be good or ill? It would be quieter to float, kinder to everybody. Thank heaven for the chances of a short life! Once in a net, desperation is graceless. We may be brutes in our earthly destinies; in our endurance of them we need not be brutish.

She was now in the luxury of passivity, when we throw our burden on the Powers above, and do not love them. The need to love them drew her out of it, that she might strive with the unbearable, and by sheer striving, even though she were graceless, come to love them humbly. It is here that the seed of good teaching supports a soul; for the condition might be mapped, and where kismet whispers us to shut eyes, and instruction bids us look up, is at a well-marked cross-road of the contest.

Quick of sensation, but not courageously resolved, she perceived how blunderingly she had acted. For a punishment, it seemed to her that she who had not known her mind must learn to conquer her nature, and submit. She had accepted Willoughby; therefore she accepted him. The fact became a matter of the past, past debating.

In the abstract, this contemplation of circumstances went well. A plain duty lay in her way. And then a disembodied thought flew round her, comparing her with Vernon to her discredit. He had for years borne much that was distasteful to him, for the purpose of studying, and with his poor income helping the poorer than himself. She dwelt on him in pity and envy; he had lived in this place, and so must she; and he had not been dishonoured

by his modesty: he had not failed of self-control, because
he had a life within. She was almost imagining she might
imitate him, when the clash of a sharp physical thought:
'The difference! the difference!' told her she was woman
and never could submit. Can a woman have an inner
life apart from him she is yoked to? She tried to nestle
deep away in herself: in some corner where the abstract
view had comforted her, to flee from thinking as her
feminine blood directed. It was a vain effort. The difference, the cruel fate, the defencelessness of women,
pursued her, strung her to wild horses' backs, tossed her
on savage wastes. In her case duty was shame: hence, it
could not be broadly duty. That intolerable difference
proscribed the word.

But the fire of a brain burning high and kindling everything, lit up herself against herself:—Was one so volatile
as she a person with a will?—Were they not a multitude
of flitting wishes, that she took for a will?—Was she,
feather-headed that she was, a person to make a stand
on physical pride?—If she could yield her hand without
reflection (as she conceived she had done, from incapacity
to conceive herself doing it reflectively), was she much
better than purchaseable stuff that has nothing to say
to the bargain?

Furthermore, said her incandescent reason, she had
not suspected such art of cunning in Willoughby. Then
might she not be deceived altogether—might she not have
misread him? Stronger than she had fancied, might he
not be likewise more estimable? The world was favourable to him: he was prized by his friends.

She reviewed him. It was all in one flash. It was not
much less intentionally favourable than the world's review and that of his friends, but, beginning with the idea
of them, she recollected—heard Willoughby's voice pro-
nouncing his opinion of his friends and the world; of
Vernon Whitford and Colonel De Craye, for example, and
of men and women. An undefined agreement to have
the same regard for him as his friends and the world had,
provided that he kept at the same distance from her,
was the termination of this phase, occupying about a

minute in time, and reached through a series of intensely
vivid pictures:—his face, at her petition to be released,
lowering behind them for a background and a comment.

'I cannot! I cannot!' she cried aloud; and it struck
her that her repulsion was a holy warning. Better be
graceless than a loathing wife: better appear inconsistent.
Why should she not appear such as she was?

Why? We answer that question usually in angry
reliance on certain superb qualities, injured fine qualities
of ours undiscovered by the world, not much more than
suspected by ourselves, which are still our fortress, where
pride sits at home, solitary and impervious as an octo-
genarian conservative. But it is not possible to answer
it so when the brain is rageing like a pine-torch and the
devouring illumination leaves not a spot of our nature
covert. The aspect of her weakness was unrelieved, and
frightened her back to her loathing. From her loathing,
as soon as her sensations had quickened to realize it, she
was hurled on her weakness. She was graceless, she was
inconsistent, she was volatile, she was unprincipled, she
was worse than a prey to wickedness—capable of it; she
was only waiting to be misled. Nay, the idea of being
misled suffused her with languor; for then the battle
would be over and she a happy weed of the sea, no longer
suffering those tugs at the roots, but leaving it to the
sea to heave and contend. She would be like Constantia then: like her in her fortunes: never so brave,
she feared.

Perhaps very like Constantia in her fortunes!

Poor troubled bodies waking up in the night to behold
visually the spectre cast forth from the perplexed
machinery inside them, stare at it for a space, till touching consciousness they dive down under the sheets with
fish-like alacrity. Clara looked at her thought, and
suddenly headed downward in a crimson gulf.

She must have obtained absolution, or else it was
oblivion, below. Soon after the plunge, her first object
of meditation was Colonel De Craye. She thought of
him calmly: he seemed a refuge. He was very nice,
he was a holiday character. His lithe figure, neat firm

footing of the stag, swift intelligent expression, and his ready frolicsomeness, pleasant humour, cordial temper, and his Irishry, whereon he was at liberty to play, as on the emblem harp of the Isle, were soothing to think of. The suspicion that she tricked herself with this calm observation of him was dismissed. Issuing out of torture, her young nature eluded the irradiating brain, in search of refreshment, and she luxuriated at a feast in considering him—shower on a parched land that he was! He spread new air abroad. She had no reason to suppose he was not a good man: she could securely think of him. Besides he was bound by his prospective office in support of his friend Willoughby to be quite harmless. And besides (you are not to expect logical sequences) the showery refreshment in thinking of him lay in the sort of assurance it conveyed, that the more she thought, the less would he be likely to figure as an obnoxious official: that is, as the man to do by Willoughby at the altar what her father would, under the supposition, be doing by her. Her mind reposed on Colonel De Craye.

His name was Horace.* Her father had worked with her at Horace. She knew most of the Odes and some of the Satires and Epistles of the poet. They reflected benevolent beams on the gentleman of the poet's name. He too was vivacious, had fun, common sense, elegance; loved rusticity, he said, sighed for a country life, fancied retiring to Canada to cultivate his own domain; 'modus agri non ita magnus':*a delight. And he, too, when in the country sighed for town. There were strong features of resemblance. He had hinted in fun at not being rich. 'Quae virtus et quanta sit vivere parvo.'* But that quotation applied to and belonged to Vernon Whitford. Even so little disarranged her meditations.

She would have thought of Vernon, as her instinct of safety prompted, had not his exactions been excessive. He proposed to help her with advice only. She was to do everything for herself, do and dare everything, decide upon everything. He told her flatly that so would she learn to know her own mind; and flatly that it was her penance. She had gained nothing by breaking down and pouring herself out to him. He would have her bring Willoughby and her father face to face, and be witness of their interview—herself the theme. What alternative was there?—obedience to the word she had pledged. He talked of patience, of self-examination and patience. But all of her—she was all marked *urgent*. This house was a cage, and the world—her brain was a cage, until she could obtain her prospect of freedom.

As for the house, she might leave it; yonder was the dawn.

She went to her window to gaze at the first colour along the grey. Small satisfaction came of gazing at that or at herself. She shunned glass and sky. One and the other stamped her as a slave in a frame. It seemed to her she had been so long in this place that she was fixed here: it was her world, and to imagine an Alp, was like seeking to get back to childhood. Unless a miracle intervened, here she would have to pass her days. Men are so little chivalrous now, that no miracle ever intervenes. Consequently she was doomed.

She took a pen and began a letter to a dear friend, Lucy Darleton, a promised bridesmaid, bidding her countermand orders for her bridal dress, and purposing a tour in Switzerland. She wrote of the mountain country with real abandonment to imagination. It became a visioned loophole of escape. She rose and clasped a shawl over her night-dress to ward off chillness, and sitting to the table again, could not produce a word. The lines she had written were condemned: they were ludicrously inefficient. The letter was torn to pieces. She stood very clearly doomed.

After a fall of tears, upon looking at the scraps, she dressed herself, and sat by the window and watched the blackbird on the lawn as he hopped from shafts of dewy sunlight to the long-stretched dewy tree-shadows, considering in her mind that dark dews are more meaningful than bright, the beauty of the dews of woods more sweet than meadow-dews. It signified only that she was quieter. She had gone through her crisis in the anticipation of it. That is how quick natures will often be cold and hard, or not much moved, when the positive crisis arrives, and why it is that they are prepared for astonishing leaps over the gradations which should render their conduct comprehensible to us, if not excuse-able. She watched the blackbird throw up his head stiff, and peck to right and left, dangling the worm each side his orange beak. Speckle-breasted thrushes were at work, and a wagtail that ran as with Clara's own little steps. Thrush and blackbird flew to the nest. They had wings. The lovely morning breathed of sweet earth into her open window and made it painful, in the dense twitter, chirp, cheep, and song of the air, to resist the innocent intoxication. O to love! was not said by her, but if she had sung, as her nature prompted, it would have been. Her war with Willoughby sprang of a desire to love repelled by distaste. Her cry for freedom was a cry to be free to love: she discovered it, half-shuddering: to love, oh! no—no shape of man, nor impalpable nature either: but to love unselfishness, and helpfulness, and planted strength in something. Then, loving and being loved a little, what strength would be hers! She could utter all the words needed to Willoughby and to her father, locked in her love: walking in this world, living in that.

Previously she had cried, despairing: If I were loved! Jealousy of Constantia's happiness, envy of her escape, ruled her then: and she remembered the cry, though not perfectly her plain-speaking to herself: she chose to think she had meant: If Willoughby were capable of truly loving! For now the fire of her brain had sunk, and refuges and subterfuges were round about it. The thought of personal love was encouraged, she chose to think, for the sake of the strength it lent her to carve her way to freedom. She had just before felt rather the reverse, but she could not exist with that feeling; and it was true that freedom was not so indistinct in her fancy as the idea of love.

Were men, when they were known, like him she knew too well?

The arch-tempter's question to her was there.

She put it away. Wherever she turned, it stood observing her. She knew so much of one man, nothing of the rest: naturally she was curious. Vernon might be sworn to be unlike. But he was exceptional. What of the other in the house?

Maidens are commonly reduced to read the masters of their destinies by their instincts; and when these have been edged by over-activity they must hoodwink their maidenliness to suffer themselves to read: and then they must dupe their minds, else men would soon see they were gifted to discern. Total ignorance being their pledge of purity to men, they have to expunge the writing of their perceptives on the tablets of the brain: they have to know not when they do know. The instinct of seeking to know, crossed by the task of blotting knowledge out, creates that conflict of the natural with the artificial creature to which their ultimately-revealed double-face, complained of by ever-dissatisfied men, is owing. Wonder in no degree that they indulge a craving to be fools, or that many of them act the character. Jeer at them as little for not showing growth. You have reared them to this pitch, and at this pitch they have partly civilized you. Supposing you to want it done wholly, you must yield just as many points in your requisitions as are needed to let the wits of young women reap their due harvest and be of good use to their souls. You will then have a fair battle, a braver, with better results.

Clara's inner eye traversed Colonel De Craye at a shot. She had immediately to blot out the vision of the Captain Oxford in him, the revelation of his laughing contempt for Willoughby, the view of mercurial principles, the scribbled histories of light love-passages.

She blotted it out, kept it from her mind: so she knew him, knew him to be a sweeter and a variable Willoughby, a generous kind of Willoughby, a Willoughby-butterfly, without having the free mind to summarize him and picture him for a warning. Scattered features of him, such as the instincts call up, were not sufficiently impressive. Besides the clouded mind was opposed to her receiving impressions.

Young Crossjay's voice in the still morning air came to her ears. The dear guileless chatter of the boy's voice! Why, assuredly it was young Crossjay who was the man she loved. And he loved her. And he was going to be an unselfish, sustaining, true strong man, the man she longed for, for anchorage. Oh the dear voice! woodpecker and thrush in one. He never ceased to chatter to Vernon Whitford walking beside him with a swinging stride off to the lake for their morning swim. Happy couple! The morning gave them both a freshness and innocence above human. They seemed to Clara made of morning air and clear lake-water. Crossjay's voice ran up and down a diatonic scale, with here and there a query in semitone and a laugh on a ringing note. She wondered what he could have to talk of so incessantly, and imagined all the dialogue. He prattled of his yesterday, to-day and to-morrow; which did not imply past and future, but his vivid present. She felt like one vainly trying to fly in hearing him; she felt old. The consolation she arrived at was to feel maternal. She wished to hug the boy.

Trot and stride, Crossjay and Vernon entered the park, careless about wet grass, not once looking at the house. Crossjay ranged ahead and picked flowers, bounding back to show them. Clara's heart beat at a fancy that her name was mentioned. If those flowers were for her she would prize them!

The two bathers dipped over an undulation.

Her loss of them rattled her chains.

Deeply dwelling on their troubles has the effect upon the young of helping to forgetfulness; for they cannot think without imagining, their imaginations are saturated with their pleasures, and the collision, though they are unable to exchange sad for sweet, distils an opiate.

'Am I solemnly engaged?' she asked herself. She seemed to be awakening.

She glanced at her bed, where she had passed the night of ineffectual moaning; and out on the high wave of grass, where Crossjay and his good friend had vanished.

Was the struggle all to be gone over again?

Little by little her intelligence of her actual position crept up to submerge her heart.

'I am in his house!' she said. It resembled a discovery, so strangely had her opiate and power of dreaming wrought through her tortures. She said it gasping. She was in his house, his guest, his betrothed, sworn to him. The fact stood out cut in steel on the pitiless daylight.

That consideration drove her to be an early wanderer in the wake of Crossjay.

Her station was among beeches on the flank of the boy's return; and while waiting there, the novelty of her waiting to waylay any one—she who had played the contrary part!—told her more than it pleased her to think. Yet she could admit that she did desire to speak with Vernon, as with a counsellor, harsh and curt, but wholesome.

The bathers reappeared on the grass-ridge, racing and flapping wet towels.

Some one hailed them. A sound of the galloping hoof drew her attention to the avenue. She saw Willoughby dash across the park-level, and dropping a word to Vernon, ride away. Then she allowed herself to be seen.

Crossjay shouted. Willoughby turned his head, but not his horse's head. The boy sprang up to Clara. He had swum across the lake and back; he had raced Mr. Whitford—and beaten him! How he wished Miss Middleton had been able to be one of them!

Clara listened to him enviously. Her thought was: We women are nailed to our sex!

She said: 'And you have just been talking to Sir Willoughby.'

Crossjay drew himself up to give an imitation of the baronet's hand-waving in adieu.

He would not have done that, had he not smelt sympathy with the performance.

She declined to smile. Crossjay repeated it, and laughed. He made a broader exhibition of it to Vernon approaching: 'I say, Mr. Whitford, who's this?'

Vernon doubled to catch him. Crossjay fled and resumed his magnificent air in the distance.

'Good morning, Miss Middleton; you are out early,' said Vernon, rather pale and stringy from his cold swim, and rather hard-eyed with the sharp exercise following it.

She had expected some of the kindness she wanted to reject, for he could speak very kindly, and she regarded him as her doctor of medicine, who would at least present the futile drug.

'Good morning,' she replied.

'Willoughby will not be home till the evening.'

'You could not have had a finer morning for your bath.'

'No.'

'I will walk as fast as you like.'

'I'm perfectly warm.'

'But you prefer fast walking.'

'Out.'

'Ah! yes, that I understand. The walk back! Why is Willoughby away to-day?'

'He has business.'

After several steps, she said: 'He makes very sure of papa.'

'Not without reason, you will find,' said Vernon.

'Can it be? I am bewildered. I had papa's promise.'

'To leave the Hall for a day or two.'

'It would have been . . .'

'Possibly. But other heads are at work as well as yours. If you had been in earnest about it, you would have taken your father into your confidence at once. That was the course I ventured to propose, on the supposition.'

'In earnest! I cannot imagine that you doubt it. I wished to spare him.'

'This is a case in which he can't be spared.'

'If I had been bound to any other! I did not know then *who* held me a prisoner. I thought I had only to speak to him sincerely.'

'Not many men would give up their prize for a word; Willoughby the last of any.'

'Prize' rang through her thrillingly from Vernon's mouth, and soothed her degradation.

She would have liked to protest that she was very little of a prize; a poor prize; not one at all in general estimation; only one to a man reckoning his property; no prize in the true sense.

The importunity of pain saved her.

'Does he think I can change again? Am I treated as something won in a lottery? To stay here is indeed more than I can bear. And if he is calculating—Mr. Whitford, if he calculates on another change, his plotting to keep me here is inconsiderate, not very wise. Changes *may* occur in absence.'

'Wise or not, he has the right to scheme his best to keep you.'

She looked on Vernon with a shade of wondering reproach.

'Why? What right?'

'The right you admit when you ask him to release you. He has the right to think you deluded; and to think you may come to a better mood if you remain—a mood more agreeable to him, I mean. He has that right absolutely. You are bound to remember also that you stand in the wrong. You confess it when you appeal to his generosity. And every man has the right to retain a treasure in his hand if he can. Look straight at these facts.'

'You expect me to be all reason!'

'Try to be. It's the way to learn whether you are really in earnest.'

'I will try. It will drive me to worse!'

'Try honestly. What is wisest now is, in my opinion, for you to resolve to stay. I speak in the character of the person you sketched for yourself as requiring. Well, then, a friend repeats the same advice. You might have gone with your father: now you will only disturb him and annoy him. The chances are, he will refuse to go.'

'Are women ever so changeable as men, then? Papa consented; he agreed; he had some of my feeling; I saw it. That was yesterday. And at night! He spoke to each of us at night in a different tone from usual. With me he was hardly affectionate. But when you advise me to stay, Mr. Whitford, you do not perhaps reflect that it would be at the sacrifice of all candour.'

'Regard it as a probational term.'

'It has gone too far with me.'

'Take the matter into the head: try the case there.'

'Are you not counselling me as if I were a woman of intellect?'

The crystal ring in her voice told him that tears were near to flowing.

He shuddered slightly. 'You have intellect,' he said, nodded, and crossed the lawn, leaving her. He had to dress.

She was not permitted to feel lonely, for she was immediately joined by Colonel De Craye.

CHAPTER XXII

The Ride

CROSSJAY darted up to her a nose ahead of the colonel.

'I say, Miss Middleton, we're to have the whole day to ourselves, after morning lessons. Will you come and fish with me and see me bird's-nest?'

'Not for the satisfaction of beholding another cracked crown, my son'; the colonel interposed: and bowing to Clara: 'Miss Middleton is handed over to my exclusive charge for the day—with her consent?'

'I scarcely know,' said she, consulting a sensation of languor that seemed to contain some reminiscence. 'If I am here. My father's plans are uncertain. I will speak to him. If I am here, perhaps Crossjay would like a ride in the afternoon.'

'Oh! yes,' cried the boy; 'out over Bournden, through Mewsey up to Closham beacon, and down on Aspenwell, where there's a common for racing. And ford the stream!'

'An inducement for you,' De Craye said to her.

She smiled and squeezed the boy's hand.

'We won't go without you, Crossjay.'

'You don't carry a comb, my man, when you bathe?'

At this remark of the colonel's, young Crossjay conceived the appearance of his matted locks in the eyes of his adorable lady. He gave her one dear look through his redness, and fled.

'I like that boy,' said De Craye.

'I love him,' said Clara.

Crossjay's troubled eyelids in his honest young face became a picture for her.

'After all, Miss Middleton, Willoughby's notions about him are not so bad, if we consider that you will be in the place of a mother to him.'

'I think them bad.'

'You are disinclined to calculate the good fortune of the boy in having more of you on land than he would have in crown and anchor buttons!'

'You have talked of him with Willoughby.'

'We had a talk last night.'

Of how much? thought she.

'Willoughby returns?' she said.

'He dines here, I know; for he holds the key of the inner cellar, and Dr. Middleton does him the honour to applaud his wine. Willoughby was good enough to tell me that he thought I might contribute to amuse you.'

She was brooding in stupefaction on her father and the wine as she requested Colonel De Craye to persuade Willoughby to take the general view of Crossjay's future and act on it.

'He seems fond of the boy, too!' said De Craye musingly.

'You speak in doubt?'

'Not at all. But is he not—men are queer fish!—make allowance for us—a trifle tyrannical, pleasantly, with those he is fond of?'

'If they look right and left?'

It was meant for an interrogation: it was not with the sound of one that the words dropped. 'My dear Crossjay!' she sighed. 'I would willingly pay for him out of my own purse, and I will do so rather than have him miss his chance. I have not mustered resolution to propose it.'

'I may be mistaken, Miss Middleton. He talked of the boy's fondness of him.'

'He would.'

'I suppose he is hardly peculiar in liking to play Pole-star.'

'He may not be.'

'For the rest, your influence should be all powerful.'

'It is not.'

De Craye looked with a wandering eye at the heavens.

'We are having a spell of weather perfectly superb. And the odd thing is, that whenever we have splendid weather at home we're all for rushing abroad. I'm booked for a Mediterranean cruise—postponed to give place to your ceremony.'

'That?' she could not control her accent.

'What worthier?'

She was guilty of a pause.

De Craye saved it from an awkward length. 'I have written half an essay on Honeymoons, Miss Middleton.'

'Is that the same as a half-written essay, Colonel De Craye?'

'Just the same, with the difference that it's a whole essay written all on one side.'

'On which side?'

'The bachelor's.'

'Why does he trouble himself with such topics?'

'To warm himself for being left out in the cold.'

'Does he feel envy?'

'He has to confess it.'

'He has liberty.'

'A commodity he can't tell the value of if there's no one to buy.'

'Why should he wish to sell?'

'He's bent on completing his essay.'

'To make the reading dull.'

'There we touch the key of the subject. For what is to rescue the pair from a monotony multiplied by two?

And so a bachelor's recommendation, when each has discovered the right sort of person to be dull with, pushes them from the Church door on a round of adventures containing a spice of peril, if 'tis to be had. Let them be in danger of their lives the first or second day. A bachelor's loneliness is a private affair of his own; he hasn't to look into a face to be ashamed of feeling it and inflicting it at the same time; 'tis his pillow; he can punch it an he pleases, and turn it over t' other side, if he's for a mighty variation; there's a dream in it. But our poor couple are staring wide awake. All their dreaming's done. They've emptied their bottle of elixir, or broken it; and she has a thirst for the use of the tongue, and he to yawn with a crony; and they may converse, they're not aware of it, more than the desert that has drunk a shower. So as soon as possible she's away to the ladies, and he puts on his Club. That's what your bachelor sees and would like to spare them; and if he didn't see something of the sort he'd be off with a noose round his neck, on his knees in the dew to the morning milkmaid.'

'The bachelor is happily warned and on his guard,' said Clara, diverted, as he wished her to be. 'Sketch me a few of the adventures you propose.'

'I have a friend who rowed his bride from the Houses of Parliament up the Thames to the Severn on into North Wales. They shot some pretty weirs and rapids.'

'That was nice.'

'They had an infinity of adventures, and the best proof of the benefit they derived is, that they forgot everything about them except that the adventures occurred.'

'Those two must have returned bright enough to please you.'

'They returned, and shone like a wrecker's beacon to the mariner. You see, Miss Middleton, there was the landscape, and the exercise, and the occasional bit of danger. I think it's to be recommended. The scene is always changeing, and not too fast; and 'tis not too sublime, like big mountains, to tire them of their everlasting big Ohs. There's the difference between going into a howling wind, and launching among zephyrs. They have fresh air and movement, and not in a railway carriage; they can take in what they look on. And she has the steering ropes, and that's a wise commencement. And my lord is all day making an exhibition of his manly strength, bowing before her some dozen to the minute; and she, to help him, just inclines when she's in the mood. And they're face to face, in the nature of things, and are not under the obligation of looking the unutterable, because, you see, there's business in hand; and the boat's just the right sort of third party, who never interferes, but must be attended to. And they feel they're labouring together to get along, all in the proper proportion; and whether he has to labour in life or not, he proves his ability. What do you think of it, Miss Middleton?'

'I think you have only to propose it, Colonel De Craye.'

'And if they capsize, why, 'tis a natural ducking!'

'You forgot the lady's dressing-bag.'

'The stain on the metal for a constant reminder of his prowess in saving it! Well, and there's an alternative to that scheme and a finer:—This, then: they read dramatic pieces during courtship, to stop the saying of things over again till the drum of the ear becomes nothing but a drum to the poor head, and a little before they affix their signatures to the fatal Registry-book of the vestry, they enter into an engagement with a body of provincial actors to join the troop on the day of their nuptials, and away they go in their coach and four, and she is Lady Kitty Caper for a month, and he Sir Harry Highflyer. See the honeymoon spinning! The marvel to me is, that none of the young couples do it. They could enjoy the world, see life, amuse the company, and come back fresh to their own characters, instead of giving themselves a dose of Africa without a savage to diversify it: an impression they never get over, I'm told. Many a character of the happiest auspices has irreparable mischief done it by the ordinary honeymoon. For my part, I rather lean to the second plan of campaign.'

Clara was expected to reply, and she said: 'Probably because you are fond of acting. It would require capacity on both sides.'

'Miss Middleton, *I* would undertake to breathe the enthusiasm for the stage and the adventure.'

'You are recommending it generally.'

'Let my gentleman only have a fund of enthusiasm. The lady will kindle. She always does at a spark.'

'If he has not any?'

'Then I'm afraid they must be mortally dull.'

She allowed her silence to speak; she knew that it did so too eloquently, and could not control the personal adumbration she gave to the one point of light revealed in, 'If he has not any.' Her figure seemed immediately to wear a cap and cloak of dulness.

She was full of revolt and anger, she was burning with her situation; if sensible of shame now at anything that she did, it turned to wrath and threw the burden on the author of her desperate distress. The hour for blaming herself had gone by, to be renewed ultimately perhaps in a season of freedom. She was bereft of her insight within at present, so blind to herself, that, while conscious of an accurate reading of Willoughby's friend, she thanked him in her heart for seeking simply to amuse her and slightly succeeding. The afternoon's ride with him and Crossjay was an agreeable beguilement to her in prospect.

Laetitia came to divide her from Colonel De Craye. Dr. Middleton was not seen before his appearance at the breakfast-table, where a certain air of anxiety in his daughter's presence produced the semblance of a raised map at intervals on his forehead. Few sights on earth are more deserving of our sympathy than a good man who has a troubled conscience thrust on him.

The Rev. Doctor's perturbation was observed. The ladies Eleanor and Isabel, seeing his daughter to be the cause of it, blamed her and would have assisted him to escape, but Miss Dale, whom he courted with that object, was of the opposite faction. She made way for Clara to lead her father out. He called to Vernon, who merely nodded while leaving the room by the window with Crossjay.

Half an eye on Dr. Middleton's pathetic exit in captivity sufficed to tell Colonel De Craye that parties divided

the house. At first he thought how deplorable it would
be to lose Miss Middleton for two days or three: and it
struck him that Vernon Whitford and Laetitia Dale were
acting oddly in seconding her, their aim not being dis-
cernible. For he was of the order of gentlemen of the
obscurely-clear in mind, who have a predetermined acuteness in their watch upon the human play, and mark men
and women as pieces of a bad game of chess, each pursuing
an interested course. His experience of a section of the
world had educated him—as gallant, frank and manly a
comrade as one could wish for—up to this point. But he
soon abandoned speculations, which may be compared to
a shaking of the anemometer, that will not let the troubled
indicator take station. Reposing on his perceptions and
his instincts, he fixed his attention on the chief persons,
only glancing at the others to establish a postulate, that
where there are parties in a house, the most bewitching
person present is the origin of them. It is ever Helen's
achievement. Miss Middleton appeared to him bewitching beyond mortal; sunny in her laughter, shadowy in
her smiling; a young lady shaped for perfect music with a
lover.

She was that, and no less, to every man's eye on earth.
High breeding did not freeze her lovely girlishness.—But
Willoughby did. This reflection intervened to blot
luxurious picturings of her, and made itself acceptable by
leading him back to several instances of an evident want
of harmony of the pair.

And now (for purely undirected impulse all within us is
not, though we may be eye-bandaged agents under direction) it became necessary for an honourable gentleman to
cast vehement rebukes at the fellow who did not comprehend the jewel he had won. How could Willoughby
behave like so complete a donkey! De Craye knew him
to be in his interior stiff, strange, exacting: women had
talked of him; he had been too much for one woman—
the dashing Constantia: he had worn one woman,
sacrificing far more for him than Constantia, to death.
Still, with such a prize as Clara Middleton, Willoughby's
behaviour was past calculating in its contemptible

absurdity. And during courtship! And courtship of that girl! It was the way of a man ten years after marriage.

The idea drew him to picture her doatingly in her young matronly bloom ten years after marriage: without a touch of age, matronly wise, womanly sweet: perhaps with a couple of little ones to love, never having known the love of a man.

To think of a girl like Clara Middleton never having, at nine and twenty, and with two fair children! known the love of a man, or the loving of a man, possibly, became torture to the Colonel.

For a pacification, he had to reconsider that she was as yet only nineteen and unmarried.

But she was engaged and she was unloved. One might swear to it, that she was unloved. And she was not a girl to be satisfied with a big house and a high-nosed husband.

There was a rapid alteration of the sad history of Clara the unloved matron solaced by two little ones. A childless Clara tragically loving and beloved, flashed across the dark glass of the future.

Either way her fate was cruel.

Some astonishment moved De Craye in the contemplation of the distance he had stepped in this morass of fancy. He distinguished the choice open to him of forward or back, and he selected forward. But fancy was dead: the poetry hovering about her grew invisible to him: he stood in the morass; that was all he knew; and momently he plunged deeper; and he was aware of an intense desire to see her face, that he might study her features again: he understood no more.

It was the clouding of the brain by the man's heart, which had come to the knowledge that it was caught.

A certain measure of astonishment moved him still. It had hitherto been his portion to do mischief to women and avoid the vengeance of the sex. What was there in Miss Middleton's face and air to ensnare a veteran handsome man of society numbering six and thirty years, nearly as many conquests? 'Each bullet has got its commission.' He was hit at last. That accident effected by Mr. Flitch

had fired the shot. Clean through the heart, does
not tell us of our misfortune till the heart is asked to
renew its natural beating. It fell into the condition of
the porcelain vase over a thought of Miss Middleton
standing above his prostrate form on the road, and
walking beside him to the Hall. Her words? What have
they been? She had not uttered words, she had shed
meanings. He did not for an instant conceive that he
had charmed her: the charm she had cast on him was too
thrilling for coxcombry to lift a head; still she had
enjoyed his prattle. In return for her touch upon the Irish
fountain in him, he had manifestly given her relief.
And could not one see that so sprightly a girl would soon
be deadened by a man like Willoughby? Deadened she
was: she had not responded to a compliment on her
approaching marriage. An allusion to it killed her smiling. The case of Mr. Flitch, with the half-wager about
his reinstation in the service of the Hall, was conclusive
evidence of her opinion of Willoughby.

It became again necessary that he should abuse Willoughby for his folly. Why was the man worrying her?
In some way he was worrying her.

What if Willoughby as well as Miss Middleton wished
to be quit of the engagement? . . .

For just a second, the handsome woman-flattered officer
proved his man's heart more whole than he supposed it.
That great organ, instead of leaping at the thought,
suffered a check.

Bear in mind, that his heart was not merely man's, it
was a conqueror's. He was of the race of amorous heroes
who glory in pursuing, overtaking, subduing: wresting
the prize from a rival, having her ripe from exquisitely
feminine inward conflicts, plucking her out of resistance
in good old primitive fashion. You win the creature in
her delicious flutterings. He liked her thus, in cooler
blood, because of society's admiration of the capturer, and
somewhat because of the strife, which always enhances
the value of a prize, and refreshes our vanity in recollection.

Moreover, he had been matched against Willoughby:

the circumstance had occurred two or three times. He could name a lady he had won, a lady he had lost. Willoughby's large fortune and grandeur of style had given him advantages at the start. But the start often means the race—with women, and a bit of luck.

The gentle check upon the galloping heart of Colonel De Craye endured no longer than a second—a simple side-glance in a headlong pace. Clara's enchantingness for a temperament like his, which is to say, for him specially, in part through the testimony her conquest of himself presented as to her power of sway over the universal heart known as man's, assured him she was worth winning even from a hand that dropped her.

He had now a double reason for exclaiming at the folly of Willoughby. Willoughby's treatment of her showed either temper or weariness. Vanity and judgement led De Craye to guess the former. Regarding her sentiments for Willoughby, he had come to his own conclusion. The certainty of it, caused him to assume that he possessed an absolute knowledge of her character: she was an angel, born supple; she was a heavenly soul, with half a dozen of the tricks of earth.. Skittish filly, was among his phrases; but she had a bearing and a gaze that forbade the dip in the common gutter for wherewithal to paint the creature she was.

Now, then, to see whether he was wrong for the first time in his life! If not wrong, he had a chance.

There could be nothing dishonourable in rescuing a girl from an engagement she detested. An attempt to think it a service to Willoughby failed midway. De Craye dismissed that chicanery. It would be a service to Willoughby in the end, without question. There was that to soothe his manly honour. Meanwhile he had to face the thought of Willoughby as an antagonist, and the world looking heavy on his honour as a friend.

Such considerations drew him tenderly close to Miss Middleton. It must, however, be confessed that the mental ardour of Colonel De Craye had been a little sobered by his glance at the possibility of both of the couple being of one mind on the subject of their betrothal.

Desireable as it was that they should be united in disagreeing, it reduced the romance to platitude, and the
third person in the drama to the appearance of a stick.
No man likes to play that part. Memoirs of the favourites
of Goddesses, if we had them, would confirm it of men's
tastes in this respect, though the divinest be the prize.
We behold what part they played.

De Craye chanced to be crossing the hall from the
laboratory to the stables when Clara shut the library-
door behind her. He said something whimsical, and did
not stop, nor did he look twice at the face he had been
longing for.

What he had seen made him fear there would be no
ride out with her that day. Their next meeting reassured
him; she was dressed in her riding-habit and wore a
countenance resolutely cheerful. He gave himself the
word of command to take his tone from her.

He was of a nature as quick as Clara's. Experience
pushed him further than she could go in fancy; but experience laid a sobering finger on his practical steps, and
bade them hang upon her initiative. She talked little.
Young Crossjay cantering ahead was her favourite
subject. She was very much changed since the early
morning; his liveliness, essayed by him at a hazard, was
unsuccessful; grave English pleased her best. The descent
from that was naturally to melancholy. She mentioned a
regret she had that the Veil was interdicted to women in
Protestant countries. De Craye was fortunately silent;
he could think of no other veil than the Moslem, and when
her meaning struck his witless head, he admitted to himself that devout attendance on a young lady's mind
stupefies man's intelligence. Half an hour later, he was
as foolish in supposing it a confidence. He was again
saved by silence.

In Aspenwell village she drew a letter from her bosom
and called to Crossjay to post it. The boy sang out:
'Miss Lucy Darleton! What a nice name!'

Clara did not show that the name betrayed anything.

She said to De Craye: 'It proves he should not be here
thinking of nice names.'

Her companion replied: 'You may be right.' He added, to avoid feeling too subservient: 'Boys will.'

'Not if they have stern masters to teach them their daily lessons, and some of the lessons of existence.'

'Vernon Whitford is not stern enough?'

'Mr. Whitford has to contend with other influences here.'

'With Willoughby?'

'Not with Willoughby.'

He understood her. She touched the delicate indication firmly. The man's heart respected her for it; not many girls could be so thoughtful or dare to be so direct; he saw that she had become deeply serious, and he felt her love of the boy to be maternal, past maiden sentiment.

By this light of her seriousness, the posting of her letter in a distant village, not entrusting it to the Hall post-box, might have import; not that she would apprehend the violation of her private correspondence, but we like to see our letter of weighty meaning pass into the mouth of the public box.

Consequently this letter was important. It was to suppose a sequency in the conduct of a variable damsel. Coupled with her remark about the Veil, and with other things, not words, breathing from her (which were the breath of her condition), it was not unreasonably to be supposed. She might even be a very consistent person. If one only had the key of her!

She spoke once of an immediate visit to London, supposing that she could induce her father to go. De Craye remembered the occurrence in the hall at night, and her aspect of distress.

They raced along Aspenwell Common to the ford; shallow, to the chagrin of young Crossjay, between whom and themselves they left a fitting space for his rapture in leading his pony to splash up and down, lord of the stream.

Swiftness of motion so strikes the blood on the brain that our thoughts are lightnings, the heart is master of them. De Craye was heated by his gallop to venture on the angling question: 'Am I to hear the names of the brides-maids?'

The pace had nerved Clara to speak to it sharply: 'There is no need.'

'Have I no claim?'

She was mute.

'Miss Lucy Darleton, for instance; whose name I am almost as much in love with as Crossjay.'

'She will not be bridesmaid to me.'

'She declines? Add my petition, I beg.'

'To all? or to her?'

'Do all the bridesmaids decline?'

'The scene is too ghastly.'

'A marriage?'

'Girls have grown sick of it.'

'Of weddings? We'll overcome the sickness.'

'With some.'

'Not with Miss Darleton? You tempt my eloquence.'

'You wish it?'

'To win her consent? Certainly.'

'The scene!'

'Do I wish that?'

'Marriage!' exclaimed Clara, dashing into the ford, fearful of her ungovernable wildness and of what it might have kindled.—You, father! you have driven me to unmaidenliness!—She forgot Willoughby in her father, who would not quit a comfortable house for her all but prostrate beseeching; would not bend his mind to her explanations, answered her with the horrid iteration of such deaf misunderstanding as may be associated with a tolling bell.

De Craye allowed her to catch Crossjay by herself. They entered a narrow lane, mysterious with possible birds' eggs in the May-green hedges. As there was not room for three abreast, the colonel made up the rear-guard, and was consoled by having Miss Middleton's figure to contemplate; but the readiness of her joining in Crossjay's pastime of the nest-hunt was not so pleasing to a man that she had wound to a pitch of excitement. Her scornful accent on 'Marriage' rang through him.

Apparently she was beginning to do with him just as she liked, herself entirely unconcerned.

She kept Crossjay beside her till she dismounted, and the colonel was left to the procession of elephantine ideas in his head, whose ponderousness he took for natural weight. We do not with impunity abandon the initiative. Men who have yielded it are like cavalry put on the defensive; a very small force with an ictus will scatter them.

Anxiety to recover lost ground reduced the dimensions of his ideas to a practical standard.

Two ideas were opposed like duellists bent on the slaughter of one another. Either she amazed him by confirming the suspicions he had gathered of her sentiments for Willoughby in the moments of his introduction to her; or she amazed him as a model for coquettes:— the married and the widowed might apply to her for lessons.

These combatants exchanged shots, but remained standing: the encounter was undecided. Whatever the result, no person so seductive as Clara Middleton had he ever met. Her cry of loathing: 'Marriage!' coming from a girl, rang faintly clear of an ancient virginal aspiration of the sex to escape from their coil, and bespoke a pure cold savage pride that transplanted his thirst for her to higher fields.

CHAPTER XXIII

Treats of the Union of Temper and Policy

Sir Willoughby meanwhile was on a line of conduct suiting his appreciation of his duty to himself. He had deluded himself with the simple notion that good fruit would come of the union of temper and policy.

No delusion is older, none apparently so promising, both parties being eager for the alliance. Yet, the theorists upon human nature will say, they are obviously of adverse disposition. And this is true, inasmuch as neither of them will submit to the yoke of an established union; as soon as they have done their mischief, they set to work tugging for a divorce. But they have attractions, the one for the other, which precipitate them to embrace whenever they meet in a breast; each is earnest with the owner of it to get him to officiate forthwith as wedding-priest. And here is the reason: temper, to warrant its appearance, desires to be thought as deliberative as policy; and policy, the sooner to prove its shrewdness, is impatient for the quick blood of temper.

It will be well for men to resolve at the first approaches of the amorous but fickle pair upon interdicting even an accidental temporary junction: for the astonishing sweetness of the couple when no more than the ghosts of them have come together in a projecting mind is an intoxication beyond fermented grapejuice or a witch's brewage; and under the guise of active wits they will lead us to the parental meditation of antics compared with which a Pagan Saturnalia* were less impious in the sight of sanity. This is full-mouthed language; but on our studious way through any human career we are subject to fits of moral elevation; the theme inspires it, and the sage residing in every civilized bosom approves it.

Decide at the outset, that temper is fatal to policy: hold them with both hands in division. One might add, be doubtful of your policy and repress your temper: it would be to suppose you wise. You can however, by incorporating two or three captains of the great army of truisms bequeathed to us by ancient wisdom, fix in your service those veteran old standfasts to check you. They will not be serviceless in their admonitions to your understanding, and they will so contrive to reconcile with it the natural caperings of the wayward young sprig Conduct, that the latter, who commonly learns to walk upright and straight from nothing softer than raps of a bludgeon on his crown, shall foot soberly, appearing at least wary of dangerous corners.

Now Willoughby had not to be taught that temper is fatal to policy; he was beginning to see in addition that the temper he encouraged was particularly obnoxious to the policy he adopted; and although his purpose in mounting horse after yesterday frowning on his bride was definite, and might be deemed sagacious, he bemoaned already the fatality pushing him even farther from her in chase of a satisfaction impossible to grasp.

But the bare fact that her behaviour demanded a line of policy crossed the grain of his temper: it was very offensive.

Considering that she wounded him severely, her reversal of their proper parts, by taking the part belonging to him, and requiring his watchfulness, and the careful dealings he was accustomed to expect from others and had a right to exact of her, was injuriously unjust. The feelings of a man hereditarily sensitive to property accused her of a trespassing impudence, and knowing himself, by testimony of his household, his tenants and the neighbourhood, and the world as well, amiable when he received his dues, he contemplated her with an air of stiff-backed ill-treatment, not devoid of a certain sanctification of martyrdom.

His bitterest enemy would hardly declare that it was he who was in the wrong.

Clara herself had never been audacious enough to say that. Distaste of his person was inconceivable to the favourite of society. The capricious creature probably wanted a whipping to bring her to the understanding of the principle called mastery, which is in man.

But was he administering it? If he retained a hold on her, he could undoubtedly apply the scourge at leisure; any kind of scourge; he could shun her, look on her frigidly, unbend to her to find a warmer place for sarcasm, pityingly smile, ridicule, pay court elsewhere. He could do these things if he retained a hold on her; and he could do them well because of the faith he had in his renowned amiability; for in doing them, he could feel that he was other than he seemed, and his own cordial nature was there to comfort him while he bestowed punishment. Cordial indeed, the chills he endured were flung from the world. His heart was in that fiction: half the hearts now beating have a mild form of it to keep them merry: and the chastisement he desired to inflict was really no more than righteous vengeance for an offended goodness of heart. Clara figuratively, absolutely perhaps, on her knees, he would raise her and forgive her. He yearned for the situation. To let her understand how little she had known him! It would be worth the pain she had dealt, to pour forth the stream of re-established confidences, to paint himself to her as he was; as he was in the spirit, not as he was to the world: though the world had reason to do him honour.

First, however, she would have to be humbled.

Something whispered that his hold on her was lost.

In such a case, every blow he struck would set her flying farther, till the breach between them would be past bridging.

Determination not to let her go, was the best finish to this perpetually revolving round which went like the same old wheel-planks of a water-mill in his head at a review of the injury he sustained. He had come to it before, and he came to it again. There was his vengeance. It melted him, she was so sweet! She shone for him like the sunny breeze on water. Thinking of her caused a catch of his breath.

The dreadful young woman had a keener edge for the senses of men than sovereign beauty.

It would be madness to let her go.

She affected him like an outlook on the great Patterne estate after an absence, when his welcoming flag wept for pride above Patterne Hall.

It would be treason to let her go.

It would be cruelty to her.

He was bound to reflect that she was of tender age, and the foolishness of the wretch was excuseable to extreme youth.

We toss away a flower that we are tired of smelling and do not wish to carry. But the rose—young woman—is not cast off with impunity. A fiend in shape of man is always behind us to appropriate her. He that touches that rejected thing is larcenous. Willoughby had been sensible of it in the person of Laetitia: and by all the more that Clara's charms exceeded the faded creature's, he felt it now. Ten thousand Furies thickened about him

at a thought of her lying by the roadside without his
having crushed all bloom and odour out of her which
might tempt even the curiosity of the fiend, man.

On the other hand, supposing her to lie there un-
touched, universally declined by the sniffing sagacious
dog-fiend, a miserable spinster for years, he could conceive notions of his remorse. A soft remorse may be
adopted as an agreeable sensation within view of the
wasted penitent whom we have struck a trifle too hard.
Seeing her penitent, he certainly would be willing to
surround her with little offices of compromising kindness.
It would depend on her age. Supposing her still youngish, there might be captivating passages between them;
as thus, in a style not unfamiliar:

'And was it my fault, my poor girl? Am I to blame,
that you have passed a lonely unloved youth?'

'No, Willoughby; the irreparable error was mine, the
blame is mine, mine only. I live to repent it. I do not
seek, for I have not deserved, your pardon. Had I it, I
should need my own self-esteem to presume to clasp it
to a bosom ever unworthy of you.'

'I may have been impatient, Clara: we are human!'

'Never be it mine to accuse one on whom I laid so
heavy a weight of forbearance!'

'Still, my old love!—for I am merely quoting history in
naming you so—I cannot have been perfectly blameless.'

'To me you were, and are.'

'Clara!'

'Willoughby!'

'Must I recognize the bitter truth that we two, once
nearly one! so nearly one! are eternally separated?'

'I have envisaged it. My friend—I may call you friend:
you have ever been my friend, my best friend! Oh, that
eyes had been mine to know the friend I had!—Willoughby, in the darkness of night, and during days that
were as night to my soul, I have seen the inexorable
finger pointing my solitary way through the wilderness
from a Paradise forfeited* by my most wilful, my wanton,
sin. We have met. It is more than I have merited. We
part. In mercy let it be for ever. Oh, terrible word!

Coined by the passions of our youth, it comes to us for our
sole riches when we are bankrupt of earthly treasures,
and is the passport given by Abnegation unto Woe that
prays to quit this probationary sphere. Willoughby, we
part. It is better so.'

'Clara! one—one only—one last—one holy kiss!'

'If these poor lips, that once were sweet to you . . .'

The kiss, to continue the language of the imaginative
composition of his time, favourite readings in which had
inspired Sir Willoughby with a colloquy so pathetic, was
imprinted.

Ay, she had the kiss, and no mean one. It was intended to swallow every vestige of dwindling attractiveness out of her, and there was a bit of scandal springing
of it in the background that satisfactorily settled her
business, and left her 'enshrined in memory, a divine
recollection, to him,' as his popular romances would say,
and have said for years.

Unhappily, the fancied salute of her lips encircled him
with the breathing Clara. She rushed up from vacancy
like a wind summoned to wreck a stately vessel.

His reverie had thrown him into severe commotion.
The slave of a passion thinks in a ring, as hares run: he
will cease where he began. Her sweetness had set him
off, and he whirled back to her sweetness: and that being
incalculable and he insatiable, you have the picture of
his torments when you consider that her behaviour made
her as a cloud to him.

Riding slack, horse and man, in the likeness of those
two ajog homeward from the miry hunt, the horse pricked
his ears, and Willoughby looked down from his road
along the hills on the race headed by young Crossjay with
a short start over Aspenwell Common to the ford. There
was no mistaking who they were, though they were well-
nigh a mile distant below. He noticed that they did not
overtake the boy. They drew rein at the ford, talking not
simply face to face, but face in face. Willoughby's novel
feeling of he knew not what drew them up to him, enabling him to fancy them bathing in one another's eyes.
Then she sprang through the ford, De Craye following,

but not close after—and why not close? She had
flicked him with one of her peremptorily saucy speeches
when she was bold with the gallop. They were not unknown to Willoughby. They signified intimacy.

Last night he had proposed to De Craye to take Miss
Middleton for a ride the next afternoon. It never came
to his mind then that he and his friend had formerly been
rivals. He wished Clara to be amused. Policy dictated
that every thread should be used to attach her to her
residence at the Hall until he could command his temper
to talk to her calmly and overwhelm her, as any man in
earnest, with command of temper and a point of vantage,
may be sure to whelm a young woman. Policy, adulter-
ated by temper, yet policy it was that had sent him on his
errand in the early morning to beat about for a house and
garden suitable to Dr. Middleton within a circuit of five,
six, or seven miles of Patterne Hall. If the Rev. Doctor
liked the house and took it (and Willoughby had seen the
place to suit him), the neighbourhood would be a chain
upon Clara: and if the house did not please a gentleman
rather hard to please (except in a venerable wine), an excuse would have been started for his visiting other houses,
and he had the response to his importunate daughter, that
he believed an excellent house was on view. Dr. Middleton had been prepared by numerous hints to meet Clara's
black misreading of a lover's quarrel, so that everything
looked full of promise as far as Willoughby's exercise of
policy went.

But the strange pang traversing him now convicted
him of a large adulteration of profitless temper with it.
The loyalty of De Craye to a friend, where a woman
walked in the drama, was notorious. It was there, and
a most flexible thing it was: and it soon resembled reason
manipulated by the sophists. Not to have reckoned on
his peculiar loyalty was proof of the blindness cast on us
by temper.

And De Craye had an Irish tongue; and he had it
under control, so that he could talk good sense and airy
nonsense at discretion. The strongest overboiling of
English Puritan contempt of a gabbler would not stop

women from liking it. Evidently Clara did like it, and Willoughby thundered on her sex. Unto such brainless things as these do we, under the irony of circumstances, confide our honour!

For he was no gabbler. He remembered having rattled in earlier days; he had rattled with an object to gain, desiring to be taken for an easy, careless, vivacious, charming fellow, as any young gentleman may be who gaily wears the golden dish of Fifty thousand pounds per annum nailed to the back of his very saintly young pate. The growth of the critical spirit in him, however, had informed him that slang had been a principal component of his rattling; and as he justly supposed it a betraying art for his race and for him, he passed through the prim and the yawning phases of affected indifference, to the pure Puritanism of a leaden contempt of gabblers.

They snare women, you see—girls! How despicable the host of girls!—at least, that girl below there!

Married women understood him: widows did. He placed an exceedingly handsome and flattering young widow of his acquaintance, Lady Mary Lewison, beside Clara for a comparison, involuntarily; and at once, in a flash, in despite of him (he would rather it had been otherwise), and in despite of Lady Mary's high birth and connections as well, the silver lustre of the maid sicklied the poor widow.

The effect of the luckless comparison was to produce an image of surpassingness in the features of Clara that gave him the final, or mace-blow. Jealousy invaded him.

He had hitherto been free of it, regarding jealousy as a foreign devil, the accursed familiar of the vulgar. Luckless fellows might be victims of the disease; he was not; and neither Captain Oxford, nor Vernon, nor De Craye, nor any of his compeers, had given him one shrewd pinch: the woman had, not the man; and she in quite a different fashion from his present wallowing anguish: she had never pulled him to earth's level, where jealousy gnaws the grasses. He had boasted himself above the humiliating visitation.

If that had been the case, we should not have needed

to trouble ourselves much about him. A run or two with the pack of imps would have satisfied us. But he desired Clara Middleton manfully enough at an intimation of rivalry to be jealous; in a minute the foreign devil had him, he was flame: flaming verdigris, one might almost dare to say, for an exact illustration; such was actually the colour; but accept it as unsaid.

Remember the poets upon Jealousy. It is to be haunted in the heaven of two by a Third; preceded or succeeded, therefore surrounded, embraced, hugged by this infernal Third: it is Love's bed of burning marl; to see and taste the withering Third in the bosom of sweetness; to be dragged through the past and find the fair Eden of it sulphurous; to be dragged to the gates of the future and glory to behold them blood: to adore the bitter creature trebly and with treble power to clutch her by the windpipe: it is to be cheated, derided, shamed, and abject and supplicating, and consciously demoniacal in treacherousness, and victoriously self-justified in revenge.

And still there is no change in what men feel, though in what they do the modern may be judicious.

You know the many paintings of man transformed to rageing beast by the curse: and this, the fieriest trial of our egoism, worked in the Egoist to produce division of himself from himself, a concentration of his thoughts upon another object, still himself, but in another breast, which had to be looked at and into for the discovery of him. By the gaping jaw-chasm of his greed we may gather comprehension of his insatiate force of jealousy. Let her go? Not though he were to become a mark of public scorn in strangling her with the yoke! His concentration was marvellous. Unused to the exercise of imaginative powers, he nevertheless conjured her before him visually till his eyeballs ached. He saw none but Clara, hated none, loved none, save the intolerable woman. What logic was in him deduced her to be individual and most distinctive from the circumstance that only she had ever wrought these pangs. She had made him ready for them, as we know. An idea of De Craye being no stranger to her when he arrived at the Hall, dashed him at De Craye for a second: it might be or might not be that they had a secret;—Clara was the spell. So prodigiously did he love and hate, that he had no permanent sense except for her. The soul of him writhed under her eyes at one moment, and the next it closed on her without mercy. She was his possession escaping; his own gliding away to the Third.

There would be pangs for him too, that Third! Standing at the altar to see her fast-bound, soul and body, to another, would be good roasting fire.

It would be good roasting fire for her too, should she be averse. To conceive her aversion was to burn her and devour her. She would then be his!—what say you? Burnt and devoured! Rivals would vanish then. Her reluctance to espouse the man she was plighted to, would cease to be uttered, cease to be felt.

At last he believed in her reluctance. All that had been wanted to bring him to the belief was the scene on the common; such a mere spark, or an imagined spark! But the presence of the Third was necessary; otherwise he would have had to suppose himself personally distasteful.

Women have us back to the conditions of primitive man, or they shoot us higher than the topmost star. But it is as we please. Let them tell us what we are to them: for us, they are our back and front of life: the poet's Lesbia, the poet's Beatrice;*ours is the choice. And were it proved that some of the bright things are in the pay of Darkness, with the stamp of his coin on their palms, and that some are the very angels we hear sung of, not the less might we say that they find us out, they have us by our leanings. They are to us what we hold of best or worst within. By their state is our civilization judged: and if it is hugely animal still, that is because primitive men abound and will have their pasture. Since the lead is ours, the leaders must bow their heads to the sentence. Jealousy of a woman, is the primitive egoism seeking to refine in a blood gone to savagery under apprehension of an invasion of rights; it is in action the tiger threatened

by a rifle when his paw is rigid on quick flesh; he tears
the flesh for rage at the intruder. The Egoist, who is our
original male in giant form, had no bleeding victim beneath his paw, but there was the sex to mangle. Much as
he prefers the well-behaved among women, who can
worship and fawn, and in whom terror can be inspired,
in his wrath he would make of Beatrice a Lesbia Quadrantaria.*

Let women tell us of their side of the battle. We are
not so much the test of the Egoist in them as they to us.
Movements of similarity shown in crowned and un-
diademed ladies of intrepid independence, suggest their
occasional capacity to be like men when it is given to
them to hunt. At present they fly, and there is the difference. Our manner of the chase informs them of the
creature we are.

Dimly as young women are informed, they have a
youthful ardour of detestation that renders them less
tolerant of the Egoist than their perceptive elder sisters.
What they do perceive, however, they have a redoubtable grasp of, and Clara's behaviour would be indefensible if her detective feminine vision might not sanction
her acting on its direction. Seeing him as she did, she
turned from him and shunned his house as the antre* of
an ogre. She had posted her letter to Lucy Darleton.
Otherwise, if it had been open to her to dismiss Colonel
De Craye, she might, with a warm kiss to Vernon's pupil,
have seriously thought of the next shrill steam-whistle
across yonder hills for a travelling companion on the way
to her friend Lucy; so abhorrent was to her the putting of
her horse's head toward the Hall. Oh, the breaking of
bread there! It had to be gone through for another day
and more: that is to say, forty hours, it might be six and
forty hours! and no prospect of sleep to speed any of
them on wings!

Such were Clara's inward interjections while poor Willoughby burnt himself out with verdigris flame having
the savour of bad metal, till the hollow of his breast was
not unlike to a corroded old cuirass found, we will assume, by criminal lantern-beams in a digging beside

green-mantled pools of the sullen soil, lumped with a
strange adhesive concrete. How else picture the sad
man?—the cavity felt empty to him, and heavy; sick of
an ancient and mortal combat, and burning; deeply-
dinted too:

> With the starry hole
> Whence fled the soul:*

very sore; impotent for aught save sluggish agony; a
specimen and the issue of strife.

Measurelessly to loathe was not sufficient to save him
from pain: he tried it: nor to despise; he went to a depth
there also. The fact that she was a healthy young
woman, returned to the surface of his thoughts like the
murdered body pitched into the river, which will not
drown and calls upon the elements of dissolution to float
it. His grand hereditary desire to transmit his estates,
wealth and name to a solid posterity, while it prompted
him in his loathing and contempt of a nature mean and
ephemeral compared with his, attached him desperately
to her splendid healthiness. The council of elders, whose
descendant he was, pointed to this young woman for his
mate. He had wooed her with the idea that they consented. O she was healthy! And he likewise; but, as
if it had been a duel between two clearly designated by
quality of blood to bid a House endure, she was the first
who taught him what it was to have sensations of his
mortality.

He could not forgive her. It seemed to him consequently politic to continue frigid and let her have a
further taste of his shadow, when it was his burning wish
to strain her in his arms to a flatness provoking his compassion.

'You have had your ride?' he addressed her politely
in the general assembly on the lawn.

'I have had my ride, yes,' Clara replied.

'Agreeable, I trust?'

'Very agreeable.'

So it appeared. Oh blushless!

The next instant he was in conversation with Laetitia,
questioning her upon a dejected droop of her eyelashes.

'I am, I think,' said she, 'constitutionally melancholy.'

He murmured to her: 'I believe in the existence of specifics, and not far to seek, for all our ailments except those we bear at the hands of others.'

She did not dissent.

De Craye, whose humour for being convinced that Willoughby cared about as little for Miss Middleton as she for him was nourished by his immediate observation of them, dilated on the beauty of the ride and his fair companion's equestrian skill.

'You should start a travelling circus,' Willoughby rejoined.

'But the idea's a worthy one!—There's another alternative to the expedition I proposed, Miss Middleton,' said De Craye. 'And I be clown? I haven't a scruple of objection. I must read up books of jokes.'

'Don't,' said Willoughby.

'I'd spoil my part! But a natural clown won't keep up an artificial performance for an entire month, you see; which is the length of time we propose. He'll exhaust his nature in a day and be bowled over by the dullest regular donkey-engine with paint on his cheeks and a nodding-topknot.'

'What is this expedition "we" propose?'

De Craye was advised in his heart to spare Miss Middleton any allusion to honeymoons.

'Merely a game to cure dulness.'

'Ah,' Willoughby acquiesced. 'A month, you said?'

'One'd like it to last for years!'

'Ah! You are driving one of Mr. Merriman's witticisms at me, Horace; I am dense.'

Willoughby bowed to Dr. Middleton and drew him from Vernon, filially taking his arm to talk with him closely.

De Craye saw Clara's look as her father and Willoughby went aside thus linked.

It lifted him over anxieties and casuistries concerning loyalty. Powder was in the look to make a warhorse breathe high and shiver for the signal.

CHAPTER XXIV

Contains an Instance of the Generosity of Willoughby

OBSERVERS of a gathering complication and a character in action commonly resemble gleaners who are intent only on picking up the ears of grain and huddling their store. Disinterestedly or interestedly they wax over-eager for the little trifles, and make too much of them. Observers should begin upon the precept, that not all we see is worth hoarding, and that the things we see are to be weighed in the scale with what we know of the situation, before we commit ourselves to a measurement. And they may be accurate observers without being good judges. They do not think so, and their bent is to glean hurriedly and form conclusions as hasty, when their business should be sift at each step, and question.

Miss Dale seconded Vernon Whitford in the occupa-tion of counting looks and tones, and noting scraps of dialogue. She was quite disinterested; he quite believed that he was; to this degree they were competent for their post; and neither of them imagined they could be per-sonally involved in the dubious result of the scenes they witnessed. They were but anxious observers, diligently collecting. She fancied Clara susceptible to his advice: he had fancied it, and was considering it one of his vanities. Each mentally compared Clara's abruptness in taking them into her confidence with her abstention from any secret word since the arrival of Colonel De Craye. Sir Willoughby requested Laetitia to give Miss Middleton as much of her company as she could; showing that he was on the alert. Another Constantia Durham seemed beating her wings for flight. The sud-denness of the evident intimacy between Clara and Colonel De Craye shocked Laetitia: their acquaintance could be computed by hours. Yet at their first interview she had suspected the possibility of worse than she now supposed to be; and she had begged Vernon not im-mediately to quit the Hall, in consequence of that faint

suspicion. She had been led to it by meeting Clara and
De Craye at her cottage-gate, and finding them as fluent
and laughter-breathing in conversation as friends. Unable to realize the rapid advance to a familiarity, more
ostensible than actual, of two lively natures, after such
an introduction as they had undergone: and one of the
two pining in a drought of liveliness: Laetitia listened to
their wager of nothing at all—a *no* against a *yes*—in the
case of poor Flitch; and Clara's, 'Willoughby will not
forgive': and De Craye's: 'Oh! he's human': and the
silence of Clara: and De Craye's hearty cry: 'Flitch shall
be a gentleman's coachman in his old seat again, or I
haven't a tongue!' to which there was a negative of
Clara's head:—and it then struck Laetitia that this
young betrothed lady, whose alienated heart acknowledged no lord an hour earlier, had met her match, and,
as the observer would have said, her destiny. She judged
of the alarming possibility by the recent revelation to
herself of Miss Middleton's character, and by Clara's
having spoken to a man as well (to Vernon), and previously. That a young lady should speak on the subject
of the inner holies to a man, though he were Vernon
Whitford, was incredible to Laetitia; but it had to be
accepted as one of the dread facts of our inexplicable life,
which drag our bodies at their wheels and leave our
minds exclaiming. Then, if Clara could speak to Vernon,
which Laetitia would not have done for a mighty bribe,
she could speak to De Craye, Laetitia thought deductively: this being the logic of untrained heads opposed
to the proceeding whereby their condemnatory deduction hangs.—Clara must have spoken to De Craye!

Laetitia remembered how winning and prevailing
Miss Middleton could be in her confidences. A gentleman hearing her might forget his duty to his friend, she
thought, for she had been strangely swayed by Clara:
ideas of Sir Willoughby that she had never before imagined herself to entertain, had been sown in her, she
thought; not asking herself whether the searchingness
of the young lady had struck them and bidden them rise
from where they lay embedded. Very gentle women

take in that manner impressions of persons, especially of the worshipped person, wounding them; like the new fortifications with embankments of soft earth, where explosive missiles bury themselves harmlessly until they are plucked out; and it may be a reason why those injured ladies outlive a Clara Middleton similarly battered.

Vernon less than Laetitia took into account that Clara was in a state of fever, scarcely reasonable. Her confidences to him he had excused, as a piece of conduct, in sympathy with her position. He had not been greatly astonished by the circumstances confided; and, on the whole, as she was excited and unhappy, he excused her thoroughly; he could have extolled her: it was natural that she should come to him, brave in her to speak so frankly, a compliment that she should condescend to treat him as a friend. Her position excused her widely. But she was not excused for making a confidential friend of De Craye. There was a difference.

Well, the difference was, that De Craye had not the smarting sense of honour with women which our meditator had: an impartial judiciary, it will be seen: and he discriminated between himself and the other justly: but sensation surging to his brain at the same instant, he reproached Miss Middleton for not perceiving that difference as clearly, before she betrayed her position to De Craye, which Vernon assumed that she had done. Of course he did. She had been guilty of it once: why, then, in the mind of an offended friend, she would be guilty of it twice. There was evidence. Ladies, fatally predestined to appeal to that from which they have to be guarded, must expect severity when they run off their railed highroad: justice is out of the question: man's brains might, his blood cannot administer it to them. By chilling him to the bone, they may get what they cry for. But that is a method deadening to their point of appeal.

In the evening Miss Middleton and the colonel sang a duet. She had of late declined to sing. Her voice was noticeably firm. Sir Willoughby said to her, 'You have recovered your richness of tone, Clara.' She smiled and appeared happy in pleasing him. He named a French ballad. She went to the music-rack and gave the song unasked. He should have been satisfied, for she said to him at the finish: 'Is that as you like it?' He broke from a murmur to Miss Dale: 'Admirable.' Some one mentioned a Tuscan popular canzone.* She waited for Willoughby's approval, and took his nod for a mandate.

Traitress! he could have bellowed.

He had read of this characteristic of caressing obedience of the woman about to deceive. He had in his time profited by it.

'Is it intuitively or by their experience that our neighbours across Channel surpass us in the knowledge of your sex?' he said to Miss Dale and talked through Clara's apostrophe to the 'Santissima Virgine Maria,' still treating temper as a part of policy, without any effect on Clara; and that was matter for sickly green reflections. The lover who cannot wound has indeed lost anchorage; he is woefully adrift: he stabs air, which is to stab himself. Her complacent proof-armour bids him know himself supplanted.

During the short conversational period before the ladies retired for the night, Miss Eleanor alluded to the wedding by chance. Miss Isabel replied to her, and addressed an interrogation to Clara. De Craye foiled it adroitly. Clara did not utter a syllable. Her bosom lifted to a wavering height and sank. Subsequently she looked at De Craye, vacantly, like a person awakened, but she looked. She was astonished by his readiness, and thankful for the succour. Her look was cold, wide, unfixed, with nothing of gratitude or of personal in it. The look however stood too long for Willoughby's endurance. Ejaculating: 'Porcelain!' he uncrossed his legs: a signal for the ladies Eleanor and Isabel to retire. Vernon bowed to Clara as she was rising. He had not been once in her eyes, and he expected a partial recognition at the good-night. She said it, turning her head to Miss Isabel, who was condoling once more with Colonel De Craye over the ruins of his wedding-present, the porcelain vase, which she supposed to have been in Willoughby's mind when he displayed the signal. Vernon walked off to his room, dark as one smitten blind: bile tumet jecur:*her stroke of neglect hit him there where a blow sends thick obscuration upon eyeballs and brain alike.

Clara saw that she was paining him and regretted it when they were separated. That was her real friend! But he prescribed too hard a task. Besides she had done everything he demanded of her, except the consenting to stay where she was and wear out Willoughby, whose dexterity wearied her small stock of patience. She had vainly tried remonstrance and supplication with her father hoodwinked by his host, she refused to consider how: through wine?—the thought was repulsive.

Nevertheless she was drawn to the edge of it by the contemplation of her scheme of release. If Lucy Darleton was at home: if Lucy invited her to come: if she flew to Lucy: Oh! then her father would have cause for anger. He would not remember that but for hateful wine! . . .

What was there in this wine of great age which expelled reasonableness, fatherliness? He was her dear father: she was his beloved child: yet something divided them; something closed her father's ears to her: and could it be that incomprehensible seduction of the wine? Her dutifulness cried violently no. She bowed, stupefied, to his arguments for remaining awhile, and rose clear-headed and rebellious with the reminiscence of the many strong reasons she had urged against them.

The strangeness of men, young and old, the little things (she regarded a grand wine as a little thing) twisting and changeing them, amazed her. And these are they by whom women are abused for variability! Only the most imperious reasons, never mean trifles, move women, thought she. Would women do an injury to one they loved for oceans of that—ah! pah!

And women must respect men. They necessarily respect a father. 'My dear, dear father!' Clara said in the solitude of her chamber, musing on all his goodness, and she endeavoured to reconcile the desperate sentiments of the position he forced her to sustain, with those of a

venerating daughter. The blow which was to fall on
him beat on her heavily in advance. 'I have not one
excuse!' she said, glancing at numbers and a mighty one.
But the idea of her father suffering at her hands cast her
down lower than self-justification. She sought to imagine
herself sparing him. It was too fictitious.

The sanctuary of her chamber, the pure white room so
homely to her maidenly feelings, whispered peace, only
to follow the whisper with another that went through her
swelling to a roar, and leaving her as a string of music
unkindly smitten. If she stayed in this house her chamber
would no longer be a sanctuary. Dolorous bondage!
Insolent death is not worse. Death's worm we cannot
keep away, but when he has us we are numb to dishonour, happily senseless.

Youth weighed her eyelids to sleep, though she was
quivering, and quivering she awoke to the sound of her
name beneath her window. 'I can love still, for I love
him,' she said, as she luxuriated in young Crossjay's
boy's voice, again envying him his bath in the lake
waters, which seemed to her to have the power to wash
away grief and chains. Then it was that she resolved to
let Crossjay see the last of her in this place. He should
be made gleeful by doing her a piece of service; he
should escort her on her walk to the railway station next
morning, thence be sent flying for a long day's truancy,
with a little note of apology on his behalf that she would
write for him to deliver to Vernon at night.

Crossjay came running to her after his breakfast with
Mrs. Montague, the housekeeper, to tell her he had
called her up.

'You won't to-morrow: I shall be up far ahead of you,'
said she; and musing on her father, while Crossjay vowed
to be up the first, she thought it her duty to plunge into
another expostulation.

Willoughby had need of Vernon on private affairs.
Dr. Middleton betook himself as usual to the library,
after answering: 'I will ruin you yet,' to Willoughby's
liberal offer to despatch an order to London for any
books he might want.

His fine unruffled air, as of a mountain in still morning
beams, made Clara not indisposed to a preliminary scene
with Willoughby that might save her from distressing
him, but she could not stop Willoughby; as little could
she look an invitation. He stood in the Hall, holding
Vernon by the arm. She passed him; he did not speak,
and she entered the library.

'What now, my dear? what is it?' said Dr. Middleton,
seeing that the door was shut on them.

'Nothing, papa,' she replied calmly.

'You've not locked the door, my child? You turned
something there: try the handle.'

'I assure you, papa, the door is not locked.'

'Mr. Whitford will be here instantly. We are engaged
on tough matter. Women have not, and opinion is
universal that they never will have, a conception of the
value of time.'

'We are vain and shallow, my dear papa.'

'No, no, not you, Clara. But I suspect you to require
to learn by having work in progress how important is . . .
is a quiet commencement of the day's task. There is not
a scholar who will not tell you so. We must have a
retreat. These invasions!—So you intend to have another
ride to-day? They do you good. To-morrow we dine
with Mrs. Mountstuart Jenkinson, an estimable person
indeed, though I do not perfectly understand our accepting.—You have not to accuse me of sitting over wine
last night, my Clara! I never do it, unless I am appealed
to for my judgement upon a wine.'

'I have come to entreat you to take me away, papa.'

In the midst of the storm aroused by this renewal of
perplexity, Dr. Middleton replaced a book his elbow had
knocked over in his haste to dash the hair off his forehead,
crying: 'Whither? To what spot? That reading of
Guide-books, and idle people's notes of Travel, and
picturesque correspondence in the newspapers, unsettles
man and maid. My objection to the living in hotels is
known. I do not hesitate to say that I do cordially abhor
it. I have had penitentially to submit to it in your dear
mother's time, καὶ τρισκακοδαίμων* up to the full ten

thousand times. But will you not comprehend that to the older man his miseries are multiplied by his years! But is it utterly useless to solicit your sympathy with an old man, Clara?'

'General Darleton will take us in, papa.'

'His table is detestable. I say nothing of that; but his wine is poison. Let that pass—I should rather say, let it not pass!—but our political views are not in accord. True, we are not under the obligation to propound them in presence, but we are destitute of an opinion in common. We have no discourse. Military men *have* produced, or diverged in, noteworthy epicures: they are often devout; they have blossomed in lettered men: they are gentlemen; the country rightly holds them in honour; but, in fine, I reject the proposal to go to General Darleton.—Tears?'

'No, papa.'

'I do hope not. Here we have everything man can desire; without contest, an excellent host. You have your transitory tea-cup tempests, which you magnify to hurricanes, in the approved historic manner of the book of Cupid. And all the better; I repeat, it is the better that you should have them over in the infancy of the alliance. Come in!' Dr. Middleton shouted cheerily in response to a knock at the door.

He feared the door was locked: he had a fear that his daughter intended to keep it locked.

'Clara!' he cried.

She reluctantly turned the handle, and the ladies Eleanor and Isabel came in, apologizing with as much coherence as Dr. Middleton ever expected from their sex. They wished to speak to Clara, but they declined to take her away. In vain the Rev. Doctor assured them she was at their service; they protested that they had very few words to say and would not intrude one moment further than to speak them.

Like a shy deputation of young scholars before the master, these very words to come were preceded by none at all; a dismal and trying pause; refreshing however to Dr. Middleton, who joyfully anticipated that the ladies could be induced to take away Clara when they had finished.

'We may appear to you a little formal,' Miss Isabel began, and turned to her sister.

'We have no intention to lay undue weight on our mission, if mission it can be called,' said Miss Eleanor.

'Is it entrusted to you by Willoughby?' said Clara.

'Dear child, that you may know it all the more earnest with us, and our personal desire to contribute to your happiness: therefore does Willoughby entrust the speaking of it to us.'

Hereupon the sisters alternated in addressing Clara, and she gazed from one to the other, piecing fragments of empty signification to get the full meaning when she might.

'—And in saying, your happiness, dear Clara, we have our Willoughby's in view, which is dependent on yours.'

'—And we never could sanction that our own inclinations should stand in the way.'

'—No. We love the old place: and if it were only our punishment for loving it too idolatrously, we should deem it ground enough for our departure.'

'—Without, really, an idea of unkindness; none, not any.'

'—Young wives naturally prefer to be undisputed queens of their own establishment.'

'—Youth and age!'

'But I,' said Clara, 'have never mentioned, never had a thought . . .'

'—You have, dear child, a lover who in his solicitude for your happiness both sees what you desire and what is due to you.'

'—And for us, Clara, to recognize what is due to you is to act on it.'

'—Besides, dear, a sea-side cottage has always been one of our dreams.'

'—We have not to learn that we are a couple of old maids, incongruous associates for a young wife in the government of a great house.'

'—With our antiquated notions, questions of domestic

management might arise, and with the best will in the world to be harmonious . . .!'

'—So, dear Clara, consider it settled.'

'—From time to time gladly shall we be your guests.'

'—Your guests, dear, not censorious critics.'

'And you think me such an Egoist!—dear ladies! The suggestion of so cruel a piece of selfishness wounds me. I would not have had you leave the Hall. I like your society; I respect you. My complaint, if I had one, would be, that you do not sufficiently assert yourselves. I could have wished you to be here for an example to me. I would not have allowed you to go. What can he think me!—Did Willoughby speak of it this morning?'

It was hard to distinguish which was the completer dupe of these two echoes of one another in worship of a family idol.

'Willoughby,' Miss Eleanor presented herself to be stamped with the title hanging ready for the first that should open her lips, 'our Willoughby is observant—he is ever generous—and he is not less forethoughtful. His arrangement is for our good on all sides.'

'An index is enough,' said Miss Isabel, appearing in her turn the monster dupe.

'You will not have to leave, dear ladies. Were I mistress here I should oppose it.'

'Willoughby blames himself for not reassuring you before.'

'Indeed we blame ourselves for not undertaking to go.'

'Did he speak of it first this morning?' said Clara; but she could draw no reply to that from them. They resumed the duet, and she resigned herself to have her ears boxed with nonsense.

'So, it is understood?' said Miss Eleanor.

'I see your kindness, ladies.'

'And I am to be Aunt Eleanor again?'

'And I Aunt Isabel?'

Clara could have wrung her hands at the impediment which prohibited her delicacy from telling them why she could not name them so, as she had done in the earlier days of Willoughby's courtship. She kissed them warmly, ashamed of kissing, though the warmth was real.

They retired with a flow of excuses to Dr. Middleton for disturbing him. He stood at the door to bow them out, and holding the door for Clara to wind up the procession, discovered her at a far corner of the room.

He was debating upon the advisability of leaving her there, when Vernon Whitford crossed the hall from the laboratory door, a mirror of himself in his companion air of discomposure.

That was not important, so long as Vernon was a check on Clara; but the moment Clara, thus baffled, moved to quit the library, Dr. Middleton felt the horror of having an uncomfortable face opposite.

'No botheration, I hope? It's the worst thing possible to work on. Where have you been? I suspect your weak point is not to arm yourself in triple brass against bother and worry; and no good work can you do unless you do. You have come out of that laboratory.'

'I have, sir.—Can I get you any book?' Vernon said to Clara.

She thanked him, promising to depart immediately.

'Now you are at the section of Italian literature, my love,' said Dr. Middleton. 'Well, Mr. Whitford, the laboratory—ah!—where the amount of labour done within the space of a year would not stretch an electric current between this Hall and the railway station: say, four miles, which I presume the distance to be. Well, sir, a dilettantism costly in time and machinery is as ornamental as foxes' tails and deers' horns to an independent gentleman whose fellows are contented with the latter decorations for their civic wreath. Willoughby, let me remark, has recently shown himself most considerate for my girl. As far as I could gather—I have been listening to a dialogue of ladies—he is as generous as he is discreet. There are certain combats in which to be the one to succumb is to claim the honours;—and that is what women will not learn. I doubt their seeing the glory of it.'

'I have heard of it; I have been with Willoughby,' Vernon said hastily, to shield Clara from her father's allusive attacks. He wished to convey to her that his interview with Willoughby had not been profitable in her interests, and that she had better at once, having him present to support her, pour out her whole heart to her father. But how was it to be conveyed? She would not meet his eyes, and he was too poor an intriguer to be ready on the instant to deal out the verbal obscurities which are transparencies to one.

'I shall regret it, if Willoughby has annoyed you, for he stands high in my favour,' said Dr. Middleton.

Clara dropped a book. Her father started higher than the nervous impulse warranted in his chair. Vernon tried to win a glance, and she was conscious of his effort, but her angry and guilty feelings prompting her resolution to follow her own counsel, kept her eyelids on the defensive.

'I don't say he annoys me, sir. I am here to give him my advice, and if he does not accept it I have no right to be annoyed. Willoughby seems annoyed that Colonel De Craye should talk of going to-morrow or next day.'

'He likes his friends about him. Upon my word, a man of a more genial heart you might march a day without finding. But you have it on the forehead, Mr. Whitford.'

'Oh! no, sir.'

'There,' Dr. Middleton drew his finger along his brows.

Vernon felt along his own, and coined an excuse for their blackness; unaware that the direction of his mind toward Clara pushed him to a kind of clumsy double meaning, while he satisfied an inward and craving wrath, as he said: 'By the way, I have been racking my head; I must apply to you, sir. I have a line, and I am uncertain of the run of the line. Will this pass, do you think?—

"In Asination's tongue he asinates":

signifying, that he excels any man of us at donkey-dialect.'

After a decent interval for the genius of criticism to seem to have been sitting under his frown, Dr. Middleton rejoined with sober jocularity: 'No, sir, it will not pass, and your uncertainty in regard to the run of the line would only be extended were the line centipedal. Our recommendation is, that you erase it before the arrival of the ferule. This might do:—

"In Assignation's name he assignats":

signifyi.ıg, that he pre-eminently flourishes hypothetical promises to pay by appointment. That might pass. But you will forbear to cite me for your authority.'

'The line would be acceptable if I could get it to apply,' said Vernon.

'Or this . . .' Dr. Middleton was offering a second suggestion, but Clara fled, astonished at men as she never yet had been. Why, in a burning world they would be exercising their minds in absurdities! And those two were scholars, learned men! And both knew they were in the presence of a soul in a tragic fever!

A minute after she had closed the door they were deep in their work. Dr. Middleton forgot his alternative line.

'Nothing serious?' he said in reproof of the want of honourable clearness on Vernon's brows.

'I trust not, sir: it's a case for common sense.'

'And you call that not serious?'

'I take Hermann's praise of the versus dochmiachus*to be not serious but unexaggerated,' said Vernon.

Dr. Middleton assented and entered on the voiceful ground of Greek metres, shoving your dry dusty world from his elbows.

CHAPTER XXV

The Flight in Wild Weather

THE morning of Lucy Darleton's letter of reply to her friend Clara was fair before sunrise with luminous colours that are an omen to the husbandman. Clara had no weather-eye for the rich Eastern crimson, nor a quiet space within her for the beauty. She looked on it as her gate of promise, and it set her throbbing with a revived relief in radiant things which she once dreamed of to surround her life, but her accelerated pulses narrowed her thoughts upon the machinery of her project. She

herself was metal, pointing all to her one aim when in
motion. Nothing came amiss to it, everything was fuel;
fibs, evasions, the serene battalions of white lies parallel
on the march with dainty rogue falsehoods. She had
delivered herself of many yesterday in her engagements
for to-day. Pressure was put on her to engage herself,
and she did so liberally, throwing the burden of deceitfulness on the extraordinary pressure. 'I want the early
part of the morning; the rest of the day I shall be at
liberty.' She said it to Willoughby, Miss Dale, Colonel
De Craye, and only the third time was she aware of the
delicious double meaning. Hence she associated it with
the Colonel.

Your loudest outcry against the wretch who breaks
your rules, is in asking how a tolerably conscientious
person could have done this and the other besides the
main offence, which you vow you could overlook but for
the minor objections pertaining to conscience, the incomprehensible and abominable lies, for example, or the
brazen coolness of the lying. Yet you know that we live
in an undisciplined world, where in our seasons of
activity we are servants of our design, and that this
comes of our passions, and those of our position. Our
design shapes us for the work in hand, the passions man
the ship, the position is their apology: and now should
conscience be a passenger on board, a merely seeming
swiftness of our vessel will keep him dumb as the unwilling guest of a pirate captain scudding from the cruiser
half in cloven brine through rocks and shoals to save his
black flag. Beware the false position.

That is easy to say: sometimes the tangle descends on
us like a net of blight on a rose-bush. There is then an
instant choice for us between courage to cut loose, and
desperation if we do not. But not many men are trained
to courage; young women are trained to cowardice. For
them to front an evil with plain speech is to be guilty of
effrontery and forfeit the waxen polish of purity, and
therewith their commanding place in the market. They
are trained to please man's taste, for which purpose they
soon learn to live out of themselves, and look on them-

selves as he looks, almost as little disturbed as he by the undiscovered. Without courage, conscience is a sorry guest; and if all goes well with the pirate captain, conscience will be made to walk the plank for being of no service to either party.

Clara's fibs and evasions disturbed her not in the least that morning. She had chosen desperation, and she thought herself very brave because she was just brave enough to fly from her abhorrence. She was light-hearted, or more truly, drunken-hearted. Her quick nature realized the out of prison as vividly and suddenly as it had sunk suddenly and leadenly under the sense of imprisonment. Vernon crossed her mind: that was a friend! Yes, and there was a guide; but he would disapprove, and even he thwarting her way to sacred liberty must be thrust aside.

What would he think? They might never meet, for her to know. Or one day in the Alps they might meet, a middle-aged couple, he famous, she regretful only to have fallen below his lofty standard. 'For, Mr. Whitford,' says she, very earnestly, 'I did wish at that time, believe me or not, to merit your approbation.' The brows of the phantom Vernon whom she conjured up were stern, as she had seen them yesterday in the library.

She gave herself a chiding for thinking of him when her mind should be intent on that which he was opposed to.

It was a livelier relaxation to think of young Crossjay's shamefaced confession presently, that he had been a laggard in bed while she swept the dews. She laughed at him, and immediately Crossjay popped out on her from behind a tree, causing her to clap hand to heart and stand fast. A conspirator is not of the stuff to bear surprises. He feared he had hurt her and was manly in his efforts to soothe: he had been up 'hours,' he said, and had watched her coming along the avenue, and did not mean to startle her: it was the kind of fun he played with fellows, and if he had hurt her, she might do anything to him she liked, and she would see if he could not stand to be punished. He was urgent with her to inflict corporal punishment on him.

'I shall leave it to the boatswain to do that when you're in the navy,' said Clara.

'The boatswain daren't strike an officer! so now you see what you know of the navy,' said Crossjay.

'But you could not have been out before me, you naughty boy, for I found all the locks and bolts when I went to the door.'

'But you didn't go to the back-door, and Sir Willoughby's private door: you came out by the hall-door; and I know what you want, Miss Middleton, you want not to pay what you've lost.'

'What have I lost, Crossjay?'

'Your wager.'

'What was that?'

'You know.'

'Speak.'

'A kiss.'

'Nothing of the sort. But, dear boy, I don't love you less for not kissing you. All that is nonsense: you have to think only of learning, and to be truthful. Never tell a story: suffer anything rather than be dishonest.' She was particularly impressive upon the silliness and wickedness of falsehood, and added: 'Do you hear?'

'Yes: but you kissed me when I had been out in the rain that day.'

'Because I promised.'

'And Miss Middleton, you betted a kiss yesterday.'

'I am sure, Crossjay—no, I will not say I am sure: but can you say you are sure you were out first this morning? Well, will you say you are sure that when you left the house you did not see me in the avenue? You can't: ah!'

'Miss Middleton, I do really believe I was dressed first.'

'Always be truthful, my dear boy, and then you may feel that Clara Middleton will always love you.'

'But, Miss Middleton, when you're married you won't be Clara Middleton.'

'I certainly shall, Crossjay.'

'No, you won't, because I'm so fond of your name!'

She considered and said: 'You have warned me, Cross-jay, and I shall not marry. I shall wait,' she was going to say, 'for you,' but turned the hesitation to a period. 'Is the village where I posted my letter the day before yesterday too far for you?'

Crossjay howled in contempt. 'Next to Clara my favourite's Lucy,' he said.

'I thought Clara came next to Nelson,' said she; 'and a long way off too, if you're not going to be a landlubber.'

'I'm not going to be a landlubber, Miss Middleton, you may be absolutely positive on your solemn word.'

'You're getting to talk like one a little now and then, Crossjay.'

'Then I won't talk at all.'

He stuck to his resolution for one whole minute.

Clara hoped that on this morning of a doubtful though imperative venture she had done some good.

They walked fast to cover the distance to the village post-office and back before the breakfast hour: and they had plenty of time, arriving too early for the opening of the door, so that Crossjay began to dance with an appetite, and was despatched to besiege a bakery. Clara felt lonely without him, apprehensively timid in the shuttered unmoving village street. She was glad of his return. When at last her letter was handed to her, on the testimony of the postman that she was the lawful appli-cant, Crossjay and she put on a sharp trot to be back at the Hall in good time. She took a swallowing glance of the first page of Lucy's writing:

'Telegraph, and I will meet you. I will supply you with everything you can want for the two nights, if you cannot stop longer.'

That was the gist of the letter. A second, less voracious, glance at it along the road brought sweetness:—Lucy wrote:

'Do I love you as I did? my best friend, you must fall into unhappiness to have the answer to that.'

Clara broke a silence.

'Yes, dear Crossjay, and if you like you shall have another walk with me after breakfast. But remember you must not say where you have gone with me. I shall give you twenty shillings to go and buy those birds' eggs and the butterflies you want for your collection; and mind, promise me, to-day is your last day of truancy. Tell Mr. Whitford how ungrateful you know you have been, that he may have some hope of you. You know the way across the fields to the railway station?'

'You save a mile; you drop on the road by Combline's mill, and then there's another five minutes' cut, and the rest's road.'

'Then, Crossjay, immediately after breakfast run round behind the pheasantry, and there I'll find you. And if any one comes to you before I come, say you are admiring the plumage of the Himalaya—the beautiful Indian bird; and if we're found together, we run a race, and of course you can catch me, but you mustn't until we're out of sight. Tell Mr. Vernon at night—tell Mr. Whitford at night you had the money from me as part of my allowance to you for pocket-money. I used to like to have pocket-money, Crossjay. And you may tell him I gave you the holiday, and I may write to him for his excuse, if he is not too harsh to grant it. He can be very harsh.'

'You look right into his eyes next time, Miss Middleton. I used to think him awful, till he made me look at him. He says men ought to look straight at one another, just as we do when he gives me my boxing-lesson, and then we won't have quarrelling half so much. I can't recollect everything he says.'

'You are not bound to, Crossjay.'

'No, but you like to hear.'

'Really, dear boy, I can't accuse myself of having told you that.'

'No, but, Miss Middleton, you do. And he's fond of your singing and playing on the piano, and watches you.'

'We shall be late if we don't mind,' said Clara, starting to a pace close on a run.

They were in time for a circuit in the park to the wild double cherry-blossom, no longer all white. Clara gazed up from under it, where she had imagined a fairer visible

heavenliness than any other sight of earth had ever given
her. That was when Vernon lay beneath. But she had
certainly looked above, not at him. The tree seemed
sorrowful in its withering flowers of the colour of trodden
snow.

Crossjay resumed the conversation.

'He says ladies don't like him much.'

'Who says that?'

'Mr. Whitford.'

'Were those his words?'

'I forget the words: but he said they wouldn't be
taught by him, like me ever since you came; and since
you came I've liked him ten times more.'

'The more you like him the more I shall like you,
Crossjay.'

The boy raised a shout and scampered away to Sir
Willoughby, at the appearance of whom Clara felt herself
nipped and curling inward. Crossjay ran up to him with
every sign of pleasure. Yet he had not mentioned him
during the walk; and Clara took it for a sign that the boy
understood the entire satisfaction Willoughby had in
mere shows of affection, and acted up to it. Hardly
blaming Crossjay, she was a critic of the scene, for the
reason that youthful creatures who have ceased to love a
person, hunger for evidence against him to confirm their
hard animus, which will seem to them sometimes, when
he is not immediately irritating them, brutish, because
they cannot analyze it and reduce it to the multitude of
just antagonisms whereof it came. It has passed by large
accumulation into a sombre and speechless load upon the
senses, and fresh evidence, the smallest item, is a champion to speak for it. Being about to do wrong, she
grasped at this eagerly, and brooded on the little of vital
and truthful that there was in the man, and how he
corrupted the boy. Nevertheless she instinctively imitated Crossjay in an almost sparkling salute to him.

'Good morning, Willoughby; it was not a morning to
lose: have you been out long?'

He retained her hand. 'My dear Clara! and you, have
you not over-fatigued yourself? Where have you been?'

'Round—everywhere! And I am certainly not tired.'

'Only you and Crossjay? You should have loosened the dogs.'

'Their barking would have annoyed the house.'

'Less than I am annoyed to think of you without protection.'

He kissed her fingers: it was a loving speech.

'The household . . .' said Clara, but would not insist to convict him of what he could not have perceived.

'If you outstrip me another morning, Clara, promise me to take the dogs; will you?'

'Yes.'

'To-day I am altogether yours.'

'Are you?'

'From the first to the last hour of it!—So you fall in with Horace's humour pleasantly?'

'He is very amusing.'

'As good as though one had hired him.'

'Here comes Colonel De Craye.'

'He must think we *have* hired him!'

She noticed the bitterness of Willoughby's tone. He sang out a good morning to De Craye, and remarked that he must go to the stables.

'Darleton? Darleton, Miss Middleton?' said the colonel, rising from his bow to her: 'A daughter of General Darleton? If so, I have had the honour to dance with her. And have not you?—practised with her, I mean; or gone off in a triumph to dance it out as young ladies do. So you know what a delightful partner she is.'

'She is!' cried Clara, enthusiastic for her succouring friend, whose letter was the treasure in her bosom.

'Oddly, the name did not strike me yesterday, Miss Middleton. In the middle of the night it rang a little silver bell in my ear, and I remembered the lady I was half in love with, if only for her dancing. She is dark, of your height, as light on her feet; a sister in another colour. Now that I know her to be your friend . . .!'

'Why, you may meet her, Colonel De Craye.'

'It'll be to offer her a castaway. And one only meets a

charming girl to hear that she's engaged! 'Tis not a line of a ballad, Miss Middleton, but out of the heart.'

'Lucy Darleton . . . You were leading me to talk seriously to you, Colonel De Craye.'

'Will you one day?—and not think me a perpetual tumbler. You have heard of melancholy clowns. You would find the face not so laughable behind my paint. When I was thirteen years younger I was loved, and my dearest sank to the grave. Since then I have not been quite at home in life; probably because of finding no one so charitable as she. 'Tis easy to win smiles and hands, but not so easy to win a woman whose faith you would trust as your own heart before the enemy. I was poor then. She said: "The day after my twenty-first birthday"; and that day I went for her, and I wondered they did not refuse me at the door. I was shown upstairs, and I saw her, and saw death. She wished to marry me, to leave me her fortune!"*

'Then never marry,' said Clara in an underbreath.

She glanced behind.

Sir Willoughby was close, walking on turf.

'I must be cunning to escape him after breakfast,' she thought.

He had discarded his foolishness of the previous days, and the thought in him could have replied: 'I am a dolt if I let you out of my sight.'

Vernon appeared, formal as usual of late. Clara begged his excuse for withdrawing Crossjay from his morning swim. He nodded.

De Craye called to Willoughby for a book of the trains.

'There's a card in the smoking-room; eleven, one, and four are the hours, if you must go,' said Willoughby.

'You leave the Hall, Colonel De Craye?'

'In two or three days, Miss Middleton.'

She did not request him to stay: his announcement produced no effect on her. Consequently, thought he—well, what? nothing: well, then, that she might not be minded to stay herself. Otherwise she would have regretted the loss of an amusing companion: that is the modest way of putting it. There is a modest and a vain for the same sentiment; and both may be simultaneously in the same breast; and each one as honest as the other; so shy is man's vanity in the presence of here and there a lady. She liked him: she did not care a pin for him—how could she? yet she liked him: O to be able to do her some kindling bit of service! These were his consecutive fancies, resolving naturally to the exclamation, and built on the conviction that she did not love Willoughby, and waited for a spirited lift from circumstances. His call for a book of the trains had been a sheer piece of impromptu, in the mind as well as on the mouth. It sprang, unknown to him, of conjectures he had indulged yesterday and the day before. This morning she would have an answer to her letter to her friend, Miss Lucy Darleton, the pretty dark girl, whom De Craye was astonished not to have noticed more when he danced with her. She, pretty as she was, had come to his recollection through the name and rank of her father, a famous general of cavalry, and tactician in that arm. The colonel despised himself for not having been devoted to Clara Middleton's friend.

The morning's letters were on the bronze plate in the hall. Clara passed on her way to her room without inspecting them. De Craye opened an envelope and went upstairs to scribble a line. Sir Willoughby observed their absence at the solemn reading to the domestic servants in advance of breakfast. Three chairs were unoccupied. Vernon had his own notions of a mechanical service—and a precious profit he derived from them! but the other two seats returned the stare Willoughby cast at their backs with an impudence that reminded him of his friend Horace's calling for a book of the trains, when a minute afterward he admitted he was going to stay at the Hall another two days, or three. The man possessed by jealousy is never in need of matter for it: he magnifies; grass is jungle, hillocks are mountains. Willoughby's legs crossing and uncrossing audibly, and his tight-folded arms and clearing of the throat, were faint indications of his condition.

'Are you in fair health this morning, Willoughby?' Dr. Middleton said to him after he had closed his volumes.

'The thing is not much questioned by those who know me intimately,' he replied.

'Willoughby unwell!' and: 'He is health incarnate!' exclaimed the ladies Eleanor and Isabel.

Laetitia grieved for him. Sunrays on a pest-stricken city, she thought, were like the smile of his face. She believed that he deeply loved Clara and had learnt more of her alienation.

He went into the hall to look up the well for the pair of malefactors; on fire with what he could not reveal to a soul.

De Craye was in the housekeeper's room, talking to young Crossjay and Mrs. Montague just come up to breakfast. He had heard the boy chattering, and as the door was ajar, he peeped in, and was invited to enter. Mrs. Montague was very fond of hearing him talk; he paid her the familiar respect which a lady of fallen fortunes, at a certain period after the fall, enjoys as a befittingly sad souvenir, and the respectfulness of the lord of the house was more chilling.

She bewailed the boy's trying his constitution with long walks before he had anything in him to walk on.

'And where did you go this morning, my lad?' said De Craye.

'Ah, you know the ground, colonel,' said Crossjay. 'I am hungry! I shall eat three eggs and some bacon, and buttered cakes, and jam, then begin again, on my second cup of coffee.'

'It's not braggadocio,' remarked Mrs. Montague. 'He waits empty from five in the morning till nine, and then he comes famished to my table, and eats too much.'

'Oh! Mrs. Montague, that is what the country people call roemancing. For, Colonel De Craye, I had a bun at seven o'clock. Miss Middleton forced me to go and buy it.'

'A stale bun, my boy?'

'Yesterday's: there wasn't much of a stopper to you in it, like a new bun.'

'And where did you leave Miss Middleton when you went to buy the bun? You should never leave a lady;

and the street of a country town is lonely at that early hour. Crossjay, you surprise me.'

'She forced me to go, colonel. Indeed she did. What do I care for a bun! And she was quite safe. We could hear the people stirring in the post-office, and I met our postman going for his letter-bag. I didn't want to go: bother the bun!—but you can't disobey Miss Middleton. I never want to, and wouldn't.'

'There we're of the same mind,' said the colonel, and Crossjay shouted, for the lady whom they exalted was at the door.

'You will be too tired for a ride this morning,' De Craye said to her, descending the stairs.

She swung a bonnet by the ribands: 'I don't think of riding to-day.'

'Why did you not depute your mission to me?'

'I like to bear my own burdens, as far as I can.'

'Miss Darleton is well?'

'I presume so.'

'Will you try her recollection of me?'

'It will probably be quite as lively as yours was.'

'Shall you see her soon?'

'I hope so.'

Sir Willoughby met her at the foot of the stairs, but refrained from giving her a hand that shook.

'We shall have the day together,' he said.

Clara bowed.

At the breakfast-table she faced a clock.

De Craye took out his watch. 'You are five and a half minutes too slow by that clock, Willoughby.'

'The man omitted to come from Rendon to set it last week, Horace. He will find the hour too late here for him when he does come.'

One of the ladies compared the time of her watch with De Craye's, and Clara looked at hers and gratefully noted that she was four minutes in arrear.

She left the breakfast-room at a quarter to ten, after kissing her father. Willoughby was behind her. He had been soothed by thinking of his personal advantages over De Craye, and he felt assured that if he could be solitary with his eccentric bride and fold her in himself, he would, cutting temper adrift, be the man he had been to her not so many days back. Considering how few days back, his temper was roused, but he controlled it.

They were slightly dissenting as De Craye stepped into the hall.

'A present worth examining,' Willoughby said to her: 'And I do not dwell on the costliness. Come presently, then. I am at your disposal all day. I will drive you in the afternoon to call on Lady Busshe to offer your thanks: but you must see it first. It is laid out in the laboratory.'

'There is time before the afternoon,' said Clara.

'Wedding presents?' interposed De Craye.

'A porcelain service from Lady Busshe, Horace.'

'Not in fragments? Let me have a look at it. I'm haunted by an idea that porcelain always goes to pieces. I'll have a look and take a hint. We're in the laboratory, Miss Middleton.'

He put his arm under Willoughby's. The resistance to him was momentary: Willoughby had the satisfaction of the thought that De Craye being with him was not with Clara; and seeing her giving orders to her maid Barclay, he deferred his claim on her company for some short period.

De Craye detained him in the laboratory, first over the China cups and saucers, and then with the latest of London—tales of youngest Cupid upon subterranean adventures, having high titles to light him. Willoughby liked the tale thus illuminated, for without the title there was no special savour in such affairs, and it pulled down his betters in rank. He was of a morality to reprobate the erring dame while he enjoyed the incidents. He could not help interrupting De Craye to point at Vernon through the window, striding this way and that, evidently on the hunt for young Crossjay. 'No one here knows how to manage the boy except myself. But go on, Horace,' he said, checking his contemptuous laugh; and Vernon did look ridiculous, out there half-drenched already in a white rain, again shuffled off by the little rascal. It seemed that he was determined to have his runaway: he struck up the avenue at full pedestrian racing pace.

'A man looks a fool cutting after a cricket-ball; but putting on steam in a storm of rain to catch a young villain out of sight, beats anything I've witnessed,' Willoughby resumed, in his amusement.

'Aiha!' said De Craye, waving a hand to accompany the melodious accent, 'there are things to beat that for fun.'

He had smoked in the laboratory, so Willoughby directed a servant to transfer the porcelain service to one of the sitting-rooms for Clara's inspection of it.

'You're a bold man,' De Craye remarked. 'The luck may be with you, though. I wouldn't handle the fragile treasure for a trifle.'

'I believe in my luck,' said Willoughby.

Clara was now sought for. The lord of the house desired her presence impatiently, and had to wait. She was in none of the lower rooms. Barclay, her maid, upon interrogation, declared she was in none of the upper. Willoughby turned sharp on De Craye: he was there.

The ladies Eleanor and Isabel, and Miss Dale, were consulted. They had nothing to say about Clara's movements, more than that they could not understand her exceeding restlessness. The idea of her being out of doors grew serious; heaven was black, hard thunder rolled, and lightning flushed the battering rain. Men bearing umbrellas, shawls, and cloaks were despatched on a circuit of the park. De Craye said: 'I'll be one.'

'No,' cried Willoughby, starting to intercept him, 'I can't allow it.'

'I've the scent of a hound, Willoughby; I'll soon be on the track.'

'My dear Horace, I won't let you go.'

'Adieu, dear boy! and if the lady's discoverable, I'm the one to find her.'

He stepped to the umbrella-stand. There was then a general question whether Clara had taken her umbrella. Barclay said she had. The fact indicated a wider stroll than round inside the park: Crossjay was likewise absent. De Craye nodded to himself.

Willoughby struck a rattling blow on the barometer.

'Where's Pollington?' he called, and sent word for his man Pollington to bring big fishing-boots and waterproof wrappers.

An urgent debate within him was in progress.

Should he go forth alone on his chance of discovering Clara and forgiving her under his umbrella and cloak? or should he prevent De Craye from going forth alone on the chance he vaunted so impudently?

'You will offend me, Horace, if you insist,' he said.

'Regard me as an instrument of destiny, Willoughby,' replied De Craye.

'Then we go in company.'

'But that's an addition of one that cancels the other by conjunction, and's worse than simple division: for I can't trust my wits unless I rely on them alone, you see.'

'Upon my word, you talk at times most unintelligible stuff, to be frank with you, Horace. Give it in English.'

' 'Tis not suited perhaps to the genius of the language, for I thought I talked English.'

'Oh! there's English gibberish as well as Irish, we know!'

'And a deal foolisher when they do go at it; for it won't bear squeezing, we think, like Irish.'

'Where!' exclaimed the ladies, 'where can she be! The storm is terrible.'

Laetitia suggested the boathouse.

'For Crossjay hadn't a swim this morning!' said De Craye.

No one reflected on the absurdity that Clara should think of taking Crossjay for a swim in the lake, and immediately after his breakfast: it was accepted as a suggestion at least that she and Crossjay had gone to the lake for a row.

In the hopefulness of the idea, Willoughby suffered De Craye to go on his chance unaccompanied. He was near chuckling. He projected a plan for dismissing Crossjay and remaining in the boathouse with Clara, luxuriating in the prestige which would attach to him for seeking and finding her. Deadly sentiments intervened. Still he might expect to be alone with her where she could not slip from him.

The throwing open of the hall-doors for the gentlemen presented a framed picture of a deluge. All the young-leaved trees were steely black, without a gradation of green, drooping and pouring, and the song of rain had become an inveterate hiss.

The ladies beholding it exclaimed against Clara, even apostrophized her, so dark are trivial errors when circumstances frown. She must be mad to tempt such weather: she was very giddy; she was never at rest. Clara! Clara! how could you be so wild! Ought we not to tell Dr. Middleton?

Laetitia induced them to spare him.

'Which way do you take?' said Willoughby, rather fearful that his companion was not to be got rid of now.

'Any way,' said De Craye. 'I chuck up my head like a halfpenny and go by the toss.'

This enraging nonsense drove off Willoughby. De Craye saw him cast a furtive eye at his heels to make sure he was not followed, and thought: 'Jove! he may be fond of her. But he's not on the track. She's a determined girl, if I'm correct. She's a girl of a hundred thousand. Girls like that make the right sort of wives for the right men. They're the girls to make men think of marrying. To-morrow! only give me the chance. They stick to you fast when they do stick.'

Then a thought of her flower-like drapery and face caused him fervently to hope she had escaped the storm.

Calling at the West park-lodge he heard that Miss Middleton had been seen passing through the gate with Master Crossjay; but she had not been seen coming back. Mr. Vernon Whitford had passed through half an hour later.

'After his young man!' said the colonel.

The lodge-keeper's wife and daughter knew of Master Crossjay's pranks; Mr. Whitford, they said, had made inquiries about him, and must have caught him and sent him home to change his dripping things; for Master Crossjay had come back, and had declined shelter in the lodge; he seemed to be crying; he went away soaking over the wet grass, hanging his head. The opinion at the lodge was, that Master Crossjay was unhappy.

'He very properly received a wigging from Mr. Whitford, I have no doubt,' said Colonel De Craye.

Mother and daughter supposed it to be the case, and considered Crossjay very wilful for not going straight home to the Hall to change his wet clothes; he was drenched.

De Craye drew out his watch. The time was ten minutes past eleven. If the surmise he had distantly spied was correct, Miss Middleton would have been caught in the storm midway to her destination. By his guess at her character (knowledge of it, he would have said), he judged that no storm would daunt her on a predetermined expedition. He deduced in consequence that she was at the present moment flying to her friend the charming brunette Lucy Darleton.

Still, as there was a possibility of the rain having been too much for her, and as he had no other speculation concerning the route she had taken, he decided upon keeping along the road to Rendon, with a keen eye at cottage and farmhouse windows.

CHAPTER XXVI

Vernon in Pursuit

THE lodge-keeper had a son, who was a chum of Master Crossjay's, and errant-fellow with him upon many adventures; for this boy's passion was to become a gamekeeper, and accompanied by one of the head-gamekeeper's youngsters, he and Crossjay were in the habit of rangeing over the country, preparing for a profession delightful to the tastes of all three. Crossjay's prospective connection with the mysterious ocean bestowed the title of captain on him by common consent; he led them, and when missing for lessons he was generally in the society of Jacob Croom or Jonathan Fernaway. Vernon made sure of Crossjay when he perceived Jacob Croom sitting on a stool in the little lodge-parlour. Jacob's appearance of a diligent perusal of a book he had presented to the lad, he took for a decent piece of trickery. It was with amazement that he heard from the mother and daughter, as well as Jacob, of Miss Middleton's going through the gate before ten o'clock with Crossjay beside her, the latter too hurried to spare a nod to Jacob. That she, of all on earth, should be encouraging Crossjay to truancy was incredible. Vernon had to fall back upon Greek and Latin aphoristic shots at the sex to believe it.

Rain was universal; a thick robe of it swept from hill to hill; thunder rumbled remote, and between the ruffled roars the downpour pressed on the land with a great noise of eager gobbling, much like that of the swine's trough fresh filled, as though a vast assembly of the hungered had seated themselves clamorously and fallen to on meats and drinks in silence, save of the chaps. A rapid walker poetically and humourously minded gathers multitudes of images on his way. And rain, the heaviest you can meet, is a lively companion when the resolute pacer scorns discomfort of wet clothes and squealing boots. South-western rain-clouds, too, are never long sullen: they enfold and will have the earth in a good strong glut of the kissing overflow; then, as a hawk with feathers on his beak of the bird in his claw lifts head, they rise and take veiled feature in long climbing watery lines: at any moment they may break the veil and show soft upper cloud, show sun on it, show sky, green near the verge they spring from, of the green of grass in early dew; or, along a travelling sweep that rolls asunder overhead, heaven's laughter of purest blue among titanic white shoulders: it may mean fair smiling for awhile, or be the lightest interlude; but the watery lines, and the drifting, the chasing, the upsoaring, all in a shadowy fingering of form, and the animation of the leaves of the trees pointing them on, the bending of the tree-tops, the snapping of branches, and the hurrahings of the stubborn hedge at wrestle with the flaws, yielding but a leaf at most, and that on a fling, make a glory of contest and wildness without aid of colour to inflame the man who is at home in them from old associa-

tion on road, heath and mountain. Let him be drenched,
his heart will sing. And thou, trim cockney, that jeerest,
consider thyself, to whom it may occur to be out in such a
scene, and with what steps of a nervous dancing master it
would be thine to play the hunted rat of the elements, for
the preservation of the one imagined dry spot about thee,
somewhere on thy luckless person! The taking of rain
and sun alike befits men of our climate, and he who would
have the secret of a strengthening intoxication must court
the clouds of the South-west with a lover's blood.

Vernon's happy recklessness was dashed by fears for
Miss Middleton. Apart from those fears, he had the
pleasure of a gull wheeling among foam-streaks of the
wave. He supposed the Swiss and Tyrol Alps to have
hidden their heads from him for many a day to come, and
the springing and chiming South-west was the next best
thing.* A milder rain descended; the country expanded
darkly defined underneath the moving curtain; the
clouds were as he liked to see them, scaling; but their
skirts dragged. Torrents were in store, for they coursed
streamingly still and had not the higher lift, or eagle ascent, which he knew for one of the signs of fairness, nor
had the hills any belt of mist-like vapour.

On a step of the stile leading to the short-cut to Rendon
young Crossjay was espied. A man-tramp sat on the top
bar.

'There you are; what are you doing there? Where's
Miss Middleton?' said Vernon. 'Now, take care before
you open your mouth.'

Crossjay shut the mouth he had opened.

'The lady has gone away over to a station, sir,' said the
tramp.

'You fool!' roared Crossjay, ready to fly at him.

'But ain't it, now, young gentleman? Can you say it
ain't?'

'I gave you a shilling, you ass!'

'You give me that sum, young gentleman, to stop here
and take care of you, and here I stopped.'

'Mr. Whitford!' Crossjay appealed to his master, and
broke off in disgust: 'Take care of me! As if anybody

who knows me would think I wanted taking care of!
Why, what a beast you must be, you fellow!'

'Just as you like, young gentleman. I chaunted you
all I know, to keep up your downcast spirits. You did
want comforting. You wanted it rarely. You cried
like an infant.'

'I let you "chaunt" as you call it, to keep you from
swearing.'

'And why did I swear, young gentleman? because I've
got an itchy coat in the wet, and no shirt for a lining. And
no breakfast to give me a stomach for this kind of weather.
That's what I've come to in this world! I'm a walking
moral. No wonder I swears, when I don't strike up a
chaunt.'

'But why are you sitting here, wet through, Crossjay?
Be off home at once, and change, and get ready for me.'

'Mr. Whitford, I promised, and I tossed this fellow a
shilling not to go bothering Miss Middleton.'

'The lady wouldn't have none o' the young gentleman, sir, and I offered to go pioneer for her to the station,
behind her, at a respectful distance.'

'As if!—you treacherous cur!' Crossjay ground his
teeth at the betrayer. 'Well, Mr. Whitford, and I didn't
trust him, and I stuck to him, or he'd have been after her
whining about his coat and stomach, and talking of his
being a moral. He repeats that to everybody.'

'She has gone to the station?' said Vernon.

Not a word on that subject was to be won from Crossjay.

'How long since?' Vernon partly addressed Mr. Tramp.

The latter became seized with shivers as he supplied
the information that it might be a quarter of an hour
or twenty minutes. 'But what's time to me, sir! If I
had reg'lar meals, I should carry a clock in my inside.
I got the rheumatics instead.'

'Way there!' Vernon cried, and took the stile at a
vault.

'That's what gentlemen can do, who sleeps in their
beds warm,' moaned the tramp. 'They've no joints.'

Vernon handed him a half-crown piece, for he had been
of use for once.

'Mr. Whitford, let me come. If you tell me to come I may. Do let me come,' Crossjay begged with great entreaty. 'I shan't see her for . . .'

'Be off, quick!' Vernon cut him short and pushed on.

The tramp and Crossjay were audible to him; Crossjay spurning the consolations of the professional sad man.

Vernon sprang across the fields, timing himself by his watch to reach Rendon station ten minutes before eleven, though without clearly questioning the nature of the resolution which precipitated him. Dropping to the road, he had better foothold than on the slippery field-path, and he ran. His principal hope was that Clara would have missed her way. Another pelting of rain agitated him on her behalf. Might she not as well be suffered to go?— and sit three hours and more in a railway-carriage with wet feet!

He clasped the visionary little feet to warm them on his breast.—But Willoughby's obstinate fatuity deserved the blow!—But neither she nor her father deserved the scandal. But she was desperate. Could reasoning touch her? If not, what would? He knew of nothing. Yesterday he had spoken strongly to Willoughby, to plead with him to favour her departure and give her leisure to sound her mind, and he had left his cousin, convinced that Clara's best measure was flight: a man so cunning in a pretended obtuseness backed by senseless pride, and in petty tricks that sprang of a grovelling tyranny, could only be taught by facts.

Her recent treatment of him, however, was very strange; so strange that he might have known himself better if he had reflected on the bound with which it shot him to a hard suspicion. De Craye had prepared the world to hear that he was leaving the Hall. Were they in concert? The idea struck at his heart colder than if her damp little feet had been there.

Vernon's full exoneration of her for making a confidant of himself, did not extend its leniency to the young lady's character when there was question of her doing the same with a second gentleman. He could suspect much: he could even expect to find De Craye at the station.

That idea drew him up in his run, to meditate on the part he should play; and by drove little Dr. Corney on the way to Rendon, and hailed him, and gave his cheerless figure the nearest approach to an Irish hug in the form of a dry seat under an umbrella and waterproof covering.

'Though it is the worst I can do for you, if you decline to supplement it with a dose of hot brandy and water at the Dolphin,' said he: 'and I'll see you take it, if you please. I'm bound to ease a Rendon patient out of the world. Medicine's one of their superstitions, which they cling to the harder the more useless it gets. Pill and priest launch him happy between them.—"And what's on your conscience, Pat?—It's whether your blessing, your Riverence, would disagree with another drop.—Then, put the horse before the cart, my son, and you shall have the two in harmony, and God speed ye!"—Rendon station, did you say, Vernon? You shall have my prescription at the Railway Arms, if you're hurried. You have the look. What is it? Can I help?'

'No. And don't ask.'

'You're like the Irish Grenadier who had a bullet in a humiliating situation. Here's Rendon, and through it we go with a spanking clatter. Here's Dr. Corney's dog-cart posthaste again. For there's no dying without him now, and Repentance is on the death-bed for not calling him in before! Half a charge of humbug hurts no son of a gun, friend Vernon, if he'd have his firing take effect. Be tender to't in man or woman, particularly woman. So, by goes the meteoric doctor, and I'll bring noses to window-panes, you'll see, which reminds me of the sweetest young lady *I* ever saw, and the luckiest man. When is she off for her bridal trousseau? And when are they spliced? I'll not call her perfection, for that's a post, afraid to move. But she's a dancing sprig of the tree next it. Poetry's wanted to speak of her. I'm Irish and inflammable, I suppose, but I never looked on a girl to make a man comprehend the entire holy meaning of the word rapturous, like that one. And away she goes! We'll not say another word. But you're a Grecian, friend Vernon. Now, couldn't you think her just a whiff of an idea of a daughter of a peccadillo-Goddess?'

'Deuce take you, Corney, drop me here; I shall be late for the train,' said Vernon, laying hand on the doctor's arm to check him on the way to the station in view.

Dr. Corney had a Celtic intelligence for a meaning behind an illogical tongue. He drew up, observing: 'Two minutes' run won't hurt you.'

He slightly fancied he might have given offence, though he was well acquainted with Vernon and had a cordial grasp at the parting.

The truth must be told, that Vernon could not at the moment bear any more talk from an Irishman. Dr. Corney had succeeded in persuading him not to wonder at Clara Middleton's liking for Colonel De Craye.

CHAPTER XXVII

At the Railway Station

CLARA stood in the waiting-room contemplating the white rails of the rain-swept line. Her lips parted at the sight of Vernon.

'You have your ticket?' said he.

She nodded, and breathed more freely; the matter of fact question was reassuring.

'You are wet,' he resumed; and it could not be denied.

'A little. I do not feel it.'

'I must beg you to come to the inn hard by: half a dozen steps. We shall see your train signalled. Come.'

She thought him startlingly authoritative, but he had good sense to back him; and depressed as she was by the dampness, she was disposed to yield to reason if he continued to respect her independence. So she submitted outwardly, resisted inwardly, on the watch to stop him from taking any decisive lead.

'Shall we be sure to see the signal, Mr. Whitford?'

'I'll provide for that.'

He spoke to the station-clerk, and conducted her across the road.

'You are quite alone, Miss Middleton?'

'I am: I have not brought my maid.'

'You must take off boots and stockings at once, and have them dried. I'll put you in the hands of the landlady.'

'But my train!'

'You have full fifteen minutes, besides fair chances of delay.'

He seemed reasonable, the reverse of hostile, in spite of his commanding air, and that was not unpleasant in one friendly to her adventure. She controlled her alert mistrustfulness and passed from him to the landlady, for her feet were wet and cold, the skirts of her dress were soiled; generally inspecting herself, she was an object to be shuddered at, and she was grateful to Vernon for his inattention to her appearance.

Vernon ordered Dr. Corney's dose, and was ushered upstairs to a room of portraits, where the publican's ancestors and family sat against the walls, flat on their canvas as weeds of the botanist's portfolio, although corpulency was pretty generally insisted on, and there were formidable battalions of bust among the females. All of them had the aspect of the national energy which has vanquished obstacles to subside on its ideal. They all gazed straight at the guest. 'Drink, and come to this!' they might have been labelled to say to him. He was in the private Walhalla* of a large class of his countrymen. The existing host had taken forethought to be of the party in his prime, and in the central place, looking fresh-flattened there, and sanguine from the performance. By-and-by a son would shove him aside; meanwhile he shelved his parent, according to the manners of energy.

One should not be a critic of our works of Art in uncomfortable garments. Vernon turned from the portraits to a stuffed pike in a glass-case, and plunged into sympathy with the fish for a refuge.

Clara soon rejoined him, saying: 'But you, you must be very wet. You are without an umbrella. You must be wet through, Mr. Whitford.'

'We're all wet through to-day,' said Vernon. 'Crossjay's wet through, and a tramp he met.'

'The horrid man! But Crossjay should have turned back when I told him. Cannot the landlord assist you? You are not tied to time. I begged Crossjay to turn back when it began to rain: when it became heavy I compelled him. So you met my poor Crossjay?'

'You have not to blame him for betraying you. The tramp did that. I was thrown on your track quite by accident. Now pardon me for using authority: and don't be alarmed, Miss Middleton; you are perfectly free for me; but you must not run a risk to your health. I met Dr. Corney coming along, and he prescribed hot brandy and water for a wet skin; especially for sitting in it. There's the stuff on the table; I see you have been aware of a singular odour; you must consent to sip some, as medicine; merely to give you warmth.'

'Impossible, Mr. Whitford: I could not taste it. But pray, obey Dr. Corney, if he ordered it for you.'

'I can't unless you do.'

'I will, then: I will try.'

She held the glass, attempted, and was baffled by the reek of it.

'Try: you can do anything,' said Vernon.

'Now that you find me here, Mr. Whitford! Anything for myself, it would seem, and nothing to save a friend. But I will really try.'

'It must be a good mouthful.'

'I will try. And you will finish the glass?'

'With your permission, if you do not leave too much.'

They were to drink out of the same glass; and she was to drink some of this infamous mixture: and she was in a kind of hotel alone with him: and he was drenched in running after her:—all this came of breaking loose for an hour!

'Oh! what a misfortune that it should be such a day, Mr. Whitford.'

'Did you not choose the day?'

'Not the weather.'

'And the worst of it is, that Willoughby will come upon

Crossjay wet to the bone, and pump him and get nothing but shufflings, blank lies, and then find him out and chase him from the house.'

Clara drank immediately, and more than she intended. She held the glass as an enemy to be delivered from, gasping, uncertain of her breath.

'Never let me be asked to endure such a thing again!'

'You are unlikely to be running away from father and friends again.'

She panted still with the fiery liquid she had gulped: and she wondered that it should belie its reputation in not fortifying her, but rendering her painfully susceptible to his remarks.

'Mr. Whitford, I need not seek to know what you think of me.'

'What I think? I don't think at all; I wish to serve you, if I can.'

'Am I right in supposing you a little afraid of me? You should not be. I have deceived no one. I have opened my heart to you, and am not ashamed of having done so.'

'It is an excellent habit, they say.'

'It is not a habit with me.'

He was touched, and for that reason, in his dissatisfaction with himself, not unwilling to hurt. 'We take our turn, Miss Middleton. I'm no hero, and a bad conspirator, so I am not of much avail.'

'You have been reserved—but I am going, and I leave my character behind. You condemned me to the poison-bowl; you have not touched it yourself.'

'In vino veritas:*if I do I shall be speaking my mind.'

'Then do, for the sake of mind and body.'

'It won't be complimentary.'

'You can be harsh. Only say everything.'

'Have we time?'

They looked at their watches.

'Six minutes,' Clara said.

Vernon's had stopped, penetrated by his total drenching.

She reproached herself. He laughed to quiet her. 'My dies solemnes* are sure to give me duckings; I'm used to them. As for the watch, it will remind me that it stopped when you went.'

She raised the glass to him. She was happier and hoped for some little harshness and kindness mixed that she might carry away to travel with and think over.

He turned the glass as she had given it, turned it round in putting it to his lips: a scarce perceptible manoeuvre, but that she had given it expressly on one side.

It may be hoped that it was not done by design. Done even accidentally, without a taint of contrivance, it was an affliction to see, and coiled through her, causing her to shrink and redden.

Fugitives are subject to strange incidents; they are not vessels lying safe in harbour. She shut her lips tight, as if they had been stung. The realizing sensitiveness of her quick nature accused them of a loss of bloom. And the man who made her smart like this was formal as a railway-official on a platform!

'Now we are both pledged in the poison-bowl,' said he. 'And it has the taste of rank poison, I confess. But the doctor prescribed it, and at sea we must be sailors. Now, Miss Middleton, time presses: will you return with me?'

'No! no!'

'Where do you propose to go?'

'To London; to a friend—Miss Darleton.'

'What message is there for your father?'

'Say, I have left a letter for him in a letter to be delivered to you.'

'To me. And what message for Willoughby?'

'My maid Barclay will hand him a letter at noon.'

'You have sealed Crossjay's fate.'

'How?'

'He is probably at this instant undergoing an interrogation. You may guess at his replies. The letter will expose him, and Willoughby does not pardon.'

'I regret it. I cannot avoid it. Poor boy! My dear Crossjay! I did not think of how Willoughby might punish him. I was very thoughtless. Mr. Whitford, my pinmoney shall go for his education. Later, when I am a little older, I shall be able to support him.'

'That's an encumbrance; you should not tie yourself to drag it about. You are inalterable, of course, but circumstances are not, and as it happens, women are more subject to them than we are.'

'But I will not be!'

'Your command of them is shown at the present moment.'

'Because I determine to be free?'

'No: because you do the contrary; you don't determine; you run away from the difficulty, and leave it to your father and friends to bear. As for Crossjay, you see you destroy one of his chances. I should have carried him off before this, if I had not thought it prudent to keep him on terms with Willoughby. We'll let Crossjay stand aside. He'll behave like a man of honour, imitating others who have had to do the same for ladies.'

'Have spoken falsely to shelter cowards, you mean, Mr. Whitford. Oh! I know.—I have but two minutes. The die is cast. I cannot go back. I must get ready. Will you see me to the station? I would rather you should hurry home.'

'I will see the last of you. I will wait for you here. An express runs ahead of your train, and I have arranged with the clerk for a signal; I have an eye on the window.'

'You are still my best friend, Mr. Whitford.'

'Though——?'

'Well, though you do not perfectly understand what torments have driven me to this.'

'Carried on tides and blown by winds?'

'Ah! you do not understand.'

'Mysteries?'

'Sufferings are not mysteries, they are very simple facts.'

'Well, then, I don't understand. But decide at once. I wish you to have your free will.'

She left the room.

Dry stockings and boots are better for travelling in than wet ones, but in spite of her direct resolve, she felt when drawing them on like one that has been tripped. The goal was desireable, the ardour was damped. Vernon's wish that she should have her free will, compelled her to sound it: and it was of course to go, to be liberated, to cast off incubus:—and hurt her father? injure Crossjay? distress her friends? No, and ten times no!

She returned to Vernon in haste, to shun the reflex of her mind.

He was looking at a closed carriage drawn up at the station-door.

'Shall we run over now, Mr. Whitford?'

'There's no signal. Here it's not so chilly.'

'I ventured to enclose my letter to papa in yours, trusting you would attend to my request to you to break the news to him gently and plead for me.'

'We will all do the utmost we can.'

'I am doomed to vex those who care for me. I tried to follow your counsel.'

'First you spoke to me, and then you spoke to Miss Dale; and at least you have a clear conscience.'

'No.'

'What burdens it?'

'I have done nothing to burden it.'

'Then it's a clear conscience?'

'No.'

Vernon's shoulders jerked. Our patience with an innocent duplicity in women is measured by the place it assigns to us and another. If he had liked he could have thought: 'You have not done but meditated something to trouble conscience.' That was evident, and her speaking of it was proof too of the willingness to be clear. He would not help her. Man's blood, which is the link with women and responsive to them on the instant for or against, obscured him. He shrugged anew when she said: 'My character would have been degraded utterly by my staying there. Could you advise it?'

'Certainly not the degradation of your character,' he said, black on the subject of De Craye, and not lightened by feelings which made him sharply sensible of the beggarly dependant that he was, or poor adventuring scribbler that he was to become.

'Why did you pursue me and wish to stop me, Mr.

Whitford?' said Clara, on the spur of a wound from his tone.

He replied: 'I suppose I'm a busybody: I was never aware of it till now.'

'You are my friend. Only you speak in irony so much. That was irony, about my clear conscience. I spoke to you and to Miss Dale: and then I rested and drifted. Can you not feel for me, that to mention it is like a scorching furnace? Willoughby has entangled papa. He schemes incessantly to keep me entangled. I fly from his cunning as much as from anything. I dread it. I have told you that I am more to blame than he, but I must accuse him. And wedding-presents! and congratulations! And to be his guest!'

'All that makes up a plea in mitigation,' said Vernon.

'It is not sufficient for you?' she asked him timidly.

'You have a masculine good sense that tells you you won't be respected if you run. Three more days there might cover a retreat with your father.'

'He will not listen to me! He confuses me; Willoughby has bewitched him.'

'Commission me: I will see that he listens.'

'And go back? Oh! no. To London! Besides there is the dining with Mrs. Mountstuart this evening; and I like her very well, but I must avoid her. She has a kind of idolatry . . . And what answers can I give? I supplicate her with looks. She observes them, my efforts to divert them from being painful produce a comic expression to her, and I am a charming "rogue," and I am entertained on the topic she assumes to be principally interesting me. I must avoid her. The thought of her leaves me no choice. She is clever. She could tattoo me with epigrams.'

'Stay: there you can hold your own.'

'She has told me you give me credit for a spice of wit. I have not discovered my possession. We have spoken of it; we call it your delusion. She grants me some beauty; that must be hers.'

'There's no delusion in one case or the other, Miss Middleton. You have beauty and wit: public opinion will say, wildness: indifference to your reputation, will be charged on you, and your friends will have to admit it. But you will be out of *this* difficulty.'

'Ah!—to weave a second?'

'Impossible to judge until we see how you escape the first.—And I have no more to say. I love your father. His humour of sententiousness and doctorial stilts is a mask he delights in, but you ought to know him and not be frightened by it. If you sat with him an hour at a Latin task, and if you took his hand and told him you could not leave him, and no tears!—he would answer you at once. It would involve a day or two further: disagreeable to you, no doubt: preferable to the present mode of escape, as I think. But I have no power whatever to persuade. I have not the "lady's tongue." My appeal is always to reason.'

'It is a compliment. I loathe the "lady's tongue."'

'It's a distinctly good gift, and I wish I had it. I might have succeeded instead of failing, and appearing to pay a compliment.'

'Surely the express train is very late, Mr. Whitford?'

'The express has gone by.'

'Then we will cross over.'

'You would rather not be seen by Mrs. Mountstuart. That is her carriage drawn up at the station, and she is in it.'

Clara looked, and with the sinking of her heart said: 'I must brave her!'

'In that case, I will take my leave of you here, Miss Middleton.'

She gave him her hand. 'Why is Mrs. Mountstuart at the station to-day?'

'I suppose she has driven to meet one of the guests for her dinner-party. Professor Crooklyn was promised to your father, and he may be coming by the down-train.'

'Go back to the Hall!' exclaimed Clara. 'How can I? I have no more endurance left in me. If I had some support!—if it were the sense of secretly doing wrong, it might help me through. I am in a web. I cannot do right, whatever I do. There is only the thought

of saving Crossjay. Yes, and sparing papa.—Good-bye,
Mr. Whitford. I shall remember your kindness gratefully. I cannot go back.'

'You will not?' said he, tempting her to hesitate.

'No.'

'But if you are seen by Mrs. Mountstuart, you must go
back. I'll do my best to take her away. Should she
see you, you must patch up a story and apply to her for
a lift. That, I think, is imperative.'

'Not to my mind,' said Clara.

He bowed hurriedly and withdrew. After her confession, peculiar to her, of possibly finding sustainment in
secretly doing wrong, her flying or remaining seemed to
him a choice of evils: and whilst she stood in bewildered
speculation on his reason for pursuing her—which was
not evident—he remembered the special fear inciting
him, and so far did her justice as to have at himself on
that subject. He had done something perhaps to save
her from a cold: such was his only consolatory thought.
He had also behaved like a man of honour, taking no
personal advantage of her situation; but to reflect on
it recalled his astonishing dryness. The strict man of
honour plays a part that he should not reflect on till
about the fall of the curtain, otherwise he will be likely
sometimes to feel the shiver of foolishness at his good
conduct.

CHAPTER XXVIII

The Return

Posted in observation at a corner of the window, Clara
saw Vernon cross the road to Mrs. Mountstuart Jenkinson's carriage, transformed to the leanest pattern of himself by narrowed shoulders and raised coat-collar. He
had such an air of saying, 'Tom's a-cold,'*that her skin
crept in sympathy.

Presently he left the carriage and went into the station:
a bell had rung. Was it her train? He approved her
going, for he was employed in assisting her to go: a

proceeding at variance with many things he had said, but he was as full of contradiction to-day as women are accused of being. The train came up. She trembled: no signal had appeared, and Vernon must have deceived her.

He returned; he entered the carriage, and the wheels were soon in motion. Immediately thereupon, Flitch's fly drove past, containing Colonel De Craye.

Vernon could not but have perceived him!

But what was it that had brought the colonel to this place? The pressure of Vernon's mind was on her and foiled her efforts to assert her perfect innocence, though she knew she had done nothing to allure the colonel hither. Excepting Willoughby, Colonel De Craye was the last person she would have wished to encounter.

She had now a dread of hearing the bell which would tell her that Vernon had not deceived her, and that she was out of his hands, in the hands of some one else.

She bit at her glove; she glanced at the concentrated eyes of the publican's family portraits, all looking as one; she noticed the empty tumbler, and went round to it and touched it, and the silly spoon in it.

A little yielding to desperation shoots us to strange distances!

Vernon had asked her whether she was alone. Connecting that inquiry, singular in itself, and singular in his manner of putting it, with the glass of burning liquid, she repeated: 'He must have seen Colonel De Craye!' and she stared at the empty glass, as at something that witnessed to something: for Vernon was not your supple cavalier assiduously on the smirk to pin a gallantry to commonplaces. But all the doors are not open in a young lady's consciousness, quick of nature though she may be: some are locked and keyless, some will not open to the key, some are defended by ghosts inside. She could not have said what the something witnessed to. If we by chance know more, we have still no right to make it more prominent than it was with her. And the smell of the glass was odious; it disgraced her. She had an impulse to pocket the spoon for a memento, to show it to grandchildren for a warning. Even the prelude to the morality to be uttered on the occasion sprang to her lips: 'Here, my dears, is a spoon you would be ashamed to use in your tea-cups, yet it was of more value to me at one period of my life than silver and gold in pointing out,' etc.: the conclusion was hazy, like the conception; she had her idea.

And in this mood she ran downstairs and met Colonel De Craye on the station steps.

The bright illumination of his face was that of the confident man confirmed in a risky guess in the crisis of doubt and dispute.

'Miss Middleton!' his joyful surprise predominated: the pride of an accurate forecast, adding: 'I am not too late to be of service?'

She thanked him for the offer.

'Have you dismissed the fly, Colonel De Craye?'

'I have just been getting change to pay Mr. Flitch. He passed me on the road. He is interwound with our fates, to a certainty. I had only to jump in; I knew it, and rolled along like a magician commanding a genie.'

'Have I been . . . ?'

'Not seriously, nobody doubts your being under shelter. You will allow me to protect you? My time is yours.'

'I was thinking of a running visit to my friend Miss Darleton.'

'May I venture? I had the fancy that you wished to see Miss Darleton to-day. You cannot make the journey unescorted.'

'Please retain the fly. Where is Willoughby?'

'He is in jack-boots. But may I not, Miss Middleton? I shall never be forgiven, if you refuse me.'

'There has been searching for me?'

'Some hallooing. But why am I rejected? Besides I don't require the fly; I shall walk if I am banished. Flitch is a wonderful conjuror, but the virtue is out of him for the next four and twenty hours. And it will be an opportunity to me to make my bow to Miss Darleton!'

'She is rigorous on the conventionalities, Colonel De Craye.'

'I'll appear before her as an ignoramus or a rebel, whichever she likes best to take in leading strings. I remember her. I was greatly struck by her.'

'Upon recollection!'

'Memory didn't happen to be handy at the first mention of the lady's name. As the general said of his ammunition and transport, there's the army!—but it was leagues in the rear. Like the footman who went to sleep after smelling fire in the house, I was thinking of other things. It will serve me right to be forgotten— if I am. I've a curiosity to know: a remainder of my coxcombry. Not that exactly: a wish to see the impression I made on your friend.—None at all? But any pebble casts a ripple.'

'That is hardly an impression,' said Clara, pacifying her irresoluteness with this light talk.

'The utmost to be hoped for by men like me! I have your permission?—one minute—I will get my ticket.'

'Do not,' said Clara.

'Your man-servant entreats you!'

She signified a decided negative with the head, but her eyes were dreamy. She breathed deep: this thing done would cut the cord. Her sensation of languor swept over her.

De Craye took a stride. He was accosted by one of the railway-porters. Flitch's fly was in request for a gentleman. A portly old gentleman bothered about luggage appeared on the landing.

'The gentleman can have it,' said De Craye, handing Flitch his money.

'Open the door,' Clara said to Flitch.

He tugged at the handle with enthusiasm. The door was open: she stepped in.

'Then, mount the box and I'll jump up beside you,' De Craye called out, after the passion of regretful astonishment had melted from his features.

Clara directed him to the seat fronting her; he protested indifference to the wet; she kept the door unshut.

His temper would have preferred to buffet the angry weather. The invitation was too sweet.

She heard now the bell of her own train. Driving beside the railway embankment she met the train: it was eighteen minutes late, by her watch. And why, when it flung up its whale-spouts of steam, she was not journeying in it she could not tell. She had acted of her free will: that she could say. Vernon had not induced her to remain; assuredly her present companion had not; and her whole heart was for flight: yet she was driving back to the Hall, not devoid of calmness. She speculated on the circumstance enough to think herself incomprehensible, and there left it, intent on the scene to come with Willoughby.

'I must choose a better day for London,' she remarked.

De Craye bowed, but did not remove his eyes from her.

'Miss Middleton, you do not trust me.'

She answered: 'Say in what way. It seems to me that I do.'

'I may speak?'

'If it depends on my authority.'

'Fully?'

'Whatever you have to say. Let me stipulate, be not very grave. I want cheering in wet weather.'

'Miss Middleton, Flitch is charioteer once more. Think of it. There's a tide that carries him perpetually to the place whence he was cast forth, and a thread that ties us to him in continuity. I have not the honour to be a friend of long standing: one ventures on one's devotion: it dates from the first moment of my seeing you. Flitch is to blame, if any one. Perhaps the spell would be broken, were he reinstated in his ancient office.'

'Perhaps it would,' said Clara, not with her best of smiles. Willoughby's pride of relentlessness appeared to her to be receiving a blow by rebound, and that seemed high justice.

'I am afraid you were right; the poor fellow has no chance,' De Craye pursued. He paused, as for decorum in the presence of misfortune, and laughed sparklingly: 'Unless I engage him, or pretend to! I verily believe that Flitch's melancholy person on the skirts of the Hall completes the picture of the Eden within.—Why will you not put some trust in me, Miss Middleton?'

'But why should you not pretend to engage him, then, Colonel De Craye?'

'We'll plot it, if you like. Can you trust me for that?'

'For any act of disinterested kindness, I am sure.'

'You mean it?'

'Without reserve. You could talk publicly of taking him to London.'

'Miss Middleton, just now you were going. My arrival changed your mind. You distrust me: and ought I to wonder? The wonder would be all the other way. You have not had the sort of report of me which would persuade you to confide, even in a case of extremity. I guessed you were going. Do you ask me, how? I cannot say. Through what they call sympathy, and that's inexplicable. There's natural sympathy, natural antipathy. People have to live together to discover how deep it is!'

Clara breathed her dumb admission of this truth.

The fly jolted and threatened to lurch.

'Flitch! my dear man!' the colonel gave a murmuring remonstrance; 'for,' said he to Clara, whom his apostrophe to Flitch had set smiling, 'we're not safe with him, however we make believe, and he'll be jerking the heart out of me before he has done.—But if two of us have not the misfortune to be united when they come to the discovery, there's hope. That is, if one has courage, and the other has wisdom. Otherwise they may go to the yoke in spite of themselves. The great enemy is Pride, who has them both in a coach and drives them to the fatal door, and the only thing to do is to knock him off his box while there's a minute to spare. And as there's no pride like the pride of possession, the deadliest wound to him is to make that doubtful. Pride won't be taught wisdom in any other fashion. But one must have the courage to do it!'

De Craye trifled with the window-sash, to give his words time to sink in solution.

Who but Willoughby stood for Pride? And who,
swayed by languor, had dreamed of a method that would
be surest and swiftest to teach him the wisdom of surrendering her?

'You know, Miss Middleton, I study character,' said
the colonel.

'I see that you do,' she answered.

'You intend to return?'

'Oh! decidedly.'

'The day is unfavourable for travelling, I must say.'

'It is.'

'You may count on my discretion in the fullest degree.
I throw myself on your generosity when I assure you
that it was not my design to surprise a secret. I guessed
the station, and went there, to put myself at your
disposal.'

'Did you,' said Clara, reddening slightly, 'chance to
see Mrs. Mountstuart Jenkinson's carriage pass you
when you drove up to the station?'

De Craye had passed a carriage. 'I did not see the
lady. She was in it?'

'Yes. And therefore it is better to put discretion on
one side: we may be certain she saw you.'

'But not you, Miss Middleton?'

'I prefer to think that I am seen. I have a description of courage, Colonel De Craye, when it is forced
on me.'

'I have not suspected the reverse. Courage wants
training, as well as other fine capacities. Mine is often
rusty and rheumatic.'

'I cannot hear of concealment or plotting.'

'Except, pray, to advance the cause of poor Flitch!'

'He shall be excepted.'

The colonel screwed his head round for a glance at his
coachman's back.

'Perfectly guaranteed to-day!' he said of Flitch's look
of solidity. 'The convulsion of the elements appears to
sober our friend; he is only dangerous in calms. Five
minutes will bring us to the park-gates.'

Clara leaned forward to gaze at the hedgeways in the

neighbourhood of the Hall, strangely renewing their familiarity with her. Both in thought and sensation she was like a flower beaten to earth, and she thanked her feminine mask for not showing how nerveless and languid she was. She could have accused Vernon of a treacherous cunning for imposing it on her free will to decide her fate.

Involuntarily she sighed.

'There is a train at three,' said De Craye, with splendid promptitude.

'Yes, and one at five. We dine with Mrs. Mountstuart to-night. And I have a passion for solitude! I think I was never intended for obligations. The moment I am bound I begin to brood on freedom.'

'Ladies who say that, Miss Middleton . . .!'

'What of them?'

'They're feeling too much alone.'

She could not combat the remark: by her self-assurance that she had the principle of faithfulness, she acknowledged to herself the truth of it:—there is no freedom for the weak! Vernon had said that once. She tried to resist the weight of it, and her sheer inability precipitated her into a sense of pitiful dependence.

Half an hour earlier it would have been a perilous condition to be traversing in the society of a closely-scanning reader of fair faces. Circumstances had changed. They were at the gates of the park.

'Shall I leave you?' said De Craye.

'Why should you?' she replied.

He bent to her gracefully.

The mild subservience flattered Clara's languor. He had not compelled her to be watchful on her guard, and she was unaware that he passed it when she acquiesced to his observation: 'An anticipatory story is a trap to the teller.'

'It is,' she said. She had been thinking as much.

He threw up his head to consult the brain comically with a dozen little blinks.

'No, you are right, Miss Middleton, inventing beforehand never prospers; 'tis a way to trip our own cleverness.

Truth and mother-wit are the best counsellors: and
as you are the former, I'll try to act up to the character
you assign me.'

Some tangle, more prospective than present, seemed to
be about her as she reflected. But her intention being to
speak to Willoughby without subterfuge, she was grateful to her companion for not tempting her to swerve.
No one could doubt his talent for elegant fibbing, and she
was in the humour both to admire and adopt the art, so
she was glad to be rescued from herself. How mother-
wit was to second truth, she did not inquire, and as she
did not happen to be thinking of Crossjay, she was not
troubled by having to consider how truth and his tale
of the morning would be likely to harmonize.

Driving down the park she had full occupation in questioning whether her return would be pleasing to Vernon,
who was the virtual cause of it, though he had done so
little to promote it: so little that she really doubted his
pleasure in seeing her return.

CHAPTER XXIX

In which the Sensitiveness of Sir Willoughby is explained: and he receives much Instruction

THE Hall-clock over the stables was then striking twelve.
It was the hour for her flight to be made known, and Clara
sat in a turmoil of dim apprehension that prepared her
nervous frame for a painful blush on her being asked by
Colonel De Craye whether she had set her watch correctly. He must, she understood, have seen through her
at the breakfast-table: and was she not cruelly indebted
to him for her evasion of Willoughby? Such perspicacity
of vision distressed and frightened her; at the same time
she was obliged to acknowledge that he had not presumed on it. Her dignity was in no way the worse for
him. But it had been at a man's mercy, and there was
the affliction.

She jumped from the fly as if she were leaving danger
behind. She could at the moment have greeted Wil-

loughby with a conventionally friendly smile. The doors were thrown open and young Crossjay flew out to her. He hung and danced on her hand, pressed the hand to his mouth, hardly believing that he saw and touched her, and in a lingo of dashes and asterisks related how Sir Willoughby had found him under the boathouse eaves and pumped him, and had been sent off to Hoppner's farm, where there was a sick child, and on along the road to a labourer's cottage: 'For I said you're so kind to poor people, Miss Middleton; that's true, now that *is* true. And I said you wouldn't have me with you for fear of contagion!' This was what she had feared.

'Every crack and bang in a boy's vocabulary?' remarked the colonel, listening to him after he had paid Flitch.

The latter touched his hat till he had drawn attention to himself, when he exclaimed with rosy melancholy: 'Ah! my lady, ah! colonel, if ever I lives to drink some of the old port wine in the old Hall at Christmastide!' Their healths would on that occasion be drunk, it was implied. He threw up his eyes at the windows, humped his body and drove away.

'Then Mr. Whitford has not come back?' said Clara to Crossjay.

'No, Miss Middleton. Sir Willoughby has, and he's upstairs in his room dressing.'

'Have you seen Barclay?'

'She has just gone into the laboratory. I told her Sir Willoughby wasn't there.'

'Tell me, Crossjay, had she a letter?'

'She had something.'

'Run: say I am here; I want the letter, it is mine.'

Crossjay sprang away and plunged into the arms of Sir Willoughby.

'One has to catch the fellow like a football'; exclaimed the injured gentleman, doubled across the boy and holding him fast, that he might have an object to trifle with, to give himself countenance: he needed it. 'Clara, you have not been exposed to the weather?'

'Hardly at all.'

'I rejoice. You found shelter?'

'Yes.'

'In one of the cottages?'

'Not in a cottage; but I was perfectly sheltered. Colonel De Craye passed a fly before he met me . . .'

'Flitch again!' ejaculated the colonel.

'Yes, you have luck, you have luck,' Willoughby addressed him, still clutching Crossjay and treating his tugs to get loose as an invitation to caresses. But the foil barely concealed his livid perturbation.

'Stay by me, sir'; he said at last sharply to Crossjay, and Clara touched the boy's shoulder in admonishment of him.

She turned to the colonel as they stepped into the hall: 'I have not thanked you, Colonel De Craye.' She dropped her voice to its lowest: 'A letter in my handwriting in the laboratory.'

Crossjay cried aloud with pain.

'I have you!' Willoughby rallied him with a laugh not unlike the squeak of his victim.

'You squeeze awfully hard, sir!'

'Why, you milksop!'

'Am I! But I want to get a book.'

'Where is the book?'

'In the laboratory.'

Colonel De Craye, sauntering by the laboratory door, sang out: 'I'll fetch you your book. What is it? EARLY NAVIGATORS? INFANT HYMNS? I think my cigar-case is in here.'

'Barclay speaks of a letter for me,' Willoughby said to Clara, 'marked to be delivered to me at noon!'

'In case of my not being back earlier: it was written to avert anxiety,' she replied.

'You are very good.'

'Oh! good! Call me anything but good. Here are the ladies. Dear ladies!' Clara swam to meet them as they issued from a morning-room into the hall, and interjections reigned for a couple of minutes.

Willoughby relinquished his grasp of Crossjay, who darted instantaneously at an angle to the laboratory, whither he followed, and he encountered De Craye coming out, but passed him in silence.

Crossjay was rangeing and peering all over the room. Willoughby went to his desk and the battery-table and the mantelpiece. He found no letter. Barclay had undoubtedly informed him that she had left a letter for him in the laboratory, by order of her mistress after breakfast.

He hurried out and ran upstairs in time to see De Craye and Barclay breaking a conference.

He beckoned to her. The maid lengthened her upper lip and beat her dress down smooth: signs of the apprehension of a crisis and of the getting ready for action.

'My mistress's bell has just rung, Sir Willoughby.'

'You had a letter for me.'

'I said . . .'

'You said when I met you at the foot of the stairs that you had left a letter for me in the laboratory.'

'It is lying on my mistress's toilet-table.'

'Get it.'

Barclay swept round with another of her demure grimaces. It was apparently necessary with her that she should talk to herself in this public manner.

Willoughby waited for her; but there was no reappearance of the maid.

Struck by the ridicule of his posture of expectation and of his whole behaviour, he went to his bedroom suite, shut himself in and paced the chambers, amazed at the creature he had become. Agitated like the commonest of wretches, destitute of self-control, not able to preserve a decent mask, he, accustomed to inflict these emotions and tremours upon others, was at once the puppet and dupe of an intriguing girl. His very stature seemed lessened. The glass did not say so, but the shrunken heart within him did, and wailfully too. Her compunction—'Call me anything but good'—coming after her return to the Hall beside De Craye, and after the visible passage of a secret between them in his presence, was a confession: it blew at him with the fury of a furnace-blast in his face. Egoist agony wrung the outcry from him that dupery is a more blest condition. He desired to be deceived.

He could desire such a thing only in a temporary transport; for above all he desired that no one should know of
his being deceived: and were he a dupe the deceiver
would know it, and her accomplice would know it, and
the world would soon know of it: that world against
whose tongue he stood defenceless. Within the shadow
of his presence he compressed opinion, as a strong frost
binds the springs of earth, but beyond it his shivering
sensitiveness ran about in dread of a stripping in a wintry
atmosphere. This was the ground of his hatred of the
world: it was an appalling fear on behalf of his naked
eidolon, the tender infant Self swaddled in his name
before the world, for which he felt as the most highly
civilized of men alone can feel, and which it was impossible for him to stretch out hands to protect. There the
poor little loveable creature ran for any mouth to blow
on; and frost-nipped and bruised, it cried to him, and
he was of no avail! Must we not detest a world that so
treats us? We loathe it the more, by the measure of our
contempt for them, when we have made the people
within the shadow-circle of our person slavish.

And he had been once a young Prince in popularity:
the world had been his possession. Clara's treatment of
him was a robbery of land and subjects. His grander
dream had been a marriage with a lady of so glowing a
fame for beauty and attachment to her lord that the
world perforce must take her for witness to merits which
would silence detraction and almost, not quite (it was
undesireable), extinguish envy. But for the nature of
women his dream would have been realized. He could
not bring himself to denounce Fortune. It had cost him a
grievous pang to tell Horace De Craye he was lucky; he
had been educated in the belief that Fortune specially
prized and cherished little Willoughby: hence of necessity his maledictions fell upon women, or he would have
forfeited the last blanket of a dream warm as poets revel in.

But if Clara deceived him, he inspired her with timidity. There was matter in that to make him wish to be
deceived. She had not looked him much in the face: she
had not crossed his eyes: she had looked deliberately

downward, keeping her head up, to preserve an exterior pride. The attitude had its bewitchingness: the girl's physical pride of stature scorning to bend under a load of conscious guilt, had a certain black-angel beauty for which he felt a hugging hatred: and according to his policy when these fits of amorous meditation seized him, he burst from the present one in the mood of his more favourable conception of Clara, and sought her out.

The quality of the mood of hugging hatred is, that if you are disallowed the hug, you do not hate the fiercer.

Contrariwise the prescription of a decorous distance of two feet ten inches, which is by measurement the delimitation exacted of a rightly respectful deportment, has this miraculous effect on the great creature man, or often it has: that his peculiar hatred returns to the reluctant admiration begetting it, and his passion for the hug falls prostrate as one of the Faithful before the shrine: he is reduced to worship by fasting.

(For these mysteries, consult the sublime chapter in the GREAT BOOK, the Seventy-First on LOVE, wherein Nothing is written, but the Reader receives a Lanthorn, a Powder-cask and a Pick-axe, and therewith pursues his yellow-dusking path across the rubble of preceding excavators in the solitary quarry: a yet more instructive passage than the over-scrawled Seventieth, or French Section, whence the chapter opens, and where hitherto the polite world has halted.)

The hurry of the hero is on us, we have no time to spare for mining-works: he hurried to catch her alone, to wreak his tortures on her in a bitter semblance of bodily worship, and satiated, then comfortably to spurn. He found her protected by Barclay on the stairs.

'That letter for me?' he said.

'I think I told you, Willoughby, there was a letter I left with Barclay to reassure you in case of my not returning early,' said Clara. 'It was unnecessary for her to deliver it.'

'Indeed? But any letter, any writing, of yours, and from you to me! You have it still?'

'No, I have destroyed it.'

'That was wrong.'

'It could not have given you pleasure.'

'My dear Clara, one line from you!'

'There were but three.'

Barclay stood sucking her lips. A maid in the secrets of her mistress is a purchaseable maid, for if she will take a bribe with her right hand she will with her left; all that has to be calculated is the nature and amount of the bribe: such was the speculation indulged by Sir Willoughby, and he shrank from the thought and declined to know more than that he was on a volcanic hillside where a thin crust quaked over lava. This was a new condition with him, representing Clara's gain in their combat. Clara did not fear his questioning so much as he feared her candour.

Mutually timid, they were of course formally polite, and no plain-speaking could have told one another more distinctly that each was defensive. Clara stood pledged to the fib; packed, sealed and posted; and he had only to ask to have it, supposing that he asked with a voice not exactly peremptory.

She said in her heart: 'It is your fault: you are relentless, and you would ruin Crossjay to punish him for devoting himself to me, like the poor thoughtless boy he is! and so I am bound in honour to do my utmost for him.'

The reciprocal devotedness moreover served two purposes: it preserved her from brooding on the humiliation of her lame flight and flutter back, and it quieted her mind in regard to the precipitate intimacy of her relations with Colonel De Craye. Willoughby's boast of his implacable character was to blame. She was at war with him, and she was compelled to put the case in that light. Crossjay must be shielded from one who could not spare an offender, so Colonel De Craye quite naturally was called on for his help, and the colonel's dexterous aid appeared to her more admirable than alarming.

Nevertheless she would not have answered a direct question falsely. She was for the fib, but not the lie; at a word she could be disdainful of subterfuges. Her look said that. Willoughby perceived it. She had written him a letter of three lines: 'There were but three': and she had destroyed the letter. Something perchance was repented by her? Then she had done him an injury! Between his wrath at the suspicion of an injury, and the prudence enjoined by his abject coveting of her, he consented to be fooled for the sake of vengeance, and something besides.

'Well! here you are, safe: I have you!' said he, with courtly exultation: 'and that is better than your handwriting. I have been all over the country after you.'

'Why did you? We are not in a barbarous land,' said Clara.

'Crossjay talks of your visiting a sick child, my love: —you have changed your dress?'

'You see.'

'The boy declared you were going to that farm of Hoppner's and some cottage. I met at my gates a tramping vagabond who swore to seeing you and the boy in a totally contrary direction.'

'Did you give him money?'

'I fancy so.'

'Then he was paid for having seen me.'

Willoughby tossed his head: it might be as she suggested; beggars are liars.

'But who sheltered you, my dear Clara? You had not been heard of at Hoppner's.'

'The people have been indemnified for their pains. To pay them more would be to spoil them. You disperse money too liberally. There was no fever in the place. Who could have anticipated such a downpour! I want to consult Miss Dale on the important theme of a dress I think of wearing at Mrs. Mountstuart's to-night.'

'Do. She is unerring.'

'She has excellent taste.'

'She dresses very simply herself.'

'But it becomes her. She is one of the few women whom I feel I could not improve with a touch.'

'She has judgement.'

He reflected and repeated his encomium.

The shadow of a dimple in Clara's cheek awakened him to the idea that she had struck him somewhere: and certainly he would never again be able to put up the fiction of her jealousy of Laetitia. What, then, could be this girl's motive for praying to be released? The interrogation humbled him: he fled from the answer.

Willoughby went in search of De Craye. That sprightly intriguer had no intention to let himself be caught solus. He was undiscoverable until the assembly sounded, when Clara dropped a public word or two, and he spoke in perfect harmony with her. After that, he gave his company to Willoughby for an hour at billiards, and was well beaten.

The announcement of a visit of Mrs. Mountstuart Jenkinson took the gentlemen to the drawing-room, rather suspecting that something stood in the way of her dinner-party. As it happened, she was lamenting only the loss of one of the jewels of the party: to wit, the great Professor Crooklyn, invited to meet Dr. Middleton at her table; and she related how she had driven to the station by appointment, the professor being notoriously a bother-headed traveller: as was shown by the fact that he had missed his train in town, for he had not arrived; nothing had been seen of him. She cited Vernon Whitford for her authority that the train had been inspected and the platform scoured to find the professor.

'And so,' said she, 'I drove home your Green Man to dry him; he was wet through and chattering; the man was exactly like a skeleton wrapped in a sponge, and if he escapes a cold he must be as invulnerable as he boasts himself. These athletes are terrible boasters.'

'They climb their Alps to crow,' said Clara, excited by her apprehension that Mrs. Mountstuart would speak of having seen the colonel near the station.

There was a laugh, and Colonel De Craye laughed loudly as it flashed through him that a quick-witted impressionable girl like Miss Middleton must, before his arrival at the Hall, have speculated on such obdurate clay as Vernon Whitford was, with humourous despair at his uselessness to her. Glancing round, he saw Vernon standing fixed in a stare at the young lady.

'You heard that, Whitford?' he said, and Clara's face betokening an extremer contrition than he thought was demanded, the colonel rallied the Alpine climber for striving to be the tallest of them—Signor Excelsior!—and described these conquerors of mountains pancaked on the rocks in desperate embraces, bleached here, burnt there, barked all over, all to be able to say they had been up 'so high'—had conquered another mountain! He was extravagantly funny and self-satisfied: a conqueror of the sex having such different rewards of enterprise.

Vernon recovered in time to accept the absurdities heaped on him.

'Climbing peaks won't compare with hunting a wriggler,' said he.

His allusion to the incessant pursuit of young Crossjay to pin him to lessons was appreciated.

Clara felt the thread of the look he cast from herself to Colonel De Craye. She was helpless, if he chose to misjudge her. Colonel De Craye did not!

Crossjay had the misfortune to enter the drawing-room while Mrs. Mountstuart was compassionating Vernon for his ducking in pursuit of the wriggler; which De Craye likened to 'going through the river after his eel': and immediately there was a cross-questioning of the boy between De Craye and Willoughby on the subject of his latest truancy, each gentleman trying to run him down in a palpable fib. They were succeeding brilliantly when Vernon put a stop to it by marching him off to hard labour. Mrs. Mountstuart was led away to inspect the beautiful porcelain service, the present of Lady Busshe. 'Porcelain again!' she said to Willoughby, and would have signalled to the 'dainty rogue' to come with them, had not Clara been leaning over to Laetitia, talking to her in an attitude too graceful to be disturbed. She called his attention to it, slightly wondering at his impatience. She departed to meet an afternoon train on the chance that it would land the professor. 'But tell Dr. Middleton,' said she, 'I fear I shall have no one worthy of him! And,' she added to Willoughby, as she walked out to her carriage, 'I shall expect you to do the great-gunnery talk at table.'

'Miss Dale keeps it up with him best,' said Willoughby.

'She does everything best! But my dinner-table is involved, and I cannot count on a young woman to talk across it. I would hire a lion of a menagerie, if one were handy, rather than have a famous scholar at my table unsupported by another famous scholar. Dr. Middleton would ride down a duke when the wine is in him. He will terrify my poor flock. The truth is, we can't leaven him: I foresee undigested lumps of conversation, unless you devote yourself.'

'I will devote myself,' said Willoughby.

'I can calculate on Colonel De Craye and our porcelain beauty for any quantity of sparkles, if you promise that. They play well together. You are not to be one of the Gods to-night, but a kind of Jupiter's cupbearer;— Juno's, if you like:'and Lady Busshe and Lady Culmer, and all your admirers shall know subsequently what you have done. You see my alarm. I certainly did not rank Professor Crooklyn among the possibly faithless, or I never would have ventured on Dr. Middleton at my table. My dinner-parties have hitherto been all successes. Naturally I feel the greater anxiety about this one. For a single failure is all the more conspicuous. The exception is everlastingly cited! It is not so much what people say, but my own sentiments. I hate to fail. However, if you are true, we may do.'

'Whenever the great gun goes off I will fall on my face, madam!'

'Something of that sort,' said the dame, smiling, and leaving him to reflect on the egoism of women. For the sake of her dinner-party he was to be a cipher in attendance on Dr. Middleton, and Clara and De Craye were to be encouraged in sparkling together! And it happened that he particularly wished to shine. The admiration of his county made him believe he had a flavour in general society that was not yet distinguished by his bride, and he was to relinquish his opportunity in order to please

Mrs. Mountstuart! Had she been in the pay of his rival she could not have stipulated for more.

He remembered young Crossjay's instant quietude, after struggling in his grasp, when Clara laid her hand on the boy: and from that infinitesimal circumstance he deduced the boy's perception of a differing between himself and his bride, and a transfer of Crossjay's allegiance from him to her. She shone; she had the gift of female beauty; the boy was attracted to it. That boy must be made to feel his treason. But the point of the cogitation was, that similarly were Clara to see her affianced shining, as shine he could when lit up by admirers, there was the probability that the sensation of her littleness would animate her to take aim at him once more. And then was the time for her chastisement.

A visit to Dr. Middleton in the library satisfied him that she had not been renewing her entreaties to leave Patterne. No, the miserable coquette had now her pastime and was content to stay. Deceit was in the air: he heard the sound of the shuttle of deceit without seeing it; but on the whole, mindful of what he had dreaded during the hours of her absence, he was rather flattered, witheringly flattered. What was it that he had dreaded? Nothing less than news of her running away. Indeed a silly fancy, a lover's fancy! yet it had led him so far as to suspect, after parting with De Craye in the rain, that his friend and his bride were in collusion, and that he should not see them again. He had actually shouted on the rainy road the theatric call 'Fooled!' one of the stage-cries which are cries of nature! particularly the cry of nature with men who have driven other men to the cry.

Constantia Durham had taught him to believe women capable of explosions of treason at half a minute's notice. And strangely, to prove that women are all of a pack, she had worn exactly the same placidity of countenance just before she fled, as Clara yesterday and to-day; no nervousness, no flushes, no twitches of the brows, but smoothness, ease of manner—an elegant sisterliness, one might almost say: as if the creature had found a midway and border-line to walk on between cruelty and kindness,

and between repulsion and attraction; so that up to the
verge of her breath she did forcefully attract, repelling at
one foot's length with her armour of chill serenity. Not
with any disdain, with no passion: such a line as she
herself pursued she indicated to him on a neighbouring
parallel. The passion in her was like a place of waves
evaporated to a crust of salt. Clara's resemblance to
Constantia in this instance was ominous. For him whose
tragic privilege it had been to fold each of them in his
arms, and weigh on their eyelids, and see the dissolving
mist-deeps in their eyes, it was horrible. Once more the
comparison overcame him. Constantia he could condemn for revealing too much to his manly sight: she had
met him almost half way: well, that was complimentary
and sanguine: but her frankness was a baldness often
rendering it doubtful which of the two, lady or gentleman,
was the object of the chase—an extreme perplexity to his
manly soul. Now Clara's inner spirit was shyer, shy as a
doe down those rose-tinged abysses; she allured both the
lover and the hunter; forests of heavenliness were in her
flitting eyes. Here the difference of these fair women
made his present fate an intolerable anguish. For if
Constantia was like certain of the ladies whom he had
rendered unhappy, triumphed over, as it is queerly
called, Clara was not. Her individuality as a woman
was a thing he had to bow to. It was impossible to roll
her up in the sex and bestow a kick on the travelling
bundle. Hence he loved her, though she hurt him.
Hence his wretchedness, and but for the hearty sincerity
of his faith in the Self he loved likewise and more, he
would have been hangdog abject.

As for De Craye, Willoughby recollected his own exploits too proudly to put his trust in a man. That fatal
conjunction of temper and policy had utterly thrown him
off his guard, or he would not have trusted the fellow
even in the first hour of his acquaintance with Clara.
But he had wished her to be amused while he wove his
plans to retain her at the Hall:—partly imagining that
she would weary of his neglect: vile delusion! In truth
he should have given festivities, he should have been the

sun of a circle, and have revealed himself to her in his more dazzling form. He went near to calling himself foolish after the tremendous reverberation of 'Fooled!' had ceased to shake him.

How behave? It slapped the poor gentleman's pride in the face to ask. A private talk with her would rouse her to renew her supplications. He saw them flickering behind the girl's transparent calmness. That calmness really drew its dead ivory hue from the suppression of them: something as much he guessed; and he was not sure either of his temper or his policy if he should hear her repeat her profane request.

An impulse to address himself to Vernon and discourse with him jocularly on the childish whim of a young lady, moved perhaps by some whiff of jealousy, to shun the yoke, was checked. He had always taken so superior a pose with Vernon that he could not abandon it for a moment: on such a subject too! Besides Vernon was one of your men who entertain the ideas about women of fellows that have never conquered one: or only one, we will say in his case, knowing his secret history; and that one no flag to boast of. Densely ignorant of the sex, his nincompoopish idealizations, at other times preposterous, would now be annoying. He would probably presume on Clara's inconceivable lapse of dignity to read his master a lecture: he was quite equal to a philippic upon woman's rights.* This man had not been afraid to say that he talked common sense to women. He was an example of the consequence!

Another result was, that Vernon did not talk sense to men. Willoughby's wrath at Clara's exposure of him to his cousin dismissed the proposal of a colloquy so likely to sting his temper, and so certain to diminish his loftiness. Unwilling to speak to anybody, he was isolated, yet consciously begirt by the mysterious action going on all over the house, from Clara and De Craye to Laetitia and young Crossjay, down to Barclay the maid. His blind sensitiveness felt as we may suppose a spider to feel when plucked from his own web and set in the centre of another's. Laetitia looked her share in the mystery. A

burden was on her eyelashes. How she could have come
to any suspicion of the circumstances, he was unable to
imagine. Her intense personal sympathy, it might be:
he thought so with some gentle pity for her—of the
paternal pat-back order of pity. She adored him, by
decree of Venus; and the Goddess had not decreed that
he should find consolation in adoring her. Nor could the
temptings of prudent counsel in his head induce him to
run the risk of such a total turnover as the incurring of
Laetitia's pity of himself by confiding in her. He checked
that impulse also, and more sovereignly. For him to be
pitied by Laetitia seemed an upsetting of the scheme of
Providence. Providence, otherwise the discriminating
dispensation of the good things of life, had made him the
beacon, her the bird: she was really the last person to
whom he could unbosom. The idea of his being in a
position that suggested his doing so, thrilled him with fits
of rage; and it appalled him. There appeared to be
another Power. The same which had humiliated him
once was menacing him anew. For it could not be Providence, whose favourite he had ever been. We must have
a couple of Powers to account for discomfort when
Egoism is the kernel of our religion. Benevolence had
singled him for uncommon benefits: malignancy was at
work to rob him of them. And you think well of the
world, do you!

Of necessity he associated Clara with the darker Power
pointing the knife at the quick of his pride. Still, he
would have raised her weeping: he would have stanched
her wounds bleeding: he had an infinite thirst for her
misery, that he might ease his heart of its charitable love.
Or let her commit herself, and be cast off! Only she must
commit herself glaringly, and be cast off by the world as
well. Contemplating her in the form of a discarded weed,
he had a catch of the breath: she was fair. He implored
his Power that Horace De Craye might not be the man!
Why any man? An illness, fever, fire, runaway horses,
personal disfigurement, a laming, were sufficient. And
then a formal and noble offer on his part to keep to the
engagement with the unhappy wreck: yes, and to lead

the limping thing to the altar, if she insisted. His imagination conceived it, and the world's applause besides.

Nausea, together with a sense of duty to his line, extinguished that loathsome prospect of a mate, though without obscuring his chivalrous devotion to his gentleman's word of honour, which remained in his mind to compliment him permanently.

On the whole, he could reasonably hope to subdue her to admiration. He drank a glass of champagne at his dressing; an unaccustomed act, but, as he remarked casually to his man Pollington, for whom the rest of the bottle was left, he had taken no horse-exercise that day.

Having to speak to Vernon on business, he went to the schoolroom, where he discovered Clara, beautiful in full evening attire, with her arm on young Crossjay's shoulder, and heard that the hard taskmaster had abjured Mrs. Mountstuart's party, and had already excused himself, intending to keep Crossjay to the grindstone. Willoughby was for the boy, as usual, and more sparklingly than usual. Clara looked at him in some surprise. He rallied Vernon with great zest, quite silencing him when he said: 'I bear witness that the fellow was here at his regular hour for lessons, and were you?' He laid his hand on Crossjay, touching Clara's hand.

'You will remember what I told you, Crossjay,' said she, rising from the seat gracefully. 'It is my command.'

Crossjay frowned and puffed.

'But only if I'm questioned,' he said.

'Certainly,' she replied.

'Then I question the rascal,' said Willoughby, causing a start. 'What, sir, is your opinion of Miss Middleton in her robe of state this evening?'

'Now, the truth, Crossjay!' Clara held up a finger; and the boy could see she was playing at archness, but for Willoughby it was earnest. 'The truth is not likely to offend you or me either,' he murmured to her.

'I wish him never, never, on any excuse, to speak anything else.'

'I always did think her a Beauty,' Crossjay growled. He hated the having to say it.

'There!' exclaimed Sir Willoughby, and bent extending an arm to her. 'You have not suffered from the truth, my Clara!'

Her answer was: 'I was thinking how he might suffer if he were taught to tell the reverse.'

'Oh! for a fair lady!'

'That is the worst of teaching, Willoughby.'

'We'll leave it to the fellow's instinct; he has our blood in him. I could convince you, though, if I might cite circumstances. Yes! But yes! And yes again! The entire truth cannot invariably be told. I venture to say it should not.'

'You would pardon it for the "fair lady"?'

'Applaud, my love.'

He squeezed the hand within his arm, contemplating her.

She was arrayed in a voluminous robe of pale blue silk vapourous with trimmings of light gauze of the same hue, gaze de Chambéry, matching her fair hair and clear skin for the complete overthrow of less inflammable men than Willoughby.

'Clara!' sighed he.

'If so, it would really be generous,' she said, 'though the teaching is bad.'

'I fancy I can be generous.'

'Do we ever know?'

He turned his head to Vernon, issuing brief succinct instructions for letters to be written, and drew her into the hall, saying: 'Know? There are people who do *not* know themselves, and as they are the majority they manufacture the axioms. And it is assumed that we have to swallow them. I may observe that I think I know. I decline to be engulphed in those majorities. "Among them, but not of them." I know this, that my aim in life is to be generous.'

'Is it not an impulse or disposition rather than an aim?'

'So much I know,' pursued Willoughby, refusing to be tripped. But she rang discordantly in his ear. His 'fancy that he could be generous,' and his 'aim at being generous,' had met with no response. 'I have given proofs,' he said briefly, to drop a subject upon which he was not permitted to dilate; and he murmured: 'People acquainted with me . . .!' She was asked if she expected him to boast of generous deeds. 'From childhood!' she heard him mutter; and she said to herself: 'Release me, and you shall be everything!'

The unhappy gentleman ached as he talked: for with men and with hosts of women to whom he was indifferent, never did he converse in this shambling, third-rate, sheepish manner, devoid of all highness of tone and the proper precision of an authority. He was unable to fathom the cause of it, but Clara imposed it on him, and only in anger could he throw it off. The temptation to an outburst that would flatter him with the sound of his authoritative voice had to be resisted on a night when he must be composed if he intended to shine, so he merely mentioned Lady Busshe's present, to gratify spleen by preparing the ground for dissension, and prudently acquiesced in her anticipated slipperiness. She would rather not look at it now, she said.

'Not now; very well,' said he.

His immediate deference made her regretful. 'There is hardly time, Willoughby.'

'My dear, we shall have to express our thanks to her.'

'I cannot.'

His arm contracted sharply. He was obliged to be silent.

Dr. Middleton, Laetitia and the ladies Eleanor and Isabel joining them in the hall found two figures linked together in a shadowy indication of halves that have fallen apart and hang on the last thread of junction. Willoughby retained her hand on his arm; he held to it as the symbol of their alliance, and oppressed the girl's nerves by contact with a frame labouring for breath. De Craye looked on them from overhead. The carriages were at the door, and Willoughby said: 'Where's Horace? I suppose he's taking a final shot at his Book of Anecdotes and neat collections of Irishisms.'

'No,' replied the colonel, descending. 'That's a spring works of itself and has discovered the secret of continuous motion, more's the pity!—unless you'll be pleased to make it of use to Science.'

He gave a laugh of good humour.

'Your laughter, Horace, is a capital comment on your wit.'

Willoughby said it with the air of one who has flicked a whip.

''Tis a genial advertisement of a vacancy,' said De Craye.

'Precisely: three parts auctioneer to one for the property.'

'Oh! if you have a musical quack, score it a point in his favour, Willoughby, though you don't swallow his drug.'

'If he means to be musical, let him keep time.'

'Am I late?' said De Craye to the ladies, proving himself an adept in the art of being gracefully vanquished and so winning tender hearts.

Willoughby had refreshed himself. At the back of his mind there was a suspicion that his adversary would not have yielded so flatly without an assurance of practically triumphing, secretly getting the better of him; and it filled him with venom for a further bout at the next opportunity: but as he had been sarcastic and mordant, he had shown Clara what he could do in a way of speaking different from the lamentable cooing stuff, gasps and feeble protestations to which, he knew not how, she reduced him. Sharing the opinion of his race, that blunt personalities, or the pugilistic form, administered directly on the salient features, are exhibitions of mastery in such encounters, he felt strong and solid, eager for the successes of the evening. De Craye was in the first carriage as escort to the ladies Eleanor and Isabel. Willoughby, with Clara, Laetitia and Dr. Middleton followed, all silent, for the Rev. Doctor was ostensibly pondering; and Willoughby was damped a little when he unlocked his mouth to say:

'And yet I have not observed that Colonel De Craye is anything of a Celtiberian Egnatius* meriting fustigation for an untimely display of well-whitened teeth, sir: "quicquid est, ubicunque est, quodcunque agit, renidet":—ha? a morbus* neither charming nor urbane to the general eye, however consolatory to the actor. But this gentleman does not offend so, or I am so strangely prepossessed in his favour as to be an incompetent witness.'

Dr. Middleton's persistent ha? eh? upon an honest frown of inquiry plucked an answer out of Willoughby that was meant to be humourously scornful and soon became apologetic under the Doctor's interrogatively grasping gaze.

'These Irishmen,' Willoughby said, 'will play the professional jester, as if it were an office they were born to. We must play critic now and then, otherwise we should have them deluging us with their Joe Millerisms.'*

'With their *O*'Millerisms you would say, perhaps?'

Willoughby did his duty to the joke, but the Rev. Doctor, though he wore the paternal smile of a man that has begotten hilarity, was not perfectly propitiated, and pursued: 'Nor to my apprehension is "the man's laugh the comment on his wit" unchallengeably new: instances of cousinship germane to the phrase will recur to you. But it has to be noted that it was a phrase of assault; it was ostentatiously battery: and I would venture to remind you, friend, that among the elect, considering that it is as fatally facile to spring the laugh upon a man as to deprive him of his life, considering that we have only to condescend to the weapon, and that the more popular necessarily the more murderous that weapon is,—among the elect, to which it is your distinction to aspire to belong, the rule holds to abstain from any employment of the obvious, the percoct,* and likewise, for your own sake, from the epitonic,* the overstrained; for if the former, by readily assimilating with the understandings of your audience are empowered to commit assassination on your victim, the latter come under the charge of unseemliness, inasmuch as they are a description of public suicide. Assuming, then, manslaughter to be your pastime, and hari-kari* not to be your bent, the phrase, to escape criminality, must rise in you as you would have it to fall on him, *ex improviso*.* Am I right?'

'I am in the habit of thinking it impossible, sir, that you can be in error,' said Willoughby.

Dr. Middleton left it the more emphatic by saying nothing further.

Both his daughter and Miss Dale, who had disapproved the waspish snap at Colonel De Craye, were in wonderment of the art of speech which could so soothingly inform a gentleman that his behaviour had not been gentlemanly.

Willoughby was damped by what he comprehended of it for a few minutes. In proportion as he realized an evening with his ancient admirers he was restored, and he began to marvel greatly at his folly in not giving banquets and Balls, instead of making a solitude about himself and his bride. For solitude, thought he, is good for the man, the man being a creature consumed by passion; woman's love, on the contrary, will only be nourished by the reflex light she catches of you in the eyes of others, she having no passion of her own, but simply an instinct driving her to attach herself to whatsoever is most largely admired, most shining. So thinking, he determined to change his course of conduct, and he was happier. In the first gush of our wisdom drawn directly from experience, there is a mental intoxication that cancels the old world and establishes a new one, not allowing us to ask whether it is too late.

CHAPTER XXX

Treating of the Dinner-Party at Mrs. Mountstuart Jenkinson's

Vernon and young Crossjay had tolerably steady work together for a couple of hours, varied by the arrival of a plate of meat on a tray for the master, and some interrogations put to him from time to time by the boy in reference to Miss Middleton. Crossjay made the discovery that if he abstained from alluding to Miss Middleton's beauty he might water his dusty path with her name nearly as much as he liked. Mention of her beauty incurred a reprimand. On the first occasion his master was wistful. 'Isn't she glorious!' Crossjay fancied he had started a sovereign receipt for blessed deviations. He tried it again, but paedagogue-thunder broke over his head.

'Yes, only I can't understand what she means, Mr. Whitford,' he excused himself. 'First I was not to tell; I know I wasn't, because she said so: she quite as good as said so. Her last words were, "Mind, Crossjay, you know nothing about me," when I stuck to that beast of a tramp, who's a "walking moral," and gets money out of people by snuffling it.'

'Attend to your lesson, or you'll be one,' said Vernon.

'Yes, but, Mr. Whitford, now I *am* to tell. I'm to answer straight out to every question.'

'Miss Middleton is anxious that you should be truthful.'

'Yes, but in the morning she told me *not* to tell.'

'She was in a hurry. She has it on her conscience that you may have misunderstood her, and she wishes you never to be guilty of an untruth, least of all on her account.'

Crossjay committed an unspoken resolution to the air in a violent sigh: 'Ah!' and said: 'If I were sure!'

'Do as she bids you, my boy.'

'But I don't know what it is she wants.'

'Hold to her last words to you.'

'So I do. If she told me to run till I dropped, on I'd go.'

'She told you to study your lessons: do that.'

Crossjay buckled to his book, invigorated by an imagination of his liege lady on the page.

After a studious interval, until the impression of his lady had subsided, he resumed: 'She's so funny! She's just like a girl, and then she's a lady too. She's my idea of a princess. And Colonel De Craye! Wasn't he taught dancing! When he says something funny he ducks and seems to be setting to his partner. I should like to be

as clever as her father. That is a clever man! I daresay
Colonel De Craye will dance with her to-night. I wish
I was there.'

'It's a dinner-party, not a dance,' Vernon forced himself to say, to dispel that ugly vision.

'Isn't it, sir? I thought they danced after dinner-
parties. Mr. Whitford, have you ever seen her run?'

Vernon pointed him to his task.

They were silent for a lengthened period.

'But does Miss Middleton mean me to speak out if Sir
Willoughby asks me?' said Crossjay.

'Certainly. You needn't make much of it. All's plain
and simple.'

'But I'm positive, Mr. Whitford, he wasn't to hear of
her going to the post-office with me before breakfast.
And how did Colonel De Craye find her and bring her
back, with that old Flitch? He's a man and can go
where he pleases, and I'd have found her too, give me the
chance. You know, I'm fond of Miss Dale, but she—
I'm very fond of her—but you can't think she's a girl as
well. And about Miss Dale, when she says a thing, there
it is, clear. But Miss Middleton has a lot of meanings.
Never mind; I go by what's inside and I'm pretty sure
to please her.'

'Take your chin off your hand and your elbow off the
book, and fix yourself,' said Vernon, wrestling with the
seduction of Crossjay's idolatry, for Miss Middleton's
appearance had been preternaturally sweet on her departure, and the next pleasure to seeing her was hearing
of her from the lips of this passionate young poet.

'Remember that you please her by speaking truth,'
Vernon added, and laid himself open to questions upon
the truth, by which he learnt, with a perplexed sense of
envy and sympathy, that the boy's idea of truth strongly
approximated to his conception of what should be agreeable to Miss Middleton.

He was lonely, bereft of the bard, when he had tucked
Crossjay up in his bed and left him. Books he could not
read; thoughts were disturbing. A seat in the library
and a stupid stare helped to pass the hours, and but for

the spot of sadness moving meditation in spite of his effort
to stun himself, he would have borne a happy resemblance to an idiot in the sun. He had verily no command
of his reason. She was too beautiful! Whatever she did
was best. That was the refrain of the fountain-song in
him; the burden being her whims, variations, inconsis-
tencies, wiles; her tremblings between good and naughty,
that might be stamped to noble or to terrible; her sincere-
ness, her duplicity, her courage, cowardice, possibilities
for heroism and for treachery. By dint of dwelling on
the theme, he magnified the young lady to extraordinary
stature. And he had sense enough to own that her character was yet liquid in the mould, and that she was a
creature of only naturally youthful wildness provoked
to freakishness by the ordeal of a situation shrewd as any
that can happen to her sex in civilized life. But he was
compelled to think of her extravagantly, and he leaned
a little to the discrediting of her, because her actual
image unmanned him and was unbearable: and to say at
the end of it 'She is too beautiful! whatever she does is
best,' smoothed away the wrong he did her. Had it been
in his power he would have thought of her in the abstract
—the stage contiguous to that which he adopted: but
the attempt was luckless; the Stagyrite* would have
failed in it. What philosopher could have set down that
face of sun and breeze and nymph in shadow as a point
in a problem?

The library-door was opened at midnight by Miss
Dale. She closed it quietly. 'You are not working, Mr.
Whitford? I fancied you would wish to hear of the
evening. Professor Crooklyn arrived after all! Mrs.
Mountstuart is bewildered: she says she expected you,
and that you did not excuse yourself to her, and she
cannot comprehend, et caetera. That is to say, she
chooses bewilderment to indulge in the exclamatory.
She must be very much annoyed. The professor did
come by the train she drove to meet!'

'I thought it probable,' said Vernon.

'He had to remain a couple of hours at the Railway
Inn: no conveyance was to be found for him. He thinks

he has caught a cold, and cannot stifle his fretfulness about it. He may be as learned as Dr. Middleton; he has not the same happy constitution. Nothing more unfortunate could have occurred; he spoilt the party. Mrs. Mountstuart tried petting him, which drew attention to him and put us all in his key for several awkward minutes, more than once. She lost her head; she was unlike herself. I may be presumptuous in criticizing her, but should not the president of a dinner-table treat it like a battle-field, and let the guest that sinks descend, and not allow the voice of a discordant, however illustrious, to rule it? Of course, it is when I see failures that I fancy I could manage so well: comparison is prudently reserved in the other cases. I am a daring critic, no doubt because I know I shall never be tried by experiment. I have no ambition to be tried.'

She did not notice a smile of Vernon's, and continued: 'Mrs. Mountstuart gave him the lead upon any subject he chose. I thought the Professor never would have ceased talking of a young lady who had been at the inn before him drinking hot brandy and water with a gentleman!'

'How did he hear of that?' cried Vernon, roused by the malignity of the Fates.

'From the landlady, trying to comfort him. And a story of her lending shoes and stockings while those of the young lady were drying. He has the dreadful snappish humourous way of recounting which impresses it; the table took up the subject of this remarkable young lady, and whether she was a lady of the neighbourhood, and who she could be that went abroad on foot in heavy rain. It was painful to me; I knew enough to be sure of who she was.'

'Did she betray it?'

'No.'

'Did Willoughby look at her?'

'Without suspicion then.'

'Then?'

'Colonel De Craye was diverting us, and he was very amusing. Mrs. Mountstuart told him afterwards that he ought to be paid salvage for saving the wreck of her party. Sir Willoughby was a little too cynical: he talked well; what he said was good, but it was not good-humoured: he has not the reckless indifference of Colonel De Craye to uttering nonsense that amusement may come of it. And in the drawing-room he lost such gaiety as he had. I was close to Mrs. Mountstuart when Professor Crooklyn approached her and spoke in my hearing of *that* gentleman and *that* young lady. They were, you could see by his nods, Colonel De Craye and Miss Middleton.'

'And she at once mentioned it to Willoughby!'

'Colonel De Craye gave her no chance, if she sought it. He courted her profusely. Behind his rattle he must have brains. It ran in all directions to entertain her and her circle.'

'Willoughby knows nothing?'

'I cannot judge. He stood with Mrs. Mountstuart a minute as we were taking leave. She looked strange. I heard her say, "The rogue." He laughed. She lifted her shoulders. He scarcely opened his mouth on the way home.'

'The thing must run its course,' Vernon said, with the philosophical air which is desperation rendered decorous. 'Willoughby deserves it. A man of full growth ought to know that nothing on earth tempts Providence so much as the binding of a young woman against her will. Those two are mutually attracted: they're both . . . They meet and the mischief's done: both are bright. He can persuade with a word. Another might discourse like an angel and it would be useless. I said everything I could think of, to no purpose. And so it is: there are those attractions!—just as, with her, Willoughby is the reverse, he repels. I'm in about the same predicament— or should be if she were plighted to me. That is, for the length of five minutes; about the space of time I should require for the formality of handing her back her freedom. How a sane man can imagine a girl like that . . .! But if she has changed, she has changed! You can't conciliate a withered affection. This detaining her, and

tricking, and not listening, only increases her aversion;
she learns the art in turn. Here she is, detained by
fresh plots to keep Dr. Middleton at the Hall. That's
true, is it not?' He saw that it was. 'No, she's not to
blame! She has told him her mind; he won't listen.
The question then is, whether she keeps to her word, or
breaks it. It's a dispute between a conventional idea
of obligation and an injury to her nature. Which is the
more dishonourable thing to do? Why, you and I see
in a moment that her feelings guide her best. It's one
of the few cases in which nature may be consulted like
an oracle.'

'Is she so sure of her nature?' said Miss Dale.

'You may doubt it; I do not. I am surprised at her
coming back. De Craye is a man of the world, and advised it, I suppose. He——well, I never had the persuasive tongue, and my failing doesn't count for much.'

'But the suddenness of the intimacy!'

'The disaster is rather famous "at first sight."'* He
came in a fortunate hour . . . for him. A pigmy's a
giant if he can manage to arrive in season. Did you not
notice that there was danger, at their second or third
glance? You counselled me to hang on here, where the
amount of good I do in proportion to what I have to
endure is microscopic.'

'It was against your wishes, I know,' said Laetitia, and
when the words were out she feared that they were tentative. Her delicacy shrank from even seeming to sound him
in relation to a situation so delicate as Miss Middleton's.

The same sentiment guarded him from betraying himself, and he said: 'Partly against. We both foresaw
the possible—because, like most prophets, we knew a
little more of circumstances enabling us to see the fatal.
A pigmy would have served, but De Craye is a handsome, intelligent, pleasant fellow.'

'Sir Willoughby's friend!'

'Well, in these affairs! A great deal must be charged
on the Goddess.'

'That is really Pagan fatalism!'

'Our modern word for it is Nature. Science condescends to speak of natural selection. Look at these! They are both graceful and winning and witty, bright to mind and eye, made for one another, as country people say. I can't blame him. Besides we don't know that he's guilty. We're quite in the dark, except that we're certain how it must end. If the chance should occur to you of giving Willoughby a word of counsel—it may—you might, without irritating him as my knowledge of his plight does, hint at your eyes being open. His insane dread of a detective world makes him artificially blind. As soon as he fancies himself seen, he sets to work spinning a web, and he discerns nothing else. It's generally a clever kind of web; but if it's a tangle to others it's the same to him, and a veil as well. He is preparing the catastrophe, he forces the issue. Tell him of her extreme desire to depart. Treat her as mad, to soothe him. Otherwise one morning he will wake a second time . . .! It is perfectly certain. And the second time it will be entirely his own fault. Inspire him with some philosophy.'

'I have none.'

'If I thought so, I would say you have better. There are two kinds of philosophy, mine and yours. Mine comes of coldness, yours of devotion.'

'He is unlikely to choose me for his confidante.'

Vernon meditated. 'One can never quite guess what he will do, from never knowing the heat of the centre in him which precipitates his actions: he has a great art of concealment. As to me, as you perceive, my views are too philosophical to let me be of use to any of them. I blame only the one who holds the bond. The sooner I am gone!—In fact, I cannot stay on. So Dr. Middleton and the Professor did not strike fire together?'

'Dr. Middleton was ready and pursued him, but Professor Crooklyn insisted on shivering. His line of blank verse: "A Railway platform and a Railway inn!" became pathetic in repetition. He must have suffered.'

'Somebody has to!'

'Why the innocent?'

'He arrives à propos.* But remember that Fridolin*

sometimes contrives to escape and have the guilty scorched. The Professor would not have suffered if he had missed his train, as he appears to be in the habit of doing. Thus his unaccustomed good fortune was the cause of his bad.'

'You saw him on the platform?'

'I am unacquainted with the Professor. I had to get Mrs. Mountstuart out of the way.'

'She says she described him to you. "Complexion of a sweetbread, consistency of a quenelle, grey, and like a saint without his dish behind the head."'

'Her descriptions are strikingly accurate, but she forgot to sketch his back, and all that I saw was a narrow sloping back and a broad hat resting the brim on it. My report to her spoke of an old gentleman of dark complexion, as the only traveller on the platform. She has faith in the efficiency of her descriptive powers, and so she was willing to drive off immediately.—The intention was a start to London. Colonel De Craye came up and effected in five minutes what I could not compass in thirty.'

'But you saw Colonel De Craye pass you?'

'My work was done; I should have been an intruder. Besides I was acting wet jacket with Mrs. Mountstuart to get her to drive off fast, or she might have jumped out in search of her Professor herself.'

'She says you were lean as a fork, with the wind whistling through the prongs.'

'You see how easy it is to deceive one who is an artist in phrases. Avoid them, Miss Dale; they dazzle the penetration of the composer. That is why people of ability like Mrs. Mountstuart see so little; they are so bent on describing brilliantly. However, she is kind and charitable at heart. I have been considering to-night that, to cut this knot as it is now, Miss Middleton might do worse than speak straight out to Mrs. Mountstuart. No one else would have such influence with Willoughby. The simple fact of Mrs. Mountstuart's knowing of it would be almost enough. But courage would be required for that. Good night, Miss Dale.'

'Good night, Mr. Whitford. You pardon me for disturbing you?'

Vernon pressed her hand reassuringly. He had but to look at her and review her history to think his cousin Willoughby punished by just retribution. Indeed for any maltreatment of the dear boy Love by man or by woman, coming under your cognizance, you, if you be of common soundness, shall behold the retributive blow struck in your time.

Miss Dale retired thinking how like she and Vernon were to one another in the toneless condition they had achieved through sorrow. He succeeded in masking himself from her, owing to her awe of the circumstances. She reproached herself for not having the same devotion to the cold idea of duty as he had; and though it provoked inquiry, she would not stop to ask why he had left Miss Middleton a prey to the sparkling colonel. It seemed a proof of the philosophy he preached.

As she was passing by young Crossjay's bedroom-door a face appeared. Sir Willoughby slowly emerged and presented himself in his full length, beseeching her to banish alarm.

He said it in a hushed voice, with a face qualified to create the sentiment.

'Are you tired? sleepy?' said he.

She protested that she was not; she intended to read for an hour.

He begged to have the hour dedicated to him. 'I shall be relieved by conversing with a friend.'

No subterfuge crossed her mind; she thought his midnight visit to the boy's bedside a pretty feature in him; she was full of pity too; she yielded to the strange request, feeling that it did not become 'an old woman' to attach importance even to the public discovery of midnight interviews involving herself as one, and feeling also that she was being treated as an old friend in the form of a very old woman. Her mind was bent on arresting any recurrence to the project he had so frequently outlined in the tongue of innuendo, of which, because of her repeated tremblings under it, she thought him a master.

He conducted her along the corridor to the private sitting-room of the ladies Eleanor and Isabel.

'Deceit!' he said, while lighting the candles on the mantelpiece.

She was earnestly compassionate, and a word that could not relate to her personal destinies refreshed her by displacing her apprehensive antagonism and giving pity free play.

CHAPTER XXXI

Sir Willoughby attempts and achieves Pathos

BOTH were seated. Apparently he would have preferred to watch her dark downcast eyelashes in silence under sanction of his air of abstract meditation and the melancholy superinducing it. Blood-colour was in her cheeks; the party had inspirited her features. Might it be that lively company, an absence of economical solicitudes and a flourishing home were all she required to make her bloom again? The supposition was not hazardous in presence of her heightened complexion.

She raised her eyes. He could not meet her look without speaking.

'Can *you* forgive deceit?'

'It would be to boast of more charity than I know myself to possess, were I to say that I can, Sir Willoughby. I hope I am able to forgive. I cannot tell. I should like to say yes.'

'Could you live with the deceiver?'

'No.'

'No. I could have given that answer for you. No semblance of union should be maintained between the deceiver and ourselves. Laetitia!'

'Sir Willoughby?'

'Have I no right to your name?'

'If it please you to . . .'

'I speak as my thoughts run, and they did not know a Miss Dale so well as a dear Laetitia: my truest friend! You have talked with Clara Middleton?'

'We had a conversation.'

Her brevity affrighted him. He flew off in a cloud.

'Reverting to that question of deceivers: is it not your opinion that to pardon, to condone, is to corrupt society by passing off as pure what is false? Do we not,' he wore the smile of haggard playfulness of a convalescent child the first day back to its toys, 'Laetitia, do we not impose a counterfeit on the currency?'

'Supposing it to be really deception.'

'Apart from my loathing of deception, of falseness in any shape, upon any grounds, I hold it an imperious duty to expose, punish, off with it. I take it to be one of the forms of noxiousness which a good citizen is bound to extirpate. I am not myself good citizen enough, I confess, for much more passive abhorrence. I do not forgive: I am at heart serious and I cannot forgive:—there is no possible reconciliation, there can be only an ostensible truce, between the two hostile powers dividing this world.'

She glanced at him quickly.

'Good and evil!' he said.

Her face expressed a surprise relapsing on the heart.

He spelt the puckers of her forehead to mean, that she feared he might be speaking unchristianly.

'You will find it so in all religions, my dear Laetitia: the Hindoo, the Persian, ours. It is universal; an experience of our humanity. Deceit and sincerity cannot live together. Truth must kill the lie, or the lie will kill truth. I do not forgive. All I say to the person is, go!'

'But that is right! that is generous!' exclaimed Laetitia, glad to approve him for the sake of blinding her critical soul, and relieved by the idea of Clara's difficulty solved.

'*Capable* of generosity perhaps,' he mused aloud.

She wounded him by not supplying the expected enthusiastic asseveration of her belief in his general tendency to magnanimity.

He said after a pause: 'But the world is not likely to be impressed by anything not immediately gratifying it. People change, I find: as we increase in years we cease to be the heroes we were! I myself am insensible to change: I do not admit the charge. Except in this, we will say: personal ambition. I have it no more. And what is it when we have it? Decidedly a confession of inferiority! That is, the desire to be distinguished is an acknowledgement of insufficiency. But I have still the craving for my dearest friends to think well of me. A weakness? Call it so. Not a dishonourable weakness!'

Laetitia racked her brain for the connection of his present speech with the preceding dialogue. She was baffled, from not knowing 'the heat of the centre in him' as Vernon opaquely phrased it in charity to the object of her worship.

'Well,' said he, unappeased, 'and besides the passion to excel, I have changed somewhat in the heartiness of my thirst for the amusements incident to my station. I do not care to keep a stud—I was once tempted: nor hounds. And I can remember the day when I determined to have the best kennels and the best breed of horses in the kingdom. Puerile! What is distinction of that sort, or of any acquisition and accomplishment? We ask! One's *self* is not the greater. To seek it, owns to our smallness, in real fact; and when it is attained, what then? My horses are good, they are admired, I challenge the county to surpass them: well? These are but my horses; the praise is of the animals, not of me. I decline to share in it. Yet I know men content to swallow the praise of their beasts and be semi-equine. The littleness of one's fellows in the mob of life is a very strange experience! One may regret to have lost the simplicity of one's forefathers, which could accept those and other distinctions with a cordial pleasure, not to say pride. As for instance, I am, as it is called, a dead shot. "Give your acclamations, gentlemen, to my ancestors, from whom I inherited a steady hand and quick sight." They do not touch *me*. Where I do not find myself—that *I* am *essentially* I—no applause can move me. To speak to you as I would speak to none, admiration—you know that in my early youth I swam in flattery—I had to swim to avoid drowning!—admiration of my personal gifts has

grown tasteless. Changed, therefore, inasmuch as there
has been a growth of spirituality. We are all in submission to mortal laws, and so far I have indeed changed.
I may add that it is unusual for country gentlemen to
apply themselves to scientific researches. These are,
however, in the spirit of the time. I apprehended that
instinctively when at College. I forsook the classics for
science. And thereby escaped the vice of domineering
self-sufficiency peculiar to classical men, of which you
had an amusing example in the carriage, on the way to
Mrs. Mountstuart's this evening. Science is modest;
slow, if you like: it deals with facts, and having mastered
them, it masters men; of necessity, not with a stupid
loud-mouthed arrogance: words big and oddly-garbed
as the Pope's body-guard!* Of course, one bows to the
Infallible;* we must, when his giant-mercenaries level
bayonets!'

Sir Willoughby offered Miss Dale half a minute that
she might in gentle feminine fashion acquiesce in the implied reproof of Dr. Middleton's behaviour to him during
the drive to Mrs. Mountstuart's. She did not.

Her heart was accusing Clara of having done it a
wrong and a hurt. For while he talked he seemed to her
to justify Clara's feelings and her conduct: and her own
reawakened sensations of injury came to the surface
a moment to look at him, affirming that they pardoned
him, and pitied, but hardly wondered.

The heat of the centre in him had administered the
comfort he wanted, though the conclusive accordant
notes he loved on woman's lips, that subservient harmony of another instrument desired of musicians when
they have done their solo-playing, came not to wind up
the performance: not a single bar. She did not speak.
Probably his Laetitia was overcome, as he had long
known her to be when they conversed; nerve-subdued,
unable to deploy her mental resources or her musical.
Yet ordinarily she had command of the latter.—Was she
too condoling? Did a reason exist for it? Had the impulsive and desperate girl spoken out to Laetitia to the
fullest?—shameless daughter of a domineering sire that

she was! Ghastlier inquiry (it struck the centre of him with a sounding ring), was Laetitia pitying him over-much for worse than the pain of a little difference be-tween lovers—for treason on the part of his bride? Did she know of a rival? know more than he?

When the centre of him was violently struck he was a genius in penetration. He guessed that she did know: and by this was he presently helped to achieve pathos.

'So my election was for Science,' he continued: 'and if it makes me, as I fear, a rara avis* among country gentlemen, it unites me, puts me in the main, I may say, in the only current of progress—a word sufficiently des-picable in their political jargon.—You enjoyed your evening at Mrs. Mountstuart's?'

'Very greatly.'

'She brings her Professor to dine here the day after to-morrow. Does it astonish you? You started.'

'I did not hear the invitation.'

'It was arranged at the table: you and I were separ-ated—cruelly, I told her: she declared that we see enough of one another, and that it was good for me that we should be separated; neither of which is true. I may not have known what is the best for me: I do know what is good. If in my younger days I egregiously erred, that, taken of itself alone, is, assuming me to have sense and feeling, the surer proof of present wisdom. I can testify in person that wisdom is pain. If pain is to add to wisdom, let me suffer! Do you approve of that, Laetitia?'

'It is well said.'

'It is felt. Those who themselves have suffered should know the benefit of the resolution.'

'One may have suffered so much as to wish only for peace.'

'True: but you! have you?'

'It would be for peace, if I prayed for an earthly gift.'

Sir Willoughby dropped a smile on her. 'I mentioned the Pope's parti-coloured body-guard just now. In my youth their singular attire impressed me. People tell me they have been re-uniformed: I am sorry. They remain one of my liveliest recollections of the Eternal City. They affected my sense of humour, always alert in me, as you are aware. We English have humour. It is the first thing struck in us when we land on the Continent: our risible faculties are generally active all through the tour. Humour, or the clash of sense with novel examples of the absurd, is our characteristic. I do not condescend to boisterous displays of it. I observe, and note the people's comicalities for my correspondence. But you have read my letters—most of them, if not all?'

'Many of them.'

'I was with you then!—I was about to say—that Swiss-guard reminded me—you have not been in Italy. I have constantly regretted it. You are the very woman, you have the soul for Italy. I know no other of whom I could say it, with whom I should not feel that she was out of place, discordant with me. Italy and Laetitia! often have I joined you together. We shall see. I begin to have hopes. Here you have literally stagnated. Why, a dinner-party refreshes you! What would not travel do, and that heavenly climate! You are a reader of history and poetry. Well, poetry! I never yet saw the poetry that expressed the tenth part of what I feel in the presence of beauty and magnificence, and when I really meditate—profoundly. Call me a positive mind. I feel: only I feel too intensely for poetry. By the nature of it, poetry cannot be sincere. I will have sincerity. Whatever touches our emotions should be spontaneous, not a craft. I know you are in favour of poetry. You would win me, if any one could. But history! there I am with you. Walking over ruins: at night: the arches of the solemn black amphitheatre pouring moonlight on us—the moonlight of Italy!'

'You would not laugh there, Sir Willoughby?' said Laetitia, rousing herself from a stupor of apprehensive amazement, to utter something and realize actual circumstances.

'Besides, you, I think, or I am mistaken in you——' he deviated from his projected speech—'you are not a victim of the sense of association, and the ludicrous.'

'I can understand the influence of it: I have at least

a conception of the humourous: but ridicule would not strike me in the Coliseum of Rome. I could not bear it, no, Sir Willoughby!'

She appeared to be taking him in very strong earnest, by thus petitioning him not to laugh in the Coliseum, and now he said: 'Besides, you are one who could accommodate yourself to the society of the ladies, my aunts. Good women, Laetitia! I cannot imagine them *de trop** in Italy, or in a household. I have of course reason to be partial in my judgement.'

'They are excellent and most amiable ladies; I love them,' said Laetitia fervently; the more strongly excited to fervour by her enlightenment as to his drift.

She read it, that he designed to take her to Italy with the ladies;—after giving Miss Middleton her liberty; that was necessarily implied. And that was truly generous. In his boyhood he had been famous for his bountifulness in scattering silver and gold. Might he not have caused himself to be misperused in later life?

Clara had spoken to her of the visit and mission of the ladies to the library: and Laetitia daringly conceived herself to be on the certain track of his meaning, she being able to enjoy their society as she supposed him to consider that Miss Middleton did not, and would not either abroad or at home.

Sir Willoughby asked her: 'You could travel with them?'

'Indeed I could!'

'Honestly?'

'As affirmatively as one may protest. Delightedly.'

'Agreed. It is an undertaking.' He put his hand out. 'Whether I be of the party or not! To Italy, Laetitia! It would give me pleasure to be with you, and it will, if I must be excluded, to think of you in Italy!'

His hand was out. She had to feign inattention or yield her own. She had not the effrontery to pretend not to see, and she yielded it. He pressed it, and whenever it shrank a quarter-inch to withdraw, he shook it up and down, as an instrument that had been lent him for due

emphasis to his remarks. And very emphatic an amorous
orator can make it upon a captive lady.

'I am unable to speak decisively on that or any subject.
I am, I think you once quoted, "tossed like a weed on
the ocean." Of myself I can speak: I cannot speak for
a second person. I am infinitely harassed. If I could
cry, "To Italy to-morrow!" Ah! . . . Do not set me
down for complaining. I know the lot of man. But Laetitia, deceit! deceit! It is a bad taste in the mouth. It
sickens us of humanity. I compare it to an earthquake: we lose all our reliance on the solidity of the
world. It is a betrayal not simply of the person; it is a
betrayal of humankind. My friend! Constant friend!
No, I will not despair. Yes, I have faults; I will remember them. Only, forgiveness is another question.
Yes, the injury I *can* forgive: the falseness never. In
the interests of humanity, no! So young, and such
deceit!'

Laetitia's bosom rose: her hand was detained: a lady
who has yielded it cannot wrestle to have it back: those
outworks which protect her, treacherously shelter the
enemy aiming at the citadel when he has taken them.
In return for the silken armour bestowed on her by our
civilization, it is exacted that she be soft and civil nigh
up to perishing-point. She breathed tremulously high,
saying on her top-breath: 'If it—it may not be so; it can
scarcely . . .' A deep sigh intervened. It saddened her
that she knew so much.

'For when I love, I love,' said Sir Willoughby; 'my
friends and my servants know that. There can be no
medium: not with me. I give all, I claim all. As I am
absorbed, so must I absorb. We both cancel and create,
we extinguish and we illumine one another. The error
may be in the choice of an object: it is not in the passion.
Perfect confidence, perfect abandonment. I repeat, I
claim it because I give it. The selfishness of love may
be denounced: it is a part of us! My answer would be,
it is an element only of the noblest of us! Love, Laetitia!
I speak of love. But one who breaks faith to drag us
through the mire, who betrays, betrays and hands us over

to the world; whose prey we become identically because of virtues we were educated to think it a blessing to possess: tell me the name for that!—Again: it has ever been a principle with me to respect the sex. But if we see women false, treacherous. . . . Why indulge in these abstract views, you would ask! The world presses them on us, full as it is of the vilest specimens. They seek to pluck up every rooted principle: they sneer at our worship: they rob us of our religion. This bitter experience of the world drives us back to the antidote of what we knew before we plunged into it: of one . . . of something we esteemed and still esteem. Is that antidote strong enough to expel the poison? I hope so! I believe so! To lose faith in womankind is terrible.'

He studied her. She looked distressed: she was not moved.

She was thinking that, with the exception of a strain of haughtiness, he talked excellently to men, at least in the tone of the things he meant to say; but that his manner of talking to women went to an excess in the artificial tongue—the tutored tongue of sentimental deference of the towering male: he fluted exceedingly; and she wondered whether it was this which had wrecked him with Miss Middleton.

His intuitive sagacity counselled him to strive for pathos to move her. It was a task; for while he perceived her to be not ignorant of his plight, he doubted her knowing the extent of it, and as his desire was merely to move her without an exposure of himself, he had to compass being pathetic as it were under the impediments of a mailed and gauntleted knight, who cannot easily heave the bosom, or show it heaving.

Moreover pathos is a tide: often it carries the awakener of it off his feet, and whirls him over and over, armour and all in ignominious attitudes of helpless prostration, whereof he may well be ashamed in the retrospect. We cannot quite preserve our dignity when we stoop to the work of calling forth tears. Moses had probably to take a nimble jump away from the rock after that venerable Law-giver had knocked the water out of it.*

However, it was imperative in his mind that he should be sure he had the power to move her.

He began: clumsily at first, as yonder gauntleted knight attempting the briny handkerchief:

'What are we! We last but a very short time. Why not live to gratify our appetites? I might really ask myself why. All the means of satiating them are at my disposal. But no: I must aim at the highest:—at that which in my blindness I took for the highest. You know the sportsman's instinct, Laetitia; he is not tempted by the stationary object. Such are we in youth, toying with happiness, leaving it, to aim at the dazzling and attractive.'

'We gain knowledge,' said Laetitia.

'At what cost!'

The exclamation summoned self-pity to his aid, and pathos was handy.

'By paying half our lives for it and all our hopes! Yes, we gain knowledge, we are the wiser; very probably my value surpasses now what it was when I was happier. But the loss! That youthful bloom of the soul is like health to the body; once gone, it leaves cripples behind. Nay, my friend and precious friend, these four fingers I must retain. They seem to me the residue of a wreck: you shall be released shortly: absolutely, Laetitia, I have nothing else remaining.—We have spoken of deception: what of being undeceived?—when one whom we adored is laid bare, and the wretched consolation of a worthy object is denied to us. No misfortune can be like that. Were it death, we could worship still. Death would be preferable. But may you be spared to know a situation in which the comparison with your inferior is forced on you to your disadvantage and your loss because of your generously giving up your whole heart to the custody of some shallow, light-minded, self——! . . . we will not deal in epithets. If I were to find as many bad names for the serpent as there are spots on his body, it would be serpent still, neither better nor worse. . . . The loneliness! And the darkness! Our luminary is extinguished. Self-respect refuses to continue worshipping, but the affection will not be turned aside. We are literally in the dust, we grovel, we would fling away self-respect if we could; we would adopt for a model the creature preferred to us; we would humiliate, degrade ourselves; we cry for justice as if it were for pardon . . .'

'For pardon! when we are straining to grant it!' Laetitia murmured, and it was as much as she could do. She remembered how in her old misery her efforts after charity had twisted her round to feel herself the sinner, and beg forgiveness in prayer: a noble sentiment, that filled her with pity of the bosom in which it had sprung. There was no similarity between his idea and hers, but her idea had certainly been roused by his word 'pardon,' and he had the benefit of it in the moisture of her eyes. Her lips trembled, tears fell.

He had heard something; he had not caught the words, but they were manifestly favourable; her sign of emotion assured him of it and of the success he had sought. There was one woman who bowed to him to all eternity! He had inspired one woman with the mysterious man-desired passion of self-abandonment, self-immolation! The evidence was before him. At any instant he could, if he pleased, fly to her and command her enthusiasm.

He had, in fact, perhaps by sympathetic action, succeeded in striking the same springs of pathos in her which animated his lively endeavour to produce it in himself.

He kissed her hand; then released it, quitting his chair to bend above her soothingly.

'Do not weep, Laetitia, you see that I do not: I can smile. Help me to bear it; you must not unman me.'

She tried to stop her crying; but self-pity threatened to rain all her long years of grief on her head, and she said: 'I must go . . . I am unfit . . . good night, Sir Willoughby.'

Fearing seriously that he had sunk his pride too low in her consideration, and had been carried farther than he intended on the tide of pathos, he remarked: 'We will speak about Crossjay to-morrow. His deceitfulness has been gross. As I said, I am grievously offended by deception. But you are tired. Good night, my dear friend.'

'Good night, Sir Willoughby.'

She was allowed to go forth.

Colonel De Craye coming up from the smoking-room, met her and noticed the state of her eyelids, as he wished her good-night. He saw Willoughby in the room she had quitted, but considerately passed without speaking, and without reflecting why he was considerate.

Our hero's review of the scene made him on the whole satisfied with his part in it. Of his power upon one woman he was now perfectly sure:—Clara had agonized him with a doubt of his personal mastery of any. One, was a poor feast, but the pangs of his flesh during the last few days and the latest hours, caused him to snatch at it, hungrily if contemptuously. A poor feast, she was yet a fortress, a point of succour, both shield and lance; a cover and an impetus. He could now encounter Clara boldly. Should she resist and defy him, he would not be naked and alone; he foresaw that he might win honour in the world's eye from his position:—a matter to be thought of only in most urgent need. The effect on him of his recent exercise in pathos was to compose him to slumber. He was for the period well-satisfied.

His attendant imps were well-satisfied likewise, and danced a round about his bed after the vigilant gentleman had ceased to debate on the question of his unveiling of himself past forgiveness of her to Laetitia, and had surrendered unto benignant sleep the present direction of his affairs.

CHAPTER XXXII

Laetitia Dale discovers a Spiritual Change and Dr. Middleton a Physical

CLARA tripped over the lawn in the early morning to Laetitia to greet her. She broke away from a colloquy with Colonel De Craye under Sir Willoughby's windows. The colonel had been one of the bathers, and he stood like a circus driver, flicking a wet towel at Crossjay capering.

'My dear, I am very unhappy!' said Clara.

'My dear, I bring you news,' Laetitia replied.

'Tell me. But the poor boy is to be expelled! He burst into Crossjay's bed-room last night and dragged the sleeping boy out of bed to question him, and he had the truth. That is one comfort: only Crossjay is to be driven from the Hall because he was untruthful previously—for me: to serve me; really, I feel it was at my command. Crossjay will be out of the way to-day and has promised to come back at night to try to be forgiven. You must help me, Laetitia.'

'You are free, Clara! If you desire it, you have but to ask for your freedom.'

'You mean . . . ?'

'He will release you.'

'You are sure?'

'We had a long conversation last night.'

'I owe it to you?'

'Nothing is owing to me. He volunteered it.'

Clara made as if to lift her eyes in apostrophe. 'Professor Crooklyn! Professor Crooklyn! I see. I did not guess that!'

'Give credit for some generosity, Clara; you are unjust.'

'By-and-by: I will be more than just by-and-by. I will practise on the trumpet: I will lecture on the greatness of the souls of men when we know them thoroughly. At present we do but half know them, and we are unjust. You are not deceived, Laetitia? There is to be no speaking to papa? nò delusions? You have agitated me. I feel myself a very small person indeed. I feel I can understand those who admire him. He gives me back my word simply? clearly? without—Oh! that long wrangle in scenes and letters? And it will be arranged for papa and me to go not later than to-morrow? Never shall I be able to explain to any one how I fell into this! I am frightened at myself when I think of it. I take the whole blame: I have been scandalous. And dear Laetitia! you came out so early in order to tell me?'

'I wished you to hear it.'

'Take my heart.'

'Present me with a part—but for good!'

'Fie! But you have a right to say it.'

'I mean no unkindness; but is not the heart you allude to an alarmingly searching one?'

'Selfish it is, for I have been forgetting Crossjay. If we are going to be generous, is not Crossjay to be forgiven? If it were only that the boy's father is away fighting for his country, endangering his life day by day, and for a stipend not enough to support his family, we are bound to think of the boy! Poor dear silly lad! with his "I say, Miss Middleton, why wouldn't (some one) see my father when he came here to call on him, and had to walk back ten miles in the rain?"—I could almost fancy that did me mischief . . . But we have a splendid morning after yesterday's rain. And we will be generous. Own, Laetitia, that it is possible to gild the most glorious day of creation.'

'Doubtless the spirit may do it and make its hues permanent,' said Laetitia.

'You to me, I to you, he to us. Well, then, if he does, it shall be one of my heavenly days. Which is for the probation of experience. We are not yet at sunset.'

'Have you seen Mr. Whitford this morning?'

'He passed me.'

'Do not imagine him ever ill-tempered.'

'I had a governess, a learned lady, who taught me in person the picturesqueness of grumpiness. Her temper was ever perfect, because she was never in the wrong, but I being so, she was grumpy. She carried my iniquity under her brows, and looked out on me through it. I was a trying child.'

Laetitia said, laughing: 'I can believe it!'

'Yet I liked her and she liked me: we were a kind of foreground and background: she threw me into relief, and I was an apology for her existence.'

'You picture her to me.'

'She says of me now, that I am the only creature she has loved. Who knows that I may not come to say the same of her?'

'You would plague her and puzzle her still.'

'Have I plagued and puzzled Mr. Whitford?'

'He reminds you of her?'

'You said you had her picture.'

'Ah! do not laugh at him. He is a true friend.'

'The man who can be a friend is the man who will presume to be a censor.'

'A mild one.'

'As to the sentence he pronounces, I am unable to speak, but his forehead is Rhadamanthine condemnation.'*

'Dr. Middleton!'

Clara looked round. 'Who? I? Did you hear an echo of papa? He would never have put Rhadamanthus over European souls, because it appears that Rhadamanthus judged only the Asiatic; so you are wrong, Miss Dale. My father is infatuated with Mr. Whitford. What can it be? We women cannot sound the depths of scholars, probably because their pearls have no value in our market; except when they deign to chasten an impertinent; and Mr. Whitford stands aloof from any notice of small fry. He is deep, studious, excellent; and does it not strike you that if he descended among us he would be like a Triton ashore?'*

Laetitia's habit of wholly subservient sweetness, which was her ideal of the feminine, not yet conciliated with her acuter character, owing to the absence of full pleasure from her life—the unhealed wound she had sustained and the cramp of a bondage of such old date as to seem iron—induced her to say, as if consenting: 'You think he is not quite at home in society?' But she wished to defend him strenuously, and as a consequence she had to quit the self-imposed ideal of her daily acting, whereby—the case being unwonted, very novel to her—the lady's intelligence became confused through the process that quickened it; so sovereign a method of hoodwinking our bright selves is the acting of a part, however naturally it may come to us! and to this will each honest autobiographical member of the animated world bear witness.

She added: 'You have not found him sympathetic? He is. You fancy him brooding, gloomy? He is the reverse; he is cheerful, he is indifferent to personal misfortune. Dr. Corney says there is no laugh like Vernon Whitford's, and no humour like his. Latterly he certainly . . . but it has not been your cruel word grumpiness. The truth is, he is anxious about Crossjay: and about other things; and he wants to leave. He is at a disadvantage beside very lively and careless gentlemen at present, but your "Triton ashore," is unfair, it is ugly. He is, I can say, the truest man I know.'

'I did not question his goodness, Laetitia.'

'You threw an accent on it.'

'Did I? I must be like Crossjay, who declares he likes fun best.'

'Crossjay ought to know him, if anybody should. Mr. Whitford has defended you against me, Clara, ever since I took to calling you Clara. Perhaps when you supposed him so like your ancient governess, he was meditating how he could aid you. Last night he gave me reasons for thinking you would do wisely to confide in Mrs. Mountstuart. It is no longer necessary. I merely mention it. He is a devoted friend.'

'He is an untiring pedestrian.'

'Oh!'

Colonel De Craye, after hovering near the ladies in the hope of seeing them divide, now adopted the method of making three that two may come of it.

As he joined them with his glittering chatter, Laetitia looked at Clara to consult her, and saw the face rosy as a bride's.

The suspicion she had nursed sprang out of her arms a muscular fact on the spot.

'Where is my dear boy?' Clara said.

'Out for a holiday,' the colonel answered in her tone.

'Advise Mr. Whitford not to waste his time in searching for Crossjay, Laetitia. Crossjay is better out of the way to-day. At least, I thought so just now. Has he pocket-money, Colonel De Craye?'

'My lord can command his inn.'

'How thoughtful you are!'

Laetitia's bosom swelled upon a mute exclamation,

equivalent to: 'Woman! woman! snared ever by the sparkling and frivolous! undiscerning of the faithful, the modest and beneficent!'

In the secret musings of moralists this dramatic rhetoric survives.

The comparison was all of her own making and she was indignant at the contrast, though to what end she was indignant she could not have said, for she had no idea of Vernon as a rival of De Craye in the favour of a plighted lady. But she was jealous on behalf of her sex: her sex's reputation seemed at stake, and the purity of it was menaced by Clara's idle preference of the shallower man. When the young lady spoke so carelessly of being like Crossjay, she did not perhaps know that a likeness, based on a similarity of their enthusiasms, loves, and appetites, has been established between women and boys. Laetitia had formerly chafed at it, rejecting it utterly, save when now and then in a season of bitterness she handed here and there a volatile young lady (none but the young) to be stamped with the degrading brand. Vernon might be as philosophical as he pleased. To her the gaiety of these two, Colonel De Craye and Clara Middleton, was distressingly musical: they harmonized painfully. The representative of her sex was hurt by it.

She had to stay beside them: Clara held her arm. The colonel's voice dropped at times to something very like a whisper. He was answered audibly and smoothly. The quick-witted gentleman accepted the correction: but in immediately paying assiduous attentions to Miss Dale, in the approved intriguer's fashion, he showed himself in need of another amounting to a reproof. Clara said: 'We have been consulting, Laetitia, what is to be done to cure Professor Crooklyn of his cold.' De Craye perceived that he had taken a wrong step, and he was mightily surprised that a lesson in intrigue should be read to him of all men. Miss Middleton's audacity was not so astonishing: he recognized grand capabilities in the young lady. Fearing lest she should proceed farther and cut away from him his vantage-ground of secrecy with her, he turned the subject and was adroitly submissive.

Clara's manner of meeting Sir Willoughby expressed a timid disposition to friendliness upon a veiled inquiry, understood by none save Laetitia, whose brain was racked to convey assurances to herself of her not having misinterpreted him. Could there be any doubt? She resolved that there could not be; and it was upon this basis of reason—that she fancied she had led him to it. Legitimate or not, the fancy sprang from a solid foundation. Yesterday morning she could not have conceived it. Now she was endowed to feel that she had power to influence him, because now, since the midnight, she felt some emancipation from the spell of his physical mastery. He did not appear to her as a different man, but she had grown sensible of being a stronger woman. He was no more the cloud over her, nor the magnet; the cloud once heaven-suffused, the magnet fatally compelling her to sway round to him. She admired him still: his handsome air, his fine proportions, the courtesy of his bending to Clara and touching of her hand, excused a fanatical excess of admiration on the part of a woman in her youth, who is never the anatomist of the hero's lordly graces. But now she admired him piecemeal. When it came to the putting of him together, she did it coldly. To compassionate him was her utmost warmth. Without conceiving in him anything of the strange old monster of earth which had struck the awakened girl's mind of Miss Middleton, Laetitia classed him with other men: he was 'one of them.' And she did not bring her disenchantment as a charge against him. She accused herself, acknowledged the secret of the change to be, that her youthfulness was dead:—otherwise could she have given him compassion, and not herself have been carried on the flood of it? The compassion was fervent, and pure too. She supposed he would supplicate; she saw that Clara Middleton was pleasant with him only for what she expected of his generosity. She grieved. Sir Willoughby was fortified by her sorrowful gaze as he and Clara passed out together to the laboratory arm in arm.

Laetitia had to tell Vernon of the uselessness of his beating the house and grounds for Crossjay. Dr. Middleton held him fast in discussion upon an overnight's classical wrangle with Professor Crooklyn, which was to be renewed that day. The Professor had appointed to call expressly to renew it. 'A fine scholar,' said the Rev. Doctor, 'but crotchety, like all men who cannot stand their Port.'

'I hear that he had a cold,' Vernon remarked. 'I hope the wine was good, sir.'

As when the foreman of a sentimental jury is commissioned to inform an awful Bench exact in perspicuous English, of a verdict that must of necessity be pronounced in favour of the hanging of the culprit, yet would fain attenuate the crime of a palpable villain by a recommendation to mercy, such foreman, standing in the attentive eye of a master of grammatical construction, and feeling the weight of at least three sentences on his brain, together with a prospect of judicial interrogation for the discovery of his precise meaning, is oppressed, himself is put on trial in turn, and he hesitates, he recapitulates, the fear of involution leads him to be involved; as far as a man so posted may, he on his own behalf appeals for mercy; entreats that his indistinct statement of preposterous reasons may be taken for understood, and would gladly, were permission to do it credible, throw in an imploring word, that he may sink back among the crowd without for the one imperishable moment publicly swinging in his lordship's estimation:—much so, moved by chivalry toward a lady, courtesy to the recollection of a hostess, and particularly by the knowledge that his hearer would expect with a certain frigid rigour charity of him, Dr. Middleton paused, spoke and paused: he stammered. Ladies, he said, were famous poisoners in the Middle Ages. His opinion was, that we had a class of manufacturing wine-merchants on the watch for widows in this country. But he was bound to state the fact of his waking at his usual hour to the minute unassailed by headache. On the other hand, this was a condition of blessedness unanticipated when he went to bed. Mr. Whitford, however, was not to think that he entertained rancour toward the wine. It was no doubt dispensed with the honourable intention of cheering. In point of flavour execrable, judging by results it was innocuous.

'The test of it shall be the effect of it upon Professor Crooklyn, and his appearance in the forenoon according to promise,' Dr. Middleton came to an end with his perturbed balancings. 'If I hear more of the eight or twelve winds discharged at once upon a railway platform, and the young lady who dries herself of a drenching by drinking brandy and water with a gentleman at a railway inn, I shall solicit your sanction to my condemnation of the wine as anti-Bacchic and a counterfeit presentment. Do not misjudge me. Our hostess is not responsible. But widows should marry.'

'You must contrive to stop the Professor, sir, if he should attack his hostess in that manner,' said Vernon.

'Widows should marry!' Dr. Middleton repeated.

He murmured of objecting to be at the discretion of a butler: unless, he was careful to add, the aforesaid functionary could boast of an University education: and even then, said he, it requires a line of ancestry to train a man's taste.

The Rev. Doctor smothered a yawn. The repression of it caused a second one, a real monster, to come, big as our old friend of the sea advancing on the chained-up Beauty.

Disconcerted by this damning evidence of indigestion, his countenance showed that he considered himself to have been too lenient to the wine of an unhusbanded hostess. He frowned terribly.

In the interval Laetitia told Vernon of Crossjay's flight for the day, hastily bidding the master to excuse him: she had no time to hint the grounds of excuse. Vernon mentally made a guess.

Dr. Middleton took his arm and discharged a volley at the crotchety scholarship of Professor Crooklyn, whom to confute by book, he directed his march to the library. Having persuaded himself that he was dyspeptic, he had grown irascible. He denounced all dining out, eulogized Patterne Hall as if it were his home, and remembered he had dreamed in the night:—a most humiliating sign of physical disturbance. 'But let me find a house in proximity to Patterne, as I am induced to suppose I shall,' he said, 'and here only am I to be met when I stir abroad.'

Laetitia went to her room. She was complacently anxious, enough to prefer solitude and be willing to read. She was more seriously anxious about Crossjay than about any of the others. For Clara would be certain to speak very definitely, and how then could a gentleman oppose her? He would supplicate, and could she be brought to yield? It was not to be expected of a young lady who had turned from Sir Willoughby. His inferiors would have had a better chance. Whatever his faults, he had that element of greatness which excludes the intercession of pity. Supplication would be with him a form of condescension. It would be seen to be such. His was a monumental pride that could not stoop. She had preserved this image of the gentleman for a relic in the shipwreck of her idolatry. So she mused between the lines of her book, and finishing her reading and marking the page, she glanced down on the lawn. Dr. Middleton was there, and alone; his hands behind his back, his head bent. His meditative pace and unwonted perusal of the turf proclaimed that a non-sentimental jury within had delivered an unmitigated verdict upon the widow's wine. Laetitia hurried to find Vernon.

He was in the hall. As she drew near him, the laboratory door opened and shut.

'It is being decided,' said Laetitia.

Vernon was paler than the hue of perfect calmness.

'I want to know whether I ought to take to my heels like Crossjay, and shun the Professor,' he said.

They spoke in undertones, furtively watching the door.

'I wish what she wishes, I am sure, but it will go badly with the boy,' said Laetitia.

'Oh, well, then I'll take him,' said Vernon, 'I would rather. I think I can manage it.'

Again the laboratory door opened. This time it shut behind Miss Middleton. She was highly flushed. Seeing them, she shook the storm from her brows, with a dead smile: the best piece of serenity she could put on for public wear.

She took a breath before she moved.

Vernon strode out of the house.

Clara swept up to Laetitia.

'You were deceived!'

The hard sob of anger barred her voice.

Laetitia begged her to come to her room with her.

'I want air: I must be by myself,' said Clara, catching at her garden-hat.

She walked swiftly to the portico-steps and turned to the right, to avoid the laboratory windows.

CHAPTER XXXIII

In which the Comic Muse has an Eye on two Good Souls

CLARA met Vernon on the bowling-green among the laurels. She asked him where her father was.

'Don't speak to him now,' said Vernon.

'Mr. Whitford, will you?'

'It is not adviseable just now. Wait.'

'Wait? Why not now?'

'He is not in the right humour.'

She choked. There are times when there is no medicine for us in sages, we want slaves; we scorn to temporize, we must overbear. On she sped, as if she had made the mistake of exchanging words with a post.

The scene between herself and Willoughby was a thick mist in her head, except the burden and result of it, that he held to her fast, would neither assist her to depart nor disengage her.

Oh, men! men! They astounded the girl; she could not define them to her understanding. Their motives, their tastes, their vanity, their tyranny, and the domino on their vanity, the baldness of their tyranny, clenched her in feminine antagonism to brute power. She was not the less disposed to rebellion by a very present sense of the justice of what could be said to reprove her. She had but one answer: 'Anything but marry him!' It threw her on her nature, our last and headlong advocate, who is quick as the flood to hurry us from the heights to our level, and lower, if there be accidental gaps in the channel. For say we have been guilty of misconduct: can we redeem it by violating that which we are and live by? The question sinks us back to the luxuriousness of a sunny relinquishment of effort in the direction against tide. Our nature becomes ingenious in devices, penetrative of the enemy, confidently citing its cause for being frankly elvish or worse. Clara saw a particular way of forcing herself to be surrendered. She shut her eyes from it: the sight carried her too violently to her escape: but her heart caught it up and huzzaed. To press the points of her fingers at her bosom, looking up to the sky as she did, and cry, 'I am not my own; I am his!' was instigation sufficient to make her heart leap up with all her body's blush to urge it to recklessness. A despairing creature then may say she has addressed the heavens and has had no answer to restrain her.

Happily for Miss Middleton she had walked some minutes in her chafing fit before the falcon-eye of Colonel De Craye spied her away on one of the beech-knolls.

Vernon stood irresolute. It was decidedly not a moment for disturbing Dr. Middleton's composure. He meditated upon a conversation, as friendly as possible, with Willoughby. Round on the front-lawn he beheld Willoughby and Dr. Middleton together, the latter having halted to lend attentive ear to his excellent host. Unnoticed by them or disregarded, Vernon turned back to Laetitia, and sauntered talking with her of things current for as long as he could endure to listen to praise of his pure self-abnegation; proof of how well he had disguised himself, but it smacked unpleasantly to him. His humourous intimacy with men's minds likened the source of this distaste to the gallant all-or-nothing of the gambler, who hates the little when he cannot have the much, and would rather stalk from the tables clean-picked than suffer ruin to be tickled by driblets of the glorious fortune he has played for and lost. If we are not to be beloved, spare us the small coin of compliments on character: especially when they compliment only our acting. It is partly endurable to win eulogy for our stately fortitude in losing, but Laetitia was unaware that he flung away a stake; so she could not praise him for his merits.

'Willoughby makes the pardoning of Crossjay conditional,' he said, 'and the person pleading for him has to grant the terms. How could you imagine Willoughby would give her up! How could he! Who! . . . He should, is easily said. I was no witness of the scene between them just now, but I could have foretold the end of it; I could almost recount the passages. The consequence is, that everything depends upon the amount of courage she possesses. Dr. Middleton won't leave Patterne yet. And it is of no use to speak to him to-day. And she is by nature impatient, and is rendered desperate.'

'Why is it of no use to speak to Dr. Middleton to-day?' said Laetitia.

'He drank wine yesterday that did not agree with him; he can't work. To-day he is looking forward to Patterne Port. He is not likely to listen to any proposals to leave to-day.'

'Goodness!'

'I know the depth of that cry!'

'*You* are excluded, Mr. Whitford.'

'Not a bit of it; I am in with the rest. Say that men are to be exclaimed at. Men have a right to expect you to know your own mind when you close on a bargain. You don't know the world or yourselves very well, it's true; still the original error is on your side, and upon that you should fix your attention. She brought her father here, and no sooner was he very comfortably established than she wished to dislocate him.'

'I cannot explain it; I cannot comprehend it,' said Laetitia.

'You are Constancy.'

'No.' She coloured. 'I am "in with the rest." I do not say I should have done the same. But I have the knowledge that I must not sit in judgement on her. I can waver.'

She coloured again. She was anxious that he should

know her to be not that stupid statue of Constancy in a corner doating on the antic Deception. Reminiscences of the interview overnight made it oppressive to her to hear herself praised for always pointing like the needle. Her newly enfranchised individuality pressed to assert its existence. Vernon, however, not seeing this novelty, continued, to her excessive discomfort, to baste her old abandoned image with his praises. They checked hers; and moreover he had suddenly conceived an envy of her life-long, uncomplaining, almost unaspiring, constancy of sentiment. If you know lovers when they have not reason to be blissful, you will remember that in this mood of admiring envy they are given to fits of uncontrollable maundering. Praise of constancy, moreover, smote shadowily a certain inconstant, enough to seem to ruffle her smoothness and do no hurt. He found his consolation in it, and poor Laetitia writhed. Without designing to retort, she instinctively grasped at a weapon of defence in further exalting his devotedness; which reduced him to cast his head to the heavens and implore them to partially enlighten her. Nevertheless, maunder he must; and he recurred to it in a way so utterly unlike himself that Laetitia stared in his face. She wondered whether there could be anything secreted behind this everlasting theme of constancy. He took her awakened gaze for a summons to asseverations of sincerity, and out they came. She would have fled from him, but to think of flying was to think how little it was that urged her to fly, and yet the thought of remaining and listening to praises undeserved and no longer flattering, was a torture.

'Mr. Whitford, I bear no comparison with you.'

'I do and must set you for my example, Miss Dale.'

'Indeed you do wrongly; you do not know me.'

'I could say that. For years . . . !'

'Pray, Mr. Whitford!'

'Well, I have admired it. You show us how self can be smothered.'

'An echo would be a retort on you!'

'On me? I am never thinking of anything else.'

'I could say that.'

'You are necessarily conscious of not swerving.'

'But I do; I waver dreadfully; I am not the same two days running.'

'You are the same, with "ravishing divisions" upon the same.'

'And you without the "divisions." I draw such support as I have from you.'

'From some simulacrum of me, then. And that will show you how little you require support.'

'I do not speak my own opinion only.'

'Whose?'

'I am not alone.'

'Again let me say, I wish I were like you!'

'Then let me add, I would willingly make the exchange!'

'You would be amazed at your bargain.'

'Others would be!'

'Your exchange would give me the qualities I am in want of, Miss Dale.'

'Negative, passive, at the best, Mr. Whitford. But *I* should have . . .'

'Oh!—pardon me. But you inflict the sensations of a boy, with a dose of honesty in him, called up to receive a prize he has won by the dexterous use of a crib.'

'And how do you suppose she feels, who has a crown of Queen o' the May forced on her head when she is verging on November?'

He rejected her analogy, and she his. They could neither of them bring to light the circumstances which made one another's admiration so unbearable. The more he exalted her for constancy, the more did her mind become bent upon critically examining the object of that imagined virtue; and the more she praised him for possessing the spirit of perfect friendliness, the fiercer grew the passion in him which disdained the imputation, hissing like a heated iron-bar that flings the water-drops to steam. He would none of it: would rather have stood exposed in his profound foolishness.

Amiable though they were, and mutually affectionate, they came to a stop in their walk, longing to separate, and not seeing how it was to be done, they had so knit themselves together with the pelting of their interlaudation.

'I think it is time for me to run home to my father for an hour,' said Laetitia.

'I ought to be working,' said Vernon.

Good progress was made to the disgarlanding of themselves thus far; yet, an acutely civilized pair, the abruptness of the transition from floweriness to commonplace affected them both, Laetitia chiefly, as she had broken the pause, and she remarked,

'I am really Constancy in my opinions.'

'Another title is customary where stiff opinions are concerned. Perhaps by-and-by you will learn your mistake, and then you will acknowledge the name for it.'

'How?' said she. 'What shall I learn?'

'If you learn that I am a grisly Egoist?'

'You? And it would not be egoism,' added Laetitia, revealing to him at the same instant as to herself, that she swung suspended on a scarce credible guess.

'—Will nothing pierce your ears, Mr. Whitford?'

He heard the intruding voice, but he was bent on rubbing out the cloudy letters Laetitia had begun to spell, and he stammered in a tone of matter-of-fact: 'Just that and no better'; then turned to Mrs. Mountstuart Jenkinson.

'—Or are you resolved you will never see Professor Crooklyn when you look on him?' said the great lady.

Vernon bowed to the Professor and apologized to him shufflingly and rapidly, incoherently, and with a red face; which induced Mrs. Mountstuart to scan Laetitia's.

After lecturing Vernon for his abandonment of her yesterday evening, and flouting his protestations, she returned to the business of the day. 'We walked from the lodge-gates to see the park and prepare ourselves for Dr. Middleton. We parted last night in the middle of a controversy and are rageing to resume it. Where is our redoubtable antagonist?'

Mrs. Mountstuart wheeled Professor Crooklyn round to accompany Vernon.

'We,' she said, 'are for modern English scholarship, opposed to the champion of German.'

'The contrary,' observed Professor Crooklyn.

'Oh. We,' she corrected the error serenely, 'are for German scholarship, opposed to English.'

'Certain editions.'

'We defend certain editions.'

'Defend, is a term of imperfect application to my position, ma'am.'

'My dear Professor, you have in Dr. Middleton a match for you in conscientious pugnacity, and you will not waste it upon me. There, there they are; there he is. Mr. Whitford will conduct you. I stand away from the first shock.'

Mrs. Mountstuart fell back to Laetitia, saying: 'He pores over a little inexactitude in phrases, and pecks at it like a domestic fowl.'

Professor Crooklyn's attitude and air were so well described that Laetitia could have laughed.

'These mighty scholars have their flavour,' the great lady hastened to add, lest her younger companion should be misled to suppose that they were not valuable to a governing hostess: 'their shadow-fights are ridiculous, but they have their flavour at a table. Last night, no: I discard all mention of last night. We failed: as none else in this neighbourhood could fail, but we failed. If we have among us a cormorant devouring young lady who drinks up all the—ha!—brandy and water—of our inns and occupies all our flys, why, our condition is abnormal, and we must expect to fail: we are deprived of accommodation for accidental circumstances. How Mr. Whitford could have missed seeing Professor Crooklyn! And what was *he* doing at the station, Miss Dale?'

'Your portrait of Professor Crooklyn was too striking, Mrs. Mountstuart, and deceived him by its excellence. He appears to have seen only the blank side of the slate.'

'Ah. He is a faithful friend of his cousin, do you not think?'

'He is the truest of friends.'

'As for Dr. Middleton,' Mrs. Mountstuart diverged from her inquiry, 'he will swell the letters of my vocabulary to gigantic proportions if I see much of him: he is contagious.'

'I believe it is a form of his humour.'

'I caught it of him yesterday at my dinner-table in my distress, and must pass it off as a form of mine, while it lasts. I talked Dr. Middleton half the dreary night through to my pillow. Your candid opinion, my dear, come! As for me, I don't hesitate. We seemed to have sat down to a solitary performance on the bass-viol. We were positively an assembly of insects during thunder. My very soul thanked Colonel De Craye for his diversions, but I heard nothing but Dr. Middleton. It struck me that my table was petrified, and every one sat listening to bowls played overhead.'

'I was amused.'

'Really? You delight me. Who knows but that my guests were sincere in their congratulations on a thoroughly successful evening? I have fallen to this, you see! And I know, wretched people! that as often as not it is their way of condoling with one. I do it myself: but only where there have been amiable efforts. But imagine *my* being congratulated for that!—Good morning, Sir Willoughby.—The worst offender! and I am in no pleasant mood with him,' Mrs. Mountstuart said aside to Laetitia, who drew back, retiring.

Sir Willoughby came on a step or two. He stopped to watch Laetitia's figure swimming to the house.

So, as, for instance, beside a stream, when a flower on the surface extends its petals drowning to subside in the clear still water, we exercise our privilege to be absent in the charmed contemplation of a beautiful natural incident.

A smile of pleased abstraction melted on his features.

CHAPTER XXXIV

Mrs. Mountstuart and Sir Willoughby

'GOOD MORNING, my dear Mrs. Mountstuart,' Sir Willoughby wakened himself to address the great lady. 'Why has she fled?'

'Has any one fled?'

'Laetitia Dale.'

'Letty Dale? Oh! if you call that flying. Possibly to renew a close conversation with Vernon Whitford, that I cut short. You frightened me with your "Shepherds-tell-me" air and tone. Lead me to one of your garden-seats: out of hearing to Dr. Middleton, I beg. He mesmerizes me, he makes me talk Latin. I was curiously susceptible last night. I know I shall everlastingly associate him with an abortive entertainment and solos on big instruments. We were flat.'

'Horace was in good vein.'

'You were not.'

'And Laetitia—Miss Dale talked well, I thought.'

'She talked with you, and no doubt she talked well. We did not mix. The yeast was bad. You shot darts at Colonel De Craye: you tried to sting. You brought Dr. Middleton down on you. Dear me, that man is a reverberation in my head. Where is your lady and love?'

'Who?'

'Am I to name her?'

'Clara? I have not seen her for the last hour. Wandering, I suppose.'

'A very pretty summer-bower,' said Mrs. Mountstuart, seating herself. 'Well, my dear Sir Willoughby, preferences, preferences are not to be accounted for, and one never knows whether to pity or congratulate, whatever may occur. I want to see Miss Middleton.'

'Your "dainty rogue in porcelain" will be at your beck—you lunch with us?—before you leave.'

'So now you have taken to quoting me, have you?'

'But, "a romantic tale on her eyelashes," is hardly descriptive any longer.'

'Descriptive of whom? Now you are upon Laetitia Dale!'

'I quote you generally. She has now a graver look.'

'And well may have!'

'Not that the romance has entirely disappeared.'

'No: it looks as if it were in print.'

'You have hit it perfectly, as usual, ma'am.'

Sir Willoughby mused.

Like one resuming his instrument to take up the melody in a concerted piece, he said: 'I thought Laetitia Dale had a singularly animated air last night.'

'Why——!' Mrs. Mountstuart mildly gaped.

'I want a new description of her. You know, I collect your mottoes and sentences.'

'It seems to me she is coming three parts out of her shell, and wearing it as a hood for convenience.'

'Ready to issue forth at an invitation? Admirable! exact!'

'Ay, my good Sir Willoughby, but are we so very admirable and exact? Are we never to know our own minds?'

He produced a polysyllabic sigh, like those many-jointed compounds of poets in happy languages, which are copious in a single expression: 'Mine is known to me. It always has been. Cleverness in women is not uncommon. Intellect is the pearl. A woman of intellect is as good as a Greek statue; she is divinely wrought, and she is divinely rare.'

'Proceed,' said the lady, confiding a cough to the air.

'The rarity of it:—and it is not mere intellect, it is a sympathetic intellect; or else it is an intellect in perfect accord with an intensely sympathetic disposition;—the rarity of it makes it too precious to be parted with when once we have met it. I prize it the more the older I grow.'

'Are we on the feminine or the neuter?'

'I beg pardon?'

'The universal or the individual?'

He shrugged. 'For the rest, psychological affinities may exist coincident with and entirely independent of material or moral prepossessions, relations, engagements, ties.'

'Well, that is not the raving of passion, certainly,' said Mrs. Mountstuart, 'and it sounds as if it were a comfortable doctrine for men. On that plea, you might all of you be having Aspasia* and a wife. We saw your fair Middleton and Colonel De Craye at a distance as we entered the park. Professor Crooklyn is under some hallucination.'

'What more likely?'

The readiness and the double-bearing of the reply struck her comic sense with awe.

'The Professor must hear that. He insists on the fly, and the inn, and the wet boots, and the warming mixture, and the testimony of the landlady and the railway porter.'

'I say, what more likely?'

'Than that he should insist?'

'If he is under the hallucination!'

'He may convince others.'

'I have only to repeat . . .!'

' "What more likely?" It's extremely philosophical. Coincident with a pursuit of the psychological affinities.'

'Professor Crooklyn will hardly descend, I suppose, from his classical altitudes to lay his hallucinations before Dr. Middleton?'

'Sir Willoughby, you are the pink of chivalry!'

By harping on Laetitia, he had emboldened Mrs. Mountstuart to lift the curtain upon Clara. It was offensive to him, but the injury done to his pride had to be endured for the sake of his general plan of self-protection.

'Simply desirous to save my guests from annoyance of any kind,' he said. 'Dr. Middleton can look "Olympus and thunder," as Vernon calls it.'

'Don't. I see him. That look! It is Dictionary-bitten! Angry, horned Dictionary!—an apparition of Dictionary in the night—to a dunce!'

'One would undergo a good deal to avoid the sight.'

'What the man must be in a storm! Speak as you please of yourself: you are a true and chivalrous knight to dread it for her. But now candidly, how is it you cannot condescend to a little management? Listen to an old friend. You are too lordly. No lover can afford to be incomprehensible for half an hour. Stoop a little. Sermonizings are not to be thought of. You can govern unseen. You are to know that I am one who disbelieves in philosophy in love. I admire the look of it, I give no credit to the assumption. I rather like lovers to be out at times: it makes them picturesque, and it enlivens their monotony. I perceived she had a spot of wildness. It's proper that she should wear it off before marriage.'

'Clara? The wildness of an infant!' said Willoughby, paternally musing over an inward shiver. 'You saw her at a distance just now, or you might have heard her laughing. Horace diverts her excessively.'

'I owe him my eternal gratitude for his behaviour last night. She was one of my bright faces. Her laughter was delicious; rain in the desert! It will tell you what the load on me was, when I assure you those two were merely a spectacle to me—points I scored in a lost game. And I know they were witty.'

'They both have wit; a kind of wit,' Willoughby assented.

'They struck together like a pair of cymbals.'

'Not the highest description of instrument. However, they amuse me. I like to hear them when I am in the vein.'

'That vein should be more at command with you, my friend. You can be perfect if you like.'

'Under your tuition.'

Willoughby leaned to her, bowing languidly. He was easier in his pain for having hoodwinked the lady. She was the outer world to him: she could tune the world's voice; prescribe which of the two was to be pitied, himself or Clara; and he did not intend it to be himself, if it came to the worst.

They were far away from that at present, and he continued: 'Probably a man's power of putting on a face is not equal to a girl's. I detest petty dissensions. Probably I show it when all is not quite smooth. Little fits of suspicion vex me. It is a weakness, not to play them off, I know. Men have to learn the arts which come to women by nature. I don't sympathize with suspicion, from having none myself.'

His eyebrows shot up. That ill-omened man Flitch had sidled round by the bushes to within a few feet of him.

Flitch primarily defended himself against the accusation of drunkenness, which was hurled at him to account for his audacity in trespassing against the interdict: but he admitted that he had taken 'something short' for a fortification in visiting scenes where he had once been happy—at Christmastide, when all the servants, and the butler at head, gray old Mr. Chessington, sat in rows, toasting the young heir of the old Hall in the old port wine! Happy had he been then, before ambition for a shop, to be his own master and an independent gentleman, had led him into his quagmire:—to look back envying a dog on the old estate, and sigh for the smell of Patterne stables: sweeter than Arabia, his drooping nose appeared to say.

He held up close against it something that imposed silence on Sir Willoughby as effectually as a cunning exordium in oratory will enchain mobs to swallow what is not complimenting them: and this he displayed, secure in its being his license to drivel his abominable pathos. Sir Willoughby recognized Clara's purse. He understood at once how the man must have come by it: he was not so quick in devising a means of stopping the tale. Flitch foiled him. 'Intact,' he replied to the question: 'What have you there?' He repeated this grand word. And then he turned to Mrs. Mountstuart to speak of Paradise and Adam, in whom he saw the prototype of himself: also the Hebrew people in the bondage of Egypt, discoursed of by the clergymen, not without a likeness to him.

'Sorrows have done me one good, to send me attentive to church, my lady,' said Flitch, 'when I might have gone to London, the coachman's home, and been driving some honourable family, with no great advantage to my morals, according to what I hear of. And a purse found under the seat of a fly in London would have a poor chance of returning *intact* to the young lady losing it.'

'Put it down on that chair; inquiries will be made, and you will see Sir Willoughby,' said Mrs. Mountstuart. 'Intact, no doubt; it is not disputed.'

With one motion of a finger she set the man rounding. Flitch halted: he was very regretful of the termination of his feast of pathos, and he wished to relate the finding of the purse, but he could not encounter Mrs. Mountstuart's look: he slouched away in very close resemblance to the ejected Adam of illustrated books.

'It's my belief that naturalness among the common people has died out of the kingdom,' she said.

Willoughby charitably apologized for him. 'He has been fuddling himself.'

Her vigilant considerateness had dealt the sensitive gentleman a shock, plainly telling him she had her ideas of his actual posture. Nor was he unhurt by her superior acuteness and her display of authority on his grounds.

He said boldly, as he weighed the purse, half tossing it: 'It's not unlike Clara's.'

He feared that his lips and cheeks were twitching, and as he grew aware of a glassiness of aspect that would reflect any suspicion of a keen-eyed woman, he became bolder still: 'Laetitia's, I know it is not. Hers is an ancient purse.'

'A present from you!'

'How do you hit on that, my dear lady?'

'Deductively.'

'Well, the purse looks as good as new in quality, like the owner.'

'The poor dear has not much occasion for using it.'

'You are mistaken: she uses it daily.'

'If it were better filled, Sir Willoughby, your old scheme might be arranged. The parties do not appear so unwilling. Professor Crooklyn and I came on them just now rather by surprise, and I assure you their heads were close, faces meeting, eyes musing.'

'Impossible.'

'Because when they approach the point, you won't allow it! Selfish!'

'Now,' said Willoughby, very animatedly, 'question Clara. Now, do, my dear Mrs. Mountstuart, do speak to Clara on that head; she will convince you I have striven quite recently:—against myself, if you like. I have instructed her to aid me, given her the fullest instructions, carte blanche.* *She* cannot possibly have a doubt. I may look to her to remove any you may entertain from your mind on the subject. I have proposed, seconded and chorussed it, and it will *not* be arranged. If you expect me to deplore that fact, I can only answer that my actions are under my control, my feelings are not. I will do everything consistent with the duties of a man of honour—perpetually running into fatal errors because he did not properly consult the dictates of those feelings at the right season. I can violate them: but I can no more command them than I can my destiny. They were crushed of old, and so let them be now. Sentiments, we won't discuss; though you know that sentiments have a bearing on social life: are factors, as they say in their later jargon. I never speak of mine. To you I could. It is not necessary. If old Vernon, instead of flattening his chest at a desk had any manly ambition to take part in public affairs, she would be the woman for him. I have called her my Egeria. She would be his Cornelia.* One could swear of her that she would have noble offspring! —But old Vernon has had his disappointment, and will moan over it up to the end. And she? So it appears. I have tried; yes, personally: without effect. In other matters I may have influence with her: not in that one. She declines. She will live and die Laetitia Dale. We are alone: I confess to you, I love the name. It's an old song in my ears. Do not be too ready with a name for *me*. Believe me—I speak from my experience hitherto— there is a fatality in these things. I cannot conceal from my poor girl that this fatality exists . . .'

'Which is the poor girl at present?' said Mrs. Mountstuart, cool in a mystification.

'And though she will tell you that I have authorized

and—Clara Middleton—done as much as man can to institute the union you suggest, she will own that she is conscious of the presence of this—fatality, I call it for want of a better title—between us. It drives her in one direction, me in another—or would, if I submitted to the pressure. She is not the first who has been conscious of it.'

'Are we laying hold of a third poor girl?' said Mrs. Mountstuart. 'Ah! I remember. And I remember we used to call it playing fast and loose in those days, not fatality. It is very strange. It may be that you were unblushingly courted in those days, and excuseable: and we all supposed . . . but away you went for your tour.'

'My mother's medical receipt for me. Partially it succeeded. She was for grand marriages: not I. I could make, I could not be, a sacrifice. And then I went in due time to Dr. Cupid on my own account. She has the kind of attraction . . . But one changes! *On revient toujours.* First we begin with a liking: then we give ourselves up to the passion for beauty: then comes the serious question of suitableness of the mate to match us: and perhaps we discover that we were wiser in early youth than somewhat later. However, she has beauty. Now, Mrs. Mountstuart, you do admire her. Chase the idea of the "dainty rogue" out of your view of her: you admire her: she is captivating; she has a particular charm of her own, nay, she has real beauty.'

Mrs. Mountstuart fronted him to say: 'Upon my word, my dear Sir Willoughby, I think she has it to such a degree that I don't know the man who could hold out against her if she took the field. She is one of the women who are dead shots with men. Whether it's in their tongues or their eyes, or it's an effusion and an atmosphere—whatever it is, it's a spell, another fatality for you!'

'Animal; not spiritual!'

'Oh! she hasn't the head of Letty Dale.'

Sir Willoughby allowed Mrs. Mountstuart to pause and follow her thoughts.

'Dear me!' she exclaimed. 'I noticed a change in

Letty Dale last night: and to-day. She looked fresher and younger; extremely well: which is not what I can say for you, my friend. Fatalizing is not good for the complexion.'

'Don't take away my health, pray!' cried Willoughby, with a snapping laugh.

'Be careful,' said Mrs. Mountstuart. 'You have got a sentimental tone. You talk of "feelings crushed of old." It is to a woman, not to a man that you speak, but that sort of talk is a way of making the ground slippery. I listen in vain for a natural tongue; and when I don't hear it, I suspect plotting in men. You show your under-teeth too at times when you draw in a breath, like a condemned high-caste Hindoo my husband took me to see in a jail in Calcutta, to give me some excitement when I was pining for England. The creature did it regularly as he breathed; you did it last night, and you have been doing it to-day, as if the air cut you to the quick. You have been spoilt. You have been too much anointed. What I've just mentioned is a sign with me of a settled something on the brain of a man.'

'The brain?' said Sir Willoughby, frowning.

'Yes, you laugh sourly, to look at,' said she. 'Mountstuart told me that the muscles of the mouth betray men sooner than the eyes, when they have cause to be uneasy in their minds.'

'But, ma'am, I shall not break my word; I shall not, not; I intend, I have resolved to keep it. I do *not* fatalize, let my complexion be black or white. Despite my resemblance to a high-class malefactor of the Calcutta prison-wards . . .'

'Friend! friend! you know how I chatter.'

He saluted her finger-ends. 'Despite the extraordinary display of teeth, you will find me go to execution with perfect calmness; with a resignation as good as happiness.'

'Like a Jacobite lord under the Georges.'*

'You have told me that you wept to read of one: like him, then. My principles have not changed, if I have. When I was younger, I had an idea of a wife who would be with me in my thoughts as well as aims: a woman with a spirit of romance, and a brain of solid sense. I shall sooner or later dedicate myself to a public life; and shall, I suppose, want the counsellor or comforter who ought always to be found at home. It may be unfortunate that I have the ideal in my head. But I would never make rigorous demands for specific qualities. The cruellest thing in the world is to set up a living model before a wife, and compel her to copy it. In any case, here we are upon the road: the die is cast. I shall not reprieve myself. I cannot release her. Marriage represents facts, courtship fancies. She will be cured by-and-by of that coveting of everything that I do, feel, think, dream, imagine . . . ta-ta-ta-ta ad infinitum. Laetitia was invited here to show her the example of a fixed character —solid as any concrete substance you would choose to build on, and not a whit the less feminine.'

'Ta-ta-ta-ta ad infinitum. You need not tell me you have a design in all that you do, Willoughby Patterne.'

'You smell the autocrat? Yes, he can mould and govern the creatures about him. His toughest rebel is himself! If you see Clara . . . You wish to see her, I think you said?'

'Her behaviour to Lady Busshe last night was queer.'

'If you will. She makes a mouth at porcelain. *Toujours la porcelaine!** For me, her pettishness is one of her charms, I confess it. Ten years younger, I could not have compared them.'

'Whom?'

'Laetitia and Clara.'

'Sir Willoughby, in any case, to quote you, here we are all upon the road, and we must act as if events were going to happen; and I must ask her to help me on the subject of my wedding-present, for I don't want to have her making mouths at mine, however pretty—and she does it prettily.'

' "Another dedicatory offering to the *rogue* in me!" she says of porcelain.'

'Then porcelain it shall not be. I mean to consult her; I have come determined upon a chat with her. I think

I understand. But she produces false impressions on those who don't know you both. "I shall have that porcelain back," says Lady Busshe to me, when we were shaking hands last night: "I think," says she, "it should have been the Willow Pattern."* And she really said: "he's in for being jilted a second time!"'

Sir Willoughby restrained a bound of his body that would have sent him up some feet into the air. He felt his skull thundered at within.

'Rather than that it should fall upon her!' ejaculated he, correcting his resemblance to the high-caste culprit as soon as it recurred to him.

'But you know Lady Busshe,' said Mrs. Mountstuart, genuinely solicitous to ease the proud man of his pain. She could see through him to the depth of the skin, which his fencing sensitiveness vainly attempted to cover as it did the heart of him. 'Lady Busshe is nothing without her flights, fads and fancies. She has always insisted that you have an unfortunate nose. I remember her saying on the day of your majority, it was the nose of a monarch destined to lose a throne.'

'Have I ever offended Lady Busshe?'

'She trumpets you. She carries Lady Culmer with her too, and you may expect a visit of nods and hints and pots of alabaster. They worship you: you are the hope of England in their eyes, and no woman is worthy of you: but they are a pair of fatalists, and if you begin upon Letty Dale with them, you might as well forbid your banns. They will be all over the country exclaiming on predestination and marriages made in heaven.'

'Clara and her father!' cried Sir Willoughby.

Dr. Middleton and his daughter appeared in the circle of shrubs and flowers.

'Bring her to me, and save me from the polyglot,' said Mrs. Mountstuart, in affright at Dr. Middleton's manner of pouring forth into the ears of the downcast girl.

The leisure he loved that he might debate with his genius upon any next step was denied to Willoughby: he had to place his trust in the skill with which he had sown

and prepared Mrs. Mountstuart's understanding to meet
the girl—beautiful abhorred that she was! detested
darling! thing to squeeze to death and throw to the dust,
and mourn over!

He had to risk it; and at an hour when Lady Busshe's
prognostic grievously impressed his intensely apprehensive nature.

As it happened that Dr. Middleton's notion of a disagreeable duty in colloquy was to deliver all that he contained, and escape the listening to a syllable of reply,
Willoughby withdrew his daughter from him opportunely.

'Mrs. Mountstuart wants you, Clara.'

'I shall be very happy,' Clara replied, and put on a
new face.

An imperceptible nervous shrinking was met by
another force in her bosom, that pushed her to advance
without a sign of reluctance. She seemed to glitter.

She was handed to Mrs. Mountstuart.

Dr. Middleton laid his hand over Willoughby's
shoulder, retiring on a bow before the great lady of the
district. He blew and said: 'An opposition of female
instincts to masculine intellect necessarily creates a corresponding antagonism of intellect to instinct.'

'Her answer, sir? Her reasons? Has she named any?'

'The cat,' said Dr. Middleton, taking breath for a sentence, 'that humps her back in the figure of the letter H,
or a Chinese bridge, has given the dog her answer and her
reasons, we may presume: but he that undertakes to
translate them into human speech might likewise venture
to propose an addition to the alphabet and a continuation of Homer. The one performance would be not more
wonderful than the other. Daughters, Willoughby,
daughters! Above most human peccancies, I do abhor
a breach of faith. She will not be guilty of that. I demand a cheerful fulfilment of a pledge: and I sigh to
think that I cannot count on it without administering a
lecture.'

'She will soon be my care, sir.'

'She shall be. Why, she is as good as married. She is

at the altar. She is in her house. She is—why, where is she not? She has entered the sanctuary. She is out of the market. This maenad shriek for freedom would happily entitle her to the Republican cap—the Phrygian* —in a revolutionary Parisian procession. To me it has no meaning: and but that I cannot credit child of mine with mania, I should be in trepidation of her wits.'

Sir Willoughby's livelier fears were pacified by the information that Clara had simply emitted a cry. Clara had once or twice given him cause for starting and considering whether to think of her sex differently or condemningly of her, yet he could not deem her capable of fully unbosoming herself even to him, and under excitement. His idea of the cowardice of girls combined with his ideal of a waxwork sex to persuade him that though they are often (he had experienced it) wantonly desperate in their acts, their tongues are curbed by rosy pudency. And this was in his favour. For if she proved speechless and stupid with Mrs. Mountstuart, the lady would turn her over, and beat her flat, beat her angular, in fine, turn her to any shape, despising her, and cordially believe him to be the model gentleman of Christendom. She would fill in the outlines he had sketched to her of a picture that he had small pride in by comparison with his early vision of a fortune-favoured, triumphing squire, whose career is like the sun's, intelligibly lordly to all comprehensions. Not like your model gentleman, that has to be expounded—a thing for abstract esteem! However, it was the choice left to him. And an alternative was enfolded in that. Mrs. Mountstuart's model gentleman could marry either one of two women, throwing the other overboard. He was bound to marry: he was bound to take to himself one of them: and whichever one he selected would cast a lustre on his reputation. At least she would rescue him from the claws of Lady Busshe, and her owl's hoot of 'Willow Pattern,' and her hag's shriek of 'twice jilted.' That flying infant Willoughby—his unprotected little incorporeal omnipresent Self (not thought of so much as passionately felt for)— would not be scoffed at as the luckless with women. A

fall indeed from his original conception of his name of
fame abroad! But Willoughby had the high consolation
of knowing that others have fallen lower. There is the
fate of the devils to comfort us, if we are driven hard.
For one of your pangs another bosom is racked by ten, we read
in the solacing Book.

With all these nice calculations at work, Willoughby
stood above himself, contemplating his active machinery,
which he could partly criticize but could not stop, in a
singular wonderment at the aims and schemes and tremours of one who was handsome, manly, acceptable in
the world's eyes: and had he not loved himself most
heartily he would have been divided to the extent of
repudiating that urgent and excited half of his being,
whose motions appeared as those of a body of insects
perpetually erecting and repairing a structure of extraordinary pettiness. He loved himself too seriously to
dwell on the division for more than a minute or so. But
having seen it, and for the first time, as he believed, his
passion for the woman causing it became surcharged
with bitterness, atrabiliar.

A glance behind him, as he walked away with Dr.
Middleton, showed Clara, cunning creature that she was,
airily executing her malicious graces in the preliminary
courtesies with Mrs. Mountstuart.

CHAPTER XXXV

Miss Middleton and Mrs. Mountstuart

'Sit beside me, fair Middleton,' said the great lady.

'Gladly,' said Clara, bowing to her title.

'I want to sound you, my dear.'

Clara presented an open countenance with a dim
interrogation on the forehead. 'Yes?' she said sub-
missively.

'You were one of my bright faces last night. I was in
love with you. Delicate vessels ring sweetly to a fingernail, and if the wit is true, you answer to it; that I can
see, and that is what I like. Most of the people one has

at a table are drums. A rub-a-dub-dub on them is the
only way to get a sound. When they can be persuaded to
do it upon one another, they call it conversation.'

'Colonel De Craye was very funny.'

'Funny, and witty too.'

'But never spiteful.'

'These Irish or half-Irishmen are my taste. If they're
not politicians, mind: I mean Irish gentlemen. I will
never have another dinner-party without one. Our
men's tempers are uncertain. You can't get them to
forget themselves. And when the wine is in them the
nature comes out, and they must be buffeting, and up
start politics, and good-bye to harmony! My husband, I
am sorry to say, was one of those who have a long account
of ruined dinners against them. I have seen him and his
friends red as the roast and white as the boiled with wrath
on a popular topic they had excited themselves over,
intrinsically not worth a snap of the fingers. In London!'
exclaimed Mrs. Mountstuart, to aggravate the charge
against her lord in the Shades.* 'But town or country,
the table should be sacred. I have heard women say it is
a plot on the side of the men to teach us our littleness.
I don't believe they have a plot. It would be to compliment them on a talent. I believe they fall upon one
another blindly, simply because they are full: which is,
we are told, the preparation for the fighting Englishman.
They cannot eat and keep a truce. Did you notice that
dreadful Mr. Capes?'

'The gentleman who frequently contradicted papa?
But Colonel De Craye was good enough to relieve us.'

'How, my dear?'

'You did not hear him? He took advantage of an
interval when Mr. Capes was breathing after a paean to
his friend, the Governor—I think—of one of the Presidencies,* to say to the lady beside him: "He was a wonderful administrator and great logician; he married an
Anglo-Indian widow, and soon after published a pamphlet in favour of Suttee." '*

'And what did the lady say?'

'She said, "Oh." '

'Hark at her! And was it heard?'

'Mr. Capes granted the widow, but declared he had never seen the pamphlet in favour of Suttee, and disbelieved in it. He insisted that it was to be named Satì. He was vehement.'

'Now I do remember:—which must have delighted the colonel. And Mr. Capes retired from the front upon a repetition of "in toto, in toto." As if "in toto"*were the language of a dinner-table! But what will ever teach these men? Must we import Frenchmen to give them an example in the art of conversation, as their grandfathers brought over marquises to instruct them in salads? And our young men too! Women have to take to the hunting-field to be able to talk with them and be on a par with their grooms. Now, there was Willoughby Patterne, a prince among them formerly. Now, did you observe him last night? did you notice how, instead of conversing, instead of assisting me—as he was bound to do doubly, owing to the defection of Vernon Whitford: a thing I don't yet comprehend—there he sat sharpening his lower lip for cutting remarks. And at my best man! at Colonel De Craye! If he had attacked Mr. Capes, with his Governor of Bomby, as the man pronounces it, or Colonel Wildjohn and his Protestant Church in Danger, or Sir Wilson Pettifer harping on his Monarchical Republic, or any other! No, he preferred to be sarcastic upon friend Horace, and he had the worst of it. Sarcasm is so silly! What is the gain if he has been smart? People forget the epigram and remember the other's good temper. On that field, my dear, you must make up your mind to be beaten by "friend Horace." I have my prejudices and I have my prepossessions, but I love good temper, and I love wit, and when I see a man possessed of both, I set my cap at him, and there's my flat confession, and highly unfeminine it is.'

'Not at all!' cried Clara.

'We are one, then.'

Clara put up a mouth empty of words: she was quite one with her. Mrs. Mountstuart pressed her hand. 'When one does get intimate with a dainty rogue!' she said. 'You forgive me all that, for I could vow that Willoughby has betrayed me.'

Clara looked soft, kind, bright, in turns, and clouded instantly when the lady resumed: 'A friend of my own sex, and young, and a close neighbour, is just what I would have prayed for. And I'll excuse you, my dear, for not being so anxious about the friendship of an old woman. But I shall be of use to you, you will find. In the first place, I never tap for secrets. In the second, I keep them. Thirdly, I have some power. And fourth, every young married woman has need of a friend like me. Yes, and Lady Patterne heading all the county will be the stronger for my backing. You don't look so mighty well pleased, my dear. Speak out.'

'Dear Mrs. Mountstuart!'

'I tell you, I am very fond of Willoughby, but I saw the faults of the boy and see the man's. He has the pride of a king, and it's a pity if you offend it. He is prodigal in generosity, but he can't forgive. As to his own errors, you must be blind to them as a saint. The secret of him is, that he is one of those excessively civilized creatures who aim at perfection: and I think he ought to be supported in his conceit of having attained it; for the more men of that class, the greater our influence. He excels in manly sports, because he won't be excelled in anything, but as men don't comprehend his fineness, he comes to us; and his wife must manage him by that key. You look down at the idea of managing. It has to be done. One thing you may be assured of, he will be proud of you. His wife won't be very much enamoured of herself if she is not the happiest woman in the world. You will have the best horses, the best dresses, the finest jewels, in England; and an incomparable cook. The house will be changed the moment you enter it as Lady Patterne. And, my dear, just where he is, with all his graces, deficient of attraction, yours will tell. The sort of Othello he would make, or Leontes,* I don't know, and none of us ever needs to know. My impression is, that if even a shadow of a suspicion flitted across him, he is a sort of man to double-dye himself in guilt by way of vengeance in anticipation of an imagined offence. Not uncommon with men. I have heard strange stories of them: and so will you in your time to come, but not from me. No young woman shall ever be the sourer for having been my friend. One word of advice now we are on the topic: never play at counter-strokes with him. He will be certain to outstroke you, and you will be driven farther than you meant to go. They say we beat men at that game, and so we do, at the cost of beating ourselves. And if once we are started, it is a race-course ending on a precipice—over goes the winner. We must be moderately slavish to keep our place; which is given us in appearance; but appearances make up a remarkably large part of life, and far the most comfortable, so long as we are discreet at the right moment. He is a man whose pride, when hurt, would run his wife to perdition to solace it. If he married a troublesome widow, his pamphlet on Suttee would be out within the year. Vernon Whitford would receive instructions about it the first frosty moon. You like Miss Dale?'

'I think I like her better than she likes me,' said Clara.

'Have you never warmed together?'

'I have tried it. She is not one bit to blame. I can see how it is that she misunderstands me: or justly condemns me, perhaps I should say.'

'The hero of two women must die and be wept over in common before they can appreciate one another. You are not cold?'

'No.'

'You shuddered, my dear.'

'Did I?'

'I do sometimes. Feet will be walking over one's grave, wherever it lies. Be sure of this: Willoughby Patterne is a man of unimpeachable honour.'

'I do not doubt it.'

'He means to be devoted to you. He has been accustomed to have women hanging around him like votive offerings.'

'I . . .!'

'You cannot: of course not: any one could see that at

a glance. You are all the sweeter to me for not being tame. Marriage cures a multitude of indispositions.'

'Oh! Mrs. Mountstuart, will you listen to me?'

'Presently. Don't threaten me with confidences. Eloquence is a terrible thing in woman. I suspect, my dear, that we both know as much as could be spoken.'

'You hardly suspect the truth, I fear.'

'Let me tell you one thing about jealous men—when they are not blackamoors married to disobedient daughters.' I speak of our civil creature of the drawing-rooms: and lovers, mind, not husbands: two distinct species, married or not:—they're rarely given to jealousy unless they are flighty themselves. The jealousy fixes them. They have only to imagine that we are for some fun likewise and they grow as deferential as my footman, as harmless as the sportsman whose gun has burst. Ah! my fair Middleton, am I pretending to teach you? You have read him his lesson, and my table suffered for it last night, but I bear no rancour.'

'You bewilder me, Mrs. Mountstuart.'

'Not if I tell you that you have driven the poor man to try whether it would be possible for him to give you up.'

'I have?'

'Well, and you are successful.'

'I am?'

'Jump, my dear!'

'He will?'

'When men love stale instead of fresh, withered better than blooming, excellence in the abstract rather than the palpable. With their idle prate of feminine intellect, and a grotto nymph, and, and a mother of Gracchi!* Why, he must think me dazed with admiration of him to talk to me! One listens, you know. And he is one of the men who cast a kind of physical spell on you while he has you by the ear, until you begin to think of it by talking to somebody else. I suppose there are clever people who do see deep into the breast while dialogue is in progress. One reads of them. No, my dear, you have very cleverly managed to show him that it isn't at all possible: he can't. And the real cause for alarm in my humble opinion is lest your amiable foil should have been a trifle, as he would say, deceived, too much in earnest, led too far. One may reprove him for not being wiser, but men won't learn without groaning, that they are simply weapons taken up to be put down when done with. Leave it to me to compose him.—Willoughby can't give you up. I'm certain he has tried; his pride has been horribly wounded. You are shrewd, and he has had his lesson. If these little rufflings don't come before marriage they come after; so it's not time lost; and it's good to be able to look back on them. You are very white, my child.'

'Can you, Mrs. Mountstuart, can you think I would be so heartlessly treacherous?'

'Be honest, fair Middleton, and answer me: Can you say you had not a corner of an idea of producing an effect on Willoughby?'

Clara checked the instinct of her tongue to defend her reddening cheeks, with a sense that she was disintegrating and crumbling; but she wanted this lady for a friend, and she had to submit to the conditions, and be red and silent.

Mrs. Mountstuart examined her leisurely.

'That will do. Conscience blushes. One knows it by the outer conflagration. Don't be hard on yourself: there you are in the other extreme. That blush of yours would count with me against any quantity of evidence—all the Crooklyns in the kingdom. You lost your purse.'

'I discovered that it was lost this morning.'

'Flitch has been here with it. Willoughby has it. You will ask him for it; he will demand payment: you will be a couple of yards' length or so of cramoisy: and there ends the episode, nobody killed, only a poor man melancholy-wounded, and I must offer him my hand to mend him, vowing to prove to him that Suttee was properly abolished. Well, and now to business. I said I wanted to sound you. You have been overdone with porcelain. Poor Lady Busshe is in despair at your disappointment. Now, I mean my wedding-present to be to your taste.'

'Madam!'

'Who is the madam you are imploring?'

'Dear Mrs. Mountstuart!'

'Well?'

'I shall fall in your esteem. Perhaps you will help me. No one else can. I am a prisoner: I am compelled to continue this imposture. Oh! I shun speaking much: you object to it and I dislike it: but I must endeavour to explain to you that I am unworthy of the position you think a proud one.'

'Tut-tut; we are all unworthy, cross our arms, bow our heads; and accept the honours. Are you playing humble handmaid? What an old organ-tune that is! Well? Give me reasons.'

'I do not wish to marry.'

'He's the great match of the county!'

'I cannot marry him.'

'Why, you are at the church-door with him! Cannot marry him?'

'It does not bind me.'

'The church-door is as binding as the altar to an honourable girl. What have you been about? Since I am in for confidences, half ones won't do. We must have honourable young women as well as men of honour. You can't imagine he is to be thrown over now, at this hour? What have you against him? come!'

'I have found that I do not . . .'

'What?'

'Love him.'

Mrs. Mountstuart grimaced transiently. 'That is no answer. The cause!' she said. 'What has he done?'

'Nothing.'

'And when did you discover this nothing?'

'By degrees: unknown to myself; suddenly.'

'Suddenly and by degrees? I suppose it's useless to ask for a head. But if all this is true, you ought not to be here.'

'I wish to go; I am unable.'

'Have you had a scene together?'

'I have expressed my wish.'

'In roundabout?—girl's English?'

'Quite clearly. Oh! very clearly.'

'Have you spoken to your father?'

'I have.'

'And what does Dr. Middleton say?'

'It is incredible to him.'

'To me too! I can understand little differences, little whims, caprices: we don't settle into harness for a tap on the shoulder, as a man becomes a knight: but to break and bounce away from an unhappy gentleman at the church-door is either madness or it's one of the things without a name. You think you are quite sure of yourself?'

'I am so sure, that I look back with regret on the time when I was not.'

'But you were in love with him.'

'I was mistaken.'

'No love?'

'I have none to give.'

'Dear me!—Yes, yes, but that tone of sorrowful conviction is often a trick, it's not new: and I know that assumption of plain sense to pass off a monstrosity.' Mrs. Mountstuart struck her lap: 'Soh! but I've had to rack my brain for it: feminine disgust? You have been hearing imputations on his past life? moral character? No? Circumstances might make him behave unkindly, not unhandsomely: and we have no claim over a man's past, or it's too late to assert it. What is the case?'

'We are quite divided.'

'Nothing in the way of . . . nothing green-eyed?'

'Far from that!'

'Then, name it.'

'We disagree.'

'Many a very good agreement is founded on disagreeing. It's to be regretted that you are not portionless. If you had been, you would have made very little of disagreeing. You are just as much bound in honour as if you had the ring on your finger.'

'In honour! But I appeal to his, I am no wife for him.'

'But if he insists, you consent!'

'I appeal to reason. Is it, madam . . .'

'But, I say, if he insists, you consent!'

'He will insist upon his own misery as well as mine.'

Mrs. Mountstuart rocked herself. 'My poor Sir Willoughby! What a fate!—And I who took you for a clever girl! Why, I have been admiring your management of him! And here am I bound to take a lesson from Lady Busshe. My dear good Middleton, don't let it be said that Lady Busshe saw deeper than I! I put some little vanity in it, I own: I won't conceal it. She declares that when she sent her present—I don't believe her—she had a premonition that it would come back. Surely you won't justify the extravagances of a woman without common reverence:—for anatomize him as we please to ourselves, he is a splendid man (and I did it chiefly to encourage and come at you). We don't often behold such a lordly-looking man: so conversable too when he feels at home; a picture of an English gentleman! The very man we want married for our neighbourhood! A woman who can openly talk of expecting him to be twice jilted! You shrink. It is repulsive. It would be incomprehensible: except, of course, to Lady Busshe, who rushed to one of her violent conclusions and became a prophetess. Conceive a woman imagining it could happen twice to the same man! I am not sure she did not send the identical present that arrived and returned once before: you know, the Durham engagement. She told me last night she had it back. I watched her listening very suspiciously to Professor Crooklyn. My dear, it is her passion to foretell disasters—her passion! And when they are confirmed, she triumphs, of course. We shall have her domineering over us with sapient nods at every trifle occurring. The county will be unendureable. Unsay it, my Middleton! And don't answer like an oracle because I do all the talking. Pour out to me. You'll soon come to a stop and find the want of reason in the want of words. I assure you that's true.—Let me have a good gaze at you. No,' said Mrs. Mountstuart, after posturing herself to peruse Clara's features, 'brains you have: one can see it by the nose and the mouth. I could vow you are the girl I thought you; you have your wits on tiptoe. How of the heart?'

'None,' Clara sighed.

The sigh was partly voluntary, though unforced; as one may with ready sincerity act a character that is our own only through sympathy.

Mrs. Mountstuart felt the extra-weight in the young lady's falling breath. There was no necessity for a deep sigh over an absence of heart or confession of it. If Clara did not love the man to whom she was betrothed, sighing about it signified—what? some pretence: and a pretence is the cloak of a secret. Girls do not sigh in that way with compassion for the man they have no heart for, unless at the same time they should be oppressed by the knowledge or dread of having a heart for some one else. As a rule, they have no compassion to bestow on him: you might as reasonably expect a soldier to bewail the enemy he strikes in action: they must be very disengaged to have it. And supposing a show of the thing to be exhibited, when it has not been worried out of them, there is a reserve in the background: they are pitying themselves under a mask of decent pity of their wretch.

So ran Mrs. Mountstuart's calculations, which were like her suspicion, coarse and broad, not absolutely incorrect, but not of an exact measure with the truth. That pin's head of the truth is rarely hit by design. The search after it of the professionally penetrative in the dark of a bosom may bring it forth by the heavy knocking all about the neighbourhood that we call good guessing, but it does not come out clean; other matter adheres to it; and being more it is less than truth. The unadulterate is to be had only by faith in it or by waiting for it.

A lover! thought the sagacious dame. There was no lover: some love there was: or rather, there was a preparation of the chamber, with no lamp yet lighted.

'Do you positively tell me you have no heart for the position of first lady of the county?' said Mrs. Mountstuart.

Clara's reply was firm: 'None whatever.'

'My dear, I will believe you on one condition.—Look at me. You have eyes. If you are for mischief, you are armed for it. But how much better, when you have won a prize, to settle down and wear it! Lady Patterne will have entire occupation for her flights and whimsies in leading the county. And the man, surely the man—he behaved badly last night: but a beauty like this,' she pushed a finger at Clara's cheek, and doated a half instant, 'you have the very beauty to break in an ogre's temper. And the man is as governable as he is presentable. You have the beauty the French call—no, it's the beauty of a queen of elves: one sees them lurking about you, one here, one there. Smile—they dance: be doleful —they hang themselves. No, there's not a trace of satanic; at least, not yet. And come, come, my Middleton, the man is a man to be proud of. You can send him into Parliament to wear off his humours. To my thinking, he has a fine style: conscious? I never thought so before last night. I can't guess what has happened to him recently. He was once a young Grand Monarque.* He was really a superb young English gentleman. Have you been wounding him?'

'It is my misfortune to be obliged to wound him,' said Clara.

'Quite needlessly, my child, for marry him you must.'

Clara's bosom rose: her shoulders rose too, narrowing, and her head fell slightly back.

Mrs. Mountstuart exclaimed: 'But the scandal! You would never never think of following the example of that Durham girl?—whether she was provoked to it by jealousy or not. It seems to have gone so astonishingly far with you in a very short time, that one is alarmed as to where you will stop. Your look just now was downright revulsion.'

'I fear it is. It is. I am past my own control. Dear madam, you have my assurance that I will not behave scandalously or dishonourably. What I would entreat of you, is to help me. I know this of myself: I am not the best of women. I am impatient, wickedly. I should be no good wife. Feelings like mine teach me unhappy things of myself.'

'Rich, handsome, lordly, influential, brilliant health, fine estates,' Mrs. Mountstuart enumerated in petulant accents as they started across her mind some of Sir Willoughby's attributes for the attraction of the soul of woman. 'I suppose you wish me to take you in earnest?'

'I appeal to you for help.'

'What help?'

'Persuade him of the folly of pressing me to keep my word.'

'I will believe you, my dear Middleton, on one condition:—your talk of no heart is nonsense. A change like this, if one is to believe in the change, occurs through the heart, not because there is none. Don't you see that? But if you want me for a friend, you must not sham stupid. It's bad enough in itself: the imitation's horrid. You have to be honest with me, and answer me right out. You came here on this visit intending to marry Willoughby Patterne.'

'Yes.'

'And *gradually* you *suddenly* discovered, since you came here, that you did not intend it, if you could find a means of avoiding it.'

'Oh! madam, yes, it is true.'

'Now comes the test. And, my lovely Middleton, your flaming cheeks won't suffice for me this time. The old serpent can blush like an innocent maid on occasion. You are to speak, and you are to tell me in six words why that was: and don't waste one on "madam," or "Oh! Mrs. Mountstuart." Why did you change?'

'I came . . . when I came I was in some doubt. Indeed I speak the truth. I found I could not give him the admiration he has, I dare say, a right to expect. I turned—it surprised me: it surprises me now. But so completely! So that to think of marrying him is . . .'

'Defer the simile,' Mrs. Mountstuart interposed. 'If you hit on a clever one, you will never get the better of it. Now, by just as much as you have outstripped my limitation of words to you, you show me you are dishonest.'

'I could make a vow.'

'You would forswear yourself.'

'Will you help me?'

'If you are perfectly ingenuous, I may try.'

'Dear lady, what more can I say?'

'It may be difficult. You can reply to a catechism.'

'I shall have your help?'

'Well, yes; though I don't like stipulations between friends. There is no man living to whom you could willingly give your hand? That is my question. I cannot possibly take a step unless I know. Reply briefly: there is or there is not.'

Clara sat back with bated breath, mentally taking the leap into the abyss, realizing it, and the cold prudence of abstention, and the delirium of the confession. Was there such a man? It resembled freedom to think there was: to avow it promised freedom.

'Oh! Mrs. Mountstuart.'

'Well?'

'You will help me?'

'Upon my word, I shall begin to doubt your desire for it.'

'*Willingly* give my hand, madam?'

'For shame! And with wits like yours, can't you perceive where hesitation in answering such a question lands you?'

'Dearest lady, will you give me your hand? may I whisper?'

'You need not whisper: I won't look.'

Clara's voice trembled on a tense chord.

'There is one . . . compared with him I feel my insignificance. If I could aid him.'

'What necessity have you to tell me more than that there is one?'

'Ah, madam, it is different: not as you imagine. You bid me be scrupulously truthful: I am: I wish you to know the different kind of feeling it is from what might be suspected from . . . a confession. To give my hand, is beyond any thought I have ever encouraged. If you had asked me whether there is one whom I admire—yes, I do. I cannot help admiring a beautiful and brave self-denying nature. It is one whom you must pity, and to pity casts you beneath him: for you pity him because it is his nobleness that has been the enemy of his fortunes. He lives for others.'

Her voice was musically thrilling in that low muted tone of the very heart, impossible to deride or disbelieve.

Mrs. Mountstuart set her head nodding on springs.

'Is he clever?'

'Very.'

'He talks well?'

'Yes.'

'Handsome?'

'He might be thought so.'

'Witty?'

'I think he is.'

'Gay, cheerful?'

'In his manner.'

'Why, the man would be a mountebank if he adopted any other. And poor?'

'He is not wealthy.'

Mrs. Mountstuart preserved a lengthened silence, but nipped Clara's fingers once or twice to reassure her without approving. 'Of course he's poor,' she said at last; 'directly the reverse of what you *could* have, it *must* be. Well, my fair Middleton, I can't say you have been dishonest. I'll help you as far as I'm able. How, it is quite impossible to tell. We're in the mire. The best way seems to me, to get this pitiable angel to cut some ridiculous capers and present you another view of him. I don't believe in his innocence. He knew you to be a plighted woman.'

'He has not once by word or sign hinted a disloyalty.'

'Then how do you know . . .?'

'I do not know.'

'He is not the cause of your wish to break your engagement?'

'No.'

'Then you have succeeded in just telling me nothing. What is?'

'Ah! madam.'

'You would break your engagement purely because the admirable creature is in existence?'

Clara shook her head: she could not say: she was dizzy. She had spoken out more than she had ever spoken to herself: and in doing so she had cast herself a step beyond the line she dared to contemplate.

'I won't detain you any longer,' said Mrs. Mountstuart. 'The more we learn, the more we are taught that we are not so wise as we thought we were. I have to go to school to Lady Busshe! I really took you for a very clever girl. If you change again, you will notify the important circumstance to me, I trust.'

'I will,' said Clara, and no violent declaration of the impossibility of her changeing again would have had such an effect on her hearer.

Mrs. Mountstuart scanned her face for a new reading of it to match with her later impressions.

'I am to do as I please with the knowledge I have gained?'

'I am utterly in your hands, madam.'

'I have not meant to be unkind.'

'You have not been unkind; I could embrace you.'

'I am rather too shattered, and kissing won't put me together. I laughed at Lady Busshe! No wonder you went off like a rocket with a disappointing bouquet when I told you you had been successful with poor Sir Willoughby and he could not give you up. I noticed that. A woman like Lady Busshe, always prying for the lamentable, would have required no further enlightenment. Has he a temper?'

Clara did not ask her to signalize the person thus abruptly obtruded.

'He has faults,' she said.

'There's an end to Sir Willoughby, then! Though I don't say he will give you up even when he hears the worst, if he must hear it, as for his own sake he should. And I won't say he ought to give you up. He'll be the pitiable angel if he does. For you—but you don't deserve compliments; they would be immoral. You have behaved badly, badly, badly. I have never had such a right-about-face in my life. You will deserve the stigma: you will be notorious: you will be called Number Two.

Think of that! Not even original! We will break the conference, or I shall twaddle to extinction. I think I heard the luncheon-bell.'

'It rang.'

'You don't look fit for company, but you had better come.'

'Oh! yes: every day it's the same.'

'Whether you're in my hands or I'm in yours, we're a couple of arch-conspirators against the peace of the family whose table we're sitting at, and the more we rattle the viler we are, but we must do it to ease our minds.'

Mrs. Mountstuart spread the skirts of her voluminous dress, remarking further: 'At a certain age our teachers are young people: we learn by looking backward. It speaks highly for me that I have not called you mad.—Full of faults, goodish-looking, not a bad talker, cheerful, poorish;—and she prefers that to this!' the great lady exclaimed in her reverie while emerging from the circle of shrubs upon a view of the Hall.

Colonel De Craye advanced to her; certainly good-looking, certainly cheerful, by no means a bad talker, nothing of a Croesus,* and variegated with faults.

His laughing smile attacked the irresolute hostility of her mien, confident as the sparkle of sunlight in a breeze. The effect of it on herself angered her on behalf of Sir Willoughby's bride.

'Good morning, Mrs. Mountstuart; I believe I am the last to greet you.'

'And how long do you remain here, Colonel De Craye?'

'I kissed earth when I arrived, like the Norman William,* and consequently I've an attachment to the soil, ma'am.'

'You are not going to take possession of it, I suppose?'

'A handful would satisfy me!'

'You play the Conqueror pretty much, I have heard. But property is held more sacred than in the times of the Norman William.'

'And speaking of property, Miss Middleton, your purse is found,' he said.

'I know it is,' she replied, as unaffectedly as Mrs. Mountstuart could have desired, though the ingenuous air of the girl incensed her somewhat.

Clara passed on.

'You restore purses,' observed Mrs. Mountstuart.

Her stress on the word, and her look, thrilled De Craye: for there had been a long conversation between the young lady and the dame.

'It was an article that dropped and was not stolen,' said he.

'Barely sweet enough to keep, then!'

'I think I could have felt to it like poor Flitch, the flyman, who was the finder.'

'If you are conscious of these temptations to appropriate what is not your own, you should quit the neighbourhood.'

'And do it elsewhere? But that's not virtuous counsel.'

'And I'm not counselling in the interests of your virtue, Colonel De Craye.'

'And I dared for a moment to hope that you were, ma'am,' he said, ruefully drooping.

They were close to the dining-room window, and Mrs. Mountstuart preferred the terminating of a dialogue that did not promise to leave her features the austerely iron cast with which she had commenced it. She was under the spell of gratitude for his behaviour yesterday evening at her dinner-table; she could not be very severe.

CHAPTER XXXVI

Animated Conversation at a Luncheon-Table

VERNON was crossing the hall to the dining-room as Mrs. Mountstuart stepped in. She called to him: 'Are the champions reconciled?'

He replied: 'Hardly that, but they have consented to meet at an altar to offer up a victim to the Gods, in the shape of modern poetic imitations of the classical.'

'That seems innocent enough. The Professor has not been anxious about his chest?'

'He recollects his cough now and then.'

'You must help him to forget it.'

'Lady Busshe and Lady Culmer are here,' said Vernon, not supposing it to be a grave announcement until the effect of it on Mrs. Mountstuart admonished him.

She dropped her voice: 'Engage my fair friend for one of your walks the moment we rise from table. You may have to rescue her; but do. I mean it.'

'She's a capital walker,' Vernon remarked in simpleton style.

'There's no necessity for any of your pedestrian feats,' Mrs. Mountstuart said, and let him go, turning to Colonel De Craye to pronounce an encomium on him: 'The most open-minded man I know! Warranted to do perpetual service and no mischief. If you were all . . . instead of catching at every prize you covet! Yes, you would have your reward for unselfishness, I assure you. Yes, and where you seek it! That is what none of you men will believe.'

'When you behold me in your own livery!' cried the colonel.

'Do I?' said she, dallying with a half-formed design to be confidential. 'How is it one is always tempted to address you in the language of innuendo? I can't guess.'

'Except that as a dog doesn't comprehend good English we naturally talk bad to him.'

The great lady was tickled. Who could help being amused by this man? And after all, if her fair Middleton chose to be a fool, there could be no gainsaying her, sorry though poor Sir Willoughby's friends must feel for him.

She tried not to smile.

'You are too absurd. Or a baby, you might have added.'

'I hadn't the daring.'

'I'll tell you what, Colonel De Craye, I shall end by falling in love with you; and without esteeming you, I fear.'

'The second follows as surely as the flavour upon a draught of Bacchus, if you'll but toss off the glass, ma'am.'

'We women, sir, think it should be first.'

' 'Tis to transpose the seasons, and give October the blossom, and April the apple, and no sweet one! Esteem's a mellow thing that comes after bloom and fire, like an evening at home; because if it went before it would have no father and couldn't hope for progeny; for there'd be no nature in the business. So please, ma'am, keep to the original order, and you'll be nature's child and I the most blest of mankind.'

'Really, were I fifteen years younger. I am not so certain . . . I might try and make you harmless.'

'Draw the teeth of the lamb so long as you pet him!'

'I challenged you, colonel, and I won't complain of your pitch. But now lay your wit down beside your candour and descend to an everyday level with me for a minute.'

'Is it innuendo?'

'No, though I dare say it would be easier for you to respond to, if it were.'

'I'm the straightforwardest of men at a word of command.'

'This is a whisper. Be alert as you were last night. Shuffle the table well. A little liveliness will do it. I don't imagine malice, but there's curiosity, which is often as bad, and not so lightly foiled. We have Lady Busshe and Lady Culmer here.'

'To sweep the cobwebs out of the sky!'

'Well, then, can you fence with broomsticks?'

'I have had a bout with them in my time.'

'They are terribly direct.'

'They "give point," as Napoleon commanded his cavalry to do.'

'You must help me to ward it.'

'They will require variety in the conversation.'

'Constant. You are an angel of intelligence, and if I have the judgeing of you, I'm afraid you'll be allowed to pass, in spite of the scandal above. Open the door; I don't unbonnet.'

De Craye threw the door open.

Lady Busshe was at that moment saying: 'And are we indeed to have you for a neighbour, Dr. Middleton?'

The Rev. Doctor's reply was drowned by the new arrivals.

'I thought you had forsaken us,' observed Sir Willoughby to Mrs. Mountstuart.

'And run away with Colonel De Craye? I'm too weighty, my dear friend. Besides, I have not looked at the wedding-presents yet.'

'The very object of our call!' exclaimed Lady Culmer.

'I have to confess I am in dire alarm about mine,' Lady Busshe nodded across the table at Clara. 'Oh! you may shake your head, but I would rather hear a rough truth than the most complimentary evasion.'

'How would you define a rough truth, Dr. Middleton?' said Mrs. Mountstuart.

Like the trained warrior who is ready at all hours for the trumpet to arms, Dr. Middleton wakened up for judicial allocution in a trice.

'A rough truth, madam, I should define to be that description of truth which is not imparted to mankind without a powerful impregnation of the roughness of the teller.'

'It is a rough truth, ma'am, that the world is composed of fools, and that the exceptions are knaves,' Professor Crooklyn furnished the example avoided by the Rev. Doctor.

'Not to precipitate myself into the jaws of the first definition, which strikes me as being as happy as Jonah's whale,* that could carry probably the most learned man of his time inside without the necessity of digesting him,' said De Craye, 'a rough truth is a rather strong charge of universal nature for the firing off of a modicum of personal fact.'

'It is a rough truth that Plato is Moses atticizing,'* said Vernon to Dr. Middleton, to keep the diversion alive.

'And that Aristotle had the globe under his cranium,' rejoined the Rev. Doctor.

'And that the Moderns live on the Ancients.'

'And that not one in ten thousand can refer to the particular treasury he filches.'

'The Art of our days is a revel of rough truth,' remarked Professor Crooklyn.

'And the literature has laboriously mastered the adjective, wherever it may be in relation to the noun,' Dr. Middleton added.

'Orson's first appearance at Court was in the figure of a rough truth, causing the Maids of Honour, accustomed to Tapestry Adams, astonishment and terror,' said De Craye.

That he might not be left out of the sprightly play, Sir Willoughby levelled a lance at the quintain, smiling on Laetitia: 'In fine, caricature is rough truth.'

She said: 'Is one end of it, and realistic directness is the other.'

He bowed: 'The palm is yours.'

Mrs. Mountstuart admired herself as each one trotted forth in turn characteristically, with one exception unaware of the aid which was being rendered to a distressed damsel wretchedly incapable of decent hypocrisy. Her intrepid lead had shown her hand to the colonel and drawn the enemy at a blow.

Sir Willoughby's 'in fine,' however, did not please her: still less did his lackadaisical Lothario-like* bowing and smiling to Miss Dale: and he perceived it and was hurt. For how, carrying his tremendous load, was he to compete with these unhandicapped men in the game of nonsense she had such a fondness for starting at a table? He was further annoyed to hear Miss Eleanor and Miss Isabel Patterne agree together, that 'caricature' was the final word of the definition. Relatives should know better than to deliver these awards to us in public.

'Well!' quoth Lady Busshe, expressive of stupefaction at the strange dust she had raised.

'Are they on view, Miss Middleton?' inquired Lady Culmer.

'There's a regiment of us on view and ready for inspection,' Colonel De Craye bowed to her, but she would not be foiled. 'Miss Middleton's admirers are always on view,' said he.

'Are they to be seen?' said Lady Busshe.

Clara made her face a question, with a laudable smoothness.

'The wedding-presents,' Lady Culmer explained.

'No.'

'Otherwise, my dear, we are in danger of duplicating and triplicating and quadruplicating, not at all to the satisfaction of the bride.'

'But there's a worse danger to encounter in the "on view," my lady,' said De Craye; 'and that's the magnetic attraction a display of wedding-presents is sure to have for the ineffable burglar, who must have a nuptial soul in him, for wherever there's that collection on view, he's never a league off. And 'tis said he knows a lady's dressing-case presented to her on the occasion, fifteen years after the event.'

'As many as fifteen?' said Mrs. Mountstuart.

'By computation of the police. And if the presents are on view, dogs are of no use, nor bolts, nor bars:—he's worse than Cupid. The only protection to be found, singular as it may be thought, is in a couple of bottles of the oldest Jamaica rum in the British Isles.'

'Rum?' cried Lady Busshe.

'The liquor of the Royal Navy, my lady. And with your permission, I'll relate the tale in proof of it. I had a friend engaged to a young lady, niece of an old sea-captain of the old school, the Benbow school,* the wooden leg and pigtail school; a perfectly salt old gentleman with a pickled tongue, and a dash of brine in every deed he committed. He looked rolled over to you by the last wave on the shore, sparkling: he was Neptune's own for humour. And when his present to the bride was opened, sure enough there lay a couple of bottles of the oldest Jamaica rum in the British Isles, born before himself, and his father to boot. 'Tis a fabulous spirit I beg you to believe in, my lady, the sole merit of the story being its portentous veracity. The bottles were tied to make them appear twins, as they both had the same claim to seniority. And there was a label on them, telling their great age, to maintain their identity. They were in truth a pair of patriarchal bottles rivalling many of the biggest houses in the kingdom for antiquity. They would have made the donkey that stood between the two bundles of hay look at them with obliquity: supposing him to have, for an animal, a rum taste, and a turn for hilarity. Wonderful old bottles! So, on the label, just over the date, was written large: UNCLE BENJAMIN'S WEDDING-PRESENT TO HIS NIECE BESSY. Poor Bessy shed tears of disappointment and indignation enough to float the old gentleman on his native element, ship and all. She vowed it was done curmudgeonly to vex her, because her uncle hated wedding-presents and had grunted at the exhibition of cups and saucers, and this and that beautiful service, and épergnes and inkstands, mirrors, knives and forks, dressing-cases, and the whole mighty category. She protested, she flung herself about, she declared those two ugly bottles should not join the exhibition in the dining-room, where it was laid out for days, and the family ate their meals where they could, on the walls, like flies. But there was also Uncle Benjamin's legacy on view, in the distance, so it was ruled against her that the bottles should have their place. And one fine morning down came the family after a fearful row of the domestics; shouting, screaming, cries for the police, and murder topping all. What did they see? They saw two prodigious burglars extended along the floor, each with one of the twin bottles in his hand, and a remainder of the horror of the midnight hanging about his person like a blown fog, sufficient to frighten them whilst they kicked the rascals entirely intoxicated. Never was wilder disorder of wedding-presents, and not one lost!—owing, you'll own, to Uncle Benjy's two bottles of ancient Jamaica rum.'

Colonel De Craye concluded with an asseveration of the truth of the story.

'A most provident far-sighted old sea-captain!' exclaimed Mrs. Mountstuart, laughing at Lady Busshe and Lady Culmer.

These ladies chimed in with her gingerly.

'And have you many more clever stories, Colonel De Craye?' said Lady Busshe.

'Ah! my lady, when the tree begins to count its gold 'tis nigh upon bankruptcy.'

'Poetic!' ejaculated Lady Culmer, spying at Miss Middleton's rippled countenance, and noting that she and Sir Willoughby had not interchanged word or look.

'But that in the case of your Patterne Port a bottle of it would outvalue the catalogue of nuptial presents, Willoughby, I would recommend your stationing some such constabulary to keep watch and ward,' said Dr. Middleton as he filled his glass, taking Bordeaux in the middle of the day, under a consciousness of virtue and its reward to come at half-past seven in the evening.

'The dogs would require a dozen of that, sir,' said De Craye.

'Then it is not to be thought of. Indeed, one!' Dr. Middleton negatived the idea.

'We are no further advanced than when we began,' observed Lady Busshe.

'If we are marked to go by stages,' Mrs. Mountstuart assented.

'Why, then, we shall be called old coaches,' remarked the colonel.

'You,' said Lady Culmer, 'have the advantage of us in a closer acquaintance with Miss Middleton. You know her tastes, and how far they have been consulted in the little souvenirs already grouped somewhere, although not yet for inspection. I am at sea. And here is Lady Busshe in deadly alarm. There is plenty of time to effect a change—though we are drawing on rapidly to the fatal day, Miss Middleton. We are, we are very near it. Oh! yes. I am one who thinks that these little affairs should be spoken of openly, without that ridiculous bourgeois affectation, so that we may be sure of giving satisfaction. It is a transaction, like everything else in life. I for my part wish to be remembered favourably. I put it as a test of breeding to speak of these things as plain matter-of-fact. You marry; I wish you to have something by you to remind you of me. What shall it be?—useful or ornamental. For an ordinary household the choice is not difficult. But where wealth abounds we are in a dilemma.'

'And with persons of decided tastes,' added Lady Busshe. 'I am really very unhappy,' she protested to Clara.

Sir Willoughby dropped Laetitia: Clara's look of a sedate resolution to preserve silence on the topic of the nuptial gifts, made a diversion imperative.

'Your porcelain was exquisitely chosen, and I profess to be a connoisseur,' he said. 'I am poor in old Saxony, as you know: I can match the county in Sèvres, and my inheritance of China* will not easily be matched in the country.'

'You may consider your Dragon vases*a present from young Crossjay,' said De Craye.

'How?'

'Hasn't he abstained from breaking them? the capital boy! Porcelain and a boy in the house together, is a case of prospective disaster fully equal to Flitch and a fly.'

'You should understand that my friend Horace—whose wit is in this instance founded on another tale of a boy—brought us a magnificent piece of porcelain, destroyed by the capsizing of his conveyance from the station,' said Sir Willoughby to Lady Busshe.

She and Lady Culmer gave out lamentable Ohs, while Miss Eleanor and Miss Isabel Patterne sketched the incident. Then the lady visitors fixed their eyes in united sympathy upon Clara: recovering from which, after a contemplation of marble, Lady Busshe emphasized: 'No, you do not love porcelain, it is evident, Miss Middleton.'

'I am glad to be assured of it,' said Lady Culmer.

'Oh! I know that face: I know that look,' Lady Busshe affected to remark rallyingly: 'it is not the first time I have seen it.'

Sir Willoughby smarted to his marrow. 'We will rout these fancies of an over-scrupulous generosity, my dear Lady Busshe.'

Her unwonted breach of delicacy in speaking publicly of her present, and the vulgar persistency of her sticking to the theme, very much perplexed him. And if he mistook her not, she had just alluded to the demoniacal Constantia Durham. It might be that he had mistaken her: he was on guard against his terrible sensitiveness. Nevertheless it was hard to account for this behaviour of a lady greatly his friend and admirer, a lady of birth. And Lady Culmer as well!—likewise a lady of birth. Were they in collusion? had they a suspicion? He turned to Laetitia's face for the antidote to his pain.

'Oh, but you are not one yet, and I shall require two voices to convince me,' Lady Busshe rejoined after another stare at the marble.

'Lady Busshe, I beg you not to think me ungrateful,' said Clara.

'Fiddle!—gratitude! it is to please your taste, to satisfy *you*. I care for gratitude as little as for flattery.'

'But gratitude is flattering,' said Vernon.

'Now, no metaphysics, Mr. Whitford.'

'But do care a bit for flattery, my lady,' said De Craye. ' 'Tis the finest of the Arts; we might call it moral sculpture. Adepts in it can cut their friends to any shape they like by practising it with the requisite skill. I myself, poor hand as I am, have made a man act Solomon by constantly praising his wisdom. He took a sagacious turn at an early period of the dose. He weighed the smallest question of his daily occasions with a deliberation truly oriental. Had I pushed it, he'd have hired a baby and a couple of mothers to squabble over the undivided morsel.'*

'I shall hope for a day in London with you,' said Lady Culmer to Clara.

'You did not forget the Queen of Sheba?'* said Mrs. Mountstuart to De Craye.

'With her appearance, the game has to be resigned to her entirely,' he rejoined.

'That is,' Lady Culmer continued, 'if you do not despise an old woman for your comrade on a shopping excursion.'

'Despise whom we fleece!' exclaimed Dr. Middleton. 'Oh, no, Lady Culmer, the sheep is sacred.'

'I am not so sure,' said Vernon.

'In what way, and to what extent, are you not so sure?' said Dr. Middleton.

'The natural tendency is to scorn the fleeced.'

'I stand for the contrary. Pity, if you like: particularly when they bleat.'

'This is to assume that makers of gifts are a fleeced people: I demur,' said Mrs. Mountstuart.

'Madam, we are expected to give; we are incited to give; you have dubbed it the fashion to give; and the person refusing to give, or incapable of giving, may anticipate that he will be regarded as benignly as a sheep of a drooping and flaccid wool by the farmer, who is reminded by the poor beast's appearance of a strange dog that worried the flock. Even Captain Benjamin, as you have seen, was unable to withstand the demand on him. The hymenaeal pair are licensed freebooters levying blackmail on us; survivors of an uncivilized period. But in taking without mercy, I venture to trust that the manners of a happier aera instruct them not to scorn us. I apprehend that Mr. Whitford has a lower order of latrons* in his mind.'

'Permit me to say, sir, that you have not considered the ignoble aspect of the fleeced,' said Vernon. 'I appeal to the ladies: would they not, if they beheld an ostrich walking down a Queen's Drawing-Room, clean-plucked, despise him though they were wearing his plumes?'

'An extreme supposition, indeed,' said Dr. Middleton, frowning over it: 'scarcely legitimately to be suggested.'

'I think it fair, sir, as an instance.'

'Has the circumstance occurred, I would ask?'

'In life? a thousand times.'

'I fear so,' said Mrs. Mountstuart.

Lady Busshe showed symptoms of a desire to leave a profitless table.

Vernon started up, glancing at the window.

'Did you see Crossjay?' he said to Clara.

'No; I must, if he is there,' said she.

She made her way out, Vernon after her. They both had the excuse.

'Which way did the poor boy go?' she asked him.

'I have not the slightest idea,' he replied. 'But put on your bonnet, if you would escape that pair of inquisitors.'

'Mr. Whitford, what humiliation!'

'I suspect you do not feel it the most, and the end of it can't be remote,' said he.

Thus it happened that when Lady Busshe and Lady Culmer quitted the dining-room, Miss Middleton had spirited herself away from summoning voice and messenger.

Sir Willoughby apologized for her absence. 'If I could be jealous, it would be of that boy Crossjay.'

'You are an excellent man, and the best of cousins,' was Lady Busshe's enigmatical answer.

The exceedingly lively conversation at his table was lauded by Lady Culmer.

'Though,' said she, 'what it all meant, and what was the drift of it, I couldn't tell to save my life. Is it every day the same with you here?'

'Very much.'

'How you must enjoy a spell of dulness!'

'If you said, simplicity and not talking for effect! I generally cast anchor by Laetitia Dale.'

'Ah!' Lady Busshe coughed. 'But the fact is, Mrs. Mountstuart is mad for cleverness.'

'I think, my lady, Laetitia Dale is to the full as clever as any of the stars Mrs. Mountstuart assembles, or I.'

'Talkative cleverness, I mean.'

'In conversation as well. Perhaps you have not yet given her a chance.'

'Yes, yes, she is clever, of course, poor dear. She is looking better too.'

'Handsome, I thought,' said Lady Culmer.

'She varies,' observed Sir Willoughby.

The ladies took seat in their carriage and fell at once into a close-bonnet colloquy. Not a single allusion had they made to the wedding-presents after leaving the luncheon-table. The cause of their visit was obvious.

CHAPTER XXXVII

*Contains clever Fencing and Intimations of the
need for it*

THAT woman, Lady Busshe, had predicted, after the
event, Constantia Durham's defection. She had also,
subsequent to Willoughby's departure on his travels,
uttered sceptical things concerning his rooted attachment
to Laetitia Dale. In her bitter vulgarity, that beaten
rival of Mrs. Mountstuart Jenkinson for the leadership of
the county had taken his nose for a melancholy prognostic
of his fortunes; she had recently played on his name:
she had spoken the hideous English of his fate. Little as
she knew, she was alive to the worst interpretation of
appearances. No other eulogy occurred to her now than
to call him the best of cousins, because Vernon Whitford
was housed and clothed and fed by him. She had
nothing else to say for a man she thought luckless! She
was a woman barren of wit, stripped of style, but she was
wealthy and a gossip—a forge of showering sparks—and
she carried Lady Culmer with her. The two had driven
from his house to spread the malignant rumour abroad:
already they blew the biting world on his raw wound.
Neither of them was like Mrs. Mountstuart, a witty
woman, who could be hoodwinked; they were dull
women, who steadily kept on their own scent of the fact,
and the only way to confound such inveterate forces was,
to be ahead of them, and seize and transform the expected fact, and astonish them, when they came up to
him, with a totally unanticipated fact.

'You see, you were in error, ladies.'

'And so we were, Sir Willoughby, and we acknowledge
it. We never could have guessed *that*!'

Thus the phantom couple in the future delivered themselves, as well they might at the revelation. He could
run far ahead.

Ay, but to combat these dolts, facts had to be encountered, deeds done, in groaning earnest. These repre-
sentatives of the pig-sconces of the population judged by

circumstances: airy shows and seems had no effect on them. Dexterity of fence was thrown away.

A flying peep at the remorseless might of dulness in compelling us to a concrete performance counter to our inclinations, if we would deceive its terrible instinct, gave Willoughby for a moment the survey of a sage. His intensity of personal feeling struck so vivid an illumination of mankind at intervals that he would have been individually wise, had he not been moved by the source of his accurate perceptions to a personal feeling of opposition to his own sagacity. He loathed and he despised the vision, so his mind had no benefit of it, though he himself was whipped along. He chose rather (and the choice is open to us all) to be flattered by the distinction it revealed between himself and mankind.

But if he was not as others were, why was he discomfited, solicitous, miserable? To think that it should be so, ran dead against his conqueror's theories wherein he had been trained, which, so long as he gained success awarded success to native merit, grandeur to the grand in soul, as light kindles light: nature presents the example. His early training, his bright beginning of life, had taught him to look to earth's principal fruits as his natural portion, and it was owing to a girl that he stood a mark for tongues, naked, wincing at the possible malignity of a pair of harridans. Why not whistle the girl away?

Why, then he would be free to enjoy, careless, younger than his youth in the rebound to happiness!

And then would his nostrils begin to lift and sniff at the creeping up of a thick pestiferous vapour. Then in that volume of stench would he discern the sullen yellow eye of malice. A malarious earth would hunt him all over it. The breath of the world, the world's view of him, was partly his vital breath, his view of himself. The ancestry of the tortured man had bequeathed him this condition of high civilization among their other bequests. Your withered contracted Egoists of the hut and the grot reck not of public opinion; they crave but for liberty and leisure to scratch themselves and soothe an excessive scratch. Willoughby was expansive, a blooming one, born to look down upon a tributary world, and to exult in being looked to. Do we wonder at his consternation in the prospect of that world's blowing foul on him? Princes have their obligations to teach them they are mortal, and the brilliant heir of a tributary world is equally enchained by the homage it brings him;—more, inasmuch as it is immaterial, elusive, not gathered by the tax, and he cannot capitally punish the treasonable recusants. Still must he be brilliant; he must court his people. He must ever, both in his reputation and his person, aching though he be, show them a face and a leg.

The wounded gentleman shut himself up in his laboratory, where he could stride to and fro, and stretch out his arms for physical relief, secure from observation of his fantastical shapes, under the idea that he was meditating. There was perhaps enough to make him fancy it in the heavy fire of shots exchanged between his nerves and the situation; there were notable flashes. He would not avow that he was in an agony: it was merely a desire for exercise.

Quintessence of worldliness, Mrs. Mountstuart appeared through his farthest window, swinging her skirts on a turn at the end of the lawn, with Horace De Craye smirking beside her. And the woman's vaunted penetration was unable to detect the histrionic Irishism of the fellow. Or she liked him for his acting and nonsense; nor she only. The voluble beast was created to snare women. Willoughby became smitten with an adoration of stedfastness in women. The incarnation of that divine quality crossed his eyes. She was clad in beauty.

A horrible nondescript convulsion composed of yawn and groan drove him to his instruments, to avert a renewal of the shock; and while arranging and fixing them for their unwonted task, he compared himself advantageously with men like Vernon and De Craye, and others of the county, his fellows in the hunting-field and on the Magistrate's bench, who neither understood nor cared for solid work, beneficial practical work, the work of Science.

He was obliged to relinquish it: his hand shook.

'Experiments will not advance much at this rate,' he said, casting the noxious retardation on his enemies.

It was not to be contested that he must speak with Mrs. Mountstuart, however he might shrink from the trial of his facial muscles. Her not coming to him seemed ominous: nor was her behaviour at the luncheon-table quite obscure. She had evidently instigated the gentlemen to cross and counter-chatter Lady Busshe and Lady Culmer. For what purpose?

Clara's features gave the answer.

They were implacable. And he could be the same.

In the solitude of his room he cried right out: 'I swear it, I will never yield her to Horace De Craye! She shall feel some of my torments, and try to get the better of them by knowing she deserves them.' He had spoken it, and it was an oath upon the record.

Desire to do her intolerable hurt became an ecstasy in his veins, and produced another stretching fit, that terminated in a violent shake of the body and limbs; during which he was a spectacle for Mrs. Mountstuart at one of the windows. He laughed as he went to her, saying: 'No, no work to-day; it won't be done, positively refuses.'

'I am taking the Professor away,' said she; 'he is fidgety about the cold he caught.'

Sir Willoughby stepped out to her. 'I was trying at a bit of work for an hour, not to be idle all day.'

'You work in that den of yours every day?'

'Never less than an hour, if I can snatch it.'

'It is a wonderful resource!'

The remark set him throbbing and thinking that a prolongation of his crisis exposed him to the approaches of some organic malady, possibly heart-disease.

'A habit,' he said. 'In there I throw off the world.'

'We shall see some results in due time.'

'I promise none: I like to be abreast of the real knowledge of my day, that is all.'

'And a pearl among country gentlemen!'

'In your gracious consideration, my dear lady. Generally speaking, it would be more adviseable to become a chatterer and keep an anecdotal note-book. I could not do it, simply because I could not live with my own emptiness for the sake of making an occasional display of fireworks. I aim at solidity. It is a narrow aim, no doubt; not much appreciated.'

'Laetitia Dale appreciates it.'

A smile of enforced ruefulness, like a leaf curling in heat, wrinkled his mouth.

Why did she not speak of her conversation with Clara?

'Have they caught Crossjay?' he said.

'Apparently they are giving chase to him.'

The likelihood was, that Clara had been overcome by timidity.

'Must you leave us?'

'I think it prudent to take Professor Crooklyn away.'

'He still . . .?'

'The extraordinary resemblance!'

'A word aside to Dr. Middleton will dispel that.'

'You are thoroughly good.'

This hateful encomium of commiseration transfixed him. Then, she knew of his calamity!

'Philosophical,' he said, 'would be the proper term, I think.'

'Colonel De Craye, by the way, promises me a visit when he leaves you.'

'To-morrow?'

'The earlier the better. He is too captivating; he is delightful. He won me in five minutes. I don't accuse him. Nature gifted him to cast the spell. We are weak women, Sir Willoughby.'

She knew!

'Like to like: the witty to the witty, ma'am.'

'You won't compliment me with a little bit of jealousy?'

'I forbear from complimenting *him*.'

'Be philosophical, of course, if you have the philosophy.'

'I pretend to it. Probably I suppose myself to succeed because I have no great requirement of it; I cannot say. We are riddles to ourselves.'

Mrs. Mountstuart pricked the turf with the point of her parasol. She looked down and she looked up.

'Well?' said he to her eyes.

'Well, and where is Laetitia Dale?'

He turned about to show his face elsewhere.

When he fronted her again, she looked very fixedly, and set her head shaking.

'It will not do, my dear Sir Willoughby!'

'What?'

'It.'

'I never could solve enigmas.'

'Playing ta-ta-ta-ta ad infinitum,* then. Things have gone far. All parties would be happier for an excursion. Send her home.'

'Laetitia? I can't part with her.'

Mrs. Mountstuart put a tooth on her under-lip as her head renewed its brushing negative.

'In what way can it be hurtful that she should be here, ma'am?' he ventured to persist.

'Think.'

'She is proof.'

'Twice!'

The word was big artillery. He tried the affectation of a staring stupidity. She might have seen his heart thump, and he quitted the mask for an agreeable grimace.

'She is inaccessible. She is my friend. I guarantee her, on my honour. Have no fear for her. I beg you to have confidence in me. I would perish rather. No soul on earth is to be compared with her.'

Mrs. Mountstuart repeated 'Twice!'

The low monosyllable, musically spoken in the same tone of warning of a gentle ghost, rolled a thunder that maddened him, but he dared not take it up to fight against it on plain terms.

'Is it for my sake?' he said.

'It will not do, Sir Willoughby!'

She spurred him to a frenzy.

'My dear Mrs. Mountstuart, you have been listening to tales. I am not a tyrant. I am one of the most easy-going of men. Let us preserve the forms due to society: I say no more. As for poor old Vernon, people call me a good sort of cousin; I should like to see him comfortably married; decently married this time. I have proposed to contribute to his establishment. I mention it to show that the case has been practically considered. He has had a tolerably souring experience of the state; he might be inclined if, say, you took him in hand, for another venture. It's a demoralizing lottery. However, Government sanctions it.'

'But, Sir Willoughby, what is the use of my taking him in hand, when, as you tell me, Laetitia Dale holds back?'

'She certainly does.'

'Then we are talking to no purpose, unless you undertake to melt her.'

He suffered a lurking smile to kindle to some strength of meaning.

'You are not over-considerate in committing me to such an office.'

'You are afraid of the danger?' she all but sneered.

Sharpened by her tone, he said: 'I have such a love of stedfastness of character, that I should be a poor advocate in the endeavour to break it. And frankly, I know the danger. I saved my honour when I made the attempt: that is all I can say.'

'Upon my word,' Mrs. Mountstuart threw back her head to let her eyes behold him summarily over their fine aquiline bridge, 'you have the heart of mystification, my good friend.'

'Abandon the idea of Laetitia Dale.'

'And marry your cousin Vernon to whom? Where are we?'

'As I said, ma'am, I am an easy-going man. I really have not a spice of the tyrant in me. An intemperate creature held by the collar may have that notion of me, while pulling to be released as promptly as it entered the noose. But I do strictly and sternly object to the scandal of violent separations, open breaches of solemn engagements, a public rupture. Put it that I am the cause, I will not consent to a violation of decorum. Is that

clear? It is just possible for things to be arranged so
that all parties may be happy in their way without much
hubbub. Mind, it is not I who have willed it so. I am,
and I am forced to be, passive. But I will not be ob-
structive.'

He paused, waving his hand to signify the vanity of the
more that might be said.

Some conception of him, dashed by incredulity, excited the lady's intelligence.

'Well!' she exclaimed, 'you have planted me in the
land of conjecture. As my husband used to say, I don't
see light, but I think I see the lynx that does. We won't
discuss it at present. I certainly must be a younger
woman than I supposed, for I am learning hard.—Here
comes the Professor, buttoned up to the ears, and Dr.
Middleton flapping in the breeze. There will be a cough,
and a footnote referring to the young lady at the station,
if we stand together, so please order my carriage.'

'You found Clara complacent? roguish?'

'I will call to-morrow. You have simplified my task,
Sir Willoughby, very much: that is, assuming that I
have not entirely mistaken you. I am so far in the dark,
that I have to help myself by recollecting how Lady
Busshe opposed my view of a certain matter formerly.
Scepticism is her forte. It will be the very oddest thing
if after all . . .! No, I shall own, romance has not
departed. Are you fond of dupes?'

'I detest the race.'

'An excellent answer. I could pardon you for it.' She
refrained from adding: 'If you are making one of me.'

Sir Willoughby went to ring for her carriage.

She knew. That was palpable: Clara had betrayed
him. 'The earlier Colonel De Craye leaves Patterne Hall
the better': she had said that: and, 'all parties would
be happier for an excursion.' She knew the position of
things and she guessed the remainder. But what she
did not know, and could not divine, was the man who
fenced her. He speculated further on the witty and the
dull. These latter are the redoubtable body. They will
have facts to convince them; they had, he confessed it

to himself, precipitated him into the novel sphere of his dark hints to Mrs. Mountstuart; from which the utter darkness might allow him to escape, yet it embraced him singularly, and even pleasantly, with the sense of a fact established.

It embraced him even very pleasantly. There was an end to his tortures. He sailed on a tranquil sea, the husband of a stedfast woman—no rogue. The exceeding beauty of stedfastness in women clothed Laetitia in graces Clara could not match. A tried stedfast woman is the one jewel of the sex. She points to her husband like the sunflower; her love illuminates him; she lives in him, for him; she testifies to his worth; she drags the world to his feet; she leads the chorus of his praises; she justifies him in his own esteem. Surely there is not on earth such beauty!

If we have to pass through anguish to discover it and cherish the peace it gives, to clasp it, calling it ours, is a full reward.

Deep in his reverie, he said his adieux to Mrs. Mountstuart, and strolled up the avenue behind the carriage-wheels, unwilling to meet Laetitia till he had exhausted the fresh savour of the cud of fancy.

Supposing it done!—

It would be generous on his part. It would redound to his credit.

His home would be a fortress, impregnable to tongues. He would have divine security in his home.

One who read and knew and worshipped him would be sitting there starlike: sitting there, awaiting him, his fixed star.

It would be marriage with a mirror, with an echo; marriage with a shining mirror, a choric echo.

It would be marriage with an intellect, with a fine understanding; to make his home a fountain of repeatable wit: to make his dear old Patterne Hall the luminary of the county.

He revolved it as a chant: with anon and anon involuntarily a discordant animadversion on Lady Busshe. His attendant imps heard the angry inward cry.

Forthwith he set about painting Laetitia in delectable human colours, like a miniature of the past century, reserving her ideal figure for his private satisfaction. The world was to bow to her visible beauty, and he gave her enamel and glow, a taller statue, a swimming air, a transcendancy that exorcised the image of the old witch who had driven him to this.

The result in him was, that Laetitia became humanly and avowedly beautiful. Her dark eyelashes on the pallor of her cheeks lent their aid to the transformation, which was a necessity to him, so it was performed. He received the waxen impression.

His retinue of imps had a revel. We hear wonders of men, and we see a lifting up of hands in the world. The wonders would be explained, and never a hand need to interject, if the mystifying man were but accompanied and reported of by that monkey-eyed confraternity. They spy the heart and its twists.

The heart is the magical gentleman. None of them would follow where there was no heart. The twists of the heart are the comedy.

'*The secret of the heart is its pressing love of self,*' says the Book.

By that secret the mystery of the organ is legible: and a comparison of the heart to the mountain rillet is taken up to show us the unbaffled force of the little channel in seeking to swell its volume, strenuously, sinuously, ever in pursuit of self; the busiest as it is the most single-aiming of forces on our earth. And we are directed to the sinuosities for the posts of observation chiefly instructive.

Few maintain a stand there. People see, and they rush away to interchange liftings of hands at the sight, instead of patiently studying the phenomenon of energy.

Consequently a man in love with one woman, and in all but absolute consciousness, behind the thinnest of veils, preparing his mind to love another, will be barely credible. The particular hunger of the forceful but adaptable heart is the key of him. Behold the mountain rillet, become a brook, become a torrent, how it inarms a handsome boulder: yet if the stone will not go with it, on it hurries, pursuing self in extension, down to where perchance a dam has been raised of a sufficient depth to enfold and keep it from inordinate restlessness. Laetitia represented this peaceful restraining space in prospect.

But she was a faded young woman. He was aware of it; and systematically looking at himself with her up-turned orbs, he accepted her benevolently, as a God grateful for worship, and used the divinity she imparted to paint and renovate her. His heart required her so. The heart works the springs of imagination; imagination received its commission from the heart, and was a cunning artist.

Cunning to such a degree of seductive genius that the masterpiece it offered to his contemplation enabled him simultaneously to gaze on Clara and think of Laetitia. Clara came through the park-gates with Vernon, a brilliant girl indeed, and a shallow one: a healthy creature, and an animal; attractive, but capricious, impatient, treacherous, foul; a woman to drag men through the mud. She approached.

CHAPTER XXXVIII

In which we take a Step to the Centre of Egoism

They met; Vernon soon left them.

'You have not seen Crossjay?' Willoughby inquired.

'No,' said Clara. 'Once more I beg you to pardon him. He spoke falsely, owing to his poor boy's idea of chivalry.'

'The chivalry to the sex which commences in lies, ends by creating the woman's hero, whom we see about the world and in certain Courts of Law.'

His ability to silence her was great: she could not reply to speech like that.

'You have,' said he, 'made a confidante of Mrs. Mountstuart.'

'Yes.'

'This is your purse.'

'I thank you.'

'Professor Crooklyn has managed to make your father acquainted with your project. That, I suppose, is the railway ticket in the fold of the purse. He was assured at the station that you had taken a ticket to London, and would not want the fly.'

'It is true. I was foolish.'

'You have had a pleasant walk with Vernon—turning me in and out?'

'We did not speak of you. You allude to what he would never consent to.'

'He's an honest fellow, in his old-fashioned way. He's a secret old fellow. Does he ever talk about his wife to you?'

Clara dropped her purse, and stooped and picked it up.

'I know nothing of Mr. Whitford's affairs,' she said, and she opened the purse and tore to pieces the railway-ticket.

'The story's a proof that romantic spirits do not furnish the most romantic history. You have the word "chivalry" frequently on your lips. He chivalrously married the daughter of the lodging-house where he resided before I took him. We obtained information of the auspicious union in a newspaper report of Mrs. Whitford's drunkenness and rioting at a London railway terminus—probably the one whither your ticket would have taken you yesterday, for I heard the lady was on her way to us for supplies, the connubial larder being empty.'

'I am sorry; I am ignorant; I have heard nothing; I know nothing,' said Clara.

'You are disgusted. But half the students and authors you hear of marry in that way. And very few have Vernon's luck.'

'She had good qualities?' asked Clara.

Her under-lip hung.

It looked like disgust; he begged her not indulge the feeling.

'Literary men, it is notorious, even with the entry to society, have no taste in women. The housewife is their object. Ladies frighten and would, no doubt, be an annoyance and hindrance to them at home.'

'You said he was fortunate.'

'You have a kindness for him.'

'I respect him.'

'He is a friendly old fellow in his awkward fashion; honourable, and so forth. But a disreputable alliance of that sort sticks to a man. The world will talk. Yes, he was fortunate so far; he fell into the mire and got out of it. Were he to marry again . . .'

'She . . ?'

'Died. Do not be startled; it was a natural death. She responded to the sole wishes left to his family. He buried the woman, and I received him. I took him on my tour. A second marriage might cover the first: there would be a buzz about the old business: the woman's relatives write to him still, try to bleed him, I dare say. However, now you understand his gloominess. I don't imagine he regrets his loss. He probably sentimentalizes, like most men when they are well rid of a burden. You must not think the worse of him.'

'I do not,' said Clara.

'I defend him whenever the matter's discussed.'

'I hope you do.'

'Without approving his folly. I can't wash him clean.'

They were at the Hall-doors. She waited for any personal communications he might be pleased to make, and as there was none, she ran upstairs to her room.

He had tossed her to Vernon in his mind not only painlessly, but with a keen acid of satisfaction. The heart is the wizard.

Next he bent his deliberate steps to Laetitia.

The mind was guilty of some hesitation; the feet went forward.

She was working at an embroidery by an open window. Colonel De Craye leaned outside, and Willoughby pardoned her air of demure amusement, on hearing him say: 'No, I have had one of the pleasantest half-hours of my life, and would rather idle here, if idle you will have it, than employ my faculties on horse-back.'

'Time is not lost in conversing with Miss Dale,' said Willoughby.

The light was tender to her complexion where she sat in partial shadow.

De Craye asked whether Crossjay had been caught. Laetitia murmured a kind word for the boy. Willoughby examined her embroidery.

The ladies Eleanor and Isabel appeared.

They invited her to take carriage-exercise with them.

Laetitia did not immediately answer, and Willoughby remarked: 'Miss Dale has been reproving Horace for idleness, and I recommend you to enlist him to do duty, while I relieve him here.'

The ladies had but to look at the colonel. He was at their disposal, if they would have him. He was marched to the carriage.

Laetitia plied her threads.

'Colonel De Craye spoke of Crossjay,' she said. 'May I hope you have forgiven the poor boy, Sir Willoughby?'

He replied: 'Plead for him.'

'I wish I had eloquence.'

'In my opinion you have it.'

'If he offends, it is never from meanness. At school, among comrades, he would shine. He is in too strong a light; his feelings and his moral nature are over-excited.'

'That was not the case when he was at home with you.'

'I am severe; I am stern.'

'A Spartan mother!'*

'My system of managing a boy would be after that model: except in this: he should always feel that he could obtain forgiveness.'

'Not at the expense of justice?'

'Ah! young creatures are not to be arraigned before the higher Courts. It seems to me perilous to terrify their imaginations. If we do so, are we not likely to produce the very evil we are combating? The alternations for the young should be school and home: and it should be in their hearts to have confidence that forgiveness alternates with discipline. They are of too tender an age for the rigours of the world; we are in danger of hardening them. I prove to you that I am not possessed of eloquence. You encouraged me to speak, Sir Willoughby.'

'You speak wisely, Laetitia.'

'I think it true. Will not you reflect on it? You have only to do so, to forgive him. I am growing bold indeed, and shall have to beg forgiveness for myself.'

'You still write? you continue to work with your pen?' said Willoughby.

'A little; a very little.'

'I do not like you to squander yourself, waste yourself, on the public. You are too precious to feed the beast. Giving out incessantly must end by attenuating. Reserve yourself for your friends. Why should they be robbed of so much of you? Is it not reasonable to assume that by lying fallow you would be more enriched for domestic life? Candidly, had I authority I would confiscate your pen: I would "away with that bauble." You will not often find me quoting Cromwell,* but his words apply in this instance. I would say rather, that lancet. Perhaps it is the more correct term. It bleeds you, it wastes you. For what? For a breath of fame!'

'I write for money.'

'And there—I would say of another—you subject yourself to the risk of mental degradation. Who knows? —moral! Trafficking the brains for money, must bring them to the level of the purchasers in time. I confiscate your pen, Laetitia.'

'It will be to confiscate your own gift, Sir Willoughby.'

'Then that proves—will you tell me the date?'

'You sent me a gold pen-holder on my sixteenth birthday.'

'It proves my utter thoughtlessness then, and later. And later!'

He rested an elbow on his knee and covered his eyes, murmuring in that profound hollow which is haunted by the voice of a contrite past: 'And later!'

The deed could be done. He had come to the conclusion that it could be done, though the effort to harmonize the figure sitting near him, with the artistic figure of his purest pigments, had cost him labour and a blinking of the eyelids. That also could be done. Her pleasant tone, sensible talk, and the light favouring her complexion, helped him in his effort. She was a sober cup; sober and wholesome. Deliriousness is for adolescence. The men who seek intoxicating cups are men who invite their fates.

Curiously, yet as positively as things can be affirmed, the husband of this woman would be able to boast of her virtues and treasures abroad, as he could not—impossible to say why not—boast of a beautiful wife or a blue-stocking wife. One of her merits as a wife would be this extraordinary neutral merit of a character that demanded colour from the marital hand, and would take it.

Laetitia had not to learn that he had much to distress him. Her wonder at his exposure of his grief counteracted a fluttering of vague alarm. She was nervous; she sat in expectation of some burst of regrets or of passion.

'I may hope that you have pardoned Crossjay?' she said.

'My friend,' said he, uncovering his face, 'I am governed by principles. Convince me of an error, I shall not obstinately pursue a premeditated course. But you know me. Men who have not principles to rule their conduct are—well, they are unworthy of a half hour of companionship with you. I will speak to you to-night. I have letters to despatch. To-night: at twelve: in the room where we spoke last. Or await me in the drawing-room. I have to attend on my guests till late.'

He bowed; he was in a hurry to go.

The deed could be done. It must be done; it was his destiny.

CHAPTER XXXIX

In the Heart of the Egoist

But already he had begun to regard the deed as his executioner. He dreaded meeting Clara. The folly of having retained her stood before him. How now to look on her and keep a sane resolution unwavering? She tempted to the insane. Had she been away, he could have walked through the performance composed by the sense of doing a duty to himself: perhaps faintly hating the poor wretch he made happy at last, kind to her in a manner, polite. Clara's presence in the house previous to the deed, and oh, heaven! after it, threatened his wits. Pride? He had none; he cast it down for her to trample it; he caught it back ere it was trodden on. Yes; he had pride: he had it as a dagger in his breast: his pride was his misery. But he was too proud to submit to misery. 'What I do is right.' He said the words, and rectitude smoothed his path, till the question clamoured for answer: Would the world countenance and endorse his pride in Laetitia? At one time, yes. And now? Clara's beauty ascended, laid a beam on him.

We are on board the labouring vessel of humanity in a storm, when cries and countercries ring out, disorderliness mixes the crew, and the fury of self-preservation divides: this one is for the ship, that one for his life. Clara was the former to him, Laetitia the latter. But what if there might not be greater safety in holding tenaciously to Clara than in casting her off for Laetitia? No, she had done things to set his pride throbbing in the quick. She had gone bleeding about first to one, then to another; she had betrayed him to Vernon, and to Mrs. Mountstuart; a look in the eyes of Horace De Craye said, to him as well: to whom not? He might hold to her for vengeance; but that appetite was short-lived in him if it ministered nothing to his purposes.

'I discard all idea of vengeance,' he said, and thrilled burningly to a smart in his admiration of the man who could be so magnanimous under mortal injury: for the

more admirable he, the more pitiable. He drank a drop
or two of self-pity like a poison, repelling the assaults of
public pity. Clara must be given up. It must be seen by
the world that, as he felt, the thing he did was right.
Laocoon* of his own serpents, he struggled to a certain
magnificence of attitude in the muscular net of constric-
tions he flung around himself. Clara must be given up.
O bright Abominable! She must be given up: but not
to one whose touch of her would be darts in the blood of
the yielder, snakes in his bed: she must be given up to an
extinguisher; to be the second wife of an old-fashioned
semi-recluse, disgraced in his first. And were it publicly
known that she had been cast off, and had fallen on old
Vernon for a refuge, and part in spite, part in shame,
part in desperation, part in a fit of good sense under the
circumstances, espoused him, her beauty would not influence the world in its judgement. The world would
know what to think. As the instinct of self-preservation
whispered to Willoughby, the world, were it requisite,
might be taught to think what it assuredly would not
think if she should be seen tripping to the altar with
Horace De Craye. Self-preservation, not vengeance,
breathed that whisper. He glanced at her iniquity for
a justification of it, without any desire to do her a permanent hurt: he was highly civilized: but with a strong
intention to give her all the benefit of the scandal, supposing a scandal, or ordinary tattle.

'And so he handed her to his cousin and secretary,
Vernon Whitford, who opened his mouth and shut his
eyes.'

You hear the world? How are we to stop it from
chattering? Enough that he had no desire to harm her.
Some gentle anticipations of her being tarnished were
imperative; they came spontaneously to him; otherwise
the radiance of that bright Abominable in loss would have
been insufferable; he could not have borne it; he could
never have surrendered her.

Moreover, a happy present effect was the result. He
conjured up the anticipated chatter and shrug of the
world so vividly that her beauty grew hectic with the

stain, bereft of its formidable magnetism. He could meet her calmly; he had steeled himself. Purity in women was his principal stipulation, and a woman puffed at, was not the person to cause him tremours.

Consider him indulgently: the Egoist is the Son of Himself. He is likewise the Father. And the son loves the father, the father the son; they reciprocate affection through the closest of ties; and shall they view behaviour unkindly wounding either of them, not for each other's dear sake abhorring the criminal? They would not injure you, but they cannot consent to see one another suffer or crave in vain. The two rub together in sympathy besides relationship to an intenser one. Are you, without much offending, sacrificed by them, it is on the altar of their mutual love, to filial piety or paternal tenderness: the younger has offered a dainty morsel to the elder, or the elder to the younger. Absorbed in their great example of devotion, they do not think of you. They are beautiful.

Yet is it most true that the younger has the passions of youth: whereof will come division between them; and this is a tragic state. They are then pathetic. This was the state of Sir Willoughby lending ear to his elder, until he submitted to bite at the fruit proposed to him—with how wry a mouth the venerable senior chose not to mark. At least, as we perceive, a half of him was ripe of wisdom in his own interests. The cruder half had but to be obedient to the leadership of sagacity for his interests to be secured, and a filial disposition assisted him; painfully indeed; but the same rare quality directed the good gentleman to swallow his pain. That the son should bewail his fate were a dishonour to the sire. He reverenced, and submitted. Thus, to say, consider him indulgently, is too much an appeal for charity on behalf of one requiring but initial anatomy—a slicing in halves —to exonerate, perchance exalt him. The Egoist is our fountain-head, primeval man: the primitive is born again, the elemental reconstituted. Born again, into new conditions, the primitive may be highly polished of men, and forfeit nothing save the roughness of his original nature. He is not only his own father, he is ours; and he is also our son. We have produced him, he us. Such were we, to such are we returning: not other, sings the poet, than one who toilfully works his shallop against the tide, 'si brachia forte remisit':—let him haply relax the labour of his arms, however high up the stream, and back he goes, 'in pejus,'* to the early principle of our being, with seeds and plants, that are as carelessly weighed in the hand and as indiscriminately husbanded as our humanity.

Poets on the other side may be cited for an assurance that the primitive is not the degenerate: rather is he a sign of the indestructibility of the race, of the ancient energy in removing obstacles to individual growth; a sample of what we would be, had we his concentrated power. He is the original innocent, the pure simple. It is we who have fallen; we have melted into Society, diluted our essence, dissolved. He stands in the midst monumentally, a landmark of the tough and honest old Ages, with the symbolic alphabet of striking arms and running legs, our early language, scrawled over his person, and the glorious first flint and arrow-head for his crest: at once the spectre of the Kitchen-midden and our ripest issue.

But Society is about him. The occasional spectacle of the primitive dangling on a rope, has impressed his mind with the strength of his natural enemy: from which uncongenial sight he has turned shuddering hardly less to behold the blast that is blown upon a reputation where one has been disrespectful of the many. By these means, through meditation on the contrast of circumstances in life, a pulse of imagination has begun to stir, and he has entered the upper sphere, or circle of spiritual Egoism: he has become the civilized Egoist; primitive still, as sure as man has teeth, but developed in his manner of using them.

Degenerate or not (and there is no just reason to suppose it), Sir Willoughby was a social Egoist, fiercely imaginative in whatsoever concerned him. He had discovered a greater realm than that of the sensual appetites, and he rushed across and around it in his conquering period with an Alexander's pride.* On these wind-like journeys he had carried Constantia, subsequently Clara; and however it may have been in the case of Miss Durham, in that of Miss Middleton it is almost certain she caught her glimpse of his interior from sheer fatigue in hearing him discourse of it. What he revealed was not the cause of her sickness: women can bear revelations—they are exciting: but the monotonousness. He slew imagination. There is no direr disaster in love than the death of imagination. He dragged her through the labyrinths of his penetralia, in his hungry coveting to be loved more and still more, more still, until imagination gave up the ghost, and he talked to her plain hearing like a monster. It must have been that; for the spell of the primitive upon women is masterful up to the time of contact.

'And so he handed her to his cousin and secretary, Vernon Whitford, who opened his mouth and shut his eyes.'

The urgent question was, how it was to be accomplished. Willoughby worked at the subject with all his power of concentration: a power that had often led him to feel and say, that as a barrister, a diplomatist, or a general, he would have won his grades: and granting him a personal interest in the business, he might have achieved eminence: he schemed and fenced remarkably well.

He projected a scene, following expressions of anxiety on account of old Vernon and his future settlement: and then—Clara maintaining her doggedness, to which he was now so accustomed that he could not conceive a change in it—says he: 'If you determine on breaking, I give you back your word *on one condition.*' Whereupon she starts: he insists on her promise: she declines: affairs resume their former footing; she frets, she begs for the disclosure: he flatters her by telling her his desire to keep her in the family: she is unilluminated, but strongly moved by curiosity: he philosophizes on marriage—'What are we? poor creatures! we must get through life as we can, doing as much good as we can to those we love; and think as you please, I love old Vernon. Am I not giving you the greatest possible proof of it?' She will not see. Then flatly out comes the one condition. That and no other. 'Take Vernon and I release you.' She refuses. Now ensues the debate, all the oratory being with him. 'Is it because of his unfortunate first marriage? You assured me you thought no worse of him': etc. She declares the proposal revolting. He can distinguish nothing that should offend her in a proposal to make his cousin happy if she will not him. Irony and sarcasm relieve his emotions, but he convinces her he is dealing plainly and intends generosity. She is confused; she speaks in maiden fashion.

He touches again on Vernon's early escapade. She does not enjoy it. The scene closes with his bidding her reflect on it, and remember the one condition of her release. Mrs. Mountstuart Jenkinson, now reduced to believe that he burns to be free, is then called in for an interview with Clara. His aunts Eleanor and Isabel besiege her. Laetitia in passionate earnest besieges her. Her father is wrought on to besiege her. Finally Vernon is attacked by Willoughby and Mrs. Mountstuart:—and here, Willoughby chose to think, was the main difficulty. But the girl has money; she is agreeable; Vernon likes her; she is fond of his 'Alps,' they have tastes in common, he likes her father, and in the end he besieges her. Will she yield? De Craye is absent. There is no other way of shunning a marriage she is incomprehensibly but frantically averse to. She is in the toils. Her father will stay at Patterne Hall as long as his host desires it. She hesitates, she is overcome; in spite of a certain nausea due to Vernon's preceding alliance, she yields.

Willoughby revolved the entire drama in Clara's presence. It helped him to look on her coolly. Conducting her to the dinner-table, he spoke of Crossjay, not unkindly; and at table he revolved the set of scenes with a heated animation that took fire from the wine and the face of his friend Horace, while he encouraged Horace to be flowingly Irish. He nipped the fellow good-humouredly once or twice, having never felt so friendly to him since the day of his arrival; but the position of critic is instinctively taken by men who do not flow: and Patterne

Port kept Dr. Middleton in a benevolent reserve when Willoughby decided that something said by De Craye was not new, and laughingly accused him of failing to consult his anecdotal note-book for the double-cross to his last sprightly sally. 'Your sallies are excellent, Horace, but spare us your Aunt Sallies!'* De Craye had no repartee, nor did Dr. Middleton challenge a pun. We have only to sharpen our wits to trip your seductive rattler whenever we may choose to think proper; and evidently, if we condescended to it, we could do better than he. The critic who has hatched a witticism is impelled to this opinion. Judging by the smiles of the ladies, they thought so too.

Shortly before eleven o'clock, Dr. Middleton made a Spartan stand*against the offer of another bottle of Port. The regulation couple of bottles had been consumed in equal partnership, and the Rev. Doctor and his host were free to pay a ceremonial visit to the drawing-room, where they were not expected. A piece of work of the elder ladies, a silken boudoir sofa-rug, was being examined, with high approval of the two younger. Vernon and Colonel De Craye had gone out in search of Crossjay, one to Mr. Dale's cottage, the other to call at the head-and under-gamekeepers. They were said to be strolling and smoking, for the night was fine. Willoughby left the room and came back with the key of Crossjay's door in his pocket. He foresaw that the delinquent might be of service to him.

Laetitia and Clara sang together. Laetitia was flushed, Clara pale. At eleven they saluted the ladies Eleanor and Isabel. Willoughby said, 'Good night' to each of them, contrasting as he did so the downcast look of Laetitia with Clara's frigid directness. He divined that they were off to talk over their one object of common interest, Crossjay. Saluting his aunts, he took up the rug, to celebrate their diligence and taste; and that he might make Dr. Middleton impatient for bed, he provoked him to admire it, held it out and laid it out, and caused the courteous old gentleman some confusion in hitting on fresh terms of commendation.

Before midnight the room was empty. Ten minutes later, Willoughby paid it a visit, and found it untenanted by the person he had engaged to be there. Vexed by his disappointment, he paced up and down, and chanced abstractedly to catch the rug in his hand; for what purpose, he might well ask himself; admiration of ladies' work, in their absence, was unlikely to occur to him. Nevertheless the touch of the warm soft silk was meltingly feminine. A glance at the mantelpiece clock told him Laetitia was twenty minutes behind the hour.

Her remissness might endanger all his plans, alter the whole course of his life. The colours in which he painted her were too lively to last; the madness in his head threatened to subside. Certain it was that he could not be ready a second night for the sacrifice he had been about to perform.

The clock was at the half hour after twelve. He flung the silken thing on the central ottoman, extinguished the lamps, and walked out of the room, charging the absent Laetitia to bear her misfortune with a consciousness of deserving it.

CHAPTER XL

Midnight: Sir Willoughby and Laetitia: with Young Crossjay under a Coverlet

Young Crossjay was a glutton at holidays and never thought of home till it was dark. The close of the day saw him several miles away from the Hall, dubious whether he would not round his numerous adventures by sleeping at an inn; for he had lots of money, and the idea of jumping up in the morning in a strange place was thrilling. Besides, when he was shaken out of sleep by Sir Willoughby, he had been told that he was to go, and not to show his face at Patterne again. On the other hand, Miss Middleton had bidden him come back. There was little question with him which person he should obey: he followed his heart.

Supper at an inn, where he found a company to listen

to his adventures, delayed him, and a short cut, intended to make up for it, lost him his road. He reached the Hall very late, ready to be in love with the horrible pleasure of a night's rest under the stars, if necessary. But a candle burned at one of the back windows. He knocked, and a kitchen-maid let him in. She had a bowl of hot soup prepared for him. Crossjay tried a mouthful to please her. His head dropped over it. She roused him to his feet, and he pitched against her shoulder. The dry air of the kitchen department had proved too much for the tired youngster. Mary, the maid, got him to step as firmly as he was able, and led him by the back-way to the hall, bidding him creep noiselessly to bed. He understood his position in the house, and though he could have gone fast to sleep on the stairs, he took a steady aim at his room and gained the door cat-like. The door resisted. He was appalled and unstrung in a minute. The door was locked. Crossjay felt as if he were in the presence of Sir Willoughby. He fled on rickety legs, and had a fall and bumps down half-a-dozen stairs. A door opened above. He rushed across the hall to the drawing-room, invitingly open, and there staggered in darkness to the ottoman and rolled himself in something sleek and warm, soft as hands of ladies, and redolent of them; so delicious that he hugged the folds about his head and heels. While he was endeavouring to think where he was, his legs curled, his eyelids shut, and he was in the thick of the day's adventures, doing yet more wonderful things.

He heard his own name: that was quite certain. He knew that he heard it with his ears, as he pursued the fleetest dreams ever accorded to mortal. It did not mix: it was outside him, and like the danger-pole in the ice, which the skater shooting hither and yonder comes on again, it recurred; and now it marked a point in his career, now it caused him to relax his pace; he began to circle, and whirled closer round it, until, as at a blow, his heart knocked, he tightened himself, thought of bolting, and lay dead-still to throb and hearken.

'Oh! Sir Willoughby,' a voice had said.

The accents were sharp with alarm.

'My friend! my dearest!' was the answer.

'I came to speak of Crossjay.'

'Will you sit here, on the ottoman?'

'No, I cannot wait. I hoped I had heard Crossjay
return. I would rather not sit down. May I entreat you
to pardon him when he comes home?'

'You, and you only, may do so. I permit none else.
Of Crossjay to-morrow.'

'He may be lying in the fields. We are anxious.'

'The rascal can take pretty good care of himself.'

'Crossjay is perpetually meeting accidents.'

'He shall be indemnified if he has had excess of punishment.'

'I think I will say good night, Sir Willoughby.'

'When freely and unreservedly you have given me
your hand.'

There was hesitation.

'To say good night?'

'I ask for your hand.'

'Good night, Sir Willoughby.'

'You do not give it. You are in doubt? Still? What
language must I use to convince you? And yet you
know me. Who knows me but you? You have always
known me. You are my home and my temple. Have
you forgotten your verses for the day of my majority?

> "The dawn-star has arisen
> In plenitude of light . . ." '

'Do not repeat them, pray!' cried Laetitia with a gasp.

'I have repeated them to myself a thousand times: in
India, America, Japan: they were like our English skylark carolling to me.

> "My heart, now burst thy prison
> With proud aerial flight!" '

'Oh! I beg you will not force me to listen to nonsense
that I wrote when I was a child. No more of those most
foolish lines! If you knew what it is to write and despise
one's writing you would not distress me. And since you
will not speak of Crossjay to-night, allow me to retire.'

'You know me, and therefore you know my contempt

for verses, as a rule, Laetitia. But not for yours to me. Why should you call them foolish? They expressed your feelings—I hold them sacred. They are something religious to me, not mere poetry. Perhaps the third verse is my favourite. . . .'

'It will be more than I can bear!'

'You were in earnest when you wrote them?'

'I was very young, very enthusiastic, very silly.'

'You were and are my image of constancy!'

'It is an error, Sir Willoughby; I am far from being the same.'

'We are all older, I trust wiser. I am, I will own; much wiser. Wise at last! I offer you my hand.'

She did not reply.

'I offer you my hand and name, Laetitia!'

No response.

'You think me bound in honour to another?'

She was mute.

'I am free. Thank heaven! I am free to choose my mate—the woman I have always loved! Freely and unreservedly, as I ask you to give your hand, I offer mine. You are the mistress of Patterne Hall; my wife!'

She had not a word.

'My dearest! do you not rightly understand? The hand I am offering you is disengaged. It is offered to the lady I respect above all others. I have made the discovery that I cannot love without respecting; and as I will not marry without loving, it ensues that I am free— I am yours. At last?—your lips move: tell me the words. *Have always loved*, I said. You carry in your bosom the magnet of constancy, and I, in spite of apparent deviations, declare to you that I have never ceased to be sensible of the attraction. And now there is not an impediment. We two against the world! we are one. Let me confess to an old foible—perfectly youthful, and you will ascribe it to youth: once I desired to absorb. I mistrusted; that was the reason: I perceive it. You teach me the difference of an alliance with a lady of intellect. The pride I have in you, Laetitia, definitely cures me of that insane passion—call it an insatiable hunger.

I recognize it as a folly of youth. I have, as it were, gone the tour, to come home to you—at last?—and live our manly life of comparative equals. At last, then! But remember, that in the younger man you would have had a despot—perhaps a jealous despot. Young men, I assure you, are orientally inclined in their ideas of love. Love gets a bad name from them. We, my Laetitia, do not regard love as a selfishness. If it is, it is the essence of life. At least it is our selfishness rendered beautiful. I talk to you like a man who has found a compatriot in a foreign land. It seems to me that I have not opened my mouth for an age. I certainly have not unlocked my heart. Those who sing for joy are not unintelligible to me. If I had not something in me worth saying, I think I should sing. In every sense you reconcile me to men and the world, Laetitia. Why press you to speak? I will be the speaker. As surely as you know me, I know you; and . . .'

Laetitia burst forth with, 'No!'

'I do not know you?' said he, searchingly mellifluous.

'Hardly.'

'How not?'

'I am changed.'

'In what way?'

'Deeply.'

'Sedater?'

'Materially.'

'Colour will come back: have no fear; I promise it. If you imagine you want renewing, *I* have the specific, I, my love, I!'

'Forgive me—will you tell me, Sir Willoughby, whether you have broken with Miss Middleton?'

'Rest satisfied, my dear Laetitia. She is as free as I am. I can do no more than a man of honour should do. She releases me. To-morrow or next day she departs. We, Laetitia, you and I, my love, are home birds. It does not do for the home bird to couple with the migratory. The little imperceptible change you allude to, is nothing. Italy will restore you. I am ready to stake my own health—never yet shaken by a doctor of medicine:—I say medicine advisedly, for there are Doctors of Divinity who would shake giants:—that an Italian trip will send you back—that I shall bring you home from Italy a blooming bride. You shake your head—despondently? My love, I guarantee it. Cannot I give you colour? Behold! Come to the light, look in the glass.'

'I may redden,' said Laetitia. 'I suppose that is due to the action of the heart. I am changed. Heart, for any other purpose, I have not. I am like you, Sir Willoughby, in this: I could not marry without loving, and I do not know what love is, except that it is an empty dream.'

'Marriage, my dearest . . .'

'You are mistaken.'

'I will cure you, my Laetitia. Look to me, I am the tonic. It is not common confidence, but conviction. I, my love, I!'

'There is no cure for what I feel, Sir Willoughby.'

'Spare me the formal prefix, I beg. You place your hand in mine, relying on me. I am pledged for the remainder. We end as we began: my request is for your hand—your hand in marriage.'

'I cannot give it.'

'To be my wife!'

'It is an honour: I must decline it.'

'Are you quite well, Laetitia? I propose in the plainest terms I can employ, to make you Lady Patterne —mine.'

'I am compelled to refuse.'

'Why? Refuse? Your reason!'

'The reason has been named.'

He took a stride to inspirit his wits.

'There's a madness comes over women at times, I know. Answer me, Laetitia:—by all the evidence a man can have, I could swear it:—but answer me: you loved me once?'

'I was an exceedingly foolish, romantic girl.'

'You evade my question: I am serious. Oh!' he walked away from her, booming a sound of utter repudiation of her present imbecility, and hurrying to her side, said:

'But it was manifest to the whole world! It was a legend. To love like Laetitia Dale, was a current phrase. You were an example, a light to women: no one was your match for devotion. You were a precious cameo, still gazing! And I was the object. You loved me. You loved me, you belonged to me, you were mine, my possession, my jewel; I was prouder of your constancy than of anything else that I had on earth. It was a part of the order of the universe to me. A doubt of it would have disturbed my creed. Why, good heaven! where are we? Is nothing solid on earth? You loved me!'

'I was childish indeed.'

'You loved me passionately!'

'Do you insist on shaming me through and through, Sir Willoughby? I have been exposed enough.'

'You cannot blot out the past: it is written, it is recorded. You loved me devotedly, silence is no escape. You loved me.'

'I did.'

'You never loved me, you shallow woman! "I did!" As if there could be a cessation of a love! What are we to reckon on as ours? We prize a woman's love; we guard it jealously, we trust to it, dream of it; *there* is our wealth; there is our talisman! And when we open the casket, it has flown!—barren vacuity!—we are poorer than dogs. As well think of keeping a costly wine in potter's clay as love in the heart of a woman! There are women—women? Oh! they are all of a stamp—coin! Coin for any hand! It's a fiction, an imposture—they cannot love! They are the shadows of men. Compared with men, they have as much heart in them as the shadow beside the body! Laetitia!'

'Sir Willoughby.'

'You refuse my offer?'

'I must.'

'You refuse to take me for your husband?'

'I cannot be your wife.'

'You have changed? . . . You have set your heart? . . . You could marry? . . . there is a man? . . . You could marry one! I will have an answer, I am sick of evasions. What was in the mind of heaven when women were created, will be the riddle to the end of the world! Every good man in turn has made the inquiry. I have a right to know who robs me—We may try as we like to solve it.—Satan is painted laughing!—I say I have a right to know who robs me. Answer me.'

'I shall not marry.'

'That is not an answer.'

'I love no one.'

'You loved me.—You are silent?—but you confessed it. Then you confess it was a love that could die! Are you unable to perceive how that redounds to my discredit? You loved me, you have ceased to love me. In other words, you charge me with incapacity to sustain a woman's love. You accuse me of inspiring a miserable passion that cannot last a life-time! You let the world see that I am a man to be aimed at for a temporary mark! And simply because I happen to be in your neighbourhood at an age when a young woman is impressionable! You make a public example of me as a man for whom women may have a caprice, but that is all; he cannot enchain them; he fascinates passingly; they fall off. Is it just, for me to be taken up and cast down at your will? Reflect on that scandal! Shadows? Why, a man's shadow is faithful to him at least. What are women? There is not a comparison in nature that does not tower above them! not one that does not hoot at them! I, throughout my life guided by absolute deference to their weakness—paying them politeness, courtesy—whatever I touch I am happy in, except when I touch women! How is it? What is the mystery? Some monstrous explanation must exist. What can it be? I am favoured by fortune from my birth until I enter into relations with women! But will you be so good as to account for it in your defence of them? Oh! were the relations dishonourable, it would be quite another matter. *Then* they . . . I could recount . . . I disdain to chronicle such victories. Quite another matter! But they are flies, and I am something more stable. They are flies. I look beyond the day; I owe a duty to my line. They are flies. I foresee it, I shall be crossed in my fate so long as I fail to shun them—flies! Not merely born for the day, I maintain that they are spiritually ephemeral.—Well, my opinion of your sex is directly traceable to you. You may alter it, or fling another of us men out on the world with the old bitter experience. Consider this, that it is on your head if my ideal of women is wrecked. It rests with you to restore it. I love you. I discover that you are the one woman I have always loved. I come to you, I sue you, and suddenly—you have changed! "I have changed: I am not the same." What can it mean? "I cannot marry: I love no one." And you say you do not know what love is—avowing in the same breath that you did love me! Am I the empty dream? My hand, heart, fortune, name, are yours, at your feet: you kick them hence. I am here—you reject me. But why, for what mortal reason am I here other than my faith in your love? You drew me to you, to repel me, and have a wretched revenge.'

'You know it is not that, Sir Willoughby.'

'Have you any possible suspicion that I am still entangled, not, as I assure you I am, perfectly free in fact and in honour?'

'It is not that.'

'Name it; for you see your power. Would you have me kneel to you, madam?'

'Oh! no; it would complete my grief.'

'You feel grief? Then you believe in my affection, and you hurl it away. I have no doubt that as a poetess, you would say, love is eternal. And you have loved me. And you tell me you love me no more. You are not very logical, Laetitia Dale.'

'Poetesses rarely are: if I am one, which I little pretend to be for writing silly verses. I have passed out of that delusion, with the rest.'

'You shall not wrong those dear old days, Laetitia. I see them now; when I rode by your cottage and you were at your window, pen in hand, your hair straying over your forehead. Romantic, yes; not foolish. Why were you foolish in thinking of me? Some day I will commission an artist to paint me that portrait of you from my description. And I remember when we first whispered . . . I remember your trembling. You have forgotten— I remember. I remember our meeting in the park on the path to church. I remember the heavenly morning of my return from my travels, and the same Laetitia meeting me, stedfast and unchangeable. Could I ever forget? Those are ineradicable scenes; pictures of my youth, interwound with me. I may say, that as I recede from them, I dwell on them the more. Tell me, Laetitia, was there not a certain prophecy of your father's concerning us two? I fancy I heard of one. There was one.'

'He was an invalid. Elderly people nurse illusions.'

'Ask yourself, Laetitia, who is the obstacle to the fulfilment of his prediction?—truth, if ever a truth was foreseen on earth! You have not changed so far that you would feel *no* pleasure in gratifying him? I go to him to-morrow morning with the first light.'

'You will compel me to follow, and undeceive him.'

'Do so, and I denounce an unworthy affection you are ashamed to avow.'

'That would be idle, though it would be base.'

'Proof of love, then! For no one but you should it be done, and no one but you dare accuse me of a baseness.'

'Sir Willoughby, you will let my father die in peace.'

'He and I together will contrive to persuade you.'

'You tempt me to imagine that you want a wife at any cost.'

'You, Laetitia, you.'

'I am tired,' she said. 'It is late, I would rather not hear more. I am sorry if I have caused you pain. I suppose you to have spoken with candour. I defend neither my sex nor myself. I can only say, I am a woman as good as dead: happy to be made happy in my way, but so little alive that I cannot realize any other way. As for love, I am thankful to have broken a spell. You have a younger woman in your mind; I am an old one: I have no ambition and no warmth. My utmost prayer is to float on the stream—a purely physical desire of life: I have no strength to swim. Such a woman is not the wife for you, Sir Willoughby. Good night.'

'One final word. Weigh it. Express no conventional regrets. Resolutely you refuse?'

'Resolutely I do.'

'You refuse?'

'Yes.'

'I have sacrificed my pride for nothing! You refuse?'

'Yes.'

'Humbled myself! And this is the answer! You do refuse?'

'I do.'

'Good night, Laetitia Dale.'

He gave her passage.

'Good night, Sir Willoughby.'

'I am in your power,' he said in a voice between supplication and menace that laid a claw on her, and she turned and replied:

'You will not be betrayed.'

'I can trust you . . . ?'

'I go home to-morrow before breakfast.'

'Permit me to escort you upstairs.'

'If you please: but I see no one here either to-night or to-morrow.'

'It is for the privilege of seeing the last of you.'

They withdrew.

Young Crossjay listened to the drumming of his head. Somewhere in or over the cavity a drummer rattled tremendously.

Sir Willoughby's laboratory-door shut with a slam.

Crossjay tumbled himself off the ottoman. He stole up to the unclosed drawing-room door, and peeped. Never was a boy more thoroughly awakened. His object was to get out of the house and go through the night avoiding everything human, for he was big with information of a character that he knew to be of the nature of gunpowder, and he feared to explode. He crossed the hall. In the passage to the scullery, he ran against Colonel De Craye.

'So there you are,' said the colonel, 'I've been hunting you.'

Crossjay related that his bed-room door was locked and the key gone, and Sir Willoughby sitting-up in the laboratory.

Colonel De Craye took the boy to his own room, where Crossjay lay on a sofa, comfortably covered over and snug in a swelling pillow; but he was restless; he wanted to speak, to bellow, to cry; and he bounced round to his left side, and bounced to his right, not knowing what to think, except that there was treason to his adored Miss Middleton.

'Why, my lad, you're not half a campaigner,' the colonel called out to him; attributing his uneasiness to the material discomfort of the sofa: and Crossjay had to swallow the taunt, bitter though it was. A dim sentiment of impropriety in unburdening his overcharged mind on the subject of Miss Middleton to Colonel De Craye, restrained him from defending himself; and so he heaved and tossed about till daybreak. At an early hour, while his hospitable friend, who looked very handsome in profile half breast and head above the sheets, continued to slumber, Crossjay was on his legs and away.

'He says I'm not half a campaigner, and a couple of hours of bed are enough for me,' the boy thought proudly, and snuffed the springing air of the young sun on the fields. A glance back at Patterne Hall dismayed him, for he knew not how to act, and he was immoderately combustible, too full of knowledge for self-containment; much too zealously-excited on behalf of his dear Miss Middleton to keep silent for many hours of the day.

CHAPTER XLI

The Rev. Dr. Middleton, Clara, and Sir Willoughby

WHEN Master Crossjay tumbled down the stairs, Laetitia was in Clara's room, speculating on the various mishaps which might have befallen that battered youngster; and Clara listened anxiously after Laetitia had run out, until she heard Sir Willoughby's voice; which in some way satisfied her that the boy was not in the house.

She waited, expecting Miss Dale to return; then undressed, went to bed, tried to sleep. She was tired of strife. Strange thoughts for a young head shot through her: as, that it is possible for the sense of duty to counteract distaste; and that one may live a life apart from one's admirations and dislikes: she owned the singular strength of Sir Willoughby in outwearying: she asked herself how much she had gained by struggling:—every effort seemed to expend her spirit's force, and rendered her less able to get the clear vision of her prospects, as though it had sunk her deeper: the contrary of her intention to make each further step confirm her liberty. Looking back, she marvelled at the things she had done. Looking round, how ineffectual they appeared! She had still the great scene of positive rebellion to go through with her father.

The anticipation of that was the cause of her extreme discouragement. He had not spoken to her since he became aware of her attempted flight: but the scene was coming; and besides the wish not to inflict it on him, as well as to escape it herself, the girl's peculiar unhappiness lay in her knowledge that they were alienated and stood opposed, owing to one among the more perplexing masculine weaknesses, which she could not hint at, dared barely think of, and would not name in her meditations. Diverting to other subjects, she allowed herself to exclaim: 'Wine! wine!' in renewed wonder of what there could be in wine to entrap venerable men and obscure their judgements. She was too young to consider that her being very much in the wrong gave all the importance to the cordial glass in a venerable gentleman's appreciation of his dues. Why should he fly from a priceless wine to gratify the caprices of a fantastical child guilty of seeking to commit a breach of faith? He harped on those words. Her fault was grave. No doubt the wine coloured it to him, as a drop or two will do in any cup: still her fault was grave.

She was too young for such considerations. She was

ready to expatiate on the gravity of her fault, so long
as the humiliation assisted to her disentanglement: her
snared nature in the toils would not permit her to reflect
on it further. She had never accurately perceived it:
for the reason perhaps that Willoughby had not been
moving in his appeals: but, admitting the charge of
waywardness, she had come to terms with conscience,
upon the understanding that she was to perceive it and
regret it and do penance for it by-and-by:—by renounc-
ing marriage altogether? How light a penance!

In the morning, she went to Laetitia's room, knocked
and had no answer.

She was informed at the breakfast-table of Miss Dale's
departure. The ladies Eleanor and Isabel feared it to
be a case of urgency at the cottage. No one had seen
Vernon, and Clara requested Colonel De Craye to walk
over to the cottage for news of Crossjay. He accepted
the commission, simply to obey and be in her service:
assuring her, however, that there was no need to be disturbed about the boy. He would have told her more,
had not Dr. Middleton led her out.

Sir Willoughby marked a lapse of ten minutes by his
watch. His excellent aunts had ventured a comment on
his appearance, that frightened him lest he himself should
be the person to betray his astounding discomfiture. He
regarded his conduct as an act of madness, and Laetitia's
as no less that of a madwoman—happily mad! Very
happily mad indeed! Her rejection of his ridiculously
generous proposal seemed to show an intervening hand
in his favour, that sent her distraught at the right
moment. He entirely trusted her to be discreet; but she
was a miserable creature, who had lost the one last
chance offered her by Providence, and furnished him
with a signal instance of the mediocrity of woman's love.

Time was flying. In a little while Mrs. Mountstuart
would arrive. He could not fence her without a design in
his head; he was destitute of an armoury if he had no
scheme: he racked the brain only to succeed in rousing
phantasmal vapours. Her infernal 'Twice'; would cease
now to apply to Laetitia: it would be an echo of Lady

Busshe. Nay, were all in the secret, *Thrice* jilted! might become the universal roar. And this, he reflected bitterly, of a man whom nothing but duty to his line had arrested from being the most mischievous of his class with women! Such is our reward for uprightness!

At the expiration of fifteen minutes by his watch, he struck a knuckle on the library-door. Dr. Middleton held it open to him.

'You are disengaged, sir?'

'The sermon is upon the paragraph which is toned to awaken the clerk,' replied the Rev. Doctor.

Clara was weeping.

Sir Willoughby drew near her solicitously.

Dr. Middleton's mane of silvery hair was in a state bearing witness to the vehemence of the sermon, and Willoughby said: 'I hope, sir, you have not made too much of a trifle.'

'I believe, sir, that I have produced an effect, and that was the point in contemplation.'

'Clara! my dear Clara!' Willoughby touched her.

'She sincerely repents her conduct, I may inform you,' said Dr. Middleton.

'My love!' Willoughby whispered. 'We have had a misunderstanding. I am at a loss to discover where I have been guilty, but I take the blame, all the blame. I implore you not to weep. Do me the favour to look at me. I would not have had you subjected to any interrogation whatever.'

'You are not to blame,' Clara said on a sob.

'Undoubtedly Willoughby is not to blame. It was not he who was bound on a runaway errand in flagrant breach of duty and decorum, nor he who inflicted a catarrh on a brother of my craft and cloth,' said her father.

'The clerk, sir, has pronounced Amen,' observed Willoughby.

'And no man is happier to hear an ejaculation that he has laboured for with so much sweat of his brow than the parson, I can assure you,' Dr. Middleton mildly groaned. 'I have notions of the trouble of Abraham. A sermon of that description is an immolation of the parent, however it may go with the child.'

Willoughby soothed his Clara.

'I wish I had been here to share it. I might have saved you some tears. I may have been hasty in our little dissensions. I will acknowledge that I have been. My temper is often irascible.'

'And so is mine!' exclaimed Dr. Middleton. 'And yet I am not aware that I made the worse husband for it. Nor do I rightly comprehend how a probably justly exciteable temper can stand for a plea in mitigation of an attempt at an outrageous breach of faith.'

'The sermon is over, sir.'

'Reverberations!' the Rev. Doctor waved his arm placably. 'Take it for thunder heard remote.'

'Your hand, my love,' Willoughby murmured.

The hand was not put forth.

Dr. Middleton remarked the fact. He walked to the window, and perceiving the pair in the same position when he faced about he delivered a cough of admonition.

'It is cruel!' said Clara.

'That the owner of your hand should petition you for it?' inquired her father.

She sought refuge in a fit of tears.

Willoughby bent above her, mute.

'Is a scene that is hardly conceivable as a parent's obligation once in a lustrum, to be repeated within the half hour?' shouted her father.

She drew up her shoulders and shook; let them fall and dropped her head.

'My dearest! your hand!' fluted Willoughby.

The hand surrendered; it was much like the icicle of a sudden thaw.

Willoughby squeezed it to his ribs.

Dr. Middleton marched up and down the room with his arms locked behind him. The silence between the young people seemed to denounce his presence.

He said cordially: 'Old Hiems has but to withdraw for buds to burst. "Jam ver egelidos refert tepores." The aequinoctial fury departs.* I will leave you for a term.'

Clara and Willoughby simultaneously raised their faces with opposing expressions.

'My girl?' her father stood by her, laying gentle hand on her.

'Yes, papa, I will come out to you,' she replied to his apology for the rather heavy weight of his vocabulary, and smiled.

'No, sir, I beg you will remain,' said Willoughby.

'I keep you frost-bound.'

Clára did not deny it.

Willoughby emphatically did.

Then which of them was the more lover-like? Dr. Middleton would for the moment have supposed his daughter.

Clara said: 'Shall you be on the lawn, papa?'

Willoughby interposed. 'Stay, sir; give us your blessing.'

'That you have.' Dr. Middleton hastily motioned the paternal ceremony in outline.

'A few minutes, papa,' said Clara.

'Will she name the day?' came eagerly from Willoughby.

'I cannot!' Clara cried in extremity.

'The day is important on its arrival,' said her father, 'but I apprehend the decision to be of the chief importance at present. First prime your piece of artillery, my friend.'

'The decision is taken, sir.'

'Then I will be out of the way of the firing. Hit what day you please.'

Clara checked herself on an impetuous exclamation. It was done that her father might not be detained.

Her astute self-compression sharpened Willoughby as much as it mortified and terrified him. He understood how he would stand in an instant were Dr. Middleton absent. Her father was the tribunal she dreaded, and affairs must be settled and made irrevocable while he was with them. To sting the blood of the girl, he called her his darling, and half enwound her, shadowing forth a salute.

She strung her body to submit, seeing her father take it as a signal for his immediate retirement.

Willoughby was upon him before he reached the door. 'Hear us out, sir. Do not go. Stay, at my entreaty. I fear we have not come to a perfect reconcilement.'

'If that is your opinion,' said Clara, 'it is good reason for not distressing my father.'

'Dr. Middleton, I love your daughter. I wooed her and won her; I had your consent to our union, and I was the happiest of mankind. In some way, since her coming to my house, I know not how—she will not tell me, or cannot—I offended. One may be innocent and offend. I have never pretended to impeccability, which is an admission that I may very naturally offend. My appeal to her is for an explanation or for pardon. I obtain neither. Had our positions been reversed, Oh! not for any real offence—not for the worst that can be imagined —I think not—I hope not—could I have been tempted to propose the dissolution of our engagement. To love is to love, with me; an engagement a solemn bond. With all my errors I have that merit of utter fidelity— to the world laughable! I confess to a multitude of errors; I have that single merit, and am not the more estimable in your daughter's eyes on account of it, I fear. In plain words, I am, I do not doubt, one of the fools among men; of the description of human dog commonly known as faithful—whose destiny is that of a tribe. A man who cries out when he is hurt is absurd, and I am not asking for sympathy. Call me luckless. But I abhor a breach of faith. A broken pledge is hateful to me. I should regard it in myself as a form of suicide. There are principles which civilized men must contend for. Our social fabric is based on them. As my word stands for me, I hold others to theirs. If that is not done, the world is more or less a carnival of counterfeits. In this instance—Ah! Clara, my love! and you have principles: you have inherited, you have been indoctrinated with them: have I, then, in my ignorance offended past penitence, that you, of all women? . . . And without being able to name my sin!—Not only for what I lose by it, but in the abstract, judicially—apart from the sentiment of personal interest, grief, pain, and the possibility of my having to endure that which no temptation would induce me to commit:—judicially;—I fear, sir, I am a poor forensic orator . . .'

'The situation, sir, does not demand a Cicero: proceed,' said Dr. Middleton, balked in his approving nods at the right true things delivered.

'Judicially, I am bold to say, though it may appear a presumption in one suffering acutely, I abhor a breach of faith.'

Dr. Middleton brought his nod down low upon the phrase he had anticipated. 'And I,' said he, 'personally, and presently, abhor a breach of faith. Judicially? Judicially to examine, judicially to condemn: but does the judicial mind detest? I think, sir, we are not on the Bench when we say that we abhor: we have unseated ourselves. Yet our abhorrence of bad conduct is very certain. You would signify, impersonally: which suffices for this exposition of your feelings.'

He peered at the gentleman under his brows, and resumed: 'She has had it, Willoughby; she has had it in plain Saxon and in uncompromising Olympian. There is, I conceive, no necessity to revert to it.'

'Pardon me, sir, but I am still unforgiven.'

'You must babble out the rest between you. I am about as much at home as a turkey with a pair of pigeons.'

'Leave us, father,' said Clara.

'First join our hands, and let me give you that title, sir.'

'Reach the good man your hand, my girl; forthright, from the shoulder, like a brave boxer. Humour a lover. He asks for his own.'

'It is more than I can do, father.'

'How, it is more than you can do? You are engaged to him, a plighted woman.'

'I do not wish to marry.'

'The apology is inadequate.'

'I am unworthy . . .'

'Chatter! chatter!'

'I beg him to release me.'

'Lunacy!'

'I have no love to give him.'

'Have you gone back to your cradle, Clara Middleton?'

'Oh! leave us, dear father.'

'My offence, Clara, my offence! What is it? Will you only name it?'

'Father, will you leave us? We can better speak together . . .'

'We have spoken, Clara, how often!' Willoughby resumed, 'with what result?—that you loved me, that you have ceased to love me: that your heart was mine, that you have withdrawn it, plucked it from me: that you request me to consent to a sacrifice involving my reputation, my life. And what have I done? I am the same, unchangeable. I loved and love you: my heart was yours, and is, and will be yours for ever. You are my affianced—that is, my wife. What have I done?'

'It is indeed useless,' Clara sighed.

'Not useless, my girl, that you should inform this gentleman, your affianced husband, of the ground of the objection you conceived against him.'

'I cannot say.'

'Do you know?'

'If I could name it, I could hope to overcome it.'

Dr. Middleton addressed Sir Willoughby.

'I verily believe we are directing the girl to dissect a caprice. Such things are seen large by these young people, but as they have neither organs nor arteries, nor brains, nor membranes, dissection and inspection will be alike profitlessly practised. Your inquiry is natural for a lover, whose passion to enter into relations with the sex is ordinarily in proportion to his ignorance of the stuff composing them. At a particular age they traffic in whims: which are, I presume, the spiritual of hysterics; and are indubitably preferable, so long as they are not pushed too far. Examples are not wanting to prove that a flighty initiative on the part of the male is a handsome corrective. In that case, we should probably have had

the roof off the house, and the girl now at your feet.
Ha!'

'Despise me, father. I am punished for ever thinking
myself the superior of any woman,' said Clara.

'Your hand out to him, my dear, since he is for a
formal reconciliation: and I can't wonder.'

'Father! I have said I do not . . . I have said I
cannot . . .'

'By the most merciful! what? what? the name for it!
words for it!'

'Do not frown on me, father. I wish him happiness.
I cannot marry him. I do not love him.'

'You will remember that you informed me aforetime
that you did love him.'

'I was ignorant . . . I did not know myself. I wish
him to be happy.'

'You deny him the happiness you wish him!'

'It would not be for his happiness were I to wed him.'

'Oh!' burst from Willoughby.

'You hear him. He rejects your prediction, Clara
Middleton.'

She caught her clasped hands up to her throat.
'Wretched, wretched, both!'

'And you have not a word against him, miserable
girl!'

'Miserable! I am.'

'It is the cry of an animal!'

'Yes, father.'

'You feel like one? Your behaviour is of that shape.
You have not a word?'

'Against myself: not against him.'

'And I, when you speak so generously, am to yield
you? give you up?' cried Willoughby. 'Ah! my love,
my Clara, impose what you will on me; not that. It is
too much for man. It is, I swear it, beyond my
strength.'

'Pursue, continue the strain: 'tis in the right key,' said
Dr. Middleton, departing.

Willoughby wheeled and waylaid him with a bound.

'Plead for me, sir; you are all-powerful. Let her be

mine, she shall be happy, or I will perish for it. I will call it on my head.—Impossible! I cannot lose her. Lose you, my love? It would be to strip myself of every blessing of body and soul. It would be to deny myself possession of grace, beauty, wit, all the incomparable charms of loveliness of mind and person in woman, and plant myself in a desert. You are my mate, the sum of everything I call mine. Clara, I should be less than man to submit to such a loss. Consent to it? But I love you! I worship you! How can I consent to lose you . . .?'

He saw the eyes of the desperately wily young woman slink sideways. Dr. Middleton was pacing at ever shorter lengths closer by the door.

'You hate me?' Willoughby sank his voice.

'If it should turn to hate!' she murmured.

'Hatred of your husband?'

'I could not promise,' she murmured more softly in her wiliness.

'Hatred?' he cried aloud, and Dr. Middleton stopped in his walk and flung up his head; 'Hatred of your husband? of the man you have vowed to love and honour? Oh! no. Once mine, it is not to be feared. I trust to my knowledge of your nature; I trust in your blood, I trust in your education. Had I nothing else to inspire confidence, I could trust in your eyes. And Clara, take the confession: I would rather be hated than lose you. For if I lose you, you are in another world, out of this one holding me in its death-like cold: but if you hate me, we are together, we are still together. Any alliance, any, in preference to separation!'

Clara listened with a critical ear. His language and tone were new; and comprehending that they were in part addressed to her father, whose phrase: 'A breach of faith': he had so cunningly used, disdain of the actor prompted the extreme blunder of her saying—frigidly though she said it:

'You have not talked to me in this way before.'

'Finally,' remarked her father, summing up the situation to settle it from that little speech, 'he talks to you in this way now; and you are under my injunction to

stretch your hand out to him for a symbol of union, or
to state your objection to that course. He, by your
admission, is at the terminus, and there, failing the why
not, must you join him.'

Her head whirled. She had been severely flagellated
and weakened previous to Willoughby's entrance. Language to express her peculiar repulsion eluded her. She
formed the words, and perceived that they would not
stand to bear a breath from her father. She perceived
too that Willoughby was as ready with his agony of
supplication as she with hers. If she had tears for a
resource, he had gestures, quite as eloquent; and a cry
of her loathing of the union would fetch a countervailing
torrent of the man's love.—What could she say? he is
an Egoist? The epithet has no meaning in such a scene.
Invent! shrieked the hundred-voiced instinct of dislike
within her, and alone with her father, alone with Willoughby, she could have invented some equivalent, to do
her heart justice for the injury it sustained in her being
unable to name the true and immense objection: but the
pair in presence paralyzed her. She dramatized them
each springing forward by turns, with crushing rejoinders. The activity of her mind revelled in giving
them a tongue, but would not do it for herself. Then
ensued the inevitable consequence of an incapacity to
speak at the heart's urgent dictate: heart and mind became divided. One throbbed hotly, the other hung
aloof; and mentally, while the sick inarticulate heart
kept clamouring, she answered it with all that she imagined for those two men to say. And she dropped poison
on it to still its reproaches: bidding herself remember her
fatal postponements in order to preserve the seeming o₁
consistency before her father; calling it hypocrite; asking
herself, what was she! who loved her! And thus beating
down her heart, she completed the mischief with a pierc-
ing view of the foundation of her father's advocacy of
Willoughby, and more lamentably asked herself what
her value was, if she stood bereft of respect for her father.

Reason, on the other hand, was animated by her better
nature to plead his case against her: she clung to her re-

spect for him, and felt herself drowning with it: and she echoed Willoughby consciously, doubling her horror with the consciousness, in crying out on a world where the most sacred feelings are subject to such lapses. It doubled her horror, that she should echo the man; but it proved that she was no better than he: only some years younger. Those years would soon be outlived: after which, he and she would be of a pattern. She was unloved: she did no harm to any one by keeping her word to this man: she had pledged it, and it would be a breach of faith not to keep it. No one loved her. Behold the quality of her father's love! To give him happiness was now the principal aim for her, her own happiness being decently buried; and here he was happy: why should she be the cause of his going and losing the poor pleasure he so much enjoyed?

The idea of her devotedness flattered her feebleness. She betrayed signs of hesitation; and in hesitating, she looked away from a look at Willoughby, thinking (so much against her nature was it to resign herself to him) that it would not have been so difficult with an ill-favoured man. With one horribly ugly, it would have been a horrible exultation to cast off her youth and take the fiendish leap.

Unfortunately for Sir Willoughby, he had his reasons for pressing impatience; and seeing her deliberate, seeing her hasty look at his fine figure, his opinion of himself combined with his recollection of a particular maxim of the Great Book to assure him that her resistance was over: chiefly owing, as he supposed, to his physical perfections.

Frequently indeed, in the contest between gentlemen and ladies, have the maxims of the Book stimulated the assailant to victory. They are rosy with blood of victims. To hear them is to hear a horn that blows the mort:* has blown it a thousand times. It is good to remember how often they have succeeded, when, for the benefit of some future Lady Vauban,* who may bestir her wits to gather maxims for the inspiriting of the Defence, the circumstance of a failure has to be recorded.

Willoughby could not wait for the melting of the snows. He saw full surely the dissolving process; and sincerely admiring and coveting her as he did, rashly this ill-fated gentleman attempted to precipitate it, and so doing arrested.

Whence might we draw a note upon yonder maxim, in words akin to these: Make certain ere a breath come from thee that thou be not a frost.

'Mine! She is mine!' he cried: 'mine once more! mine utterly! mine eternally!' and he followed up his devouring exclamations in person as she, less decidedly, retreated. She retreated as young ladies should ever do, two or three steps, and he would not notice that she had become an angry Dian, all arrows:*her maidenliness in surrendering pleased him. Grasping one fair hand, he just allowed her to edge away from his embrace, crying: 'Not a syllable of what I have gone through! You shall not have to explain it, my Clara. I will study you more diligently, to be guided by you, my darling. If I offend again, my wife will not find it hard to speak what my bride withheld—I do not ask why: perhaps not able to weigh the effect of her reticence: not at that time, when she was younger and less experienced, estimating the sacredness of a plighted engagement. It is past, we are one, my dear sir and father. You may leave us now.'

'I profoundly rejoice to hear that I may,' said Dr. Middleton.

Clara writhed her captured hand.

'No, papa, stay. It is an error, an error. You must not leave me. Do not think me utterly, eternally, belonging to any one but you. No one shall say I am his but you.'

'Are you quicksands, Clara Middleton, that nothing can be built on you? Whither is a flighty head and a shifty will carrying the girl?'

'Clara and I, sir,' said Willoughby.

'And so you shall,' said the Doctor, turning about.

'Not yet, papa': Clara sprang to him.

'Why, you, you, you, it was you who craved to be alone with Willoughby!' her father shouted; 'and here we are rounded to our starting-point, with the solitary difference that now you do not want to be alone with Willoughby. First I am bidden go; next I am pulled back; and judging by collar and coat-tail, I suspect you to be a young woman to wear an angel's temper threadbare before you determine upon which one of the tides driving him to and fro you intend to launch on yourself. Where is your mind?'

Clara smoothed her forehead.

'I wish to please you, papa.'

'I request you to please the gentleman who is your appointed husband.'

'I am anxious to perform my duty.'

'That should be a satisfactory basis for you, Willoughby;—as girls go!'

'Let me, sir, simply entreat to have her hand in mine before you.'

'Why not, Clara?'

'Why an empty ceremony, papa?'

'The implication is, that she is prepared for the important one, friend Willoughby.'

'Her hand, sir; the reassurance of her hand in mine under your eyes:—after all that I have suffered, I claim it, I think I claim it reasonably, to restore me to confidence.'

'Quite reasonably; which is not to say, necessarily; but, I will add, justifiably; and it may be, sagaciously, when dealing with the volatile.'

'And here,' said Willoughby, 'is my hand.'

Clara recoiled.

He stepped on. Her father frowned. She lifted both her hands from the shrinking elbows, darted a look of repulsion at her pursuer, and ran to her father, crying: 'Call it my mood! I am volatile, capricious, flighty, very foolish. But you see that I attach a real meaning to it, and feel it to be binding: I cannot think it an empty ceremony, if it is before you. Yes, only be a little considerate to your moody girl. She will be in a fitter state in a few hours. Spare me this moment; I must collect myself. I thought I was free; I thought he would not press me. If I give my hand hurriedly now, I shall, I know, immediately repent it. There is the picture of me! But, papa, I mean to try to be above that, and if I go and walk by myself, I shall grow calm to perceive where my duty lies . . .'

'In which direction shall you walk?' said Willoughby.

'Wisdom is not upon a particular road,' said Dr. Middleton.

'I have a dread, sir, of that one which leads to the railway-station.'

'With some justice!' Dr. Middleton sighed over his daughter.

Clara coloured to deep crimson: but she was beyond anger, and was rather gratified by an offence coming from Willoughby.

'I will promise not to leave his grounds, papa.'

'My child, you have threatened to be a breaker of promises.'

'Oh!' she wailed. 'But I will make it a vow to you.'

'Why not make it a vow to me this moment, for this gentleman's contentment, that he shall be your husband within a given period!'

'I will come to you voluntarily. I burn to be alone.'

'I shall lose her!' exclaimed Willoughby in heartfelt earnest.

'How so?' said Dr. Middleton. 'I have her, sir, if you will favour me by continuing in abeyance.—You will come within an hour voluntarily, Clara: and you will either at once yield your hand to him, or you will furnish reasons, and they must be good ones, for withholding it.'

'Yes, papa.'

'You will?'

'I will.'

'Mind, I say *reasons*.'

'Reasons, papa. If I have none . . .'

'If you have none that are to my satisfaction, you implicitly, and instantly, and cordially obey my command.'

'I will obey.'

'What more would you require?' Dr. Middleton bowed to Sir Willoughby in triumph.

'Will she . . .'

'Sir! Sir!'

'She is your daughter, sir. I am satisfied.'

'She has perchance wrestled with her engagement, as the aboriginals of a land newly discovered by a crew of adventurous colonists do battle with the garments imposed on them by our considerate civilization;—ultimately to rejoice with excessive dignity in the wearing of a battered cocked-hat and trowsers not extending to the shanks: but she did not break her engagement, sir; and we will anticipate, that moderating a young woman's native wildness, she may, after the manner of my comparison, take a similar pride in her fortune in good season.'

Willoughby had not leisure to sound the depth of Dr. Middleton's compliment. He had seen Clara gliding out of the room during the delivery; and his fear returned on him that, not being won, she was lost.

'She has gone'; her father noticed her absence. 'She does not waste time in the mission to procure that astonishing product of a shallow soil, her reasons; if such be the object of her search. But no: it signifies that she deems herself to have need of composure—nothing more. No one likes to be turned about; we like to turn ourselves about: and in the question of an act to be committed, we stipulate that it shall be our act—girls and others. After the lapse of an hour, it will appear to her as her act.—Happily, Willoughby, we do not dine away from Patterne to-night.'

'No, sir.'

'It may be attributable to a sense of deserving, but I could plead guilty to a weakness for old Port to-day.'

'There shall be an extra bottle, sir.'

'All going favourably with you, as I have no cause to doubt,' said Dr. Middleton, with the motion of wafting his host out of the library.

CHAPTER XLII

Shows the Divining Arts of a Perceptive Mind

STARTING from the Hall, a few minutes before Dr. Middleton and Sir Willoughby had entered the drawing-room overnight, Vernon parted company with Colonel De Craye at the park-gates, and betook himself to the cottage of the Dales, where nothing had been heard of his wanderer; and he received the same disappointing reply from Dr. Corney, out of the bed-room window of the genial physician, whose astonishment at his covering so long a stretch of road at night for news of a boy like Crossjay—gifted with the lives of a cat—became violent and rapped Punch-like blows on the window-sill at Vernon's refusal to take shelter and rest. Vernon's excuse was that he had 'no one but that fellow to care for,' and he strode off, naming a farm five miles distant. Dr. Corney howled an invitation to early breakfast to him, in the event of his passing on his way back, and retired to bed to think of him. The result of a variety of conjectures caused him to set Vernon down as Miss Middleton's knight, and he felt a strong compassion for his poor friend. 'Though,' thought he, 'a hopeless attachment is as pretty an accompaniment to the tune of life as a gentleman might wish to have, for it's one of those big doses of discord which make all the minor ones fit in like an agreeable harmony, and so he shuffles along as pleasantly as the fortune-favoured, when they come to compute!'

Sir Willoughby was the fortune-favoured in the little doctor's mind; that high-stepping gentleman having wealth, and public consideration, and the most ravishing young lady in the world for a bride. Still, though he reckoned all these advantages enjoyed by Sir Willoughby at their full value, he could imagine the ultimate balance of good fortune to be in favour of Vernon. But to do so, he had to reduce the whole calculation to the extreme abstract, and feed his lean friend, as it were, on dew and roots; and the happy effect for Vernon lay in a distant future, on the borders of old age, where he was to be blest with his lady's regretful preference, and rejoice in the fruits of good constitutional habits. The reviewing mind was Irish. Sir Willoughby was a character of man profoundly opposed to Dr. Corney's nature; the latter's instincts bristled with antagonism—not to his race, for Vernon was of the same race, partly of the same blood, and Corney loved him: the type of person was the annoyance. And the circumstance of its prevailing successfulness in the country where he was placed, while it held him silent as if under a law, heaped stores of insurgency in the Celtic bosom. Corney contemplating Sir Willoughby, and a trotting kern governed by Strongbow, have a point of likeness between them; with the point of difference, that Corney was enlightened to know of a friend better adapted for eminent station, and especially better adapted to please a lovely lady—could these high-bred Englishwomen but be taught to conceive another idea of manliness than the formal carved-in-wood idol of their national worship!

Dr. Corney breakfasted very early, without seeing Vernon. He was off to a patient while the first lark of the morning carolled above, and the business of the day, not yet fallen upon men in the shape of cloud, was happily intermixed with nature's hues and pipings. Turning off the highroad up a green lane, an hour later, he beheld a youngster prying into a hedge head and arms, by the peculiar strenuous twist of whose hinder parts, indicative of a frame plunged on the pursuit in hand, he clearly distinguished young Crossjay. Out came eggs. The doctor pulled up.

'What bird?' he bellowed.

'Yellowhammer,' Crossjay yelled back.

'Now, sir, you'll drop a couple of those eggs in the nest.'

'Don't order me,' Crossjay was retorting: 'Oh! it's you, Dr. Corney. Good morning. I said that, because I always do drop a couple back. I promised Mr. Whitford I would, and Miss Middleton too.'

'Had breakfast?'

'Not yet.'

'Not hungry?'

'I should be if I thought about it.'

'Jump up.'

'I think I'd rather not, Dr. Corney.'

'And you'll just do what Dr. Corney tells you; and set your mind on rashers of curly fat bacon and sweetly-smoking coffee, toast, hot cakes, marmalade and damson-jam. Wide go the fellow's nostrils, and there's water at the dimples of his mouth! Up, my man.'

Crossjay jumped up beside the doctor, who remarked, as he touched his horse: 'I don't want a man this morning, though I'll enlist you in my service if I do. You're fond of Miss Middleton?'

Instead of answering, Crossjay heaved the sigh of love that bears a burden.

'And so am I,' pursued the doctor: 'You'll have to put up with a rival. It's worse than fond: I'm in love with her. How do you like that?'

'I don't mind how many *love* her,' said Crossjay.

'You're worthy of a gratuitous breakfast in the front parlour of the best hotel of the place they call Arcadia. And how about your bed last night?'

'Pretty middling.'

'Hard, was it, where the bones haven't cushion?'

'I don't care for bed. A couple of hours, and that's enough for me.'

'But you're fond of Miss Middleton anyhow, and that's a virtue.'

To his great surprise, Dr. Corney beheld two big round tears force their way out of this tough youngster's eyes, and all the while the boy's face was proud.

Crossjay said, when he could trust himself to disjoin his lips: 'I want to see Mr. Whitford.'

'Have you got news for him?'

'I've something to ask him. It's about what I ought to do.'

'Then, my boy, you have the right name addressed in the wrong direction: for I found you turning your shoulders on Mr. Whitford. And he has been out of his bed, hunting you all the unholy night you've made it for him. That's melancholy. What do you say to asking my advice?'

Crossjay sighed. 'I can't speak to anybody but Mr. Whitford.'

'And you're hot to speak to him?'

'I want to.'

'And I found you running away from him. You're a curiosity, Mr. Crossjay Patterne.'

'Ah! so'd anybody be who knew as much as I do,' said Crossjay, with a sober sadness that caused the doctor to treat him seriously.

'The fact is,' he said, 'Mr. Whitford is beating the country for you. My best plan will be to drive you to the Hall.'

'I'd rather not go to the Hall,' Crossjay spoke resolutely.

'You won't see Miss Middleton anywhere but at the Hall.'

'I don't want to see Miss Middleton, if I can't be a bit of use to her.'

'No danger threatening the lady, is there?'

Crossjay treated the question as if it had not been put.

'Now, tell me,' said Dr. Corney, 'would there be a chance for me, supposing Miss Middleton were disengaged?'

The answer was easy. 'I'm sure she wouldn't.'

'And why, sir, are you so cock sure?'

There was no saying; but the doctor pressed for it, and at last Crossjay gave his opinion that she would take Mr. Whitford.

The doctor asked why; and Crossjay said it was because Mr. Whitford was the best man in the world. To which, with a lusty 'Amen to that,' Dr. Corney remarked: 'I should have fancied Colonel De Craye would have had the first chance: he's more of a lady's man.'

Crossjay surprised him again by petulantly saying: 'Don't.'

The boy added: 'I don't want to talk, except about

birds and things. What a jolly morning it is! I saw the
sun rise. No rain to-day. You're right about hungry,
Dr. Corney!'

The kindly little man swung his whip. Crossjay informed him of his disgrace at the Hall, and of every
incident connected with it, from the tramp to the
baronet, save Miss Middleton's adventure, and the night-
scene in the drawing-room. A strong smell of something
left out struck Dr. Corney, and he said: 'You'll not let
Miss Middleton know of my affection. After all, it's only
a little bit of love. But, as Patrick said to Kathleen,
when she owned to such a little bit, "that's the best bit
of all!" and he was as right as I am about hungry.'

Crossjay scorned to talk of loving, he declared. 'I
never tell Miss Middleton what I feel. Why, there's
Miss Dale's cottage!'

'It's nearer to your empty inside than my mansion,'
said the doctor, 'and we'll stop just to inquire whether a
bed's to be had for you there to-night, and if not, I'll
have you with me, and bottle you and exhibit you, for
you're a rare specimen. Breakfast, you may count on,
from Mr. Dale. I spy a gentleman.'

'It's Colonel De Craye.'

'Come after news of you.'

'I wonder!'

'Miss Middleton sends him; of course she does.'

Crossjay turned his full face to the doctor. 'I haven't
seen her for such a long time! But he saw me last night,
and he might have told her that, if she's anxious.—
Good morning, colonel. I've had a good walk and a
capital drive, and I'm as hungry as the boat's crew of
Captain Bligh.'*

He jumped down.

The colonel and the doctor saluted smiling.

'I've rung the bell,' said De Craye.

A maid came to the gate, and upon her steps appeared
Miss Dale, who flung herself at Crossjay, mingling kisses
and reproaches. She scarcely raised her face to the
colonel more than to reply to his greeting, and excuse the
hungry boy for hurrying indoors to breakfast.

'I'll wait,' said De Craye. He had seen that she was paler than usual. So had Dr. Corney; and the doctor called to her concerning her father's health. She reported that he had not yet risen, and took Crossjay to herself.

'That's well,' said the doctor, 'if the invalid sleeps long. The lady is not looking so well, though. But ladies vary; they show the mind on the countenance, for want of the punching we meet with to conceal it; they're like military flags for a funeral or a gala; one day furled, and next day streaming. Men are ships' figure-heads, about the same for a storm or a calm, and not too handsome, thanks to the ocean. It's an age since we encountered last, colonel: on board the Dublin boat, I recollect, and a night it was!'

'I recollect that you set me on my legs, doctor.'

'Ah, and you'll please to notify that Corney's no quack at sea, by favour of the monks of the Chartreuse, whose elixir has power to still the waves.* And we hear that miracles are done with!'

'Roll a physician and a monk together, doctor!'

'True: it'll be a miracle if they combine. Though the cure of the soul is often the entire and total cure of the body: and it's maliciously said, that the body given over to our treatment is a signal to set the soul flying. By the way, colonel, that boy has a trifle on his mind.'

'I suppose he has been worrying a farmer or a game-keeper.'

'Try him. You'll find him tight. He's got Miss Middleton on the brain. There's a bit of a secret; and he's not so cheerful about it.'

'We'll see,' said the colonel.

Dr. Corney nodded. 'I have to visit my patient here presently. I'm too early for him: so I'll make a call or two on the lame birds that are up,' he remarked, and drove away.

De Craye strolled through the garden. He was a gentleman of those actively perceptive wits which, if ever they reflect, do so by hops and jumps: upon some dancing mirror within, we may fancy. He penetrated a

plot in a flash; and in a flash he formed one; but in both
cases, it was after long hovering and not over-eager
deliberation, by the patient exercise of his quick perceptives. The fact that Crossjay was considered to have
Miss Middleton on the brain, threw a series of images of
everything relating to Crossjay for the last forty hours into
relief before him: and as he did not in the slightest degree
speculate on any one of them, but merely shifted and
surveyed them, the falcon that he was in spirit as well as
in his handsome face leisurely allowed his instinct to
direct him where to strike. A reflective disposition has
this danger in action, that it commonly precipitates
conjecture for the purpose of working upon probabilities
with the methods and in the tracks to which it is accustomed: and to conjecture rashly is to play into the
puzzles of the maze. He who can watch circling above it
awhile, quietly viewing, and collecting in his eye, gathers
matter that makes the secret thing discourse to the brain
by weight and balance; he will get either the right clue or
none; more frequently none; but he will escape the en-
tanglement of his own cleverness, he will always be
nearer to the enigma than the guesser or the calculator,
and he will retain a breadth of vision forfeited by them.
He must, however, to have his chance of success, be
acutely besides calmly perceptive, a reader of features,
audacious at the proper moment.

De Craye wished to look at Miss Dale. She had returned home very suddenly, not, as it appeared, owing
to her father's illness: and he remembered a redness of
her eyelids when he passed her on the corridor one night.
She sent Crossjay out to him as soon as the boy was well
filled. He sent Crossjay back with a request. She did not
yield to it immediately. She stepped to the front door
reluctantly, and seemed disconcerted. De Craye begged
for a message to Miss Middleton. There was none to
give. He persisted. But there was really none at present,
she said.

'You won't entrust me with the smallest word?' said he,
and set her visibly thinking whether she could despatch a
word. She could not; she had no heart for messages.

'I shall see her in a day or two, Colonel De Craye.'

'She will miss you severely.'

'We shall soon meet.'

'And poor Willoughby!'

Laetitia coloured and stood silent.

A butterfly of some rarity allured Crossjay.

'I fear he has been doing mischief,' she said. 'I cannot get him to look at me.'

'His appetite is good?'

'Very good indeed.'

De Craye nodded. A boy with a noble appetite is never a hopeless lock.

The colonel and Crossjay lounged over the garden.

'And now,' said the colonel, 'we'll see if we can't arrange a meeting between you and Miss Middleton. You're a lucky fellow, for she's always thinking of you.'

'I know I'm always thinking of her,' said Crossjay.

'If ever you're in a scrape, she's the person you must go to.'

'Yes, if I know where she is!'

'Why, generally she'll be at the Hall.'

There was no reply: Crossjay's dreadful secret jumped to his throat. He certainly was a weaker lock for being full of breakfast.

'I want to see Mr. Whitford so much,' he said.

'Something to tell him?'

'I don't know what to do: I don't understand it!' The secret wriggled to his mouth. He swallowed it down: 'Yes, I want to talk to Mr. Whitford.'

'He's another of Miss Middleton's friends.'

'I know he is. He's true steel.'

'We're all her friends, Crossjay. I flatter myself I'm a Toledo when I'm wanted. How long had you been in the house last night before you ran into me?'

'I don't know, sir: I fell asleep for some time, and then I woke . . .!'

'Where did you find yourself?'

'I was in the drawing-room.'

'Come, Crossjay, you're not a fellow to be scared by

ghosts? You looked it when you made a dash at my midriff.'

'I don't believe there are such things. Do you, colonel? You can't!'

'There's no saying. We'll hope not; for it wouldn't be fair fighting. A man with a ghost to back him'd beat any ten. We couldn't box him, or play cards, or stand a chance with him as a rival in love. Did you, now, catch a sight of a ghost?'

'They weren't ghosts!' Crossjay said what he was sure of, and his voice pronounced his conviction.

'I doubt whether Miss Middleton is particularly happy,' remarked the colonel. 'Why? Why, you upset her, you know, now and then.'

The boy swelled. 'I'd do . . . I'd go . . . I wouldn't have her unhappy . . . It's that! that's it! And I don't know what I ought to do. I wish I could see Mr. Whitford.'

'You get into such headlong scrapes, my lad.'

'I wasn't in any scrape yesterday.'

'So you made yourself up a comfortable bed in the drawing-room? Lucky Sir Willoughby didn't see you.'

'He didn't, though!'

'A close shave, was it?'

'I was under a cover of something silk.'

'He woke you?'

'I suppose he did. I heard him.'

'Talking?'

'He was talking.'

'What! talking to himself?'

'No.'

The secret threatened Crossjay to be out or suffocate him. De Craye gave him a respite.

'You like Sir Willoughby, don't you?'

Crossjay produced a still-born affirmative.

'He's kind to you,' said the colonel; 'he'll set you up and look after your interests.'

'Yes, I like him,' said Crossjay, with his customary rapidity in touching the subject; 'I like him; he's kind, and all that, and tips and plays with you, and all that;

but I never can make out why he wouldn't see my father when my father came here to see him ten miles, and had to walk back ten miles in the rain, to go by rail a long way, down home, as far as Devonport, because Sir Willoughby wouldn't see him, though he was at home, my father saw. We all thought it so odd: and my father wouldn't let us talk much about it. My father's a very brave man.'

'Captain Patterne is as brave a man as ever lived,' said De Craye.

'I'm positive you'd like him, colonel.'

'I know of his deeds, and I admire him, and that's a good step to liking.'

He warmed the boy's thoughts of his father.

'Because, what they say at home is, a little bread and cheese, and a glass of ale, and a rest, to a poor man—lots of great houses will give you that, and we wouldn't have asked for more than that. My sisters say they think Sir Willoughby must be selfish. He's awfully proud; and perhaps it was because my father wasn't dressed well enough. But what can we do? We're very poor at home, and lots of us, and all hungry. My father says he isn't paid very well for his services to the Government. He's only a marine.'

'He's a hero!' said De Craye.

'He came home very tired, with a cold, and had a doctor. But Sir Willoughby did send him money, and mother wished to send it back, and my father said she was not like a woman—with our big family. He said he thought Sir Willoughby an extraordinary man.'

'Not at all; very common; indigenous,' said De Craye. 'The art of cutting, is one of the branches of a polite education in this country, and you'll have to learn it, if you expect to be looked on as a gentleman and a Patterne, my boy. I begin to see how it is Miss Middleton takes to you so. Follow her directions. But I hope you did not listen to a private conversation. Miss Middleton would not approve of that.'

'Colonel De Craye, how could I help myself? I heard a lot before I knew what it was. There was poetry!'

'Still, Crossjay, if it was important!—was it?'

The boy swelled again, and the colonel asked him: 'Does Miss Dale know of your having played listener?'

'She!' said Crossjay. 'Oh! I couldn't tell *her*.'

He breathed thick: then came a threat of tears. 'She wouldn't do anything to hurt Miss Middleton. I'm sure of that. It wasn't her fault. She—there goes Mr. Whitford!' Crossjay bounded away.

The colonel had no inclination to wait for his return. He walked fast up the road, not perspicuously conscious that his motive was to be well in advance of Vernon Whitford: to whom after all, the knowledge imparted by Crossjay would be of small advantage. That fellow would probably trot off to Willoughby to row him for breaking his word to Miss Middleton! There are men, thought De Craye, who see nothing, feel nothing.

He crossed a stile into the wood above the lake, where, as he was in the humour to think himself signally lucky, espying her, he took it as a matter of course that the lady who taught his heart to leap should be posted by the Fates. And he wondered little at her power, for rarely had the world seen such union of princess and sylph as in that lady's figure. She stood holding by a beech-branch, gazing down on the water.

She had not heard him. When she looked she flushed at the spectacle of one of her thousand thoughts, but she was not startled; the colour overflowed a grave face.

'And 'tis not quite the first time that Willoughby has played this trick!' De Craye said to her, keenly smiling with a parted mouth.

Clara moved her lips to recall remarks introductory to so abrupt and strange a plunge.

He smiled in that peculiar manner of an illuminated comic perception: for the moment he was all falcon; and he surprised himself more than Clara, who was not in the mood to take surprises. It was the sight of her which had animated him to strike his game; he was down on it.

Another instinct at work (they spring up in twenties oftener than in twos when the heart is the hunter)

prompted him to directness and quickness, to carry her
on the flood of the discovery.

She regained something of her mental self-possession as
soon as she was on a level with a meaning she had not yet
inspected; but she had to submit to his lead, distinctly
perceiving where its drift divided to the forked currents
of what might be in his mind and what was in hers.

'Miss Middleton, I bear a bit of a likeness to the
messenger to the glorious despot—my head is off if I
speak not true! Everything I have is on the die.* Did I
guess wrong your wish?—I read it in the dark, by the
heart. But here's a certainty: Willoughby sets you free.'

'You have come from him?' she could imagine nothing
else, and she was unable to preserve a disguise; she
trembled.

'From Miss Dale.'

'Ah!' Clara drooped: 'she told me that once.'

''Tis the fact that tells it now.'

'You have not seen him since you left the house?'

'Darkly: clear enough: not unlike the hand of destiny
—through a veil. He offered himself to Miss Dale last
night, about between the witching hours of twelve and
one.'

'Miss Dale . . .?'

'Would she other? Could she? The poor lady has
languished beyond a decade. She's love in the feminine
person.'

'Are you speaking seriously, Colonel De Craye?'

'Would I dare to trifle with you, Miss Middleton?'

'I have reason to know it cannot be.'

'If I have a head, it is a fresh and blooming truth.
And more—I stake my vanity on it!'

'Let me go to her.' She stepped.

'Consider,' said he.

'Miss Dale and I are excellent friends. It would not
seem indelicate to her. She has a kind of regard for me,
through Crossjay.—Oh! can it be? There must be some
delusion. You have seen—you wish to be of service to
me; you may too easily be deceived. Last night?—he
last night . . .? And this morning!'

''Tis not the first time our friend has played the trick, Miss Middleton.'

'But this is incredible: that last night . . . and this morning, in my father's presence, he presses! . . . You have seen Miss Dale?—Everything is possible of him: they were together, I know. Colonel De Craye, I have not the slightest chance of concealment with you. I think I felt that when I first saw you. Will you let me hear why you are so certain?'

'Miss Middleton, when I first had the honour of looking on you, it was in a posture that necessitated my looking up, and morally so it has been since. I conceived that Willoughby had won the greatest prize on earth. And next I was led to the conclusion that he had won it to lose it. Whether he much cares, is the mystery I haven't leisure to fathom. Himself is the principal consideration with himself, and ever was.'

'You discovered it!' said Clara.

'He uncovered it,' said De Craye. 'The miracle was, that the world wouldn't see. But the world is a piggy-wiggy world for the wealthy fellow who fills a trough for it, and that he has always very sagaciously done. Only women besides myself have detected him. I have never exposed him; I have been an observer pure and simple: and because I apprehended another catastrophe—making something like the fourth, to my knowledge, one being public . . .'

'You knew Miss Durham?'

'And Harry Oxford too. And they're a pair as happy as blackbirds in a cherry-tree, in a summer sunrise, with the owner of the garden asleep. Because of that apprehension of mine, I refused the office of best man till Willoughby had sent me a third letter. He insisted on my coming. I came, saw, and was conquered.* I trust with all my soul I did not betray myself. I owed that duty to my position of concealing it. As for entirely hiding that I had used my eyes, I can't say: they must answer for it.'

The colonel was using his eyes with an increasing suavity that threatened more than sweetness.

'I believe you have been sincerely kind,' said Clara. 'We will descend to the path round the lake.'

She did not refuse her hand on the descent, and he let it escape the moment the service was done. As he was performing the admirable character of the man of honour, he had to attend to the observance of details; and sure of her though he was beginning to feel, there was a touch of the unknown in Clara Middleton which made him fear to stamp assurance; despite a barely resistible impulse, coming of his emotions and approved by his maxims. He looked at the hand, now a free lady's hand. Willoughby settled, his chance was great. Who else was in the way? No one. He counselled himself to wait for her: she might have ideas of delicacy. Her face was troubled, speculative; the brows clouded, the lips compressed.

'You have not heard this from Miss Dale?' she said.

'Last night they were together: this morning she fled. I saw her this morning distressed. She is unwilling to send you a message: she talks vaguely of meeting you some days hence. And it is not the first time he has gone to her for his consolation.'

'That is not a proposal,' Clara reflected. 'He is too prudent. He did not propose to her at the time you mention. Have you not been hasty, Colonel De Craye?'

Shadows crossed her forehead. She glanced in the direction of the house, and stopped her walk.

'Last night, Miss Middleton, there was a listener.'

'Who?'

'Crossjay was under that pretty silk coverlet worked by the Miss Patternes. He came home late, found his door locked, and dashed downstairs into the drawing-room, where he snuggled up and dropped asleep. The two speakers woke him; they frightened the poor dear lad in his love for you, and after they had gone, he wanted to run out of the house, and I met him, just after I had come back from my search, bursting, and took him to my room, and laid him on the sofa, and abused him for not lying quiet. He was restless as a fish on a bank. When I woke in the morning he was off. Dr. Corney came across him somewhere on the road and drove him to the cottage. I was ringing the bell. Corney told me the boy had you on his brain, and was miserable, so Crossjay and I had a talk.'

'Crossjay did not repeat to you the conversation he had heard?' said Clara.

'No.'

She smiled rejoicingly, proud of the boy, as she walked on.

'But you'll pardon me, Miss Middleton—and I'm for him as much as you are—if I was guilty of a little angling.'

'My sympathies are with the fish.'

'The poor fellow had a secret that hurt him. It rose to the surface crying to be hooked, and I spared him twice or thrice, because he had a sort of holy sentiment I respected, that none but Mr. Whitford ought to be his father confessor.'

'Crossjay!' she cried, hugging her love of the boy.

'The secret was one not to be communicated to Miss Dale of all people.'

'He said that?'

'As good as the very words. She informed me too, that she couldn't induce him to face her straight.'

'Oh! that looks like it. And Crossjay was unhappy? Very unhappy?'

'He was just where tears are on the brim, and would have been over, if he were not such a manly youngster.'

'It looks . . .' She reverted in thought to Willoughby, and doubted, and blindly stretched hands to her recollection of the strange old monster she had discovered in him. Such a man could do anything.

That conclusion fortified her to pursue her walk to the house and give battle for freedom. Willoughby appeared to her scarce human, unreadable, save by the key that she could supply. She determined to put faith in Colonel De Craye's marvellous divination of circumstances in the dark. Marvels are solid weapons when we are attacked by real prodigies of nature. Her countenance cleared. She conversed with De Craye of the polite and the political world, throwing off her personal burden completely, and charming him.

At the edge of the garden, on the bridge that crossed the haha from the park, he had a second impulse, almost a warning within, to seize his heavenly opportunity to ask for thanks and move her tender lowered eyelids to hint at his reward. He repressed it, doubtful of the wisdom.

Something like 'heaven forgives me!' was in Clara's mind, though she would have declared herself innocent before the scrutator.

CHAPTER XLIII

In which Sir Willoughby is led to think that the Elements have conspired against him

CLARA had not taken many steps in the garden before she learnt how great was her debt of gratitude to Colonel De Craye. Willoughby and her father were awaiting her. De Craye, with his ready comprehension of circumstances, turned aside unseen among the shrubs. She advanced slowly.

'The vapours, we may trust, have dispersed?' her father hailed her.

'One word, and these discussions are over, we dislike them equally,' said Willoughby.

'No scenes,' Dr. Middleton added. 'Speak your decision, my girl, pro formâ,* seeing that he who has the right demands it, and pray release me.'

Clara looked at Willoughby.

'I have decided to go to Miss Dale for her advice.'

There was no appearance in him of a man that has been shot.

'To Miss Dale?—for advice?'

Dr. Middleton invoked the Furies. 'What is the signification of this new freak?'

'Miss Dale must be consulted, papa.'

'Consulted with reference to the disposal of your hand in marriage?'

'She must be.'

'Miss Dale, do you say?'

'I do, papa.'

Dr. Middleton regained his natural elevation from the bend of body habitual with men of an established sanity, paedagogues and others, who are called on at odd intervals to inspect the magnitude of the infinitesimally absurd in human nature: small, that is, under the light of reason, immense in the realms of madness.

His daughter profoundly confused him. He swelled out his chest, remarking to Willoughby: 'I do not wonder at your scared expression of countenance, my friend. To discover yourself engaged to a girl as mad as Cassandra, without a boast of the distinction of her being sun-struck, can be no specially comfortable enlightenment. I am opposed to delays, and I will not have a breach of faith committed by daughter of mine.'

'Do not repeat those words,' Clara said to Willoughby.

He started. She had evidently come armed. But how, within so short a space? What could have instructed her? And in his bewilderment he gazed hurriedly above, gulped air, and cried: 'Scared, sir? I am not aware that my countenance can show a scare. I am not accustomed to sue for long: I am unable to sustain the part of humble supplicant. She puts me out of harmony with creation—We are plighted, Clara. It is pure waste of time to speak of soliciting advice on the subject.'

'Would it be a breach of faith for me to break my engagement?' she said.

'You ask?'

'It is a breach of sanity to propound the interrogation,' said her father.

She looked at Willoughby! 'Now?'

He shrugged haughtily.

'Since last night?' said she.

'Last night?'

'Am I not released?'

'Not by me.'

'By your act.'

'My dear Clara!'

'Have you not virtually disengaged me?'

'I who claim you as mine?'

'Can you?'

'I do and must.'

'After last night?'

'Tricks! shufflings! Jabber of a barbarian woman upon the evolutions of a serpent!' exclaimed Dr. Middleton. 'You were to capitulate, or to furnish reasons for your refusal. You have none. Give him your hand, girl, according to the compact. I praised you to him for returning within the allotted term, and now forbear to disgrace yourself and me.'

'Is he perfectly free to offer his? Ask him, papa.'

'Perform your duty. Do let us have peace!'

'Perfectly free! as on the day when I offered it first,' Willoughby frankly waved his honourable hand.

His face was blanched: enemies in the air seemed to have whispered things to her: he doubted the fidelity of the Powers above.

'Since last night?' said she.

'Oh! if you insist, I reply, since last night.'

'You know what I mean, Sir Willoughby.'

'Oh! certainly.'

'You speak the truth?'

' "*Sir* Willoughby"!' her father ejaculated in wrath. 'But will you explain what you mean, epitome that you are of all the contradictions and mutabilities ascribed to women from the beginning! "Certainly," he says, and knows no more than I. She begs grace for an hour, and returns with a fresh store of evasions, to insult the man she has injured. It is my humiliation to confess that our share in this contract is rescued from public ignominy by his generosity. Nor can I congratulate him on his fortune, should he condescend to bear with you to the utmost; for instead of the young woman I supposed myself to be bestowing on him, I see a fantastical planguncula* enlivened by the wanton tempers of a nursery chit. If one may conceive a meaning in her, in miserable apology for such behaviour, some spirit of jealousy informs the girl.'

'I can only remark, that there is no foundation for it,' said Willoughby. 'I am willing to satisfy you, Clara. Name the person who discomposes you. I can scarcely imagine one to exist: but who can tell?'

She could name no person. The detestable imputation of jealousy would be confirmed if she mentioned a name: and indeed Laetitia was not to be named.

He pursued his advantage: 'Jealousy is one of the fits I am a stranger to,—I fancy, sir, that gentlemen have dismissed it. I speak for myself.—But I can make allowances. In some cases, it is considered a compliment; and often a word will soothe it. The whole affair is so senseless! However, I will enter the witness-box, or stand at the prisoner's bar! Anything to quiet a distempered mind.'

'Of you, sir,' said Dr. Middleton, 'might a parent be justly proud.'

'It is not jealousy; I could not be jealous!' Clara cried, stung by the very passion; and she ran through her brain for a suggestion to win a sign of meltingness if not esteem from her father. She was not an iron maiden, but one among the nervous natures which live largely in the moment, though she was then sacrificing it to her nature's deep dislike. 'You may be proud of me again, papa.'

She could hardly have uttered anything more impolitic.

'Optume: but deliver yourself ad rem,' he rejoined, alarmingly pacified. 'Firmavit fidem.* Do you likewise, and double on us no more like puss in the field.'

'I wish to see Miss Dale,' she said.

Up flew the Rev. Doctor's arms in wrathful despair resembling an imprecation.

'She is at the cottage. You could have seen her,' said Willoughby.

Evidently she had not.

'Is it untrue, that last night, between twelve o'clock and one, in the drawing-room, you proposed marriage to Miss Dale?'

He became convinced that she must have stolen downstairs during his colloquy with Laetitia, and listened at the door.

'On behalf of old Vernon?' he said, lightly laughing. 'The idea is not novel, as you know. They are suited, if they could see it.—Laetitia Dale and my cousin Vernon Whitford, sir.'

'Fairly schemed, my friend, and I will say for you, you have the patience, Willoughby—of a husband!'

Willoughby bowed to the encomium, and allowed some fatigue to be visible. He half yawned: 'I claim no happier title, sir,' and made light of the weariful discussion.

Clara was shaken: she feared that Crossjay had heard incorrectly, or that Colonel De Craye had guessed erroneously. It was too likely that Willoughby should have proposed Vernon to Laetitia.

There was nothing to reassure her save the vision of the panic amazement of his face at her persistency in speaking of Miss Dale. She could have declared on oath that she was right, while admitting all the suppositions to be against her. And unhappily all the Delicacies (a doughty battalion for the defence of ladies until they enter into difficulties and are shorn of them at a blow, bare as dairy-maids), all the body-guard of a young gentlewoman,* the drawing-room sylphides, which bear her train, which wreathe her hair, which modulate her voice and tone her complexion, which are arrows and shield to awe the creature man, forbade her utterance of what she felt, on pain of instant fulfilment of their oft-repeated threat of late to leave her to the last remnant of a protecting sprite. She could not, as in a dear melodrama, from the aim of a pointed finger denounce him, on the testimony of her instincts, false of speech, false in deed. She could not even declare that she doubted his truthfulness. The refuge of a sullen fit, the refuge of tears, the pretext of a mood, were denied her now by the rigour of those laws of decency which are a garment to ladies of pure breeding.

'One more respite, papa,' she implored him, bitterly conscious of the closer tangle her petition involved, and, if it must be betrayed of her, perceiving in an illumination how the knot might become so woefully Gordian* that haply in a cloud of wild events the intervention of a gallant gentleman out of heaven, albeit in the likeness of one of earth, would have to cut it: her cry within, as she succumbed to weakness, being fervider: 'Anything but marry this one!' She was faint with strife and dejected, a condition in the young when their imaginative energies hold revel uncontrolled and are projectively desperate.

'No respite!' said Willoughby genially.

'And I say, no respite!' observed her father. 'You have assumed a position that has not been granted you, Clara Middleton.'

'I cannot bear to offend you, father.'

'Him! Your duty is not to offend him. Address your excuses to him. I refuse to be dragged over the same ground, to reiterate the same command perpetually.'

'If authority is deputed to me, I claim you,' said Willoughby.

'You have not broken faith with me?'

'Assuredly not, or would it be possible for me to press my claim?'

'And join the right hand to the right,' said Dr. Middleton: 'no, it would not be possible. What insane root she has been nibbling, I know not, but she must consign herself to the guidance of those whom the gods have not abandoned, until her intellect is liberated. She was once . . . there: I look not back:—if she it was, and no simulacrum of a reasonable daughter. I welcome the appearance of my friend Mr. Whitford. He is my sea-bath and supper on the beach of Troy,* after the day's battle and dust.'

Vernon walked straight up to them: an act unusual with him, for he was shy of committing an intrusion.

Clara guessed by that, and more by the dancing frown of speculative humour he turned on Willoughby, that he had come charged in support of her. His forehead was curiously lively, as of one who has got a surprise well under, to feed on its amusing contents.

'Have you seen Crossjay, Mr. Whitford?' she said.

'I've pounced on Crossjay; his bones are sound.'

'Where did he sleep?'

'On a sofa, it seems.'

She smiled, with good hope—Vernon had the story.

Willoughby thought it just to himself that he should defend his measure of severity.

'The boy lied; he played a double game.'

'For which he should have been reasoned with at the Grecian portico of a boy,'*said the Rev. Doctor.

'My system is different, sir. I could not inflict what I would not endure myself.'

'So is Greek excluded from the later generations; and you leave a field, the most fertile in the moralities in youth, unploughed and unsown. Ah! well. This growing too fine is our way of relapsing upon barbarism. Beware of over-sensitiveness, where nature has plainly indicated her alternative gateway of knowledge. And now, I presume, I am at liberty.'

'Vernon will excuse us for a minute or two.'

'I hold by Mr. Whitford now I have him.'

'I'll join you in the laboratory, Vernon,' Willoughby nodded bluntly.

'We will leave them, Mr. Whitford. They are at the time-honoured dissension upon a particular day, that for the sake of dignity, blushes to be named.'

'What day?' said Vernon, like a rustic.

'*The* day, these people call it.'

Vernon sent one of his vivid eyeshots from one to the other. His eyes fixed on Willoughby's with a quivering glow, beyond amazement, as if his humour stood at furnace heat, and absorbed all that came.

Willoughby motioned to him to go.

'Have you seen Miss Dale, Mr. Whitford?' said Clara.

He answered: 'No. Something has shocked her.'

'Is it her feeling for Crossjay?'

'Ah,' Vernon said to Willoughby, 'your pocketing of the key of Crossjay's bedroom door was a masterstroke!'

The celestial irony suffused her, and she bathed and swam in it, on hearing its dupe reply: 'My methods of discipline are short. I was not aware that she had been to his door.'

'But I may hope that Miss Dale will see me,' said Clara. 'We are in sympathy about the boy.'

'Mr. Dale might be seen. He seems to be of a divided mind with his daughter,' Vernon rejoined. 'She has locked herself up in her room.'

'He is not the only father in that unwholesome predicament,' said Dr. Middleton.

'He talks of coming to you, Willoughby.'

'Why to me?' Willoughby chastened his irritation: 'He will be welcome, of course. It would be better that the boy should come.'

'If there is a chance of your forgiving him,' said Clara.

'Let the Dales know I am prepared to listen to the boy, Vernon. There can be no necessity for Mr. Dale to drag himself here.'

'How are Mr. Dale and his daughter of a divided mind, Mr. Whitford?' said Clara.

Vernon simulated an uneasiness. With a vacant gaze that enlarged around Willoughby and was more discomforting than intentness, he replied: 'Perhaps she is unwilling to give him her entire confidence, Miss Middleton.'

'In which respect, then, our situations present their solitary point of unlikeness in resemblance, for I have it in excess,' observed Dr. Middleton.

Clara dropped her eyelids for the wave to pass over. 'It struck me that Miss Dale was a person of the extremest candour.'

'Why should we be prying into the domestic affairs of the Dales!' Willoughby interjected, and drew out his watch, merely for a diversion; he was on tiptoe to learn whether Vernon was as well instructed as Clara, and hung to the view that he could not be, while drenching in the sensation that he was:—and if so, what were the Powers above but a body of conspirators? He paid Laetitia that compliment. He could not conceive the human betrayal of the secret. Clara's discovery of it had set his common sense adrift.

'The domestic affairs of the Dales do not concern me,' said Vernon.

'And yet, my friend,' Dr. Middleton balanced himself, and with an air of benevolent slyness, the import of which did not awaken Willoughby until too late, remarked: 'They might concern you. I will even add, that there is a probability of your being not less than the fount and origin of this division of father and daughter, though Willoughby in the drawing-room last night stands accuseably the agent.'

'Favour me, sir, with an explanation,' said Vernon, seeking to gather it from Clara.

Dr. Middleton threw the explanation upon Willoughby.

Clara communicated as much as she was able in one of those looks of still depth which say, Think! and without causing a thought to stir, take us into the pellucid mind.

Vernon was enlightened before Willoughby had spoken. His mouth shut rigidly, and there was a springing increase of the luminous wavering of his eyes. Some star that Clara had watched at night was like them in the vivid wink and overflow of its light. Yet, as he was perfectly sedate, none could have suspected his blood to be chasing wild with laughter, and his frame strung to the utmost to keep it from volleying. So happy was she in his aspect, that her chief anxiety was to recover the name of the star whose shining beckons and speaks, and is in the quick of spirit-fire. It is the sole star which on a night of frost and strong moonlight preserves an indomitable fervency: that she remembered, and the picture of a hoar earth and a lean Orion in flooded heavens, and the star beneath, Eastward* of him: but the name! the name!—She heard Willoughby indistinctly.

'Oh, the old story; another effort; you know my wish; a failure, of course, and no thanks on either side. I suppose I must ask your excuse.—They neither of them see what's good for them, sir.'

'Manifestly, however,' said Dr. Middleton, 'if one

may opine from the division we have heard of, the father is disposed to back your nominee.'

'I can't say; as far as I am concerned, I made a mess of it.'

Vernon withstood the incitement to acquiesce, but he sparkled with his recognition of the fact.

'You meant well, Willoughby.'

'I hope so, Vernon.'

'Only you have driven her away.'

'We must resign ourselves.'

'It won't affect me, for I'm off to-morrow.'

'You see, sir, the thanks I get.'

'Mr. Whitford,' said Dr. Middleton, 'you have a tower of strength in the lady's father.'

'Would you have me bring it to bear upon the lady, sir?'

'Wherefore not?'

'To make her marriage a matter of obedience to her father?'

'Ay, my friend, a lusty lover would have her gladly on those terms, well knowing it to be for the lady's good. What do you say, Willoughby?'

'Sir! Say? What can I say? Miss Dale has not plighted her faith. Had she done so, she is a lady who would never dishonour it.'

'She is an ideal of constancy, who would keep to it though it had been broken on the other side,' said Vernon, and Clara thrilled.

'I take that, sir, to be a statue of constancy, modelled upon which, a lady of our flesh may be proclaimed as graduating for the condition of idiocy,' said Dr. Middleton.

'But faith is faith, sir.'

'But the broken is the broken, sir, whether in porcelain or in human engagements: and all that the one of the two continuing faithful, I should rather say, regretful, can do, is to devote the remainder of life to the picking up of the fragments; an occupation properly to be pursued, for the comfort of mankind, within the enclosure of an appointed asylum.'

'You destroy the poetry of sentiment, Dr. Middleton.'

'To invigorate the poetry of nature, Mr. Whitford.'

'Then you maintain, sir, that when faith is broken by one, the engagement ceases, and the other is absolutely free?'

'I do; I am the champion of that platitude, and sound that knell to the sentimental world; and since you have chosen to defend it, I will appeal to Willoughby, and ask him if he would not side with the world of good sense in applauding the nuptials of man or maid married within a month of a jilting?'

Clara slipped her arm under her father's.

'Poetry, sir,' said Willoughby, 'I never have been hypocrite enough to pretend to understand or care for.'

Dr. Middleton laughed. Vernon too seemed to admire his cousin for a reply that rang in Clara's ears as the dullest ever spoken. Her arm grew cold on her father's. She began to fear Willoughby again.

He depended entirely on his agility to elude the thrusts that assailed him. Had he been able to believe in the treachery of the Powers above, he would at once have seen design in these deadly strokes, for his feelings had rarely been more acute than at the present crisis; and he would then have led away Clara, to wrangle it out with her, relying on Vernon's friendliness not to betray him to her father: but a wrangle with Clara promised no immediate fruits, nothing agreeable; and the lifelong trust he had reposed in his protecting genii, obscured his intelligence to evidence he would otherwise have accepted on the spot, on the faith of his delicate susceptibility to the mildest impressions which wounded him. Clara might have stooped to listen at the door: she might have heard sufficient to create a suspicion. But Vernon was not in the house last night; she could not have communicated it to him, and he had not seen Laetitia, who was besides trustworthy, an admirable if a foolish and ill-fated woman.

Preferring to consider Vernon a pragmatical moralist played upon by a sententious drone, he thought it politic to detach them, and vanquish Clara while she was in the beaten mood, as she had appeared before Vernon's vexatious arrival.

'I'm afraid, my dear fellow, you are rather too dainty and fussy for a very successful wooer,' he said. 'It's beautiful on paper, and absurd in life. We have a bit of private business to discuss. We will go inside, sir, I think. I will soon release you.'

Clara pressed her father's arm.

'More?' said he.

'Five minutes. There's a slight delusion to clear, sir. My dear Clara, you will see with different eyes.'

'Papa wishes to work with Mr. Whitford.'

Her heart sank to hear her father say: 'No, 'tis a lost morning. I must consent to pay tax of it for giving another young woman to the world. I have a daughter! You will, I hope, compensate me, Mr. Whitford, in the afternoon. Be not downcast. I have observed you meditative of late. You will have no clear brain so long as that stuff is on the mind. I could venture to propose to do some pleading for you, should it be needed for the prompter expedition of the affair.'

Vernon briefly thanked him, and said:

'Willoughby has exerted all his eloquence, and you see the result: you have lost Miss Dale and I have not won her. He did everything that one man can do for another in so delicate a case: even to the repeating of her famous birthday verses to him, to flatter the poetess. His best efforts were foiled by the lady's indisposition for me.'

'Behold,' said Dr. Middleton, as Willoughby, electrified by the mention of the verses, took a sharp stride or two, 'you have in him an advocate who will not be rebuffed by one refusal, and I can affirm that he is tenacious, pertinacious as are few. Justly so. Not to believe in a lady's No, is the approved method of carrying that fortress built to yield. Although unquestionably to have a young man pleading in our interests with a lady, counts its objections. Yet Willoughby being notoriously engaged, may be held to enjoy the privileges of his elders.'

'As an engaged man, sir, he was on a level with his elders in pleading on my behalf with Miss Dale,' said Vernon.

Willoughby strode and muttered. Providence had grown mythical in his thoughts, if not malicious: and it is the peril of this worship, that the object will wear such an alternative aspect when it appears no longer subservient.

'Are we coming, sir?' he said, and was unheeded. The Rev. Doctor would not be defrauded of rolling his billow.

'As an honourable gentleman faithful to his own engagement and desirous of establishing his relatives, he deserves, in my judgement, the lady's esteem as well as your cordial thanks; nor should a temporary failure dishearten either of you, notwithstanding the precipitate retreat of the lady from Patterne, and her seclusion in her sanctum on the occasion of your recent visit.'

'Supposing he had succeeded,' said Vernon, driving Willoughby to frenzy, 'should I have been bound to marry?'

Matter for cogitation was offered to Dr. Middleton.

'The proposal was without your sanction?'

'Entirely.'

'You admire the lady?'

'Respectfully.'

'You do not incline to the state?'

'An inch of an angle would exaggerate my inclination.'

'How long are we to stand and hear this insufferable nonsense you talk?' cried Willoughby.

'But if Mr. Whitford was not consulted . . .' Dr. Middleton said, and was overborne by Willoughby's hurried: 'Oblige me, sir.—Oblige me, my good fellow!' he swept his arm to Vernon, and gestured a conducting hand to Clara.

'Here is Mrs. Mountstuart!' she exclaimed.

Willoughby stared. Was it an irruption of a friend or a foe? He doubted, and stood petrified between the double-question.

Clara had seen Mrs. Mountstuart and Colonel De

Craye separating: and now the great lady sailed along the sward like a royal barge in festival trim.

She looked friendly, but friendly to everybody, which was always a frost on Willoughby, and terribly friendly to Clara.

Coming up to her she whispered: 'News indeed! Wonderful! I could not credit his hint of it yesterday. Are you satisfied?'

'Pray, Mrs. Mountstuart, take an opportunity to speak to papa,' Clara whispered in return.

Mrs. Mountstuart bowed to Dr. Middleton, nodded to Vernon, and swam upon Willoughby, with: 'Is it? But *is* it? Am I really to believe? You have? My dear Sir Willoughby? Really?'

The confounded gentleman heaved on a bare plank of wreck in mid sea.

He could oppose only a paralyzed smile to the assault.

His intuitive discretion taught him to fall back a step, while she said: 'So!' the plummet word of our mysterious deep fathoms; and he fell back further, saying: 'Madam?' in a tone advising her to speak low.

She recovered her volubility, followed his partial retreat and dropped her voice:

'Impossible to have imagined it as an actual fact! You were always full of surprises, but this! this! Nothing manlier, nothing more gentlemanly has ever been done: nothing: nothing that so completely changes an untenable situation into a comfortable and proper footing for everybody. It is what I like: it is what I love:— sound sense! Men are so selfish: one cannot persuade them to be reasonable in such positions. But you, Sir Willoughby, have shown wisdom and sentiment: the rarest of all combinations in men.'

'Where have you . . .?' Willoughby contrived to say.

'Heard? The hedges, the house-tops, everywhere. All the neighbourhood will have it before nightfall. Lady Busshe and Lady Culmer will soon be rushing here, and declaring they never expected anything else, I do not doubt. I am not so pretentious. I beg your excuse for that "twice" of mine yesterday. Even if it hurt my vanity, I should be happy to confess my error: I was utterly out. But then I did not reckon on a fatal attachment, I thought men were incapable of it. I thought we women were the only poor creatures persecuted by a fatality. It *is* a fatality! You tried hard to escape, indeed you did. And she will do honour to your final surrender, my dear friend. She is gentle, and very clever, very: she is devoted to you: she will entertain excellently. I see her like a flower in sunshine. She will expand to a perfect hostess. Patterne will shine under her reign; you have my warrant for that. And so will you. Yes, you flourish best when adored. It must be adoration. You have been under a cloud of late. Years ago I said it was a match, when no one supposed you could stoop. Lady Busshe would have it was a screen, and she was deemed high wisdom. The world will be with you. All the women will be: excepting, of course, Lady Busshe, whose pride is in prophesy; and she will soon be too glad to swell the host. There, my friend, your sincerest and oldest admirer congratulates you. I could not contain myself; I was compelled to pour forth. And now I must go and be talked to by Dr. Middleton. How does he take it? They leave?'

'He is perfectly well,' said Willoughby, aloud, quite distraught.

She acknowledged his just correction of her for running on to an extreme in low-toned converse, though they stood sufficiently isolated from the others. These had by this time been joined by Colonel De Craye, and were all chatting in a group—of himself, Willoughby horribly suspected.

Clara was gone from him! Gone! but he remembered his oath and vowed it again: not to Horace De Craye! She was gone, lost, sunk into the world of waters of rival men, and he determined that his whole force should be used to keep her from that man: the false friend who had supplanted him in her shallow heart, and might, if he succeeded, boast of having done it by simply appearing on the scene.

Willoughby intercepted Mrs. Mountstuart as she was

passing over to Dr. Middleton: 'My dear lady! spare me a minute.'

De Craye sauntered up, with a face of the friendliest humour: 'Never was man like you, Willoughby, for shaking new patterns in a kaleidoscope.'

'Have you turned punster, Horace?' Willoughby replied, smarting to find yet another in the demon secret, and he drew Dr. Middleton two or three steps aside, and hurriedly begged him to abstain from prosecuting the subject with Clara. 'We must try to make her happy as we best can, sir. She may have her reasons—a young lady's reasons!' He laughed, and left the Rev. Doctor considering within himself under the arch of his lofty frown of stupefaction.

De Craye smiled slyly and winningly as he shadowed a deep droop on the bend of his head before Clara, signifying his absolute devotion to her service, and this present good fruit for witness of his merits.

She smiled sweetly though vaguely. There was no concealment of their intimacy.

'The battle is over,' Vernon said quietly, when Willoughby had walked some paces beside Mrs. Mountstuart, adding: 'You may expect to see Mr. Dale here. He knows.'

Vernon and Clara exchanged one look, hard on his part, in contrast with her softness, and he proceeded to the house.

De Craye waited for a word or a promising look. He was patient, being self-assured, and passed on.

Clara linked her arm with her father's once more, and said, on a sudden brightness: 'Sirius, papa!'*

He repeated it in the profoundest manner: 'Sirius! And is there,' he asked, 'a feminine scintilla of sense in that?'

'It is the name of the star I was thinking of, dear papa.'

'It was the star observed by King Agamemnon before the sacrifice in Aulis. You were thinking of that? But, my love, my Iphigeneia, you have not a father who will insist on sacrificing you.'

'Did I hear him tell you to humour me, papa?'

Dr. Middleton humphed.

'Verily the dog-star rages in many heads,' he responded.

CHAPTER XLIV

Dr. Middleton: the Ladies Eleanor and Isabel: and Mr. Dale

CLARA looked up at the flying clouds. She travelled with them now, and tasted freedom, but she prudently forebore to vex her father; she held herself in reserve.

They were summoned by the mid-day bell.

Few were speakers at the meal, few were eaters. Clara was impelled to join it by her desire to study Mrs. Mountstuart's face. Willoughby was obliged to preside. It was a meal of an assembly of mutes and plates, that struck the ear like the well-known sound of a collection of offerings in church after an impressive exhortation from the pulpit. A sally of Colonel De Craye's met the reception given to a charity-boy's muffled burst of animal spirits in the silence of the sacred edifice. Willoughby tried politics with Dr. Middleton, whose regular appetite preserved him from uncongenial speculations when the hour for appeasing it had come; and he alone did honour to the dishes, replying to his host:

'Times are bad, you say, and we have a Ministry doing with us what they will. Well, sir, and that being so, and opposition a manner of kicking them into greater stability, it is the time for wise men to retire within themselves, with the steady determination of the seed in the earth to grow. Repose upon nature, sleep in firm faith, and abide the seasons. That is my counsel to the weaker party.'

The counsel was excellent, but it killed the topic.

Dr. Middleton's appetite was watched for the signal to rise and breathe freely; and such is the grace accorded to a good man of an untroubled conscience engaged in doing his duty to himself, that he perceived nothing of the general restlessness; he went through the dishes calmly, and as calmly he quoted Milton to the ladies Eleanor and Isabel, when the company sprang up all at once upon his closing his repast. Vernon was taken away from him by Willoughby. Mrs. Mountstuart beckoned covertly to Clara. Willoughby should have had something to say to him, Dr. Middleton thought: the position was not clear. But the situation was not disagreeable; and he was in no serious hurry, though he wished to be enlightened.

'This,' Dr. Middleton said to the spinster aunts, as he accompanied them to the drawing-room, 'shall be no lost day for me if I may devote the remainder of it to you.'

'The thunder, we fear, is not remote,' murmured one.

'We fear it is imminent,' sighed the other.

They took to chanting in alternation.

'—We are accustomed to peruse our Willoughby, and we know him by a shadow.'

'—From his infancy to his glorious youth and his established manhood.'

'—He was ever the soul of chivalry.'

'—Duty: duty first. The happiness of his family: the well-being of his dependents.'

'—If proud of his name, it was not an over-weening pride; it was founded in the conscious possession of exalted qualities.'

'—He could be humble when occasion called for it.'

Dr. Middleton bowed to the litany, feeling that occasion called for humbleness from him.

'Let us hope . . .!' he said, with unassumed penitence on behalf of his inscrutable daughter.

The ladies resumed:

'—Vernon Whitford, not of his blood, is his brother!'

'—A thousand instances! Laetitia Dale remembers them better than we.'

'—That any blow should strike him!'

'—That another should be in store for him!'

'—It seems impossible he can be quite misunderstood!'

'Let us hope . . .!' said Dr. Middleton.

'—One would not deem it too much for the dispenser of goodness to expect to be a little looked up to!'

'—When he was a child he one day mounted a chair, and there he stood in danger, would not let us touch him, because he was taller than we, and we were to gaze. Do you remember him, Eleanor? "I am the sun of the house!" It was inimitable!'

'—Your feelings; he would have your feelings! He was fourteen when his cousin Grace Whitford married, and we lost him. They had been the greatest friends; and it was long before he appeared among us. He has never cared to see her since.'

'—But he has befriended her husband. Never has he failed in generosity. His only fault is—'

'—His sensitiveness. And that is—'

'—His secret. And that—'

'—You are not to discover! It is the same with him in manhood. No one will accuse Willoughby Patterne of a deficiency of manliness: but what is it?—he suffers, as none suffer, if he is not loved. He himself is inalterably constant in affection.'

'—What it is no one can say. We have lived with him all his life, and we know him ready to make any sacrifice: only, he does demand the whole heart in return. And if he doubts, he looks as we have seen him to-day.'

'—Shattered: as we have never seen him look before.'

'We will hope,' said Dr. Middleton, this time hastily. He tingled to say 'what it was': he had it in him to solve perplexity in their inquiry. He did say, adopting familiar speech to suit the theme: 'You know, ladies, we English come of a rough stock. A dose of rough dealing in our youth does us no harm, braces us. Otherwise we are likely to feel chilly: we grow too fine where tenuity of stature is necessarily buffeted by gales, namely, in our self-esteem. We are barbarians, on a forcing soil of wealth, in a conservatory of comfortable security; but still barbarians. So, you see, we shine at our best when we are plucked out of that, to where hard blows are given, in a state of war. In a state of war we are at home, our men are high-minded fellows, Scipios and good legionaries.*

In the state of peace we do not live in peace: our native roughness breaks out in unexpected places, under extraordinary aspects—tyrannies, extravagances, domestic exactions: and if we have not had sharp early training . . . within and without . . . the old fashioned island-instrument to drill into us the civilization of our masters, the ancients, we show it by running here and there to some excess. Ahem. Yet,' added the Rev. Doctor, abandoning his effort to deliver a weighty truth obscurely for the comprehension of dainty spinster ladies, the super-abundance of whom in England was in his opinion largely the cause of our decay as a people, 'yet I have not observed this ultra-sensitiveness in Willoughby. He has borne to hear more than I, certainly no example of the frailty, could have endured.'

'He concealed it,' said the ladies. 'It is intense.'

'Then is it a disease?'

'It bears no explanation; it is mystic.'

'It is a cultus, then, a form of self-worship.'

'Self!' they ejaculated. 'But is not Self indifferent to others? Is it Self that craves for sympathy, love and devotion?'

'He is an admirable host, ladies.'

'He is admirable in all respects.'

'Admirable must he be who can impress discerning women, his life-long housemates, so favourably. He is, I repeat, a perfect host.'

'He will be a perfect husband.'

'In all probability.'

'It is a certainty. Let him be loved and obeyed, he will be guided. That is the secret for her whom he so fatally loves. That, if we had dared, we would have hinted to her. She will rule him through her love of him, and through him all about her. And it will not be a rule he submits to, but a love he accepts. If she could see it!'

'If she were a metaphysician!' sighed Dr. Middleton.

'—But a sensitiveness so keen as his might—'

'—Fretted by an unsympathizing mate—'

'—In the end become, for the best of us is mortal—'

'—Callous!'

'—He would feel perhaps as much—'

'—Or more!—'

'—He would still be tender—'

'—But he might grow outwardly hard!'

Both ladies looked up at Dr. Middleton, as they revealed the dreadful prospect.

'It is the story told of corns!' he said, sad as they.

The three stood drooping: the ladies with an attempt to digest his remark; the Rev. Doctor in dejection lest his gallantry should no longer continue to wrestle with his good sense.

He was rescued.

The door opened and a footman announced:

'Mr. Dale.'

Miss Eleanor and Miss Isabel made a sign to one another of raising their hands.

They advanced to him, and welcomed him.

'Pray be seated, Mr. Dale. You have not brought us bad news of our Laetitia?'

'So rare is the pleasure of welcoming you here, Mr. Dale, that we are in some alarm, when, as we trust, it should be matter for unmixed congratulation.'

'Has Dr. Corney been doing wonders?'

'I am indebted to him for the drive to your house, ladies,' said Mr. Dale, a spare, close-buttoned gentleman, with an Indian complexion deadened in the sickchamber. 'It is unusual for me to stir from my precincts.'

'The Rev. Dr. Middleton.'

Mr. Dale bowed. He seemed surprised.

'You live in a splendid air, sir,' observed the Rev. Doctor.

'I can profit little by it, sir,' replied Mr. Dale. He asked the ladies: 'Will Sir Willoughby be disengaged?'

They consulted: 'He is with Vernon. We will send to him.'

The bell was rung.

'I have had the gratification of making the acquaintance of your daughter, Mr. Dale, a most estimable lady,' said Dr. Middleton.

Mr. Dale bowed. 'She is honoured by your praises,

sir. To the best of my belief—I speak as a father—she merits them. Hitherto I have had no doubts.'

'Of Laetitia?' exclaimed the ladies; and spoke of her as gentleness and goodness incarnate.

'Hitherto I have devoutly thought so,' said Mr. Dale.

'Surely she is the very sweetest nurse, the most devoted of daughters!'

'As far as concerns her duty to her father, I can say she is that, ladies.'

'In all her relations, Mr. Dale!'

'It is my prayer,' he said.

The footman appeared. He announced that Sir Willoughby was in the laboratory with Mr. Whitford, and the door locked.

'Domestic business,' the ladies remarked. 'You know Willoughby's diligent attention to affairs, Mr. Dale.'

'He is well?' Mr. Dale inquired.

'In excellent health.'

'Body and mind?'

'But, dear Mr. Dale, he is never ill.'

'Ah! For one to hear that who is never well! And Mr. Whitford is quite sound?'

'Sound? The question alarms me for myself,' said Dr. Middleton. 'Sound as our Constitution, the Credit of the country, the reputation of our Prince of poets. I pray you to have no fears for him.'

Mr. Dale gave the mild little sniff of a man thrown deeper into perplexity.

He said: 'Mr. Whitford works his head; he is a hard student; he may not be always, if I may so put it, at home on worldly affairs.'

'Dismiss that defamatory legend of the student, Mr. Dale; and take my word for it, that he who persistently works his head has the strongest for all affairs.'

'Ah! Your daughter, sir, is here?'

'My daughter is here, sir, and will be most happy to present her respects to the father of her friend Miss Dale.'

'They are friends?'

'Very cordial friends.'

Mr. Dale administered another feebly pacifying sniff to himself.

'Laetitia!' he sighed in apostrophe, and swept his forehead with a hand seen to shake.

The ladies asked him anxiously whether he felt the heat of the room; and one offered him a smelling-bottle.

He thanked them. 'I can hold out until Sir Willoughby comes.'

'We fear to disturb him when his door is locked, Mr. Dale; but, if you wish it, we will venture on a message. You have really no bad news of our Laetitia? She left us hurriedly this morning, without any leave-taking, except a word to one of the maids, that your condition required her immediate presence.'

'My condition! And now her door is locked to me! We have spoken through the door, and that is all. I stand sick and stupefied between two locked doors, neither of which will open, it appears, to give me the enlightenment I need more than medicine.'

'Dear me!' cried Dr. Middleton, 'I am struck by your description of your position, Mr. Dale. It would aptly apply to our humanity of the present generation; and were these the days when I sermonized, I could propose that it should afford me an illustration for the pulpit. For my part, when doors are closed I try not their locks; and I attribute my perfect equanimity, health even, to an uninquiring acceptation of the fact that they are closed to me. I read my page by the light I have. On the contrary, the world of this day, if I may presume to quote you for my purpose, is heard knocking at those two locked doors of the secret of things on each side of us, and is beheld standing sick and stupefied because it has got no response to its knocking. Why, sir, let the world compare the diverse fortunes of the beggar and the postman: knock to give, and it is opened unto you: knock to crave, and it continues shut. I say, carry a letter to your locked door, and you shall have a good reception: but there is none that is handed out. For which reason . . .'

Mr. Dale swept a perspiring forehead, and extended

his hand in supplication; 'I am an invalid, Dr. Middleton,' he said. 'I am unable to cope with analogies. I have but strength for the slow digestion of facts.'

'For facts, we are bradypeptics* to a man, sir. We know not yet if nature be a fact or an effort to master one. The world has not yet assimilated the first fact it stepped on. We are still in the endeavour to make good blood of the fact of our being.'

Pressing his hand to his temples, Mr. Dale moaned: 'My head twirls; I did unwisely to come out. I came on an impulse; I trust, honourable. I am unfit—I cannot follow you, Dr. Middleton. Pardon me.'

'Nay, sir, let me say, from my experience of my countrymen, that, if you do not follow me, and can abstain from abusing me in consequence, you are magnanimous,' the Rev. Doctor replied, hardly consenting to let go the man he had found to indemnify him for his gallant service of acquiescing as a mute to the ladies, though he knew his breathing robustfulness to be as an East wind to weak nerves, and himself an engine of punishment when he had been torn for a day from his books.

Miss Eleanor said: 'The enlightenment you need, Mr. Dale? Can we enlighten you?'

'I think not,' he answered faintly. 'I think I will wait for Sir Willoughby . . . or Mr. Whitford. If I can keep my strength. Or could I exchange—I fear to break down —two words with the young lady who is, was . . .?'

'Miss Middleton, my daughter, sir? She shall be at your disposition; I will bring her to you.' Dr. Middleton stopped at the window. 'She, it is true, may better know the mind of Miss Dale than I. But I flatter myself I know the gentleman better. I think, Mr. Dale, addressing you as the lady's father, you will find me a persuasive, I could be an impassioned, advocate in his interests.'

Mr. Dale was confounded; the weakly sapling caught in a gust falls back as he did.

'Advocate?' he said. He had little breath.

'His impassioned advocate, I repeat: for I have the highest opinion of him. You see, sir, I am acquainted with the circumstances. I believe,' Dr. Middleton half-turned to the ladies, 'we must, until your potent inducements, Mr. Dale, have been joined to my instances, and we overcome what feminine scruples there may be, treat the circumstances as not generally public. Our Strephon* may be chargeable with shyness. But if for the present it is incumbent on us, in proper consideration for the parties, not to be nominally precise, it is hardly requisite in this household that we should be. He is now for protesting indifference to the state. I fancy we understand that phase of amatory frigidity. Frankly, Mr. Dale, I was once in my life myself refused by a lady, and I was not indignant, merely indifferent to the marriage-tie.'

'My daughter *has* refused him, sir?'

'Temporarily it would appear that she has declined the proposal.'

'He was at liberty? . . . he could honourably . . .?'

'His best friend and nearest relative is your guarantee.'

'I know it; I hear so: I am informed of that; I have heard of the proposal, and that he could honourably make it. Still, I am helpless, I cannot move, until I am assured that my daughter's reasons are such as a father need not underline.'

'Does the lady, perchance, equivocate?'

'I have not seen her this morning; I rise late. I hear an astounding account of the cause for her departure from Patterne, and I find her door locked to me—no answer.'

'It is that she has no reasons to give, and she feared the demand for them.'

'Ladies!' dolorously exclaimed Mr. Dale.

'We guess the secret, we guess it!' they exclaimed in reply; and they looked smilingly, as Dr. Middleton looked.

'She had no reasons to give?' Mr. Dale spelt these words to his understanding. 'Then, sir, she knew you not adverse?'

'Undoubtedly, by my high esteem for the gentleman, she must have known me not adverse. But she would not consider me a principal. She could hardly have conceived me an obstacle. I am simply the gentleman's friend. A zealous friend, let me add.'

Mr. Dale put out an imploring hand; it was too much for him.

'Pardon me; I have a poor head. And your daughter the same, sir?'

'We will not measure it too closely, but I may say, my daughter the same, sir. And likewise—may I not add?—these ladies.'

Mr. Dale made sign that he was overfilled. 'Where am I! And Laetitia refused him?'

'Temporarily, let us assume. Will it not partly depend on you, Mr. Dale!'

'But what strange things have been happening during my daughter's absence from the cottage!' cried Mr. Dale, betraying an elixir in his veins. 'I feel that I could laugh if I did not dread to be thought insane. She refused his hand, and he was at liberty to offer it? My girl! We are all on our heads. The fairy-tales were right and the lesson-books were wrong. But it is really, it is really very demoralizing. An invalid—and I am one, and no momentary exhilaration will be taken for the contrary —clings to the idea of stability, order. The slightest disturbance of the wonted course of things unsettles him. Why, for years I have been prophesying it! and for years I have had everything against me, and now when it is confirmed, I am wondering that I must not call myself a fool!'

'And for years, dear Mr. Dale, this union, in spite of counter-currents and human arrangements, has been our Willoughby's constant preoccupation,' said Miss Eleanor.

'His most cherished aim,' said Miss Isabel.

'The name was not spoken by me,' said Dr. Middleton. 'But it is out, and perhaps better out, if we would avoid the chance of mystifications. I do not suppose we are seriously committing a breach of confidence, though he might have wished to mention it to you first himself. I have it from Willoughby that last night he appealed to your daughter, Mr. Dale—not for the first time, if I apprehend him correctly; and unsuccessfully. He despairs. I do not: supposing, that is, your assistance vouchsafed to us. And I do not despair, because the gentleman is a gentleman of worth, of acknowledged worth. You know him well enough to grant me that. I will bring you my daughter to help me in sounding his praises.'

Dr. Middleton stepped through the window to the lawn on an elastic foot, beaming with the happiness he felt charged to confer on his friend Mr. Whitford.

'Ladies! it passes all wonders,' Mr. Dale gasped.

'Willoughby's generosity does pass all wonders,' they said in chorus.

The door opened: Lady Busshe and Lady Culmer were announced.

CHAPTER XLV

The Patterne Ladies: Mr. Dale: Lady Busshe and Lady Culmer: with Mrs. Mountstuart Jenkinson

LADY BUSSHE and Lady Culmer entered spying to right and left. At the sight of Mr. Dale in the room, Lady Busshe murmured to her friend: 'Confirmation!'

Lady Culmer murmured: 'Corney is quite reliable.'

'The man is his own best tonic.'

'He is invaluable for the country.'

Miss Eleanor and Miss Isabel greeted them.

The amiability of the Patterne ladies, combined with their total eclipse behind their illustrious nephew, invited enterprising women of the world to take liberties, and they were not backward.

Lady Busshe said: 'Well? the news! we have the outlines. Don't be astonished: we know the points: we have heard the gun. I could have told you as much yesterday. I *saw* it. And I guessed it the day before. Oh! I do believe in fatalities now. Lady Culmer and I agree to take that view: it is the simplest. Well, and are you satisfied, my dears?'

The ladies grimaced interrogatively. 'With what?'

'With it! with all! with her! with him!'

'Our Willoughby?'

'Can it be possible that they require a dose of Corney?' Lady Busshe remarked to Lady Culmer.

'They play discretion to perfection,' said Lady Culmer. 'But, my dears, we are in the secret.'

'How did she behave?' whispered Lady Busshe. 'No high flights and flutters, I do hope. She was well-connected, they say; though I don't comprehend what they mean by a line of scholars—one thinks of a row of pinafores: and she was pretty. That is well enough at the start. It never will stand against brains. He had the two in the house to contrast them, and . . . the result! A young woman with brains—in a house—beats all your Beauties. Lady Culmer and I have determined on that view. He thought her a delightful partner for a dance, and found her rather tiresome at the end of the gallopade. I saw it yesterday, clear as daylight. She did not understand him, and he did understand her. That will be our report.'

'She is young: she will learn,' said the ladies, uneasily, but in total ignorance of her meaning.

'And you are charitable, and always were. I remember you had a good word for that girl Durham.'

Lady Busshe crossed the room to Mr. Dale, who was turning over leaves of a grand book of the heraldic devices of our great Families.*

'Study it,' she said, 'study it, my dear Mr. Dale; you are in it, by right of possessing a clever and accomplished daughter. At page 300 you will find the Patterne crest. And mark me, she will drag you into the Peerage before she has done—relatively, you know. Sir Willoughby and wife will not be contented to sit down and manage the estates. Has not Laetitia immense ambition? And very creditable, I say.'

Mr. Dale tried to protest something. He shut the book, examined the binding, flapped the cover with a finger, hoped her ladyship was in good health, alluded to his own and the strangeness of the bird out of the cage.

'You will probably take up your residence here, in a larger and handsomer cage, Mr. Dale.'

He shook his head. 'Do I apprehend . . .?' he said.

'I *know*,' said she.

'Dear me, can it be?'

Mr. Dale gazed upward, with the feelings of one awakened late to see a world alive in broad daylight.

Lady Busshe dropped her voice. She took the liberty permitted to her with an inferior in station, while treating him to a tone of familiarity in acknowledgement of his expected rise: which is high breeding, or the exact measurement of social dues.

'Laetitia will be happy, you may be sure. I love to see a long and faithful attachment rewarded—love it! Her tale is the triumph of patience. Far above Grizzel!* No woman will be ashamed of pointing to Lady Patterne. You are uncertain? You are in doubt? Let me hear— as low as you like. But there is no doubt of the new shifting of the scene?—no doubt of the proposal? Dear Mr. Dale! a very little louder. You are here because—? of course you wish to see Sir Willoughby. She? I did not catch you quite. She? . . . it seems, you say . . .?'

Lady Culmer said to the Patterne ladies:

'You must have had a distressing time. These affairs always mount up to a climax, unless people are very well bred. We saw it coming. Naturally we did not expect such a transformation of brides: who could? If I had laid myself down on my back to think, I should have had it. I am unerring when I set to speculating on my back. One is cooler: ideas come; they have not to be forced. That is why I am brighter on a dull winter afternoon, on the sofa, beside my tea-service, than at any other season. However, your trouble is over. When did the Middletons leave?'

'The Middletons leave?' said the ladies.

'Dr. Middleton and his daughter.'

'They have not left us.'

'The Middletons are here?'

'They are here, yes. Why should they have left Patterne?'

'Why?'

'Yes. They are likely to stay some days longer.'

'Goodness!'

'There is no ground for any report to the contrary, Lady Culmer.'

'No ground!'

Lady Culmer called out to Lady Busshe.

A cry came back from that startled dame.

'She has refused him!'

'Who?'

'*She* has!'

'She?—Sir Willoughby?'

'Refused!—declines the honour.'

'Oh! never! No, that carries the incredible beyond romance! But is he perfectly at . . .?'

'Quite, it seems. And she was asked in due form and refused.'

'No, and no again!'

'My dear, I have it from Mr. Dale.'

'Mr. Dale, what can be the signification of her conduct?'

'Indeed, Lady Culmer,' said Mr. Dale, not unpleasantly agitated by the interest he excited, in spite of his astonishment at a public discussion of the matter in this house, 'I am in the dark. Her father should know, but I do not. Her door is locked to me; I have not seen her. I am absolutely in the dark. I am a recluse. I have forgotten the ways of the world. I should have supposed her father would first have been addressed.'

'Tut-tut. Modern gentlemen are not so formal; they are creatures of impulse and take a pride in it. He spoke. We settle that. But where did you get this tale of a refusal?'

'I have it from Dr. Middleton.'

'From Dr. Middleton!' shouted Lady Busshe.

'The Middletons are here,' said Lady Culmer.

'What whirl are we in?' Lady Busshe got up, ran two or three steps and seated herself in another chair. 'Oh! do let us proceed upon system. If not, we shall presently be rageing; we shall be dangerous. The Mid-

dletons are here, and Dr. Middleton himself communi-
cates to Mr. Dale that Laetitia Dale has refused the hand
of Sir Willoughby, who is ostensibly engaged to his own
daughter! And pray, Mr. Dale, how did Dr. Middleton speak of it? Compose yourself; there is no violent
hurry, though our sympathy with you and our interest
in all the parties does perhaps agitate us a little. Quite at
your leisure—speak!'

'Madam . . . Lady Busshe.' Mr. Dale gulped a ball
in his throat. 'I see no reason why I should not speak.
I do not see how I can have been deluded. The Miss
Patternes heard him. Dr. Middleton began upon it, not
I. I was unaware, when I came, that it was a refusal.
I had been informed that there was a proposal. My
authority for the tale was positive. The object of my
visit was to assure myself of the integrity of my daughter's
conduct. She had always the highest sense of honour.
But passion is known to mislead, and there was this most
strange report. I feared that our humblest apologies were
due to Dr. Middleton and his daughter. I know the
charm Laetitia can exercise. Madam, in the plainest
language, without a possibility of my misapprehending
him, Dr. Middleton spoke of himself as the advocate of
the suitor for my daughter's hand. I have a poor head.
I supposed at once an amicable rupture between Sir
Willoughby and Miss Middleton, or that the version
which had reached me of their engagement was not
strictly accurate. My head is weak. Dr. Middleton's
language is trying to a head like mine; but I can speak
positively on the essential points: he spoke of himself as
ready to be the impassioned advocate of the suitor for my
daughter's hand. Those were his words. I understood
him to entreat me to intercede with her. Nay, the name
was mentioned. There was no concealment. I am certain there could not be a misapprehension. And my
feelings were touched by his anxiety for Sir Willoughby's
happiness. I attributed it to a sentiment upon which I
need not dwell. Impassioned advocate, he said.'

'We are in a perfect maelstrom!' cried Lady Busshe,
turning to everybody.

'It is a complete hurricane!' cried Lady Culmer.

A light broke over the faces of the Patterne ladies. They exchanged it with one another.

They had been so shocked as to be almost offended by Lady Busshe, but their natural gentleness and habitual submission rendered them unequal to the task of checking her.

'Is it not,' said Miss Eleanor, 'a misunderstanding that a change of names will rectify?'

'This is by no means the first occasion,' said Miss Isabel, 'that Willoughby has pleaded for his cousin Vernon.'

'We deplore extremely the painful error into which Mr. Dale has fallen.'

'It springs, we now perceive, from an entire misapprehension of Dr. Middleton's.'

'Vernon was in his mind. It was clear to us.'

'Impossible that it could have been Willoughby!'

'You see the impossibility, the error!'

'And the Middletons here!' said Lady Busshe. 'Oh! if we leave unilluminated we shall be the laughing-stock of the county. Mr. Dale, please, wake up. Do you see? You may have been mistaken.'

'Lady Busshe,' he woke up; 'I may have mistaken Dr. Middleton; he has a language that I can compare only to a review-day of the field forces. But I have the story on authority that I cannot question: it is confirmed by my daughter's unexampled behaviour. And if I live through this day I shall look about me as a ghost to-morrow.'

'Dear Mr. Dale!' said the Patterne ladies compassionately.

Lady Busshe murmured to them: 'You know the two did not agree; they did not get on: I saw it; I predicted it.'

'She will understand him in time,' said they.

'Never. And my belief is, they have parted by consent, and Letty Dale wins the day at last. Yes, now I do believe it.'

The ladies maintained a decided negative, but they

knew too much not to feel perplexed, and they betrayed it, though they said: 'Dear Lady Busshe! is it credible, in decency?'

'Dear Mrs. Mountstuart!' Lady Busshe invoked her great rival appearing among them: 'You come most opportunely; we are in a state of inextricable confusion: we are bordering on frenzy. You, and none but you, can help us. You know, you always know; we hang on you. Is there any truth in it? a particle?'

Mrs. Mountstuart seated herself regally. 'Ah! Mr. Dale!' she said, inclining to him. 'Yes, dear Lady Busshe, there is a particle.'

'Now, do not roast us! You can; you have the art. I have the whole story. That is, I have a part. I mean, I have the outlines. I cannot be deceived, but you can fill them in, I know you can. I saw it yesterday. Now, tell us, tell us. It must be quite true or utterly false. Which is it?'

'Be precise.'

'His fatality! you called her. Yes, I was sceptical. But here we have it all come round again, and if the tale is true, I shall own you infallible. Has he?—and she?'

'Both.'

'And the Middletons here? They have not gone; they keep the field. And more astounding, she refuses him! And to add to it, Dr. Middleton intercedes with Mr. Dale for Sir Willoughby!'

'Dr. Middleton intercedes!' This was rather astonishing to Mrs. Mountstuart.

'For Vernon,' Miss Eleanor emphasized.

'For Vernon Whitford, his cousin,' said Miss Isabel, still more emphatically.

'Who,' said Mrs. Mountstuart, with a sovereign lift and turn of her head, 'speaks of a refusal?'

'I have it from Mr. Dale,' said Lady Busshe.

'I had it, I thought, distinctly from Dr. Middleton,' said Mr. Dale.

'That Willoughby proposed to Laetitia for his cousin Vernon, Dr. Middleton meant,' said Miss Eleanor.

Her sister followed: 'Hence this really ridiculous

misconception!—sad indeed,' she added, for balm to
Mr. Dale. 'Willoughby was Vernon's proxy. His cousin,
if not his first, is ever the second thought with him.'

'But can we continue . . .?'

'Such a discussion!'

Mrs. Mountstuart gave them a judicial hearing. They
were regarded in the county as the most indulgent of
nonentities, and she as little as Lady Busshe was restrained from the burning topic in their presence. She
pronounced:

'Each party is right and each is wrong.'

A cry: 'I shall shriek!' came from Lady Busshe.

'Cruel!' groaned Lady Culmer.

'Mixed, you are all wrong. Disentangled, you are
each of you right. Sir Willoughby does think of his
cousin Vernon; he is anxious to establish him; he is the
author of a proposal to that effect.'

'We know it!' the Patterne ladies exclaimed. 'And
Laetitia rejected poor Vernon once more!'

'Who spoke of Miss Dale's rejection of Mr. Whitford?'

'Is he not rejected?' Lady Culmer inquired.

'It is in debate, and at this moment being decided.'

'Oh! do be seated, Mr. Dale,' Lady Busshe implored
him, rising to thrust him back to his chair if necessary.
'Any dislocation, and we are thrown out again! We
must hold together if this riddle is ever to be read. Then,
dear Mrs. Mountstuart, we are to say that there is no
truth in the other story?'

'You are to say nothing of the sort, dear Lady Busshe.'

'Be merciful! And what of the fatality?'

'As positive as the Pole to the needle.'

'She has not refused him?'

'Ask your own sagacity.'

'Accepted?'

'Wait.'

'And all the world's ahead of me! Now, Mrs. Mountstuart, you are oracle. Riddles, if you like—only speak!
If we can't have corn, give us husks.'

'Is any one of us able to anticipate events, Lady
Busshe?'

'Yes. I believe that you are. I bow to you. I do sincerely. So it's another person for Mr. Whitford? You nod. And it is our Laetitia for Sir Willoughby? You smile. You would not deceive me? A very little, and I run about crazed and howl at your doors. And Dr. Middleton is made to play blind man in the midst? And the other person is—now I see day! An amicable rupture, and a smooth new arrangement! She has money; she was never the match for our hero; never; I saw it yesterday, and before, often: and so he hands her over—tuthe-rum-tum-tum, tuthe-rum-tum-tum.' Lady Busshe struck a quick march on her knee: 'Now isn't that clever guessing? The shadow of a clue for me! And because I know human nature. One peep, and I see the combination in a minute. So he keeps the money in the family, becomes a benefactor to his cousin by getting rid of the girl, and succumbs to his fatality. Rather a pity he let it ebb and flow so long. Time counts the tides, you know. But it improves the story. I defy any other county in the kingdom to produce one fresh and living to equal it. Let me tell you I suspected Mr. Whitford, and I hinted it yesterday.'

'Did you indeed!' said Mrs. Mountstuart, humouring her excessive acuteness.

'I really did. There is that dear good man on his feet again. And looks agitated again.'

Mr. Dale had been compelled both by the lady's voice and his interest in the subject, to listen. He had listened more than enough: he was exceedingly nervous. He held on by his chair, afraid to quit his moorings, and: 'Manners!' he said to himself unconsciously aloud, as he cogitated on the libertine way with which these chartered great ladies of the district discussed his daughter. He was heard and unnoticed. The supposition, if any, would have been that he was admonishing himself.

At this juncture Sir Willoughby entered the drawing-room by the garden-window, and simultaneously Dr. Middleton by the door.

CHAPTER XLVI

The Scene of Sir Willoughby's Generalship

HISTORY, we may fear, will never know the qualities of leadership inherent in Sir Willoughby Patterne to fit him for the post of Commander of an army, seeing that he avoided the fatigues of the service and preferred the honours bestowed in his country upon the quiet administrators of their own estates: but his possession of particular gifts, which are military, and especially of the proleptic mind, which is the stamp and sign-warrant of the heaven-sent General, was displayed on every urgent occasion when, in the midst of difficulties likely to have extinguished one less alert than he to the threatening aspect of disaster, he had to manœuvre himself.

He had received no intimation of Mr. Dale's presence in his house, nor of the arrival of the dreaded women Lady Busshe and Lady Culmer: his locked door was too great a terror to his domestics. Having finished with Vernon, after a tedious endeavour to bring the fellow to a sense of the policy of the step urged on him, he walked out on the lawn with the desire to behold the opening of an interview not promising to lead to much, and possibly to profit by its failure. Clara had been prepared, according to his directions, by Mrs. Mountstuart Jenkinson, as Vernon had been prepared by him. His wishes, candidly and kindly expressed both to Vernon and Mrs. Mountstuart, were, that since the girl appeared disinclined to make him a happy man, she would make one of his cousin. Intimating to Mrs. Mountstuart that he would be happier without her, he alluded to the benefit of the girl's money to poor old Vernon, the general escape from a scandal if old Vernon could manage to catch her as she dropped, the harmonious arrangement it would be for all parties. And only on the condition of her taking Vernon, would he consent to give her up. This he said imperatively: adding, that such was the meaning of the news she had received relating to Laetitia Dale. From what quarter had she received it? he asked. She shuffled in her reply, made a gesture to signify that it was in the air, universal, and fell upon the proposed arrangement. He would listen to none of Mrs. Mountstuart's woman-of-the-world instances of the folly of pressing it upon a girl who had shown herself a girl of spirit. She foretold the failure. He would not be advised; he said: 'It is my scheme'; and perhaps the look of mad benevolence about it induced the lady to try whether there was a chance that it would hit the madness in our nature, and somehow succeed or lead to a pacification. Sir Willoughby condescended to arrange things thus for Clara's good; he would then proceed to realize his own. Such was the face he put upon it. We can wear what appearance we please before the world until we are found out, nor is the world's praise knocking upon hollowness always hollow music; but Mrs. Mountstuart's laudation of his kindness and simplicity disturbed him; for though he had recovered from his rebuff enough to imagine that Laetitia could not refuse him under reiterated pressure, he had let it be supposed that she was a submissive handmaiden throbbing for her elevation; and Mrs. Mountstuart's belief in it afflicted his recent bitter experience; his footing was not perfectly secure. Besides, assuming it to be so, he considered the sort of prize he had won; and a spasm of downright hatred of a world for which we make mighty sacrifices to be repaid in a worn, thin, comparatively valueless coin, troubled his counting of his gains. Laetitia, it was true, had not passed through other hands in coming to him, as Vernon would know it to be Clara's case: time only had worn her: but the comfort of the reflection was annoyed by the physical contrast of the two. Hence an unusual melancholy in his tone that Mrs. Mountstuart thought touching. It had the scenic effect on her which greatly contributes to delude the wits. She talked of him to Clara as being a man who had revealed an unsuspected depth.

Vernon took the communication curiously. He seemed readier to be in love with his benevolent relative than with the lady. He was confused, undisguisedly moved, said the plan was impossible, out of the question, but thanked Willoughby for the best of intentions, thanked him warmly. After saying that the plan was impossible, the comical fellow allowed himself to be pushed forth on the lawn to see how Miss Middleton might have come out of her interview with Mrs. Mountstuart. Willoughby observed Mrs. Mountstuart meet him, usher him to the place she had quitted among the shrubs, and return to the open turf-spaces. He sprang to her.

'She will listen,' Mrs. Mountstuart said: 'she likes him, respects him, thinks he is a very sincere friend, clever, a scholar, and a good mountaineer; and thinks you mean very kindly. So much I have impressed on her, but I have not done much for Mr. Whitford.'

'She consents to listen,' said Willoughby, snatching at that as the death-blow to his friend Horace.

'She consents to listen, because you have arranged it so that if she declined she would be rather a savage.'

'You think it will have no result?'

'None at all.'

'Her listening will do.'

'And you must be satisfied with it.'

'We shall see.'

' "Anything for peace," she says: and I don't say that a gentleman with a tongue would not have a chance. She wishes to please you.'

'Old Vernon has no tongue for women, poor fellow! You will have us be spider or fly, and if a man can't spin a web, all he can hope is not to be caught in one. She knows his history too, and that won't be in his favour. How did she look when you left them?'

'Not so bright: like a bit of china that wants dusting. She looked a trifle *gauche*, it struck me; more like a country girl with the hoyden taming in her than the well-bred creature she is. I did not suspect her to have feeling. You must remember, Sir Willoughby, that she has obeyed your wishes, done her utmost: I do think we may say she has made some amends: and if she is to blame she repents, and you will not insist too far.'

'I do insist,' said he.

'Beneficent, but a tyrant!'

'Well, well.' He did not dislike the character.

They perceived Dr. Middleton wandering over the lawn, and Willoughby went to him to put him on the wrong track: Mrs. Mountstuart swept into the drawing-room. Willoughby quitted the Rev. Doctor, and hung about the bower where he supposed his pair of dupes had by this time ceased to stutter mutually:—or what if they had found the word of harmony? He could bear that, just bear it. He rounded the shrubs, and behold, both had vanished. The trellis decorated emptiness. His idea was, that they had soon discovered their inability to be turtles:* and desiring not to lose a moment while Clara was fretted by the scene, he rushed to the drawing-room with the hope of lighting on her there, getting her to himself, and finally, urgently, passionately offering her the sole alternative of what she had immediately rejected. Why had he not used passion before, instead of limping crippled between temper and policy? He was capable of it: as soon as imagination in him conceived his personal feelings unwounded and unimperilled, the might of it inspired him with heroical confidence, and Clara grateful, Clara softly moved, led him to think of Clara melted. Thus anticipating her he burst into the room.

One step there warned him that he was in the jaws of the world. We have the phrase, that a man is himself, under certain trying circumstances. There is no need to say it of Sir Willoughby: he was thrice himself when danger menaced, himself inspired him. He could read at a single glance the Polyphemus eye* in the general head of a company. Lady Busshe, Lady Culmer, Mrs. Mountstuart, Mr. Dale, had a similarity in the variety of their expressions that made up one giant eye for him, perfectly, if awfully, legible. He discerned the fact that his demon secret was abroad, universal. He ascribed it to fate. He was in the jaws of the world, on the world's teeth. This time he thought Laetitia must have betrayed him, and bowing to Lady Busshe and Lady Culmer, gallantly pressing their fingers and responding to their becks and archnesses, he ruminated on his defences before he should accost her father. He did not want to be alone with the man, and he considered how his presence might be made useful.

'I am glad to see you, Mr. Dale. Pray, be seated. Is it nature asserting her strength? or the efficacy of medicine? I fancy it can't be both. You have brought us back your daughter?'

Mr. Dale sank into a chair, unable to resist the hand forcing him.

'No, Sir Willoughby, no. I have not; I have not seen her since she came home this morning from Patterne.'

'Indeed? She is unwell?'

'I cannot say. She secludes herself.'

'Has locked herself in,' said Lady Busshe.

Willoughby threw her a smile. It made them intimate. This was an advantage against the world, but an exposure of himself to the abominable woman.

Dr. Middleton came up to Mr. Dale to apologize for not presenting his daughter Clara, whom he could find neither in nor out of the house.

'We have in Mr. Dale, as I suspected,' he said to Willoughby, 'a stout ally.'

'If I may beg two minutes with you, Sir Willoughby,' said Mr. Dale.

'Your visits are too rare for me to allow of your numbering the minutes,' Willoughby replied. 'We cannot let Mr. Dale escape us now that we have him, I think, Dr. Middleton.'

'Not without ransom,' said the Rev. Doctor.

Mr. Dale shook his head. 'My strength, Sir Willoughby, will not sustain me long.'

'You are at home, Mr. Dale.'

'Not far from home, in truth, but too far for an invalid beginning to grow sensible of weakness.'

'You will regard Patterne as your home, Mr. Dale,' Willoughby repeated for the world to hear.

'Unconditionally?' Dr. Middleton inquired with a humourous air of dissenting.

Willoughby gave him a look that was coldly courteous, and then he looked at Lady Busshe. She nodded imperceptibly. Her eyebrows rose, and Willoughby returned a similar nod.

Translated, the signs ran thus:

'—Pestered by the Rev. gentleman:—I see you are. Is the story I have heard correct?—Possibly it may err in a few details.'

This was fettering himself in loose manacles.

But Lady Busshe would not be satisfied with the compliment of the intimate looks and nods. She thought she might still be behind Mrs. Mountstuart; and she was a bold woman, and anxious about him, half-crazed by the riddle of the pot she was boiling in, and having very few minutes to spare.

Not extremely reticent by nature, privileged by station, and made intimate with him by his covert looks, she stood up to him. 'One word to an old friend. Which is the father of the fortunate creature? I don't know how to behave to them.'

No time was afforded him to be disgusted with her vulgarity and audacity.

He replied, feeling her rivet his gyves: 'The house will be empty to-morrow.'

'I see. A decent withdrawal, and very well cloaked. We had a tale here of her running off to decline the honour, afraid, or on her dignity or something.'

How was it that the woman was ready to accept the altered posture of affairs in his house—if she had received a hint of them? He forgot that he had prepared her in self-defence.

'From whom did you have that?' he asked.

'Her father. And the lady aunts declare it was the cousin she refused!'

Willoughby's brain turned over. He righted it for action, and crossed the room to the ladies Eleanor and Isabel. His ears tingled. He and his whole story discussed in public! Himself unroofed! And the marvel that he of all men should be in such a tangle, naked and blown on, condemned to use his cunningest arts to unwind and cover himself, struck him as though the lord of his kind were running the gauntlet of a legion of imps. He felt their lashes.

The ladies were talking to Mrs. Mountstuart and Lady Culmer of Vernon and the suitableness of Laetitia to a scholar. He made sign to them, and both rose.

'It is the hour for your drive. To the cottage! Mr. Dale is ill. She must come. Her sick father! No delay, going or returning. Bring her here at once.'

'Poor man!' they sighed: and 'Willoughby,' said one, and the other said: 'There is a strange misconception you will do well to correct.'

They were about to murmur what it was. He swept his hand round, and excusing themselves to their guests, obediently they retired.

Lady Busshe at his entreaty remained, and took a seat beside Lady Culmer and Mrs. Mountstuart.

She said to the latter: 'You have tried scholars. What do you think?'

'Excellent, but hard to mix,' was the reply.

'I never make experiments,' said Lady Culmer.

'Some one must!' Mrs. Mountstuart groaned over her dull dinner-party.

Lady Busshe consoled her. 'At any rate, the loss of a scholar is no loss to the county.'

'They are well enough in towns,' Lady Culmer said.

'And then I am sure you must have them by themselves.'

'We have nothing to regret.'

'My opinion.'

The voice of Dr. Middleton in colloquy with Mr. Dale swelled on a melodious thunder: 'For whom else should I plead as the passionate advocate I proclaimed myself to you, sir? There is but one man known to me who would move me to back him upon such an adventure. Willoughby, join me. I am informing Mr. Dale . . .'

Willoughby stretched his hands out to Mr. Dale to support him on his legs, though he had shown no sign of a wish to rise.

'You are feeling unwell, Mr. Dale.'

'Do I look very ill, Sir Willoughby?'

'It will pass. Laetitia will be with us in twenty minutes.'

Mr. Dale struck his hands in a clasp. He looked alarmingly ill, and satisfactorily revealed to his host how he could be made to look so.

'I was informing Mr. Dale that the petitioner enjoys our concurrent good wishes: and mine in no degree less than yours, Willoughby,' observed Dr. Middleton, whose billows grew the bigger for a check. He supposed himself speaking confidentially. 'Ladies have the trick; they have, I may say, the natural disposition for playing enigma now and again. Pressure is often a sovereign specific. Let it be tried upon her all round, from every radiating line of the circle. You she refuses. Then I venture to propose myself to appeal to her. My daughter has assuredly an esteem for the applicant that will animate a woman's tongue in such a case. The ladies of the house will not be backward. Lastly, if necessary, we trust the lady's father to add his instances. My prescription is, to fatigue her negatives; and where no rooted objection exists, I maintain it to be the unfailing receipt for the conduct of a siege. No woman can say No for ever. The defence has not such resources against even a single assailant, and we shall have solved the problem of continuous motion before she will have learnt to deny in perpetuity. That I stand on.'

Willoughby glanced at Mrs. Mountstuart.

'What is that?' she said. 'Treason to our sex, Dr. Middleton?'

'I think I heard, that no woman can say No for ever!' remarked Lady Busshe.

'To a loyal gentleman, ma'am: assuming the field of the recurring request to be not unholy ground; consecrated to affirmatives rather.'

Dr. Middleton was attacked by three angry bees. They made him say Yes and No alternately so many times that he had to admit in men a shiftier yieldingness than women were charged with.

Willoughby gesticulated as mute chorus on the side of the ladies; and a little show of party spirit like that, coming upon their excitement under the topic, inclined them to him genially.

He drew Mr. Dale away while the conflict subsided in sharp snaps of rifles and an interval rejoinder of a cannon.

Mr. Dale had shown by signs that he was growing fretfully restive under his burden of doubt.

'Sir Willoughby, I have a question. I beg you to lead me where I may ask it. I know my head is weak.'

'Mr. Dale, it is answered when I say that my house is your home, and that Laetitia will soon be with us.'

'Then this report is true!'

'I know nothing of reports. You are answered.'

'Can my daughter be accused of any shadow of falseness, dishonourable dealing?'

'As little as I.'

Mr. Dale scanned his face. He saw no shadow.

'For I should go to my grave bankrupt if that could be said of her; and I have never yet felt poor, though you know the extent of a pensioner's income. Then this tale of a refusal . . . ?'

'Is nonsense.'

'She has accepted?'

'There are situations, Mr. Dale, too delicate to be clothed in positive definitions.'

'Ah, Sir Willoughby, but it becomes a father to see that his daughter is not forced into delicate situations. I hope all is well. I am confused. It may be my head. She puzzles me. You are not . . . Can I ask it here? You are quite? . . . Will you moderate my anxiety? My infirmities must excuse me.'

Sir Willoughby conveyed by a shake of the head and a pressure of Mr. Dale's hand, that he was not, and that he was quite.

'Dr. Middleton?' said Mr. Dale.

'He leaves us to-morrow.'

'Really!' The invalid wore a look as if wine had been poured into him. He routed his host's calculations by calling to the Rev. Doctor. 'We are to lose you, sir?'

Willoughby attempted an interposition, but Dr. Middleton crashed through it like the lordly organ swallowing a flute.

'Not before I score my victory, Mr. Dale, and establish my friend upon his rightful throne.'

'You do not leave to-morrow, sir?'

'Have you heard, sir, that I leave to-morrow?'

Mr. Dale turned to Sir Willoughby.

The latter said: 'Clara named to-day. To-morrow, I thought preferable.'

'Ah?' Dr. Middleton towered on the swelling exclamation, but with no dark light. He radiated splendidly. 'Yes, then, to-morrow. That is, if we subdue the lady.'

He advanced to Willoughby, seized his hand, squeezed it, thanked him, praised him. He spoke under his breath, for a wonder; but: 'We are in your debt lastingly, my friend,' was heard, and he was impressive, he seemed subdued, and saying aloud: 'Though I should wish to aid in the reduction of that fortress,' he let it be seen that his mind was rid of a load.

Dr. Middleton partly stupefied Willoughby by his way of taking it, but his conduct was too serviceable to allow of speculation on his readiness to break the match. It was the turning-point of the engagement.

Lady Busshe made a stir.

'I cannot keep my horses waiting any longer,' she said, and beckoned. Sir Willoughby was beside her immediately. 'You are admirable! perfect! Don't ask me to hold my tongue. I retract, I recant. It *is* a fatality. I have resolved upon that view. You could stand the shot of beauty, not of brains. That is our report. There! And it's delicious to feel that the county wins you. No tea. I cannot possibly wait. And, oh! here she is. I must have a look at her. My dear Laetitia Dale!'

Willoughby hurried to Mr. Dale.

'You are not to be excited, sir: compose yourself. You will recover and be strong to-morrow: you are at home; you are in your own house; you are in Laetitia's drawing-room. All will be clear to-morrow. Till to-morrow we talk riddles by consent. Sit, I beg. You stay with us.'

He met Laetitia and rescued her from Lady Busshe, murmuring, with the air of a lover who says, 'my love!

my sweet!' that she had done rightly to come and come at once.

Her father had been thrown into the proper condition of clammy nervousness to create the impression. Laetitia's anxiety sat prettily on her long eyelashes as she bent over him in his chair.

Hereupon Dr. Corney appeared; and his name had a bracing effect on Mr. Dale. 'Corney has come to drive me to the cottage,' he said. 'I am ashamed of this public exhibition of myself, my dear. Let us go. My head is a poor one.'

Dr. Corney had been intercepted. He broke from Sir Willoughby with a dozen little nods of accurate understanding of him, even to beyond the mark of the communications. He touched his patient's pulse lightly, briefly sighed with professional composure, and pronounced: 'Rest. Must not be moved. No, no, nothing serious,' he quieted Laetitia's fears, 'but rest, rest. A change of residence for a night will tone him. I will bring him a draught in the course of the evening. Yes, yes, I'll fetch everything wanted from the cottage for you and for him. Repose on Corney's forethought.'

'You are sure, Dr. Corney?' said Laetitia, frightened on her father's account and on her own.

'Which aspect will be the best for Mr. Dale's bedroom?' the hospitable ladies Eleanor and Isabel inquired.

'South-east, decidedly: let him have the morning sun: a warm air, a vigorous air and a bright air, and the patient wakes and sings in his bed.'

Still doubtful whether she was in a trap, Laetitia whispered to her father of the privacy and comforts of his home.

He replied to her that he thought he would rather be in his own home.

Dr. Corney positively pronounced No to it.

Laetitia breathed again of home, but with the sigh of one overborne.

The ladies Eleanor and Isabel took the word from Willoughby, and said: 'But you are at home, my dear.

This is your home. Your father will be at least as well attended here as at the cottage.'

She raised her eyelids on them mournfully, and by chance diverted her look to Dr. Middleton, quite by chance.

It spoke eloquently to the assembly of all that Willoughby desired to be imagined.

'But there is Crossjay,' she cried. 'My cousin has gone, and the boy is left alone. I cannot have him left alone. If we, if, Dr. Corney, you are sure it is unsafe for papa to be moved to-day, Crossjay must . . . he cannot be left.'

'Bring him with you, Corney,' said Sir Willoughby: and the little doctor heartily promised that he would, in the event of his finding Crossjay at the cottage, which he thought a distant probability.

'He gave me his word he would not go out till my return,' said Laetitia.

'And if Crossjay gave you his word,' the accents of a new voice vibrated close by, 'be certain that he will not come back with Dr. Corney unless he has authority in your handwriting.'

Clara Middleton stepped gently to Laetitia, and with a manner that was an embrace, as much as kissed her for what she was doing on behalf of Crossjay. She put her lips in a pouting form to simulate saying: 'Press it.'

'He is to come,' said Laetitia.

'Then, write him his permit.'

There was a chatter about Crossjay and the sentinel true to his post that he could be, during which Laetitia distressfully scribbled a line for Dr. Corney to deliver to him. Clara stood near. She had rebuked herself for a want of reserve in the presence of Lady Busshe and Lady Culmer, and she was guilty of a slightly excessive containment when she next addressed Laetitia. It was, like Laetitia's look at Dr. Middleton, opportune: enough to make a man who watched as Willoughby did, a fatalist for life: the shadow of a difference in her bearing toward Laetitia sufficed to impute acting either to her present coolness or her previous warmth. Better still, when

Dr. Middleton said: 'So we leave to-morrow, my dear, and I hope you have written to the Darletons,' Clara flushed and beamed, and repressed her animation on a sudden, with one grave look, that might be thought regretful, to where Willoughby stood.

Chance works for us when we are good captains.

Willoughby's pride was high, though he knew himself to be keeping it up like a fearfully dexterous juggler, and for an empty reward: but he was in the toils of the world.

'Have you written? The post-bag leaves in half an hour,' he addressed her.

'We are expected, but I will write,' she replied: and her not having yet written counted in his favour.

She went to write the letter. Dr. Corney had departed on his mission to fetch Crossjay and medicine. Lady Busshe was impatient to be gone. 'Corney,' she said to Lady Culmer, 'is a deadly gossip.'

'Inveterate,' was the answer.

'My poor horses!'

'Not the young pair of bays?'

'Luckily, my dear. And don't let me hear of dining to-night!'

Sir Willoughby was leading out Mr. Dale to a quiet room, contiguous to the invalid gentleman's bed-chamber. He resigned him to Laetitia in the hall, that he might have the pleasure of conducting the ladies to their carriage.

'As little agitation as possible. Corney will soon be back,' he said, bitterly admiring the graceful subservience of Laetitia's figure to her father's weight on her arm.

He had won a desperate battle, but what had he won? What had the world given him in return for his efforts to gain it? Just a shirt, it might be said: simple scanty clothing, no warmth. Lady Busshe was unbearable; she gabbled; she was ill-bred, permitted herself to speak of Doctor Middleton as ineligible, no loss to the county. And Mrs. Mountstuart was hardly much above her, with her inevitable stroke of caricature:—'You see Dr. Middleton's pulpit scampering after him with legs!' Perhaps the Rev. Doctor did punish the world for his having forsaken his pulpit, and might be conceived as haunted by it at his heels, but Willoughby was in the mood to abhor comic images: he hated the perpetrators of them and the grinners. Contempt of this laughing empty world, for which he had performed a monstrous immolation, led him to associate Dr. Middleton in his mind, and Clara too, with the desireable things he had sacrificed— a shape of youth and health; a sparkling companion; a face of innumerable charms; and his own veracity; his inner sense of his dignity; and his temper, and the limpid frankness of his air of scorn, that was to him a visage of candid happiness in the dim retrospect. Haply also he had sacrificed more; and looked scientifically into the future: he might have sacrificed a nameless more. And for what? he asked again. For the favourable looks and tongues of these women whose looks and tongues he detested!

'Dr. Middleton says he is indebted to me: I am deeply in *his* debt,' he remarked.

'It is we who are in *your* debt for a lovely romance, my dear Sir Willoughby,' said Lady Busshe, incapable of taking a correction, so thoroughly had he imbued her with his fiction, or with the belief that she had a good story to circulate.

Away she drove rattling her tongue to Lady Culmer.

'A hat and horn, and she would be in the old figure of a post-boy on a hue-and-cry sheet,'*said Mrs. Mountstuart.

Willoughby thanked the great lady for her services, and she complimented the polished gentleman on his noble self-possession. But she complained at the same time of being defrauded of her 'charmer' Colonel De Craye since luncheon. An absence of warmth in her compliment caused Willoughby to shrink and think the wretched shirt he had got from the world no covering after all: a breath flapped it.

'He comes to me, to-morrow, I believe,' she said, reflecting on her superior knowledge of facts in comparison with Lady Busshe, who would presently be hearing of something novel, and exclaiming: 'So, *that* is why you patronized the colonel!' And it was nothing of the sort, for Mrs. Mountstuart could honestly say she was not the woman to make a business of her pleasure.

'Horace is an enviable fellow,' said Willoughby, wise in The Book, which bids us ever, for an assuagement, to fancy our friend's condition worse than our own, and recommends the deglutition of irony as the most balsamic for wounds in the whole moral pharmacopœia.

'I don't know,' she replied with a marked accent of deliberation.

'The colonel is to have you to himself to-morrow!'

'I can't be sure of what I shall have in the colonel!'

'Your perpetual sparkler?'

Mrs. Mountstuart set her head in motion. She left the matter silent.

'I'll come for him in the morning,' she said, and her carriage whirled her off.

Either she had guessed it, or Clara had confided to her the treacherous passion of Horace De Craye!

However, the world was shut away from Patterne for the night.

CHAPTER XLVII

Sir Willoughby and his Friend Horace De Craye

WILLOUGHBY shut himself up in his laboratory to brood awhile after the conflict. Sounding through himself, as it was habitual with him to do, for the plan most agreeable to his taste, he came on a strange discovery among the lower circles of that microcosm. He was no longer guided in his choice by liking and appetite: he had to put it on the edge of a sharp discrimination and try it by his acutest judgement before it was acceptable to his heart: and knowing well the direction of his desire, he was nevertheless unable to run two strides on a wish. He had learnt to read the world: his partial capacity for reading persons had fled. The mysteries of his own bosom were bare to him; but he could comprehend

them only in their immediate relation to the world outside. This hateful world had caught him and transformed him to a machine. The discovery he made was,
that in the gratification of the egoistic instinct we may
so beset ourselves as to deal a slaughtering wound upon
Self to whatsoever quarter we turn.

Surely there is nothing stranger in mortal experience.
The man was confounded. At the game of Chess it is the
dishonour of our adversary when we are stale-mated:
but in life, combating the world, such a winning of the
game questions our sentiments.

Willoughby's interpretation of his discovery was
directed by pity: he had no other strong emotion left
in him. He pitied himself, and he reached the conclusion
that he suffered because he was active; he could not be
quiescent. Had it not been for his devotion to his house
and name, never would he have stood twice the victim
of womankind. Had he been selfish, he would have been
the happiest of men! He said it aloud. He schemed
benevolently for his unborn young, and for the persons
about him: hence he was in a position forbidding a step
under pain of injury to his feelings. He was generous: otherwise would he not in scorn of soul, at the
outset, straight off, have pitched Clara Middleton to the
wanton winds? He was faithful in affection: Laetitia
Dale was beneath his roof to prove it. Both these women
were examples of his power of forgiveness, and now a
tender word to Clara might fasten shame on him—such
was her gratitude! And if he did not marry Laetitia,
laughter would be devilish all around him—such was the
world's! Probably Vernon would not long be thankful
for the chance which varied the monotony of his days.
What of Horace? Willoughby stripped to enter the ring
with Horace: he cast away disguise. That man had
been the first to divide him in the all but equal slices of
his egoistic from his amatory self: murder of his individuality was the crime of Horace De Craye. And further,
suspicion fixed on Horace (he knew not how, except that
The Book bids us be suspicious of those we hate) as the
man who had betrayed his recent dealings with Laetitia.

Willoughby walked the thoroughfares of the house to meet Clara and make certain of her either for himself or, if it must be, for Vernon, before he took another step with Laetitia Dale. Clara could reunite him, turn him once more into a whole and an animated man; and she might be willing. Her willingness to listen to Vernon promised it. 'A gentleman with a tongue would have a chance,' Mrs. Mountstuart had said. How much greater the chance of a lover! For he had not yet supplicated her: he had shown pride and temper. He could woo, he was a torrential wooer. And it would be glorious to swing round on Lady Busshe and the world, with Clara nestling under an arm, and protest astonishment at the erroneous and utterly unfounded anticipations of any other development. And it would righteously punish Laetitia.

Clara came downstairs, bearing her letter to Miss Darleton.

'*Must* it be posted?' Willoughby said, meeting her in the hall.

'They expect us any day, but it will be more comfortable for papa,' was her answer. She looked kindly in her new shyness.

She did not seem to think he had treated her contemptuously in flinging her to his cousin, which was odd!

'You have seen Vernon?'

'It was your wish.'

'You had a talk?'

'We conversed.'

'A long one?'

'We walked some distance.'

'Clara, I tried to make the best arrangement I could.'

'Your intention was generous.'

'He took no advantage of it?'

'It could not be treated seriously.'

'It was meant seriously.'

'There I see the generosity.'

Willoughby thought this encomium, and her consent to speak on the subject, and her scarcely embarrassed air and richness of tone in speaking, very strange: and strange was her taking him quite in earnest. Apparently she had no feminine sensation of the unwontedness and the absurdity of the matter!

'But, Clara! am I to understand that he did not speak out?'

'We are excellent friends.'

'To miss it, though his chance were the smallest!'

'You forget that it may not wear that appearance to him.'

'He spoke not one word of himself?'

'No.'

'Ah! the poor old fellow was taught to see it was hopeless—chilled. May I plead? Will you step into the laboratory for a minute? We are two sensible persons . . .'

'Pardon me, I must go to papa.'

'Vernon's personal history perhaps . . .?'

'I think it honourable to him.'

'Honourable!—'hem!'

'By comparison.'

'Comparison with what?'

'With others.'

He drew up to relieve himself of a critical and condemnatory expiration of a certain length. This young lady knew too much. But how physically exquisite she was!

'Could you, Clara, could you promise me—I hold to it. I must have it, I know his shy tricks—promise me to give him ultimately another chance? Is the idea repulsive to you?'

'It is one not to be thought of.'

'It is not repulsive?'

'Nothing could be repulsive in Mr. Whitford.'

'I have no wish to annoy you, Clara.'

'I feel bound to listen to you, Willoughby. Whatever I can do to please you, I will. It is my life-long duty.'

'Could you, Clara, could you conceive it, could you simply conceive it;—give him your hand?'

'As a friend, Oh! yes.'

'In marriage.'

She paused. She, so penetrative of him when he

opposed her, was hoodwinked when he softened her feelings: for the heart,—though the clearest, is not the most constant instructor of the head; the heart, unlike the often obtuser head, works for itself and not for the commonwealth.

'You are so kind . . . I would do much . . .' she said.

'Would you accept him—marry him? He is poor.'

'I am not ambitious of wealth.'

'*Would* you marry him?'

'Marriage is not in my thoughts.'

'But could you marry him?'

Willoughby expected no. In his expectation of it he hung inflated.

She said these words: 'I could engage to marry no one else.'

His amazement breathed without a syllable.

He flapped his arms, resembling for the moment those birds of enormous body which attempt a rise upon their wings and achieve a hop.

'Would you engage it?' he said, content to see himself stepped on as an insect if he could but feel the agony of his false friend Horace—their common pretensions to win her were now of that comparative size.

'Oh! there can be no necessity. And an oath—no!' said Clara, inwardly shivering at a recollection.

'But you could?'

'My wish is to please you.'

'You could?'

'I said so.'

It has been known of the patriotic mountaineer of a hoary pile of winters, with little life remaining in him, but that little on fire for his country, that by the brink of the precipice he has flung himself on a young and lusty invader, dedicating himself exultingly to death if only he may score a point for his country by extinguishing in his country's enemy the stronger man. So likewise did Willoughby, in the blow that deprived him of hope, exult in the toppling over of Horace De Craye. They perished together, but which one sublimely relished the headlong descent? And Vernon taken by Clara would be Vernon simply tolerated. And Clara taken by Vernon would be Clara previously touched, smirched. Altogether he could enjoy his fall.

It was at least upon a comfortable bed, where his pride would be dressed daily and would never be disagreeably treated.

He was henceforth Laetitia's own. The bell telling of Dr. Corney's return was a welcome sound to Willoughby, and he said good-humouredly: 'Wait, Clara, you will see your hero Crossjay.'

Crossjay and Dr. Corney tumbled into the hall. Willoughby caught Crossjay under the arms to give him a lift in the old fashion pleasing to Clara to see. The boy was heavy as lead.

'I had work to hook him and worse to net him,' said Dr. Corney. 'I had to make him believe he was to nurse every soul in the house, you among them, Miss Middleton.'

Willoughby pulled the boy aside.

Crossjay came back to Clara heavier in looks than his limbs had been. She dropped her letter in the hall-box, and took his hand to have a private hug of him. When they were alone, she said: 'Crossjay, my dear, my dear! You look unhappy.'

'Yes, and who wouldn't be, and you're not to marry Sir Willoughby!' his voice threatened a cry. 'I know you're not, for Dr. Corney says you are going to leave.'

'Did you so very much wish it, Crossjay?'

'I should have seen a lot of you, and I shan't see you at all, and I'm sure if I'd known I wouldn't have——, and he has been and tipped me this.'

Crossjay opened his fist in which lay three gold pieces.

'That was very kind of him,' said Clara.

'Yes, but how can I keep it?'

'By handing it to Mr. Whitford to keep for you.'

'Yes, but, Miss Middleton, oughtn't I to tell him? I mean Sir Willoughby.'

'What?'

'Why, that I,' Crossjay got close to her, 'why, that I, that I—you know what you used to say. I wouldn't tell a lie, but oughtn't I, without his asking . . . and this money! I don't mind being turned out again.'

'Consult Mr. Whitford,' said Clara.

'I know what you think, though.'

'Perhaps you had better not say anything at present, dear boy.'

'But what am I to do with this money?'

Crossjay held the gold pieces out as things that had not yet mingled with his ideas of possession.

'I listened, and I told of him,' he said. 'I couldn't help listening, but I went and told; and I don't like being here, and his money, and he not knowing what I did. Haven't you heard? I'm certain I know what you think, and so do I, and I must take my luck, I'm always in mischief, getting into a mess or getting out of it. I don't mind, I really don't, Miss Middleton, I can sleep in a tree quite comfortably. If you're not going to be here, I'd just as soon be anywhere. I must try to earn my living some day. And why not a cabin-boy? Sir Cloudesley Shovel* was no better. And I don't mind his being wrecked at last, if you're drowned an admiral. So I shall go and ask him to take his money back, and if he asks me I shall tell him, and there. You know what it is: I guessed that from what Dr. Corney said. I'm sure I know you're thinking what's manly. Fancy me keeping his money, and you not marrying him! I wouldn't mind driving a plough. I shouldn't make a bad game-keeper. Of course I love boats best, but you can't have everything.'

'Speak to Mr. Whitford first,' said Clara, too proud of the boy for growing as she had trained him, to advise a course of conduct opposed to his notions of manliness, though now that her battle was over she would gladly have acquiesced in little casuistic compromises for the sake of the general peace.

Some time later Vernon and Dr. Corney were arguing upon the question. Corney was dead against the senti-mental view of the morality of the case propounded by Vernon as coming from Miss Middleton and partly shared by him. 'If it's on the boy's mind,' Vernon said,

'I can't prohibit his going to Willoughby and making a
clean breast of it, especially as it involves me, and sooner
or later I should have to tell him myself.'

Dr. Corney said no at all points. 'Now hear me,' he
said finally. 'This is between ourselves, and no breach
of confidence, which I'd not be guilty of for forty friends,
though I'd give my hand from the wrist-joint for one—
my left, that's to say. Sir Willoughby puts me one or
two searching interrogations on a point of interest to him,
his house and name. Very well, and good night to that,
and I wish Miss Dale had been ten years younger, or had
passed the ten with no heartstrings and sinkings wearing
to the tissues of the frame and the moral fibre to boot.
She'll have a fairish health, with a little occasional
doctoring; taking her rank and wealth in right earnest,
and shying her pen back to Mother Goose.* She'll do.
And, by the way, I think it's to the credit of my sagacity
that I fetched Mr. Dale here fully primed, and roused the
neighbourhood, which I did, and so fixed our gentleman,
neat as a prodded eel on a pair of prongs—namely, the
positive fact and the general knowledge of it. But mark
me, my friend. We understand one another at a nod.
This boy, young Squire Crossjay, is a good stiff hearty
kind of a Saxon boy, out of whom you may cut as gallant
a fellow as ever wore epaulettes. I like him, you like
him, Miss Dale and Miss Middleton like him; and Sir
Willoughby Patterne of Patterne Hall and other places
won't be indisposed to like him mightily in the event of
the sun being seen to shine upon him with a particular
determination to make him appear a prominent object,
because a solitary, and a Patterne.' Dr. Corney lifted
his chest and his finger: 'Now, mark me, and verbum
sap:*Crossjay must not offend Sir Willoughby. I say no
more. Look ahead. Miracles happen, but it's best to
reckon that they won't. Well, now, and Miss Dale.
She'll not be cruel.'

'It appears as if she would,' said Vernon, meditating
on the cloudy sketch Dr. Corney had drawn.

'She can't, my friend. Her position's precarious;
her father has little besides a pension. And her writing

damages her health. She can't. And she likes the
baronet. Oh, it's only a little fit of proud blood. She's
the woman for him. She'll manage him—give him an
idea that he has got a lot of ideas. It'd kill her father
if she was obstinate. He talked to me, when I told him
of the business, about his dream fulfilled, and if the
dream turns to vapour, he'll be another example that
we hang more upon dreams than realities for nourishment, and medicine too. Last week I couldn't have got
him out of his house with all my art and science. Oh,
she'll come round. Her father prophesied this, and I'll
prophesy that. She's fond of him.'

'She was.'

'She sees through him?'

'Without quite doing justice to him now,' said Vernon.
'He can be generous—in his way.'

'How?' Corney inquired, and was informed that he
should hear in time to come.

Meanwhile Colonel De Craye, after hovering over the
park and about the cottage for the opportunity of poun-
cing on Miss Middleton alone, had returned, crest-fallen
for once, and plumped into Willoughby's hands.

'My dear Horace,' Willoughby said, 'I've been looking
for you all the afternoon. The fact is—I fancy you'll
think yourself lured down here on false pretences: but
the truth is, I am not so much to blame as the world will
suppose. In point of fact, to be brief, Miss Dale and I
. . . I never consult other men how they would have
acted. The fact of the matter is, Miss Middleton . . . I
fancy you have partly guessed it.'

'Partly,' said De Craye.

'Well, she has a liking that way, and if it should turn
out strong enough, it's the best arrangement I can
think of.'

The lively play of the colonel's features fixed in a blank
inquiry.

'One can back a good friend for making a good husband,' said Willoughby. 'I could not break with her in
the present stage of affairs without seeing to that. And
I can speak of her highly, though she and I have seen in

time that we do not suit one another. My wife must have brains.'

'I have always thought it,' said Colonel De Craye, glistening and looking hungry as a wolf through his wonderment.

'There will not be a word against her, you understand. You know my dislike of tattle and gossip. However, let it fall on me; my shoulders are broad. I have done my utmost to persuade her, and there seems a likelihood of her consenting. She tells me her wish is to please me, and this will please me.'

'Certainly. Who's the gentleman?'

'My best friend, I tell you. I could hardly have proposed another. Allow this business to go on smoothly just now.'

There was an uproar within the colonel to blind his wits, and Willoughby looked so friendly that it was possible to suppose the man of projects had mentioned his best friend to Miss Middleton.

And who was the best friend?

Not having accused himself of treachery, the quick-eyed colonel was duped.

'Have you his name handy, Willoughby?'

'That would be unfair to him at present, Horace—ask yourself—and to her. Things are in a ticklish posture at present. Don't be hasty.'

'Certainly. I don't ask. Initials'll do.'

'You have a remarkable aptitude for guessing, Horace, and this case offers you no tough problem—if ever you acknowledge toughness. I have a regard for her and for him—for both pretty equally; you know I have, and I should be thoroughly thankful to bring the matter about.'

'Lordly!' said De Craye.

'I don't see it. I call it sensible.'

'Oh! undoubtedly. The style, I mean. Tolerably antique?'

'Novel, I should say, and not the worse for that. We want plain practical dealings between men and women. Usually we go the wrong way to work. And I loathe sentimental rubbish.'

De Craye hummed an air. 'But the lady?' said he.

'I told you, there seems a likelihood of her consenting.'

Willoughby's fish gave a perceptible little leap now that he had been taught to exercise his aptitude for guessing.

'Without any of the customary preliminaries on the side of the gentleman?' he said.

'We must put him through his paces, friend Horace. He's a notorious blunderer with women; hasn't a word for them, never marked a conquest.'

De Craye crested his plumes under the agreeable banter. He presented a face humourously sceptical.

'The lady is positively not indisposed to give the poor fellow a hearing?'

'I have cause to think she is not,' said Willoughby, glad of acting the indifference to her which could talk of her inclinations.

'Cause?'

'Good cause.'

'Bless us!'

'As good as one can have with a woman.'

'Ah?'

'I assure you.'

'Ah! Does it seem like her, though?'

'Well, she wouldn't engage herself to accept him.'

'Well, that seems more like her.'

'But she said she could engage to marry no one else.'

The colonel sprang up, crying: 'Clara Middleton said it?' He curbed himself. 'That's a bit of wonderful compliancy.'

'She wishes to please me. We separate on those terms. And I wish her happiness. I've developed a heart lately and taken to think of others.'

'Nothing better. You appear to make cock sure of the other party—our friend?'

'You know him too well, Horace, to doubt his readiness.'

'Do *you*, Willoughby?'

'She has money and good looks. Yes, I can say I do.'

'It wouldn't be much of a man who'd want hard pulling to that lighted altar!'

'And if he requires persuasion, you and I, Horace, might bring him to his senses.'

'Kicking, 'twould be!'

'I like to see everybody happy about me,' said Willoughby, naming the hour as time to dress for dinner.

The sentiment he had delivered was De Craye's excuse for grasping his hand and complimenting him; but the colonel betrayed himself by doing it with an extreme fervour almost tremulous.

'When shall we hear more?' he said.

'Oh, probably to-morrow,' said Willoughby. 'Don't be in such a hurry.'

'I'm an infant asleep!' the colonel replied, departing.

He resembled one, to Willoughby's mind: or a traitor drugged.

'There is a fellow I thought had some brains!'

Who are not fools to be set spinning if we choose to whip them with their vanity! It is the consolation of the great to watch them spin. But the pleasure is loftier, and may comfort our unmerited misfortune for a while, in making a false friend drunk.

Willoughby, among his many preoccupations, had the satisfaction of seeing the effect of drunkenness on Horace De Craye when the latter was in Clara's presence. He could have laughed. Cut in keen epigram were the marginal notes added by him to that chapter of The Book which treats of friends and a woman: and had he not been profoundly preoccupied, troubled by recent intelligence communicated by the ladies, his aunts, he would have played the two together for the royal amusement afforded him by his friend Horace.

CHAPTER XLVIII

The Lovers

THE hour was close upon eleven at night. Laetitia sat in the room adjoining her father's bed-chamber. Her elbow was on the table beside her chair, and two fingers pressed her temples. The state between thinking and feeling, when both are molten and flow by us, is one of our nature's intermissions, coming after thought has quieted the fiery nerves, and can do no more. She seemed to be meditating. She was conscious only of a struggle past.

She answered a tap at the door, and raised her eyes on Clara.

Clara stepped softly. 'Mr. Dale is asleep?'

'I hope so.'

'Ah! dear friend.'

Laetitia let her hand be pressed.

'Have you had a pleasant evening?'

'Mr. Whitford and papa have gone to the library.'

'Colonel De Craye has been singing?'

'Yes—with a voice! I thought of you upstairs, but could not ask him to sing piano.'

'He is probably exhilarated.'

'One would suppose it: he sang well.'

'You are not aware of any reason?'

'It cannot concern me.'

Clara was in rosy colour, but could meet a steady gaze.

'And Crossjay has gone to bed?'

'Long since. He was at dessert. He would not touch anything.'

'He is a strange boy.'

'Not very strange, Laetitia.'

'He did not come to me to wish me good night.'

'That is not strange.'

'It is his habit at the cottage and here; and he professes to like me.'

'Oh! he does. I may have wakened his enthusiasm, but you he loves.'

'Why do you say it is not strange, Clara?'

'He fears you a little.'

'And why should Crossjay fear me?'

'Dear, I will tell you. Last night—You will forgive him, for it was by accident: his own bed-room door was locked and he ran down to the drawing-room and curled himself up on the ottoman, and fell asleep, under that padded silken coverlet of the ladies—boots and all, I am afraid!'

Laetitia profited by this absurd allusion, thanking Clara in her heart for the refuge.

'He should have taken off his boots,' she said.

'He slept there, and woke up. Dear, he meant no harm. Next day he repeated what he had heard. You will blame him. He meant well in his poor boy's head. And now it is over the county. Ah! do not frown.'

'That explains Lady Busshe!' exclaimed Laetitia.

'Dear, dear friend,' said Clara. 'Why—I presume on your tenderness for me; but let me: to-morrow I go— why will you reject your happiness? Those kind good ladies are deeply troubled. They say your resolution is inflexible; you resist their entreaties and your father's. Can it be that you have any doubt of the strength of this attachment? I have none. I have never had a doubt that it was the strongest of his feelings. If before I go I could see you . . . both happy, I should be relieved, I should rejoice.'

Laetitia said quietly: 'Do you remember a walk we had one day together to the cottage?'

Clara put up her hands with the motion of intending to stop her ears.

'Before I go!' said she. 'If I might know this was to be, which all desire, before I leave, I should not feel as I do now. I long to see you happy . . . him, yes, him too. Is it like asking you to pay my debt? Then, please! But, no; I am not more than partly selfish on this occasion. He has won my gratitude. He can be really generous.'

'An Egoist?'

'Who is?'

'You have forgotten our conversation on the day of our walk to the cottage?'

'Help me to forget it—that day, and those days, and all those days! I should be glad to think I passed a time beneath the earth, and have risen again. I was the Egoist. I am sure, if I had been buried, I should not have stood up seeing myself more vilely stained, soiled, dis-figured—oh! Help me to forget my conduct, Laetitia. He and I were unsuited—and I remember I blamed my-self then. You and he are not: and now I can perceive the pride that can be felt in him. The worst that can be said is, that he schemes too much.'

'Is there any fresh scheme?' said Laetitia.

The rose came over Clara's face.

'You have not heard? It was impossible, but it was kindly intended. Judging by my own feeling at this moment, I can understand his. We love to see our friends established.'

Laetitia bowed. 'My curiosity is piqued, of course.'

'Dear friend, to-morrow we shall be parted. I trust to be thought of by you as a little better in grain than I have appeared, and my reason for trusting it is, that I know I have been always honest—a boorish young woman in my stupid mad impatience; but not insincere. It is no lofty ambition to desire to be remembered in that character, but such is your Clara, she discovers. I will tell you. It is his wish . . . his wish that I should promise to give my hand to Mr. Whitford. You see the kindness.'

Laetitia's eyes widened and fixed:

'You think it kindness?'

'The intention. He sent Mr. Whitford to me, and I was taught to expect him.'

'Was that quite kind to Mr. Whitford?'

'What an impression I must have made on you during that walk to the cottage, Laetitia! I do not wonder; I was in a fever.'

'You consented to listen?'

'I really did. It astonishes me now, but I thought I could not refuse.'

'My poor friend Vernon Whitford tried a love speech.'

'He? no: Oh! no.'

'You discouraged him?'

'I? no.'

'Gently, I mean.'

'No.'

'Surely you did not dream of trifling? He has a deep heart.'

'Has he?'

'You ask that: and you know something of him.'

'He did not expose it to me, dear; not even the surface of the mighty deep.'

Laetitia knitted her brows.

'No,' said Clara, 'not a coquette: she is not a coquette, I assure you.'

With a laugh, Laetitia replied: 'You have still the "dreadful power" you made me feel that day.'

'I wish I could use it to good purpose!'

'He did not speak?'

'Of Switzerland, Tyrol, the Iliad, Antigone.'

'That was all?'

'No, Political Economy.* Our situation, you will own, was unexampled: or mine was. Are you interested in me?'

'I should be, if I knew your sentiments.'

'I was grateful to Sir Willoughby: grieved for Mr. Whitford.'

'Real grief?'

'Because the task imposed on him of showing me politely that he did not enter into his cousin's ideas, was evidently very great, extremely burdensome.'

'You, so quick-eyed in some things, Clara!'

'He felt for me. I saw that, in his avoidance of . . . And he was, as he always is, pleasant. We rambled over the park for I know not how long, though it did not seem long.'

'Never touching that subject?'

'Not ever neighbouring it, dear. A gentleman should esteem the girl he would ask . . . certain questions. I fancy he has a liking for me as a volatile friend.'

'If he had offered himself?'

'Despising me?'

'You can be childish, Clara. Probably you delight to tease. He had his time of it, and it is now my turn.'

'But he must despise me a little.'

'Are you blind?'

'Perhaps, dear, we both are, a little.'

The ladies looked deeper into one another.

'Will you answer me?' said Laetitia.

'Your if? If he had, it would have been an act of condescension.'

'You are too slippery.'

'Stay, dear Laetitia. He was considerate in forbearing to pain me.'

'That is an answer. You allowed him to perceive that it would have pained you.'

'Dearest, if I may convey to you what I was, in a simile for comparison: I think I was like a fisherman's float on the water, perfectly still, and ready to go down at any instant, or up. So much for my behaviour.'

'Similes have the merit of satisfying the finder of them, and cheating the hearer,' said Laetitia. 'You admit that your feelings would have been painful.'

'I was a fisherman's float: please, admire my simile: any way you like, this way or that, or so quiet as to tempt the eyes to go to sleep. And suddenly I might have disappeared in the depths, or flown in the air. But no fish bit.'

'Well, then, to follow you, supposing the fish or the fisherman, for I don't know which is which . . . Oh! no, no: this is too serious for imagery. I am to understand that you thanked him at least for his reserve.'

'Yes.'

'Without the slightest encouragement to him to break it?'

'A fisherman's float, Laetitia!'

Baffled and sighing, Laetitia kept silence for a space. The simile chafed her wits with a suspicion of a meaning hidden in it.

'If he had spoken?' she said.

'He is too truthful a man.'

'And the railings of men at pussy women who wind about and will not be brought to a mark, become intelligible to me.'

'Then, Laetitia, if he had spoken, if, and one could have imagined him sincere . . .'

'So truthful a man?'

'I am looking at myself. If!—why, then, I should have burnt to death with shame. Where have I read?— some story—of an inextinguishable spark. That would have been shot into my heart.'

'Shame, Clara? You are free.'

'As much as remains of me.'

'I could imagine a certain shame, in such a position, where there was no feeling but pride.'

'I could not imagine it where there was no feeling but pride.'

Laetitia mused: 'And you dwell on the kindness of a proposition so extraordinary!' Gaining some light, impatiently she cried: 'Vernon loves you.'

'Do not say it!'

'I have seen it.'

'I have never had a sign of it.'

'There is the proof.'

'When it might have been shown again and again!'

'The greater proof!'

'Why did he not speak when he was privileged?—strangely, but privileged.'

'He feared.'

'Me?'

'Feared to wound you—and himself as well, possibly. Men may be pardoned for thinking of themselves in these cases.'

'But why should he fear?'

'That another was dearer to you?'

'What cause had I given . . . Ah! see! He could fear that; suspect it! See his opinion of me! Can he care for such a girl? Abuse me, Laetitia. I should like a good round of abuse. I need purification by fire. What have I been in this house? I have a sense of whirling through it like a madwoman. And to be loved, after it all!—No! we must be hearing a tale of an antiquary prizing a battered relic of the battle-field that no one else would look at. To be loved, I see, is to feel our littleness, hollowness—feel shame. We come out in all our spots. Never to have given me one sign, when a lover would have been so tempted! Let me be incredulous, my own dear Laetitia. Because he is a man of honour, you would say! But are you unconscious of the torture you inflict? For if I am—you say it—loved by this gentleman, what an object it is he loves—that has gone clamouring about more immodestly than women will bear to hear of, and she herself to think of! Oh! I have seen my own heart. It is a frightful spectre. I have seen a weakness in me that would have carried me anywhere. And truly I shall be charitable to women—I have gained that. But, loved! by Vernon Whitford! The miserable little me to be taken up and loved after tearing myself to pieces! Have you been simply speculating? You have no positive knowledge of it! Why do you kiss me?'

'Why do you tremble and blush so?'

Clara looked at her as clearly as she could. She bowed her head. 'It makes my conduct worse!'

She received a tenderer kiss for that. It was her avowal, and it was understood: to know that she had loved, or had been ready to love him, shadowed her in the retrospect.

'Ah! you read me through and through,' said Clara, sliding to her for a whole embrace.

'Then there never was cause for him to fear?' Laetitia whispered.

Clara slid her head more out of sight. 'Not that my heart ... But I said I have seen it; and it is unworthy of him. And if, as I think now, I could have been so rash, so weak, wicked, unpardonable—such thoughts were in me!—then to hear him speak, would make it necessary for me to uncover myself and tell him—incredible to you, yes!—that while ... yes, Laetitia, all this is true: and thinking of him as the noblest of men, I could have welcomed any help to cut my knot. So there,' said Clara, issuing from her nest with winking eyelids, 'you see the pain I mentioned.'

'Why did you not explain it to me at once?'

'Dearest, I wanted a century to pass.'

'And you feel that it has passed?'

'Yes; in Purgatory—with an angel by me. My report of the place will be favourable. Good angel, I have yet to say something.'

'Say it, and expiate.'

'I think I did fancy once or twice, very dimly, and especially to-day ... properly I ought not to have had any idea: but his coming to me, and his not doing as another would have done, seemed . . . A gentleman of real nobleness does not carry the common light for us to read him by. I wanted his voice; but silence, I think, did tell me more: if a nature like mine could only have had faith without hearing the rattle of a tongue.'

A knock at the door caused the ladies to exchange looks.

Laetitia rose as Vernon entered.

'I am just going to my father for a few minutes,' she said.

'And I have just come from yours,' Vernon said to Clara.

She observed a very threatening expression in him.

The sprite of contrariety mounted to her brain to indemnify her for her recent self-abasement. Seeing the bed-room door shut on Laetitia, she said: 'And of course papa has gone to bed': implying 'otherwise . . .'

'Yes, he has gone. He wished me well.'

'His formula of good-night would embrace that wish.'

'And failing, it will be good night for good to me!'

Clara's breathing gave a little leap. 'We leave early to-morrow.'

'I know. I have an appointment at Bregenz for June.'

'So soon? With papa?'

'And from there we break into Tyrol, and round away to the right, Southward.'

'To the Italian Alps! And was it assumed that I should be of this expedition?'

'Your father speaks dubiously.'

'You have spoken of me, then?'

'I ventured to speak of you. I am not over-bold, as you know.'

Her lovely eyes troubled the lids to hide their softness.

'Papa should not think of my presence with him dubiously.'

'He leaves it to you to decide.'

'Yes, then: many times: all that can be uttered.'

'Do you consider what you are saying?'

'Mr. Whitford, I shut my eyes and say Yes.'

'Beware. I give you one warning. If you shut your eyes . . .'

'Of course,' she flew from him, 'big mountains must be satisfied with my admiration at their feet.'

'That will do for a beginning.'

'They speak encouragingly.'

'One of them.' Vernon's breast heaved high.

'To be at your feet makes a mountain of you?' said she.

'With the heart of a mouse if that satisfies me!'

'You tower too high; you are inaccessible.'

'I give you a second warning. You may be seized and lifted.'

'Some one would stoop, then.'

'To plant you like the flag on the conquered peak!'

'You have indeed been talking to papa, Mr. Whitford.' Vernon changed his tone.

'Shall I tell you what he said?'

'I know his language so well.'

'He said——'

'But you have acted on it.'

'Only partly. He said——'

'You will teach me nothing.'

'He said . . .'

'Vernon, no! oh! not in this house!'

That supplication coupled with his name confessed the end to which her quick vision perceived she was being led, where she would succumb.

She revived the same shrinking in him from a breath of their great word yet: not here; somewhere in the shadow of the mountains.

But he was sure of her. And their hands might join. The two hands thought so, or did not think, behaved like innocents.

The spirit of Dr. Middleton, as Clara felt, had been blown into Vernon, rewarding him for forthright outspeaking. Over their books, Vernon had abruptly shut up a volume and related the tale of the house. 'Has this man a spice of religion in him?' the Rev. Doctor asked midway. Vernon made out a fair general case for his

cousin in that respect. 'The complemental dot on his i
of a commonly civilized human creature!' said Dr.
Middleton, looking at his watch and finding it too late to
leave the house before morning. The risky communication was to come. Vernon was proceeding with the
narrative of Willoughby's generous plan when Dr. Middleton electrified him by calling out: 'He whom of all
men living I should desire my daughter to espouse!' and
Willoughby rose in the Rev. Doctor's esteem: he praised
that sensibly minded gentleman, who could acquiesce in
the turn of mood of a little maid, albeit Fortune had
withheld from him a taste of the switch at school. The
father of the little maid's appreciation of her volatility
was exhibited in his exhortation to Vernon to be off to
her at once with his authority to finish her moods and
assure him of peace in the morning. Vernon hesitated.
Dr. Middleton remarked upon being not so sure that
it was not he who had done the mischief. Thereupon
Vernon, to prove his honesty, made his own story bare.
'Go to her,' said Dr. Middleton. Vernon proposed a
meeting in Switzerland, to which Dr. Middleton assented, adding: 'Go to her': and as he appeared a total
stranger to the decorum of the situation, Vernon put his
delicacy aside, and taking his heart up, obeyed. He too
had pondered on Clara's consent to meet him after she
knew of Willoughby's terms, and her grave sweet manner
during the ramble over the park. Her father's breath
had been blown into him; so now, with nothing but the
faith lying in sensation to convince him of his happy
fortune (and how unconvincing that may be until the
mind has grasped and stamped it, we experience even
then when we acknowledge that we are most blest), he
held her hand. And if it was hard for him, for both, but
harder for the man, to restrain their particular word from
a flight to heaven when the cage stood open and nature
beckoned, he was practised in self-mastery, and she loved
him the more.

Laetitia was a witness of their union of hands on her
coming back to the room.

They promised to visit her very early in the morning,

neither of them conceiving that they left her to a night
of storm and tears.

She sat meditating on Clara's present appreciation of
Sir Willoughby's generosity.

CHAPTER XLIX

Laetitia and Sir Willoughby

WE cannot be abettors of the tribes of imps whose
revelry is in the frailties of our poor human constitution.
They have their place and their service, and so long as
we continue to be what we are now, they will hang on to
us, restlessly plucking at the garments which cover our
nakedness, nor ever ceasing to twitch them and strain at
them until they have fairly stripped us for one of their
horrible Walpurgis nights;*when the laughter heard is of
a character to render laughter frightful to the ears of men
throughout the remainder of their days. But if in these
festival hours under the beams of Hecate they are uncontrollable by the Comic Muse, she will not flatter them
with her presence during the course of their insane and
impious hilarities, whereof a description would out-
Brocken Brockens*and make Graymalkin and Paddock*
too intimately our familiars.

It shall suffice to say that from hour to hour of the midnight to the grey-eyed morn, assisted at intervals by the
ladies Eleanor and Isabel, and by Mr. Dale awakened
and reawakened—hearing the vehemence of his petitioning outcry to soften her obduracy—Sir Willoughby
pursued Laetitia with solicitations to espouse him, until
the inveteracy of his wooing wore the aspect of the life-
long love he raved of aroused to a state of mania. He
appeared, he departed, he returned; and all the while
his imps were about him and upon him, riding him,
prompting, driving, inspiring him with outrageous
pathos, an eloquence to move any one but the dead,
which its object seemed to be in her torpid attention. He
heard them, he talked to them, caressed them; he flung
them off and ran from them, and stood vanquished for

them to mount him again and swarm on him. There are
men thus imp-haunted. Men who, setting their minds
upon an object, must have it, breed imps. They are
noted for their singularities, as their converse with the
invisible and amazing distractions are called. Willoughby became aware of them that night. He said to
himself, upon one of his dashes into solitude: I believe I
am possessed! And if he did not actually believe it, but
only suspected it, or framed speech to account for the
transformation he had undergone into a desperately beseeching creature, having lost acquaintance with his
habitual personality, the operations of an impish host
had undoubtedly smitten his consciousness.

He had them in his brain: for while burning with an
ardour for Laetitia, that incited him to frantic excesses of
language and comportment, he was aware of shouts of
the names of Lady Busshe and Mrs. Mountstuart Jenkinson, the which, freezing him as they did, were directly
the cause of his hurrying to a wilder extravagance and
more headlong determination to subdue before break of
day the woman he almost dreaded to behold by daylight,
though he had now passionately persuaded himself of
his love of her. He could not, he felt, stand in the daylight without her. She was his morning. She was, he
raved, his predestined wife. He cried: 'Darling!' both
to her and to solitude. Every prescription of his ideal of
demeanour as an example to his class and country, was
abandoned by the enamoured gentleman. He had lost
command of his countenance. He stooped so far as to
kneel, and not gracefully. Nay, it is in the chronicles of
the invisible host around him, that in a fit of supplication,
upon a cry of 'Laetitia!' twice repeated, he whimpered.

Let so much suffice. And indeed not without reason
do the multitudes of the servants of the Muse in this land
of social policy avoid scenes of an inordinate wantonness,
which detract from the dignity of our leaders and menace
human nature with confusion. Sagacious are they who
conduct the individual on broad lines, over familiar
tracks, under well-known characteristics. What men will
do, and amorously minded men will do, is less the

question than what it is politic that they should be shown to do.

The night wore through. Laetitia was bent, but had not yielded. She had been obliged to say—and how many times, she could not bear to recollect: 'I do not love you; I have no love to give'; and issuing from such a night to look again upon the face of day, she scarcely felt that she was alive.

The contest was renewed by her father with the singing of the birds. Mr. Dale then produced the first serious impression she had received. He spoke of their circumstances, of his being taken from her and leaving her to poverty, in weak health; of the injury done to her health by writing for bread; and of the oppressive weight he would be relieved of by her consenting. He no longer implored her; he put the case on common ground.

And he wound up: 'Pray do not be ruthless, my girl.'

The practical statement, and this adjuration incongruously to conclude it, harmonized with her disordered understanding, her loss of all sentiment and her desire to be kind. She sighed to herself: 'Happily, it is over!'

Her father was too weak to rise. He fell asleep. She was bound down to the house for hours; and she walked through her suite, here at the doors, there at the windows, thinking of Clara's remark 'of a century passing.' She had not wished it, but a light had come on her to show her what she would have supposed a century could not have effected: she saw the impossible of overnight a possible thing: not desireable, yet possible, wearing the features of the possible. Happily, she had resisted too firmly to be again besought.

Those features of the possible once beheld allured the mind to reconsider them. Wealth gives us the power to do good on earth. Wealth enables us to see the world, the beautiful scenes of the earth. Laetitia had long thirsted both for a dowering money-bag at her girdle, and the wings to fly abroad over lands which had begun to seem fabulous in her starved imagination. Then, moreover, if her sentiment for this gentleman was gone, it was only a delusion gone; accurate sight and know-ledge of him would not make a woman the less helpful mate. That was the mate he required: and he could be led. A sentimental attachment would have been service-less to him. Not so the woman allied by a purely rational bond: and he wanted guiding. Happily, she had told him too much of her feeble health and her lovelessness to be reduced to submit to another attack.

She busied herself in her room, arranging for her departure, so that no minutes might be lost after her father had breakfasted and dressed.

Clara was her earliest visitor, and each asked the other whether she had slept, and took the answer from the face presented to her. The rings of Laetitia's eyes were very dark. Clara was her mirror, and she said: 'A singular object to be persecuted through a night for her hand! I know these two damp dead leaves I wear on my cheeks to remind me of midnight vigils. But you have slept well, Clara.'

'I have slept well, and yet I could say I have not slept at all, Laetitia. I was with you, dear, part in dream and part in thought: hoping to find you sensible before I go.'

'Sensible. That is the word for me.'

Laetitia briefly sketched the history of the night; and Clara said, with a manifest sincerity that testified of her gratitude to Sir Willoughby: 'Could you resist him, so earnest as he is?'

Laetitia saw the human nature without sourness: and replied: 'I hope, Clara, you will not begin with a large stock of sentiment, for there is nothing like it for making you hard, matter-of-fact, worldly, calculating.'

The next visitor was Vernon, exceedingly anxious for news of Mr. Dale. Laetitia went into her father's room to obtain it for him. Returning she found them both with sad visages, and she ventured, in alarm for them, to ask the cause.

'It's this,' Vernon said: 'Willoughby will everlast-ingly tease that boy to be loved by him. Perhaps, poor fellow, he had an excuse last night. Anyhow he went into Crossjay's room this morning, woke him up and talked to him, and set the lad crying, and what with one thing and another Crossjay got a berry in his throat, as he calls it, and poured out everything he knew and all he had done. I needn't tell you the consequence. He has ruined himself here for good, so I must take him.'

Vernon glanced at Clara. 'You must indeed,' said she. 'He is my boy as well as yours. No chance of pardon?'

'It's not likely.'

'Laetitia!'

'What can I do?'

'Oh! what can you not do?'

'I do *not* know.'

'Teach him to forgive!'

Laetitia's brows were heavy and Clara forebore to torment her.

She would not descend to the family breakfast-table. Clara would fain have stayed to drink tea with her in her own room, but a last act of conformity was demanded of the liberated young lady. She promised to run up the moment breakfast was over. Not unnaturally, therefore, Laetitia supposed it to be she to whom she gave admission, half an hour later, with a glad cry of, 'Come in, dear.'

The knock had sounded like Clara's.

Sir Willoughby entered.

He stepped forward. He seized her hands. 'Dear!' he said. 'You cannot withdraw that. You called me dear. I am, I must be dear to you. The word is out, by accident or not, but, by heaven, I have it and I give it up to no one. And love me or not—marry me, and my love will bring it back to you. You have taught me I am not so strong. I must have you by my side. You have powers I did not credit you with.'

'You are mistaken in me, Sir Willoughby,' Laetitia said feebly, outworn as she was.

'A woman who can resist me by declining to be my wife, through a whole night of entreaty, has the quality I need for my house, and I batter at her ears for months, with as little rest as I had last night, before I surrender my chance of her. But I told you last night I want you within the twelve hours. I have staked my pride on it. By noon you are mine: you are introduced to Mrs. Mountstuart as mine, as the lady of my life and house. And to the world! I shall not let you go.'

'You will not detain me here, Sir Willoughby?'

'I will detain you. I will use force and guile. I will spare nothing.'

He raved for a term, as he had done overnight.

On his growing rather breathless, Laetitia said: 'You do not ask me for love?'

'I do not. I pay you the higher compliment of asking for *you*, love or no love. My love shall be enough. Reward me or not. I am not used to be denied.'

'But do you know what you ask for? Do you remember what I told you of myself? I am hard, materialistic; I have lost faith in romance, the skeleton is present with me all over life. And my health is not good. I crave for money. I should marry to be rich. I should not worship you. I should be a burden, barely a living one, irresponsive and cold. Conceive such a wife, Sir Willoughby!'

'It will be you!'

She tried to recall how this would have sung in her ears long back. Her bosom rose and fell in absolute dejection. Her ammunition of arguments against him had been expended overnight.

'You are so unforgiving,' she said.

'Is it I who am?'

'You do not know me.'

'But you are the woman of all the world who knows *me*, Laetitia.'

'Can you think it better for you to be known?'

He was about to say other words: he checked them. 'I believe I do not know myself. Anything you will, only give me your hand; give it; trust to me; you shall direct me. If I have faults, help me to obliterate them.'

'Will you not expect me to regard them as the virtues of meaner men?'

'You will be my wife!'

Laetitia broke from him, crying: 'Your wife, your

critic! Oh! I cannot think it possible. Send for the ladies. Let them hear me.'

'They are at hand,' said Willoughby, opening the door.

They were in one of the upper rooms anxiously on the watch.

'Dear ladies,' Laetitia said to them, as they entered. 'I am going to wound you, and I grieve to do it: but rather now than later, if I am to be your housemate. He asks me for a hand that cannot carry a heart, because mine is dead. I repeat it. I used to think the heart a woman's marriage portion for her husband. I see now that she may consent, and he accept her, without one. But it is right that you should know what I am when I consent. I was once a foolish romantic girl; now I am a sickly woman, all illusions vanished. Privation has made me what an abounding fortune usually makes of others— I am an Egoist. I am not deceiving you. That is my real character. My girl's view of him has entirely changed; and I am almost indifferent to the change. I can endeavour to respect him, I cannot venerate.'

'Dear child!' the ladies gently remonstrated.

Willoughby motioned to them.

'If we are to live together, and I could very happily live with you,' Laetitia continued to address them, 'you must not be ignorant of me. And if you, as I imagine, worship him blindly, I do not know how we are to live together. And never shall you quit this house to make way for me. I have a hard detective eye. I see many faults.'

'Have we not all of us faults, dear child?'

'Not such as he has; though the excuses of a gentleman nurtured in idolatry may be pleaded. But he should know that they are seen, and seen by her he asks to be his wife, that no misunderstanding may exist, and while it is yet time he may consult his feelings. He worships himself.'

'Willoughby?'

'He is vindictive.'

'Our Willoughby?'

'That is not your opinion, ladies. It is firmly mine.

Time has taught it me. So, if you and I are at such variance, how can we live together? It is an impossibility.'

They looked at Willoughby. He nodded imperiously.

'We have never affirmed that our dear nephew is devoid of faults. If he is offended . . . And supposing he claims to be foremost, is it not his rightful claim, made good by much generosity? Reflect, dear Laetitia. We are your friends too.'

She could not chastise the kind ladies any further.

'You have always been my good friends.'

'And you have no other charge against him?'

Laetitia was milder in saying; 'He is unpardoning.'

'Name one instance, Laetitia.'

'He has turned Crossjay out of his house, interdicting the poor boy ever to enter it again.'

'Crossjay,' said Willoughby, 'was guilty of a piece of infamous treachery.'

'Which is the cause of your persecuting me to become your wife!'

There was a cry of 'Persecuting!'

'No young fellow behaving so basely can come to good,' said Willoughby, stained about the face with flecks of redness at the lashings he received.

'Honestly,' she retorted. 'He told of himself: and he must have anticipated the punishment he would meet. He should have been studying with a master for his profession. He has been kept here in comparative idleness to be alternately petted and discarded: no one but Vernon Whitford, a poor gentleman doomed to struggle for a livelihood by literature—I know something of that struggle—too much for me!—no one but Mr. Whitford for his friend.'

'Crossjay is forgiven,' said Willoughby.

'You promise me that?'

'He shall be packed off to a crammer at once.'

'But my home must be Crossjay's home.'

'You are mistress of my house, Laetitia.'

She hesitated. Her eyelashes grew moist. 'You can be generous.'

'He is, dear child!' the ladies cried. 'He is. Forget his errors in his generosity, as we do.'

'There is that wretched man Flitch.'

'That sot has gone about the county for years to get me a bad character,' said Willoughby.

'It would have been generous in you to have offered him another chance. He has children.'

'Nine. And I am responsible for them?'

'I speak of being generous.'

'Dictate.' Willoughby spread out his arms.

'Surely now you should be satisfied, Laetitia?' said the ladies.

'Is *he*?'

Willoughby perceived Mrs. Mountstuart's carriage coming down the avenue.

'To the full.' He presented his hand.

She raised hers with the fingers catching back before she ceased to speak and dropped it;—

'Ladies, you are witnesses that there is no concealment, there has been no reserve, on my part. May heaven grant me kinder eyes than I have now. I would not have you change your opinion of him; only that you should see how I read him. For the rest, I vow to do my duty by him. Whatever is of worth in me is at his service. I am very tired. I feel I must yield or break. This is his wish, and I submit.'

'And I salute my wife,' said Willoughby, making her hand his own, and warming to his possession as he performed the act.

Mrs. Mountstuart's indecent hurry to be at the Hall before the departure of Dr. Middleton and his daughter, afflicted him with visions of the physical contrast which would be sharply perceptible to her this morning of his Laetitia beside Clara.

But he had the lady with brains! He had: and he was to learn the nature of that possession in the woman who is our wife.

CHAPTER L

Upon which the Curtain falls

'PLAIN sense upon the marriage question is my demand upon man and woman, for the stopping of many a tragedy.'

These were Dr. Middleton's words in reply to Willoughby's brief explanation.

He did not say that he had shown it parentally while the tragedy was threatening, or at least there was danger of a precipitate descent from the levels of comedy. The parents of hymenaeal men and women he was indisposed to consider as dramatis personae. Nor did he mention certain sympathetic regrets he entertained in contemplation of the health of Mr. Dale, for whom, poor gentleman, the proffer of a bottle of the Patterne Port would be an egregious mockery. He paced about, anxious for his departure, and seeming better pleased with the society of Colonel De Craye than with that of any of the others. Colonel De Craye assiduously courted him, was anecdotal, deferential, charmingly vivacious, the very man the Rev. Doctor liked for company when plunged in the bustle of the preliminaries to a journey.

'You would be a cheerful travelling comrade, sir,' he remarked, and spoke of his doom to lead his daughter over the Alps and Alpine lakes for the Summer months.

Strange to tell, the Alps for the Summer months, was a settled project of the colonel's.

And thence Dr. Middleton was to be hauled along to the habitable quarters of North Italy in high Summertide.

That also had been traced for a route on the map of Colonel De Craye.

'We are started in June, I am informed,' said Dr. Middleton.

June, by miracle, was the month the colonel had fixed upon.

'I trust we shall meet, sir,' said he.

'I would gladly reckon it in my catalogue of pleasures,'

the Rev. Doctor responded: 'for in good sooth it is conjectureable that I shall be left very much alone.'

'Paris, Strasburg, Basle?' the colonel inquired.

'The Lake of Constance, I am told,' said Dr. Middleton.

Colonel De Craye spied eagerly for an opportunity of exchanging a pair of syllables with the third and fairest party of this glorious expedition to come.

Willoughby met him, and rewarded the colonel's frankness in stating that he was on the look-out for Miss Middleton to take his leave of her, by furnishing him the occasion. He conducted his friend Horace to the Blue Room, where Clara and Laetitia were seated circling a half embrace with a brook of chatter, and contrived an excuse for leading Laetitia forth. Some minutes later Mrs. Mountstuart called aloud for the colonel, to drive him away. Willoughby, whose good offices were unabated by the services he performed to each in rotation, ushered her into the Blue Room, hearing her say, as she stood at the entrance: 'Is the man coming to spend a day with me with a face like that?'

She was met and detained by Clara.

De Craye came out.

'What are you thinking of?' said Willoughby.

'I was thinking,' said the colonel, 'of developing a heart like you, and taking to think of others.'

'At last!'

'Ah, you're a true friend, Willoughby, a true friend. And a cousin to boot!'

'What! has Clara been communicative?'

'The itinerary of a voyage Miss Middleton is going to make.'

'Do you join them?'

'Why, it would be delightful, Willoughby, but it happens I've got a lot of powder I want to let off, and so I've an idea of shouldering my gun along the sea-coast and shooting gulls: which'll be a harmless form of committing parricide and matricide and fratricide—for there's my family, and I come of it!—the gull! And I've to talk lively to Mrs. Mountstuart for something like a matter of twelve hours, calculating that she goes to bed at midnight: and I wouldn't bet on it; such is the energy of ladies of that age!'

Willoughby scorned the man who could not conceal a blow, even though he joked over his discomfiture.

'Gull!' he muttered.

'A bird that's easy to be had, and better for stuffing than for eating,' said De Craye. 'You'll miss your cousin.'

'I have,' replied Willoughby, 'one fully equal to supplying his place.'

There was confusion in the hall for a time, and an assembly of the household to witness the departure of Dr. Middleton and his daughter. Vernon had been driven off by Dr. Corney, who further recommended rest for Mr. Dale, and promised to keep an eye for Crossjay along the road.

'I think you will find him at the station, and if you do, command him to come straight back here,' Laetitia said to Clara.

The answer was an affectionate squeeze, and Clara's hand was extended to Willoughby, who bowed over it with perfect courtesy, bidding her adieu.

So the knot was cut. And the next carriage to Dr. Middleton's was Mrs. Mountstuart's, conveying the great lady and Colonel De Craye.

'I beg you not to wear that face with me,' she said to him. 'I have had to dissemble, which I hate, and I have quite enough to endure, and I must be amused, or I shall run away from you and enlist that little countryman of yours, and him I can count on to be professionally restorative. Who can fathom the heart of a girl! Here is Lady Busshe right once more! And I was wrong. She must be a gambler by nature. I never should have risked such a guess as that. Colonel De Craye, you lengthen your face preternaturally, you distort it purposely.'

'Ma'am,' returned De Craye, 'the boast of our army is never to know when we are beaten, and that tells of a great-hearted soldiery. But there's a field where the Briton must own his defeat, whether smiling or crying, and I'm not so sure that a short howl doesn't do him honour.'

'She was, I am certain, in love with Vernon Whitford all along, Colonel De Craye!'

'Ah!' the colonel drank it in. 'I have learnt that it was not the gentleman in whom I am chiefly interested. So it was not so hard for the lady to vow to friend Willoughby she would marry no one else!'

'Girls are unfathomable! And Lady Busshe—I know she did not go by character—shot one of her random guesses, and she triumphs. We shall never hear the last of it. And I had all the opportunities. I'm bound to confess I had.'

'Did you by chance, ma'am,' De Craye said with a twinkle, 'drop a hint to Willoughby of her turn for Vernon Whitford?'

'No,' said Mrs. Mountstuart, 'I'm not a mischief-maker; and the policy of the county is to keep him in love with himself, or Patterne will be likely to be as dull as it was without a lady enthroned. When his pride is at ease he is a prince. I can read men. Now, Colonel De Craye, pray, be lively.'

'I should have been livelier, I'm afraid, if you had dropped a bit of a hint to Willoughby. But you're the magnanimous person, ma'am, and revenge for a stroke in the game of love shows us unworthy to win.'

Mrs. Mountstuart menaced him with her parasol. 'I forbid sentiments, Colonel De Craye. They are always followed by sighs.'

'Grant me five minutes of inward retirement, and I'll come out formed for your commands, ma'am,' said he.

Before the termination of that space De Craye was enchanting Mrs. Mountstuart, and she in consequence was restored to her natural wit.

So, and much so universally, the world of his dread and his unconscious worship wagged over Sir Willoughby Patterne and his change of brides, until the preparations for the festivities of the marriage flushed him in his county's eyes to something of the splendid glow he had worn on the great day of his majority. That was upon the season when two lovers met between the Swiss and Tyrol Alps over the Lake of Constance. Sitting beside them the Comic Muse is grave and sisterly. But taking a glance at the others of her late company of actors, she compresses her lips.

EXPLANATORY NOTES

MEREDITH'S dense prose makes the task of providing explanatory annotation a particularly taxing one, and I have been mindful of the various implications for an editor of Laetitia Dale's observation that 'Similes have the merit of satisfying the finder of them, and cheating the hearer' (p. 528). In the case of *The Egoist*, Meredith's esoteric vocabulary causes unusual difficulties: I have generally included a note on the meaning of an individual word when it is to be found only in the *Oxford English Dictionary* and not in the *Shorter Oxford English Dictionary* or the *Concise Oxford Dictionary*. I am grateful for the help of Dexter Hoyos, Department of Latin, University of Sydney, in identifying Meredith's quotations from classical texts; and also acknowledge the assistance I have derived from the work of previous editors of *The Egoist*: Lionel Stevenson (Boston, Mass.: Houghton Mifflin Riverside edition, 1958), George Woodcock (Harmondsworth: Penguin, 1968), and Robert M. Adams (New York: Norton Critical Edition, 1979).

The following abbreviations are used: *Letters* for *The Letters of George Meredith*, ed. C. L. Cline, 3 vols. (Oxford, 1970); and *Notebooks* for *The Notebooks of George Meredith*, ed. Gillian Beer and Margaret Harris (Salzburg, 1983). Quotations from 'Essay: On the Idea of Comedy and of the Uses of the Comic Spirit' use the familiar title *Essay on Comedy* and refer to the text in *Miscellaneous Prose*, vol. xxiii of Constable's Memorial Edition of Meredith's work (London, 1910).

1 *Comedy . . . the representation convincing*: Meredith delivered a lecture on comedy to the London Institution on 1 February 1877, which was afterwards published as 'On the Idea of Comedy, and of the Uses of the Comic Spirit', *New Quarterly Magazine*, 8 (April 1877), 1–40; and as a separate volume, *An Essay on Comedy and the Uses of the Comic Spirit*, in 1897. Some of his notes for the lecture are preserved: *Notebooks*, 73–5 and 186–7. He also wrote an 'Ode: To the Comic Spirit', published in *Poems: The Empty Purse* (1892). As discussed in the Introduction, his concept of the Comic Spirit and its civilizing power, developed in the lecture, is further exemplified in *The Egoist*. See *Essay on Comedy*, 44–5, for a passage analogous to the opening paragraph of the novel; and pp. 46–7 for a description of the Comic Spirit ('It has the sage's brows, and the sunny malice of a faun lurks at the corners of the half-closed lips').

1 *the watchmaker's eye*: an oblique allusion to the argument from analogy designed to prove the existence of God which opens William Paley's *Natural Theology* (1802). A watch found upon a heath may be assumed to have had a maker: so therefore must the natural world be the result of divine design.

their speech: the manuscript of *The Egoist*, fo. 2, includes the following passage which Meredith scored through. It is interesting principally for its avowed resistance to the conventions of realistic and of sentimental fiction; and also for the withdrawn clue to a major image in the mention of Sir Willoughby's China. I am grateful to the Beinecke Rare Book and Manuscript Library, Yale University Library, for permission to publish this passage.

Thus we are without a map of the county where Sir Willoughby Patterne lived, though we are to understand that he occupied it; and also a plan of Patterne Hall, his ancestral mansion and the scene of the hunting of him, is denied to us. Only a faint sketch of the memorable place is granted, quite incidentally: and we must suppose either that the comic spirit is no landscape painter, or that he is too hot upon his quarry to be heedful of the circumstantial. In like manner he is as indifferent to the marking down of trifles as he is disdainful of playing the part of poker of the domestic emotions. The fount of tears is untroubled, he will not fly you the wet handkerchief of fireside Pathos; and Sir Willoughby's hat, gloves, coat, boots, are more or less left to imagination: his China too, and his pictures, and the furniture of his house, the family relics and the heirlooms. Nothing is touched that does not come in the way of the chase. For being a spirit, he hunts the spirit in men . . .

the biggest book on earth . . . the Book of Egoism: Meredith frequently incorporates a tutelary text in his novels, such as Sir Austin Feverel's *Pilgrim's Scrip* in *The Ordeal of Richard Feverel* (1859). In this instance, the Book of Egoism is a metaphor for human nature. John Goode points out that in the 1870s, ' "Egoism" belongs to a technical context', where the term was used most extensively by Henry Sidgwick, 'who was concerned to take it seriously as a positive moral attitude'; and used most significantly by Spencer and Comte, 'as a biological/psychological term, with, to be sure, moral implications' ('*The Egoist*: Anatomy or Striptease?', in Ian Fletcher (ed.), *Meredith Now: Some Critical Essays*, London, 1971, 207). See *Notebooks*, 4, and also the note to p. 4 on 'Egoist'.

1 *the Lizard*: the southernmost point of England, a headland in south-western Cornwall.

2 *Who, says the notable humourist . . . solitary majestic outsider?*: I am unable satisfactorily to paraphrase these dense sentences. It is heartening to find a contemporary reviewer, in a laudatory account of the novel, quoting this as 'the only passage which fairly baffles all comprehension' (unsigned review, *New Quarterly Magazine*, NS 3, 1880, quoted in Ioan Williams (ed.), *Meredith: The Critical Heritage*, London, 1971, 233). The reviewer suggests 'Mr Meredith's style is a cross between Mr Carlyle's and Mr Browning's . . . The simplest statement becomes an epigram in his hands.' Meredith himself in 1898 pointed out to Henry-D. Davray, who proposed translating *The Egoist* into French: 'You will find the introductory chapter rather stiff work, and should be told that the pretended testimony to the merits of Comedy is in the vein of Carlyle' (*Letters*, 1295). Certainly 'the notable humourist' is rendered in a tortuous, near-apocalyptic manner very like that of Carlyle, whose impassioned prophetic spirit pervades the 'Prelude'. Moreover, in *Essay on Comedy* Meredith refers admiringly but not uncritically to Carlyle as 'a living great, though not creative, humourist' who 'is often wanting in proportion and in discretion' (p. 44). The most comprehensive discussion of the relationship of Meredith's work to Carlyle's is Lionel Stevenson, 'Carlyle and Meredith', in John Clubbe (ed.), *Carlyle and his Contemporaries* (Durham, NC, 1976), 257–79.

the cliff you ken of at Dover: there is possibly an allusion here to *King Lear*, IV. vi, in which Edgar describes an imagined cliff and the scene below to the blind Gloucester, who tries to throw himself from it. They are subsequently joined by the mad King Lear.

That is all we got from Science: this paragraph alludes to the controversies in evolutionary theory consequent upon the publication in 1859 of Charles Darwin's *On the Origin of Species By Means of Natural Selection, or the Preservation of Favoured Races in the Struggle for Life*. In particular, there is reference to the debate at a meeting of the British Association for the Advancement of Science at Oxford University in 1860 between T. H. Huxley (Darwin's 'bulldog') and Bishop Wilberforce, who was outraged at the notion that humankind is descended from the apes. Meredith relishes the paradox that Science, regarded as the means of achieving progress and as exemplifying the objectivity of reason, should require civilized nineteenth-century citizens to acknowledge their animal qualities and thus in a sense regress to the primitive. Gillian Beer points out that 'The basis of the novel is the struggle between the instinctual demands of a man or woman's nature and the social forms they adopt by demand or as disguise' (*Meredith: A Change of Masks*, London, 1970, 127).

the broad Alpine survey . . . the Comic Spirit?: compare a paragraph in the *Essay on Comedy*: 'O for a breath of Aristophanes, Rabelais, Voltaire, Cervantes, Fielding, Molière! These are spirits that, if you know them well, will come when you do call. You will find the very invocation of them act on you like a renovating air—the South-west coming off the sea, or a cry in the Alps' (p. 33). See also notes to pp. 54 and 275.

3 *stillatory*: (obsolete) distillery.

Bacchus: Roman god of wine. In *Essay on Comedy* Meredith associates Bacchanalian revelry with comedy and its status relative to tragedy: 'Comedy, we have to admit, was never one of the most honoured of the Muses . . . The light of Athene over the head of Achilles illuminates the birth of Greek Tragedy. But Comedy rolled in shouting under the divine protection of the Son of the Wine-jar' (p. 5).

gallop to Hymen, gallop to Hades: the Greek gods respectively of marriage and of the infernal regions.

Amphitrite: a sea-nymph, consort of Neptune, the god of the sea.

a sweet cook: this sentence and the preceding one are very close in content and expression to propositions advanced in *Essay on Comedy*, especially in the gastronomic analogy of its closing paragraph (pp. 54–5).

4 *Ariel . . . Sycorax*: in Shakespeare's *The Tempest*, when Prospero came to the island he freed Ariel from Sycorax and took the sprite into his own service.

Egoist: the first definition of 'egoist' given in *OED* is 'A sect . . . called Egoists, who maintained that we have no evidence of the existence of any but ourselves.' The second sense is 'One who makes regard to his own interest the guiding principle of his conduct', and a review of *The Egoist* is cited: 'He is . . . thoroughly selfish, an "egoist", as Mr. Meredith, adopting current slang, writes the word which used to be "egotist" ' (*Saturday Review*, 15 November 1879). John Goode in an important discussion of the novel which sets it in various of its contemporary intellectual contexts, refers to the *OED* definitions of 'egoist', 'emphasizing

. . . that "egoist" re-enters the English language between the mid-fifties and mid-seventies with a renewed connotative force—linking it with the attempt to find a basis for human conduct in empirical scientific discourse' (*The Egoist*: Anatomy or Striptease?', 207). It should be recalled in addition that Meredith encountered current ideas and concerns in personal contexts. His friend Leslie Stephen (from whom Vernon Whitford is drawn: see note to p. 10), in an essay on 'Humour' published in the *Cornhill Magazine* for March 1876, observed that 'the humorist must also be an egotist. The oddities of his own character give him the utmost delight' (quoted by Robert Bernard Martin, *The Triumph of Wit: A Study of Victorian Comic Theory*, Oxford, 1974, 88). Meredith's comment in a letter to Robert Louis Stevenson, 'It is a Comedy, with only half of me in it'—*Letters*, 569—may be pertinent; likewise Meredith's observation to Stevenson concerning Sir Willoughby Patterne, 'my dear fellow, . . . he is all of us' ('Books Which Have Influenced Me', 1887, in *Meredith: The Critical Heritage*, ed. Ioan Williams, London, 1971, 521). Martin elsewhere points out that Stephen's essay, and another, 'Ridicule and Truth' by James Sully—who was also known to Meredith—published in the *Cornhill Magazine* in May 1877, 'may well have contributed to George Meredith's consideration of comedy' (p. 15).

to strip himself stark naked: an echo of the clothes imagery so prominent in Carlyle's *Sartor Resartus* (1833–4), and in Meredith's earlier novel *Evan Harrington; or, He would be a Gentleman* (1860), in which the titular hero is ashamed of being descended from a tailor. A number of entries in the *Notebooks* are similarly preoccupied with the idea of the naked truth: e.g. 'Facts are like men, they may be born naked; but they are soon compelled to wear the clothing. They make us sinners respectable. At the first birth they are bear [*sic*], but to repeat, what is called naked fact is very blameable' (p. 2).

6 *Willoughby . . . Patterne*: see the Introduction for discussion of the significance of the name and its allusion to the story of the Willow Pattern plate. Lionel Stevenson in his Riverside edition of *The Egoist* offers a conjecture, which he attributes to Nevil Coghill, about the unusual name Crossjay, given to Willoughby's kinsman who appears in the next paragraph: it 'may refer to the identifying mark of two Js, crossed back to back, used on Minton china. In this sense the Crossjay Patternes, father and son, might represent the solid English virtues in contrast with Willoughby's

artificiality' (Boston, Mass., 1958, p. xviii). See further comments on names in notes to pp. 9, 10, 13, 18, 32, 178, and 211.

death to younger sons: the law of primogeniture, the custom by which property or a title descends to the eldest son, was introduced into England at the Norman Conquest. It is intended to prevent fragmentation of property.

the Marines: the Royal Marine was established by Charles II in 1664, specially recruited troops being trained for service at sea and in land operations carried out in connection with naval campaigns. Its status relative to the Navy is indicated by the colloquial saying, expressing incredulity, 'That will do for the marines, but the sailors won't believe it' (*OED*, citation from 1823).

the storming . . . the coast of China: British military and mercantile forces combined to penetrate China in the mid-nineteenth century. Lieutenant Patterne's exploit, as part of an attack on a fortification situated on the bank of a river, would have taken place during the Second Chinese (Opium) War of 1856–8, or the third in 1860.

7 *the great dispensary*: as is spelt out on the next page, this is Willoughby's term for chance or fate—a phrase which, though it has a connotation from alchemy, attempts to contain and regulate the apparently irrational within verifiable scientific procedures such as are carried out in dispensing medicines.

the black dragon on a yellow ground: the armies of the Qing dynasty which ruled China from the seventeenth century to 1911 were organized under banners (companies). The dragon, along with clouds, waves, and mountains, was a frequent ceremonial emblem. Yellow was the emperor's colour.

celestial prisoners: the use of 'celestial' to mean 'Chinese' derives from a translation of one of the native names for the Chinese Empire.

a Tudor . . . a Plantagenet: the Tudors reigned in England and Wales from 1485 (Henry VII) to 1603 (Elizabeth I); the Plantagenets reigned in England from 1154 (Henry II) to 1485 (Richard III). Descendants of these royal houses may now be butchers or furniture-makers.

8 '*on his hat, his coat, his feet, or anything that was his*': an echo of the tenth commandment as phrased in the Anglican catechism ('Thou shalt not covet thy neighbour's house, thou shalt not

covet thy neighbour's wife, nor his servant, nor his maid, nor his ox, nor his ass, nor any thing that is his').

9 *the day of Sir Willoughby's majority*: his coming of age at the age of 21, and entering into full control of his property. Significant birthdays of the heir figure also in Meredith's earlier novel *The Ordeal of Richard Feverel*.

the remembered, if not the right, thing: Meredith's fascination with the power of epithet was intense. Compare the reflections in his notebooks: 'A brilliant saying arrests thought: a simple observation instigates it: an idea that fixes the mind to itself cannot be of entire truth: one that leads it forth, altho' it be into the darkness, is the better guide. What we desire to hit is around us, not ahead, and moving with us, around us' (*c.*1862; *Notebooks*, 50).

Laetitia Dale: another significantly named character—her given name is Latin, 'gladness'; her family name signifies someone who lives in a valley (and by implication, in seclusion).

10 *Vernon Whitford: . . . 'a Phoebus Apollo turned fasting friar'*: Phoebus (expressing the brightness of the sun) and Apollo are alternative names for the Greek god of music, poetry, and all the fine arts, as well as of medicine. The character of Vernon Whitford was drawn—at least in some aspects—from Leslie Stephen (1832–1904), whom Meredith had met in Vienna in 1866. See *Letters*, 658: 'If you remember Vernon Whitford of the *Egoist*, it is a sketch of L. Stephen, but merely a sketch, not doing him full justice, though the strokes within and without are correct' (8 April 1882). See Norman Kelvin, *A Troubled Eden: Nature and Society in the Works of George Meredith* (Stanford, Calif., 1961), 110–12, for discussion of Meredith's transformation of his rationalist friend. At the time when *The Egoist* was written, Stephen was well established in the world of letters. Among other books he had published a collection of essays on the pleasures of the Alps, *The Playground of Europe* (1871). He had been appointed editor of the *Cornhill Magazine* in 1871, a position he relinquished in 1882 when he undertook what is generally regarded as his major achievement, the editorship of the *Dictionary of National Biography*. In 1879 Stephen was a prime mover in arranging the 'Sunday Tramps', a group which walked the Surrey countryside, Meredith among them. His first wife, 'Minny' (neé Harriet Marian Thackeray), died in 1875. Stephen wrote of her, 'My Minny shared my love of the Alps. She was not, indeed, a walker but she heartily enjoyed the life and the scenery. We spent our honeymoon in

Switzerland' (*Sir Leslie Stephen's Mausoleum Book*, ed. Alan Bell, Oxford, 1977, p. 20; see also p. xvii for Bell's comments on the way in which for Stephen 'The Alps became a holy place largely because of their close connection with the "saints" he married'). It would seem that Minny's attachment to the Alps may inform the depiction of Clara Middleton. Meredith's work on the novel almost exactly coincided with the period of Stephen's widowerhood: on 26 March 1878 he married the widow Julia Duckworth (née Jackson, 1846–95). The four children of this union included Virginia Woolf, who took her father as the basis for the character of Mr Ramsay in her novel *To the Lighthouse* (1927).

Vernon as a Christian name, said to derive from the Greek word for the alder tree, came into use in the late nineteenth century (*The Oxford Dictionary of English Christian Names*, ed. E. G. Withycombe, 1945; 3rd edn. 1977, mentions Vernon Whitford as an early example). The surname Whitford means 'white ford', reinforcing the character's association with the natural world.

Ciceronian eulogy: Marcus Tullius Cicero (106–43 BC) was Rome's greatest orator, and a staunch upholder of republican principles. Cicero is referred to again on pp. 12 and 197, and quoted at p. 203.

Hebe: Greek goddess of youth, for a time cup-bearer to the gods.

Mrs. Mountstuart's quiet little touch of nature: an echo of a phrase of Shakespeare's Ulysses in *Troilus and Cressida*, III. iii. 175, 'One touch of nature makes the whole world kin'.

Alcibiades: a brilliant but unscrupulous Athenian politician and military commander (c.460–404 BC).

Louis XIV perruquier: a wig-maker (perruquier) working in the style of the French King Louis XIV would produce abundant and opulent curls. Louis XIV, the Sun King (1638–1715), remains a symbol of absolute monarchy, and of the splendour of the baroque style. The association of Willoughby with this figure is developed later in the novel: see e.g. pp. 141, 171, and 379.

11 *Arcadian*: Arcadia, a mountainous district in ancient Greece, was proverbial for the contented pastoral simplicity of its people (cf. p. 450).

the Martyr Charles . . . reigned: Charles I (1600–49) was martyred (in the eyes of his Royalist followers) when executed by Oliver Cromwell's Puritans. His son, Charles II (1630–85), 'the Merry Monarch', was restored to the throne in 1660, and his court was the scene of much greater licence than had prevailed during

Cromwell's Protectorate. The conflict of Cavalier and Roundhead significantly represents not only oppositions of sexual and social styles, but also the political opposition, fought over in the Civil Wars of 1640–60, between the divine right of kings upheld by the Royalists, and the rights of the people, upheld by the Roundhead parliamentarians.

an English cavalier: the term 'cavalier' derives from the Italian for horseman or knight, and carries overtones of courtly gallantry. The supporters of Charles I in the English Civil War were known as Cavaliers.

12 *the leg of Rochester, Buckingham, Dorset, Suckling*: all English men of letters of the seventeenth century. John Wilmot, second earl of Rochester (1647–80), George Villiers, second duke of Buckingham (1628–87), and Charles Sackville, sixth earl of Dorset (1638–1706), were favourites of Charles II; Sir John Suckling (1609–41) was one of the most brilliant of the witty Cavalier poets associated with the court of Charles I. Here as elsewhere throughout the passage on the leg, there is play on the expression, 'to make a leg', meaning to bow deeply.

valiance: (archaic) a valiant act or deed; a feat of valour or bravery (*OED*: this usage is cited).

Jove playing carpet-knight: Jove is one of the names of Jupiter, the most powerful of all the gods of classical mythology. 'Carpet-knight' is a contemptuous term for a warrior whose achievements belong to 'the carpet', the domestic scene, rather than to the field of battle. The *double entendre* of the whole passage is reinforced by the implication that a limb capable of great actions is not utilized to its full potential.

13 *Constantia Durham (whom Mrs. Mountstuart called 'The Racing Cutter')*: Mrs. Mountstuart's epithet perhaps shares the cynical, bawdy spirit of Restoration comedy as well as echoing Mirabel's description of Millamant in Congreve's *The Way of the World* (1700), quoted by Meredith in *Essay on Comedy*: 'Here she comes, i' faith, full sail, with her fan spread, and her streamers out, and a shoal of fools for tenders' (p. 20). Cf. the description of Clara at pp. 175–6. The association of women with yachts under sail occurs elsewhere in Meredith's fiction, a notable instance being the description of the *Esperanza* and her owner Cecilia Halkett in chapter XV of *Beauchamp's Career* (1876). Although a craft designed for speed, like a cutter, can be a splendid sight under sail, it is none the less subject to wind and current: hence the

image conveys woman's dependence on a guiding (male) power. Constantia of course belies her given name by proving inconstant to Willoughby.

Indian Gods: probably Buddhas, or various Hindu gods.

16 *Theseus . . . Ariadne*: Theseus, one of the most celebrated heroes of antiquity, was rescued from the maze of the Minotaur by following a thread laid by Ariadne, daughter of Minos, King of Crete.

a 'salvage,' or green, man: the conventional representation of a savage in heraldry and pageants; a human figure naked or enveloped in foliage.

Sir Roger de Coverley: an air and a country dance after which a character in the early eighteenth-century *Spectator* papers of Addison and Steele is named.

a widow unmarried a second time: Willoughby's phobia about widows is vehemently expressed here and subsequently (for example, see p. 50; also note to p. 20). Meredith's notebooks contain a number of entries to do with widows, an obsession connected with his unhappy first marriage to the young widow Mary Ellen Peacock Nicolls: see *Notebooks*, 136–7.

17 *slings and arrows*: alludes to 'The slings and arrows of outrageous fortune' considered by Prince Hamlet in *Hamlet*, III. i. 58.

metropolitan conquests, not to be recited: the sexual double standard is evident here. Willoughby's amorous exploits with London women (ladies of easy virtue?) need not be taken into account as he plans marriage, while the virginal purity of any potential bride is paramount to him.

18 *A young Captain Oxford*: 'Captain Oxford is named after the University and a street in central London, both societies where Willoughby's peculiar predominance is subject to challenge' (Norton Critical Edition). Clara attributes further significance to this name by her confusion of it with 'Whitford': see pp. 129–30 and 136.

19 *the devotee of Juggernaut*: Jaganath, 'lord of the world', is the form under which the Hindu god Krishna is worshipped in his temple of Puri. His devotees were popularly supposed to fling themselves under the wheels of the wagon carrying his image on his feast day.

20 *a woman to be burnt*: the allusion is to the Hindu practice of suttee, in which the widow incinerates herself on her husband's funeral pyre. See *Notebooks*, 31, 39, and 136–7; and see note to p. 369.

22 *hussar*: a member of a light cavalry regiment. Hussars had a glamorous image, partly because of their brightly coloured and elaborate uniforms, and also because of their tactical role as skirmishers.

23 *a Samaritan soul*: the parable of the good Samaritan, who stopped to help an injured man by the roadside when others of higher standing had passed him by, is told in Luke 10: 25–37.

24 *the Infernal of Paris*: Robert M. Adams in his Norton Critical Edition says that 'The "Infernal of Paris" was the ruling clique of the French Revolution', but I have been unable to find independent corroboration for this claim, or any more plausible explanation than that the phrase refers in a general way to the diabolic aspects of Parisian life (French, *l'enfer*, hell, the nether world).

25 *The President*: it is reasonable to assume that Willoughby's travels took place during the term of office of the eighteenth President, Ulysses S. Grant (1869–77). Grant's father was a tanner; Grant himself a military man who led the Union forces to victory in the Civil War. His presidency was plagued by administrative and financial scandal.

to lash terga cauda: to lash from side to side—a pig-Latin expression.

26 *He found . . . squeezed him passionately*: this telling image of Willoughby's egoism alludes to the myth of the beautiful youth Narcissus, who fell in love with his own reflection in a fountain and eventually killed himself because he could never seize the object of his desire.

31 *yaffles*: green woodpeckers.

32 *her Christian name was Clara*: again there is insistence on the significance of names. For all her bright beauty, Clara is not as clear and transparent as Sir Willoughby thinks.

34 *her of Ephesus*: a reference to a tale told by Eumolpus, in Petronius' *Satyricon* 111–12, about a widow of Ephesus who devotedly mourned by her dead husband's body for five days, until a sentry ordered to guard the crucified bodies of three criminals persuaded her to eat, and then to enjoy with him other pleasures of the flesh. During the soldier's absence from guard duty, one of the bodies was removed from the cross: in order to save her lover from punishment, the widow gave over the corpse of her husband to hang in its place.

34 *'Platonism'*: the Greek philosopher Plato originally formulated in the context of a homosexual relationship the idea of a love which could rise above sexual desire, but by the sixteenth century the sense in which 'Platonism' is used here, of a spiritualized heterosexual love, was recognized.

36 *Egeria*: a nymph who inspired the Roman philosopher-king Numa (*fl. c.*700 BC), second of the seven kings of Rome. According to Ovid, after the death of Numa Egeria melted into tears and was changed into a fountain by the goddess Diana (*Metamorphoses* 15). Egeria is invoked again on p. 361.

37 *A deeper student of Science*: the ruminations attributed to Willoughby in this paragraph suggest his acquaintance with evolutionary ideas. He offers a version of Charles Darwin's theories of Natural Selection, as propounded in *The Origin of Species* (1859: see especially the account of sexual selection in bantams in chapter IV), and further developed in later works like *The Descent of Man* (1871). It is not clear how much of Darwin Meredith had actually read, though the extent of his interest in evolution is abundantly clear from his writing.

40 *a babe's caul against shipwreck*: the caul is the thin membrane, which, if covering a child's head at birth, is supposed to bring good luck and to be an infallible preservative against drowning.

the fair western-eastern: George Eliot, reviewing Meredith's *The Shaving of Shagpat*, compared his use of Oriental forms to Goethe's in his cycle of love poems, *West-östlicher Divan* (1819): 'thoroughly Western in spirit, though Eastern in its forms' (*Leader*, 5 January 1856). The phrase here seems to refer to a contest of west and east in which male tendencies to primitive oriental behaviour have been overcome by civilized, occidental, female powers.

41 *'a dainty rogue in porcelain'*: 'rogue', in addition to its usual sense of a dishonest person, a vagabond, someone of a mischievous disposition, has a biological usage, i.e. an individual varying markedly from the normal, usually inferior—as in the expression 'rogue elephant' to indicate one who lives apart from the herd, of a savage disposition.

42 *the women of Leonardo, the angels of Luini*: the painter Bernardino Luini (d. 1532) was influenced by Leonardo da Vinci (1452–1519) during the latter's second stay in Milan, 1506–13. Luini frequently painted the Virgin Mary; Leonardo's best-known female subject is of course the *Mona Lisa*.

47 *basiation's obscurity*: in effect, kissing in dark corners. The sole *OED* citation for *basiation* is this passage: the word derives ultimately from Latin, and means 'kissing'.

retro Sathanas!: (Latin) get thee behind me, Satan!: Matthew 16: 23, Mark 8: 33.

52 *father-in-law*: now used only in the sense of the father of one's husband or wife; but well into the nineteenth century the term was used as here to mean stepfather.

54 *and see the Alps*: Meredith's own pleasure in the Alps is amply attested: see *Letters*, 90–116, describing the first of his extended visits (in particular, p. 93: 'My first sight of the Alps has raised odd feelings. Here at last seems something more than earth, and visible, if not tangible'); also *Notebooks*, 47–8 and 60–1. Throughout his fiction from *The Ordeal of Richard Feverel* (1859) to *The Amazing Marriage* (1895), Meredith used Alpine settings, mainly for scenes of particular significance.

60 *Dian-like*: like a representation of the chaste goddess Diana. See note to p. 444.

67 *like the mythological Titan at war with Jove*: Jupiter, while still a child, conquered the gigantic Titans who had imprisoned his father Saturn for breaking a vow to raise no male children.

70 *Mary Ambree . . . the Amazons*: an anthology of redoubtable women. Mary Ambree was a legendary English heroine supposed to have taken part in the Siege of Ghent in 1584, when that town was held by the Spaniards: her exploits form the subject of a ballad published in 1680. Hannah Snell (1723–92) enlisted as a soldier and received a pension after being wounded on service at Pondicherry, a French colony on the coast south of Madras in India; she also served in the fleet and appeared on the stage in the mid-1750s to sing about her nautical adventures as James Gray. The William Taylor in question is likely to be the fortunate husband of Elizabeth. Their story is told in a song dating from the early eighteenth century, 'The Female Sailor's Garland'. As they were on the point of marriage, William was seized by the press-gang, whereupon Elizabeth dressed as a man and signed on as a sailor. She was eventually discovered, but so impressed the captain that he used his influence to find William and arrange their wedding. Joan of Arc (1412–31) contributed to the liberation of France from the English in the reign of Charles VII. Meredith made notes for a play about her in the 1850s—see *Notebooks*, 31–4, and 137–8. Boadicea was queen of the Iceni in the

east of Britain, who fought against the Romans in the first century AD. The Amazons were a legendary race of female warriors said to live in Scythia, a region which would now form part of Russia.

the glorious Valentine's day of our naval annals: 14 February 1797, when the British fleet under Admiral Sir John Jervis in his flagship the *Captain*, defeated the Spanish in the battle of Cape St Vincent.

71 *half-crown pieces . . . sovereigns*: the half-crown coin was worth two shillings and sixpence; there were eight of them to the pound sterling (sovereign coin). A tabulation of average weekly male wages in England and Wales in 1867 gives the wage of a sailor as from fifteen shillings to one pound (Geoffrey Best, *Mid-Victorian Britain 1851–75*, London, 1971, 97): a tip of a sovereign to young Crossjay, then, can fairly be thought of as equivalent to the weekly earnings of his father the marine.

72 *Robinson Crusoe's old goat in the cavern*: in the twenty-third year of his residence on the island, Robinson Crusoe—in Daniel Defoe's 1719 novel of that name—finds a cave in the earth. Exploring it, he is frightened by 'two broad shining Eyes of some Creature, whether Devil or Man I knew not' (World's Classics edition, ed. J. Donald Crowley, Oxford, 1981, 177). The creature turns out to be a dying billy-goat.

74 *Flibbertigibbet*: the name of a devil or fiend.

Mont Blanc: the highest peak in the Alps. The first recorded ascent was in 1786.

billman: a footsoldier armed with a bill—that is, a shafted weapon with a broad hook-shaped blade and a spike at the back.

75 *"mulier formosa"*: the reference is to the opening sentence of Horace's *Ars Poetica* which ridicules the incongruity of a figure which 'at the top is a lovely woman', passes through the neck of a horse and feathered limbs, and 'ends below in a black and ugly fish'. Horace is making the point that painters and poets have a creative licence, but within certain limits.

78 *Vestal*: consecrated to Vesta, goddess of the hearth and hearth fire; the Vestal virgins were priestesses of ancient Rome, robed always in white.

80 *Busby*: Dr Richard Busby was headmaster of Westminster School from 1638 to 1695, and notorious for flogging.

Horse him and birch him: have the boy to be flogged with birch rods lie over the back of another or over a chair.

81 *Prussians that must both march and think in step*: the effectiveness of the Prussian armies had been demonstrated during the Seven Weeks War of 1866, against Austria, and more recently in the Franco-Prussian War of 1870–1, which had been followed by the unification of Germany under Prussian leadership. Otto von Bismarck, in 1871 appointed first Chancellor of the German empire, initiated a series of reforms designed to achieve uniformity: a common currency, a central bank, and a single code of civil law for Germany.

84 *ad nauseam*: (Latin) to a disgusting extent.

88 *judgement before the wise King*: Solomon, who proposed that a child whose parentage was being disputed by two women should be cut in half (1 Kings 3: 16–28). The same incident is referred to on p. 394.

90 *his Etruscans or his Dorians*: his Latin and Greek studies (from Etruria, a region of Italy whose inhabitants were particularly noted for superstition and for opposition to the power of Rome; and Doria, a region of Greece near Athens).

98 *hommes d'esprit*: (French) men of spirit and wit. Meredith's own wit is at work with a kind of pun on the name of the cook, who serves the inner man but is called Dehors (French, 'outside').

99 *There's a French philosopher . . . who takes April 1st*: Auguste Comte (1798–1857), the founder of the philosophy of Positivism, which recognizes only positive facts and observable phenomena. Comte's influence in England in the 1860s and 1870s was profound, and at the time Meredith was working on *The Egoist* he was in close contact with English positivists such as Frederic Harrison, John Morley, and Leslie Stephen. Comte proposed that the calendar of his Religion of Humanity—a religion which took as its object of worship Humanity conceived as a single corporate being—should celebrate benefactors of the human race: Willoughby here mocks the idea, narrowing the field to three French men of letters— Jean-Jacques Rousseau (1712–78); Voltaire (1694–1778); Jean Racine (1639–99)—who have in common a satiric and democratic spirit derived from their opposition to the civil and ecclesiastical establishments of their day. 1 April, April Fool's Day, gives licence for practical jokes and such misrule, and is therefore, Willoughby implies, an especially appropriate date for inclusion in so ridiculous a calendar as Comte's seems to him to be.

105 *Perseus*: in classical mythology, Perseus delivered Andromeda, who had been tied naked to a rock, from a sea-monster. The same

myth is alluded to on pp. 158 and 345. Joseph A. Kestner's discussion of the ways British painters used classical motifs and legends in representing women in *Mythology and Misogyny: The Social Discourse of Nineteenth-century British Classical-Subject Painting* (Madison, Wis., 1989) is relevant to a consideration of Meredith's classical allusions.

106 *another name for Oxford*: a Freudian slip before Freud. Clara's slip of the tongue betrays the growth of her feeling for Vernon Whitford, who is to come to stand in the same relation to her as Harry Oxford to Constantia Durham. See also pp. 129–30; and Sir Willoughby's dismissive association of Oxford and Whitford, p. 19. Freud in the chapter on 'Slips of the Tongue' in *The Psychopathology of Everyday Life* quotes extensively from Ernest Jones's discussion of this passage, and may be taken to indicate tacit agreement with Jones's description of *The Egoist* as 'the masterpiece of the greatest English novelist, George Meredith' (Standard Edition of the Complete Psychological Works of Sigmund Freud, ed. James Strachey, London, 1960, vi. 98).

119 *Melusine*: a water-sprite of French legend, part woman, part fish. She married a mortal, and turned into a serpent when he broke a promise to her.

120 *Piedmontese Bersaglieri*: infantrymen from the Piedmont region of northern Italy.

122 *Styria*: an Alpine province of Austria.

130 *barouche*: a four-wheeled carriage with a seat outside for the driver, seats in the body of the carriage for two couples facing, and a folding hood,.

137 *Possession without obligation . . . approaches felicity*: a version of one of Meredith's favourite apophthegms. Compare ' "Sentimentalists," says THE PILGRIM'S SCRIP, "are they who seek to enjoy Reality without incurring the Immense Debtorship for a thing done" ' (*The Ordeal of Richard Feverel*, World's Classics edition, ed. John Halperin, Oxford, 1984, 213). This sententia is slightly adapted as a telegram in James Joyce's *Ulysses*: '*The sentimentalist is he who would enjoy without incurring the immense debtorship for a thing done.* Signed: Dedalus' (1922; Penguin edition, ed. Hans Walter Gabler, 1986, 164).

(sauf votre respect): (French) begging your pardon.

Parsee: a descendant of those Persians who fled to India in the seventh and eighth centuries to escape Muslim persecution and preserve their Zoroastrian religion. The following sentences refer to the dualism of Zoroastrianism, and, in the reference to the sun, to its fire-worship (of which Meredith had made much in *The Ordeal of Richard Feverel*).

138 *emulgence*: the action of milking out. The *OED* has two citations for this word, the present instance and one from 1674.

142 *under Moslem law*: a basic social precept of Islam is that marriage should be encouraged, to which end polygamy is permitted. The number of wives a man may have at any one time is limited to four. See also note to p. 205.

156 *Heinsius*: Daniel Heinsius (1580–1665) was a Dutch scholar and editor of Aristotle. His son Nicholas (1620–81) was also a famous classical scholar.

158 *the hero . . . the yawning mouth-abyss*: again, the myth of Perseus, flying with Mercury's wings to the rescue of Andromeda. See notes to pp. 105 and 345.

171 *the Gallican courtier of any period from Louis Treize to Louis Quinze*: a member of the French court between the beginning of the reign of Louis XIII in 1610 and the end of the reign of Louis XV in 1774. The system of royal absolutism against which the revolution of 1789 was directed began under Louis XIII and developed fully in the long reign (1643–1715) of his son Louis XIV—to whom Sir Willoughby is elsewhere likened (e.g. p. 379). See Meredith's comments on the court of Louis XIV in *Essay on Comedy*, p. 12 (quoted in the Introduction).

175 *ad inferas*: (Latin) to the infernal regions, hell.

Calypso-clad: dressed like the nymph who beguiled Odysseus.

176 *above the breeze*: see notes to pp. 13 and 275.

177 *the Loves. Not the Graces*: in classical mythology, the Graces were the goddesses, usually three in number, who bestowed beauty and charm: Aglaia (brightness), Euphrosyne (joyfulness), and Thalia (bloom).

178 *I've a superstition that Flitch ought to drive you from the church-door*: the name of the banished coachman means literally a side of bacon. De Craye's 'superstition' may well derive from the custom, begun in the Essex village of Dunmow in the thirteenth century and revived in 1855, of awarding a flitch of bacon (the Dunmow Flitch) to a married couple who will take an oath that they have lived through the year without strife.

179 *these fits of Irish*: Meredith, who was proud of his own Welsh and Irish ancestry, made much of the temperamental differences between the mercurial Celt and other more phlegmatic races, like the Saxon (as at p. 191), generally privileging the superior intuitive powers of the Celt. See *Notebooks* 150; and *Essay on Comedy*, 52–3, where the French are seen as having access to the Comic Spirit in a way denied to the Germans.

184 *fire rather than ice*: Clara's self-analysis here draws on the belief in ancient and medieval philosophy that all material bodies are compounded of four elements: earth, water, air, and fire.

185 *quid femina possit*: what a woman is capable of. From a sentence in Virgil's *Aeneid*, v, which translates as 'Knowledge of what a woman can do in the madness of dishonoured love aroused uneasy forebodings in the Trojan's hearts.'

   semper eadem: (Latin) always the same.

   "this the seat, this mournful gloom for that celestial light?": Satan speaking in Milton's *Paradise Lost*:

   Is this the Region, this the Soil, the Clime,
   Said then the lost Archangel, this the seat
   That we must change for Heav'n, this mournful gloom
   For that celestial light?
   (Oxford Standard Authors edition, ed. Helen Darbishire,
                               1958, Book I, ll. 242–5).

186 *"Quod autem . . . puto medicum"*: Dr Middleton translates his quotations from Petronius, *Satyricon* 56. As is the case with several of the learned doctor's classical quotations, he alludes to a situation in which a licence of a kind intolerable to Sir Willoughby is permitted—here, to the orgy of Trimalchio's feast. The phrases quoted immediately follow a poem addressed to luxury which refers to an unfaithful wife. The second part of the quotation is selective: Trimalchio says, '*ego puto medicum et nummularium*' ('I think the doctor and the money-lender').

188 *'Factum est; laetus est; amantium irae, etc.'*: the first two clauses appear to be Dr Middleton's own Latin phraseology: 'It is done; he is happy.' He then alludes to Terence, *Andria* 555: '*Amantium irae amoris integratio est*' ('Lovers' quarrels are the renewal of love').

191 *Rowena*: the fair Saxon lady in Scott's *Ivanhoe* (1819).

   'Are you of the rebel party, Colonel de Craye?': that is, are you seeking self-government for Ireland? The issue of Home Rule was to

become prominent in the 1880s, though at the time the novel was being written it was already of active concern. Charles Stewart Parnell, who was to become identified with the cause, was elected MP for Meath in 1875 and president of the Irish National Land League in 1878.

192 *a two-act piece*: by the time of the action of *The Egoist*, the practice of including more than one play on an evening's bill was beginning to decline, at least in London. The 'two-act piece' concocted here is a farce, or after-piece, picking up on the convention of the comic stage-Irishman which dates at least from the eighteenth century. *The Irishman in Spain* has a faint affinity (through the Irish hero) with Meredith's posthumously-published novel, *Celt and Saxon* (1910, but begun in the 1870s), and also (through the name Don Beltran) with his play, *The Satirist*, written in the late 1870s, at about the same time as *The Egoist*: see Gillian Beer, 'George Meredith and *The Satirist*', *Review of English Studies*, 15 (1964), 283–95, and *Notebooks*, 88 and 196. Willoughby is conspicuously absent from the cast, lacking the facility to adopt any other persona.

the Prado: the fashionable promenade of Madrid.

the last portrait of Britannia: his last penny—from the image of Britannia on the English coin.

194 *the sentinel at Pompeii*: a man who stayed at his post during the eruption of Vesuvius in AD 79. Excavation of the site of the ancient city fourteen miles south-east of Naples began in 1709, but was put on a systematic basis in 1860 by the Italian archaeologist Giuseppe Fiorelli. Among other things, Fiorelli developed a technique for making casts of bodies on the site by pouring cement into the hollows formed in the volcanic ash when the bodies disintegrated.

solde: pay, especially of soldiers.

196 *nugae*: trifling jests.

a comfortable pride in his digestion: Dr Middleton, scholar and epicure, has affinities with Adrian Harley in Meredith's early novel, *The Ordeal of Richard Feverel*. There may be some envy on Meredith's part, since one of his friends coined the nickname 'the Dyspeptic' for him.

197 *Cicero's Tullia*: Tullia was a thrice-married daughter of the Roman orator and statesman (see note to p. 10) to whom he was devoted. She died in childbirth in 45 BC.

198 *senior Hocks*: considerable correspondence was generated in the *Times Literary Supplement* by a letter from Lord Simon asking 'What were these hocks whose lasting powers could be compared by Dr Middleton with those of port?' (12 February 1971, 183). Lord Simon said that 'The 1921 hocks lasted well up to the beginning of the war of 1939 (and possibly, for all I know, even longer).' Other correspondents wrote in about their experiences of aged white wines, with a number of drinkable wines around forty years old being reported (26 February, 5 and 12 March). Julian Jeffs (5 March, 271) explained that 'The taste for fresh, young German wines is a comparatively recent one. In the last century age was esteemed in white wines, particularly those of Germany, and in Champagne', adding a quotation from Thomas George Shaw's *Wine, the Vine, and the Cellar* (1864), on the manufacture by the addition of burnt sugar or fortified wine of 'what is called "old brown hock", formerly in great repute in this country, but now replaced by purer, young wines'.

the Idaean Three: the goddesses Aphrodite, Athene, and Hera, who on Mount Ida near Troy competed for a prize of a golden apple, awarded by the mortal Paris to the most beautiful.

Port is the Homeric hexameter, Burgundy the Pindaric dithyramb: Dr Middleton enlists his passion for classical scholarship to rank other objects of his passions. His favourite wine, port, has the supreme status of the epics attributed to Homer, the *Iliad* and the *Odyssey*, which are written in lines of six metric feet (hexameters). Burgundy has fine but lesser qualities, likened to the works of the Greek lyric poet Pindar (*c*.522–443 BC). The dithyramb is a choral lyric, originally in honour of Dionysus or Bacchus, and hence vehement and wild.

"Graiis, . . . praeter laudem, nullius avaris": Horace, *Ars Poetica*, ll. 323–4: 'To the Greeks, who craved naught but glory'.

202 *a wine for Tithonus*: Aurora, goddess of the dawn, was enamoured of the Trojan Tithonus, whom she made immortal, without granting him also eternal youth. Willoughby does not apprehend Dr Middleton's jocund suggestion that the old wine has great potency.

203 *Hippocrene*: a fountain sacred to the Muses.

"Mulier tum bene olet": a modification of a line from Cicero's *Letters to Atticus*, ii, which Dr Middleton translates in the following sentence.

203 *"Ut flos . . . Sic virgo, dum . . ."*: 'As the flower is born unseen in an enclosed garden . . . So a virgin . . .' (Catullus, *Carmina*, lxii, 39, 45). The passage adverted to by Dr Middleton reflects on the loss of favour among her family and friends experienced by a maiden who surrenders her virginity.

205 *yet are we not turbaned Orientals . . . Moslem*: a further reference to the inferior status and treatment of women in the Orient at large and in the Islamic world in particular (see e.g. note to p. 142). In the *Essay on Comedy* 30–1 there is explicit discussion of attitudes to women among Arabs.

206 *I am fitter to drive the horses of the sun*: Dr Middleton expresses his ecstatic response to the wine by reference to Phaethon who was permitted by Phoebus to drive the flying horses of the sun for just one day. Phaethon forgot his instructions, the sun went off course, and Jupiter had to intervene to save the world from incineration.

211 *His name was Horace*: the Roman poet (65–8 BC), whose works were among the standard texts for a classical education in England. The induction of Clara into such studies was not of course typical of the education of a Victorian girl—and elsewhere in the novel classical quotation and reference are largely the preserve of Dr Middleton and Vernon Whitford.

'*modus agri non ita magnus*': 'a piece of land, not so very large' (Horace, *Satires*, II. vi. 1). The poet Horace retired to his farm in the Sabine Hills, near Rome, in 32 BC; the military Horace, in considering emigration, may be influenced by Canada's having achieved the status of a Dominion in 1867.

'*Quae virtus et quanta sit vivere parvo*': Clara's recollection is of Horace, *Satires*, II. ii. 1, 'What and how great, my friends, is the virtue of frugal living'—a line reminiscent also of *Odes*, II. xvi, where the poet claims to 'live well on a little'.

233 *Saturnalia*: festival in honour of the god Saturn, celebrated in mid-December, and notable for the abandonment of most customary constraints.

236 *my solitary way . . . Paradise forfeited*: the closing lines of Milton's *Paradise Lost* are significantly recalled in the speech of contrition Willoughby is attributing to Clara:

> The World was all before them, where to choose
> Thir place of rest, and Providence thir guide:
> They hand in hand with wandring steps and slow,

Through *Eden* took thir solitarie way.
(Oxford Standard Authors edition, ed. Helen Darbishire,
1958, Book XII, ll. 646–9)

241 *the poet's Lesbia, the poet's Beatrice*: the Roman poet Catullus (*c*.84–*c*.54 BC) addressed many of his verses to the carnal Lesbia (see also note to p. 242). The Florentine Dante Alighieri (1265–1321) celebrates Beatrice in the *Vita Nuova* and the *Divina Commedia* as the quintessence of womanly spirituality.

242 *Lesbia Quadrantaria*: Lesbia was the name by which Catullus addressed his mistress Clodia in love poems. The women in question was thought to be so depraved as to sell herself very cheaply: the term 'Quadrantaria' means something like 'worth a farthing'.

antre: cave.

243 *With . . . the soul*: I cannot identify a source for these lines.

244 *Mr. Merriman's witticisms*: presumably from one of the books of jokes referred to above.

248 *a Tuscan popular canzone*: the air Clara chooses appears to have a religious theme, suggested by the reference to 'the most holy Virgin Mary' below.

249 *bile tumet jecur*: the liver swells with bile (Horace, *Odes*, I. xiii. 4). The phrase has the sense of being in a rage.

251 *και τρισκακοδαίμων*: (Greek) 'and three bad devils', triply unfortunate.

257 *Hermann's praise of the versus dochmiachus*: Gottfried Hermann (1772–1848) wrote a book on Greek metres, of which the dochmiac is one frequently used by the dramatists.

265 *to leave me her fortune*: a kind of situation that interested Meredith. Similar macabre accounts of thwarted marriages or inheritances are to be found in the *Notebooks*: see especially 68.

275 *the springing and chiming South-west was the next best thing*: again the association of the Alps and the south-west wind (see note to p. 2). The tonic effects of the south-westerly are favourites of Meredith as well as of Vernon: see *Letters*, e.g. pp. 591 and 1071, where he quotes Catullus as does Dr Middleton on p. 435; and also cf. note to p. 54 and the description of Clara on p. 176. The panegyric on the storm in the previous paragraph has counterparts among his poems, notably 'South-West Wind in the Woodland' (published in *Poems*, 1851) and 'The South-Wester' (in *A Reading of Earth*,

1888), both of which extol the wind as one which enables appreciation of the unity of the natural world.

280 *Walhalla*: in Scandinavian mythology, Valhalla is the hall in the celestial regions where the souls of heroes slain in battle spend eternity fighting and feasting.

282 *In vino veritas*: a venerable Latin tag, 'in wine is truth'.

dies solemnes: (Latin) literally 'solemn days', also meaning holidays.

288 *'Tom's a-cold'*: the phrase is repeatedly used in *King Lear*, III. iv, of Edgar on the heath disguised as a madman.

304 *your Green Man*: see note to p. 16.

306 *a kind of Jupiter's cupbearer:—Juno's if you like*: Ganymede was the best-known of Jupiter's cupbearers, thought to have ambiguous sexual preferences. Mrs Mountstuart's suggestion that De Craye may prefer to be Juno's cupbearer, however, probably recognizes his support for Clara, and could allude also to Juno's continual unhappiness on account of Jupiter's infidelities.

309 *a philippic upon woman's rights*: a bitter attack on a topical subject. The term 'philippic' is derived from the orations of Demosthenes against Philip of Macedon in defence of Athenian liberty in the fourth century BC. Activity directed towards establishing both the rights of Woman and of women intensified as the nineteenth century progressed, and by the 1870s, issues to do with the suffrage, education, and property rights, had emerged as matters of particular concern.

312 *gaze de Chambéry*: translucent gauzy fabric, named for the place in the south of France where it is woven.

314 *a Celtiberian Egnatius*: Catullus' poem xxxix is an attack on one of Lesbia's lovers (for Lesbia, see note to p. 242). Egnatius is presumably from a Roman family settled in Spain, and for Catullus' vituperative purposes it is convenient to describe him as connected with the savage Celtiberi, a people of north central Spain subdued with difficulty by Rome in the second century BC. Dr Middleton in this speech develops a web of allusions to Catullus' poem, which opens with a sneer at Egnatius' relentless smiling. He quotes ll. 6–7 ('Whatever time, whatever place, whatever he is doing, he grins'), and freely translates the following lines in the rest of the sentence. The poem alleges that the Celtiberi maintain their white teeth and pink gums by brushing their teeth with their own urine.

315 *morbus*: disease.

315 *Joe Millerisms*: *Joe Miller's Jests: or the wit's vade-mecum* (1739) was a jest-book assembled by John Mottley, and named after Joseph Miller (1684–1738), an actor in the Drury Lane company.

percoct: overdone, hackneyed. This passage is cited along with two seventeenth-century usages in the *OED*.

epitoniç: overstrained. This passage is the sole citation in the *OED*.

hari-kari: corruption of *hara-kiri*, the Japanese custom of suicide by disembowelment, particularly to avoid disgrace.

316 *ex improviso*: (Latin) on the spur of the moment.

319 *the Stagyrite*: the great philosopher Aristotle (384–322 BC), born at Stagira in Macedon.

322 *"at first sight"*: 'Who ever loved, that loved not at first sight?': Marlowe, *Hero and Leander*, i. 176.

323 *à propos*: (French) to the purpose, opportunely.

Fridolin: a page in *Der Gang nach der Eisenhammer*, by Schiller (1759–1805), who is unjustly accused of making love to his mistress, the Countess Cunigond. His accuser, the Count, plots to have Fridolin burnt alive, but is himself incinerated.

329 *oddly-garbed as the Pope's body-guard*: the Swiss Guard is a corps established by Pope Julius II in the early sixteenth century. It is recruited from among Swiss citizens and charged especially with the protection of the person of the pontiff. The Guard has several uniforms of which the best-known, referred to here, was designed by Michelangelo at the request of Julius II. It consists of a voluminous doublet and breeches striped in dark blue, red, and yellow.

the Infallible: the doctrine of the primacy and infallibility of the Pope was proclaimed by Pius IX in 1870, during the first Vatican Council. This doctrine accords the pontiff assurance against error when teaching the whole church on issues of faith and morals. Within three months of its proclamation, the last of the Papal States was annexed to the newly unified Italy by Victor Emmanuel II, leaving the Vatican politically impotent, and the Pope a prisoner in it.

330 *rara avis*: (Latin) rare bird.

332 *de trop*: (French) in excess, in the way.

334 *Moses . . . out of it*: it is perhaps significant that the context of this reference requires divine intervention to support the authority of

a leader. At a time during their wanderings in the desert when the Israelites were rebellious because they had no water, God instructed Moses to smite a rock, out of which water gushed (Exodus 17: 6).

340 *Rhadamanthine condemnation*: Rhadamanthus is a figure in classical mythology best known as judge of the underworld. However, as Clara points out, he also ruled some islands in the Aegean and many of the Greek cities in Asia.

a Triton ashore: the Tritons were sea-deities, half-man, half-fish.

345 *the chained-up Beauty*: another allusion to the predicament of Andromeda: see notes to pp. 105 and 158.

357 *Aspasia*: a mistress. A notable Aspasia was mistress to the Athenian statesman Pericles (d. 429 BC).

361 *carte blanche*: (French) white card; in English usage, unconditional authority.

my Egeria . . . his Cornelia: for Egeria, see note to p. 36. Cornelia, a member of the Roman family of the Scipios, was celebrated for her piety and learning. She had twelve children of whom only two sons and one daughter lived to adulthood. After the death of her husband in 154 BC, she refused an offer of marriage from Ptolemy VIII of Egypt in order to devote herself to her sons, the Gracchi. Both Tiberius (c.163–133 BC) and Gaius (153–121 BC) held office and attempted reforms in republican Rome. The daughter married the mighty Scipio Africanus.

362 *On revient toujours*: (French) one always comes back.

363 *a Jacobite lord under the Georges*: the Jacobites were followers of the House of Stuart, whose claims to the throne of Britain were finally destroyed in the rising of 1745. Several Scottish Jacobites were executed for their part in the rising against the authority of King George II. His father, George I of the German House of Hanover, had succeeded Queen Anne, the last Stuart monarch, in 1714; his grandson George III and great-grandson George IV provided the sequence of four Georges which ended with the succession of William IV in 1830.

364 *Toujours la porcelaine!*: (French) always porcelain!

365 *"it should have been the Willow Pattern"*: because of the likeness of the action being played out at Patterne Hall to the story depicted on Willow Pattern china. See Introduction and notes to pp. 1 and 6.

367 *the Republican cap—the Phrygian*: during the French Revolution of 1789, the long loose Phrygian cap was worn by many of the revolutionaries. Phrygia was a territory in Asia Minor in ancient times.

369 *in the Shades*: among the dead.

one of the Presidencies: each of the three divisions of the East India Company's territory on the Indian subcontinent was originally under the administration of a president.

in favour of Suttee: Meredith here uses a note made many years earlier: 'one who married a widow, and afterwards wrote a treatise on the virtue and morality of "Suttee" (GM)' (*Notebooks*, 31 and 136–7; and see notes to pp. 16 and 20).

370 *in toto*: (Latin) entirely.

371 *The sort of Othello . . . or Leontes*: both Shakespearian characters whose jealousy has dreadful consequences for their wives. The death of Desdemona is irrevocable; Hermione in *The Winter's Tale* is restored to life and to her husband Leontes.

373 *jealous men . . . disobedient daughters*: a reference to Desdemona's having married Othello without her father's knowledge or consent.

a mother of Gracchi!: Cornelia: see note to p. 361.

379 *a young Grand Monarque*: Louis XIV: see note to p. 10.

384 *Croesus*: a king of Lydia, sixth century BC, thought to be fabulously wealthy.

the Norman William: legend has it that William the Conqueror stumbled and fell as he was coming ashore at Pevensey Bay in Sussex on 28 September 1066. He turned to good account what might have been taken as an ill omen by holding up fistfuls of sand and declaring: 'A good omen: thus do I seize the earth of England!'

388 *Jonah's whale*: as punishment for disobeying God, Jonah was swallowed by a whale in a storm at sea. The experience caused him to repent (Jonah 1 and 2).

'It is a rough truth that Plato is Moses atticizing': the Greek philosopher has much in common with the Hebrew prophet.

389 *Orson's first appearance at Court*: uncouth, since he had been raised by a bear. The reference is to the early French romance, *Valentine and Orson*.

389 *Lothario-like*: a jaunty libertine, a rake; named after a character in *The Fair Penitent* (1722) by Nicholas Rowe.

390 *the Benbow school*: Bessy's Uncle Benjamin is of the ilk of John Benbow (1653–1702), who ran away to sea and rose to non-commissioned rank in the Royal Navy before being court-martialled for disparaging the captain. He then set up as a trader, and when his vessel was attacked by Moorish pirates off Cadiz in 1685, fought them off and pickled the heads of the thirteen pirates killed in the action in order that he might claim a reward. He subsequently rejoined the Navy and rose to the rank of Admiral. Although his leg was shattered in an action against the French in the Caribbean in 1702, he fought on and at the end of the battle ordered that seven officers be tried on charges which included cowardice in the face of the enemy.

393 *old Saxony . . . Sèvres . . . China*: Willoughby evaluates his collection of porcelain. China made at Meissen in southern Germany was known as Dresden or *porcelaine de Saxe*. It was regarded as the finest in Europe until about 1766, when Sèvres became pre-eminent. Like Meissen, Sèvres (named after the suburb of Paris where it originated) is a hard-paste porcelain, of which eighteenth-century examples are particularly prized. The term 'China', now used generically for various types of earthenware, comes from a Persian word for porcelain, and here refers to the kind of semi-transparent earthenware originally manufactured in China and brought to Europe by the Portuguese in the sixteenth century.

Dragon vases: a kind of porcelain decorated with designs of dragons.

394 *undivided morsel*: see note to p. 88.

the Queen of Sheba: the Queen of Sheba came to Jerusalem to find out whether King Solomon was as wise and as prosperous as she had heard tell. She returned richly fêted to her own country, convinced (1 Kings 10: 1–13).

395 *latrons*: robbers, brigands. *OED* cites this passage.

402 *ad infinitum*: (Latin) to infinity, forever.

410 *'A Spartan mother!'*: Sparta was one of the leading city-states of ancient Greece, whose inhabitants were noted for their courage, frugality, and discipline. It was a Spartan mother who on handing her son the shield he was to carry into battle said that he was to come back either with it or on it.

411 *"away with that bauble."* . . . *quoting Cromwell*: Oliver Cromwell (1599–1658), soldier, politician, and from 1653 to 1658, Lord Protector of England, when dismissing Parliament on 20 April 1653 is reported to have instructed a soldier 'Take away that bauble', referring to the Mace as an emblem of royal sovereignty.

414 *Laocoon*: a priest in Troy who was sacrificing a bullock to Neptune when two enormous sea-serpents set upon his two sons. His attempts to rescue them were unavailing, and all three were squeezed to death.

416 *'si brachia forte remisit'* . . . *'in pejus'*: Dr Middleton roughly paraphrases a passage from Virgil's *Georgics*, i. 199–203. The first phrase means, 'if he has by chance relaxed his efforts'; the second, 'for the worse'.

417 *an Alexander's pride*: the conquests of Alexander the Great (356–322 BC) included Egypt and Persia.

419 *'Your sallies . . . Aunt Sallies!'*: Willoughby's ponderous joke depends on his bringing together 'sallies', in the sense of brilliant remarks, and 'Aunt Sallies', referring to figures who are the butt of jibes and insults.

a Spartan stand: see note to p. 410.

434 *the trouble of Abraham*: the most relevant of Abraham's many troubles are probably those of finding a wife for his son Isaac (Genesis 24).

435 *Old Hiems . . . The aequinoctial fury departs*: Dr Middleton paraphrases the opening of Catullus' poem xlvi, in which the poet celebrates his departure from Bithynia, referring to the end of winter ('hiems', Latin, winter). He quotes the first line ('Now spring brings back its balmy warmth'), and translates the following one.

443 *a horn that blows the mort*: a hunting custom, in which a horn is sounded when the quarry is killed.

Lady Vauban: the Seigneur de Vauban was an expert in defensive fortifications, military engineer to Louis XIV. The hypothetical 'future Lady Vauban' is attributed power of resistance to male onslaught.

444 *an angry Dian, all arrows*: Diana, the goddess of hunting, protector of women, is frequently represented with a bow and quiver of arrows.

449 *a trotting kern governed by Strongbow*: a primitive Irish foot-soldier subject to the might of English rule.

450 *Arcadia*: see note to p. 11.

452 *the boat's crew of Captain Bligh*: on 28 April 1789, Captain William Bligh and eighteen men were cast adrift from Tahiti in an open boat after the crew of the *Bounty* had mutinied. They reached Timor on 14 June, after a journey of 5,600 km.

453 *the monks of the Chartreuse, whose elixir has power to still the waves*: at La Grande-Chartreuse, the head monastery of the Carthusians, near Grenoble, a brandy-based liqueur is made, to which Dr Corney here attributes the power to stop sea-sickness.

459 *on the die*: depending on the cast of the dice.

460 *I came, saw, and was conquered*: De Craye modifies the boast displayed in the triumphal procession of Julius Caesar after his defeat of Mithridates, king of Pontus, in 76 BC, *'veni, vidi, vici'* ('I came, I saw, I conquered').

463 *pro formâ*: (Latin) according to the protocol, formally.

464 *Cassandra*: a Trojan princess, who agreed to yield to the sun-god Apollo if he would grant her the gift of prophecy. He bestowed the gift, but she withheld her favours whereupon he modified the gift so that no one would believe her predictions even when they were accurate. She was looked upon by the Trojans as insane: Dr Middleton makes a learned joke in attributing her derangement to her being 'sun-struck'.

465 *planguncula*: a wax effigy, usually associated with sorcery.

466 *Optume . . . fidem*: (Latin) 'optume', excellent; 'ad rem', to the point; 'firmavit fidem', he has given his word.

467 *all the body-guard of a young gentlewoman*: this passage alludes to the supernatural machinery of Pope's mock heroic *The Rape of the Lock* (1714), in which there are also references to breaking china: e.g. Canto ii, ll. 105–6; Canto iii, ll. 159–60. For discussion of reminiscences of Pope's poem in *The Egoist*, see Michael Wheeler, *The Art of Allusion in Victorian Fiction* (London, 1979), 105–7.

468 *the knot . . . Gordian*: one of the exploits of Alexander the Great was to cut with his sword the intricate knot tied by Gordius at Gordium in Asia Minor. There was a belief that whoever could untie the knot would take the empire of Asia.

on the beach of Troy: the city of Troy was on an eminence near Mount Ida, about four miles from the shore of the Hellespont. Dr

Middleton's description of the refreshment Vernon's company brings him may obliquely refer to the circumstances of the Trojan War, fought to recover the Greek Helen from Paris, the son of the king of Troy.

469 *the Grecian portico of a boy*: Dr Middleton is offering an elaborate variation on the saying 'Spare the rod and spoil the child'.

471 *a lean Orion . . . the star beneath, Eastward*: the constellation of Orion the hunter, and Sirius, the dog-star: see note to p. 478.

478 *Sirius, papa!*: as the subsequent dialogue indicates, Clara's difficulty in recalling the name of the star may have to do with its prominence in the opening lines of Euripides' play, *Iphigenia in Aulis*. In the play, Agamemnon threatens to sacrifice his daughter Iphigenia on the altar. Sirius is the brightest of the fixed stars whose influence when rising about the same time as the sun was supposed to cause excessive heat during the dog-days, noted from ancient times as the most unwholesome part of the year (in the latitude of Greenwich, around the middle of August).

481 *Scipios and good legionaries*: the Scipios were a celebrated family in Rome under the republic, notable for military exploits and also for sexual purity.

486 *bradypeptics*: slow of digestion. This is the sole usage cited in the *OED*. Cf. comments on Dr Middleton's digestion at p. 196.

487 *Strephon*: a conventional name for a rustic lover.

490 *a grand book of the heraldic devices of our great Families*: Burke's *Peerage (A Genealogical and Heraldic History of the Peerage and Baronetage of the United Kingdom)* first appeared in 1826, and has been published annually since 1847.

491 *Far above Grizzel!*: a reference to patient Griselda as the type of long-suffering wifely fortitude. Boccaccio treated the subject in the *Decameron*, as did Chaucer in 'The Clerk's Tale'.

501 *turtles*: (archaic) turtle-doves; and hence love-birds.

the Polyphemus eye: in classical antiquity, a race of giant Cyclops each of whom had a single eye in the middle of the forehead was thought to inhabit western Sicily. Polyphemus was their king.

511 *the old figure of a post-boy on a hue-and-cry sheet*: a post-boy is a letter carrier or a swift messenger, and hence an appropriate illustration for official publications which included details of offences committed and names or descriptions of wanted criminals.

518 *Sir Cloudesley Shovel*: Sir Cloudesley Shovell (1650–1707) rose
from the ranks to the office of Admiral. His ship foundered and
sank with all hands off the Scilly Isles in 1707.

519 *Mother Goose*: Laetitia has written stories for children, which
Corney categorizes using the name derived originally from
Perrault's *Contes de ma mère l'oye* (*Tales of my mother the goose*, 1697).
In English, the term was first used in *Songs for the Nursery: or,
Mother Goose's Melodies*, published in Boston, Mass., in 1719.

verbum sap: (Latin) *verbum sapientiae*, a word to the wise.

527 *Switzerland . . . Political Economy*: Vernon's conversation has ranged
from the classic and sublime to contemporary social science. The
sublimity of the Alps is juxtaposed to two great Greek works, one
epic (the *Iliad* of Homer) and one tragic (Sophocles' *Antigone*),
and to the more modern study of Political Economy (from our
perspective, 'classical' economics). The term originally referred
to the practice of managing a national economy, then came to
designate the theory dealing with the laws that regulate the
production and distribution of wealth.

531 *Bregenz*: a town in Austria, on Lake Constance.

534 *Walpurgis nights*: the night of 30 April, when witches are said to
hold revels in honour of Satan at various appointed places
including the Brocken (see note below).

out-Brocken Brockens: the Brocken, the highest peak of the Harz
range in Saxony, has various associations with the supernatural.
Witches are supposed to dance there on *Walpurgisnacht* (see note
above). The Spectre of the Brocken is an optical illusion in which
spectators' shadows, greatly magnified, are projected on the mists
about the summit of the mountain opposite.

Graymalkin and Paddock: Greymalkin or Grimalkin, a grey cat;
Paddock, a toad—both commonly associated with witches (as in
Macbeth, 1. i. 8–9).

THE WORLD'S CLASSICS

A Select List

The Two Drovers and Other Stories
Edited by Graham Tulloch
Introduction by Lord David Cecil

Sir Philip Sidney:
The Countess of Pembroke's Arcadia (The Old Arcadia)
Edited by Katherine Duncan-Jones

Tobias Smollett: The Expedition of Humphry Clinker
Edited by Lewis M. Knapp
Revised by Paul-Gabriel Boucé

Robert Louis Stevenson: Treasure Island
Edited by Emma Letley

Anthony Trollope: The American Senator
Edited by John Halperin